BLACK FLAGGED APEX

a novel by

Steven Konkoly

Book Three in the Black Flagged Series

First edition

For information, contact skonkoly@earthlink.net

ISBN-13: 978-1481294881
ISBN-10: 1481294881

Dedication

For Kosia, Matthew and Sophia. Still my favorite people in the whole world.

Acknowledgments

In the spirit of tighter writing, I'm going to keep the acknowledgments to a minimum. This is also an effort to keep them on one page (or two), instead of ten, which is where they were headed.

First and foremost to my wife, who spent countless hours reading and taking notes. Once again, she provided several essential course corrections that better served the storyline, and you can thank her for the twist at the very end. She has become my primary sounding board for story ideas and a continuous voice of reason throughout the writing process. Best of all, she can't avoid me.

To the beta reader crew. Bill for his "Caesar-like" thumbs up or thumbs down assessment. I'm always tense waiting to hear from him. Trent and Nancy for reading with enthusiasm and providing an exhaustive list of typos, word suggestions and reality checks. Joe S. for keeping me from writing a novel within a novel. You can thank him for *Black Flagged VEKTOR*, the next book in the series. Bruce, Marcia and Glen for their read through and suggestions, despite their insanely busy schedules. Jon, for his valued insight as a one of my earliest readers and reviewers. I believe he read this book somewhere in the Bering Straits. To everyone in my writing group, which has served as a guiding light for the critical aspects of character development and narrative. Beyond the furious gun battles and technological intrigue, the Black Flagged series is driven by characters, which is all too easy to forget. Finally, I want to welcome Joe Bunich to the crew. He volunteered to "informally" proof all three of my previous books, and caught errors missed by everyone. He is living proof that the "right" extra set of eyes can make a huge difference.

To the formal production crew, starting with Felicia A. Sullivan, my ever faithful editor. She's been really patient with all of my covert ops, technothriller stuff…and my deadlines. Jeroen ten Berge for the overall Black Flagged series cover concept. I can't wait to see all three covers side by side. Stef for professionally formatting all versions of this novel, in addition to my entire backlist. Trust me, we all win with Stef on the job. His product is flawless. Pauline for proofing all of my books. She's proofed over 500K words for me at this point. Just the thought of that makes me want to turn off my computer.

About the author

Steven Konkoly graduated from the United States Naval Academy and served for eight years in various roles within the Navy and Marine Corps. He currently lives with his family on the coast of southern Maine.

He published his first novel, *The Jakarta Pandemic*, in 2010, followed by *Black Flagged* in 2011 and *Black Flagged Redux in 2012.* An excerpt from his apocalyptic thriller, *The Jakarta Pandemic*, can be found at the back of this book, along with a with a bonus excerpt from the next book in *Black Flagged* series, *Black Flagged VEKTOR*

Please visit Steven's blog for updates and information regarding all of his works: www.stevenkonkoly.com

About Black Flagged Apex

Black Flagged Apex takes place on the heels of *Black Flagged Redux*. Admittedly, I took a little heat for ending *Redux* with the virus canisters unrecovered and Petrovich's team still pursuing leads related to Al Qaeda's possible intention to unleash the virus in the United States. For me, this was a logical cut off point for the novel, since most of the conflict had been resolved in the novel, and I couldn't go any further without locking myself into another 500 pages. I'm not ready to present a one thousand-page novel to readers, and I assume that many of you feel the same. As you read *Apex*, I think you'll better understand why I separated the two stories. They are uniquely different in many ways. For those that found the *Redux* ending to be abrupt, I thank you for persevering to read the series.

Like *Black Flagged Redux*, keep in mind that the scenes occur in chronological order and are labeled in local time. Here is a short list of the time zone differences between the locations featured in the *Black Flagged Apex* and the U.S. East Coast: Argentina +2 hours, Moscow +9 hours, Germany +6 hours, Novosibirsk +11 hours, Sweden +6 hours.

Finally, don't forget about the character list, which you can also print from my blog www.stevenkonkoly.com. I'm not saying you'll need it, but *Black Flagged Apex* adds to the memorable character list from *Black Flagged Redux*.

Character List

In alphabetical order

Mohamed Abusir – Al Qaeda cell leader, Newark, New Jersey

Ramish Banergee "Mish" – Black Flag Electronic Warfare Team, Europe

Alvaro Batista "Alvin" – Black Flag Electronic Warfare Team, Europe

Audra Bauer – CIA, Deputy Director, National Clandestine Service

Kerem Demir – FBI, Task Force Scorpion, Investigative Lead

Karl Berg – CIA, Assistant Deputy Director, National Clandestine Service

Tyrell Bishop – True America, Hacker Valley Compound Leader

Michael Brooks – True America, Head of Security, Poconos Lab Unit

Tommy Brown – True America, Militant Arm Commander

Jason Carnes – True America, Head of Laboratory Operations, Poconos Lab Unit

Dihya Castillo – Black Flag, Middle Eastern Group

Robert Copely – CIA Director

Rear Admiral Mark DeSantos – DIA, Strategic Services Branch Director

Miguel Estrada – True America, Militant Arm Leadership

Richard Farrington – Black Flag, European Group Leader

Aleem Fayed – Black Flag, Middle Eastern Group Leader

Luc Fortier "Luke" – Black Flag Electronic Warfare Team, Europe

Joel Garrity – Director of the National Counter Terrorism Center

Lieutenant General Frank Gordon – Commander Joint Special Operations Command

Timothy Graves – Black Flag Electronic Warfare Team, U.S.

Jackson Greely – True America, Co-founder of Militant Arm

Julius Grimes – True America, Militant Arm Operative

Salvador Guerrero – Homeland Security liaison to NCTC

Anish Gupta – Black Flag Electronic Warfare Team, U.S.

Ashraf Haddad – Black Flag Middle Eastern Group

Colonel Jeff Hanson – SOCOM liaison to NCTC

Lee Harding – True America, Co-founder of Militant Arm

Konrad Hubner "Fritz" – Black Flag, European Group

Darryl Jackson – Brown River Security Corporation executive

Alexei Kaparov – Federal Security Service, Russian Federation

Damon Katsoulis – FBI Task Force Scorpion, Tactical Lead

Major General Bob Kearney – Defense Intelligence Agency Director
Sarah Kestler – White House Counterterrorism Director

Reinhard Klinkman "Klink" – Black Flag European Group

Thomas Manning – CIA, Director National Security Branch

Enrique Melendez "Rico" – Black Flag Americas Group

Frank Mendoza – FBI, Task Force Scorpion Assistant Leader

Owen Mills – CEO Crystal Source Water, True America Militant Arm

Joseph Morales – Assistant Attorney General for National Security

Kathryn Moriarty – FBI, Task Force Scorpion Mobile Commander.

Imam Hamid Abdul Muhammad – Al Qaeda recruiter, Newark, New Jersey
Jeffrey Munoz – Black Flag Americas Group

Dana O'Reilly – FBI, Task Force Scorpion Lead Data Analyst

Tariq Paracha – Black Flag Middle Eastern Group

Anne Renee Paulson – True America, Militant Arm, Distribution Phase Leader

Daniel Petrovich – Black Flag, Americas Group

Jessica Petrovich – Black Flag, Americas Group

James Quinn – National Security Advisor

Jacob Remy – White House Chief of Staff

Anatoly Reznikov – Former scientist at VECTOR labs in Russia

Brigadier General Terrence Sanderson - Black Flag Leader

Abraham Sayar – Black Flag, Middle Eastern Group

Ryan Sharpe – FBI Task Force Scorpion Leader

Frederick Shelby – FBI Director

Callie Stewart – Black Flag liaison to NCTC

Marianne Templeton – Secretary of Homeland Security

Jason Volk – NCTC Watch Supervisor

Kathleen Walker – White House Senior Counsel

Abdul Waseer – Black Flag, Middle Eastern Group

Bob Wilkins – Crystal Source Distribution Center Manager

Benjamin Young – True America fundraiser/contribution manager

APEX:

"Apex – Latin, meaning

high point or culmination."

BLACK VEIL

Late April 2008

Chapter 1

6:42 AM
South 20th Street
Newark, New Jersey

Special Agent Ethan Reeves rubbed his eyes and took a sip of bitter coffee from a worn blue travel mug. Sunlight crept through the open doorway connecting the front room of the apartment to the kitchen, spreading along the worn gray carpeting. Through the opening, he heard Special Agent Dave Howard rummage noisily through cabinets and drawers. Muttered obscenities floated into the quiet room, causing a barely discernible grin to form on his face.

"The sugar's gone," said Reeves.

"What happened to the rest of the packets?"

"You forgot to put them in the fridge last night. The mice showed up again. Crapped all over the kitchen table too," said Reeves.

"Sorry about that. I'll head out a little later. This place is fucking disgusting. Did I mention that before?" groaned Howard.

"That's the first time today. I'll call the incoming team and let them know what they need to bring," he said blandly.

Reeves shook his wireless mouse and brought one of the computer monitors back to life. He leaned back and slouched in the stiff, inexpensive office chair that the Newark field office had finally approved. Before these arrived, they had suffered through the day on folding chairs, frequently standing up to stretch out ever tightening backs and hamstrings.

By mid-afternoon, he usually spent more time standing than sitting. At the end of a week's rotation, Reeves felt twice his age. His body would slowly recover over the weekend, eventually returning to normal before he reported to the Newark field office on Monday. There, he would enjoy a few days of slightly less mundane work, constantly dreading the arrival of Friday morning, when he would report for another week of duty holed up in their surveillance post. One week on. One week off. Pure agony.

So far, the realities of stakeout duty had met few of his preconceived notions. Instructors at the FBI Academy tried to manage every new agent's expectations about the job, but they had failed miserably to prepare him for the inevitable stakeout assignment. Reeves stubbornly held onto his pre-academy fantasies; daydreams that put him in a desperate position to singlehandedly apprehend one of the nation's most wanted terrorists and stop the next 9/11. He needed to cling to this delusion, because after five months of reviewing digital feeds and adjusting surveillance equipment, cynicism had started to blanket his romantic notions about life as a special agent in the FBI.

His partner, an even keeled, fifteen-year veteran of the Bureau, did his best to maintain an enthusiastic façade, but Reeves could sense that Special Agent Howard's FBI spark had been extinguished long ago. Howard quickly steered their conversations away from work, focusing on family, friends, hobbies, vacations...anything but FBI work. Luckily for Reeves, Dave was an entertaining and comical storyteller, because as a single, newly minted agent, their lives had little in common beyond their FBI credentials.

He activated two more monitors and searched the first screen for the 'digital highlights' function. Despite the FBI's frugal interior decorating job, the surveillance package deployed in the apartment was state-of-the-art. Little expense had been spared to provide a nearly automated system, which made their jobs infinitely easier than any of their predecessors'. Long gone were the days spent coordinating bathroom breaks and snapping pictures through a 35mm camera equipped with a telephoto lens. Ironically, they rarely looked out of the apartment windows at their surveillance target. They could watch everything from the monitors.

The new system employed four digital cameras, providing continuous, automated coverage of the target house. The powerful night vision equipped cameras worked simultaneously from different windows to capture each and every detail. The system even provided limited thermal detection capability, which could roughly pinpoint the location of any human or large dog within the house. Laser microphones continuously scanned exposed windows for vibrations and automatically recorded the conversations within.

All of this information was continuously uploaded to a location unknown to either agent, where it was closely analyzed on a timeline determined by investigative prioritization algorithms. Based on their extensive experience at this location, the data review for the first floor occupants of 32A, South 20th Street, started later in the morning. They had never been contacted by the Data Analysis Group (DAG) prior to lunch today.

Even with all of this automation, their duties included a cursory review of the video and audio surveillance recordings. Since neither of them spoke Arabic, their only responsibility regarding the audio involved reviewing "irregularities." These included arguments, languages other than Arabic, or female voices. Even that job was simplified by the software, which screened the different feeds and highlighted these portions for them based on embedded protocols. The video review required a little more effort.

They typically reviewed the night's digital highlights before breakfast, quickly catching up to near "real time" on the daily feeds. The system flawlessly drew their attention to anomalies detected by the sensors: late night visitors, lights at unusual hours and telephone calls after the team recorded "all quiet" in the house. The suspects in the target apartment kept a pretty tight schedule, which made the job simple. Reeves or Howard would check the highlights, if there were any, and together they would conduct a fast speed scan through the video, further searching for any obvious irregularities.

They weren't required to remain awake once they logged "all quiet," since their stakeout was classified as an intelligence gathering activity. The four men living together in 32A had raised enough red flags to warrant further investigation, but hadn't been classified as an immediate or developing threat.

When the digital highlights screen appeared, Reeves first thought the system had experienced a glitch. Five months of reviewing night feeds had never yielded anything more interesting than an aborted break-in attempt through one of the building's side windows. Annoyed, he sat up in the chair. The system had highlighted multiple audio, video, and thermal irregularities. In fact, the Windows based system provided a two-page list of anomalies for him to review.

He clicked the first one in the queue, which started a recorded digital feedback stamped "2:24 AM," sending video to two of his screens. He watched the screen on the right, which showed three figures emerge from the back of the target building's backyard and approach the rear deck. The second screen zoomed in on each of the figures in rapid succession, intelligently deciding to capture close up images. Oddly, all of them were dressed in dark clothing, wearing ski masks.

"What the hell?" he muttered.

"You say something?" Howard called from the kitchen.

"Dave, get over here!"

Reeves leaned forward in the chair and watched the three figures pause at the bottom of the deck on the screen.

Howard appeared in the opening and leaned against the white, paint-chipped doorframe. "What?"

"Take a look at this. I think our friends had visitors...holy fuck! Someone took out our guys!" he yelled and shot up from the chair.

"Take it easy, Ethan. What did you see?" said Howard, who calmly walked over to the card table hosting all of their computer equipment.

"Multiple flashes inside the house. We need to get over there now!"

Reeves scrambled around the chair and moved quickly across the room. He reached into a black and gray nylon backpack lying next to the opened sleeper couch, removing his badge, service pistol and a spare magazine from a hidden compartment. Howard leaned over the table and started working the computer mouse.

"Will you settle down? What are we looking at...what the?"

His voice trailed off as he replayed the video and watched the figures disappear from sight. The camera panned out and everything looked normal for a few seconds. The first flash came from the front window, followed immediately by flashes from the side windows, which they had previously determined were bedrooms.

"Shit!" yelled Howard.

He nearly fell backward over the chair, colliding with Reeves as they both sprinted for the kitchen. Howard grabbed his holster and badge from one of the kitchen cabinets, and followed Reeves out the back door and down the crumbling stairway to the cracked, weed filled concrete patio. They sprinted across the street with their guns drawn and approached the rear deck.

"We're fucked," hissed Reeves when they reached the back door.

"Nobody's fucked here. This..."

"This kind of shit happens all the time? You were about to say that, weren't you?" said Reeves.

"Maybe. Let's throttle back and do this by the book. I'll go first, staying low. You cover. We'll work our way through the rooms. No assumptions. Someone might still be alive in the house, and they won't be happy to see us," said Howard.

Reeves took a deep breath.

"Got it. I'm good," he said and adjusted the grip on his Glock 23.

"Ready?" said Howard.

"Ready."

Reeves watched Howard turn the doorknob and push the weathered door inward. They both braced themselves against the doorframe and aimed into the duplex. The door led into the kitchen.

"You smell that?" whispered Howard.

"Smells like someone took a shit on the floor," replied Reeves.

"That's what dead people smell like, before they start rotting. Cover me."

Howard crouched and moved slowly through the kitchen, aiming at the only doorway leading further into the house. When he reached the doorway, he took up a position on the left side of the door, staying low. Reeves followed the same path and stacked up behind Howard. Once in position, Howard aimed through the opening into a long hallway. Reeves stood up and aimed over Howard's head. He saw two doors on the left, which they knew were bedrooms, and a door on the right, which had to be a bathroom. Howard edged into the hallway and nodded at the first door on the right. They moved up to the closed door. Once in position, Reeves pressed up against the left side of the hall and aimed down the hallway. Howard slowly worked the doorknob before quickly pushing the door open, pistol extended forward with both hands.

"Bathroom's clear," he whispered, leaving the door open.

He turned to face the first door on the left, repeating the process as soon as Reeves took up a position on the right side of the hallway. Instead of pausing at the door, he followed it into the room, feet scuffling just out of Reeves' sight.

"Clear," he heard from inside the room.

Reeves moved into the bedroom doorway and braced his forearms against the doorframe, focused on the hallway leading to the front room.

"One of our subjects is dead. Al Farouq. Two shots to the forehead. We call this in and wait," said Howard.

The smell of feces had worsened after Howard opened the door, activating his gag reflex. Reeves turned his head and glanced into the room, taking small breaths through his mouth. He had to see this. He'd imagined shooting these guys in several of his daydream scenarios, and simply couldn't believe someone had actually beat him to it. The image took his breath away, almost forcing his coffee back up.

A single figure lay on the bed, perfectly arranged for sleep. The pillow looked dark brown under Farouq's head, clearly soaked with coagulating blood. The fitted mattress sheet at the head of the bed was similarly stained, along with the top sheet, which was still pulled up to the man's chin. A small puddle of blood had started to form on the floor under the corner of the loosely hanging top sheet. He could imagine a much larger pool spreading under the bed, where the blood had surely soaked through the mattress. He snapped his head back to the hallway, which Howard was counting on him to cover.

"Shit. We're screwed," whispered Reeves.

"This is not going to be good. That's for sure," replied Howard.

"What do we do?"

"Not much we *can* do. We call this in and check the rest of the bodies."

"Look on the bright side," said Howard.

"There's a bright side to this?" asked Reeves.

"Yeah, we won't have to spend another night in that rat infested shithole. Let's get this over with," he said and moved back into the hall.

They had three more dead bodies to confirm.

Chapter 2

7:25 AM
White House Situation Room
Washington D.C.

Frederick Shelby sat in one of the prime seats at the long conference table. Two seats away from the President of the United States, he was content to be included in the upper echelon of attendees. The conference table had been reconfigured to seat an expanded group of the most important people in the U.S. government, in what could easily be described as the most important conference room in the entire world. Technicians had worked feverishly yesterday to configure the room exclusively for the command and control of the government's response to the terrorist plot uncovered by the CIA.

Video conference cameras adorned the table, next to each imbedded computer terminal. Flat screen monitors covered nearly every square inch of eye-level wall space, each presenting a different map, data table or news report. The constant flow of information on the screens brought the static walls alive with vivid, high definition colors. The information flowing to these screens was controlled by analysts sitting at the mobile "Watch Floor" station at the far corner of the room.

This two-tiered hub consisted of four stations packed closely together, each housing three flat screen monitors for operators to analyze and manipulate. The mobile station's electronics suite had been modified to communicate with the nerve centers of every agency and unit involved in the operation. All crisis related communications sent to the White House would filter through the station and be appropriately disseminated. In anticipation of the complicated, multi-agency effort required to handle the crisis, the president decided to transfer complete responsibility for information management from the White House Situation Room's central

Watch Floor to the mobile hub. If necessary, Situation Room technicians could add another mobile station and double the conference room's information management capacity.

He stared down the long table, very much enjoying the picture he saw. The generals and admirals were about as far away as possible from the president, without putting them at a kiddie table, which was where they belonged in his opinion. Especially after last night's debacle and the clear implication that someone in their ranks had tipped off Sanderson. He had been so close to catching Sanderson, only to have the rug pulled out from under him, in what could only be described as a calculated, carefully planned publicity stunt. Fortunately, he had kept his cool. A few more choice words the other night, and he might be a lot further away from the president. Everyone sat quietly as the flat screen monitors simultaneously changed to a CNN broadcast.

"CNN ran this twenty-five minutes ago and we're already getting hit left and right with domestic requests for information and civil emergency funding. Pay attention," said the president.

International news correspondent, Michael Foreman, appeared on the screen next to an inset map of western Russia. As he started speaking, the map zoomed in to the Kola Peninsula and the location of Monchegorsk appeared. The words "Breaking News" were stacked above the CNN tagline, "Civil Unrest Reported in Russia."

"This is Michael Foreman with breaking news in Russia. A shockingly bizarre Reuters news story is quickly shaping into a potential nightmare for the world community. Samantha Rivers reports live from St. Petersburg."

"Thank you Michael. I'm standing outside of St. Petersburg square, next to a group of protesters that will join thousands of their fellow countrymen inside the square to demand open access to Monchegorsk. As it stands, only military traffic is allowed on the main highway leading out of St. Petersburg to the beleaguered city, strictly enforced at checkpoints and by ominous patrols of armored vehicles. Until earlier today, most of the media crews had been operating out of Petrozavodsk, a little over two hundred kilometers to the north. Hundreds of military vehicles poured through the small city on their way north to Monchegorsk, which is another two hundred and fifty kilometers north. Abruptly, military and police units forced all media crews back to St. Petersburg, where we have been told to remain indefinitely.

"Confirmed news from the area is scarce, but persistent rumors of a deadly epidemic continue to surface. So far, nobody has been able to confirm the shocking and unbelievable

footage sent anonymously to Reuters, suggesting that the Russian military is systematically destroying the city and killing its inhabitants. Russian officials have made no comment. One thing is for certain, the Russian government has taken extraordinary measures to seal off the area surrounding Monchegorsk. What is truly frightening is the fact that the world hasn't seen an emergency government response on this scale from the Russian government since Chernobyl."

"Thank you, Samantha. And now we turn to CNN's very own national security advisor, Brett Russell."

The screen froze and the president returned his gaze to the table.

"And therein lies our problem. The media didn't skip a beat making this a national security issue, and they don't know the half of it...yet. We need to accelerate our efforts to safeguard the American public, and I'm not sure it can be done without drawing attention to the fact that the Monchegorsk situation is directly related to our national security and could very well be the tip of the iceberg. I want to leave this room with an effective, short-term strategy that we can improve upon for the long term. Here's what I think. We can't deploy the National Guard to watch over the nation's water treatment plants without answering some difficult questions. Homeland is already getting crushed with inquiries from state and local law enforcement agencies. We prudently raised the threat level to Orange, without providing details about the threat. This is highly unusual. We've only raised the threat level this high five times on a national level, and we've always provided details. I don't feel this strategy is sustainable beyond noon today. I want to hear your thoughts."

Frederick Shelby made a quick decision to jump into the thick of things. The FBI's taskforce stood at the vanguard of efforts to stop whatever might be headed to U.S. shores and he wanted to make sure everyone in the room understood that fact. The squeaky wheel got the grease, or in this case, the resources.

"Yes, Mr. President. I think we all need more information on the incoming threat. What exactly are we dealing with? I've read the reports, but the information is vague at best. I think we could better shape the nation's response with more precise information," said Shelby.

Many of the attendees muttered agreement with his comment, while a few displayed mildly disapproving faces. He committed these to memory. It was always good to know who might not be on your side when things went sideways. the Secretary of State, Secretary of Defense, White House Chief of Staff and, no surprise here, the Director of the CIA. Even Sarah Kestler, the White House Counterterrorism Director looked a little annoyed.

"Our CDC liaison answers the technical questions about the Zulu Virus," said the president.

"Zulu Virus?" said one of the Generals.

A tall man with exceedingly dark hair and matching eyebrows stood up from the far end of the table. He looked nothing like a scientific type to Shelby.

"Good morning. I'm Dr. Marston Phillips, assistant deputy director for the CDC's Office of Infectious Diseases. This is my colleague, Dr. Pradeep Chandrashekar, who heads the Office of Public Health Preparedness and Response," he said, gesturing to the man in a dark blue suit seated next to him at the conference table.

"So, to answer your question briefly, we are looking at a weaponized form of herpes simplex encephalitis, genetically modified to aggressively attack the brain's temporal lobe. Worse yet, we suspect that the modification has reduced the virus's lethality."

"Isn't that a good thing?" interjected James Quinn, National Security Advisor.

"Normally, yes. Left untreated, herpes simplex encephalitis has a high fatality rate. Near seventy percent."

The entire room broke into murmurs at the presentation of that statistic.

"Treated aggressively, we can reduce this to thirty percent," continued the scientist.

"Thirty? That's still extremely high," the National Security Advisor said.

"Correct. For an infectious disease, this is a worst-case scenario in terms of lethality, but keep in mind that viral encephalitis is not a highly transmittable disease, like the Avian Flu. This is partly why cases of viral encephalitis are still extremely rare," said Phillips.

"So this should be relatively easy to contain if released on U.S. soil?" asked the Homeland Security Director.

"May I?" asked Pradeep Chandrashekar.

"Please," said Phillips, who sat down to let his colleague continue.

"If the Zulu Virus is released into a public water source, containment of the disease itself will not be our biggest challenge. Physical containment of the impacted community and the management of information will be your biggest priority. Weaponized encephalitis is the ultimate biological weapon."

"But if it's not contagious, at worst we're looking at highly localized terrorist incidents. Tragic and horrific, but manageable," said the White House Chief of Staff.

"You're missing the bigger picture here, Mr. Remy. Herpes simplex encephalitis does more than produce casualties, and if the virus in question has been modified as suggested, the impact of its release can't be understated. Here are the statistics for the unmodified virus. In those treated aggressively, less than three percent regain normal brain function. This can vary from very mild to severe impairment, depending upon several factors. Early treatment with high dose, intravenous acyclovir is the only modifiable factor scientists have identified. However, this may not be an option in our situation. Testing isn't complete, but the initial research conducted by Edgewood indicates that the weaponized strain in question races to the temporal lobe, leaving little hope of recovery."

"How can you know that for sure?" asked Shelby.

"We can't, but based on the information surrounding the current situation, we have to assume a worst case scenario," interjected Phillips.

"And what is that?" continued Shelby.

"If released in a municipal water supply, unknown to the population, it has the potential to affect nearly everyone. Take a small town of twenty thousand people. Even if we discovered the attack immediately after the virus circulated through the drinking water and treated everyone in the town with acyclovir, 95% of them will suffer neurological impairment at varying levels. 19,000 citizens. Neurological impairment will range from..." he paused and glanced at the president and the Director of the CIA, who shared a glance and nod almost imperceptibly toward Phillips.

"Full homicidal rage and hyper-aggressive behavior to minor seizures. Brain damage in almost every case. Edgewood's initial report indicated that we would likely be dealing with the more serious end of that spectrum. The reports gathered by..." he stopped again and looked to the CIA Director.

Shelby started to get even further annoyed. He could tell that Phillips was uncomfortable taking the conversation any further and he knew exactly why. Prior to entering the conference room, Shelby had been cornered by the National Security Advisor, who informed him that there could be no direct mention of Sanderson's team during the meeting. They could be called "intelligence assets in Europe" or "onsite ground assets" but specific reference beyond that was forbidden.

They didn't have time for the paperwork before the meeting, but information regarding Sanderson's present and future involvement with the government would be classified Compartmentalized Information Security (CIS) Category One. The Black Flag program was once again one of the most highly classified secrets of the United States government. Obviously, Phillips had been given the same speech. He wondered who else had been yanked aside by the National Security Advisor. Not everyone, or they wouldn't have to dance around this issue during the meeting. The president ended the uncomfortable pause.

"The effects of the virus in question have been confirmed firsthand in Russia. We are dealing with the worst end of that spectrum. I don't mean to cut you off, Dr. Phillips, but let me say what needs to be said. If that virus is released, we face the likelihood of trying to contain an entire city or township of brain damaged citizens, many of them mentally deranged and violent, who face no hope of recovery. I can't even begin to fathom how we would handle 19,000 cases like Dr. Phillips suggested in just a small township. People would have to be detained and treated compassionately, even the ones that would require maximum security institutionalization. Imagine this happening simultaneously in fifty-eight separate cities across America. This is the ultimate terrorist weapon, with the potential to tear apart the fabric of American society.

"I want to focus on taking steps to protect our citizens from the release of this virus in the United States, while responsibly and cautiously preparing them for the possibility of an attack. The joint FBI and Homeland Security taskforce based out of our National Counterterrorism Center is already fast at work tracking down domestic leads. We have assets doing the same thing abroad. So, how do we start preparing the public, while not hindering investigative progress?" said the president.

"We have to be careful with raising the threat level. Orange is significant, but taking it to Red could tip off the group preparing to attack. Possibly accelerate their timeline or cause them to go to ground. Whatever we do, we can't tip them off until the investigation has reached a critical mass," said Shelby.

"But going to Red would leave no question in anyone's mind that this was the real deal. If we're planning to activate the National Guard, I don't see how we can avoid it," said Marianne Templeton, Secretary of Homeland Security.

"Going to Red will cause a widespread panic. We need to slowly ease into this, based on the immediacy of the threat. We can activate the National Guard without going to Red," said the White House Chief of Staff.

"I don't think we can get away with that for very long, Dr. Chandrashekar. Where does the CDC stand in terms of a response?" asked Templeton.

"We're already assembling first response teams and deploying them nationwide so they can reach anywhere within the continental U.S. within a few hours. These teams will confirm the presence of the virus and allow full scale resources to be deployed. We'll coordinate with Health and Human Services to educate the public as determined by the administration. We're working up media packages, public education announcements, and response guidelines for first responders," responded Chandrashekar.

"Pauline, what can we expect from your department at the outset?" asked the president.

Pauline Rosenberg, Secretary of the Department of Health and Human Services leaned forward to see around Director Shelby.

"Mr. President, my department will work closely with the CDC to ensure the rapid and targeted deployment of our National Disaster Medical System assets. Under your recent directive, we have created and disseminated several National Planning Scenarios intended to guide federal, state and local disaster planning efforts. Unfortunately, efforts to implement the recommendations proposed by these scenarios are still in their infancy at the state and local levels. The sooner we alert state and local governments, the better. These scenarios are designed to focus response efforts for geographically limited disasters projected to produce significant casualties in the tens of thousands. A bioweapons attack is one of the scenarios. State governments need to start readying a response."

"I agree with you, Ms. Rosenberg, but we need to figure out how to do this without creating a panic," said the president.

"What are we doing directly on a federal level?" he asked.

"On a federal level, we are preparing all of our deployable medical response assets. We have fifty-five Disaster Medical Assistance Teams and thirty-one Federal Medical Stations that can be deployed within twenty-four hours. All of the equipment and personnel are being assembled as we speak. Once CDC identifies a hot zone, we will commit these additional assets and start intensively coordinating with local medical and law enforcement authorities. Nineteen thousand patients will require an incredible effort at every level, which will quickly outstrip local resources. Mr. President, you should be prepared to immediately declare any area hit as a federal disaster."

"Nineteen thousand was only an example. The number could be in the hundreds of thousands, depending on the target city," Dr. Chandrashekar informed them.

"What about the Strategic National Stockpile and Project BioShield? We've spent close to forty billion dollars on bioweapons defense since 9/11 and the anthrax attacks. Five billion alone for vaccines," said the White House Chief of Staff.

"Unfortunately, most of that money went to purchasing and stockpiling vaccines and drugs to counter anthrax and smallpox, which have always been considered to be the most likely bioterrorism threats. We've also put a considerable amount of funding into research for an antidote to botulism toxins. The rest went to research to improve treatments to exposure to chemical and radiological weapons. We have no stockpile of anti-virals suited to treat a weaponized version, or any version of herpes simplex encephalitis."

"What about the drug companies that make the ones we need?" asked the Chief of Staff.

"We're in contact with them right now, to see how quickly they can increase production of these drugs. The production of oral valacyclovir can likely be increased immediately, but the intravenous acyclovir will present a problem. Unfortunately, the intravenous solution is the standard of treatment for HSE. High doses of orally administered valacyclovir are only theoretically effective in this case."

"Shit. We have nothing stockpiled to defend against this?" the Chief of Staff asked.

"Not at the moment."

"I'll get on the phone to the CEO's of these companies as soon as I leave the room and make sure you have their undivided attention," said the president.

"Where do we stand right now in the investigation?" asked Sarah Kestler, White House Counterterrorism Director.

This was Shelby's chance to shine, though he knew that most of his own Task Force's success depended heavily on Sanderson's team's efforts in

Europe. All of this was a cruel twist of fate and irony for Shelby, one that scorched his very soul with the fires of mistrust and suspicion. Sanderson had burned them all twice now; two years ago by destroying the HYDRA investigation for his own selfish purposes, and one day ago by forcing the president to grant his entire band of criminals a blanket immunity agreement. Each scenario had been carefully crafted and manipulated by Sanderson.

Deep down inside, he wasn't completely convinced that this whole terrorist threat wasn't Sanderson's plan from the very beginning. He would never forgive Sanderson for the two high profile embarrassments placed in his lap, and despite the immunity agreement, he *would* have his revenge. He'd have to be patient and extremely cautious, but he'd find a way to send that traitorous bastard to prison for the rest of his life. He already knew where to start the process.

He stared down at Major General Bob Kearney and nodded. He hadn't been surprised to see his friend in the meeting, but the presence of Rear Admiral DeSantos seemed unusual. Why the Strategic Services Branch (SSB) needed to sit in on one of the most important meetings in history was lost on him, unless the SSB was Sanderson's new home. Kearney would be seething if this turned out to be the case, but the arrangement might prove useful. Kearney was an ally that might prove instrumental to bringing Sanderson down. If Sanderson's crew was attached to the SSB, a subordinate command to Kearney's DIA, Shelby's commitment to bringing Sanderson down might be easier than expected.

Clearing his throat, he stood up to address the president.

"Task Force Scorpion will focus investigative efforts in two directions. Since Al Qaeda operatives were last in possession of the virus in Europe, our primary focus is on suspected Al Qaeda cells in the U.S. These cells typically operate independently, but based on the coordinated plan foiled in Europe, we suspect that this will be a coordinated effort here at home. The larger the network, the more likely we will pick up leads right away. I have tripled the number of agents to the International Terrorism Operations Section assigned to Al Qaeda and made this the FBI's number one investigative priority. Homeland Security has made a similar shift in its resources," said Shelby, nodding to Marianne Templeton.

"Our second focus is on domestic terrorism networks. Intelligence gathered in Europe indicated the remote possibility that one of our homegrown terrorist groups may be involved, though this has not been confirmed, and the extent of their involvement is unknown. Special Agent Ryan Sharpe, Task Force Scorpion's leader, has worked extensively within the Domestic Terrorism section for the past few years and is intimately familiar with all of these groups. His assistant, Special Agent Frank Mendoza, is a rising star within the Al Qaeda investigative section. I've put our best people on deck for this and am confident that we'll start making significant progress immediately," he finished.

"And our overseas assets? How do they fit into this?" asked the National Security Advisor.

Both Shelby and the Director of the CIA started to answer this question at the same time, neither one of them wanting to back down.

"General Copley?" said the president.

"Thank you, Mr. President. Intelligence suggests that Al Qaeda planned to use a medical supply distribution company in Germany to ship the remaining virus to the U.S. Discreet assets are moving quickly to that site and—"

"Should I be worried about this?" interrupted the Secretary of State, Colin Hyde.

Shelby chuckled to himself and had to exercise every last bit of restraint not to visibly show his amusement. Should he be worried? Hadn't he seen the results of the CIA's discreet assets in Stockholm? They nearly destroyed half of a city block in broad daylight. The Black Flag teams were the Secretary of State's worst nightmare. An international incident steamroller on autopilot to tear up as much of Europe as humanly possible. He should be very worried.

"We can talk about that a little later, Colin. Based on the information we've shared with Germany already, I don't think they'll have a problem with what we have in mind," said the president, nodding for General Copley to finish.

Shelby couldn't constrain himself and barely managed to turn an outright laugh into a cough.

"If we're lucky, the virus may still be sitting in Europe. If not, they'll do everything possible to figure out where these canisters were shipped. Evidence found in Europe indicated that several Al Qaeda cells made hasty exits from the European scene. If the canisters were shipped recently, as suspected, Task Force Scorpion might have a chance of grabbing it all at once on the ground here."

"You mean we're not even 100% sure this is inbound?" said Joseph Morales, speaking up for the first time.

Morales was the Department of Justice's Assistant Attorney General for National Security (AAG-NS) and directed three other AAG's within the National Security Division that handled the legal aspects of counterterrorism, counterespionage and intelligence gathering. Shelby rarely clashed with Morales, since his position was newly appointed by the president, and they mostly saw eye to eye on issues regarding domestic counterintelligence and counterterrorism. Most importantly, his attorneys spent most of their time focusing on foreign intelligence gathering methods. Frankly, he was surprised that the president had included him in this meeting, as he could imagine no circumstance on earth under which the administration would bring him up to speed on the details of their most current foreign intelligence gathering asset's origins. Morales would be another ally Shelby could rely upon when things started to get dicey.

"We should have a yes or no answer on that within a few hours," said Copley.

"I don't want to overstep my area of expertise, Madame Secretary," said Morales, gesturing toward Pauline Rosenberg from Health and Human Services, "but there are certain actions that won't be retractable. Maybe we should wait for word from our overseas assets, before we start contacting state governors and ramping up bioterrorism resources. It won't take much for the media to start piecing this all together, especially with the news from Russia."

"I tend to agree with this course of action," said Marianne Templeton. "If this isn't inbound, an overreaction on our part will unnecessarily panic the public."

Sarah Kestler stood up, scowling with pursed lips. She always wore a severe looking face, but this new look gave her an entirely new dimension of seriousness.

"Nobody is suggesting that we shut down FEDEX and UPS, or confiscate every package delivered within the last week. Some basic steps are prudent. It sounds like the virus could already be here. The European cells vanished within the last four days, right?"

"So it appears from the foreign law enforcement reports," said Shelby.

"Al Qaeda isn't going to wait for us to gather the next report. Four days ago? Give them a day to consolidate the virus at the shipping facility, maybe another day to pack and ship. Until proven otherwise, I recommend that we start taking steps based on the assumption that U.S. based Al Qaeda cells are in possession of fifty-eight bioweapons canisters. Or at least someone is in possession of these weapons. Given the fact that they abandoned Europe, likely in response to the news pouring out of the Kola Peninsula, I don't think they plan to sit around and stare at the canisters for very long. This is a bold plan that took years to coordinate. They're shifting tactics and strategy quickly. Frankly, I'd be surprised if they hadn't already carried out their mission here. We need the National Guard and local law enforcement out protecting our water supply right now. European authorities didn't waste any time securing and testing their water supplies."

"It's just that once we start this ball rolling, it'll be hard to stop," added the Secretary of Homeland Security.

"She's right. Once we start making calls at the state level, this thing will take on a life of its own," said the Health and Human Services Secretary.

"I think we'll have much bigger problems if Al Qaeda manages to release the virus. Each canister can poison a city," said Kestler.

"Our intelligence indicates that they would use more than one per city," added the CIA Director.

"Fair enough. Twenty cities...even one city will create an unstoppable panic, well beyond any scare caused by preparing for an attack. It sounds like the right steps are being taken by every agency at the federal level. I just think it's time to get local and state authorities involved. We need to start securing water supply points and testing water."

"Does anyone firmly disagree with this strategy?" asked the president.

"I still think we should wait until the threat is confirmed. If we immediately take the steps that Ms. Kestler recommends, we have to raise the threat level to Red. There is no going back from there. It has only been done once since 9/11."

"I can live with that," said Kestler.

"You don't have to deal with the impact on the nation's transportation system, airports, borders...this goes far beyond just sliding the color over to Red."

"Just one successful attack will change the nation forever, Mr. President. This has the potential to make 9/11 look like a pipe bomb," replied Kestler.

Shelby liked the way she thought and acted. No nonsense, action oriented.

"Alright. Ms. Kennedy?" said the president.

"Sir?" said Sandra Kennedy, the Deputy Secretary of Defense, leaning her head inward to make eye contact with the president.

"Let's activate the Army National Guard and Army Reserve immediately. Do whatever needs to be done to coordinate with each state. Make sure they understand that this is a nationally directed deployment."

"Understood, Mr. President."

"If we're lucky, we'll find out in a few hours that the virus never left Europe. I'm willing to deal with the fallout of putting the Guard and the appropriate government agencies on high alert. The situation in Monchegorsk is a nightmare. Even before Russia's unforgiveable wholesale slaughter of the population, it was—"

"Unverified at the moment," interrupted the Secretary of State.

"It's been verified, Colin. However, I understand your concerns regarding the Russians," he said, shooting the Secretary of State a harsh look.

"Marianne, let's move the Homeland Security Advisory System threat level to Red. Severe risk of attack," the president decided.

The president started going down the line, tasking the members, but Shelby was distracted by an alert on the built-in tabletop computer monitor in front of him. The monitor at his seat had been configured for him to send and receive intranet traffic from his own office to provide a way for his staff and immediate subordinates to pass him information while he was stuck in the White House situation room. So far, the messages had been routine, intended for him to review in between sessions. A Flash Priority message caught his eye at the top of the queue and all of his other message traffic stopped. He noticed that one of the president's aides, sitting at a chair behind the president, received a cell phone call. Even Shelby wasn't allowed to bring a cell phone into the Situation Room, so he knew this must have been an internal communication. The aide stood up and walked along the outside wall of the room toward him.

"Director Shelby, I've been informed that you have a Flash message," he stated.

"Thank you. I just saw it."

This exchange went mostly unnoticed in the room. It wasn't uncommon for senior government officials to receive critical messages while in the audience of the president. Shelby's eyes narrowed as he read the contents of the message. When he shifted his gaze to the president, he noticed that all eyes were focused on him. The president had stopped talking and was waiting for Shelby.

"What happened?" said the president.

"Six of the seven suspected Al Qaeda cells under surveillance in the greater New York/New Jersey metro area were taken out last night. Massacred in their sleep. I think it's fair to assume that some of the virus is here already," said Shelby, clearly shaken by the news.

"What about the other cell?" asked Marianne Templeton.

"Missing. They shook ground surveillance and never returned to their apartment last night," said Shelby.

"Shit. How the hell could this have happened right under your peoples' noses? They were under surveillance, right?" snapped Jacob Remy.

"Easy, Jacob," said the president.

"Simultaneous strikes around 2:30 in the morning. This is surveillance, not protective duty. These groups never move at night. They follow unvarying routines throughout the day and wake up in the middle of the night to pray. We listen to every conversation they have and analyze every aspect of their lives."

"But someone can walk inside and kill them without anyone knowing?" pressed the White House Chief.

"We can figure this out later. Do you have any leads? Anything that can move us in the right direction?" said the president.

"We got lucky at one of the sites," said Shelby.

Jacob Remy huffed at this comment.

"One of the killers removed his mask prematurely, within view of our cameras. We're working on identifying him. Surveillance records indicate that all of the sites received multiple FEDEX packages yesterday," said Shelby.

"Are you fucking kidding me?" yelled Jacobs.

"How long would it have taken for that information to raise an alarm? This is unreal!"

"Maybe if you'd quit withholding funds from my agency, I could hire more agents to watch these pricks...and upgrade the systems used by our analysts to filter through the thousands of reports that are filed on an hourly basis from law enforcement agencies nationwide."

"Now this is my fault?" said Jacobs.

"It's Al Qaeda's fault, gentlemen. That's it. Let's get the investigation moving with the new information," said the president.

He turned to Director Copley.

"I still want your people moving on the medical supply company in Germany. Seven cells with suspicious activity isn't the full extent of this. There would have to be more. We need to figure out who hit them."

"Probably the domestic group referenced by our intelligence source," interrupted the CIA Director.

"Let's figure that out. I can't imagine this domestic group got every canister. We need to approach this from both angles," said the president.

"General Gordon, I am invoking my authority under the Insurrection Act to deploy active military units in support of domestic law enforcement agencies. My own counsel and the Attorney General agree that this level of coordinated terrorist activity on U.S. soil warrants my authority in this case."

"What did you have in mind, Mr. President?"

"Special Forces. Tier One units and all other direct action capable Special Forces teams. Full helicopter support. I want our best teams available to support Task Force Scorpion."

"Sir, we have the same capabilities within the FBI. Coupled with local SWAT assets, this should be more than enough to cover any possible contingencies," said Director Shelby.

"I'm not casting any doubt on your agency's capabilities. I want to plan for the worst-case scenario. We get all of our best operators into the game. I will only authorize the use of U.S. Special Forces as a last option."

"I'll get the units ready and coordinate with Task Force Scorpion regarding geographic deployment. If you don't mind, Director Shelby, I'd like to assign a liaison to your task force," said Lieutenant General Gordon.

"The more the merrier," said Shelby, not really meaning what he said.

"We have a long day ahead of us. I don't want to hold any of you up any longer. Make sure you coordinate your agency's press releases with my office. We need to be on the same page when communicating to the press and the public. Any last concerns?"

"Good. Get to it," said the president.

He immediately left the room with his entourage, which included the Chief of Staff, his secret service detail, a few aides and the Director of the CIA. Major General Bob Kearney and Rear Admiral DeSantos vanished just as quickly out of a door on the other side of the conference room. The noise level instantly rose to a level making it nearly impossible to carry on a conversation. Shelby yelled across to Marianne Templeton.

"Are you scheduled to meet with the president after this?"

"No. I need to get out of here and get this nightmare rolling. I still think we should wait for further confirmation. You won't be able to buy groceries tonight on your way home after this news hits," said Templeton.

"Or bottled water. I wouldn't worry about heading home tonight. Nobody's leaving his or her office in the foreseeable future. I'll catch up with you later," he said, moving swiftly toward the door.

He reached the conference room exit and stepped outside, searching for any signs of the president's entourage. He spotted General Kearney and Admiral DeSantos headed in the direction of the president's private office on the other side of the Watch Floor. Tracking their progress, he pushed through an endless gaggle of seemingly inconsequential aides and government staffers waiting to rendezvous with someone important in the conference room he just departed. He watched as Secret Service agents stationed outside of the office admitted the two flag ranked officers and pulled the office door shut.

Through the two windows, he could see the president seated behind a desk and Director Copley sitting directly across from him. The president motioned with his hand and the two officers sat down on chairs squeezed into the office next to the CIA director. The president reached behind him and the windows suddenly fogged, obscuring Shelby's view inside the office.

He knew this had something to do with Sanderson. The president was taking an extreme risk sanctioning the use of these assets. Less than twenty-eight hours ago, Sanderson's organizations had been classified as a terrorist organization. He couldn't afford a screw up that would draw the public's attention to that fact. The president was probably spelling out exactly what he expected in terms of Sanderson's continued involvement on foreign soil. Shelby didn't like guessing. Sanderson's operatives had been assigned to Task Force Scorpion, and he still didn't have a good handle on their rules of engagement or the scope of their authority. He was told to wait on this, until a DIA liaison was assigned to the NCTC.

As Director of the FBI, in charge of the nation's premiere law enforcement and domestic surveillance apparatus, the term "need to know basis" didn't apply to him. He needed to know everything. His only consolation in this case was the fact that he had a man on the inside, talking with the president while he was jostled around by this endless tide of servants waiting eagerly to serve their masters.

Chapter 3

9:25 AM
Acassuso Barrio
Buenos Aires, Argentina

Jessica leaned into the vanity mirror and gently applied the concealer stick to the remaining dark purple areas under her left eye. She held the stick between her index finger and thumb, patting the application lightly with her pinky finger to blend it into the foundation. She had spent the better half of an hour applying makeup to her bruised and battered face. The process was taking her twice as long without the use of her left hand, which sat uselessly in a tight gauze wrap on the brown speckled granite countertop.

Concealing signs of physical abuse surfaced deep, distant emotions that Jessica had spent the last ten years pushing further and further into her subconscious. She was no stranger to "making herself look pretty again" after silently enduring repeated beatings at the hand of Srecko Hadzic's associates in Serbia.

The physical abuse hadn't been the worst part. In fact, it had barely bothered her at all. She had a built-in tolerance for physical pain. One of the many "gifts" she had acquired living under the constant threat of her father's wildly unpredictable, alcohol fueled rampages. Taking a closed fist high on the cheekbone or a backhand to the mouth was something she had learned to live with.

She had thought all of that would change when she reported to Langley. Ironically, she couldn't have been further mistaken. Instead, they would turn her into one of the most lethal operatives in recent CIA history and put her into a situation where she was forbidden to use those skills to defend herself. She had developed dozens of coping mechanisms as a helpless child, none of which could help her deal with the fact that she had become a predator, but she would still be abused nonetheless. This burden had slowly unraveled her in Belgrade, nearly killing her.

Finding Daniel in that hellhole had certainly saved her from herself. Daniel insisted that they had saved each other, but she knew better. That was something he said to ease her emotional pain. She had no doubt that Daniel would have survived his "tour of duty" in Serbia. He was one of life's guaranteed survivors, and staying close to him would always be her best chance to survive too.

She touched up the last remaining evidence of the desperate struggle that had almost ended her life and leaned back to take in her handiwork. She had to give them credit; even Daniel might not recognize her at first glance. Thanks to a discreet team of beauty consultants, who specialized in hiding wealthy victims of abuse within plain sight, she could effortlessly walk into Ministro Pistarini International Airport and board a plane headed anywhere in the world.

Her long, lustrous jet-black hair had been replaced by a dark brown, short pixie-cropped style that accentuated the strong, angular contours of her face and freshly lifted eyebrows. She had changed her eye color from dark brown to deep blue, with the help of custom vanity contact lenses that also hid the temporary damage to the blood vessels in her left eye. Balanced collagen injections helped her lips appear normal against the persistent swelling on the left side of her face. She had changed her appearance as much as possible without plastic surgery or Hollywood-level special effects makeup. Only a close examination by a seasoned social services case-worker could detect her secret. Even her bandaged hand would be disguised in a sleek, medical grade plastic hand splint that would require little more than a quick explanation about a recent "tennis" accident.

In a few minutes she would complete the transformation with a dark gray, Ralph Lauren sleeveless turtleneck dress that would cover the extensive abrasions and cuts from the piano wire that had nearly severed her carotid artery five days earlier. She had to hand it to the small group of stylists that took over her bedroom for several hours yesterday. They may have cost a fortune, but they didn't mess around. She felt "pretty" again.

Her cellphone rang from somewhere deeper in the house, most likely from the kitchen where she had prepared an espresso earlier. She had carried the phone around with her, hoping to hear from Daniel before he became too involved in his next job for Sanderson. She didn't have many details regarding his next operation in Germany, but he had made it sound like routine work. She was certain that there would be nothing routine about his day, but at least it wouldn't involve penetrating a "rabid zombie" infested city to retrieve a human head, or driving full speed into a Spetznaz crossfire. Whatever the mission, she knew it wasn't a good idea to distract him, but she needed more than a call every two or three days while he was away. Especially after what almost happened in their Buenos Aires high-rise. She *needed* to talk to him every hour if possible, but would settle for once a day.

She started to form the words to call her two unwilling manservants, Munoz and Melendez, but quickly remembered they had departed soon after she treated them to the most expensive dinner she could import into the safe house. It was the smallest token of gratitude she could offer the two men that had saved her from Srecko's beasts. The duo had even started to lighten up a little, which probably had less to do with her charming personality and everything to do with the availability of an exquisitely smooth Malbec vintage, and the dawning realization that they would be taking the next available private flight back to Sanderson's mountain hideaway. Either way, she enjoyed seeing them let their guard down just a little and finally relax. She owed them everything.

She had oddly come to terms with her own death at the apartment. On some level, she had felt relieved that her struggle was finally finished. At least she had convinced herself that she had accepted her death. All she had to do was relax her muscles and take a little weight off her tensed midsection. The thin piano wire would have cut a few more millimeters into her neck, effectively opening her carotid artery. It might have been a bad decision given the Celox Munoz had found in Josef Hadzic's torture kit, but she somehow doubted they could have kept her alive for more than a minute or two jamming hemostatic powder into her neck. What they had planned to do to her corpse afterward, on camera for their boss, hadn't mattered to her either, so she thought.

Ultimately, all of those thoughts proved false. When Melendez's bullet removed her captor's head, she sprang into action with no hesitation, leaving little doubt about her decision to live or die.

She put down the concealer stick and walked across the cool, gray marble tile to the kitchen. She hadn't expected to hear from Daniel until later in the afternoon. His group had an operation planned for the evening, which always shut him down externally. She read the caller ID, not recognizing the number, which could only mean one thing. The last person she really wanted to talk to right now. Three people had the number for this throw away phone. Daniel, Munoz, and her least favorite person in the world. She accepted the call.

"Do I need to get a restraining order?" she said by way of greeting.

"I highly doubt that would be possible, since you officially no longer exist as an Argentinian citizen," said General Sanderson.

"That was fast. Can I pick up the new paperwork this morning? There's room on a flight leaving at 12:15," said Jessica.

"So now you're happy to hear from me? Your passport will be delivered within the hour by a trusted member of the U.S. Embassy. One of Karl Berg's friends. That might give you enough time to book that flight."

"I'm impressed," she said.

"I'll take that as a compliment, though I must admit that having a little leverage over the White House helps work wonders with the State Department. The passport has been issued in the name Jessica Petrovich, and will contain an entry stamp for your vacation to Argentina. Once you get out of Argentina, you're home free. Your names have been removed from every U.S. generated international and domestic watch list. The Petroviches are free and clear as far as the U.S. government is concerned."

"Do you trust them?"

"For now, but I'd recommend having a backup plan ready at all times. I'll help you get a second set of papers, just in case. Have Daniel pass on the details when the two of you have talked about it."

"We'll be sure to get in touch," said Jessica.

"Why do I get the feeling the two of you already have a plan to disappear?"

"Because you know us too well? Who knows, we might sign on with you as a *Mr. and Mrs. Smith* freelance team. No promises, but all options are still on the table."

"Now that is a pleasant surprise coming from you. Even hearing you mention the possibility gives me hope. I was utterly convinced that I'd never see the two of you again."

"You might not..." she said and paused. "But sometimes life makes the choices for you."

"In my experience, it's most of the time. The two of you will always be welcome here. Don't ever forget that," Sanderson said.

"Somehow, I don't think you'll let us forget."

"We all know each other too well. Enjoy your time together. The two of you have earned it. I expect to hear from Daniel early this evening. Sounds like they are close to wrapping up their work in Germany. Of course, it all depends on his ability to get some very stubborn people to talk."

"I'm sure Daniel will be on one of the first flights out of Germany tomorrow."

"A lot of highly placed, extremely anxious government officials in D.C. are counting on that very same assessment."

"Daniel never disappoints."

"No. He doesn't. Good luck, Jessica," Sanderson said, and the call disconnected.

She placed the phone on the cold granite countertop and glanced at a two-thirds empty bottle of last night's Malbec standing next to the sink. Was nine-thirty in the morning too early for a glass of wine? Probably. Plus, she needed something stronger to deal with the anxiety stirred up from talking to Sanderson. He'd ruined their lives for his own selfish gain, though the entire situation was certainly more complex. Without the general's new initiative, who knows what the world might have faced in the upcoming weeks. The limited reports streaming out of Russia painted an extremely bleak picture. Without Daniel, the world may never have discovered the truth about what happened in Monchegorsk. She felt her mind spinning again and glanced at the bottle of wine. Still not a good idea. Maybe a little closer to eleven o'clock.

Chapter 4

7:38 PM
Gallusviertel District "Gallus"
Frankfurt, Germany

"We stick out like a sore thumb around here," muttered Daniel from the rear bench row of their Ford Transit van.

"At least nobody will call the cops," said Konrad Hubner.

"That's because we look like the cops," said Daniel.

"We're fine. This isn't a high crime area. The immigrants take care of this place," said Reinhard Klinkman.

Klinkman had met them in Hamburg, after they had travelled separately by car through Sweden and Denmark. Thanks to the Schengen Agreement, neither of their cars was subjected to more than a visual check at reduced speed, at either the Danish or German border. Introduced in 1985, the Schengen Agreement gradually abolished border controls throughout the European Union, making it possible to drive from Stockholm to Spain without ever displaying a passport or enduring customs searches. If you held a passport from a non-Schengen Area country, all you had to do was gain admittance to the European continent, legally or illegally, and you could travel freely without question or fear of discovery.

Once Petrovich's team landed in Stockholm a few days earlier, they were more or less guaranteed access to the rest of Europe. Of course, the matter of their involvement in a running gun battle on the streets of Stockholm had the potential to complicate this freedom, but once they escaped the city, they saw no sign of an enhanced security presence in any part of Sweden.

Klinkman had arranged for them to return their rental cars in Hamburg and take possession of two used vans, which they drove to Frankfurt. One van, with darkened rear windows, would be used by the assault team. The windowless, second van gave Sanderson's Electronic Warfare (EW) team a private cargo area to turn the van into a mobile electronics suite.

Three members of this newly formed group had joined them in Frankfort, having arrived from various parts of Europe. Utilizing laptop equipment and wireless technology worth five times the amount of their van, they had easily hacked into Frankfurt's Deutsche BioMedizinische (DBM) database, sending the data to the CIA. Although theoretically unnecessary in this case, since most of the cyber work could be done from the U.S., Sanderson wanted to put this team in the field alongside the clandestine operatives. Apparently, Berg hadn't argued with the idea, since it would provide one more layer of separation between his agency and German authorities should the unthinkable transpire. Berg seemed to be all about these layers, which Petrovich could appreciate. All of his own layers had been peeled away recently, leaving him completely exposed.

The electronic warfare team had another goal that had been cautiously revealed by their team leader, "Luke." The Frenchman had disclosed the fact that they would try to hack the CIA's system and either download the terrorist databases or install a backdoor that they could access later. Sanderson didn't want the team constrained by nervous decision makers when national security matters were at stake. Daniel had no doubt that the electronics team had been given orders to go deeper than just the terrorist databases. Sanderson never passed up an opportunity to expand his influence, and if the CIA let their collective guard down for a second while linking with Luke's team, the General would take full advantage of the situation. Sanderson never ceased to amaze and disgust Petrovich.

"There's the apartment block. Lots of shady looking faces around here. Are you sure the van won't disappear? That would pose a real fucking problem," said Farrington.

"It's not like the States. You don't find the same level of crime. There are plenty of rougher, all white neighborhoods further west," said Hubner.

"I don't want to have to walk him to the nearest U-bahn station if our van disappears," replied Farrington.

"It won't be a problem," muttered Hubner.

"I still think we should deal with him in his apartment. Fewer variables," said Klinkman.

"This is a tightly knit immigrant community. Word will get around fast and eventually make its way to the real police, who will be quick to respond. There's no federal police bureaucracy working in our favor. We need to get Sahil into the van as quickly as possible," said Hubner.

Hubner was right. No broad federal law enforcement agency existed in Germany, so they couldn't flash federal badges and buy time like in the U.S or Russia. Nearly all law enforcement tasks fell under territorial German State Police, which were administered separately by each region. The only federal police apparatus in Germany was the Bundespolizei (BPOL), which didn't include any specialized units that would typically conduct an urban based raid. Most BPOL units served federal internal security or border supervision roles.

They had thought about posing as members of Germany's counterterrorism forces, GSG-9, a specialized branch of the BPOL, but decided against the idea. The mere suggestion of a GSG-9 operation would raise every law enforcement alarm in the region. Their hastily provided identification badges indicated that they were members of the Hesse Landeskriminalamt (LKA), or State Investigative Bureau, which made enough sense to silence most curious onlookers. The LKA specialized in investigating and preventing politically motivated crimes. Four bulky LKA investigators dragging a young Muslim man into a van wouldn't be the most unusual law enforcement spectacle seen in this neighborhood.

Daniel glanced around at his surroundings as the van pulled into an empty space next to a large green, graffiti covered dumpster on Idsteiner Strasse. The northern Gallus neighborhood was dominated by rows of long, nondescript, three story apartment blocks, each extending at least one hundred meters from Idsteiner Strasse. If Sahil's apartment was at the end of one of these blocks, they might have to reposition the car. The van was parked in front of a low hedge, between two of the buildings. Beyond the hedge, lay a grassy courtyard, which was outlined by a continuation of the hedge and covered with rectangular clothes drying poles. Spaced closely together, the poles resembled crudely erected, miniature soccer goals. Only a few were still adorned by drying laundry this close to sunset and presented another possible complication upon exit with their man. Entrance doorways to both buildings were visible on the outer edges of the long courtyard, spaced evenly down the entire block.

He shifted nearly all of his attention to the apartment building on the left side of the courtyard. 85 Idsteiner. Upon arrival, he had noted that the target building featured no balconies on either side, just bare faced walls containing small windows. They wouldn't have to post someone in the adjacent courtyard to prevent a jumper. The target's apartment designation was 2F, which they had presumed to mean second floor. Counting doorways, the apartment was most likely located halfway down the building, which meant a long transit dragging a feisty terrorist. They didn't have much time to spend in the apartment, but he wasn't opposed to spending a few precious moments convincing Sahil that resistance would be met by severe, unthinkable pain. He glanced behind him into the cargo hold area at a large black nylon bag. He wouldn't need the contents of this bag to convince Sahil. The bag could wait for later, when they had more time.

Farrington patted Klinkman on the shoulder and turned to face Daniel and Hubner.

"Alright. Let's do this. I want to be out of here within five minutes. Daniel and I will handle any law enforcement interference."

He locked eyes with Daniel.

"Use your compressed air pistol first. You'll have five separate shots. Each dart will instantly paralyze your targ—"

"I'm familiar with the effects," he interrupted bitterly.

"The darts will not penetrate a ballistic vest. Your best bet will be to hit an arm or leg," said Farrington without changing his expression.

"Or the face," added Petrovich.

"Don't shoot for the face. You'll puncture an eye. At twenty five meters, the air pistols are extremely accurate. Don't shoot for the neck either," he said, maintaining the emotionless face.

Petrovich had at least expected a smile considering the fact that Farrington had zapped him with the same neurotoxin two years ago in the middle of Georgetown University, but this was Farrington's first operation as team leader. Petrovich would play a support role and observe. If Farrington performed as expected, Sanderson would detach Petrovich, leaving Farrington in charge of European operations. Daniel had every intention of making sure Farrington succeeded. He wanted to put as much of this behind him as possible and get back to Jessica.

"Let's hit it," said Farrington.

The four of them simultaneously opened their doors and stepped onto the pavement. Walking briskly, they scanned the courtyard and street for any signs of trouble. Nothing raised any sort of internal alarm for Daniel as they turned onto the narrow sidewalk running parallel to 85 Idsteiner. The first doorway confirmed the apartment numbering scheme. "Apartments 1-3A." Five more doorways to the entrance for 1-3F. 2F would be on the second floor. Upon a casual glance at the first door, Klinkman turned his head to Farrington.

"Ten seconds to pick the lock," he said casually.

They filed down the sidewalk until arriving at the door marked "Apartments 1-3F." Hubner walked past the doorway, leaning against the wall just short of the nearest first floor window. Farrington took a few steps into the courtyard, through a break in the hedgerow, and examined the opposite building's facade. Klinkman immediately went to work on the door with a tool extracted from a small kit he had kept concealed under his black leather jacket. Petrovich concentrated on the street, particularly the area around the van. So far, he hadn't detected any unwanted attention. One pedestrian crossed the opening between buildings, but never glanced in their direction.

Unfortunately, interested pedestrians posed the least of their problems. The real threat came from paranoid neighbors peeking through windows. It didn't take a master's degree in criminology to figure out that Daniel's team was attempting an unauthorized entry. Klinkman was fast, but few citizens kneeled down to insert their keys. A quick scan of the balconies revealed that they were empty, which surprised him given the warm temperature. Then again, most of the working class denizens of the Gallus didn't have time to lounge around mid-week and breathe in the spring air.

"We're in," said Klinkman.

The team disappeared into 85 Idsteiner with one purpose: to extract Sahil Mazari from the apartment. Mazari worked as a computer network programmer at Deutsche BioMedizinische, assigned specifically to support DBM's distribution department. Mazari had been the only employee at DBM's Frankfurt facility flagged in the CIA database, which made him their most logical starting point. A Pakistani born immigrant, he had taken several trips back to Pakistan within the past year, which raised red flags given his previous association with Al Qaeda extremists. The sudden, increased number of visits to Pakistan fit a pattern identified by the CIA. A dangerous precursor for escalated participation in extremist activity. Similar patterns had been identified prior to hundreds of attempted or completed terrorist attacks in the past.

Even more condemning, he had twice travelled back with known Al Qaeda extremists based out of Hamburg. Both of these suspected operatives had attended Technische Universität Hamburg-Harburg (TUHH) with Mazari, and one of them had even completed the same computer information technology degree. Dubbed "Terrorist U" by the CIA's Middle East analysts, former TUHH students could be found at the top of every "known terrorist" watch list around the world. A claim to fame that did not appear as a selling point on any of the university's marketing brochures.

Hamburg continued to serve as a hotbed of Muslim extremist activity, long after the infamous "Hamburg Cell" had changed the world on 9/11 under the leadership of Mohamed Atta. Atta had also been a "student" at TUHH, disappearing from Germany for extended periods of time to travel to Afghanistan. He continued his studies at leisure, while plotting the most diabolical terrorist attack in history. The CIA had no intention of letting any more TUHH "graduates" conduct attacks against the United States. Mazari's web of connections in Hamburg barred him from entering the United States, and put him on a growing list of "likely terrorists."

Farrington approached the door marked 2F, and the rest of the team fanned out along the walls of the cramped stairway vestibule. Each apartment had its own small landing. Two old, rusted bicycles were stacked against the far wall, causing Petrovich to squeeze by to get behind Farrington. They all withdrew HK P2000 SK (subcompact) pistols from their waistline holsters and stood silent, taking in any noise from the apartment and stairway. Laughter vibrated from 2F. They would soon put an end to that.

Petrovich took a six-inch suppressor out of an inside pocket on his jacket and started screwing it onto the custom threaded barrel. He would be first in the door, tasked with neutralizing any threat that stood in the way of abducting Mazari. They didn't have a wealth of information about his roommates, but couldn't discount the possibility that this could be a den of extremism.

Farrington tapped his right ear and nodded at Hubner, who quickly gave him a thumbs up. Hubner was the only member of the group wearing an earpiece, connecting the assault group with the mobile surveillance team. Luke and his group were scanning local police channels, searching for any indication that the team might have unwelcome visitors. Apparently, the police channels were still clear. Farrington pointed at the door, which put Klinkman into action.

Klinkman placed a small electronic device at the top right corner of the door, next to the frame, and slid the device down to the door knob. The device displayed a green LED, which turned red about halfway down the door. He pressed a small button on the device with his thumb as it turned red, leaving a small black dot on the white door. He repeated the process under the doorknob, moving the device to the floor without a break in the green LED color.

He reached down into a small bag attached to his waist and pulled out a small thumb sized charge, called a "popper." He placed the malleable charge over the small black dot and pressed it against the frame. If affixed correctly, the low grade plastic explosive would "pop" the deadbolt identified by Klinkman's device. The noise level created by the small explosion would sound like a very angry husband slamming the door to an apartment. He pushed a small, preset timer into the charge and started to work on the doorknob with his toolkit.

Seven seconds later, he glanced up at Farrington. A quick nod was all it took to start the countdown. Klinkman flipped a small switch on the side of the timer and pressed the single button on its face before clearing to the side of the door.

Immediately following the sudden, explosive crack, Petrovich delivered a strong frontal kick to the weakened door. Klinkman turned the doorknob just in time to ensure that the kick knocked the door open with enough force to embed the inner doorknob into the drywall. Petrovich raced into the apartment with his gun raised, followed by Farrington. Within a second they had identified their target, who was holding an Xbox controller in his hand, flanked on a small green couch by two dark skinned men, each holding a paper plate containing a partially eaten slice of pizza. One of the young men held an amber beer bottle frozen to his lips. A fourth roommate stood frozen over an open cardboard pizza box on a table behind the couch. All of them had frozen in place, staring wide eyed at the men holding pistols aimed at their heads. Klinkman yanked the door out of the wall and slammed it shut. A science fiction fantasy game displayed on the forty-inch flat screen TV mounted on the wall behind Farrington made the only sound in the room. Mazari paused the game and the room quieted. Hubner broke the deathly silence with a calm, authoritative voice.

"Sahil Mazari. Drop the controller and place your hands high above your head. If anyone moves, they will be shot in the head," he said in German.

"We don't really speak much German," Mazari said in broken German.

"Do you speak Russian?" asked Petrovich.

"Is he speaking Russian? Why would the police use Russian?" said the man holding the beer to the left of Mazari in Indian accented English.

He had purposely used Russian to add another layer of confusion to the situation. Now these terrorists would be even more stressed about their fate. Russians operating in Germany spelled bad news for a Muslim extremist, though Petrovich had to admit that the beer and pizza scene seemed completely out of place. The three roommates looked distinctly Indian, and all of them looked "soft," especially Mazari. He was at least forty pounds overweight and had an extremely slack look on his face. He looked nothing like any of the criminal element Petrovich had seen in his notorious career. Somehow *this* guy spent several months training in the hills of Afghanistan?

Klinkman restated his request in English and Mazari dropped the Xbox controller and moved his hands high.

"I think this is a mistake of some kind...officers?" said Mazari.

"No mistake. Stand up from the couch and walk forward, keeping your hands above your head," stated Farrington.

"Can we just talk about this first? We're all here on work visas," persisted Mazari.

"Can I move?" said the man holding the beer bottle.

His arm was already shaking from keeping the position for several seconds. Petrovich started to get the distinct feeling that Mazari was not their man.

"Nobody moves but Mazari. Stand up and walk toward me slowly, or we'll kill your two friends and grab you ourselves," said Farrington.

"The neighbors won't hear a thing," said Petrovich, aiming the suppressed pistol at the young man to the right of Mazari.

"Dude. Get up from the couch. He's fucking aiming that thing right at my head," said the man to Mazari's right, barely moving his lips.

"You need to go with them," the man frozen over the pizza box piped in.

All of their English was Hindi accented, including Mazari's.

Mazari complied with their request and found himself zip tied with a bag over his head within seconds. He was out the door and on his way down the stairs a few seconds after that, escorted by Klinkman and Hubner.

"What about the rest of them?" said Petrovich, lingering in the doorway to speak with Farrington in private.

"I don't think they pose a threat. Something's off here. Make sure they don't fuck with us. Grab Mazari's laptop," whispered Farrington.

Petrovich was relieved that Farrington had sensed the same incongruity. If Mazari was involved in the plot to ship the virus to the United States, he may have been an unknowing accomplice. Petrovich took a few steps back into the room. They were still frozen in place, which would make his job easier.

"Let me keep this as simple as possible. If you call the police, we will kill your friend and then kill you. We're monitoring all police channels and have another team watching the building. Don't leave your apartment either. You didn't see a badge tonight, because there are no badges. Your friend may be involved in something really nasty. Something you want to stay as far away from as possible. Mazari will likely end up floating in the Main river tomorrow...without a head. You do anything to alert the authorities and it'll be a busy day for the Frankfurt central morgue. Understood?"

They all nodded and he had little doubt that the message was received.

"Does Mazari have a laptop?"

They all nodded and their eyes shifted toward the counter separating the kitchen from the family room. Four laptops were stuffed onto the crowded Formica counter.

"Get his laptop. Does he have a security token? Something that generates a password?"

"It's on his key chain. In his pocket. Can I put the beer down?"

He grabbed the laptop out of the man's hands, aiming carefully at his head.

"I'd finish the beer first. Remember what I said about ending up in the river."

Petrovich stepped out and closed the door, listening intensely for movement inside. Nothing. Perfect. He sprinted down the stairs to rejoin the team.

Chapter 5

1:52 PM
CIA Headquarters
McLean, Virginia

Audra Bauer paced through the "Fishbowl" in the CIA operations center, anxious to hear from Sanderson's team in Germany. Mazari's abduction had gone smoothly. The team hadn't attracted any law enforcement attention grabbing him from the apartment and they were now on the way to a small, privately accessed home north of Frankfurt. She was always amazed at how easy it was to make someone disappear, especially an enemy of the United States. She couldn't say for sure what would happen to Mazari, but one thing was certain, if he was connected to the virus canisters, he would never taste freedom again.

The operations center's watch officer turned her head and nodded to Bauer.

"The director is inbound. Just passed through ops center security."

"Thank you, Karen. Is Manning with him?"

"No. Just the director."

The last thing she needed was the director watching over her shoulder. Whatever Farrington and Petrovich had in store for Mazari was very likely not on the CIA's menu of acceptable prisoner handling techniques. Then again, the president himself had sanctioned the continued use of these assets to prosecute the leads uncovered in Stockholm, so perhaps a little high level visibility would help ease some of the tensions in the operations center. She had a full complement of analysts and technicians rotating through the center in twelve hour shifts. Too many eyes and ears in her opinion. The director's presence during this critical phase might reinforce the fact that this operation came from the very top.

She saw General Copley's face on one of the screens near the watch officer's station. The watch officer typed a code into a small keyboard, which was immediately followed by a pneumatic hiss from the door cut into the center of the obscured glass wall separating the "fishbowl" from the rest of the operations floor.

"General Copley, glad you could join us," she said, walking over to meet him.

"No you're not, but I figured with Berg on a field trip, you could use some extra company. For a few minutes at least," he said.

Berg's mission to retrieve Anatoly Reznikov was a secret shared by very few at this point. The scientist's miraculous survival at the hands of Petrovich and Farrington had been kept offline. As far as she knew, everyone within the operations center thought Reznikov had died in the Stockholm safe house. Petrovich and the attending physician had confirmed his demise to the entire operations center via satellite phone, leaving little doubt that Sanderson's team had killed Reznikov, while torturing him for information. Despite the value and importance of the information gained, they were all well aware that the House and Senate Intelligence Oversight Committees were unlikely to sweep aside the methods used to gain the information. She had seen a few tense looks when Farrington announced that they would start Mazari's interrogation in the van, on the way to the safe house. Twelve long minutes had passed since that report.

"What's the status of our team?" asked Copley.

"Sanitary pickup of Mazari. The team is transporting him to the safe house. Interrogation in progress."

Copley nodded. "Good. The team understands the stakes?"

"Without a doubt. This crew works fast. Very efficient," she said, resisting the temptation to look at one of the more nervous analysts.

"So I've heard," said Copley.

"Call coming through from the team in Frankfurt. Speaker or private?" announced the watch officer.

"Speaker," said Bauer.

"You're connected," said the watch officer into her ear microphone.

"I think we have the wrong guy," Farrington's voice said over the line. "Mazari's been crying like a bitch ever since we stuffed him in the van. He says that the frequent travel to Pakistan was to visit his sick grandfather. Congestive heart failure. He traveled back with his cousin on two occasions to visit. He's scheduled to travel again in two weeks, without the cousin. He said that they don't get along very well, mainly because the cousin is...I quote...'pushy with the mosques.' If Mazari's an extremist, he's at the very low end of the totem pole."

"Can he provide information to help us verify his story?" asked Bauer.

"I just fired off a secure email with everything he provided. I got tired of typing. He was about to provide his entire life story. When we busted into his apartment, he was playing video games and drinking beer with three other equally soft looking techies. My gut says he's a dead end. I think we should cut his throat and dump him on the side of the road. Minimize our losses."

Farrington's voice rose as he made the last statement, turning nearly every head in the operations center, including Copley's.

"If you think he's a dead end, then dump him in the river," she said.

"Understood. We'll snip his fingers and cut off his face to buy us some time," said Farrington.

"What the fuck?" said one of the analysts near Bauer.

Bauer held out a finger to the analyst and cocked her head. They could all hear some pleading and fast-talking from the Frankfurt end of the connection, followed by an angry, muffled voice. Ten seconds later, Farrington's voice echoed through the operations center.

"He thinks he knows the group we're looking for at DBM, and I don't think he's connected with them. He seems more concerned that the group will retaliate against him," said Farrington.

"You can assure him that the group won't be a problem. Give me some time to verify Mazari's story. Can your team work with Mazari to identify the others?"

"Affirmative. We have full access to DBM thanks to Mazari's laptop...hold on a second...we have an address. All four of them are listed at the same location."

"How far away are you?" said Bauer.

"Not far. Ten minutes," replied Farrington.

"Excellent. Do whatever it takes to secure information regarding the shipments. Keep in mind that the FBI has tracked down two of the shipment batches, accounting for thirty-eight of the fifty-eight canisters Reznikov claims to have produced. Reznikov used two canisters in Russia, leaving eighteen shipped to an unknown location. You might be able to leverage the fact that several Al Qaeda cells in the U.S. were terminated by an unknown group. No canisters were recovered at any of the locations," said Bauer.

"Understood. I'll advise when we are in position. What do you really want me to do with Mazari?" said Farrington.

"Let me verify enough of his story to justify his release. I'm not sure how our system missed the fact that one of the Al Qaeda travelling companions is his cousin. Be prepared to drop him off with cab fare."

"Sounds like a plan. We're headed to the new target location," said Farrington, ending the call.

Copley muffled a laugh.

"You had me worried there for a few seconds," he said.

"I'm starting to gain a better understanding and appreciation for how Sanderson's people work," said Bauer, wondering if that statement would ever resurface in a Congressional hearing.

"Keep a tight leash on that crew. Get the information required and pull them out. Their presence on foreign soil is a major liability for us, and it's only a matter of time before Stockholm catches up to them...and us," said Copley.

"I understand, sir."

Copley nodded his approval before turning to the watch officer, who quickly authorized his departure from the "fishbowl." Bauer let out a sigh of relief. She could feel the tension ease in the room as the door hissed shut, sealing them off from their director. His visit had been perfectly timed, leaving no doubt in her mind that it had been purposely planned. She constantly updated the director's digital feed from her computer terminal, so he would have known that Manning was in a separate meeting, and that the operation was in a critical phase requiring an enhanced level of accountability.

His presence had assured everyone in the room that he directly approved the methods employed by Sanderson's team, thereby diverting the undercurrent of doubt that had started to rise within the operations center.

Like static electricity, this undercurrent would slowly build up again and be discharged by another well timed visit. Even as the deputy director of the National Clandestine Service, she didn't have the clout or seniority to diffuse it herself. She just hoped that her boss, Thomas Manning, could do it. She didn't relish the prospect of frequent visits from Copley.

Chapter 6

8:32 PM
Niederrad District
Frankfurt, Germany

Reinhard Klinkman turned the van off Goldstein Strasse and eased into a parking space just past the corner of Schwarzwald Strasse.

"Drop him off here," said Farrington, glancing behind them at the intersection.

Petrovich opened the right side sliding door and gestured to the open pavement.

"Here? We're south of the river?" said Mazari, hesitant to step out of the van.

"Would you prefer we dump you in the river?" said Petrovich.

"Fuck you guys," he said, hopping out of the van.

"I don't suppose I'll be getting my laptop back?"

Petrovich slid the door shut in the middle of Mazari's sentence.

"I'd get as far from here as possible. Remember, the river is always an option if you decide to contact the police. Take the train back to your apartment and stay there until it's time for work tomorrow. Fuck with me on this and you're a dead man. Got it?" said Farrington through the front passenger window.

"Yeah, I understand," said Mazari, barely raising his head to display a combined look of contempt and fear. "Not every Muslim is a terrorist."

"No. But every terrorist seems to be a Muslim," said Farrington, tossing Mazari's wallet out of the window onto the sidewalk.

The van sped away toward the new target building a few blocks west, which would prove to be a more complicated operation than Mazari's abduction. They now possibly faced an organized, highly trained Al Qaeda cell. Using Mazari's laptop as a breach point, the electronics warfare team based out of the second van had gained full, permanent access to DBM's computer network. Database records showed that the three men identified by Mazari lived in the same apartment on Jugenheimer Strasse. Two of them worked in the same department. Shipping. The third held a late shift job in the medical specimen-packaging department.

One of the two men, Naeem Hassan, worked in a supervisory role within the shipping and distribution department, which identified him as the most likely leader of the suspected terrorist cell. Of the three Egyptian men, he was the only one that had finished college, earning an engineering degree in Cairo. Six years later, he moved to Hamburg and started work on an advanced degree in construction engineering at "Terrorist U," but discontinued studies upon accepting his current position at Deutsche BioMedizinische.

Hassan's travel pattern didn't raise the same red flags as Mazari's, but a search of Egyptian databases showed that Hassan had bounced around from one unemployment line to the next during his six years in Egypt. Six long years of social humiliation, no doubt blamed on the West by the dangerous proliferation of radical Mullahs preaching jihad. Plenty of time to be radicalized by Al Qaeda recruiters and sent forth into Europe.

At this point, Hassan had been in Germany for nearly three years, while the other two men had been issued student visas last summer to attend Frankfurt Technical College. A quick search through the college's registrar database showed that the two had been dropped from student rolls after they failed to register for classes by mid-September. Notifications had been sent to German immigration authorities, but little would be done to track them. Petrovich wondered how many of these thirty year old college "students" simply disappeared into Europe, never to attend a single class. Too many, according to Audra Bauer.

Based on the information available, they would focus on Hassan. Ozier el-Masri worked in the same department as Hassan and would serve as their secondary focus. That left them with Hanif Akhnaten, who worked in the medical specimen packing department, which was a subsidiary of the Laboratory Group and a separate department altogether. His role had likely been limited to providing the appropriate packing supplies and medical labels to properly camouflage the shipments.

Working together, Hassan and el-Masri were perfectly situated to manifest and hide the shipments among the thousands of deliveries transported daily to the FEDEX hub on the outskirts of Frankfurt International Airport. Nearly two thousand shipments had been delivered to the United States on the day in question, and FEDEX delivery records for the seven known Al Qaeda cell locations didn't provide the FBI with a discernible package manifest pattern. Each of the addresses had received four separate shipments over the course of the day, giving them twenty-eight shipping records to examine.

Unfortunately, the twenty-eight shipments had originated from twenty-eight separate batches, which had been received by the Frankfurt FEDEX hub over a forty-eight hour period. The deliveries had been scheduled to leave DBM's shipping facility in a manner that had kept most of the canisters on separate planes while crossing the Atlantic, which appeared to be no easy task. FBI investigators concluded that this kind of timing would require a detailed level of information only available within the FEDEX hub, suggesting the presence of another Al Qaeda conspirator.

Given that neither FEDEX nor the FBI could discern a pattern in the shipments, Task Force Scorpion would rely on "overseas assets" to help them connect the dots. Petrovich glanced back at the black nylon bag sitting against the wheel well. He could definitely see using the contents of this bag within the next thirty minutes. He reached back and pulled the bag closer. Once again, they wouldn't have much time on site, but he would make that time count. Whoever left the apartment alive with them would be taken to the safe house, where they could go to work extracting detailed information. He wasn't hopeful that they would unravel the entire shipping pattern.

So far, the task force could officially account for the suspected delivery of only twenty-eight out of fifty-eight canisters, but they had no further leads. They just needed to extract enough information to get the FBI into the game. Even one more shipment location might tip the balance. It was all a numbers game. One link leads to the next. So far, the FBI had no links, which was an extremely frightening thought.

The team drove in silence for several minutes, arriving in front of 31 Jugenheim. Petrovich found himself once again staring down a long courtyard at what seemed like an endless sea of apartment blocks. Unlike Mazari's Gallus residence, the trees and shrubs on the street and in the courtyard blocked much of their view. Farrington talked with the surveillance team as Klinkman found a questionable parking space one building down from their target building. Farrington disconnected the call as Klinkman wedged the van into a parallel spot on the Jugenheim.

"What are we looking at?" said Petrovich.

"Luke says all three of our guys are inside. They ran traces on cell phone numbers recorded in DBM's HR database. GPS trace confirms that the phones are located about 70 meters from our current position. Fifth floor," said Farrington.

"Not good. We'll have to drag at least two of them down to ground level, and I doubt either of them will come along willingly," said Petrovich.

"Maybe we should tranquilize them upon entry. Klink can move the van up to the door through the courtyard. There's plenty of room to maneuver the van on the grass," said Hubner.

"If we drive the van up, we're going to attract a lot of attention, and Herr Klinkman will not be able to help with the takedown. We're talking about three guys up there, all likely Al Qaeda operatives. If we hit them with the neurotoxins, we'll have to wait a few hours to start the interrogation. We'll need some immediate shock and awe to impress this crew. From my experience with interrogations, the most useful information comes in the first few minutes, before the subject gets their shit together. It's either that or weeks of isolation and subtle mental games. We don't have a big window of time here. We go in hot," said Farrington.

Daniel couldn't have said this better himself. He agreed completely. They needed to jar the information out of them within the next few minutes. Even taking them to the safe house would decrease the likelihood of producing timely, accurate information. Daniel had witnessed some terrifyingly cruel torture based interrogations during his two years in Serbia, but most of these sessions had been designed to force a confession. Easy work compared to extracting truthful information.

"We'll need Klinkman in the apartment. If we decide to move them, we can send him down for the van. It won't take more than three of us to get these assholes down to the ground level. We'll have gravity on our side. Just don't get the fucking van stuck in the courtyard," said Petrovich.

"A little more credit for my driving please? I can pull the van through the opening between those trash dumpsters. It'll be a tight fit, but I can get this thing up into the courtyard. Straight shot down the middle. Looks clear on the other end. The only problem I see is that I'll have to turn us around in the courtyard. The other end looks blocked. It would be very easy for the police to bottle us up in this courtyard," said Klinkman

"It's our best option at the moment. We'll know if the police are alerted and can adjust accordingly. I'm hoping to get what we need inside the apartment," said Farrington.

"Don't count on it. If Al Qaeda trusted this crew with the virus shipment, they're likely to be among the best operatives in the Al Qaeda inventory," said Petrovich.

"Agreed. We hit their door in exactly six minutes. They're about two minutes from settling in on their mats for maghrib. Sunset prayer. Luke's team will confirm that they are deeply into reciting their verses before we hit the door. If they try to resist when we bust inside, Petrovich will use his pistol to disable or kill Hanif Akhnaten. That'll give us a two to one ratio to get the others under control. Stay alert inside the apartment. We need to keep Hassan and Ozier el-Masri alive for interrogation under any circumstance. The FBI is missing a big piece of the puzzle. This crew might be the only hope of piecing the whole thing together. Any questions?"

"Silencers for everyone?" asked Hubner.

"Negative. Just Petrovich. He's the only shooter unless something is really off in the apartment. Are we good?"

They all nodded and waited to hear from Luke's team.

⁂

Luke Fortier sat on the edge of a cheap plastic folding chair and listened intently to the array of police scanners arranged on the makeshift desk bolted into the back of the Ford transporter van. The entire cargo area behind the driver and passenger seat had been hastily converted for their use during this operation. A thick padded curtain separated the two areas, providing the team with complete privacy from anyone staring through the windshield or front side windows. From the outside, the van resembled every other compact van found throughout Europe, with the exception of the unique antenna array located toward the back. A trained observer would note that this very average van had an enhanced Wi-Fi and satellite communications capability, in addition to a combined UHF/VHF landmobile radio system. Fortier's job was to communicate with Farrington's team and scan every possible police frequency for any indication of a law enforcement response to the team's entry to the target building. The other two members of the team got to do the fun work on this operation.

He turned his head toward Ramish "Mish" Banergee and Alvaro "Alvin" Batista, who were huddled around three laptop computers sitting on the metal table jammed into the left side of the van. Wires poured down the back of the table, splitting into thick tentacles that snaked off in several directions along the carpeted floor, sending information to various electronics components buried in shock absorbent foam cases designed expressly for the purpose of mobile surveillance. Mish kneeled at the desk and typed a string of commands into the left most laptop. The middle screen changed to a view of the brightly lit, sparsely decorated room. Three men appeared near the bottom of the screen, facing away from the door. They all bowed in unison and stood back up, before dropping to their knees and prostrating with their heads touching the floor.

"Look at this shit. I'm a genius," crowed Mish.

"You got lucky. One in a thousand that they'd leave a laptop open for us. We have eyes and ears on target, Luke," said Batista.

"Looks like they're into a rhythm. Are they faced away from the door?"

"Yep. Facing southeast. Pointing directly at our van, ironically."

"I think they're planning on taking a trip. I see a few suitcases along the far wall. Check it out," said Banergee.

The screen zoomed in on three pieces of luggage stacked along the wall leading to a different room.

"The team is at the door. I'm clearing them for entry. Do you see anything on the screen that might get in their way?"

"I don't see any weapons or furniture obstructions. No unusual RF activity from the building or surrounding area. The team is clear," said Mish.

"Give me an identification line up," said Luke.

Banergee typed furiously and worked the mouse, isolating images and sending them to Batista's laptop on the right side of the table. Batista matched the pictures taken from the hijacked laptop with employee identification photos taken at DBM. The entire process took five seconds.

"From the team's frame of reference. Left to right. El-Masri. Hassan. Akhnaten.

"Alright. I'm clearing the team. Keep your eyes glued to that screen," said Luke.

He pressed a small button attached to a wire connecting his earpiece to a handheld VHF radio clipped to his belt.

"Room looks clear for entry. No obstructions. Three targets facing away from door. All identities confirmed. Upon entry you'll find el-Masri on the left, Hassan in the middle and Akhnaten on the right. Police channels are clear. They're roughly four minutes into prayer. Do you want to breach while they're on the floor?" said Luke.

"They're praying, right?" whispered Hubner.

"Yes. But the prayer cycle involves standing, kneeling, prostrating. Your choice," replied Luke.

"We'll take prostrated. Charges are set. Ready to go when they hit the floor," said Hubner.

"Stand by."

Fortier moved from his chair to a position directly behind Banergee and Batista, cramming himself against the side of the van behind their chairs and leaning forward until he could see the middle screen between their heads. Watching a live operation was an extremely rare event, and he had no intention of missing this one. Petrovich's reputation for ruthless brutality far preceded him, and given this terrorist cell's intentions, he hoped Petrovich wouldn't disappoint them.

"Put this on speaker," he said to Batista.

He watched the three men stand up as Quranic verses suddenly filled the van. He pressed the talk button for his handheld radio.

"Five seconds estimated. Three. Two. Breach!" he hissed.

The apartment door exploded inward, just as the three terrorists touched their foreheads to the floor. Petrovich slid into view first, with a suppressed pistol extended forward. Luke heard the distinctive pop of the suppressor as the screen became a tangle of human bodies vying for physical dominance. When the action settled, the three suspected terrorists were arranged neatly in a line, secured tightly to chairs taken from the kitchen table. One of them, possibly Akhnaten, was bleeding profusely from a shoulder wound. A thick line of silver duct tape crossed each of their mouths.

"Christ. That was quick. I wouldn't have wanted to be on the wrong side of that door," said Luke.

"This crew doesn't fuck around," Batista said incredulously.

&

Petrovich glanced back at the door, which remained open. Hubner caught his glance and quickly slammed it shut, relocking the knob. They hadn't detected a deadbolt, so it turned out to be one of the easiest breach jobs yet. A simple lock pick exercise and a kick. They had considered using a charge just to further disorient the three men, but given the fact that the men would be deep in prayer, they had opted for the quietest entry possible to avoid a call to the police. The apartment building on Jugenheim was different than Mazari's. The hallway extended the length of the building, giving them less privacy.

Once the door was shut, Farrington nodded to Hubner, who would lead the interrogation. Neither Farrington nor Petrovich could speak German, which was the only language beyond Arabic that was listed on their human resources files at DBM. Farrington suspected that their German would be rough, but given the fact that nobody on Farrington's team spoke Arabic, German would be their only common ground. Luke's team had a sophisticated translation program, but they wanted to keep this a secret from the men for now. Huebner addressed Hassan in German.

"Naeem Hassan, I will make this very simple for you. You have been betrayed by those you trusted. They led us directly to your apartment."

Petrovich studied their eyes. Hassan and el-Masri kept the same defiant sneer. Akhnaten's grimace of pain didn't shift, though he didn't exude the same purposeful menace as his co-conspirators. He was slowly bleeding to death from the bullet that shattered his shoulder.

"Your brothers in America have all been killed, and the virus canisters that you shipped to them have been stolen. This had been their plan all along. You were pawns in their game. Your leadership made a grave mistake trusting this group. Trusting anyone outside of Al Qaeda. Even the scientist who created the virus betrayed you."

Farrington nodded at Klinkman, who ripped the tape away from Hassan's mouth.

"Your brothers' plan for the virus in America is finished. All of them are dead. I can help you to avenge your brothers. I need to know the destinations for all of the shipments. I can account for twenty-eight of your shipments. Dr. Anatoly Reznikov assured us that there were fifty-eight."

Hassan's eyes just barely betrayed his surprise at the mention of the total canister count. Petrovich caught this and winked at Farrington, who tore the tape from el-Masri's lips, followed by Hassan's.

"I need an answer from you, Mr. Hassan. Will you help us? If you make this easy for us, I'll personally ensure that you get to meet the men that betrayed your brothers. I'll make sure that you are all sent to the same prison. You'll have the chance to avenge their deaths with your own hands. All of you. What do you think about this offer?" said Hubner.

"Infidel pigs. You are lying through your teeth," spat Hassan.

With Luke feeding him the information through his earpiece, Hubner recited the list of known FEDEX shipment addresses for each of the terrorist cells in the tri-city New York area. El-Masri's eyes widened and he spoke in rapid Arabic. He was instantly silenced by an order from Hassan, who barked at Hubner, "My brothers will not fail."

"Hassan, they've already failed. I'm not making any of this up. We may only know seven of your brothers' addresses, but I think it's pretty clear that the rest are dead and probably rotting as we speak. The bodies recovered by the FBI will be given a proper Muslim burial. You should honor the rest of your brothers with this courtesy," said Klinkman, in a calm, friendly tone.

"Your people will rape their corpses and defile them. This is what my brothers can expect in America."

Klinkman stepped forward within a few feet of the seated men and brought himself to one knee. He stared at el-Masri and spoke in the same soft tone.

"Last chance, gentlemen. If you don't cooperate, you will be tortured, killed and desecrated in a manner that will prevent you from entering paradise. You will be cremated and your ashes will be mixed with hot pig lard to coagulate and sit in a jar until reheated and served to the next group of Jihadis that we catch. I have a funeral home waiting for your bodies as we speak."

"Nothing can prevent us from entering paradise. We are pure," spoke el-Masri.

"You don't sound convinced," hissed Hubner.

"Do it," said Farrington.

Everyone moved at once. Petrovich raised his silenced pistol and shot Akhnaten once in each shoulder. The man screamed, but the duct tape turned the sound into a muffled, high-pitched moan. Hubner flicked open a four-inch serrated blade, which had been concealed in his right hand. He pounced on el-Masri as Klinkman yanked the man's hair down from behind, causing him to scream in agony and buck in his chair. Hubner braced el-Masri's head and started to cut off his left ear.

Hassan growled and tried to stand with the chair, but Farrington pistol-whipped him across the temple, collapsing him back into the chair. Hassan turned to look at Akhnaten, who was struggling wildly in his chair. He watched Petrovich fire a third bullet between the Akhnaten's's eyes, spraying the gray wall and flimsy window curtain with a mosaic of bright red clumps.

ক

Luke couldn't believe his eyes. Everyone in the van turned away from the screen, but the screams echoed through the van, providing a grim reminder of the work they ultimately supported on behalf of General Sanderson. When he finally decided to look back, the view provided by the hijacked computer webcam had been partially obscured by what he could only assume was splatter from Akhnaten's head.

"Turn the volume down at least," said Luke. "Focus on your jobs."

He turned around to keep a close eye on his own laptop screen, which monitored every local law enforcement radio signal they could find scanning UHF and VHF frequencies. The software he used would monitor and detect keywords inputted by Luke. He could also listen to the primary channels himself through his headset, which provided a split feed that he could control from the computer. One feed connected him to the team in the apartment and the other filled his right ear with police chatter. He turned up the volume for the primary police dispatch channel. Hubner's channel was silent, but that didn't surprise Luke at the moment. The crazy German was busy slicing off el-Masri's ear. He'd be shocked if someone didn't report this to the police.

"Shit. He just tore off the rest of the ear and tried to jam it down Hassan's throat," said Batista.

"Can I cut the feed to the webcam? We can do our jobs without it," said Banergee in a disgusted tone.

"Cut it. Keep the cell phone live."

Luke wondered what they had gotten themselves into with Sanderson. He had been approached thirteen months earlier by Klinkman, with an interesting proposal. Klinkman would facilitate the immediate funding of their startup computer security business, in return for discreet cyber services. They were told that the team would be used for "off the books" clandestine work related to EU security. Klinkman had been upfront about the legal issues raised by the kind of service required of the team, but this didn't bother Luke's crew. Even Banergee, who had started out working as a "white hat" hacker for computer technology powerhouse SCC Global, had no issue with the work. He had traded his "white hat" status for the less defined "gray hat" to join Luke and Batista in their startup venture.

The entire team had been flown out to the training compound in Argentina, to meet Sanderson and receive two weeks of intensive personal defense and firearms training. Luke had been extremely impressed by Sanderson's operation and the operatives chosen to fill the ranks. Research into Sanderson's past gave them no pause. As computer security specialists, a polite term for hacker, they were considered rogues by outsiders. Aligning with Sanderson further reinforced this notion. If Sanderson were a hacker, he would be the king of all "gray hats."

For the first time since initially meeting with Klinkman, Luke could tell they were all having serious doubts about their involvement. They had expected to violate multiple cyber laws in support of Sanderson's team, along with some basic privacy violations, but nothing could have prepared them for what they had all just witnessed. They could only hope that Sanderson's crew would get everything they needed out of Hassan, and that this would be their last stop in Frankfurt.

❧

Hubner backed away from Hassan after delivering a stiff punch to the terrorist's solar plexus. The man moaned in an attempt to regain his breath. Petrovich aimed his pistol at Hassan's right shoulder and fired, grazing the top and splattering el-Masri's face with blood. Klinkman brought a closed fist down on Hassan's wounded shoulder, causing the terrorist to scream and buck in his chair. Everyone backed away and let the situation settle for several seconds. Hassan raised his head with defiant eyes and Petrovich could tell that they wouldn't get any information out of him in this apartment. Hassan was a long-term project. El-Masri was their only hope of an immediate payoff.

El-Masri whimpered and rocked in his chair. The entire left side of his head was a gory mess from Hubner's crude ear amputation. Blood covered the side of his neck and saturated the shoulder of his white collared shirt. He wouldn't raise his head to look at them, which told Petrovich that they were close to breaking him. They needed to do it fast, before he became emboldened by Hassan's stoicism.

"Cut off his other ear," said Petrovich.

Hubner repeated the order in German and raised the knife. El-Masri protested in Arabic and German, begging them not to cut him again. Hassan stared lifelessly at Petrovich, while Hubner explained their situation.

"This keeps going until one of you gives us the addresses."

Hassan spit at Petrovich, hitting him in the leg.

"I guess your friend loses the other ear," said Hubner.

While Hubner removed el-Masri's remaining ear, Farrington slid the chair with Akhnaten's lifeless body in front of the two terrorists. He stepped behind the chair and reached into Petrovich's black nylon bag, removing a hacksaw. He nodded at Hubner, who explained what they planned to do next.

"Before we cremate your bodies, we're going to saw them into pieces to ensure there is no way for you to reach paradise and your seventy-two virgins."

This comment caused Hassan's eyes to narrow, which Petrovich noted with some satisfaction. This could be useful if they needed to continue the interrogation later.

"Mr. Hassan, you can stop his pain by giving us the address. I don't see why you're doing this to him on behalf of the people who betrayed you. Give us the information, and I'll carry through on my promise to let you avenge your brothers."

"I will never betray my brothers. Allahu Akbar! You will all die!"

"Wrong answer. Hit his ears," said Hubner.

Klinkman simultaneously slapped both hands against the sides of el-Masri's head. The man writhed in pain and Klinkman repeated the process. After the first few hits, El-Masri started to growl more like Hassan. He screamed angry Arabic phrases, which Hubner ignored.

"You're not going to have much of a face left in a few minutes. I want the addresses!" bellowed Hubner.

El-Masri growled words back at him. Whatever he said caused Hassan to break eye contact with Petrovich and turn his head.

❧

Batista leaned his face into the computer screen.

"Check this out. Translation of what El-Masri just screamed: 'Hassan will shit the addresses down your throat.' Do you think Hassan ate the address list?"

Luke spun in his chair and read the screen. The translation software was a top shelf program, leaving little to question about the substance of El-Masri's comment. He typed a few search strings into his own computer, looking for context. A few seconds later, he contacted Hubner.

"Fritz, El-Masri just screamed…and I quote, 'Hassan will shit the addresses down your throat.' I think he may have eaten the list. I can't find any Arab insults specific to defecation. This may have been a literal comment," said Luke.

"Only one way to find out," said Hubner.

The channel went silent, but they could all hear the verbal exchanges through Akhnaten's hijacked cell phone.

"Did Hassan eat the list?" they heard Hubner ask.

The van remained silent for a few seconds. None of them could see the response from Hassan or El-Masri, but judging by Petrovich's sinister laugh, Luke was very glad that they had stopped the web cam feed. He just hoped they would show some mercy and kill Hassan before they started cutting him open.

Chapter 7

9:20 PM
Gulfstream V Aircraft
Somewhere over the UK

Karl Berg drummed his fingers on the top of his armrest, staring at Anatoly Reznikov. The scientist sat upright in a hospital bed, his wrists and ankles restrained by thick plastic straps bolted to the metal bed. Two IV drips hung over his right shoulder, clipped into the bed so they wouldn't roll with the movement of the Gulfstream V. A portable diagnostic machine and defibrillator had been attached to the cabin near the foot of his bed, monitoring his vitals. A Langley physician sat in the row nearest to Reznikov, keeping an eye on the man's pulse, and occasionally checking his blood pressure. Reznikov was in poor shape to travel, but Berg wanted get him out of Sweden as soon as possible. Russian intelligence services were extremely well connected in the northern countries of Europe and he couldn't take any risks that could connect the U.S. to his abduction.

Part of him wished the Swedish doctor hadn't managed to revive the scientist. Reznikov had enabled terrorists to pursue one of the most twisted conspiracies in recent human history, all for his own gain. According to his most recent conversation with Audra, U.S. authorities had made little progress in their efforts to recover the virus canisters. If released by Al Qaeda, or whoever planned to use them, dozens of U.S. cities would suffer the same fate as the Russian city, Monchegorsk. Another reason to jettison Reznikov over the Atlantic and be done with him. The thought of U.S. taxpayers footing the bill to keep this psychopath alive didn't sit well with him, but for some odd reason, he couldn't order the man's execution. Berg couldn't shake the feeling that there was more to Reznikov's story, and he intended to hear the rest of it before the putting this mad Russian down.

"No drink service on an agency plane?" said the woman sitting diagonally across from him.

"Agency policy," he said and paused before continuing. "But I've been known to violate procedure from time to time."

He pulled his dark brown leather satchel down from the overhead compartment and unlatched the thick straps holding the cover flap securely in place. He reached in and raised a bottle of light brown liquid from the depths of the leather sanctuary.

"I hope you don't mind expensive whiskey."

"I'd drink moonshine at this point. It's been a long twenty-four hours floating around Stockholm like a refugee."

He studied Erin Foley's features for a moment. Her straight shoulder-length hair showed signs of waviness. He imagined she spent a significant part of her morning flattening and styling her uncooperative blond locks. She was attractive, in her early thirties, with soft facial features that wouldn't draw second look on the streets of Stockholm, or any Scandinavian city. Exactly what the CIA looked for in an active operative. No second glances. She'd been silent until now, which had suited Berg fine. The last thing he needed on this flight was a chatterbox. This one displayed a reserve he admired, especially given the bragging rights she had earned.

"Sorry about that, but we couldn't leave you in circulation. Not after you killed a Zaslon. The Russians will put this one together pretty quickly. He was the only one knifed on the street. It screams CIA," said Berg, removing two short crystal tumblers from a compartment along the aircraft's inner hull.

"I can't imagine the Russians could hold any leverage over us. It would put them in an awkward position," she replied, eyeing the glasses.

"Very awkward, but the Zaslon group is different. They won't let this one go so easily. Your image was recorded on at least two security cameras leaving Bondegatan Street. If you had stayed in Stockholm, they would have found you," he said.

Berg poured two fingers of the whiskey into each tumbler and set the bottle on the seat next to him. He handed her one of the glasses and raised his own for a toast.

"To a job exceptionally well done."

She raised her eyebrow at the toast and the two glasses clinked together. She downed half of her tumbler in one swallow, showing no sign of the whiskey burning her throat on the way down. She stared at the drink, clearly contemplating doing the same with the rest of it.

"You do realize that you just fired down one of the finest whiskeys every made. This particular single pot still was distilled at the B-Daly Distillery in Tullamore, which closed a long time ago. Not many bottles of this lying around anymore," he said, taking a measured sip.

She raised the glass again and threw back the rest of her $200 drink before staring out of the window into the darkness.

"Sorry. I never really acquired the taste."

Berg could see that she had finally realized what this plane ride back to the states meant for her career.

"You're not the first field agent to suddenly change career tracks. It's not an easy pill to swallow, but most covert agents find themselves sent home for mundane reasons. Blown cover, a misspoken word to the wrong foreign national…not many are sent home for taking out a Zaslon operative. You could have walked away from that street. Your job was done."

"I didn't see it that way," she said, placing her glass back down on Berg's faux wooden seat tray.

He poured her another drink and leaned back in his seat.

"I guess we got lucky. The one black-ops trained agent assigned to the Stockholm embassy finds herself in the middle of the blackest op in recent history. Drinks are on me," he said and raised his glass again.

"I'll take one of those," boomed a Russian speaking voice.

"Looks like our friend is awake. Please excuse me for a moment," said Berg.

The doctor barely glanced at Reznikov's vitals as Berg made his way down the cramped aisle. The scientist pulled at his restraints a few times and smiled.

"Where could I possibly go? This is uncivil," he said.

"I wanted to make it easier to wheel you out of the door over the Atlantic," replied Berg, dusting off his fluent Russian.

"Such harsh treatment at the hands of my new friends. I assume we are friends?"

Berg shook his head, wondering if the doctor would protest if he slammed his fist down on Reznikov's stomach.

"How's my new friend looking?" he said to the doctor instead.

The gray haired, tired looking physician opened a small black notebook and looked up at him.

"He appears stable. His heart's electrophysiology is back to normal, though I wouldn't recommend giving him a drink. I predict a successful delivery."

"Delivery? What am I, a slab of meat?" Reznikov said and pulled at his restraints again.

"That can be arranged if necessary. Enjoy the sunrise, if you get to see one during the trip. It'll be your last. I've arranged a dark cell for you. Well off the grid. You're about to disappear forever, after a lengthy visit from your new friends," said Berg.

"I told them everything," said Reznikov.

"They were working under a timeline back in Stockholm. They won't be in any rush this time."

"You already know everything. I sold the virus to Al Qaeda. The distribution center in Germany, the lists of addresses....everything. You stopped the plot, I assume. What the fuck else do you want from me?"

Reznikov's heart rate had nearly doubled in the past fifteen seconds, indicating that Berg had hit a nerve.

"We stopped the plot in Europe, but most of the virus canisters made it to the U.S. Your twisted ego and blatant insanity has put millions of American lives at risk. This doesn't put you in a good position. My superiors want to make sure you aren't hiding anything."

"I'm not insane," said Reznikov.

Berg could see that this was another raw nerve to be played. Reznikov didn't see himself as deranged. If he had any intention of discussing what Reznikov did to Monchegorsk, he was certain that the scientist would provide a "rational" explanation. The fact that he treated the sale of the virus to Al Qaeda so flippantly was a sure sign of his detachment from reality. He'd be sure to pass these observations to the interrogation team assigned to tear Reznikov apart mentally and physically.

"Tell it to your interrogators," said Berg.

He started to walk back to his seat to enjoy the rest of his drink, but Reznikov's next comment stopped him in his tracks.

"The program isn't dead."

He turned around slowly, pretending not to care. "What program?"

"The Russian bioweapons program. Weaponized encephalitis is just the tip of the iceberg."

"Are you saying that the VEKTOR labs has a full scale, active bioweapons program?"

"Why do you think they wanted me dead so badly? Why they're doing everything in their power to cover up Monchegorsk and blame the city's demise on an insurgent uprising. That's pure nonsense."

"What else are they working on?" said Berg, realizing that he sounded way too eager.

"I think we need to discuss my future living arrangements before I go into any more detail."

"A deal? You want some kind of a deal? We can torture the information out of you. It would be a lot less expensive, and wouldn't leave me with a bad taste in my mouth," said Berg.

"You can't torture that level of detail out of me, and you'll want the details. I can deliver the entire program. The major players, the facility, history, current programs…everything. All I ask in return is a comfortable place to live out my remaining years, and access to vodka. Good vodka, not the cheap shit. I've always wanted to live in the mountains."

Berg noticed that Reznikov's heart rate had almost returned to normal, which struck him as pure irony given the fact that he could feel his own heart through his throat. This confirmed what one of the Edgewood scientists had suspected, but only hinted about. There was no way that Reznikov had genetically modified basic encephalitis samples in a makeshift laboratory on Kazakhstan soil. The laboratory site discovered in the middle of the former Semipalatinsk nuclear testing grounds had been used to grow a virus Reznikov had stolen from VEKTOR. No wonder the Russians seemed willing to stop at nothing to kill Reznikov and keep samples of the virus out of western hands.

Berg suddenly felt exposed in the private jet. The Russians hadn't hesitated to shoot down the last private CIA charter to depart for the United States. He fought the urge to look out of the small oval window over Reznikov's head. They were as safe as possible over the United Kingdom, escorted by two Royal Air Force Typhoon fighter jets. The high performance fighter aircraft would accompany them as far as possible over the Atlantic, before returning to their base. They would fly unescorted for several hundred miles until met by a pair of F-15 Strike Eagles launched from Langley Air Force base.

He looked down at Reznikov, who wore a smug look on his pale face, wondering if they could torture this out of him. He certainly deserved to endure some serious discomfort for engineering the tragedy in Monchegorsk and exposing the rest of the world to his madness. Unfortunately, Reznikov was right about the details. Just knowing the basics about the Russian bioweapons program wouldn't be enough. They needed actionable intelligence, the kind of information that would require a comfortable setting and legal assurances.

"I have an idea that might agree with you," he muttered.

"No prison cells," stated Reznikov.

"No. This is a very different kind of place. More of a house arrest type of situation with a view. Small population. Clean air. If I swing this, you have to give me everything."

"You might not want to hear everything. How about that drink? Vodka is more of my drink, but I'm not feeling picky right now," said Reznikov.

"Sorry. I need to deliver you alive. Doctor's orders. Plus, I have no intention of sitting here and putting a cup to your lips like you're a nursing home patient. If the right people buy off on what I have in mind, you'll be swimming in vodka."

"I expect the good stuff. Smirnoff doesn't count."

Berg returned to his seat without acknowledging Reznikov's comment. He moved next to the window so he couldn't see the man's disgusting face while he tried to process the next move. Foley continued to stare out into the darkness, giving him a moment to himself. He'd have to contact Audra immediately to see if the Agency would trade a "retirement package" at Mountain Glen for Reznikov's information. He couldn't imagine the director turning down the deal. Until moments ago, even the CIA had no idea that the Russian bioweapons program still existed. He let his mind wander for a moment, performing an "all possibilities" assessment of the situation. A faint smile began to form as he delved deeper into one of the ideas. He grabbed his glass of whiskey and downed the contents. He felt the burn in his throat, followed by the warm rush that spread upward to his head. Maybe Ms. Foley had the right idea.

"That's a dangerous looking smile," said Foley.

"You have no idea. You speak fluent Russian, right?" he said.

She barely nodded.

"I need to make a private phone call," he said, suddenly getting up from his seat.

He walked toward the front of the jet and took a seat in a small alcove designed for privacy. He wished it was enclosed, and briefly considered taking a seat in the lavatory. The thought of sitting inside the cramped space for this phone call didn't last very long. He had enough privacy here, as long as he kept his voice low. He used the cordless phone to dial a number he had memorized and waited for the Gulfstream's MCS-7000 Satellite Communications System to connect the call. He purposely did not utilize the CIA's secure channel to route the call. He liked to maintain plausible deniability until the very last moment, and what he was about to suggest would require an incredible amount of deniability. Until the time was right, he didn't want any record of this call to exist. The line connected.

"Karl. I hadn't expected to hear from you this soon. Everything proceeded according to plan in Frankfurt. I just spoke with Farrington and they were able to extract a working list of shipping addresses for the virus canisters," said General Sanderson.

"That quickly? Maybe I should recommend that we send a few of our interrogators down to Argentina for some training. I expected this to take a few days," he said in a hushed tone.

"They got lucky. Let's leave it at that. To what do I owe the pleasure of your call? I have a feeling this isn't a social call."

"I wish this could be a friendly chat between two veterans of the war on terror, but I've just been told some very disturbing news. Reznikov claims that the Russians never really stopped their bioweapons program at VEKTOR. He alluded to the fact that he had been a part of the program before he went rogue. We had it all wrong. We thought Reznikov had been banned from VEKTOR for trying to informally revive the bioweapons program. I think he stole fully weaponized viral encephalitis samples that he helped them create. He said this was just the tip of the iceberg at VEKTOR labs."

"Jesus. Is there any way he might be bluffing? I assume he's looking for a deal in exchange for information," said Sanderson.

"Of course. We can't let him walk, but I have something in mind that should be acceptable to him. He won't give me any more details until the deal is finalized. If what he says is true, I might need you to loan us a few more 'Russians.'"

"How many are you thinking?" said Sanderson.

"Enough to penetrate VEKTOR, permanently destroy their bioweapons program and kill everyone directly involved in the program."

"This is going to take time. I'll start assembling a team on my end. I have two deep cover operatives within Russia that can start surveillance in Novosibirsk. They've been with me since the beginning. I can send five more trained 'Russians,' in addition to Farrington. I gather that Farrington's current team will do us little good on this job?"

"Unless they speak perfect Russian and can blend into the population. I don't think Novosibirsk is a melting pot of Europeans."

"Then I can send some of my greener operatives to augment the team," said Sanderson.

"It might not be necessary. Let's get a report from your operatives in place. Eight operatives might be enough, plus I have an agent that I can loan you. She's proven herself to be quite resourceful and deadly. She might be an asset for taking down laboratory personnel outside of the facility," said Berg.

"Sounds like a plan. I'll get everyone moving in the right direction. The Russians have really served us a shit sandwich here. The investigation stateside is about to intensify. The addresses acquired by the Frankfurt team will likely correspond with the assassinated Al Qaeda cells, and maybe give us a few that nobody has uncovered. We're working behind the scenes to augment the FBI's intelligence gathering efforts."

"Are they aware of your behind the scenes help?"

"Not exactly. Some of our methods are not on the approved FBI tactics list," said Sanderson.

"I don't envy your tightrope position over the FBI. One wrong step and you could find yourself back on the shit list," said Berg.

"Who's kidding who? My name is still on that shit list. They just won't admit it to my face. I just hope our covert assistance will be enough to help them stop this nightmare plot, before it becomes a reality like Monchegorsk."

"Well, you're not on the CIA's shit list, I can guarantee that. Without your help, I'd still be trying to push a crazy theory up the chain-of-command, while our government remained blissfully unaware of the looming terrorist threat. Be careful with the feds, you can't afford a misstep with them. None of us can afford that misstep."

"Thanks for the warning, and the kind words. I'll watch my back with the FBI. Apparently, I've made the FBI director's personal enemy list again."

"Not a good list to be on. That man has a long memory," said Berg.

"Tell me about it. I'll keep you posted on our progress. Will you be able to leverage any more help from your contact in Moscow?" said Sanderson.

Berg didn't like hearing Sanderson casually reference his contact. It was no secret that someone on the inside had given them Reznikov's location, but he didn't like to hear any speculation or assumptions regarding Kaparov's identity.

"I'll reach out and see what they can do for us."

"Understood. One of these days, I hope we can sit down and sip a good scotch. We both lost good people in this fight," said Sanderson.

"I look forward to it. Watch you back, General," he said and disconnected the call.

He returned to his seat and met Erin Foley's suspicious gaze.

"How would you feel about taking a trip to Russia?" said Berg.

"I was afraid you'd ask me that. Do I have a choice in the matter?"

"There's always a choice, but I really need your help."

"What happened to the Zaslon group that would stop at nothing to find and kill me?" said Foley.

"We'll have to drastically change your look and give you a false identity. I think the work I have in mind will suit you," said Berg.

"Dare I ask?"

"You have no idea exactly how critical your actions were yesterday. Killing that Zaslon operative enabled a chain of events that could prevent one of the most devastating terrorist attacks in history. If you agree to help me with this, I'll give you the whole story. We still have a long flight ahead of us," said Berg.

"I'm in."

Chapter 8

4:27 PM
National Counterterrorism Center (NCTC)
McLean, Virginia

Special Agent-in-Charge Ryan Sharpe stood ready to address Task Force Scorpion on the ground level of the National Counterterrorism Center's Watch Floor. NCTC's Director, Joel Garrity, had made significant changes to the floor's configuration for the purpose of accommodating Sharpe's task force. Garrity integrated his own personnel into the task force, to ensure a smooth transition for the multi-agency team working under Sharpe's direction, but still retained enough space and manpower to carry out the terrorist intelligence and analysis functions assigned to him by the Director of National Intelligence. Given the scope of the potential terrorist threat posed by the Zulu Virus, most of the center's energy and resources would be committed to Task Force Scorpion.

Sharpe looked up at the second floor scaffolding that ringed the entire Watch Floor. The second floor mostly contained offices that would be occupied by the various liaisons assigned to the task force, giving each separate agency a reasonable modicum of privacy. Despite the overall spirit of cooperation and transparency fostered by the open NCTC layout, each liaison would be given the privacy to communicate freely with their parent organization. In addition to a massive FBI contingent, his task force was comprised of representatives from the Department of Defense, CIA, Homeland Security, White House, Department of Energy, Department of Health and Human Services, Centers for Disease Control, National Security Agency and the Department of Justice. Garrity had run out of offices to house each separate entity and had modified a few of the smaller conference rooms to suit their purposes.

Keeping this task force focused would prove difficult at best, but Director Shelby had made it clear to him that the president wanted "all hands communicating" for this one. "No secrets." Sharpe had been kept in the dark about the attempted raid on Sanderson's compound, however, he now understood how close the raid had come to possibly derailing the CIA's efforts to track down the Zulu Virus in Europe. As much as he despised Sanderson and didn't trust the CIA, their work had uncovered and stopped the first phase of Al Qaeda's twisted plan. But had it been Al Qaeda's plan from the beginning? Information passed to him minutes ago by Phillip Duncan, the task force's CIA liaison, suggested otherwise.

"Do we have everyone? Mobile HQ?" he said to Special Agent Mendoza.

Mendoza nodded and pointed to an immense projection screen to their right, as they faced the group assembled in the middle of the Watch Floor.

"Mobile HQ is up. Everyone is present."

The screen showed a grainy, live image of the Task Force Scorpion's mobile HQ leadership team. The screen was one of several mounted to the second floor decking. The largest screen, twice the size of the others, loomed directly above and behind their heads. It contained a map of the east coast, featuring the New York tri-state area to the far right. All of the known Al Qaeda cell locations within the tri-state area were mapped in red, along with several yellow markers indicating locations of interest. He'd explain these to the group. A lone red marker suddenly appeared on the far left edge of the screen, in Harrisburg, Pennsylvania.

Sharpe was about to begin, but instead focused on an Admiral standing to the far right of the group. Next to him stood an intense looking blond woman wearing a dark gray suit.

"Who's the pair on the far right? The Admiral and…"

"They just arrived. The woman is Sanderson's liaison to your task force. Callie Stewart. The Navy SEAL is Rear Admiral Mark DeSantos, Director of the DIA's Strategic Services Branch. He's accepted full accountability for the integration of Sanderson's people into the task force," said Mendoza.

Sharpe kept his gaze focused on Admiral DeSantos, receiving a quick nod from the SEAL, which he returned.

"Damn it, I'm not comfortable with Sanderson's people on the task force. Especially someone right in the nerve center," muttered Sharpe.

"How do you think O'Reilly feels? She nearly lost an arm thanks to these assholes," replied Mendoza.

"Keep O'Reilly and Ms. Stewart as far apart as humanly possible. You know how O'Reilly can get."

"Better than anyone. I'm not too worried. None of the operatives provided by Sanderson had any involvement with the events two years ago. Agent Demir was seriously impressed with the team assigned to Mobile HQ. Moriarty liked what she saw too."

"I'm less concerned about the field operatives. Let's keep a tight watch on Ms. Stewart. I find it odd that Sanderson would insist on placing a liaison with us. Call me paranoid," said Sharpe.

"I feel the same way. I'll make sure they understand the ground rules when your briefing is finished."

"I want to talk to her myself," he said, turning his stare toward Mendoza.

Mendoza nodded as Sharpe addressed the group. As soon as it was apparent that he would speak, the entire Watch Floor quieted.

"We have a few new developments. Intelligence provided a few minutes ago by the CIA has identified and confirmed all of the addresses that received canisters of the Zulu Virus. Eleven in total. Ten of the addresses are located in the tri-state area. We already knew about seven of these locations. The eleventh address is in Harrisburg, Pennsylvania. FEDEX. Agent Moriarty, I want FBI rapid response teams at the three remaining tri-state area locations immediately. The data just went live on your feed. I'll coordinate a response for the Harrisburg location."

Kathryn Moriarty, Special Agent-in-Charge of Task Force Scorpion's Mobile HQ, acknowledged Sharpe's order with the word "understood." She didn't waste words or time like so many other agents of her tenure, which was one of the primary reasons that Sharpe had chosen her as Field Lead for the task force. Like Agent Mendoza, she was also one of the most capable and decisive agents he had ever met. He had considered sending Mendoza out into the field to lead the team, but felt his skills would be better served helping him run the show at NCTC. He had worked extensively with Mendoza on Task Force Hydra and had grown comfortable with the agent's unflappable sense of guarded optimism.

Mendoza had talked him off the ledge more than once. If the Zulu Virus conspiracy was about to take the turn he suspected, he'd need Mendoza more than ever before.

"At this point, we haven't recovered a single canister of the virus. We know that four canisters were shipped to each location around New York and that the rest were likely sent to Pennsylvania. Let's get with our FEDEX contacts and confirm this," said Sharpe.

"Already on it, sir," replied Special Agent O'Reilly.

"It appears that forty canisters went to Al Qaeda cells clustered in the tri-state area. Seven of these cells were already under FBI surveillance. A coordinated strike by an unknown force took down six of them. No canisters were recovered. One cell is missing and presumably retained their canister. We'll see what we find at the other three locations. Surveillance records have provided us with a possible avenue to investigate. One of the killers removed his ski mask at the wrong time and we captured an image of his face. This person has just been identified as Julius Grimes, a member of the fringe political group True America. A connection between True America and the virus is speculative at this point, but I want to dig deeper into this organization. True America is one of several groups that my team has tracked for the past year, and I don't believe this is a coincidence. They've been stockpiling high-end weaponry and recruiting ex-military types. Apparently, Grimes is a Best Buy manager by day and an assassination team leader by night."

"What is his status at the moment?" asked Jason Volk, NCTC Watch Floor Supervisor.

"Missing. He didn't report for work this morning. I have a feeling we won't catch any easy breaks on this one, ladies and gentlemen."

"Will we be putting other possible True America militants under surveillance? How extensive is the list that you've developed?" asked Salvador Guerrero, Homeland Security's primary liaison to the NCTC.

"Yes. That'll be one of our primary tasks. We'll start to break down these assignments immediately. My list of possible militants is a short one. As a legitimate political movement, True America has rapidly expanded over the past three years, with political action offices in every major city and thousands of volunteers. The early extremist views and calls for a government overthrow were quickly moderated as its popularity grew. Lee Harding, one of the group's founders, used to give speeches every week, espousing a violent overthrow of the government. Same with Jackson. As it stands, we rarely ever see True America's original leadership council. They've been replaced by a growing number of governors, legislators and public sector types that have pledged to support the movement to retake America in 2008."

"This is a vast, well connected organization. We'll need to move cautiously in the direction of True America," added Dan Moreno, counsel for the Department of Justice.

"Mr. Moreno is right. True America is a multi-faceted organization, with over twenty million supporters and thousands of grassroots volunteers. We'll need more than Grimes' involvement to take this outside of the task force. Currently, there is no detectable nexus between the militant arm and the mainstream political movement. We tried to tie the two together, but the sidelining of Greely and Harding severely hampered our efforts. We don't know if their vanishing act was purposely orchestrated to draw attention away from the extremist elements of the organization or if it was a forced 'retirement' imposed by mainstream leadership. Either way, it doesn't matter. The militant arm has been stockpiling sophisticated weaponry through several known arms dealers. They're up to something. Grimes' appearance at an Al Qaeda safe house wasn't a coincidence. More like an extremely bad omen. We'll start with the list my team has cultivated and see where it takes us. Special Agent O'Reilly will take the lead on this and provide tasking," he said, nodding to O'Reilly.

"The majority of this task force will continue to investigate leads related to the confirmed Al Qaeda network in the New York tri-state area. At least three of the cells are connected to Imam Hamid Abdul Mohammed, the radical founder of Masjid Muhammad, his own mosque right in the heart of these neighborhoods. Hamid Mohammed is without a doubt connected to Muslim extremists and has been under surveillance for years. He's been preaching to young Muslims since he arrived in the U.S. from Saudi Arabia six years ago and he is suspected of recruiting at least one of the men involved in plotting to blow up a police station in Philadelphia. The White House has been looking for a reason to send him to Guantanamo Bay ever since he landed on U.S. soil."

"This should be more than enough to bring him in for questioning," said Guerrero from Homeland, glancing over at the representative from the Department of Justice.

"We'd love to bring him in, but he never returned to his apartment after leaving his mosque on the night of the killings. According to the Newark field office, he vanished without a trace," said Sharpe.

"Has the FBI searched the mosque?" yelled Callie Stewart from the back of the room.

Agent Sharpe glanced sharply in her direction and responded.

"On what grounds? I would need a warrant to authorize a search of the mosque, and as it stands, I don't think there's a judge out there that would issue one based on my strong suspicion that Muhammad is connected to some of the men killed yesterday. The men attended his mosque, but beyond that, we have no evidence that the men are directly connected to the Imam. Quite frankly, we had no evidence that the men under surveillance in the houses were connected to Al Qaeda."

"Then how could the FBI authorize the surveillance?" she persisted.

"The Patriot Act provides us with an expanded range of options for intelligence gathering, with fewer restrictions. However, it does not give us the right to search Hamid Muhammed's mosque. Unless Justice can find me a judge that will approve a warrant to enter one of the most controversial mosques in the country," said Sharpe.

Before Dan Moreno from the Department of Justice could answer Sharpe's rhetorical question, Stewart continued.

"What if you suspected that some of the canisters might be hidden in the mosque? Are any of the missing cells connected to Hamid Muhammed?"

"None of them directly. The three cells with solid ties were eliminated last night. Special Agent Moriarty and her crew will turn Newark inside out to find Mr. Muhammed. If he's alive, we'll find him shortly," he said, not exactly sure why he was answering to one of Sanderson's lackeys.

"Unless he's hiding in his own mosque. I'd keep a close watch for anyone bringing takeout orders to 38 Jay Street," she said and whispered something to Admiral DeSantos.

"Since a warrant to raid any of the area mosques is off the table, we need to focus on finding Hamid Muhammed and the missing cell. Like Mr. Muhammed, the cell under surveillance on Sherman Avenue never returned to their apartment after sunset prayer at the Islamic Cultural Center. We have three additional addresses to investigate, which will add more names to the list."

"I have SWAT assets headed to each site. They should all be secured in under ten minutes," said Agent Moriarty through the teleconference feed displayed on the large screen to his right.

"We'll hit a good lead if we keep adding more data to the crunch pile. Any last questions? Good," he said, without really waiting for anyone to respond.

"I want to give Agent Moriarty something solid to pursue by tomorrow morning. It's going to be a long night."

Sharpe watched the crowd of agents, analysts and technicians head to their assigned stations on the floor. He was amazed how nearly seventy people could be swallowed whole by the vast Watch Floor. Once the group assembled in front of him had dispersed, the room fell silent again, giving him the false sense that nothing would be accomplished here. He missed the crowded, poorly ventilated operations rooms at the J. Edgar Hoover building, where he couldn't yell across the room and expect to be heard above the din of activity and voices.

Everything was different here. Everyone wore Bluetooth earpieces, which connected each person to both their desk node and NCTC issued touch screen phone. Using the NCTC application on the touch screen phone, they could access the approved external and internal directories from anywhere inside NCTC, allowing them to quickly communicate with any other station in the building or place a secured call outside of NCTC. The level of activity in the room would soon rival the New York Stock Exchange trading floor, yet he still felt like he might be interrupting someone's concentration if he used a normal voice to talk to Agent Mendoza, who stood right next to him waiting for his marching orders.

"Frank. Get O'Reilly moving in the right direction with True America and stand by to hit the ground running with any new leads from the three new Al Qaeda locations. We need to turn something over quickly," he said, glancing in Callie Stewart's direction.

"You could have just texted me that message with your new gadget," said Mendoza.

"You know damned well I don't know how to send a text message. And I have no intention of looking like one of those idiots talking to himself," said Sharpe.

Sharpe's earpiece emitted a soft electronic tone, which only he could hear. His touch phone vibrated at the same time.

"Looks like you have a call," said Mendoza.

Sharpe pulled the phone out of his NCTC issued holster and read the screen. "Special Agent O'Reilly." A green button on the screen said "Press to Accept."

"I just press the button on the screen?" said Sharpe.

"Jesus. Haven't you seen an iPhone before? How old is your daughter?"

"Fourteen. She has my wife's old phone," said Sharpe.

"Getting a little old for hand-me-down phones," said Mendoza. "Better get that call," he added.

Sharpe pressed the button on the screen.

"How can I help you, Dana?"

"No. I don't need anything. Just wanted to say hi," she said, waving from her station fifteen feet away.

"Are you kidding me?" he yelled across to her, attracting everyone's attention.

"You don't need to speak that loudly. The earpiece is really sensitive," she said.

"I can hear you talking at your station," he said, directing the comment at her crescent shaped work area.

"Frank, square her away. I need to speak with our new friends before they disappear," he said, brushing past Mendoza.

Stewart and Admiral DeSantos had started walking with an Army colonel to the closest staircase, most likely with the intent of disappearing into the Defense Intelligence Agency's office to discuss their apparent non-role in the task force. As far as he was concerned, Department of Defense (DoD) assets would be used as a last resort. He hadn't been comfortable giving them full access to the NCTC Watch Floor and their data stream, but the order to fully integrate DoD assets had trickled down from the very top.

Still, he needed to establish a few ground rules with Stewart and her minders. Director Shelby had given him a positive appraisal of the admiral, but was suspicious of the DIA's involvement. Shelby was suspicious of everyone, which was probably why he had survived the administrative and political game at the Bureau long enough to be named Director. He had good reason to be wary of DeSantos.

The SEAL admiral ran the Defense Intelligence Agency's Strategic Services Branch (SSB), which was essentially a legalized, "on the books" version of Sanderson's original Black Flag program. The SSB rose from the ashes of Sanderson's disgraced Black Flag program, allowing the Department of Defense to retain their own field intelligence gathering capability. Strict legislative oversight ensured that the SSB would never morph back into the black hole of misappropriated funding and undocumented intelligence activity that defined the Black Flag program. Old habits died hard, and Shelby didn't want Sanderson's people infecting Task Force Scorpion. The director already suspected that Sanderson had some key allies inside the Beltway. Allies that appeared enthusiastic about his return.

"Admiral DeSantos, Ms. Stewart, may I have a quick word with you in my office?" he said, before they started to ascend the stairs.

"Absolutely. I wasn't sure how you wanted to handle introductions, so we thought we'd sneak off and seek you out a little later when everything had settled down," said DeSantos.

"I appreciate your understanding of the situation, Admiral, but we need to go over a few things before the investigation starts to build momentum. My office is right here," said Sharpe.

He walked past the staircase to a wall of glass under the second floor catwalk. The glass spanned the entire back wall of the room, only interrupted by four evenly spaced handles protruding gently from the shiny surface. Upon first glance, the handles looked misplaced, but as Sharpe approached the wall, the vague outlines of doors became apparent.

The first level of the NCTC Watch Floor contained only four offices, two of which were permanently occupied by NCTC staff. The Watch Floor Director, Karen Wilhelm, occupied one of these offices. She was directly supported by six Watch Floor supervisors, who maintained stations on the floor and alternated shifts to keep the floor running twenty-four hours a day. In reality, she was the only senior level NCTC employee that required an office here, however, Joel Garrity, NCTC Director, also maintained a rarely used office.

Even today Garrity wouldn't spend much of his time on the floor. For the most part, his center would continue with business as usual. Hundreds of offices and cubicles forming the rest of NCTC would have no direct involvement in Task Force Scorpion's desperate mission. Garrity's Watch Floor had been essentially commandeered to house the multi-agency task force, which was neither unusual nor unwelcome for Garrity. Upon their arrival, he'd admitted to Sharpe that they needed to host more operations like this to justify the continued existence of their high tech center. For most of the year, he said the Watch Floor served as one of the most expensive offices in the country, with most of the analysts and techs working on tasks that could just as easily be accomplished in the cubicle blocks of the main building.

The third office was reserved for the president or members of the National Security Council. This room remained locked and empty most of the year, since visits to the Watch Floor by anyone from this senior group seemed limited to the occasional speaking event that needed a high tech background to impress upon the world that the United States took terrorism seriously.

That left one office for the task force leader, which could be reconfigured in any way to accommodate the person who would briefly occupy the space. He had asked that the office be configured for two people—himself and Mendoza, though he suspected that Mendoza would spend most of his time on the floor managing the task force. He felt that it was important for Mendoza to share the office. Though Sharpe was technically the task force leader, they had been called in together to form the task force and Sharpe wouldn't have been the least bit surprised if Shelby had given command of Scorpion to Mendoza. Mendoza had recently been promoted to a position within the Terrorist Operations Division that clearly outranked Sharpe's sidelined assignment to the Domestic Terrorism Branch, but the FBI still informally followed a set of antiquated rules that often rewarded seniority and favors over performance. He wanted to send a clear message to the task force that Mendoza was just as much in command of Task Force Scorpion as himself.

He swiped his NCTC key card over a faint blue light that materialized in the glass by the handle as he neared. The light turned green and he pulled it open for his visitors, who filed inside the office and stood to the right of the door as he entered. Sharpe moved past them and pressed a button on his desk, which brightened the lighting in the room, while simultaneously clouding the windows. Stewart noticed the change, glancing furtively at the windows while raising an approving eyebrow.

"I bet you don't have anything like that back in Argentina," said Sharpe, wondering how she would respond.

"It turned out to be a little more rustic than I had anticipated. This is more my style," she replied, smiling.

He eyed Stewart for a brief second, before the Admiral could introduce them. Callie Stewart returned his gaze with deep brown eyes that blazed with warmth and intelligence. He had expected the same cold, emotionless stare perfected by the rest of the Sanderson's rogue's gallery. The interrogation videos and surveillance shots collected two years ago still haunted him. Munoz never changed his expression once during his short stint in captivity. Images of Farrington and Petrovich proved even more disturbing, betraying no emotional response to murders committed minutes before.

Despite her slightly disarming smile, he suspected she was just as lethal and unreadable as the rest of Sanderson's crew. He could tell by the cut of her suit and the way she carried herself that she had an athletic, well-toned physique. Her blond hair was cropped just above the light blue, starched collar protruding from her gray blazer. Instead of suit pants, she wore a conservative length matching skirt. She was by far the most sharply dressed, attractive woman on the watch floor. He surmised it to be a carefully crafted look. She was already turning heads on the Watch Floor. He'd have to keep a close watch on her to figure out exactly why Sanderson had sent her. He still didn't buy off on Sanderson's sudden goodwill mission.

"Agent Sharpe, this is Callie Stewart. Former Marine Corps counterintelligence officer. She'll serve as our direct liaison to assets provided by General Terrence Sanderson. I've already gone over the ground rules," said DeSantos.

"Welcome aboard, Ms. Stewart," he said, extending his hand.

"If you don't mind, I'd like to go over them again. Please take a seat," he said.

Stewart spoke as she moved one of the chairs closer to Sharpe's desk. "I completely understand, Agent Sharpe. My role is limited to interaction between your task force and the operatives assigned to work with Special Agent Kerem Demir."

"Perfect. Everyone is extremely impressed with your team…"

"Thank you, sir. They're capable of undercov—"

"And everyone is extremely wary of exactly how this will work."

Stewart's expression changed slightly. He couldn't tell much from the shift, but she certainly didn't appreciate being interrupted with a vague accusation.

"Understandable. This is untested ground for both of our organizations, and given the history between Sanderson and Task Force Hydra, I can't imagine this sits well with anyone here. We're onboard to augment your street level investigative and intelligence gathering capabilities. The team we have provided to the mobile task force is impressive on many levels. Please don't let your reservations sideline them. Get them out on the streets. Get them into that mosque and—"

"I can't put your people into that mosque. I can't put anyone in that mosque right now, especially operatives that I am not yet comfortable with. Your people are part of an official law enforcement operation targeting Islamic extremists in the area. We'll work on getting a warrant that could enable this, but I wouldn't raise your hopes too high. Welcome to my world, Ms. Stewart. As much as I'd like to march into Hamid Muhammed's mosque and tear the place apart looking for him, we have laws to obey and procedures to follow. I get the distinct feeling that General Sanderson doesn't place very much emphasis on these concepts."

She regarded him carefully and he could sense that she would restrain her response.

"It's a different world for us, yes," she conceded, "but we'll play by your rules."

"As long as your people understand that, this joint venture should be a success. I have a few more ground rules for you. No weapons of any kind."

"For me or the field team?" she immediately responded.

"For either."

"That's unacceptable for the field team. If they're put into harm's way, they need to be able to defend themselves."

"This is non-negotiable. I have agents on this task force that have been shot by Sanderson's people. If we use your operatives, their involvement will be strictly limited to undercover work alongside real law enforcement agents. My agents will ensure their safety, and if they can't…then your people will not be utilized."

"I'll have to speak with Sayar about this. He's the team leader, so this will be his call," said Stewart.

Dressed to blend in with the local Arab immigrant population, Abraham Sayar and three operatives from Sanderson's Middle East team sat ignored in a corner office at the Newark Field Office, having tried unsuccessfully to interject themselves into the Task Force Scorpion's Mobile Investigative Team. So far, Special Agent Kerem Demir had been highly impressed with their potential for undercover work, expressing an early interest in deploying them near the Hamid Abdul Muhammad's mosque to start working the locals, but his enthusiasm had apparently been quelled by someone higher up in the food chain. Sayar suspected that the task force's commander, Special Agent-in-Charge Moriarty, didn't share in Demir's excitement. She had read him the same ground rules upon their arrival at the field office from Newark Liberty International Airport.

"As long as he understands that it's not his call to procure weapons for this operation. If they are found with any weapons, they will be arrested," said Sharpe.

"Even if they have legal permits to carry the weapons?" said Stewart.

"I'm well aware of your organization's seemingly epic ability to procure documents, but that isn't the point. If I say they don't carry weapons, then they don't carry weapons. Period. If I banned a special agent from carrying a weapon on an operation, then the same rules would apply," said Sharpe.

"I know your back is up against the wall on this. I saw the looks cast in my direction and yours when I walked onto the Watch Floor. Everyone will be keeping a close eye on how you handle the rogues. I get it. Will you at least promise to personally review the roles our operatives may be assigned, and see if carrying a weapon can be allowed? Just keep the option open. My people can be very discreet."

"I'll consider this request. Either myself or Special Agent Mendoza will review the circumstances surrounding their field deployments and make the call. You've been awfully quiet, Admiral. What do you think?"

"I think Ms. Stewart's suggestion makes sense. No weapons as a general rule. Each field situation could be proactively reviewed and the policy reassessed. I do think they should at least be allowed to carry discreet knives at all times in the field. A knife can be a great equalizer for an undercover operative if a situation takes an unexpected turn."

"I've seen firsthand what Sanderson's people can do with knives. No weapons unless approved by Agent Mendoza or me," said Sharpe.

"Understood," said Stewart.

"The second ground rule regards communications. All contact with the outside is subject to strict monitoring. No exceptions. I assume they confiscated your cell phone upon check-in and transferred all of your contacts to the new phone?"

"Yes. That was very nice of them," she said.

"If you want to talk to Sanderson or your field team, you'll have to route through a special channel that has been created just for you. One of my agents will monitor all of your calls. You'll pass no operational information to Sanderson. He's not part of the task force. Special Agent Demir will pass information to your field team, so there really isn't a need for you to do that either," he said.

"That's fine. I may check in once or twice with Sanderson, but I'll probably do this via email, which should make it even easier for your techs to monitor. As for the field team, Sayar is in charge of executing whatever tasks they are given. If he's not getting the information he needs, he'll let me know, and I'll bring it up with you or agent Mendoza," she said.

"Why exactly are you here?" said Sharpe.

"Because someone at a much higher pay grade than either of us thinks that Sanderson's assets could prove decisive to the task force's success. I'm here to make sure they're employed at these decisive moments."

"Which brings me to ground rule number three. I don't want you walking the floor and sticking your nose into everyone's business. These people still see you as an agent of the enemy, presidential pardon aside. Barely two years ago, Sanderson crippled the most promising counterterrorist investigation in FBI history, severely injuring dozens of FBI agents and police officers in the process. On top of that, his agents ruthlessly killed an off duty police officer, several civilian military contractors and a loyal DIA employee in the process of accomplishing Sanderson's mission, which turned out to be little more than a cover up of information," he said, turning to DeSantos.

"The less time you spend out there, the better. You can access all posted workflow from the Department of Defense's office on the second level. I expect you to stay close to that office. If we need your expertise in a planning session, I'll teleconference you into the meeting. I need to keep the task force focused on the investigation, and your presence here is already enough of a distraction. Stay out of sight."

"I hope to find bathrooms on the second floor, where I will be sequestered. I don't want to have to use the office waste can out of desperation. I've used worse in the field, but this is such a nice place," she said.

Admiral DeSantos stifled a laugh, but couldn't suppress a sly smile.

"Figures. All of the women assigned to my task force are professional comedians."

"I thought they beat that out of probationary agents in Quantico," said Stewart.

"And I thought the same about the Marine Corps," he said.

"Some personality traits can't be removed, no matter how hard they try. I won't get in your way here. If it makes a difference to your team, you can let them know that I joined Sanderson's crew four months ago as a consultant. I've spent about three weeks at his compound, where his planning staff brought me up to speed on their capabilities, and I briefly joined teams in the field to make a firsthand assessment. I was contacted yesterday regarding this assignment."

"Where do you currently work? I didn't see that in your background," asked Sharpe.

"A small think tank right here in D.C. That's all I can say," she said.

"Great. More secrets. Are we clear on the ground rules?"

"Crystal clear, Agent Sharpe."

"Perfect. Admiral DeSantos, will you be staying with us for the duration?"

"Negative. Colonel Hanson, the Special Operations liaison, will remain onsite to represent the Department of Defense. I'll get her settled in upstairs before I leave. I'll be back and forth as my schedule permits," he said.

"Very well. I'll get to work on a snack station with coffee for you on the second floor. Toilets are up there, to the right of the staircase you were about to use," said Sharpe.

Stewart nodded and smiled, before following DeSantos out of the office. Sharpe was surprised that she agreed to his stipulations so easily. He had expected more resistance to this demand. In truth, the entire conversation had played out more smoothly than he had envisioned. He had secretly hoped that she would refuse to abide by his rules, giving him solid ground to remove her from NCTC. Instead, she had been agreeable, almost pleasant even.

He had been surprised to learn that she wasn't a permanent part of Sanderson's entourage and still wasn't sure what to make of this disclosure. Her current employer was a mystery that a basic background check hadn't resolved, though her security clearance had sailed through without issue. She had provided his administrative personnel with a phone number that had apparently satisfied all of their requirements, without disclosing any information. He'd asked O'Reilly to dig further, but she came back with the same results. She'd never seen anything like this before, but agreed that it was completely legitimate. Callie Stewart, former Marine counterintelligence officer, worked for a highly secretive, extremely well connected private group within the Beltway. He didn't like it.

He activated his computer screen and selected O'Reilly's name from the communications directory. His earpiece came to life with the sound of a ring tone.

"Panera Bread. Will this be for pickup?" he heard.

"I'm sorry. What the…I think…"

"Just messing with you, boss. What's up?" she said.

"Do you see the two walking up the stairs by my office?"

"The snake charmer and his cobra?"

"Don't worry. Admiral DeSantos will make sure she stays in her basket," he said.

"Good. Because if I run into her in the bathroom down here, I might not be able to restrain myself.".

"She'll be using the second floor bathroom."

"You better keep the ladies room down here clear for me. You don't want me wandering upstairs."

"She's under orders to steer clear of the task force personnel, and you're now under orders to stay away from her. Are we clear on that?" he said.

"Yes. Is that why you called, sir?"

"No. I need you to personally track her communications. I don't trust her any more than you do. You can tap into her communications node. I don't expect you to monitor her calls and emails live, but I want you to review them as soon as possible. She's not to pass operational information to Sanderson. If she violates that rule, she's out of here. I also want to know what she's telling the field team."

"Easy enough. I'll brief you as soon as I review any outgoing communications."

"Thank you, Dana. I'll be out on the floor in a few minutes," he said.

"Sir, I think the whole purpose of this communication system is to keep you in your office."

"Am I really that bad?"

"Better than Mendoza," she admitted.

"I presume he's standing right next to you?"

"Of course. I just texted him the context of our conversation. He looks confused. This is too much fun for me. Technology is like old guys' kryptonite. You should see him fumbling with his phone, while trying to interpret my veiled insults. How long are we going to be trapped in this room?"

"Too long. Now get back to work."

Callie Stewart walked along the second floor catwalk with Admiral DeSantos. Neither of them said a word until they had entered the Department of Defense's assigned office and closed the door. The office had been configured with two sparse inward facing workstations that occupied the rear half of the space. One of the workstations had been labeled with a placard reading "DIA," which she would share with DeSantos, and the other read "SOCOM." A small couch had been pushed up against the floor to ceiling window at the front, crowded against a small wire and glass end table. She stepped several feet into the crowded office and turned to the window, hoping the glass had been equipped with the same privacy feature as Sharpe's office.

"How was my performance?"

"Convincing. I think he expected more of a fight, but that would have given him a reason to boot you off the task force. I think you skirted the line appropriately with a few well placed, sarcastic comments. I guarantee they'll be watching your calls closely."

"Our people have full access to their system, so they won't be able to spy on me unless I want them to," she said.

"Already?" he said, staring at her with a look of disbelief.

"I'm pretty sure Sanderson's people had full access even before we went into Sharpe's office."

"I probably don't want to know how you pulled that off."

One of her first acts of subterfuge upon arriving was a little sleight of hand trick. She knew about NCTC procedure better than most of the members of the task force, having spent plenty of time here in the course of her duties at Aegis Corporation. Of course, nobody assigned to Task Force Scorpion was aware of this, and any of the duty personnel assigned to NCTC would be strictly forbidden to mention it. She knew that the NCTC check-in technicians would kindly transfer all of her cell phone contacts to the "loaner" phone provided by NCTC. She also knew that this would be one of the last parts of the check-in process, which would provide her with the opportunity to pull her trick.

The cell phone she brought with her had been equipped with a sophisticated bar code scanner, which she used to scan her security pass card. Prior to surrendering the phone, she insisted on placing one call to her office, to give them her "loaner" cell phone number. She told NCTC personnel that her office colleagues might not answer a strange number and the task force couldn't afford to waste time squaring away the situation in the middle of this crisis. Everyone at NCTC knew what was at stake on the Watch Floor, so her request drew no attention from the technicians. Her call transmitted the security pass card's data to a Black Flag cyber operations team that had set up shop within a small office in nearby Merrifield, Virginia. The team wasn't sure if this would be enough for them to hack into NCTC's system, so they had given her other options.

One of the "contacts" transferred from her phone to the NCTC "loaner" contained a designer virus engineered to access NCTC's computer network. The virus would install a backdoor into the system for the waiting cyber ops team, while covering its own tracks with the latest generation rootkit software. Once the team had access to the system, they would download a more sophisticated and robust kernel-mode rootkit to conceal their direct access to the operating system. Since kernel-mode rootkits operated at the same security level as the operating system itself, they were difficult to detect and nearly impossible to remove without rebooting the entire system.

Activation of the virus had been simple. Before walking onto the Watch Floor with Admiral DeSantos, she placed a quick "check in" call to General Sanderson on her new phone, which was digitally routed through NCTC's computer system. Once her "loaner" phone started negotiating NCTC network protocols, the virus took off for its destination and her job was done. She chatted with Sanderson for less than thirty seconds, which was twenty-nine seconds longer than necessary.

She had checked the contact list on her NCTC phone upon leaving Sharpe's office, noticing that the contact containing the virus had disappeared. The cyber team had told her that they would erase the contact once they had full access. At this point, she could place and receive calls on her phone, which would remain invisible to Sharpe's surveillance efforts. She could also access Sharpe's desktop, eavesdrop on his calls and "attend" all of his videoconferences. She wouldn't have to do any of this, of course, since Sanderson had over a dozen operatives tracking Task Force Scorpion from his own operations center at the headquarters lodge in Argentina.

At this point, her job was to maintain a semblance of legitimacy for Sanderson's organization. She'd push the envelope a few times, as would be expected by Sharpe's team, but overall she'd demonstrate respect for his ground rules. Ground rules that had been rendered meaningless by Sanderson's cyber warfare operations, but would appear to remain intact.

"Sorry. Trade secret. And you never know when I might have to pay the DIA a little visit for Sanderson."

"I'll make sure we confiscate your cell phone before issuing a security badge."

"You saw that? Impressive."

"I'll be back later tonight with some dinner. The food here sucks and I'd hate to think of you eating alone. I'm not even sure Colonel Hanson will want to be seen with you. Looks like he's made himself at home in one of the conference rooms."

"And you don't mind being seen with me?"

"Well, it's too late to save my reputation. I was seen escorting you into the building," he said.

"Poor you."

"Someone has to take the dirty jobs," he said.

"They really hate Sanderson that badly?" she said.

"With a passion. All they remember is what he did two years ago. Fucking over the FBI was bad enough, but that's not what everyone remembers. He made a huge mistake killing Derren McKie inside the Pentagon. McKie had sold him out to General Tierney, who in turn blew the lid on the Black Flag program, so I can understand the feeling of betrayal…but he had the man killed right inside the Pentagon. Pretty high profile to say the least.

"Then one of his operatives accidentally kills an off duty police officer the same night, in the middle of massacring several Brown River contractors at a grocery store in Silver Spring. Not a good public relations night for Sanderson. He's back in the fold because they need him. Beyond that, nobody will touch him."

"I think they'll always need someone like Sanderson," she said.

"You're absolutely right, but I don't think the general will ever get to point where he can put a For Sale sign up in Argentina. He's stuck there. So, I'll be back around 7 p.m. with some Thai food."

"I can't wait," she said.

"Stay out of trouble."

"That's what I do best."

"We'll see," DeSantos said and left.

As soon as the door closed, Stewart (or Callie?) searched her desk for the controls to obscure the window. The last thing she needed was for someone suspicious like O'Reilly to glance up and see her talking on a call that didn't show up in the NCTC system. She looked around the room until she spotted a second light switch near the door. She flipped the switch down, and the glass fogged, leaving a translucent screen to cover the front of her office. Satisfied with her privacy, she dialed Sanderson's number, which was instantaneously masked within the system. Her call was connected within seconds.

"Nice job. I have full access to the system. I saw a request go to the Department of Justice to authorize surveillance at Muhammad's mosque."

"Sharpe and I had a little talk about putting people on the inside. He didn't seem optimistic about the chances of securing a warrant."

"At least he's not opposed to the idea. We can still get a head start on finding Muhammad with the two operatives working outside of the task force."

Sanderson had wisely chosen to send two of his best Al Qaeda Group operatives ahead of the Sayar's group, traveling under their flawlessly crafted false identities, well below FBI radar. Aleem Fayed, of Saudi descent, was the head of the Middle East-Al Qaeda (MEAQ) group. A former army intelligence officer, he had been marginalized for years until 9/11 brought the war on terror into focus. Fortunately for Sanderson,

Fayed had resigned his commission in May 2001, opting to help a forward thinking Sanderson recruit operatives for the Middle East Group.

Tariq Paracha, a native born Pakistani, was the second operative to join Sanderson, recruited by Fayed while still in college. Paracha's family had moved to the U.S. when he was ten; leaving Pakistan behind to put their engineering degrees to work, while removing their son from the ever tightening clutches of the Pakistani madrasa system. Tariq had been approached by Fayed in 2002, during the spring of his senior year at the University of Colorado Boulder. By July he was back in Pakistan, attending Madrasa school for six months to bring back everything he learned.

"I'll put Fayed into the mosque for now and keep the mobile surveillance team close by. Paracha is with the surveillance group and can join Fayed at a moment's notice if necessary. Unmask your phone and contact Sayar to explain the official situation to him. He'll put up a fight, you'll agree; but in the end, everyone will respect and observe the FBI's lead on this one."

"I know the drill."

"I'm sure you do. We'll keep you posted through emails to your phone. They'll look like basic updates to anyone that grabs the phone out of your hand, but one of the words will be linked to the real message. Anything that requires immediate attention will be preceded by an innocuous check-in call from me or someone at my ops center. Other than that, have fun on your little vacation."

"This is what I do for a living, General."

"Until I can convince you to join us full time down in Argentina," said Sanderson.

"Offering a full time paycheck would be a good start. I'll be in touch," Stewart said and hung up.

She had a good feeling about Sanderson. Everything about his group was run professionally, leaving nothing to chance, and she liked his philosophy. He was a rogue, a fallen angel thrown out of paradise for refusing to sacrifice his ideals in a world that rewarded compromise. He wasn't afraid to bend the rules to make the hard decisions that everyone else avoided, or tell the truths that needed to be heard to make progress. He told her from the very start that he "makes a living in that gray area, where the best decisions rarely sit well with anyone."

She liked the idea of working on the "outside," and secretly hoped that Sanderson would make her an offer she couldn't refuse. She worked on a consulting basis for the Aegis Group, so she could most likely fit her work for Sanderson into that schedule, but eventually she would run into a conflict. She'd risk her job with Aegis every time she stepped into Sanderson's world. D.C. was a small world, especially among private contractors working the counterintelligence circles. Worst case scenario, she would be "outed" to the Aegis Group, and they would blackball her in D.C., forcing her to join Sanderson's merry band of outlaws living in the pristine wilderness of western Argentina. She could think of worse outcomes.

She turned her attention back to the task at hand and dialed the six-digit prefix that would "unmask" her call to Abraham Sayar from the watchful eyes of Task Force Scorpion.

Chapter 9

8:25 PM
Mt. Arlington, New Jersey

Abdul Mohammed Abusir drove the stolen Honda Odyssey minivan down Howard Boulevard searching for the turn onto Old Drakeville Road, which would lead them to the service road that reached the Mt. Arlington pump station. They had driven past the entrance to the service road earlier, but couldn't make any sort of assessment about the level of security guarding their target. The Mount Arlington pump station was one of four targets originally assigned to his cell. It wasn't his primary target, but a drive by the Morristown pump station left him feeling uneasy.

The pump station had been located in a busy section of the township, well within sight of regular traffic. They could see a police cruiser parked inside the gate leading to the complex, which was a new development. This was not the standard procedure in America, and they had never seen a law enforcement presence during any of their previous reconnaissance visits to the four targets assigned to their cell. His two remaining cell members agreed that they should choose a more secluded target. All of them immediately suggested Mt. Arlington, located in the thick woods off Lake Hopatcong.

When Ghazi Hamar failed to show up for evening prayer at the Islamic Center, Abusir had placed a call to Hamid Muhammad's mosque and listened to the prerecorded message on the answering machine. The message contained none of the emergency code words he had memorized, but he still felt that something was wrong. Hamar had left the el-Halal variety store, one of their usual hangouts, in the middle of the afternoon to visit a nephew that lived in Elizabeth. He'd done this before on several occasions, successfully rejoining them for evening prayer. He had never missed Maghrib before. This was the one time they gathered without fail to pray together as brothers for the strength and wisdom to strike a devastating blow to their sworn enemy, the United States.

That evening's Maghrib was to be their most significant. Earlier that morning, Abusir had received a call on his cell phone that he had anticipated for months. He immediately recognized the number, which he had memorized in the hills of Kandahar several months earlier. The caller simply told him that the package would arrive at his apartment before noon. He knew what this meant for his team.

They would each take one of the canisters and hide it in a location unknown to the rest of the cell. This would ensure the continued survival of their plan if any of them were captured. As far as he was concerned, the arrival of the virus canisters signified the imminent destruction of America. He would take no chances with the weapons provided by Allah himself.

Hamar's failure to show up that night had been too much of a coincidence for him. He ordered the rest of his cell into hiding, to be contacted the following morning. He gave each one of them an envelope of cash and told them each to take a taxi to a motel and await instructions. In the morning, he called Hamid Muhammad's mosque and listened to the pre-recorded message on the answering machine. Something had definitely gone wrong the night before. The code words imbedded in the message told him to execute his plan immediately. He could only assume that the sudden order was somehow related to Hamar's disappearance.

It didn't matter. They would succeed regardless of the obstacles placed before them. They had been chosen by Allah to carry Jihad straight into the heart of enemy territory, and it was God's will that they would succeed. This much had always been clear to Abusir, even if their directions from Imam Muhammad had been murky at times. The Imam had served as a conduit of information from their network overseas, directing them through files imbedded in links accessible through the mosque's website or more urgently through the answering machine.

The recent slew of messages and activity gave him the sense that the timeline for their mission had been compressed. Two days ago, he had been instructed to retrieve an Internet document detailing several methods they might employ to deliver the virus at each target site. Over the past three weeks, they had familiarized themselves with the areas around each pump station, but beyond that, they knew very little about what they would find at each site. Specific details seemed nearly impossible to acquire. They had a black nylon gym bag filled with tools that they might need to access the water supply, and would have to rely upon the use of generic schematics to determine the type of system they might find at the site. Once they agreed on the system, they could trace the right schematic to determine the easiest points of access to deliver the canister's deadly contents into the water supply.

He turned the car onto Old Drakeville Road and slowed. Old Drakeville Road was an unlit side road and the service entrance came up quickly on the right side. He wasn't sure they could easily see the Morris County Municipal Utility Authority sign in the dark. The sign had been difficult enough to find in broad daylight.

"Watch for the sign," he commanded.

He had full faith in his brothers, but as soon as he received the attack order, he ceased to be their friend. He was their commander, to whom they had sworn their undying loyalty, and as such, he didn't *ask* them to do things. He *commanded* them. A few tense moments passed as they cruised slower than the speed limit. Fortunately, Old Drakeville Road was a little used side road running roughly parallel to Howard Boulevard and providing access to several smaller businesses that were closed in the evening. They were lucky in this regard. The area along Howard Boulevard was packed with restaurants and retail outlets, all doing a brisk business. Interstate 80 was less than a full kilometer away providing them with a quick escape, if Allah willed it. Abdul was not afraid to die on this mission. He had long ago prepared himself for this eventuality. There was no uncertainty regarding his place alongside fallen brothers in paradise, where a blissful eternity awaited the faithful.

"There it is!" yelled Ibrahim Salih, pointing toward a small, unlit sign partially obscured by thick bushes.

Abdul Abusir applied the brake and took the turn slowly, feeling the crunch of the minivan's suspension as they dropped off the well-maintained blacktop road onto an uneven gravel surface. Google Earth satellite photos showed him that the pump station was located roughly one hundred and fifty meters down the service road, which wound forty five degrees to the right approximately two thirds of the way to the station. Allah had smiled upon him again. He would be able to use lights up until the turn, without alerting anyone at the station. They would cruise the last fifty meters of the road relying upon the ambient light provided by the station. They would emerge into the pump station's parking lot without warning, achieving complete surprise. He couldn't imagine that the Mt. Arlington pump station would be more heavily guarded than the Morristown water complex. Even if there were three cars instead of one, they would cut through these infidel defenders with ease.

"Prepare for heavy contact in the parking lot. When we start shooting, I want it to be over in seconds. A prolonged firefight will attract unwanted attention and alert any pump station duty personnel."

"Allahu Akbar. We cannot fail," said Fahid Atef from the back seat.

Abdul glanced back into the minivan's darkened passenger compartment and saw Fahid cradle the shape of a compact AK-47 assault rifle. Upon returning his attention to the dusty gravel road, he heard Fahid retract and release the rifle's bolt mechanism, seating a 7.62mm round in the weapon's chamber. Fahid passed the rifle to Ibrahim in the front passenger seat and repeated the process with two more rifles. Whatever waited for them at the pump station didn't stand a chance. He was excited to the point of delirium that their final mission was at hand.

"Allahu Akbar!" he yelled.

<>

Miguel Estrada watched the minivan turn off Old Drakeville Road onto the Mt. Arlington pump station service road. Once the minivan's taillights disappeared into the trees, he opened the driver's door of the Explorer and stepped out into the cool air. The area was silent except for the distant symphony of spring peepers. He rested an arm on the open door and remained perfectly still.

"Do we call it in now?" asked his partner.

"Negative. We give this a minute or two," he said.

He took a deep breath and exhaled slowly. Abusir's team had been slightly craftier than they had expected, almost evading his surveillance team in Parsippany. Estrada's team had planted a GPS tracking device on the car Abusir had secretly kept in a storage facility on the outskirts of East Orange. They had discovered the car three months ago when surveillance teams started following Abusir's group. In Parsippany, the team drove into a corporate parking garage and ditched their Nissan Sentra. The move had been planned in advance, since entry into the business park's garage required a pass card. Estrada's team covered both possible exits and waited. Ten minutes later, they spotted Abusir driving a dark blue Honda Odyssey minivan. He couldn't express how relieved he had been to hear that they had reacquired Abusir. Losing him would have put Estrada in a tough situation.

They had little doubt that Abusir's group had been activated to carry out their mission, but knew nothing about their specific target selection. Figuring out Abusir's target was critical to his organization's plan. They had watched him investigate a pump station in Morristown, but nobody had been surprised when the terrorist cell passed on the opportunity. The pump station was located on a busy road, highly visible from every direction, with a police cruiser parked inside the gated facility.

Estrada had put his money on the Mt. Arlington pump station, after Abusir had conducted his own surveillance run down Old Drakeville Road two hours earlier. He had been so confident in his guess, that he had returned at dusk and backed the Explorer into a spot twenty feet into the trees and bushes, where he could observe the service road entrance without being detected by cars coming from either direction.

"What are we waiting for? We need to call this in and get the fuck out of here," said his partner.

"Patience, my friend. Just another minute."

They had chosen Abusir's cell for a reason. The Egyptian born terrorist ran things differently than the other terrorist cells they had uncovered. He insisted that they all live separately and take daytime jobs. Many of the other cells lived together in the same apartment and did nothing but wait around and draw suspicion from the FBI. Most importantly, Abusir's cell had not been detected by the FBI. Leadership had figured correctly that Abusir would take immediate action to preserve his cell when Ghazi Hamar didn't show up for evening prayer.

This had been important to leadership, since they had little intelligence regarding the interconnectivity between terrorist cells, or the FBI's penetration of the tri-state area Al Qaeda network. They had determined that most of the cells were under routine twenty-four hour surveillance, but they didn't know if the greater network had been penetrated. They were almost certain that Abusir's cell hadn't been discovered, but they couldn't take even the slightest chance. Once the FBI woke up to discover their handiwork throughout the tri-state area, any surviving cells under immediate surveillance would be locked down. They needed at least one cell to remain operational and receive Imam Muhammad's inevitable orders. This was critical to a plan that had been set into motion nearly a year ago.

Estrada's thoughts were interrupted by staccato bursts of distant gunfire. No doubt he was hearing AK-47's. He knew their sound all too well. The automatic gunfire echoed through the trees, distinctive enough at this distance, but unlikely to attract any serious attention from someone waiting for a table outside of the Cracker Barrel back toward the highway on Howard Boulevard. He'd have to make sure the local authorities took notice.

He reached into one of the pockets on his jacket and produced a disposable cell phone, which he used to dial 911. The call was immediately connected.

"I just heard automatic weapons fire coming from the Mt. Arlington pump station! It sounded like a fucking invasion!" he yelled at the dispatcher.

Within thirty seconds the call was complete, and he was headed back to Howard Boulevard. Both of his additional surveillance teams placed a similar call to 911. As he turned south toward the interstate, he dialed the News 12 New Jersey Tip Line, which would be the first of several calls placed to the media to make sure every American knew that their country was under attack again, and that business as usual in Washington wouldn't be enough to protect the public from their greatest fears. This would be the first step on a long, difficult journey to bring this once great nation back to a position of power and respect both here and abroad. Back to the True America our founding fathers had envisioned.

Chapter 10

9:11 PM
National Counterterrorism Center (NCTC)
McLean, Virginia

Sharpe sat in a chair next to Special Agent Hesterman, vying for room to examine his screen. Even with three wide screen monitors at the station, there was little room for him to see around Hesterman. He wasn't even sure how O'Reilly could see the screens through the massive agent. He must have been a linebacker at Michigan.

"Eric, can you shift about thirty feet to the left? I can't see the screen on the right."

O'Reilly immediately laughed. "How do you think I feel?"

"*I* feel like I'm being harassed again," said Hesterman, staring intently at the screen.

"Bring it up with the director if you're not happy. I hear he's looking for an agent-intern to work out of his office. Be a great career move," said Sharpe.

"Shit. I'd rather lick one of these crime scenes clean than hang out in his office for the day," said Hesterman.

"Speaking of crime scenes. Anything new with any of the addresses?"

"Well, I might have something. One of the new addresses is different. It's a small apartment with only one occupant listed on the lease, and Mr. Abdul Mohammed Abusir was not found with his brains adorning the walls."

"That makes two missing terrorist cells," stated O'Reilly.

"And still no sign of the virus canisters. Wonderful," muttered Sharpe.

"Whoever hit Al Qaeda didn't leave a trace, beyond Mr. Grimes removing his mask in front of our cameras," said O'Reilly.

"Still no sign of Grimes?"

"Negative. We're watching his house and the Best Buy in Union, New Jersey. I think half of the customers in the Union store right now are federal employees. The phone tap on his house hasn't produced anything useful. His wife has placed several worried calls to friends and family, but nothing that would indicate that she knows his current location. We're checking out anyone she called for a possible connection to True America," said O'Reilly.

"This is not good. Shelby's been all over me to make some progress here. If we don't shake something loose soon, I might consider..."

One of the screens at the workstation suddenly displayed an incoming high level alert, which stopped him from completing his sentence. The appearance of the message coincided with the buzzing of the NCTC mobile phone on his hip. He could hear several nearby phones buzzing, especially O'Reilly's, which was sitting on the workstation desk. Oddly enough, the buzzing was almost equally as annoying as the ring tones he had forbidden within the Watch Floor. Another damn "emergency alert," the thirtieth of the day that the White House situation room had relayed, containing information they already knew or didn't need to know. At least they were actively participating, instead of simply demanding updates all day.

"It's started!" yelled one of the NCTC analysts at a nearby station.

"Homeland Security just received an alert from the Morris County Sheriff's Department. The pump station at Mt. Arlington was attacked by three suspects at roughly 8:45 P.M. The suspects killed two Mt. Arlington police officers stationed in the parking lot and one Morris County SWAT officer before they were gunned down and killed by SWAT. Two Morris County Utilities technicians were found shot inside the pump station. They found three of the canisters at the scene."

The room burst into a hectic cacophony of questions and phone calls as Sharpe read the rest of the report.

"The canisters were empty. Jesus," he said, turning around to face the Homeland Security station. "The canisters are empty!" he said to Salvador Guerrero, Homeland's NCTC liaison.

"They know. Everyone's already moving on this. DHS, FEMA, Homeland...everyone," said Guerrero.

"Eric, inform Agent Moriarty immediately. I want one of our investigative teams out there as soon as possible. Dana, put me in touch with whoever is in charge at the scene. We need to make sure they know this is our show. They've lost officers and emotions will be running high. I need them to preserve the evidence for our own crime scene techs."

He reread the dispatch on the screen, but didn't see any reference to the suspects' physical characteristics. O'Reilly spun her chair to face Sharpe.

"I have Lieutenant David McKay on the line. You can pick up the call on your phone," she said and spun back around.

He took his phone out of the holster on his belt and pressed the green button to accept the transferred call.

"Lieutenant McKay, This is Ryan Sharpe with the FBI. I'm in charge of the task force responsible for finding the rest of the canisters and preventing more attacks. I'm really sorry for the loss of your men. I can't imagine how devastating this will be to the families involved. Let me know if there is anything I can do in the future to make sure they're taken care of. This is technically a federal operation and I want to make sure they get the proper recognition. I don't know what to say beyond that," said Sharpe.

"Thank you, Agent Sharpe. I'll take you up on that offer if necessary, and I appreciate the fact that you didn't start off the conversation telling me how I'm no longer in charge here."

"I can't tell you how relieved I was to hear that we had a Lieutenant on-scene. I can't go into details, but I need the scene preserved. I'm sending one of our crime scene units and several investigators out to the pump station. Right now I need to know if the suspects looked Arab."

"The only way these three could look more Arab was if they had wrapped towels around their heads. They look like stand-ins for the 9/11 hijackers. Why wouldn't they look Arab?"

"I can't talk about that right now. Thank you, Lieutenant. I wish we could have headed off this attack. I feel terrible for the families of the men lost tonight."

"Men and women. One of the Mt. Arlington officers was married with three kids. She and her partner were riddled with bullets sitting in their cruiser. Fucking savages," said McKay.

"Savages indeed. It's going to be a long night. Thank you in advance for the hospitality out there. I wish it were under better circumstances."

"Me too. I'll keep an eye out for your people."

The call disconnected and Sharpe patted Hesterman's right shoulder.

"How are we doing?"

"Moriarty is assembling the team as we speak. She hopes to have them out there before 10:30. She's keeping Demir in Newark to continue working Al Qaeda."

"Good. Mt. Arlington might generate a lead, but it will likely direct us right back to Newark. I still haven't heard a word from Justice about getting people inside the mosque. My biggest concern right now is that this attack may have just made our jobs even more difficult. There's no way the White House will be able to contain this. They'll have to declare Morris County a disaster area and go door to door to keep people from drinking the water. I don't know how they're going to figure that out."

"Kind of makes our job not seem so bad," said O'Reilly.

"Except we'll be the ones that get blamed for not stopping the attack, or any future attacks," he said.

Salvador Guerrero had managed to sneak beside them unnoticed. His voice startled Sharpe.

"They can shove the blame right up the administration's ass. One car with two officers guarding the pump station? What the fuck do they expect?"

"They're looking at too many points of vulnerability to guard. Water towers. Pipelines. Some towns have multiple pump stations. Every law enforcement officer in America would be occupied. The president activated the National Guard and Army Reserve, but the attack came too fast," said Sharpe.

"They could have directed state and local authorities to properly defend these sites while the Guard and Reserves mobilized. Wait until you see what happens next. Once this hits the media, they'll start stationing infantry platoons at each site. Standby for operation knee jerk. This is going to be a complete fiasco by the time we wake up tomorrow."

"Who said we'd be going to sleep?" said Sharpe.

"Good point. Let me know if there's anything I can do on my end. The best we can do is figure out how to stop the next imminent attack. There's still one more terrorist cell missing," said Guerrero.

"We're still missing fifty-five canisters. I hate to say it, but one missing Al Qaeda cell is the least of our problems," said Sharpe.

"True. But I get the feeling we'll have some time before we have to worry about the majority of those canisters. The cell that hit Mt. Arlington either panicked and struck early, or was given last minute orders based on the near elimination of the entire network. My money is on the latter option. The remaining cell could be out there right now casing their target…or targets."

"Hopefully, we'll get something from Mt. Arlington that will put the last Al Qaeda cell out of business, so we can concentrate on the extent of True America's involvement," said Sharpe.

"You know that group better than anyone in this room. If True America is involved, we have an even bigger problem. Only God himself knows what they might have planned for those canisters."

"My hope is that they plan to hand the canisters over to the government. The best-case scenario is that they orchestrated this as a huge publicity stunt to show the American people that they are truly America's new heroes. We have an election year coming up, and the word on the street is that they are consolidating political power to make a move in 2008."

"What's the worst case scenario?" said Guerrero.

"The worst case scenario is they are planning to destabilize the country through terrorism."

"Which one is your money on?"

"Somewhere between the two, leaning toward the worst case scenario. True America's spin-doctors have done a great job distancing the movement's public face from the group's original founders. Just five years ago, Jackson Greely and Lee Harding regularly took to the streets decrying government tyranny and demanding a quick, violent overthrow. We found literature published by these two going back decades. They've been on Uncle Sam's radar for a long time as domestic terrorist threats. Over the past three to four years, the two have faded into the sunset, orchestrated by the more savvy visible leadership currently cruising around the country in their True America tour buses."

"Why would they agree to step down if this was their movement from the beginning?"

"My sources say they haven't stepped down from anything, aside from the podium. True America's political action arm takes in millions of dollars in grass roots donations every month. There's a sea of people hungry for the kind of change at the core of True America's manifesto, but Greely and

Harding's visions of a violent overthrow kept the organization pinned to the ground. Wallets have a tendency to snap shut when either of those two appears in front of the True America banner. If Greely or Harding is behind the theft of the virus canisters, I wouldn't expect True America to hand them over in an expression of good will."

His cell phone buzzed in his hand and he glanced at the message on its screen.

"Any word on the mosque request?" read the message sent from Callie Stewart.

Sharpe glanced up at the black metal catwalk and saw Stewart leaning on the rail, smiling down on him from a distance and waving with her phone. He shook his head and typed a quick response. He hadn't heard anything from Justice. Two additional requests had been sent up through their NCTC liaison, but nothing had come back. Maybe the recent attack on the Mt. Arlington pump station would loosen their interpretations of the Patriot Act. He looked up at Stewart again, secretly wishing he could authorize her to send some of Sanderson's operatives into the mosque. He hated himself for thinking this, but he had an extremely bad feeling about the next few days. Mt. Arlington had the potential to be the very beginning of a national nightmare.

He felt slightly lucky at the moment. There was little they could have done to prevent the attack, and the emergency response was out of his hands. He didn't envy the task lying ahead for the state and federal agencies responsible for safeguarding the lives of the citizens who might have been exposed to the contaminated water from the Mt. Arlington station. His job was to prevent the next attack.

Chapter 11

9:20 PM
Masjid (Mosque) Muhammad
Newark, New Jersey

Aleem Fayed remained seated long after the last of the mosque's devoted had left the modest building. He raised his head and glanced casually in the direction of the Mihrab, a small, curved alcove in the northeast wall, indicating the direction of Mecca. The Mihrab appeared modestly decorated in comparison to some of the larger mosques he had visited, adorned with paint instead of expensively arranged mosaic tile. Everything about Hamid Muhammad's mosque emphasized simplicity. The small prayer hall could hold roughly eighty worshippers, shoulder to shoulder on the dark hard wood floor. He didn't see a separate prayer area for women, which didn't surprise him. Hamid Muhammad's brand of Islam didn't accommodate women, or most Muslims for that matter.

His Friday noon sermons were widely known as the most anti-western tirades on the east coast, often packing the mosque to twice its advertised capacity in the afternoon. According to FBI and police intelligence, Friday wasn't the only day he conducted a sermon. Two or three times a week, he would hold a more private sermon in one of the back rooms for potential terror candidates. Young men attending Muhammad's mosque had a propensity for appearing on the front lines in Afghanistan or Iraq, or in many cases, joining the ever growing population of Jihadist prisoners rotting in Guantanamo Bay. All the U.S. government could do was try to catalogue the men coming and going from the mosque, in the hopes of alerting allied authorities to the potential trouble headed in their direction.

Unfortunately, too many of the young attendees had simply vanished into thin air over the past few years

Tonight, all of that would change, if his hunch proved correct. He had attended all the day's prayers so far, from dawn to sunrise, trying to get a feel for the mosque's regular attendees. Attendance had surprised him at Fajr (pre-sunrise), consisting of a few dozen men who had clearly been there for some time. The number of worshipers increased drastically for Zuhr (noon prayer), but dropped off considerably for Asr (afternoon) and Maghrib (sunset) prayer. He overheard grumblings about the absence of Imam Hamid Muhammad, who had never missed noon or afternoon prayer unannounced, since anyone could remember. He attributed the lower numbers to their Imam's absence.

He had lingered in the mosque after Asr and noticed a group of three men waiting near an open door on the left side of the prayer hall. He saw a few desks inside the room, indicating that this could be the mosque's Quranic study room. A true believer would never put their Quran on the floor, and he had no doubt that the men Hamid allowed in that room were "true believers" in the most literal sense of the word. Of course, he doubted the men had come for Quranic study.

They looked edgy and impatient, continuously stealing glances past the minbar, the traditional raised platform for sermons, at the door on the right side of the prayer hall. He assumed this door led to the Imam's office. Their glances started to shift in his direction, taking on more of an angry impatience. The disdainful looks gave him the distinct impression that their new master didn't plan to make an appearance until the mosque was cleared. He gladly obliged the men and walked out of the front door, taking a left on Irvine Turner Boulevard. He doubled back ten minutes later to find the mosque's front doors locked.

Aleem stood up from the prayer sitting position and started to roll up his prayer mat. He glanced at the door in the far right corner of the room. In a few seconds, he would take the day's fight through that door, directly to the enemy. First, he needed to take care of a few impediments that had unwisely chosen to stay past Mahgrib.

"You forgot the final rakat," issued a voice from behind him.

"And you forgot your manners," Aleem replied in an Arabic dialect that would identify him as a connected member of a Saudi society.

He turned to face the three men he had seen waiting for the Imam earlier in the day. Through their loose fitting clothes he could tell that the men had not undergone any serious physical training in their lives. A fact that would soon change when they reported to whatever training camp Hamid Muhammad arranged for them. Three to six months of intensive mental and physical drills would transform these raw recruits into lethal instruments for Al Qaeda. Slightly more lethal, at least. Aleem Fayed stared at them, waiting for a response.

"Your family name means nothing here," spat the tallest of the three.

"And your family name means nothing there. It'll never mean anything, anywhere. I'd rather feast on a pig than shake your filthy hand," replied Aleem, stepping closer to the man.

He could tell that his comments had cut straight to this young fundamentalist's core. His ego was still in a fragile state, having most likely come from a lower class family in Riyadh. The incredible disparity between classes in Saudi Arabia fueled the fire that forged angry, bitter young men like the one standing before him. The Imams of the Kingdom had become experts in harnessing that anger and turning it against the west, blaming all of their ills on America and its allies. They preached their own ultra-conservative form of Islamic doctrine, known as Saudi Wahhabism, as the one true path for Islam to rise above corrupt western influences and regain dominance. On sermon days, the mosques overflowed into the streets with disenfranchised young men listening to the Imams blame America and Israel for all of their troubles. Frighteningly, this phenomenon was not limited to Saudi Arabia. Similar scenes proliferated throughout the Middle East, extending along the Indian Ocean to South West Asia.

"Watch what you say here! You can't hide behind the corrupt police and your inbred family here. This is our mosque. What do you want here?"

The two men behind the leader started to spread out slowly, in an attempt to intimidate him. The man to his right looked slightly overweight, wearing khaki pants and an off white, cotton button down shirt. His black hair was longer than the others', giving him a slightly unkempt look. Aleem wondered what the Imam thought of that. Aleem, however, was more concerned with the man approaching him from the left side with a murderous glare and a modicum of caution. Cautious confidence. It probably wouldn't matter in the end, but it was something for him to consider.

"I want the same thing you want," said Aleem.

"And what is that?"

"I need to speak with the Hamid Muhammad."

"The Imam doesn't speak with pigs like you," said the man.

"Is that any way to treat a fellow Muslim? The Quran commands you to treat people of all beliefs and cultures peacefully, and with kindness. I bet your false Imam didn't focus on that aspect of Islam," said Aleem.

The three continued to stare him down, moving slowly into what they perceived as the best position to attack him.

"Paradise awaits us as a reward for our faith."

"Oddly enough, I think you might still reach paradise. I think the Prophet will make an exception in your cases. This really isn't your fault," said Aleem, gesturing to the prayer hall.

The man on his right lunged forward in a terribly timed attempt to grab Aleem for his compatriots. Aleem dodged the initial attack, snagging the man's left arm and twisting it into an extremely painful position that he could use to maneuver the hefty kid to block the others. The leader sprang forward at a perceived gap that Aleem had purposefully allowed to exist, only to be slammed to the ground by the useless weight of his friend's spiraling body.

Aleem pounded his elbow into the fixed arm of the first attacker, cracking his elbow inward and eliciting a blood-curdling scream. He pivoted around the incapacitated man and delivered an upward sweeping kick into the leader's throat while the man was still on all fours from the sudden collision with his overweight friend. The sheer force of the kick crushed his larynx and dislodged his upper vertebrae, rendering him paralyzed. He would asphyxiate within minutes, unable to bring his hands to his neck.

He kept a close eye on the remaining attacker, who proved to be cautious as well as confident, staying out of Aleem's immediate hand-to-hand combat range. Taking advantage of the man's hesitation, he briefly turned his attention back to the screaming man on the floor clutching his elbow. A quick stomp to the man's knee brought both hands downward, exposing his upper body to extreme violence.

Aleem collapsed onto the man, bringing his right elbow down on the man's neck with the full force of his own body, instantly killing him. He was back on his feet within a fraction of a second, in time to see the third and final assailant back out of a halfhearted attack. The man had just witnessed the near instantaneous death of his friends at the hand of an enemy that spoke perfect Arabic. Aleem could tell the man's confidence had evaporated, replaced by utter confusion.

"Smart move. The Imam has betrayed the cause. You can't even begin to comprehend the level of his betrayal. My orders are to return him so we can learn the true extent of the damage. Can you help me with this? If not, you will join your friends."

The man stuttered, clearly in complete shock at the sudden turn of events. He saw the doubt flash across the man's face. His world had unraveled too quickly for rational thought. The next few moments would be critical for Aleem.

"What do you need?"

"Is Hamid here at the mosque?"

In the background, they could both hear the group's leader struggle to force air through his destroyed windpipe, an involuntary and useless attempt by the man's body to survive.

"Can he be saved?" asked the man.

"He won't be saved. Where is Hamid?"

"Through that door somewhere."

"Did you copy that? Any movement at the side exit?" Aleem said aloud, waiting for a response in his earpiece.

"Copy. Tariq is en route. Thirty seconds. Negative movement. If the Imam was in the building, he's still there. Sensors detect a cell phone within the confines of the building. Low-level emission."

"Who are you talking to?" demanded the man.

Aleem smiled at him.

"My colleagues. Who else?"

He saw the final realization flash in the terrorist recruit's eyes. When presented with another conflicting batch of information, his confused psyche had simply fallen back on what he wanted to believe, which in this case was completely correct—that Aleem worked for the enemies of Allah and had tricked him into betraying the Imam. He burst forward, quickly engaging Aleem before a sharp pain to his solar plexus dropped him to his knees with a sudden thud. Aleem kicked him in the back, pushing him down to join his friends on the floor. A pool of bright red blood spread rapidly underneath the pile. Aleem leaned over to wipe a small, serrated blade clean on the back of the dying man's, crisp white shirt before walking over to unlock the front door for Tariq.

Tariq Paracha slipped through the door, carrying a black nylon duffel bag. The pair immediately locked and bolted the door to prevent any unwanted guests.

"Allah won't be pleased," said Tariq, pulling a silenced pistol from the duffel bag and tossing it to Aleem.

"He'll get over it. Through that door. Did Graves find schematics for the building?" said Aleem.

"No. But one of the businesses a few doors down submitted a plan that required a zoning change, so he was able to download the scanned document. Looks like a similar layout from the front. We can expect a basement," said Tariq.

"Good. I'd prefer to do our work in the building. I hope it's a deep basement. If our Imam doesn't feel like chatting, we'll need to compel him."

Tariq hefted the bag up and down, shaking the assortment of metal tools contained within. "I brought everything we should need."

"Let's find this missing Imam, shall we?" said Aleem.

They approached the closed door on the far right side of the cramped prayer hall, ready to do whatever was necessary to produce a viable lead for Task Force Scorpion. Given the fact that Aleem and Tariq could proceed unhampered by legal or moral restrictions, they stood an excellent chance of success.

Chapter 12

11:14 PM
Wayne County
Pennsylvania

Julius Grimes had long ago lost track of where his van was headed. They had turned off Interstate 87, headed west on I-84 in Pennsylvania. The van had exited the interstate deep in the Pocono Mountains region, taking several obscure paved roads that eventually led to unmarked gravel roads travelling deep into the rolling foothills. He had been told by the driver of the van that they were headed to one of True America's most closely guarded sites, which added to his already highly elevated anxiety level.

He knew that he'd seriously fucked up at the target site. He hadn't taken his mask off on purpose, but it didn't matter to his team leader, Kathy Nadeau. She didn't say a word until they were several miles away from the scene. Even then, she simply turned in the front passenger seat of the car and suddenly extended the business end of her silenced pistol against his forehead. He had carefully weighed his options in the milliseconds that followed.

He could have slammed her hand against the headrest, likely dislocating her elbow and disarming her, but that would have put him in an even worse situation. Instead of becoming a fugitive from both the U.S. government and the most powerfully connected shadow network in America, he did nothing as Nadeau hissed a few berating words and removed the pistol from his face. She placed a quick phone call and announced that he would have to go into hiding until they could determine the extent of the damage he had caused. She never looked at him again, which gave him an uneasy feeling about his future in True America.

His fears were somewhat eased early the next morning in one of True America's tri-state area safe houses. He received instructions to await pickup by one the delivery vans that would deliver a consolidated shipment of canisters to a secret location out of state. He was told to take a few days off from work, while senior leadership decided how to handle his situation. They made it clear that he couldn't contact his family, since his identity might be compromised. He felt terrible as he thought he might have possibly dragged his family into a potential nightmare by his carelessness. However, the risks had always been clear to Julius. He had made a conscious decision to play a critical role in reshaping America, understanding that revolution often came with a hefty price tag.

He just hadn't expected to start paying so early. He'd made an adrenaline filled, rookie error back at the target site. The mask he had been given for the operation had been a few sizes too small, squeezing his head and causing him to sweat profusely. Stepping back into the cool night air, his first instinct had been to get the damn ski mask off his head. The cocktail of natural stimulants flowing through his system had dampened his common sense. One little mistake and his life had been permanently changed. In the grand scheme of things it wouldn't matter. He was part of a more important change, and when the transformation was complete, he would be rewarded. He had been assured of this.

The van bumped along a pitch-black road, eventually stopping at a large, neglected wooden gate placed across the road. In the harsh glare of the van's headlights, the gate looked ancient, yet formidable. Rising six feet high and joining the thick forest on either side of the van, the fence looked out of place for such a remote location. A simple fence would have drawn less attention, but Julius had to remind himself that it would be highly unlikely for anyone to stumble on this location by accident.

The driver lowered his window and turned on the interior lights. Julius glanced back at their precious cargo. Twenty canisters, seated in two specially designed crates, were hidden in compartments nestled underneath several pallets of bottled water. He felt exposed in the light, presuming that a camera was confirming their identities at this very moment. Several seconds later, the rickety barrier in front of the van started to slide out of the way. He suspected that there was more to the fence than rotten wood. His nervousness started to give way to excitement at the prospect of being exposed to more of True America's plan for "The Rising".

The van's rough transit smoothed out just past the gate, and they travelled for several minutes until Julius could see lights ahead. He leaned forward and watched as they approached a long, one story, flat-roofed structure. From what he could tell, this was the only structure within sight. The sheer darkness surrounding the building swallowed up the meager glow cast by a small light fixture to the right of a single loading bay. The van pulled up to a point roughly ten feet from the building. When it stopped, the loading bay door rolled open, exposing the inside of the facility.

Through the window, Julius could see several hundred pallets of water bottles stacked inside the bay, which appeared much deeper than he had initially estimated. Based on what he saw, the building must extend at least a hundred feet back. A few men appeared in the bay and hopped down from the concrete loading platform. He could barely believe he was now a part of an even more secretive arm of True America.

"Everyone out. They'll take over from here," said the driver.

Julius opened the van door and was immediately greeted by an intense glaring Caucasian man he had never seen before. In the faded light, he could see that the man had a military style tattoo on his right bicep, partially visible underneath a black polo style shirt.

"Mr. Grimes, my name is Michael Brooks. Head of security. Your identity has been compromised, so it looks like you'll be joining us here. This site will be extremely busy over the next few weeks and we can use another set of hands."

"How long will I have to stay? I was told that my family might be able to join me; I didn't really have this in mind," said Julius.

He was starting to feel like more of a prisoner than an elite member of True America's militant arm. He could be stuck here indefinitely without seeing his family.

"We know that your family is under surveillance. Since the FBI hasn't approached them, we can only assume that they are waiting for you. We suspect that you may be their only lead at this point. Consider yourself lucky."

"Lucky? To be imprisoned here indefinitely?"

"To be alive. Work hard and keep your mouth shut here. You won't be given another warning. Understood?"

Julius thought about the pistol he still had tucked into his jeans. Nobody had suggested that he surrender the Beretta, so he'd kept it near him at all times. He wasn't sure what he'd do if they asked for it.

"Understood. Where exactly am I?"

"At our lab, pretty much in the middle of nowhere. Let's head inside and get you situated."

Julius followed Brooks to a door on the right side of the loading bay. Two more men jumped down onto a concrete strip below the bay's lip. The security man opened the windowless door, exposing a well-lit room. He gestured for Julius to enter and stood back a few feet. A small set of concrete stairs led Julius to the door and into the room. When he saw his team leader standing inside the empty space, his heart sank. He knew exactly why they had brought him to the middle of nowhere. He remembered back to the beginning. One of True America's key tenets was "we take care of our own." The saying had more than one meaning. He had been constantly reminded of this in the early phase of his recruitment, when the question of his loyalty hadn't yet to be fully answered.

He turned and leapt out of the doorway, landing on the moist, root infested dirt with two feet. He reached for the Beretta secured against the small of his back and started sprinting toward the darkness. If he could make it to the woods, he could hide until he figured out his next move. His only thought at the moment was to just survive. He cursed himself for not trusting his earlier instincts.

Looking around as he ran, Julius extended the pistol toward Brooks and pulled the trigger. Nothing happened. He faltered in his run, pulling the pistol's slide back to chamber another round. He did this flawlessly, watching the unfired bullet eject from the pistol before he depressed the trigger again. Brooks stared at him and shook his head. Julius stopped running in the middle of the dirt field. He repeated the process, aiming at Karen Nadeau, who had appeared in the doorway, blocking most of the light from inside. The hammer fell, but the pistol failed to discharge.

"We took the liberty of replacing your Beretta while you were deep in a drug induced sleep at the safe house!" yelled Brooks.

Julius tried one more time, aiming at Brook's head. He wasn't sure how they drugged him, but sleep had come easily enough. He had no reason to doubt what the man had said, so he tossed the pistol to the ground.

"This is your version of gratitude, Mr. Grimes? Fuck up one of the most important jobs we can give you and shoot your way free when the terms of your punishment aren't acceptable?" said Brooks.

"Should I have dug my own grave for you too? Or is a pre-dug hole part of the 'we take care of our own' motto."

"Grave? Kathy's not here to kill you, Grimes. I took your entire team out of circulation to minimize the damage. Ward Young is here as well. I can't take the risk of the possible connections."

Both of his teammates stepped down from the building and stood near Brooks. He whispered something to them and they started walking over to the loading bay. Julius stood there, stunned by the revelation.

"Now I have a real problem, Julius. I can't trust anyone on this team anymore."

Kathy Nadeau and Ward Young stopped in their tracks and turned their heads toward Brooks. Before either of them could protest, suppressed automatic weapons fire erupted from the loading bay and smaller doorway, puncturing their bodies and dropping them to the recently cleared forest floor. Aerosolized blood mist from their exit wounds lingered in the air above them, illuminated by the door's light fixture.

"Go fuck yourself. I get the distinct feeling nobody is going to leave this compound alive. Good luck to the rest of you! This is how True America rewards loyalt—"

A single gunshot passed through his head, putting an end to a line of reasoning that Michael Brooks didn't want him to continue in front of too many people.

Chapter 13

12:08 AM
Masjid (Mosque) Mohammad
Newark, New Jersey

Aleem Fayed sat in a chair they had dragged down from the classroom attached to the prayer hall. He faced Hamid Abdul Muhammad, who sat unharmed on a small wooden stool they had found in the basement. His hands and feet were tied to the stool, to prevent him from doing anything more than hurt himself if he should try to stand up. The basement had proved to be the best possible location they could have secured on short notice. They could have rented a hotel room by the hour in one of the seediest sections of town, where strange noises and even screams wouldn't raise any eyebrows. Or they could have used the rental house that had been secured this morning in an equally questionable part of town. The house had a basement and might become their only option if the Imam proved resistant to their accelerated mental and physical torture routine.

He suspected that they would have more success with physical torture. The Imam had grown soft in America, having expanded his waist at a rate that must have alarmed his handlers in the Middle East. When he arrived to preach hate and recruit terrorists eight years ago, he looked slim and fit in his traditional white garments. Now, he more closely resembled a bearded version of the late John Belushi. His white prayer robes must have gone through several alterations to cover the man sweating in the chair in front of them.

They hadn't spoken a word to him since finding him jammed into a cabinet in his upstairs office. He had left the basement door open, hoping to trick them into hastily plunging down the stairs, but Tariq had noticed two formidable slide bolts on the back of the door. If they had thoughtlessly rushed into the basement, Hamid could have easily barricaded the door and tried to escape. The single, bare light bulb in the basement was controlled from a switch inside of his office, which would have compounded their problem. They would have been locked inside an unfamiliar, pitch-black basement with the success of their mission now hinged upon the three technicians sitting in a van two blocks away. Sanderson would have never forgiven them if they had lost the Imam.

Tariq called down from the office above.

"It looks like we're ready to go."

Aleem smiled at Hamid and started phase two of their plan to get him talking quickly. He hoped to have this wrapped up in under two hours. The silent treatment was just a short tension builder. Done properly, they would isolate Hamid for as long as it would take to get him to initiate contact. Tonight, they didn't have that kind of time.

"Imam Muhammad, As-Salaam Alaikum. You're in a deep pile of shit right now. You understand that, right?"

Hamid didn't respond in any way. His expression remained the same and his gaze focused on an indeterminate point beyond Aleem. Tariq descended the stairs with their black duffle bag and walked behind the Imam. He dropped the bag to the ground and unzipped it.

"Eventually you'll talk. They all do."

Silence penetrated the room and the Imam didn't waver. Aleem nodded imperceptibly to Tariq, who had removed a can of hair spray, a lighter and a black cloth bag. Less than a second later, Hamid Muhammad's head was engulfed in flames from the aerosol can. He immediately panicked and screamed, trying desperately to stand. Tariq had anticipated his sudden movement and forced the black bag down over his head, pulling down on the sides of the bag.

The bag served two purposes. The first was to extinguish the flames and the second was to keep him from tipping over. Tariq held the bag in place while Aleem beat the sides of the hood to ensure the fire had been stopped. Hamid stopped thrashing and started to recover his composure, just as Tariq pulled the bag's drawstrings tight.

The calmness slowly morphed back into desperation, as Hamid struggled to breathe what little oxygen had slipped into the bag. He gave it another twenty seconds for him to take in the stench of his own burnt hair and singed skin before giving Tariq the signal to remove the hood. When the hood was yanked off his head, the Imam's smug look was gone, replaced by sheer panic. Besides some burnt hair that still smoldered, there appeared to be little physical damage from the fire.

"Do I have your attention now, or do I need to light your head on fire again? This time I'll start with your beard."

"You're not the police!" he gasped.

"No. I'm about as far from the police as you can get."

"Then who are you? Mossad?"

"You might wish we were the Mossad at some point tonight. Even the Mossad has a few rules," said Aleem.

Hamid regarded him with a concerned look, which gave Aleem some hope that they might be able to wrap this up quickly. They had quickly broken the impassive wall the Imam had erected to stall them.

"You have a big problem, Hamid," said Aleem.

"And what might that be?"

"You betrayed your own cause. Shameful really. An entire network of Al Qaeda sleeper cells wiped out because of your greed and immorality."

"What are you talking about?" said Hamid, trying to glance behind him.

"Let's not fuck around here. We know that the European network shipped fifty-eight canisters of a very nasty virus to the United States. Originally, there were several targets in Europe, but the Russian scientist went rogue and panicked your colleagues overseas. Forty of them went directly to your cells and eighteen went to True America, who then turned right around and betrayed you. Two of your cells survived, but one was just slaughtered trying to deliver the virus to their target. America is on high alert. The only targets you might have left are a few lemonade stands in your very own Muslim neighborhoods, because I think the tolerance level for sweaty Arabs in most neighborhoods just hit an all-time low."

Hamid looked surprised at the level of information provided by Aleem.

"What does this have to do with greed?"

"You're the one that fucked over your own people. How else could the FBI roll up the conspiracy so quickly? Facing charges of collecting and disseminating child pornography, you tried to strike a deal with True America to finance your disappearance to a comfortable compound in Mexico. In exchange for the remaining virus canisters, three million dollars appears in a Cayman Islands account with your name on it, but is suddenly seized by the same agency that made the deposit. Surprise. You made the deal with undercover FBI agents posing as members of True America. Imagine the FBI's surprise when suddenly confronted with Al Qaeda's conspiracy to poison U.S. cities. And they just thought you might be running some kind of child trafficking ring with domestic extremists. This is going to be a hard story to explain to your colleagues in the Guantanamo Bay Detention Camp. Especially with all of the sordid details we can selectively leak into your cell block."

"The True America pigs are the ones that betrayed me. This is a fact," Hamid spat.

"Fact. Fiction. Details really. We can make this look like whatever we want. We have all of the addresses for your sleeper cell network. We'll publish this list. Trust me, your friends will wonder how in the hell we could have acquired this. Of course, the cell responsible for shipping the virus in Frankfurt disappeared without a trace, as they had no doubt been instructed."

"It won't matter. The faithful will never believe what you throw into your false media."

"You'll spend so much of your time explaining these amazing circumstances that I doubt there will be any time left for your duties as an Imam. You'll meet some of your former recruits, who will remember you as a defiant firebrand Imam. Imagine what they'll think when you show up to join them. They'll see you as a soft, corrupted traitor that capitulated to western excess and sin."

"When my plan succeeds, I will be hailed as the greatest hero. The one who struck the most vicious blow against the Great Satan. You have no true idea how many canisters are still in circulation. Your government can't protect everyone.

"Would you like me to show you the actual list? I have a picture of it on my phone. It's a little hard to read. One of my operatives cut it out of Naeem Hassan's stomach. He swallowed the list. Can you believe that? Completely unexpected. This left us wondering how many other Al Qaeda operatives carried secrets to their graves. Disembowelment and an invasive stomach search is now part of our standard operating procedure. You can thank Mr. Hassan for that."

Hamid sighed, which Aleem knew was a subtle sign of resignation. Aleem had been watching him closely.

"Hamid, eight out of the ten sites were taken down by True America. Turn on the news and you'll see what happened to the ninth team. Give me the tenth team and any information related to your contact with True America, and I will arrange your immediate transit to Saudi Arabia, where you can start over. You have been betrayed by True America. Frankly, we don't know their motivations for stealing all of the virus. I need links to the group, contact information. Some kind of way to set up a meeting to deliver the remaining virus canisters. I need the last cell to make this happen. I need their identities so we can pose as this team and resurface. I also need to be able to report to my people that we are only facing one threat. You'll have to sacrifice this team."

"I'll never betray my brothers," said Hamid.

"They've already been betrayed. If you don't help us with this, you'll go to Guantanamo as a filthy child pornographer and traitor to your own cause. We'll put together a scenario that will be impossible for you to explain. Trust me on this."

Hamid remained silent.

"This will be easy for you. You'll report that the ninth cell was killed trying to accomplish their mission and that the final cell has been killed by True America. We'll make it look like the other attacks. Nobody will know the difference and you'll vanish, only to reappear at some later date. We'll keep you hidden from the government until we can verify your information. Once verified, we'll start the process of getting you out of the country. Wherever you choose."

"It won't be that easy. I can't just go running back to the mosques in Saudi Arabia. It would make no sense. And I can't simply appear in Pakistan or anywhere for that matter. If the plan failed, they'll be looking for me."

"That's not my problem. I can only guarantee to get you to your chosen destination."

"How do I know you won't shoot me in the back of the head after I tell you what you want to know?"

"I swear by Allah."

"And your friend?"

"I swear by Allah as well," said Tariq.

"This is no coincidence, Hamid. I'm not the most faithful Muslim, but I am a Muslim. The Prophet has given you another chance. Before we arrived, you had nothing. Your last remaining operational cell is useless given the circumstances. All is lost and I guarantee there is no way you could escape the country without our help. Maybe you'll disappear and never be heard from again, or maybe you'll continue the fight. That's not for me to decide. It is His will, and we are all given different paths."

"It is truly His will," conceded Hamid.

"We'll need to move you to a more secure location. The FBI is working on a warrant to enter the mosque. Right now it's under surveillance from the outside. We've identified two vans and an apartment with a view of the front and back doors," he said.

"How will you get me out of here?"

"Easy enough, I hope. Just follow our directions without question. Understood?" said Aleem.

Hamid nodded. He directed Tariq to join him in the upstairs office to coordinate the escape, which would require the surveillance team to earn their paycheck. When they arrived at the top of the stairs, Tariq turned to Aleem and whispered.

"What was that speech all about?"

Aleem grabbed his arm and moved him toward the back of the office, away from the stairwell.

"Hope. Without hope, he'll put up another barrier. We don't have time for that."

"Well my hope is that you don't really plan to let him go free," said Tariq.

"Of course not, he's dead as soon as we confirm the information needed to move the investigation forward."

❧

Ten minutes later, Special Agent Janice Riehms stared through her binoculars at a van approaching Masjid Muhammad's side entrance on Sussex Avenue. The white Dodge Sprinter van drove at a normal speed as it neared the last remaining stop sign separating it from the mosque. From her observation post in the front window of a third story apartment at the intersection of Jay and Sussex, she had a clear view of the mosque's front and side entrances. Since Hamid Muhammad had become the center of the FBI's attention, four additional agents had been assigned to the two-bedroom apartment, shrinking the space considerably, but ensuring that they could accurately screen every person coming in and out of the mosque.

Attendance had dropped considerably throughout the day, making their jobs slightly easier. The facial recognition software tied to their surveillance cameras gave them an initial "probability of match" analysis within a second of a face appearing at the door. If any of the faces were obscured from sight, back up cameras installed on the roofs of two additional locations along Jay Street would ensure they could capture a digital image. Failing that, undercover FBI agents mobilized along Jay and Sussex during prayer times could approach the suspect and confirm their identity. They had coordinated three on street "interactions" today, which likely explained the shrinking number of attendees at the mosque. Word travelled quickly throughout the Muslim community.

"I have a van approaching from the west on Sussex. White with no rear windows. Looks like a cargo van," she said to the two agents watching the flat screen monitors.

Two additional agents appeared in the doorway to observe. Tensions had been heating up all day, but sunset prayer put them all on high alert. The three young men that always stayed behind in the mosque had been joined by two additional men. One of them had entered for sunset prayer and failed to emerge an hour later. The other appeared two blocks away on Jay Street and waited outside of the front door for a few minutes before entering. Nearly three hours later, none of them had exited the mosque, which gave special agent Riehms the impression that they were plotting to help the Imam escape.

"Notify Mobile SWAT units," she ordered.

"Got it. Units notified. I have the van leaving the stop sign. We'll be watching closely," replied one of the agents in front of the monitors.

The entire internal bedroom wall had been occupied with long folding tables and computer equipment. Four flat screen monitors showed the separate surveillance feeds and one larger monitor held their command and control interface. The agent who had just responded typed the SWAT notification, which was instantly transferred to both of the Suburbans. The SUVs were parked one block away, effectively sandwiching Jay Street. Each vehicle carried five SWAT agents, including the driver, and could move into a blocking position to prevent the escape of a vehicle leaving the mosque.

"Confirmed. Van is approaching the mosque," Riehms said.

She watched the van pass the side entrance and suddenly stop. Three figures darted from the mosque's door, disappearing behind the van.

"Fuck! They're loading him into the van!" she said, continuing to watch.

"I have the van stopped at the intersection of Jay and Sussex, turning left onto Jay. I didn't see it stop," said the agent watching the screen.

Another agent mumbled agreement. Through her binoculars, she saw the van speed through the intersection and turn right onto Jay Street. She ran from the window to the computer monitor.

"What the fuck are you talking about? I just watched it pick up three men and turn right onto Jay. Get SWAT moving south to intercept!"

"The van turned left. Take a look. Nobody left the mosque," said the agent.

"I saw it with my own fucking eyes. We're going to lose the Imam. Send SWAT south. The van has to turn on Central Ave. Either way, one of our teams can intercept!"

There was a two second delay as puzzled agents traded glances. She didn't like the fact that they were questioning her judgment, but she could understand their confusion. The computer monitor playback clearly showed the van turning left. Something was wrong here.

"Open a channel to SWAT," Riehms said as the agent typed her initial intercept request into the computer.

"I just fired off the order. They'll have plenty of time to intercept if the van went right. Should I notify non-tactical units to proceed north, just to cover our asses?"

"Fine. Send them north," she said, grabbing the headset offered to her by the agent. "SWAT Mobile this is Overlook. Proceed south to intercept a white Dodge Sprinter van. No back windows. Minimum of four onboard, possibly including our target. How copy, over?"

A static filled voice responded, "This is SWAT Mobile. My unit has just passed Dickerson Street. Less than five seconds away from a blocking position on Central Avenue. Sister unit is approaching Central along Hudson. Stand by for visual confirmation."

A few tense seconds passed as they waited for the truth. Agent Riehms thought about contacting the non-tactical units, but decided against it. She had seen the van turn right; there was no point contacting them, unless the van didn't show up on Central Avenue. There was no way for the van to break through Jay onto one of the adjoining streets and double back. They had confirmed this during a tactical assessment of the neighborhood. If the van didn't appear on Central, the only possible explanation was that it had stopped.

"Can you call up a map that shows our units' positions? We might need to guide them if the van tries to double back."

"One second," replied the agent, typing away.

All of the agents assigned to the stakeout were huddled around the computer monitor, blocking her view of the larger, central screen. She moved to a more centralized location to view the map.

"Agent Bedford, take these and make sure the van doesn't come back down Jay Street," she said, giving the binoculars to the newest agent to join her team.

"Yes, ma'am."

When the agent reached the window, her headset came to life.

"Suspect van just turned left onto Central Avenue. Moving forward to block. My second unit is less than fifty feet behind them. Send back up units! The van just slowed and is now turning into oncoming traffic! Unit two just rammed them from behind. Stand by. Out."

The line went dead.

"Send FBI and police units to their location, Central Avenue between Norfolk and Hudson. Give them one of our radio frequencies for coordination. What the fuck? Why does this map show all of our units headed north? You ordered SWAT south, right?"

"Yes! You just talked to them! Where did they say they were?"

"On Central Avenue," she muttered, utterly confused.

"SWAT Mobile, this is Overlook. What is your status, over?"

"Overlook. This is SWAT Mobile. I just turned left on Orange. No sign of the suspect van. Approaching Jay Street. Do you want me to turn down Jay and start searching? I can keep unit two at the top of the street to prevent an escape."

"SWAT Mobile. You just reported to me that you had engaged the suspect van on Central Avenue? Confirm your location again?" she said.

"I'm at the top of Jay Street. I've been taking my orders from the mobile tablet. I haven't sent an update since we started driving north," replied the voice.

"They drove north? Shit!" she yelled.

"His GPS location matches. According to the system, both SWAT Mobile units are at the northern end of Jay Street."

"Something is wrong with the system. Can you play back my conversation with SWAT Mobile?" she said.

"Which one?"

"The one supposedly on Central Avenue. Put it on speaker," she ordered.

Three seconds later, her conversation echoed through the room, filling her with dread. There was a stark difference between the two voices and the quality of the transmission. Her conversation with the SWAT leader on Central Avenue had been full of static and there was something off with the voice.

"What do you hear in that conversation?" she asked the other agents.

"I don't mean this to sound like a racial comment, but it sounded like you were on a bad connection with Dell technical support in Bangalore, India."

Nobody laughed at his comment.

"Is it possible for this system to be hijacked or hacked?" asked agent Riehms.

"It's not *im*possible," conceded the agent sitting in front of the command screen.

"Shit. Communicate with cell phones only, until we figure out what happened. I want all units headed south. We have to assume they're already on Central Avenue. I want blocks set up at every entrance to Interstate 280 for ten miles in either direction. Can you give us a directory of cell phone numbers for everyone assigned to our group?"

The agent typed a few commands and a list appeared. He ordered the computer to print several copies. Agent Riehms entered the numbers for the SWAT team leader's cell phone and pressed send. A second later, she heard a buzzing sound coming from Agent Bedford, who was dutifully watching Jay Street through his binoculars. He reached for his belt and took out his Blackberry. When he read the screen, he lowered the binoculars and held up the phone so she could see the screen.

"I think it's safe to assume that our system was hacked," said Agent Bedford, "unless you misdialed an entire cell phone number."

Aleem Fayed hit the van's sliding door and toppled to the carpeted floor, keeping a grip on Hamid Muhammad's arm. Tariq had fared better during the wild turn, having immediately grabbed the only permanently affixed passenger seat available in the back of the converted van. Tariq had expressed his concern about using the surveillance team for this kind of a precision timed maneuver, but they really didn't have a choice. If he had left the mosque at midnight to join up with the van, there was a solid chance that the FBI would follow him. The van took another sharp turn, which elicited a few excited hollers and sent Aleem careening into Tariq and Hamid.

"Take it easy, Graves! We're clear! The last thing we need is to attract any local police attention. Cars speeding around corners at midnight attract a lot of attention! Slow the fuck down!"

"Alright! Alright! I just wanted to get us off Central Avenue. We're fine. Right in the middle of Rutgers University. I'll cruise us through campus and we'll head south," said Timothy Graves.

Graves was the leader and default driver for the team, which had fallen short by one over the course of the past week. They had lost their secondary hacker, Benjamin Weindorf, to a startup computer security company that had just secured several million dollars of funding from the U.S. Navy. Tariq had personally visited Weindorf upon arriving in the States, to impress upon the young man that any mention of his previous "benefactor" would result in an early burial. Graves had been unable to find a trustworthy replacement in such a short period of time, but they might not need one in the future. Their primary systems hacker seemed more than capable of handling the excess workload.

Anish Gupta raised his hands above his head, palms facing upward, and slowly pumped his arms up and down.

"Raise the roof bitches! Those motherfuckers have no idea what just hit them. Watch this!" he said, typing a command on his keyboard.

"All mobile units, this is over watch. Suspect van spotted heading north on Mount Prospect Ave. Local units in pursuit. Proceed down Clifton Avenue to Bloomfield Avenue for intercept. Set up a block at intersection of Clifton and Bloomfied."

Through the speaker, they all heard several units responding affirmatively to his command.

"I'm tracking them by individual cell phone. Every FBI unit is headed north on Clifton. Local police are a different story. Agents at over watch successfully made several calls to 911," said Gupta. "He doesn't look too badly burned," he added, nodding at Hamid.

The Imam lay flat on the van floor with a fresh band of duct tape over his mouth. They had kept the duct tape off while transporting him to the van, in order to maintain the appearance that his escorted departure was an escape. Aleem sat on his chest, keeping him pinned to the floor until they were far enough away to risk propping him up in a seat.

"How long until they get their shit together?" asked Aleem.

"Not long. They'll unscrew the cell phone issue shortly. I just scrambled their directories, so if they didn't have a number memorized, they'd dial the wrong number. I didn't mess with their back up system at the field office, so they'll probably get a data refresh. Depends on who's working IT at the field office. If it was me, I would sever all connection to the mobile site. I'd order them to physically cut the fucking cable modem wires. Not that it would matter. I already have full access to the field office. This was more fun than I had anticipated."

"He's going to drive me crazy. Isn't he?" Aleem asked Graves.

"You get used to it. He's one of the best in the business...and he actually seems to enjoy this cloak and dagger shit," said Graves.

"Good. Because this looks like the very beginning of a long operation. We'll need to do something with this van before we reach the safe house. How portable is all of your equipment?"

"Thirty minutes to strip it down, including the antenna and satellite rig. We'll probably have to burn the van," said Gupta.

"Really? Now our friend here is operational?" said Aleem, eliciting a laugh from everyone in the van that didn't have his mouth taped.

"Just saying," Gupta responded. "Our fingerprints and DNA are all over this biatch."

"Where did you find a gangsta Hindu computer hacker?" asked Tariq.

"He found me, and this is nothing by the way. He's actually behaving for you guys," replied Graves, turning the van gently onto a crowded urban street.

"Wonderful," said Aleem.

Tariq and Aleem watched the traffic around the van closely for signs of unwanted law enforcement attention. Aleem spotted a three-story parking garage coming up on the opposite side of the road, which appeared to be connected to the Sheraton hotel towering over it.

"Graves, let's pull into that parking garage and find a new ride. We won't last much longer on the road if they successfully issue an APB. There's too much traffic out here," said Aleem.

"I can take care of the APB. I'm tapped into the State Police and local Newark Police network," said Gupta.

"Forget it. You'll lose satellite as soon as we duck into the garage. Start disassembling the gear," said Aleem.

"Can I call you Aleem G? It's so close to Ali G. You know who I'm talking about, right? HBO series?" said Gupta.

Aleem regarded the young Indian man strapped into a swivel bucket seat that had been bolted into the middle of the rear cargo compartment. Both of his hands typed away at one of the keyboards on the metal cargo table. He could see that the heavy-duty table had been welded to the left side of the van at several points. All of the equipment had been secured in custom made metal holsters and strapped down with industrial grade Velcro straps. The entire set up, Anish Gupta included, looked like it could survive a multiple rollover accident. It was hard to get mad at someone who looked so ridiculous and so serious at the same time.

"No. To all of your questions," said Aleem.

"Maybe I can just call you G?"

"How about you start getting all of this equipment ready for transfer and I'll think of a name. It'll probably sound a lot like Aleem."

"No sense of humor. Fuck. I get it. Mouth shut," said the young man.

Aleem continued to stare past Gupta, examining traffic through the rear window. He knew the young techie understood the stakes up front, but from behind his computers, this was still more or less a game to him. He didn't see the dead bodies in the mosque and he wasn't there when they engulfed Hamid's head in flames. And he wouldn't be there when they put a bullet in the terrorist's head. Hopefully, this would continue to feel like somewhat of a game for him. A game at this point that would land him in federal prison as an accessory to murder, among dozens of additional charges related to interfering with a federal investigation and hacking federal databases…and this was only the beginning.

Chapter 14

12:57 AM
National Counterterrorism Center
Washington D.C.

Special Agent Sharpe hung up the phone and stood up from his desk. Frank Mendoza gave him one of his patented raised eyebrows looks. For a moment, he stared past his friend at the NCTC Watch Floor. All of the displays full of information, maps and charts gave the impression that they were on top of the situation. Analysts and technicians moved back and forth between stations, trading conversations, which to the untrained eye would appear to be a good sign of productive activity. Sharpe knew better.

The watch floor had been designed to keep analysts and agents at their well separated work stations, where they could work relatively undisturbed, while still maintaining the critical "we all sink or swim" aura. Most of the agents filling temporary stations were tech savvy and figured out how to make use of the NCTC system within the first few hours of taking their posts. The fact that even the NCTC analysts were out of their chairs meant they didn't have enough to propel the investigation forward. The information passed to him through several phone calls would only make matters worse.

"It's not good, Frank. They lost the van. Disappeared into thin air along with Hamid Muhammad. All right in front of the FBI team assigned to watch the mosque," said Sharpe.

"We had people on that team?" said Frank.

"The Newark field office ran the stakeout. I just spoke with the senior agent at the site, Janice Riehms. Top notch agent. Sounds like she ran it by the book, but they suffered from some kind of major cyber electronics attack during the breakout. Completely compromised their communications and digital feed. She said they've never seen anything like this before. All of their vehicles were sent in the wrong direction. She mentioned something about their cell phones being rerouted too. Headquarters is sending a cyber operations team to Newark to investigate their systems for further evidence of a breach. They're concerned about the level of sophistication demonstrated by this attack."

"Any good news?" said Mendoza.

"Three dead terrorist suspects were found in the mosque. The Newark field office suspects that this was Hamid Muhammad's next batch of recruits."

"Any chance this was the missing cell?"

"No such luck. This is a major setback. Now we have the most radical Imam in America loose with his last terrorist cell. Unfucking real. I need to brief the team. We may have to concentrate more on our True America leads."

"What leads?" asked Mendoza.

"We'll have to start turning over information on every member of True America associated with their militant arm. Anyone ever seen in public or private sector with Jackson Greely or Lee Harding. Maybe we can find a connection to the delivery address in Harrisburg. Right now all we have there is a burned down house in foreclosure. The owners moved to Florida over a year ago and don't appear connected in any way."

"This is all very thin," Mendoza remarked.

"Tell me about it. If we don't produce something by tomorrow morning, we'll start to have visitors. High ranking visitors."

Chapter 15

4:22 AM
Corner of East 4th Street and Hobart Ave.
Bayonne, New Jersey

Special Agent Damon Katsoulis opened the front passenger door of the suburban and stepped out into the chilly air. A stiff breeze from the Upper Bay rustled through the young trees across the street, carrying a hint of saltiness over the pollution spewing into the air from the industrial wasteland that defined Bayonne's southeastern tip. Task Force Scorpion's Tactical Group sat quietly in several positions within the neighborhood, waiting for agent Katsoulis's command to pounce on apartment #2B at 98 Hobart Ave. He jogged over to the street corner and joined two tactical agents leaned up against a gray brick storefront that looked like it had been boarded up for years. Weeds poked through the concrete on both sides of the store.

"Anything unusual?" he asked.

"Negative," said the agent closest to the corner. "My only concern is the lighting situation for the approach. There are several industrial grade sodium lamps directly across from the target building at the back entrance gate to Hamm Brands. Nothing we can do about those, unless we try to contact security at Hamm and get them to douse the lights."

"No. We have an hour until dawn and even less time until civil twilight. We need to hit them now. They'll be up for prayer in thirty minutes or so," said Katsoulis.

"We won't be exposed for long. I'm just concerned that they might have a lookout posted. Two of the apartment windows face the street. Luckily, we have two healthy trees on the street corner in front of the building that partially obscure those windows."

"Alright. Two minute warning," he said.

Katsoulis reached up to his vest and depressed a button that opened his communication channel to the team leaders.

"Back Door, this is Lead. Two minute warning for the approach. Advise when in position, over."

A clear voice replied in his headset, acknowledging the warning order. Katsoulis peeked around the corner and saw what the team leader had described. The entire street corner formed by the intersection of George and Hobart was bathed in an artificial orange glow from several lights set along the gate and two-story structure. He could imagine that the residents loved having twenty-four hour daylight compliments of Hamm Brands.

He pulled his head back and swung his M4 Carbine around to a ready position along his chest. He started to check all of his equipment, while the three SUV's double parked along East 4th Street emptied ten additional SWAT agents into the quiet neighborhood. The agents started assembling near the corner, checking their own weapons and communications gear, while making sure they had unhindered access to flashbang grenades and spare ammunition magazines. A similar scene would unfold somewhere down George Street, putting over two dozen heavily armed tactical agents at his command for the takedown.

Finishing his personal check, there was only one more thing to do. Katsoulis checked his weapon's safety, ensuring that it was engaged, and chambered a round with the charging handle. The sound of his rifle's bolt slamming home echoed against the concrete, signaling for the rest of the team to do the same in rapid succession. "Front door" was ready for action.

He saw several investigative agents exit their cars and start to wander toward the corner, keeping their distance. They would stand guard over the cars and wait for him to give the "all clear" signal over the communications net. At that point, the tactical team would be charged with transporting the prisoners back to the field office, where legendary FBI interrogator Gregory Carlisle would start the long process of extracting useful information. Katsoulis imagined that Carlisle would start with the fact that people from their own community had turned against them.

The Newark field office had received an extremely detailed, late night tip regarding three young men who just recently moved into an apartment that had remained conspicuously unoccupied for thirteen months. Three dark skinned men, "definitely Arab and new to the community," had arrived yesterday morning, wearing only backpacks. The caller requested to remain anonymous, in fear of possible retribution by more conservative members of "their community." Caller ID at the field office and FBI phone tracing efforts placed the call to the apartment directly above the suspects.

Investigative agents quickly pieced together what the caller meant by "their community." Bayonne, New Jersey was home to a small but robust Muslim community that had successfully integrated with the rest of the immigrant groups in the area years before 9/11. The last thing any of them wanted was a group of suspected terrorists to tarnish the community's reputation, though the caller pointed out that not everyone in the community shared the same view. The field office also suspected that the call was motivated by the late night coverage of the "possible terrorist attack" in Mt. Arlington. Media coverage of the safe house attacks had so far been successfully avoided, but word of what happened in Mt. Arlington was quickly spreading. It was a little hard to conceal the fact that authorities were trying to keep nearly one hundred thousand citizens from drinking water provided by the Morris County Municipal Utilities Authority.

He glanced at his watch and saw that nearly two minutes had elapsed.

"Back Door, Lead. Proceed to breach position," he said, receiving an immediate response.

"Let's go," he whispered to the team leader standing next to him, slapping the man on the back.

He watched the twelve men file past, carrying a variety of weapons and breaching gear. They all wore full Level IIIA body armor, fitted with hardened ceramic plates capable of stopping armor-piercing rounds. Despite the impression of invulnerability, the body armor couldn't protect the men from every type of round at every angle. There were plenty of gaps and seams for mindless bullets to penetrate, leaving the wearer severely wounded or dead. The plates were designed to intercept the most probable center mass hits in the back or chest and would do little to stop an impact outside of these zones. Still, the ceramic plates remained a statistically good bet, since data supported the fact that most shooters under stress will aim for center mass and hope for the best.

When the last agent turned the corner, he joined the line, which snaked down the cracked sidewalk under the harsh orange glow cast by the overpowering sodium vapor lights. The tactical team traversed the distance between the two street corners, arriving at the front door in less than twenty seconds. The agents stacked up against the front wall of the apartment, crouched below the barred first floor windows, and waited for the breach team to analyze the front door. He monitored their hushed conversations over the tactical net. Both the front and side doors were locked. Katsoulis walked up the line of agents pressed against the vinyl siding and kneeled behind the team leader. He didn't say a word.

A tense minute passed while the agents tried unsuccessfully to pick the lock. The team leader discussed options with the agent manipulating the tools for a few seconds. He whispered orders into his headset, bringing one of the agents out of the stack with their portable battering ram. The agent trying to open the lock felt confident that the door would give in with a low intensity hit from the battering ram. Katsoulis wondered if they might be better off with a full strike, leaving nothing to chance.

The target apartment was on the second floor directly above them, so any level of impact might alert the suspects, which would leave them with little time to reach the apartment and gain entry. Unfortunately, the last minute nature of the "anonymous" tip had prevented them from setting up the best possible surveillance of the target building. They had agents with powerful night vision equipped optics watching the windows from cars on the street, but beyond that, they had no way to tell what was going on inside the apartment. The team leader turned to him and whispered.

"Upon hitting this door, it'll take us less than ten seconds to get flashbangs into the target apartment. This team will reach the apartment first, based on the location of the stairs. We won't have any time to assess the apartment door. We'll use shotgun breach loads and the ram at the same time. I don't see a way around this. It's a gamble on which door to use. My assumption is that the windows right above us are for a common area. They're bigger than the side windows above my other team. Based on that assumption, hitting this door will put the impact sound furthest away from the bedrooms."

"It's your call. Sounds like a solid plan based on what we were given. As long as they hit the door upstairs fast and furious, we'll surprise the shit out of them," said Katsoulis.

The team leader wasted no time continuing the conversation. He had over twenty agents exposed on the street.

"Back Door, this is Lead. Front Door will breach using the ram. Your breach will be delayed to keep the element of surprise. We suspect that the bedrooms are right above your door. Send four men around to secure the front entrance and have the remaining eight ready to immediately breach the side door to back up the primary assault team."

"Lead, this is Back Door. We just got the door open."

"Roger. Forget that plan. Proceed with entire team to target door and wait for me to arrive. I'm sending a backup team around the side to cover the entrance and street," he said and turned to face Katsoulis.

"We caught a break. We'll have the element of surprise on the target door. Agent Pruitt, I'm taking the last three from your stack to cover the side door. I'll open your door from the inside prior to the main breach. Keep half of your team here to secure the door and send the rest up as back up. Got it?" said the team leader.

Pruitt acknowledged the team leader's order by immediately briefing his team. The three agents from the end of the line along the building jogged to meet Katsoulis, who was already around the corner.

&

Jafal el-Sharif had finally fallen asleep in the extremely uncomfortable wooden chair that he had dragged from the kitchen table to his bedroom. His head leaned precariously against the paint chipped window framing, half shaded by the orange light that invaded his family's apartment. His head twitched within moments of his eyes closing, slamming his head against the sharp edge of the wood frame and causing him to briefly cry out in pain. Fortunately, his wife and children were not in the apartment to hear him. He had sent them to stay with her sister after receiving a strange request from a member of his mosque.

He had been asked to watch the street around his apartment for any suspicious law enforcement activity. With the recent discovery that the New York City Police department had been profiling local Muslim communities, activists within the Bayonne Muslim society had started to vocalize their opposition to further cooperation with local police. The man had told Jafal that his assistance was critical to proving that the federal and local law enforcement agencies were illegally targeting Muslims for discrimination.

"They" suspected that a major operation was underway in Bayonne, possibly in his own neighborhood, and they wanted to send the media down to intercept the police at the scene. He had been warned to be especially vigilant at night, when the police liked to terrorize members of the community, before disappearing back into the night. Some members of the community had supposedly vanished in these raids, only to reappear behind bars in Guantanamo Bay. Something had to be done to stop this harassment, and Jafal would be their first line of defense. He had a cell phone number to call if the police showed up on his street.

He shook his head from the impact and cursed himself for falling asleep. He figured he had only been out for a few seconds. He took a deep breath and leaned forward to take in more of the street. His eyes caught movement to the far right, and he immediately inched forward in the chair. What he saw nearly caused him to fall onto the floor in front of the window. Two heavily armed police officers disappeared into the side door of the apartment building on the opposite side of George Street. They were right! They moved so quickly and quietly that he had almost missed them. Allah had woken him at just the right moment! He grabbed the cell phone resting on the windowsill and dialed the number he had programmed into his phone.

"Allahu Akbar," he whispered gleefully, hoping to strike a small blow against the oppressive American regime.

&

"We have a possible problem," said Anish Gupta.

He leaned forward, staring at a lone laptop screen set on a folding table at the safe house in New Brunswick. They had moved all of the computer equipment from the van into the house, where it would remain until they acquired a new van with the required internal configuration to continue mobile field operations. Anish had been confident that they could carry out the necessary surveillance from the small house. Once Graves and Tariq had positioned themselves on the roof of a nearby Hamm Brands warehouse, all he claimed to need was uninterrupted high-speed internet access and his decked out laptop.

The surveillance post was close enough for their wireless signal mapper to detect and pinpoint passive cell phone transmissions within the vicinity of the target building. It could also transmit enough power to perform a few highly classified snooping tricks. Thanks to Hamid Muhammad's confession, they had been able to turn one of the terrorist's cell phones into a bug. Hamid didn't think any of the previously known numbers would be active, but one of the men had apparently violated strict security procedures and kept his old phone. This had been one of the ways they had corroborated Hamid's information. One of the cell phone numbers matched an active phone located at 98 Hobart Avenue, which was where Hamid swore they would find the missing terrorist cell.

"What's up?" muttered Aleem, physically exhausted from the evening's activities.

"I have two cell phones operational within fifty feet of each other. I can hear one of them ringing from our co-opted phone in the target apartment. The other is located across the street. I think it's a lookout. We're live with Tariq and Graves," he said, pointing to a microphone mounted on the table.

Aleem sat up at the dining room table, his mind scrambling to figure out what they could do to covertly assist the FBI SWAT team. Hamid didn't think they would be armed with much more than knives and pistols, but he also wasn't sure to what extent that the cell would be supported by his loyal followers within the Bayonne Muslim community. The apartment had been secretly rented by Hamid a year earlier and kept vacant for the purpose of temporarily hiding a cell in plain sight. He had given the apartment key to one of his followers to deliver to the cell's leader, with sealed instructions. This had been followed by another sealed message to be carried to his contact in Bayonne. He had been forthcoming with this information, clearly wanting to avoid a sudden inferno engulfing his head again. Aleem had no reason to believe that Hamid knew about the lookout in the adjacent apartment. In any event, he would use this information to further terrorize the Imam.

"Tariq. Can you see any movement on infrared? You should have a clear line of sight to the apartment's front door," said Aleem.

Aleem had wanted the surveillance team to transmit the feed to their safe house, but Graves didn't want to overcomplicate the communications rig they needed to erect on the warehouse roof in order to support mission essentials. The anonymous tip to the FBI had been placed before the surveillance team had figured out how they would get into Hamm Brand's sprawling complex and onto the roof of the massive building. The trip back to Bayonne from the safe house in New Brunswick had put them on a tight schedule.

"Nothing yet. SWAT teams are in the front and side doors. Hold on. Shit, I have multiple heat signatures in the common area. They're up. I have no way to engage," he heard on the speaker.

"There's nothing you can do. Anish, can you provide a distraction? Ring their phones?"

"I can ring the number we have...or I can activate the camera's flash."

"Do both. Coordinate the flash with SWAT's countdown," said Aleem.

Gupta had scanned all active VHF frequencies before and after the FBI SWAT team's arrival, quickly determining which frequencies were used for the tactical team's P25 Digital Encrypted radios. He had access to an extremely proprietary brute force key recovery program that could provide him with the encryption key and in an act of sheer desperation, he could try to "rekey" all of the radios using a program that Graves had acquired from sources that Gupta had worried about more than Sanderson. Neither of these methods had been necessary, since their illicit access to the multiple FBI networks provided them with the "key" used by Task Force Scorpion's tactical units. He had enjoyed using the same technology to co-opt the Newark field office's radios during their escape with the Imam for Masjid Muhammad.

Gupta typed furiously at the keyboard, while monitoring the SWAT team.

"Three second countdown. Damn they moved fast. Two, one..."

"I just saw a flash," said Tariq.

"The phone should be ringing too. Wow! I just lost my hearing," he said, snatching the headphones from his head.

"Three flashbangs. Windows shattered. No gunshots. Lots of yelling," reported Tariq.

"You just heard the bang part of the flashbang," said Aleem.

"Thanks for the warning."

"Imagine what it's like on the receiving end."

Gupta replaced the headset and listened intently to the radio chatter. He didn't hear any transmissions indicating a "man down." He started to hear reports of "clear" from several team members.

"I didn't hear any gunshots, but they could have been mixed in with the flashbangs," said Tariq.

"From what I can tell, no shots were fired. They recovered four canisters. The HAZMAT truck should be pulling up any second," said Gupta.

"Looks like it just arrived," added Tariq.

"Nice job, Anish. You probably saved an FBI agent's life today," said Aleem.

"Maybe. But that life would have never been in danger if we didn't place the call in the first place," said Gupta, obviously mulling over his own logic.

"I'm not getting into another logic trap debate with you. This day has been long enough. Good work. Leave it at that. Let's send everything we have to Insider," said Aleem.

Insider was their codename for Callie Stewart within the NCTC. Sanderson's plan to accelerate the investigation on behalf of the FBI had only just begun. The next phase sounded dicey in Aleem's opinion, but might help them skip a few steps and bring everyone closer to finding the remaining virus canisters. Hamid Muhammad might live to see another day.

Chapter 16

10:45 AM
Berlin Tegel International Airport
Berlin, Germany

Daniel Petrovich took his new passport from the smartly dressed customs agent and tucked it into the interior breast pocket of his black wool pea coat.

"You can proceed to the waiting lounge, or if you prefer, a private room. All areas are fully equipped for your business needs. The aircraft just arrived, so it may take a few minutes to refuel and re-inspect. Enjoy your flight, Mr. Petrovich."

"Thank you. The crew can find me in the lounge," he said.

He pulled his carry-on luggage to a comfortable seating area at the front of the private terminal lobby. The three serious looking operatives stood in unison as he approached.

"I guess this is goodbye. No tears please. Look at the positive side of my departure. One less smelly body driving around Europe in a rental van," said Petrovich.

"And just as I was starting to get used to you," said Farrington.

"My infectious charm rubs off on everyone," said Petrovich, extending his right hand.

The two men shook hands vigorously.

"Take care of this guy. He's Sanderson's protégé," he said to Hubner and Klinkman.

"That's a relief. We were worried you might be his protégé," said Klinkman.

They all laughed at Klinkman's rare display of humor.

"What now, Mr. Petrovich? Sounds like there's plenty of unfinished business back in the states. You might be better off vacationing somewhere else. Plus, you're a little overdressed," said Farrington, pulling Daniel's left collar.

"Rest and recuperation. Jessica's choice. I'll follow her wherever she chooses. Gentlemen."

He exchanged firm handshakes with Hubner and Klinkman.

"Don't drink the water," added Hubner.

"That's what you say for Mexico," said Klinkman.

"Not anymore," replied Hubner.

"I'll stick to bottled water for now," he said, turning to Farrington.

"Good luck with the German comedy duo. I foresee long, painful car rides in your future," said Petrovich.

"See you around," said Farrington.

"No offense, but hopefully not."

Farrington smiled and slapped him on the shoulder.

"I hope you're right."

Petrovich nodded to the group and made his way to the door leading to the private terminal's lounge. He fought the urge to glance back at them, as if doing so would catapult him back into Sanderson's world. He had been disturbed to learn that Farrington, and presumably Sanderson, knew where he was headed. He had booked the Gulf Stream V with his own funds and had expected his destination to remain a secret. Maybe Farrington had taken a stab in the dark. If so, he had fallen for the oldest trick in the book and confirmed the destination. Then again, if Farrington had been fishing for information, he'd have to assume that anything Daniel said would be a subterfuge. He could go on and on with this logic, until he came full circle.

He couldn't wait to be out of this business. He'd spend a week or two relaxing with Jessica on the beach before they started to make plans to vanish again. This time, they'd fully cover their tracks. Daniel and Jessica Petrovich would cease to exist in the eyes of General Terrence Sanderson and the rest of the world, leaving them at peace to live normal lives. The kind of normal that more than thirty million dollars can buy.

He took a seat in the empty lounge and stared out of the window at the shiny, sleek Gulf Stream V taxiing to rest fifty meters beyond the glass. Roughly eight hours from now, the jet would land in Charleston, South Carolina, where he would meet Jessica and drive to a rental villa on Fripp

Island, just outside of Beaufort. He couldn't imagine that Al Qaeda had any plans to poison the water supply of a private beach resort community on the South Carolina coast. He checked his watch. It was still a little early to call Jessica.

She had arrived in Charleston yesterday afternoon, promptly checking into a suite at the Charleston Place, the most luxurious hotel within the city's historic downtown district. He'd call her from the aircraft and coordinate his arrival. He'd rented a four door, soft-top Jeep Wrangler for the upcoming weeks. He couldn't wait to drive through the warm Atlantic air with the top down, taking in the simplicity of the low country with Jessica.

They had spent a considerable amount of time vacationing in Hilton Head while they lived in Maine, taking full advantage of the warm weather and southern hospitality. For this trip, they had opted to steer clear of their usual resort in Hilton Head due to their recently erased celebrity criminal status. They had become regulars at some of Hilton Head's finest restaurants, similarly establishing their presence in nearby Savannah. This time, they would explore new territory in Beaufort and Charleston, while anonymously enjoying the same ocean on Fripp Island. Two weeks to enjoy one of their favorite stateside refuges for the last time. They'd make the best of it, before Daniel reached out to some of his past acquaintances. Acquaintances in the business of finding new identities for wealthy clients.

Chapter 17

5:03 AM
National Counterterrorism Center
Washington D.C.

Special Agent Sharpe finished giving his pep talk to the exhausted task force personnel and started to make his rounds to all of the stations. Special Agent Mendoza would start making arrangements to have the personnel rotate through mandatory rest periods, where they would make use of the limited onsite sleeping quarters. NCTC designers had assumed correctly that certain operations might keep watch floor users tied to the building for several days, however, they had grossly underestimated the possible size of these groups. Sharpe would likely have to authorize the use of several rooms at a nearby Marriott.

The investigation's pace had picked up over the past few hours, and would likely build more momentum as the day unfolded. They now had full access to Hamid Muhammad's mosque and apartment. Both qualified as federal crime scenes when Agent Janice Riehms found three dead bodies in the middle of the prayer hall. Riehms had carefully crafted her request to enter the mosque on the premise that the Imam's sudden departure more resembled an abduction than an escape. Two men pushing another man into the back of a van at midnight. Sharpe authorized her to search the mosque for signs of foul play, which they immediately discovered. In many ways, the loss of the Imam opened investigative avenues previously blocked by the Justice Department's restrictions.

The biggest break came from the "anonymous" tip that led to the successful capture of the missing terrorist cell. Four virus canisters had been recovered from a cooler in one of the bedrooms. From what

Homeland's bioweapons team could tell, each of the canisters appeared to contain their original payload. Removing four canisters from terrorist hands signified a major win for Task Force Scorpion, however, fifty canisters still remained at large, which was not a comforting thought. Sharpe figured he'd better have someone make the Marriott arrangements immediately. They had just scratched the surface of this investigation.

He could feel Callie Stewart's eyes following him as he worked his way through the last few stations. So far, she had proved to be unobtrusive, simply observing the action from her perch. He had expected her to frequently descend the stairs to share her thoughts, but she only seemed interested in pestering him with text messages about putting undercover agents in the mosque. Those messages had mercifully stopped after the Imam's spectacular escape.

❧

Callie Stewart watched Special Agent Sharpe disappear under the catwalk. She was a little nervous about what General Sanderson wanted her to do. Sharpe might arrest her on the spot, though he had no real charges to levy against her, or he might simply ban her from NCTC. Either option would render her mission incapable. Even if she were to convince him to follow Sanderson's plan, he might change his mind at any moment and exercise his options to have her removed.

Her boss felt confident that Sharpe would bite at the proposal. This wouldn't be Sharpe's first walk into the gray area. He'd taken a step out onto that ledge earlier tonight, when he had authorized Agent Riehms to enter the mosque. Sanderson had assured her that the FBI agent had other skeletons hidden in his closet, and fed her the lines she would need to sway Sharpe. He expected her to improvise the rest to earn her exorbitant fee for this job.

She made her way down the stairs, drawing a few stares from both NCTC and Task Force personnel. She could sense a combination of enmity and pure attraction. She locked eyes with Special Agent Mendoza and flicked her head, hoping he would understand this subtle gesture. She needed him in the room with Sharpe when she made her proposal. If Sharpe went along with it, she needed Mendoza's approval to seal the deal among the rest of the task force. A one-on-one meeting would raise too many suspicions, especially with Special Agent O'Reilly.

Sanderson's cyber team had already defeated several attempts by O'Reilly to electronically eavesdrop on her office. She didn't blame the agent for her suspicion and anger. Sanderson's operatives had severely wounded three agents assigned to Sharpe two years ago, including O'Reilly. She had spent several weeks in recovery, trying to regain full use of her left arm. A 5.56mm bullet had separated the forearm muscle from the bone. From her perch on the catwalk, she could clearly see that O'Reilly had not fully recovered; she frequently removed her left hand from the keyboard, continuing only with her right hand while she gave the left forearm a break.

Stewart reached Sharpe's door, which was open, and knocked on the frame. Agent Mendoza closed in on her from behind.

"Come in," Sharpe said, without looking up.

She stepped inside his office, and when he finally lifted his head, she could tell that he wished it were possible to rescind the invitation. Agent Mendoza squeezed by her without any sort of pleasantry and stood near the left front corner of Sharpe's desk. Mendoza swept his right hand back slightly, clearing enough of his jacket to ensure quick, smooth access to his service pistol.

"How may I help you, Ms. Stewart?" asked Sharpe.

"May I close the door? You can keep the windows transparent, so O'Reilly doesn't get too worried," she said.

"Sure," Sharpe conceded.

Once the door was shut, she wasted no time getting to the point.

"Now that you've more or less neutralized the Al Qaeda side of the threat, we need to focus on the real problem. True America..."

"We? The task force is doing just fine without your help. We'll let you know when Congress, the Department of Justice, the Supreme Court and the president have authorized us to ignore the laws of the land, thereby approving the methods your organization might employ. If that's all, I'm a little busy processing all of our new leads."

"No word on the warrants from Justice?" she prodded.

"I don't need the warrants anymore. The mosque is a federal crime scene."

"That's right. The Imam was abducted," she said flatly.

"We found three bodies inside the mosque. Arabs. Turns out one of them was on the watch list with ties to known Al Qaeda operatives in Europe."

"But you found them after you conspired with Agent Riehms to classify the Imam's departure as an abduction."

"Agent Riehms applied sixteen years of FBI experience to reach that conclusion. I trust her judgment."

"Especially since it allowed you access to the mosque you've been begging Justice to let you enter. And I'm sure Agent Riehms had every reason to make a sound, objective assessment, given the fact that she just lost the primary focus of the task force's investigation. Put the two together, and it sounds like a compelling reason to break a few rules."

"That's your interpretation," said Sharpe.

"Let's just hope it stays that way."

Sharpe simply stared at her, shaking his head. "I'm really not worried about it."

"Which is exactly why you need to hear what I'm proposing, Agent Sharpe. You've made some gains stepping over the line, but you'll have to do it again to break into True America. We need to start working our way up their human network; capture personnel on the ground. Right now, all you have is a tenuous link to True America with Julius Grimes. He's disappeared, and I can guarantee that you'll never see him again."

"The Imam made contact with True America at some point to coordinate the specifics of the delivery to Harrisburg. It looks like Al Qaeda was keeping their end of the bargain, so there's bound to be more. I guarantee we'll find something at the mosque or in his apartment that will give us the jumpstart we need," said Sharpe.

"You won't. Our people have scoured his computer and the mosque. There's nothing useful in his apartment either. And Al Qaeda had no intention of keeping their end of the bargain. I can give you an address in Middletown, Pennsylvania that contains five decomposing Middle Eastern men. This was the hit squad assigned by Al Qaeda to recover the Harrisburg delivery. Both of these organizations were running a double cross from the start," said Stewart.

"Really? And exactly how do you know this?" interjected Mendoza.

"Because we have the Imam."

Agent Sharpe rose swiftly, and for a brief moment, Stewart thought she might have to physically defend herself. Mendoza's hand flashed to his gun, pulling it three quarters of the way out of its holster.

"You're in way over your head here, Ms. Stewart. I hope you're fucking with me right now, because if you aren't...I'll have your ass dragged off in handcuffs."

"Sanderson wants to use the Imam to draw True America into the open. Whether you arrest me or not, the Imam will start placing calls this morning to his True America contacts," she said.

"He'll never be able to convince them to come out of hiding. True America is done with Al Qaeda."

"Maybe. According to the Imam, True America tipped him off about the FBI raids," said Stewart.

"This morning's raid?" said Mendoza.

"No. He claims to have received a call at about 3:30 in the morning, on the night that most of his teams were hit by True America. He was told to go into hiding at the mosque, where the FBI couldn't touch him," said Stewart.

"This doesn't make a lot of sense. How confident are you in the Imam's information?" said Sharpe.

"His babysitters are fairly certain he's telling the truth, though I agree that something doesn't add up."

"Either way, Ms. Stewart, by now True America has to realize that Mr. Muhammad uncovered the truth. I doubt very much that they would agree to meet with him," said Sharpe.

"You're absolutely right," she said and paused before continuing. "He's not going to try and set up a meeting. He'll threaten to expose Al Qaeda's collaboration with True America. The Imam hasn't coughed up any big picture details, but I think it's fair to assume that True America had a hand in funding this operation from the very beginning. He can use Grime's name to establish some credibility. Say that he has additional assets that have managed to track some of their operatives. You'll release news of the last cell being captured, so the Imam's desperation will make sense. He has no more virus in his possession, so he'll expose them if they don't give him ten canisters to continue his mission against the Infidels. Something convincing like that."

"They'll never give him the canisters. He's dead if they can draw him out of hiding," said Sharpe.

"Huh," muttered Mendoza, drawing a strange look from Sharpe.

"You're starting to get the picture, Agent Mendoza. The calls will be traceable. The location is a logical fit for where the Imam might hide. We sit and wait for them to send a team to eliminate the Imam," Stewart said.

"Since I haven't been arrested yet, is it fair to assume that you're interested?"

"Intrigued is a better word. I can't put undercover FBI agents in a situation where they are guaranteed to be attacked," said Sharpe.

"You don't have to. Our undercover team will cover ground zero. Trust me, they're a lot more convincing undercover than your people. The FBI can provide sniper support and SWAT backup. If True America takes the bait, you'll be able to start pulling at True America's threads. Sooner or later, you'll start to unravel their cover."

"What do you think, Frank?" Sharpe asked, turning to Mendoza.

"I was really hoping you wouldn't ask me that," replied Mendoza.

"All of your bases will be covered on this one. How well do you trust Kerem Demir, your investigative lead?" asked Stewart.

"Implicitly. He's a loyal agent," said Sharpe without hesitation.

"I'm not talking about loyalty. I'm talking about doing you a favor and keeping it quiet."

"I don't like where this is going," said Mendoza.

"All I'm suggesting is that you have him prioritize the analysis of the cell phones recovered in Bayonne. A few calls were placed to a market on Coney Island Avenue in Brooklyn. Several dozen shops on that street cater to the massive Muslim community in Kensington. If I were the Imam, this would be a decent place for me to hole up and plan the next move."

"These guys are careful. Why would they make a call to a physical location that could jeopardize the safety of the Imam?"

"Why would the original World Trade Center bombers try to get their deposit back for a rental van that they exploded in the attack? I think you might be giving these people a little more credit than they deserve. One of the terrorists in Bayonne was carrying a cell phone that should have been destroyed prior to arriving at the safe house. Not to mention the fact that eight out of the ten terrorist cells associated with this plot were taken down by True America."

Sharpe shook his head slowly as his eyes narrowed. He sat down at his desk and typed a message.

"Done. The cell phones have been given the highest priority. What else does Sanderson have up his sleeve? I assume the anonymous tip about the safe house in Bayonne was graciously provided by your organization?"

"The Imam gave us the location, which we immediately passed on to your task force. Sanderson's efforts are focused on helping you move the investigation forward."

"As you can well imagine, I don't trust him any more than I trust the Imam. He's a master manipulator and an engineer of chaos. If I sense at any point that he's playing a game here, I'll pull the plug on your organization's participation and detain everyone until I sort it out. Is that understood?"

"Perfectly. Just think of where your investigation stands right now compared to last night. This is the kind of progress you can expect to continue making with Sanderson's support."

"When can we expect the Imam to fall into our lap?" Mendoza asked.

"When he's no longer useful to the investigation," said Stewart blankly.

"Very funny. Why do I get the distinct impression that Hamid Muhammad will never be seen again?" asked Sharpe.

"Do you really want to see him sipping tea in an interrogation cell?"

"Not really," mumbled Mendoza.

"Neither does Sanderson. You don't need to worry about the Imam. He's our problem. It's better that way. How long until Agent Demir comes up with the Brooklyn location?" said Stewart.

"I have a videoconference with the White House situation room in two hours. I'd like to include this in my briefing. He'll send the data directly here for analysis. If I haven't seen anything in thirty minutes, I'll have O'Reilly request it, if she hasn't already."

"Why didn't you send the request directly to O'Reilly in the first place?" asked Stewart.

"Because if I had sent her this request while meeting with you, she'd put two and two together before you walked out of the door."

Callie Stewart nodded. "I'll notify Sanderson. He'll contact our team at the field office in Newark and—"

"And the rest of the team you concealed from me?" said Sharpe.

"They'll get to work scouting the location before this becomes official. Lines of sight for your stake out teams; optimal sniper positions; avenues of approach, all that. They should have most of it figured out by the time your first units arrive on the scene. The Imam should place his first call by mid-morning at the latest, so your people will need to hustle. If True America traces the call, they could have people on the scene within minutes."

Mendoza started to say something, but stopped before uttering a word. Sharpe flashed him a look, which she recognized immediately.

"Don't get any crazy ideas, gentlemen. The Imam will not be present at the site."

"I never said—" Mendoza started.

"You didn't have to," Stewart interrupted, heading toward the door. "Woman's intuition. Which reminds me…you might want to consider bringing O'Reilly in on the secret sooner rather than later. She'll become a liability if she discovers that you cut her out of the loop."

"O'Reilly isn't your concern," said Sharpe.

Stewart raised an eyebrow in response to his comment and exited the office displaying a half smirk. Upon leaving, she stared up at one of the larger flat screen displays near O'Reilly's workstation. Through her peripheral vision, she could see Agent Hesterman tracking her movement toward the stairs, which meant that O'Reilly was trying to be discreet. O'Reilly had the potential to become a massive problem if not handled correctly. They needed to bring her in at the ground level on this one.

Sanderson had identified O'Reilly as the other potential player on the task force. She had conspired with Sharpe two years ago to pass highly classified information to a less than scrupulous field agent, in an ill-fated attempt to turn Jessica Petrovich against her husband. Jessica had played Special Agent Edwards in order to steal the agent's computer and password, granting Sanderson's crew full access to the task force's database. What she did to Agent Edwards afterward went down in FBI history as a textbook case of how not to interact with a witness under any circumstance.

Sharpe's only luck that day stemmed from the fact that Edwards had been given a relatively high dose of a date rape drug, and couldn't remember much beyond his alcohol laden, expensive dinner with the femme fatale. The uproar surrounding Edward's thoroughly incompetent and embarrassing screw up lasted long enough for O'Reilly to remove the incriminating emails from the inside. In Sanderson's opinion, O'Reilly would support Sharpe on a slight divergence from procedure, or a major one if the end justified the means, and it didn't directly endanger other agents.

BLACK WATER

Chapter 18

7:00 AM
The Jacksons' Residence
Fredericksburg, Virginia

Darryl Jackson took a bite out of his meticulously prepared English muffin and savored the melted butter that oozed from the perfectly crisped top. Sweet juices from a thin slice of warmed tomato competed with the butter and perfectly contrasted the sharp taste of sprinkled asiago cheese. Cheryl had created another masterpiece. Damn he loved that woman.

"Liz will be finished with her finals on May 10th. It'll be nice to have her around here for the summer. Sounds like most of her friends are coming home too," said Cheryl.

His wife was dressed in dark gray slacks and a light pink blouse. Her matching gray jacket hung neatly over the back of a low backed chair pushed up against their kitchen island. This would be her second year as Deputy Superintendent of Fredericksburg's Public Schools. He always marveled at her energy level. She had effortlessly balanced the demands of parenthood and an ambitious career within the Fredericksburg school district. She had started off teaching high school English, while simultaneously pursuing a master's degree in school administration. Five years later, she had secured a position as principal of Walker-Grant Middle School, beating out candidates from all over the region.

Nobody had been surprised that she would seek the big position, and serving as Deputy Superintendent was the only way to eventually secure the Superintendent position without an education doctorate. She faced long odds without the coveted doctorate, which was considered a resume requirement for most superintendent positions nationwide, but she felt confident that her work on the ground as a teacher, principal and Deputy would overshadow the proliferation of education doctorates acquired by out of work teachers.

"The sooner the better. I wish we could convince Emily to postpone her trip to France," he said, watching the television mounted under a row of kitchen cabinets visible from the table in their breakfast nook.

"It was either one month in the French countryside during the summer, or an entire semester right outside of Paris. I think we dodged a bullet with the summer program," she said.

He looked at her and smiled. "I know you're right, but things seem unsettled out there…do you mind if I turn this up?"

The television in their kitchen was small and mainly viewed from the kitchen island, but Darryl had incredibly acute vision at longer distances, a genetic gift that had fortunately saved his life more than once in the field. They normally kept the volume down for breakfast, relying on his hawk eyes to spot anything important to them. What he saw on the screen made him lunge for the remote and raise the volume. As the newscast unfolded, they both listened intently…

"…area around the Mount Arlington station is sealed off for nearly a mile and authorities are keeping a tight lid on any information flowing to the media. Local hospital officials also declined to comment on the nature of the emergency. Witnesses standing outside of a nearby restaurant said they heard distant gunfire at around 8:30 last night, but dismissed the sound as fireworks. A large police response, consisting of SWAT units, descended on the access road to the pump station at 9 PM.

"Local and federal law enforcement officials would not comment on the nature of the police action in Mount Arlington, but affiliate news correspondents have confirmed that a widespread government effort to stop citizens from drinking public water began at 10:15 PM last evening and continues at this very moment. The efforts appear concentrated on Morris County Municipal Utilities customers, who are served by a series of pumps and wells located in northern New Jersey. Townships served by water pumped by the Morris County Municipal Utilities Authority include, Denville, Jefferson, Mine Hill, Mount Arlington, Parsippany-Troy Hills, Randolph, Roxbury, Wharton Borough and Southeast Morris County. Citizens in these affected areas have been warned not to drink water from any public source until further notice. Anyone that drank public water after 9 PM is encouraged to immediately call 911 or report to the nearest hospital."

Darryl lowered the English muffin to his plate and stood up from the table. Liz lived in a dormitory at Princeton University, located less than fifty miles from Parsippany. He didn't need NBC to connect the dots for him. This sounded like a terrorist attack on the water supply, and he wasn't naïve enough to hope that it was an isolated attack. He grabbed his cell phone off the kitchen island and had dialed his daughter before his wife reached his side. While the phone rang, he listened to the rest of Matt Lauer's report and heard him speculate about a link between recent police raids throughout Europe. He also raised the specter of a possible connection to the mysterious tragedy in Monchegorsk. Mention of the Russian city grabbed Darryl's attention and he listened intently while he waited for Liz to answer her phone.

"...and international news agencies have made little progress in the Kola Peninsula. Restricted to St. Petersburg, foreign correspondents and diplomats have been unable to gain even the foggiest picture of what has unfolded in the northern city. Russian internal security forces have reportedly used heavy-handed tactics to keep foreigners from seeking information beyond the city. Located 750 miles north of St. Petersburg along a single highway, the Russian government has effectively sealed off all access to Monchegorsk. Only military vehicles have been seen heading north into the Kola Peninsula, casting serious questions about the Russian government's assertion that the situation in Monchegorsk is under control."

His daughter wasn't answering her phone. He speed dialed the number for the resident assistant on her floor. She was going to flip out when she discovered that he had acquired this number on a visit to her dorm, but he had a bad feeling about the news coming out of Mount Arlington.

"...the release of shocking video footage acquired by the Reuters news agency from a source deep within the city, Russian officials acknowledged the deployment of armored military units to wrest control of the city from an insurgent group. Officials declined to give any details regarding the insurgency, only sharing the fact that insurgents had caused significant damage to the city's critical industrial infrastructure. Norval Nickel, the world's leading producer of nickel and palladium, maintains an immense mining and smelting operation in Monchegorsk.

"Russian area experts have cast serious doubts on the likelihood that an insurgency could develop so suddenly without warning signs. Aspects of the Reuters video suggest a massive medical crisis, resulting in a widespread pattern of bizarre behavior in the city. Watch groups here at home have demanded immediate transparency in the handling of the Mount Arlington situation, suggesting the possibility of a biological attack on our nation's water supply that may be linked to Monchegorsk."

Darryl struggled to keep calm. He knew this had to be related to Berg's recent request for weapons in Kazakhstan. He disconnected the call to Liz's resident assistant.

"Nobody's answering," he said.

"She'll be fine, honey. The area affected is limited to upper Morris County. Princeton's water supply can't be connected in any way. We'll get a hold of her and make sure she buys enough bottled water to get her through the next two weeks."

"If she's not out buying water right now, there's not much of a chance she'll get her hands on any," said Darryl.

"Then I'll buy it down here and drive it up to her. Easy fix," Cheryl said.

"I'll head out right now to buy the water."

"It sounds like some kind of terrorist attack to me. I think the whole Monchegorsk angle is fear mongering, though," said Cheryl, turning off the television.

"I don't know. It may not be that farfetched. I might know someone with inside information," Darryl said, wishing he hadn't made the statement.

"You're not calling him."

"If anyone knows, it'll be him. If they expect more attacks, we need to know."

His wife stared at him for five long seconds with an impassive face. Darryl didn't like seeing this face, and could imagine the effect it would have on her staff or co-workers. She finally spoke to him.

"No requests or favors. Berg has two strikes against him at this point. One more and you're out."

"You mean *he's* out."

"I didn't misspeak. One more strike and you're out. Make sure to get a hold of Emily. She's on the other side of the country, but now you have me nervous," Cheryl said.

"I'll call her before I call Berg."

"Just hearing that name makes me cringe. I need to get moving here. I have a feeling we'll have more to discuss today than next year's curriculum and staffing levels. Keep me in the loop," Cheryl said and leaned over to kiss him goodbye.

"I will. Have a great day, my love," he said, returning the kiss.

His wife could be a real hard-ass at times, which was why he loved her even more. She'd set him straight a number of times, saving his ass from bad career moves and bad associations. The one bad habit she had never been able to break was his friendship with Karl Berg. They had a bond that could never be broken. Darryl walked through the kitchen into the den and opened one of his desk drawers, removing a "throwaway" cell phone. He dialed Berg's cell phone and waited. His friend answered on the third ring. Ten minutes later, Darryl Jackson called his wife and told her that he would take the day off and drive up to New Jersey to deliver their daughter as much bottled water as he could fit in their Suburban. He confirmed that Mount Arlington had experienced a terrorist attack on its water supply, but decided to omit the part about how the FBI and CIA couldn't account for fifty canisters of the same virus used to poison the city of Monchegorsk and turn it into a scene that would make George Romero jealous.

Chapter 19

7:11 AM
White House Situation Room
Washington D.C.

Sharpe sat next to Mendoza at the head of a large conference table in the largest interior room attached to the NCTC's watch floor. The camera imbedded into the table transmitted a digital video feed of the two agents to the White House situation room, where their bright, smiling faces would be plastered on the largest flat screen monitor available within sight of the president and most of his senior staff. To Sharpe's left, just out of camera view, sat O'Reilly, who would simultaneously transmit support media to another screen within the situation room. Ideally, she would display maps or diagrams that would provide a visual reinforcement of his talking points. They had discussed the synchronization of a few slides with his highlights immediately prior to the videoconference, but he wanted her to use her own judgment, which he trusted implicitly.

Then again, she hadn't been happy to hear about their illicit affair with General Sanderson's gang. He wouldn't be surprised to see his senior year high school portrait appear during the presentation, or much worse. O'Reilly's talent for data analysis was matched only by her proficiency with digital imaging software. He tried not to think of what might appear on the White House situation room screen if she was still as pissed off as she had been when Mendoza nearly had to drag her back into Sharpe's office. He'd hit the button to fog the windows like a panicky bank teller during a robbery, hoping that the windows were somewhat soundproof in addition to shatter resistant. He was pretty sure she would test all of those performance parameters after being pulled by her arm back in by Mendoza.

They all waited nervously, trying not to fidget or touch their faces. The director of FEMA, along with the Secretary of Homeland security, provided an update regarding efforts to contain the poisoning of a portion of Morris County Municipal Utilities Authority's water supply system through the Mt. Arlington pump station. Confirming what he already knew, FEMA's director explained how a critical error in Al Qaeda's target selection had likely spared them a major disaster. The Morris County Municipal Utilities Authority served as an indirect supplier of water to local water companies. None of the water that passed through their pump stations went directly to consumers. It was all stored in tanks owned by the townships or water companies, and subsequently piped to residents, creating a significant delay. CDC personnel, supported by state health officials, had been testing community water throughout the night, and hadn't detected signs that the Zulu Virus had been distributed. This had been a lucky break for Morris County residents. Their counterpart utilities provider in southern Morris County piped water directly to consumers. If the terrorists had chosen a pump station connected to the southern Morris County loop, they would be facing a catastrophe.

The president finally asked Director Shelby for an update regarding the Task Force's investigation. Joel Garrity, NCTC Director, looked up from his terminal at the other end of the table. The technician next to him nodded, which prompted Garrity to give Sharpe a "thumbs up." They were live.

"Mr. President, Deputy Assistant Director Ryan Sharpe will brief us on Task Force Scorpion's progress. Agent Sharpe, you have the floor."

"You can skip all of the formalities, Agent Sharpe. This is a brass tacks meeting," said the president. "Where do we stand?"

"Yes, sir. Shortly after midnight, Hamid Muhammad, the Imam with known ties to at least three of the terrorist cells assassinated yesterday, escaped from a site under active and direct FBI surveillance. He may have been abducted. The disappearance was timed with a sophisticated cyber attack on FBI computer equipment at the stakeout site."

"He's gone? How could he have escaped?" demanded Jacob Remy, White House Chief of Staff.

"I'll get to that very shortly, sir. The good news is that we received an anonymous tip a few hours later that led to the apprehension of the last terrorist cell. They were hiding out in an apartment on the edge of a well-established Muslim community in Bayonne, New Jersey. We recovered four virus canisters from this site. This still leaves fifty canisters unaccounted for, but given the intelligence provided to us by the CIA, these were the last canisters in Al Qaeda's possession. We can now focus our investigation on the domestic terror network, True America. As you know, we've identified one of the previous evening's murderers as Julius Grimes, a known True America militant."

"You still haven't answered my question, Agent Sharpe," insisted Remy.

"I apologize, sir. One of the cell phones recovered in Bayonne showed calls to a landline inside an Arab market in Brooklyn. The market is located on Coney Island Avenue, Kensington. This is one of the biggest Muslim communities in the tri-state area. We're putting this site under surveillance as we speak. The calls were placed yesterday, prior to noon prayer. We think someone at the market coordinated the pedestrian delivery of a message to the Imam, who was hiding in the mosque at the time."

"The Imam was hiding in his own mosque and you lost him? I think it's time for a sweeping look at FBI surveillance procedures. I can't believe this!" fumed Remy.

"If this is the first you've heard of Hamid Muhammad hiding in his own mosque, then I suggest the problem might lie at your own feet, Jacob. We've been working every angle possible for the past two days trying to get agents into that mosque! So far, Justice is dragging their feet and my requests through your office appear to have vaporized into thin air! No offense, Joe. I know this is above your pay grade back in those hallowed halls," said Shelby.

Joseph Morales, the Department of Justice's Assistant Attorney General for National Security raised both of his hands in a mock defeated gesture.

"None taken, of course."

"Gentlemen! We can work this out later. Agent Sharpe, do you think the Imam is hiding at the location you described?"

"It's possible, sir. We'll have the market under surveillance within the hour."

"I don't want to wait. Send in the troops. I'm comfortable hiding behind the Patriot Act on this one and the next one. No more waiting around for warrants to track down these psychopaths," said the president.

"But, Mr. President—"

"No buts, Mr. Morales. We have fifty canisters of an apocalyptic level virus out there somewhere. If I had known we were waiting around for a warrant to enter that mosque, I would have grabbed some of the generals and admirals sitting at this table and driven down there myself to kick the door down."

"The market is one thing. The mosque is an entirely different story," interjected the president's chief of staff.

"Not anymore. We have several million taxpaying citizens in New Jersey staring at their water faucets in disbelief. The news agencies are all over this. Can anyone guess the lead segment on every radio and television news broadcast this morning? Worse yet, they're starting to crack the code linking Monchegorsk to last night's attack.

"It's a little hard to conceal the fact that I've ordered the National Guard and local law enforcement agencies to secure the water supply system. Convoys of heavily armed Humvee's tend to draw attention from a public unaccustomed to seeing .50 caliber machine guns on Main Street. We can all guess where this will go very shortly, ladies and gentlemen. The Russian crackdown, despite the human rights horror involved, has bought us some valuable time. Time that's running out. We need to reassure the American people that the situation is under control. Agent Sharpe, how long until we can have a tactical unit inside that market?"

"Not long, sir. Ten minutes. May I make a proposal, Mr. President? One that will better serve the investigation."

"If you're worried about the legal ramifications, I can promise you it will not be an issue for you or anyone on your task force," the president assured him.

"I'm not worried about that, sir. Here's the problem. I'm fairly confident that Al Qaeda's role is finished. What we desperately need are some True America leads. According to the intelligence shared with my task force, the Imam collaborated with True America to gain funding for the development of the virus, in exchange for a portion of the final product. It appears True America never had any intention of honoring the deal, which makes sense. The last thing True America needs is to be connected in any way with the most reviled terrorist network in history. The Imam is the last remaining link between True America and Al Qaeda. If I were sitting on the throne at True America, I'd want him dead. They can't afford to have this nexus confirmed and made public. The Imam' network has been sloppy, as evidenced by the fact that eight out of ten cells were taken out. It's only a matter of time before True America finds him, and when they do, we'll be there. I plan to put the market under full tactical surveillance with snipers and an army of SWAT agents ready to storm the building."

Jacob Remy started to open his mouth to make what Sharpe could only assume was a crack about the task force's recent surveillance record, but the president intervened.

"Shelby, make this happen. I like the way this agent thinks. Good luck, Agent Sharpe."

"Thank you, Mr. President."

"Agent Sharpe, I'll be in touch shortly to discuss the assets involved," added Director Shelby.

The NCTC technician gave a hand signal indicating that the videoconference was finished.

"That's it. Let me know if you need anything else. I'll have the screens configured for side-by-side video streams within the hour. My techs just need the feed protocols from the field tactical teams to make it happen," said Joel, the watch floor director.

"Thanks, Joel. When the teams are set, I'll make sure they get the right protocols," said O'Reilly.

"Good luck today. Should be interesting," he said.

"Let's hope so," added Sharpe.

When Garrity and his technician closed the door, Mendoza made the first comment.

"I can't wait for Shelby's call. Assets involved? I can't believe they're going to keep this a secret. Do you think Jacob Remy knows we're using Black Flag assets?"

"Be careful with those words," warned Sharpe.

"The use of Sanderson's people has been sanctioned by the president. No limitations. I can't imagine Remy was left out of that decision."

"One thing is clear. We better not fuck up the market operation," said O'Reilly.

"I still think we need the Imam at the market," said Mendoza.

"You want to put that request through Ms. Stewart? Maybe they can drug him unconscious and sit him at a stool inside the market. Carry him around like *Weekend at Bernie's*," said Sharpe.

"Except he wouldn't be dead. Might work," added O'Reilly.

They all laughed briefly, then Sharpe got serious.

"At least we assume he isn't dead. Director Shelby never gave me the full details behind Sanderson's sudden return to the government's good graces, but it apparently involved a level of deception and manipulation similar to the stunt he pulled two years ago. He did tell me not to get comfortable with Sanderson's people," said Sharpe.

"He doesn't need to tell us that. The good general flushed nearly three years' worth of work down the toilet. Not to mention the fact that I almost lost my arm," said O'Reilly.

"He wasn't suggesting that we cozy up to the man. I think he suspects that Sanderson might somehow be involved in the virus threat. He didn't come out and say that, but I could read it from him. We need to be extremely cautious with Sanderson's people, and make no assumptions," said Sharpe.

"I'll second that," said Mendoza.

"Alright. I'll be in my office waiting for Shelby to call. Frank, would you walk up and notify Ms. Stewart? I'll contact Kathryn Moriarty and start the ball rolling in Newark. Dana, I want to be fully linked into the mobile task force on this one. Anything they can see, I want to see. I'll let Moriarty and her supervisory special agents call the shots, but I want the ability to command by negation in real time. I'll explain this to Moriarty."

The two agents nodded and wished him good luck talking to the director. He felt extremely fortunate to have them both on the task force. The three of them had a history together going back nearly five years, since the beginning of Task Force Hydra. They had started to go their separate ways after Hydra was unceremoniously destroyed by Sanderson's successful ploy to bury the rest of the Black Flag files. The setback had been costly to the American people. Sharpe didn't have time to pore over the connections, but he wondered if Sanderson's actions had enabled the very crisis they were facing.

His task force had mapped Al Qaeda's financial network in the U.S., and had already initiated the surveillance of several suspected terror cells connected with the network. All of that disappeared within the span of twelve hours on May 26, 2005, compliments of General Terrence Sanderson. Now the same man was helping them stop a terrorist plot that may never have developed without his interference. Sharpe hoped the irony of the situation wasn't lost on anyone that had sanctioned the use of Sanderson's assets.

It certainly hadn't been lost on Director Shelby. Sharpe had withheld Shelby's more caustic comments from Mendoza and O'Reilly on purpose. The director questioned Sanderson's involvement to the very core of this entire crisis. Shelby had no doubt lost much of his ability to judge the situation objectively, but even a hardened investigator like Sharpe couldn't quite shake the feeling that the director's theory held some merit. Shelby never laid it all out in front of Sharpe, but he asked some highly disturbing questions:

Don't you find it odd that all of our key intelligence came from Sanderson's people? The list of Al Qaeda addresses. Reznikov's details. Intelligence from the Kurchatov lab. Details from Monchegorsk. The Imam's sudden cooperation. Where is this Reznikov? Is the Imam really alive? Have we sent our own people to Kurchatov? How hard could it be to get our own live intel on Monchegorsk?

The more Sharpe listened, the more he started to question General Sanderson's involvement. He needed to strike a balance between pursuing the leads that made sense and protecting his own people. He couldn't expose Mendoza or O'Reilly to the director's core suspicions without risking a complete breakdown within the task force. With fifty canisters of Reznikov's designer encephalitis virus in enemy hands, he couldn't afford the slightest glitch in his team. It would remain his burden alone to harbor Shelby's suspicions.

Chapter 20

8:16 AM
Wayne County
Pennsylvania

Jackson Greely hopped down from his black 1993 Chevy Suburban 2500 and slammed the door shut. He stood nearly six feet tall on a muscular frame that would normally spill out of any oversized SUV…but not this monster. The drop from the running boards had been increased by an additional eighteen inches due to a custom drilled six-inch lift kit, bearing Goodyear R18 Kevlar tires. When it came to his transportation, Greely didn't mess around, and he'd just as soon put his concealed Smith and Wesson .357 revolver in his mouth and pull the trigger than purchase one of those Nissan or Toyota knockoff versions like the Titan or Tundra. Sure, they were built in America, but the profits flowed right out of the door to Japan. Soon enough, all of that would change.

He walked toward the open door to the right of the closed loading bay doors, noting several cars parked on the grass. As the de facto leader of True America, they had left an open path along the gravel driveway for his SUV, parking the rest of the vehicles on the far side of the driveway or in the field. Only his good friend Lee Harding dared park in front of him, and he hadn't arrived. Harding was about five minutes out, having travelled all night from their training compound. He wanted to oversee the final stage of the compound's enhanced security preparations, and ensure that Tyrell Bishop handled the next phase of their operation flawlessly.

He was greeted by Michael Brooks as he approached the door. Greely had requested a quick word with Brooks before the meeting began. Both men walked several feet away from the opening.

"Did you take care of the problem?" asked Greely.

"Last night. He almost got away on us. Bolted toward that tree line when he saw his team leader."

"Why didn't you kill him as soon as he stepped out of the van?"

"Carnes can use the help around here. The lab complex is a little short-handed, given the circumstances. The place is secure. They weren't going anywhere."

"Were there witnesses?"

"Just the security manager and his team. Everyone else was busy in the lab, which is on the far side of the complex. A five hundred pound bomb could hit your truck and nobody inside the lab would hear it," said Brooks. "Sorry. That was probably a bad choice for an example," he added.

"You're fucking right it was. If I didn't count you in my close circle of friends, I'd consider that a veiled threat."

"Sorry," repeated Brooks.

"Next time I tell you to do something, don't get creative. They should have been executed upon arrival or somewhere else. We can't afford to have rumors floating around here, not when sacrifices like these are only the beginning. We still have a long road ahead of us," Greely said, staring at the cars parked where the team was executed. "Looks like everyone except Lee is present."

"Everyone arrived within the last hour or so. Lee will be here in a few minutes," said Brooks.

Greely abruptly started to walk back toward the door.

"Jackson, before we head in…" Brooks said carefully, "What are your thoughts about Benjamin Young?"

"He still puts a lot of corporate money into our coffers. Is he showing signs of strain?" asked Greely.

"His lifestyle puts him at risk. Makes him vulnerable. He cheats on his wife daily, drinks heavily and has started to increase his cocaine habit. I'm not seeing a pretty end here."

"Send him another message. He's too damn good at wrangling money out of the Beltway and Wall Street," said Greely.

"We've already sent him two. Now there's the prostitution thing. He's flying them to his apartments in Manhattan, Atlanta and D.C. The only place he's not seen with them is during the few hours a week he spends with his wife and kids," said Brooks.

"Keep a close eye on him for now. I'll work on finding a replacement, which won't be easy. Ben is a fucking genius when it comes to schmoozing money out of people. If you detect an immediate problem, terminate his association with True America," said Greely.

"Understood."

Just as they started to walk back, a mud encrusted, hard top Jeep Wrangler skidded to a halt less than three feet from Greely's SUV, sending a cloud of gravel dust over the shiny black behemoth. Lee Harding emerged from the cloud and bounded over to greet them. In stark contrast to Jackson Greely's tall, muscular frame; Harding resembled a wiry, compact runner. He wore a loose fitting gray polo style shirt tucked into naturally faded jeans. A thick brown belt, adorned with a sizable bronze buckle plate kept the jeans affixed to his lean frame. A few steps away from Greely and Brooks, he turned around to view his handiwork.

"Sorry to get your baby a little dusty. How many times a week do you take that through the car wash?" he said, grinning.

"Only when your momma's too busy with her other chores," said Greely.

The two men shook hands and exchanged firm, yet brief man hugs. Brooks accepted a strong handshake as Greely brought him up to speed on the previous night's debacle.

"Done deal then. Michael. Keep your eyes and ears on the key players. We're in a critical, yet vulnerable phase right now. Anyone showing signs of wear and tear needs to disappear."

"Everyone's holding up so far. No indications of a problem, aside from Mr. Young. He'll be spending the next week in Atlanta near his family, so maybe things will cool down with him. Either way, we'll be watching," said Brooks.

"Shall we?" said Greely, waving his hand toward the door.

They entered the sparse complex and navigated through two empty rooms to a hallway that led deeper into the structure. The building's air temperature felt cool, with no detectable humidity, which matched the sterile appearance of the building's interior. The building still smelled like recent construction to Greely. He vividly remembered standing on the wild parcel of land currently occupied by the building, surveying the area. Just fourteen months ago, this place was a blueprint. He could barely believe that their vision for America stood a solid chance of becoming a reality. Years of rhetoric assembled in a single bold plan to propel True America into the spotlight as the nation's only hope of redemption. He marveled at the simplicity of the building. Good old fashioned building materials made right here in America. Steel imported all the way from a Wheeling-Pittsburg plant in eastern Ohio. Soon enough, the steel belt would be revived. America would be revived. Pulled right out of its grave.

He felt electrified walking through the door to the conference room. Greely remained standing as the other members of True America's secret leadership cabal settled into their chairs. He scanned their faces, looking for hints of nervousness, and found none. The group exuded confidence and purpose. Perfect for those charged with reshaping America's destiny.

"You all know I'm not big on speeches…anymore," he said, incurring a few chuckles.

He turned to face one of the team members. Tommy Brown ran the tactical side of True America's militant arm. A former Green Beret, he had retired from military service after spending most of his twenty-year career bouncing back and forth between Africa and Central America as a military advisor. Lee Harding had recruited him nearly a decade earlier, after a heated discussion about the Iran-Contra debacle.

Brown had approached him immediately after one of his rousing speeches at the Crossroads of the West Gun Show. They talked for nearly two hours about the decline of America, which Brown claimed to have seen firsthand on active duty. He wouldn't divulge the details of his involvement in Nicaragua, but the intense Jamaican-born American made it clear to Harding that he was disgusted by the government's role in the fiasco. He cited Iran-Contra as the first in a series of government sponsored disasters that had tarnished America's image abroad and weakened the nation's leverage. Harding liked what he heard and offered him a job in his fledgling political movement. Brown had proven to be one of their most loyal plank owners.

"Tommy, this is your first trip to the lab, right?"

"Yes, sir. Been a little busy at the compound," Brown said in his usual gruff voice.

"Welcome to ground zero," Greely said, shifting his gaze to a blond woman dressed in a casual gray suit.

"Anne Renee, always a pleasure. From this point forward, you'll be dividing your time between Mr. Mill's distribution center and the lab. I can't stress how important your job will be."

"I'm honored to be given this responsibility."

"You've earned it. I'll probably never understand the intricacies that went into unraveling the Al Qaeda network, but your group performed a miracle."

"Thank you, sir. I can assure you that the distribution operation will be given the same careful planning and security."

Anne Renee Paulson had been another gift from the heavens. A former Army Master Sergeant, Paulson had served as an intelligence specialist, finishing her career at Forward Operating Base Falcon just outside of Baghdad, where she put her intelligence training to work scouring the new base for security threats. Greely nodded at her before continuing.

"The final shipments arrived last night. I've asked Jason Carnes to give you all a quick rundown of our projected timeline. Jason?"

A lanky, brown haired man wearing a white lab coat over jeans and a brown shirt stood up to address the group. Carnes was their lead scientist, charged with the responsibility of overseeing production of the final product.

"The contents of all fifty canisters have been separated from their gel coatings. We are ready to mix the virus concentrate with avian blood, to promote the growth of more virus. We've tested this procedure with excellent results. Within two days, we will have enough biologically infected material to proceed with the bottling phase, though I will need at least the same amount of time to prepare the material and bottle it."

"Jason, will you explain how this works again? Why don't we just put it right into the water? I don't like the idea of preparing the material. You're planning to render it partially inert, right?"

"Correct. The biggest challenge we face is the amount of time the bottles may sit at an uncontrolled temperature. Until the moment the crates roll off our trucks, they will be kept at an optimal temperature that will ensure the virus's survival. Beyond that, we can't make any assumptions.

The mixture I plan to put into the caps will contain live virus and partially inert virus. The partially inert portion will be enveloped in dried animal feces. Virology research has proven that humans have been infected with forms of equine encephalitis through breathing in the dust from dried feces. I've tested our combined delivery method extensively over the past month, and it never fails to ensure the delivery of a contaminant level exposure. Once the bottle cap is twisted, the protective seal is breached. When the target takes a sip and replaces the cap, the virus will be mixed into the water. Trust me, Lee. This will work flawlessly."

"Unless they drink the whole bottle without replacing the cap," said Greely.

"Yes. If they don't replace the cap, then the virus won't mix," said Carnes.

"Or if they place the bottle down carefully. Doesn't water have to splash on the inside of the cap?" asked Owen Mills, owner of Crystal Source.

Mills had come up with the bottled water idea in the first place, funding a majority of the current plot from the vast fortune he made as the owner of northeastern Pennsylvania's most successful bottled water company. Crystal Source had been in his family for several decades and dominated the market in the Poconos region. Mills had secretly joined forces with Greely and Harding in the early 1990's, lured in by the promise of a seat at the big table when True America rose from the ashes.

"We've been through this already, gentlemen. Most consumers of bottled water replace the cap and toss the bottle in a backpack or car seat. I suppose if you planned to hand these out at the end of a 10K road race, you might want to reconsider the plan. I get the feeling that's not the case," said Carnes.

"We were just trying to shake the tree a little, Jason. I had to be sure of your confidence level in this design," said Harding.

"It's an effective design. Mr. Mills can attest to that," said Carnes.

"Jason worked with some of our engineers to create the cap, under the guise of research into a flavored water delivered by the same method. The only drawback I can see is the need for the water to hit the cap. He's right about the research. I funded it," said Owen Mills.

"Alright. Sorry for the theatrics, Jason. I'm hearing four days until the bottles are ready to roll?" said Greely.

"Four days minimum on this end. The bottling assembly line is a miniaturized version of what they use at any of the big plants. We have one line dedicated to removing the caps from the bottles we've stockpiled, and another to replace the caps with our own. We have the machinery to label and wrap the bottles in new pallets right here. I'm including this process in the eight day estimate."

"We've been diverting pallets of water for over two months. Nothing that would raise eyebrows in accounting," Mills stated.

"Then we have to transport it by smaller trucks and vans to the distribution hub in Honesdale, to be loaded onto larger, refrigerated trucks. One day total to move the product. Once it leaves here, it's out of my hands," said Carnes.

"Everything is set at the distribution center. I've arranged for two private docking bays, not that anything would appear unusual. I'll talk with the site supervisor to make sure nobody gets in the way. Once the pallets are delivered and staged according to their final destination, we'll bring in the trucks. I figure it'll take them the better part of a work day to get the trucks loaded and on the streets," said Mills.

"I wish we could load it here. Too much back and forth bullshit," Greely griped.

"We're looking at massive, one time deliveries requiring the use of refrigerated semi-trailers. We could never get anything that big in here."

"I know. It worries me. Tommy, we'll be leaning heavily on your friend here. Tactical and operational security will be critical at that site and everywhere in between. I can't stress the importance of your job, Renee. Once the product starts to leave this lab, we enter the final, tactical phase of the operation."

"I understand, sir. Mr. Brown and I have selected the best operatives for the job. The loading bays are isolated and secure. All of the paperwork is in order. Everyone has been briefed and rebriefed. We're ready to execute the mission," said Paulson.

"Excellent. I'm not detecting any impediments to our progress at this point, however, since we're here, I'd like to discuss an opportunity to completely close the link between True America and Hamid Muhammad. Tommy, how confident are you that our friend escaped FBI surveillance?"

"Extremely," Brown answered. "FBI agents turned the mosque inside out last night, around midnight. One of the undercover SWAT units took off like a bat out of hell in pursuit of something just before the raid. A white van sped off from the scene, just before SWAT responded. Regular police radio traffic indicated a massive response in support of federal agents. He's still out there."

"Which concerns me," said Greely.

"We should have killed him earlier," Mills chimed in.

"We needed him to go to ground and activate the remaining cell," said Harding.

"Cells," Brown corrected.

Anne Renee Paulson shot him a confused look, followed by the rest of the group. He tapped his iPhone screen.

"Breaking news," he read. "FBI officials just announced that they have captured the last remaining cell in the terrorist network responsible for the water supply attack at Mt. Arlington pump station. Based on foreign and domestic intelligence sources, they are confident that the captured cell represents the last of the Al Qaeda network involved in a recently uncovered plot to poison multiple water sources. Hamid Muhammad, 'the radical Imam,' is wanted in a possible connection to the plot. His whereabouts are currently unknown."

"He's a slippery son-of-a-bitch. We need to find him before the FBI does," said Harding.

"Renee, I'm going to keep Mr. Estrada's team in place within the tri-state area. Killing Hamid Muhammad takes priority. The Imam will turn up shortly, and we'll be there to remove him from the equation. Tommy, make sure Estrada's group is ready to roll at a moment's notice, no subtlety necessary. The media will attribute his execution to a radical anti-Muslim group. Just find him and kill him," said Greely.

"We'll start actively turning over his known hideouts," said Brown.

"Just make sure not to attract any FBI attention," Greely ordered.

"Understood. We'll be using the best technology money can buy to track the FBI."

"The best that *I* can buy," said Mills, and they all laughed.

"All right. This will probably be our last face-to-face meeting for quite a while. We all go our separate ways and communicate by secure satellite phone only. If the FBI is looking in our direction, they're not going to find anything. Let's not give them something to work with. That's it, everyone. A new dawn awaits us in about three weeks."

"To a new America," boasted Mills.

"To the True America," responded everyone.

"Michael, can you stick around for a second?" said Greely, nodding to Harding.

"Sure."

Greely and Harding made their way around the room, shaking hands and patting backs, before closing the door and returning to Brooks.

"How are things going with our special surveillance project?" Greely asked.

"Making progress. I've narrowed the selection down to three possible candidates. I can't rush this one. Once the offer is made, the candidate either accepts or has to disappear. Just one disappearance could jeopardize the project. I need to choose the candidate carefully," said Brooks.

"Take your time, but don't take forever. We need better FBI intelligence. We'll proceed with the next phase in three days. I need your special project operational by that time. Things will move fast after the next attack."

"I can do it in three days."

"I wasn't giving you the option to take longer," said Greely. "We've waited long enough to see this day."

"We'll approach the candidate within two days. This is going to be an amazing few weeks," said Brooks.

"Scary as all hell," Harding said, "but worth every bit of sacrifice."

Greely couldn't have agreed more. He was ready to sacrifice his own life if necessary to bring the United States of America back to its former glory. The next three weeks would prove pivotal to their efforts to bring about The New Recovery, True America's primary goal for the American people.

Dissatisfied with the costs associated with America's present role as the world's police force and frustrated by politicians that continued to turn a blind eye to the economic warfare being waged against the U.S. through uneven trade relationships; more and more Americans were looking for an alternative. The New Recovery would usher in a new era of strength, prosperity and independence for the American people. Two decades of "deterrent isolationism" to rebuild America's infrastructure, reinvest in U.S. industry and restructure foreign policy. The United States would emerge from The New Recovery as an ultra-super power, with few of the ties currently hindering its prosperity and security.

He swelled with pride at the thought of playing a role in the nation's transformation. While their extreme plan would be disavowed by the mainstream True America political movement, the aftershock would enable True America political leaders to topple the two-party system and offer a new option for True Americans. At first he'd be declared an outlaw, but as America transformed, the history books would change to reflect their greatness…and how True America's founders, like Romulus and Remus, had changed the course of human history.

Chapter 21

3:55 PM
Charleston International Airport
Charleston, South Carolina

Arranging to meet Jessica in the private lounge had turned out to be one of his better ideas. If she had been given the opportunity to blend into a larger group in the "arrivals" area, he may not have recognized her. She wore a stylish, colorful sleeveless turtleneck top with designer jeans and black narrow strap sandals. As always, she looked stunning, but he wasn't sure if he cared for her short hair.

"Like my new hairstyle?" she asked, immediately testing him.

"It looks incredible. I never pictured you with short hair, but it really works," Daniel said, dropping his carry-on bag.

"Bullshit."

He embraced her, mindful of her injuries, and kissed her passionately. He wished that they could fully test the privacy of this lounge. He'd been gone for seven days, but it felt like a lifetime. He couldn't imagine how Jessica felt. Despite her advertised self-reliance and confidence, he knew that she depended on him emotionally. Sanderson had been wise to keep the details of her attack a secret until the Stockholm operation had run its course. He would have left the operation to Farrington and jumped on the next plane to Buenos Aires, which could have led to disastrous results across the board. The mission might have failed and he would more than likely have been picked up at the Buenos Aires airport.

By the time Sanderson had shared the details of Jessica's harrowing experience, she had recovered enough to convince him that he could shepherd the last stage of the mission in Germany. He felt guilty delaying his return, but she sounded stable, and he trusted Munoz and Melendez implicitly to guard her. He eased his embrace, but she showed no sign of releasing him.

"You're back," she whispered, resting her head on his shoulder.

"I'm back."

She let go and backed up a few steps to look him over.

"Not a scratch? Amazing."

"A few scratches and bruises, but nothing more than that."

He didn't dare go any further. He'd been chased down by Mi-28 Havoc helicopters, ambushed by a regional Spetznaz platoon, fired upon at point blank range by armored vehicles, swarmed by virus-crazed "zombies," and caught in a crossfire by Zaslon operatives. All of this, however, paled in comparison to Jessica's ordeal. She had narrowly escaped a fate worse than death—being gang-raped for hours by the most detestable, heartless group of men to ever walk the planet. He would never leave her side again, except for one final mission to kill Srecko Hadzic. He'd make that one exception.

"I'm so glad you're back. We can't be apart again. Ever. It's not good for me," she said.

He could see her eyes watering, and felt his own start to moisten.

"Never again. We're a team," he said and kissed her lips.

"I'm really digging the new look. Seriously. Sexy and smart," he said.

"Unlike before?"

"I think I'll shut up for now. How's your hand?"

He took her left hand gently in his own and examined the tight bandage.

"Not so bad. It's healing pretty quickly. I can bend the fingers without too much pain. Looks like hell underneath the bandages."

"And your neck?" he said, gently caressing the soft skin just under her right cheek.

"Turtlenecks are my new fashion. I even found a bathing suit. Looks a little retro, but it works."

"Let's get out of here. I rented a Jeep for us," he said, and paused to hold her again. "I missed you so much. I love you more than you could possibly know."

"I love you even more," she said.

They held each other for another minute, before slowly letting go.

"A jeep? I was thinking more like a convertible BMW. Less jostling around."

"Whatever you desire my beloved princess."

"Right now I want to get us checked into our villa. I have a few desires that can't be fulfilled in this lobby," she said.

"Maybe we should rent a van," he suggested.

"I figured you'd be sick of vans at this point," she said.

"Good point. We can wait."

❧

Several hours later, Jessica and Daniel lay next to each other, listening to the surf crash onto the beach in front of their villa. Naked in a tangle of sheets, their breathing slowly returned to normal after another intense session exploring each other's bodies. He didn't want her to feel rushed, and would have been fine waiting as long as she needed, but she didn't hesitate. They had picked up Thai takeout and a few bottles of white wine on the way back in their BMW 3 Series convertible, enjoying a private dinner on the small wooden deck overlooking the Atlantic Ocean. Warm sea breezes washed over them, fueling their desires as the wine magnified the experience. Halfway through dinner, Jessica had grabbed his hand and pulled him through the sliding door to the bedroom. They had started off tentatively, as he had expected, but this uncertainty dissolved quickly as passion and arousal smothered them unchecked. Neither of them seemed to notice that night had descended, and they still hadn't cleaned up dinner when the moon finally made an appearance over the eastern horizon, casting a pale blue light onto their bed. He rolled over and held her tightly. She sighed and didn't say a word.

Daniel woke up as the first tendrils of sunlight reached the wicker headboard of their cottage bed. He was lying next to Jessica, both of them buried under the sheets and blankets that had been tossed from the bed at some point the night before. The temperature had dipped significantly after midnight, changing the breezes that flowed freely off the ocean into their cottage. He vaguely remembered picking up the bed linens and haphazardly tucking them back into the bed before closing the patio slider.

Jessica lay asleep on her side, facing his side of the bed. Her makeup had faded during the night, and he could see the black eye that dominated the right side of her face. She had removed her contacts at some point in the evening, which exposed the broken blood vessels surrounding her naturally brown iris. He felt anger and guilt rising within him, which was never a good combination for Daniel. Her neck was the worst part. Several horizontal scabs marked the ordeal that had nearly killed her. They must have restrained her by the neck with piano wire, or some kind of game fish line. Still rubbed raw, a band of red puffy skin and dark scabs circled her entire neck. Srecko would suffer a painful death for putting her through this. Anger and guilt. Bad for Daniel, but even worse for Srecko.

He reached out and caressed her left cheek. She settled into a smile, keeping her eyes closed.

"How does Frankenbride look without her disguise?"

"Positively beautiful, as always," he said, without hesitation.

"Uh-huh. What time is it?" she muttered, finally opening her eyes.

"Ten after seven. The sun just peeked over the water. I'll make us some coffee if you're getting up."

"That sounds nice. I'll get dressed and meet you out on the patio," she said.

"Are you trying to get rid of me?" Daniel said, kissing her inviting lips.

"Yes. You may not have a problem with the way I look, but I do. Quick change and makeup job. I promise."

"I meant what I said. You look beautiful."

Jessica sat up in the bed, pulling the sheets up to her chin. "I know you did. I just don't feel right displaying my injuries to the public."

"Who cares?"

"I do. I don't play the role of victim very well. It's hard not to feel like a full time victim bearing these scars. Plus, everyone will think you're a wife beater."

He stared at her for a moment, neither pitying her nor trying to process her logic. He just wanted to gaze at the woman he loved, and would sacrifice anything to protect. His love for her had no boundaries and no other loyalties. He knew this would be tested again, but from this point forward, they would remain together. He had long ago committed to spending the rest of his life with her, no matter what the circumstances. Long before either of them had been swallowed up by devils disguised as government agents and military heroes.

He'd started carrying a small diamond ring around with him during the spring of their final semester of college. He kept waiting for the right moment to spring the question, thinking he had all the time in the world. When she said goodbye and suddenly disappeared from his life a few days after graduation, he'd been devastated. He regretted waiting more than anything in his life. The ring could have changed everything, and put them on a path that didn't consume them from the inside, corrupting their morality and burying the deepest scars in their subconscious. All of this was his fault for waiting to make a decision that he knew was inevitable.

"You there, Danny?" she said, waving a hand in front of him.

He nodded and shook his head at the same time.

"Yep. Sort of. Sorry. I was just thinking out everything at one time. Not a good idea for this tiny brain," he said and leaned over to kiss her on the forehead.

"We'll have plenty of time to think through all of this. Just you and me," she said.

"I like the sound of that. See you on the patio."

Chapter 22

8:47 PM
Coney Island Avenue
Brooklyn, New York

Abraham Sayar sat quietly at a round marble topped table near the expansive front window of the El Halal Middle Eastern Market. The window covered most of the store's frontage, extending from the left most side of the market to the glass and metal door packed against the right side wall. Bathed in bright fluorescent lighting, with his back against a poster-covered wall, he concentrated on his tea and tried not to think about how exposed he felt in front of the window. He was the market's lone table customer, drawing an occasional stare from the sparse foot traffic on Coney Island Avenue.

Typically, all of the tables would be crowded with loud groups sipping tea like Sayar, serving as a spirited backdrop for the numerous patrons who stopped by to grab freshly prepared Middle Eastern dishes and imported sundries. Word had leaked over the course of the day that something big was happening at El Halal, and it was best to avoid the place for now. All of this had been engineered by Sayar and his team, through the Imam.

They wanted to avoid civilian casualties at all costs and avoid complications, but most importantly, they wanted to give the market a strong aura to observers on the street. Anyone asked would recommend steering clear of El Halal tonight, which was exactly the kind of publicity Sayar wanted to convey to any True America reconnaissance teams. He was trying to give True America the strong impression that El Halal had a secret. They had no idea if the terror group could track the Imam's calls, but if they arrived anywhere in Kensington, all signs would lead to their trap.

Sayar hadn't moved from his table for most of the day, marking him as part of the Imam's personal security detail. He wore western style street clothes, which made him even more conspicuous. He had traded the traditional loose fitting clothing for dark khaki pants, a white button down oxford and an outdated Members Only style, waist level jacket, which he hadn't removed since he arrived. His muscular frame added to the menace he exuded with his tense body posture and permanently affixed scowl.

The rest of his team was scattered throughout the store. Diyah Castillo sat behind the cash register, looking bored and pretending to text friends on her cell phone. She was dressed more traditionally, better reflecting the Muslim values of the community, without going overboard. Her head was loosely wrapped in a light blue hijab, exposing only her face. The rest of her outfit consisted of dark blue jeans and a light brown, patterned blouse. It was a stylish representation of the women's Muslim dress code that had become more common with the Muslim youth in America.

The last visible member of the team wandered through the store, lingering in different sections to handle the merchandise for a few minutes before moving on. He took a few breaks from this routine throughout the day, to join Sayar for tea and food. This marked him as part of the security team, if there had been any doubt before, which was all part of the desired effect.

Abdul Waseer remained upstairs, monitoring the surveillance feeds from a camera hidden in the alley and another attached to a light post in front of the market. Thanks to the electronic warfare team sitting in a van nearby, he could also listen to FBI radio traffic. His primary job was to give the team downstairs an advanced warning of an attack. This task would be critical to their survival. Once detected, he would descend the stairs and reinforce efforts to repel the assault. His arrival would be a welcome sight to the three vulnerable operatives sitting exposed in the market. Their defensive situation hadn't materialized like Sayar had hoped.

They wore level-two body armor under their clothing, which would protect them from most submachine gun and sidearm rounds, but they had been under- equipped for the mission with FBI issued Glock 23 pistols. Sayar had lobbied for more firepower, but his request had been met with considerable resistance by the mobile task force commander, Special Agent-in-Charge, Kathryn Moriarty. Special Agent Damon Katsoulis had started to protest, but Moriarty had shut him down quickly. Apparently, the "powers-that-be" in the FBI still didn't fully trust Sanderson's people. He shared a few knowing looks with Katsoulis, as Moriarty lectured Sayar and his team of operatives. At least he had one possible ally in the FBI. Since Katsoulis's snipers and assault teams covered the market, this made him breathe a little easier through Moriarty's condescending diatribe.

At length, she "reminded" him that their sole purpose was to lure True America into the open. At least she acknowledged the reality of their precarious situation in the store, though she grossly overestimated her own units' response time. They all agreed that the attack would come fast and furious, but Moriarty insisted that they would only need enough firepower to slow the initial attack. FBI snipers and tactical units would "go to work" on hostile forces as soon as they were detected. Sayar saw the logic of this approach, but still requested two semi-automatic shotguns—one to cover each entrance to the market. FBI intelligence indicated that True America had access to some serious weaponry and body armor, representing a combination that would be hard to stop with pistols. His request was immediately denied. Even Katsoulis nearly shook his head in front of his boss.

He still had some hope that a direct attack on the market might never materialize. Sanderson' electronic warfare team had a solid chance to detect and identify the assault units on the street, giving the FBI and Sayar's team fair warning about their approach. Of course, the existence of Sanderson's electronics laden mini-van remained a secret from the FBI, so they would have to be extremely creative with how they alerted the FBI. He had been assured by his counterpart, Aleem Fayed, that the techs had a solid plan. He just hoped that the plan would give the FBI enough time to make a difference in the fight.

ởỡ

Timothy Graves caught himself holding his breath again. In extremely tense situations, he had a bad habit of not breathing. Anish Gupta interrupted his concentration.

"You're holding your breath again."

"No shit. It helps me think," said Graves, shifting uncomfortably in his folding chair.

"Actually, you're depriving your brain of oxygen, which accomplishes the opposite," said Gupta.

"No. Depriving my body of oxygen vasodilates the blood vessels, allowing a better perfusion of oxygen when I breathe again. It gives me a heightened state of awareness," said Graves, not sure if his nonsense would pass muster with Gupta.

"The blood vessels in the lungs vasoconstrict during hypoxia, which renders your proposed theory ineffective," Gupta countered.

"Do you know everything?"

"Pretty much," replied Gupta.

They both stared at the various screens, searching for anything that might indicate an imminent attack on the El Halal market. So far, the only encrypted radio traffic near the target area belonged to the FBI. One of their computer screens tracked and sorted the data transmitted by the FBI's P25 equipped radios. This data included locations. Graves had installed two battery powered "pinging" relays on nearby rooftops prior to the FBI's mid-morning arrival. Once the FBI's operating frequencies had been established, they had actively "pinged" the data layer and catalogued the automated responses. The radio users didn't have to transmit a radio message to appear on their "radar." Even non-transmitting radios would respond to their undetectable "pings."

Within seconds of the FBI's arrival on and around Coney Island Avenue, Gupta had mapped the entire task force. Once all of the FBI units had settled into their positions, he activated the two remote relays and tasked the system to simultaneously "ping" the entire task force twice every second. The silent responses allowed them to triangulate the position of each FBI radio, and more importantly, each agent. The computer screen displayed a map of the streets surrounding El Halal Market, marking their locations.

The FBI occupied the only vacant apartment on the street within view of El Halal Market. With a diagonal view, the apartment served as the FBI's sniper nest and headquarters. They counted ten radios in the building, four of which they had identified as either a sniper or spotter. The remaining six radios were by far the most active of the task force. Overall, the FBI had lucked out with their temporary lodging.

Situated on the corner of Coney Island Avenue and Foster Avenue, less than one hundred meters from the market, the third floor corner unit commanded an expansive southbound view of Coney Island Avenue. The view stretched nearly an entire city block, giving the sharpshooters perfect firing trajectories at potential threats nearly one hundred meters from the market, in any direction on the street. If confirmed threats approached from the south, snipers could engage at further distances.

The FBI's view of the northern approach was limited by the shallow angle of the street facing windows along Coney Island Avenue. FBI observers could not effectively see beyond the intersection of Foster and Coney Island. Fortunately, their position north of the market gave them ample time to respond to any threats coming in from the north.

The only other road emptying into this crowded stretch of Coney Island Avenue was Glenwood Road, which passed just under the FBI apartment, and was under direct surveillance by a large contingent of FBI SWAT vehicles hidden at the edge of a church parking lot fifty meters back from Coney Island Avenue. They counted fourteen radios at that location. Radio traffic indicated that this would be the primary response team. Three additional teams sat hidden in similar locations off Coney Island Avenue, each consisting of eight SWAT agents in two vehicles. One would seal Foster Avenue to the north, and another would block the south, emerging from a hidden location in a funeral home on H Avenue.

The third team had the most difficult job. Eight agents had to cover the claustrophobic alleyway approach, that had multiple points of access leading into the darkened, trash strewn space from the driveways and homes on the residential street behind the market. They could only rely on these agents to provide an early warning. There were too many points of entry and positions of cover in the alley to effectively engage a trained terrorist group without the assurance of friendly casualties, or the deployment of thirty additional agents. The FBI's tactical team leader had been uncomfortable spreading his agents so thin along the rear approach, especially since they would not be "geared up" like the rest of his agents. They would be in street clothes, equipped with compact submachine guns and concealable body armor. He needed them to somewhat blend into the neighborhood, even if they were just sitting in cars or hanging back in the shadows. The agents watching the alley would rally together and respond on foot once the entire threat picture developed.

From Graves' point of view, the FBI's deployment looked solid. This assessment had been slightly reassuring to Sayar, who might have to rely upon the FBI's response to stay alive. Sayar would need to keep True America's assault team at bay for at least thirty seconds, until the FBI arrived. As always, this assumed that the FBI assault teams hadn't been detected. If True America ran interference against the responding agents, Sayar and his team could find themselves in an even more desperate situation. He hoped they could give the FBI advanced warning. It could mean the difference between life and death for Sayar's crew. Early detection hinged on the same method used to identify and map the FBI's deployment.

Graves watched Gupta's eyes shift between the two screens in front of him. Aside from his fingers tapping at a thin silver wireless keyboard, nothing else moved. He sat locked into the chair, intensely focused on their mission, taking only a fraction of a second away from the task to deliver the occasional, well-deserved sarcastic comment. Normally, these comments would flow freely, but under pressure, Gupta became tolerable inside the cramped utility van. Blessed silence let Graves know that Gupta was ultra-focused.

Graves noticed a change on one of the screens. Gupta's fingers started typing before he could form the thought to speak.

"What's that?"

"Working on it. We might have an encrypted transmission," said Gupta.

Their system continuously scoured the airwaves for encrypted and "in the clear" radio signals, processing each transmission's electronic characteristics through protocols designed to detect an inbound covert operation. The system was intimately familiar with all of the "background" noise within a three block radius of El Halal Market. Wireless routers, personal handheld radios, local police channels, cordless telephones, cell phone towers…all of it categorized by the antenna Grave's had installed on the roof of the apartment building currently used by the FBI on Coney Island Avenue. The sensitive, multi-spectrum receiver had "listened" to the neighborhood for nearly twelve hours, passing information to the van. The data processed and catalogued by their software provided an intimate look at the area's electronic signature. After twelve hours, any new transmissions stood out like a sore thumb. A previously undetected P25 encryption protocol suddenly appeared on his screen.

"Market, this is Over Watch. Possible assault inbound. We are in the process of confirming," said Graves.

He received acknowledgements from the team in the market and Sayar. Fayed sat with Tariq Paracha in a stolen Honda Accord three blocks away from the market, waiting to play their role.

Gupta furiously typed commands, trying to stay a few steps ahead of the incoming data analysis. He didn't bother telling the computer to break the encryption code. The coroner would be zipping up body bags by the time their proprietary blunt force crypto-hack program provided the intruder system's encryption protocols. All he really needed was to determine locations, which would be simple. The system isolated the data layer used by the encrypted signal, and Gupta ordered the remote relays to repeatedly "ping" all users within that layer. As the new radios silently responded to his "ping" request, the digital street map of the neighborhood changed, and Graves stopped breathing. They would have seconds instead of minutes to make a difference.

&

Special Agent Shawn Barber stared out of the third story bedroom window at the El Halal Market storefront. From his position in one of the apartment's south facing windows, he could see the sidewalks on both sides of the street. Several sodium vapor street lamps cast ample light onto the busy street, eliminating his need for the tripod-mounted night vision scope pushed into the corner next to him.

His eyes flickered to the left, catching the faint outline of Special Agent Stephan Woods on the other side of the darkened room. The young agent sat forward in a folding chair, staring through the enormous night vision scope attached to his bolt-action Remington M40A1 .308 sniper rifle. The rifle, with its bipod extended, rested on a small table pushed against the wall under the other south facing window.

Barber's weapon hung by a combat sling designed to keep the weapon diagonal across the front of his chest. His right hand rested on the rifle's pistol grip, ready to release the safety and put the weapon into action in a moment's notice. He heard talking from one of the rooms adjacent to the bedroom, but didn't turn to look. The task force's leadership team had occupied the rest of the apartment, setting up a disorganized gaggle of folding tables and chairs to hold up the computers that they seemed dependent upon to breathe. He had been with the FBI long enough to know a time when everything didn't depend on internet protocols and email. A time when the job didn't require four technicians to support every agent in the field.

He had joined the Bureau after returning from the first Gulf War. His Boston based Marine Corps reserve unit had been activated in the fall of 1990, just a few months after he completed his bachelor's degree at Stonehill College. As the platoon's only "officially" trained sniper, Staff Sergeant Barber spent most of Operation Desert Storm attached to his battalion's reconnaissance element, riding in an open HUMVEE well forward of the front lines. Upon returning to the States in April, 1991, he applied for a job with the FBI, hitting the post-Vietnam federal retirement wave perfectly. He found himself back in Quantico, Virginia just in time for an unmistakably miserable mid-Atlantic summer.

Barber took in the entire scene on Coney Island Avenue. Every minute, no fewer than a dozen cars passed the market, coming from either direction. The stoplight at the intersection of Foster and Coney Island didn't seem to have the slightest impact on the traffic. Pedestrian traffic in the immediate vicinity had lightened significantly from rush hour. The bus stop directly across from the apartment had stopped disgorging riders, which eased the flow of pedestrians wandering the streets. Occasionally, one or two passengers would loiter at the stop, and board an outbound bus. Still, he counted eight civilians within the designated engagement zone.

He stifled a yawn, turning it into an arm stretch. Just as his arms extended outward, his radio crackled and came to life.

"Two cars approaching. Weapons visible. Right in front of the market!"

The transmission was followed by Supervisory Special Agent Katsoulis's voice and the sound of panicked footsteps rushing into the bedroom.

"Unit transmitting. Identify yourself."

Barber didn't have time to fully process Katsoulis's request. By the time he had shouldered his weapon and kneeled, bracing the rifle's vertical grip against the windowsill, it didn't matter who had given the warning. He watched the street over the scope, not wanting to limit his situational awareness, and saw the attack unfold. The maneuver was brilliant.

A northbound SUV veered left, crossing the median and jumping the curb in front of the El Halal Market. The massive vehicle struck a fire hydrant and smashed into the far right corner of the market, sending a thick column of water skyward. The sharp, staccato crackling of automatic weapons fire immediately filled the street. As the market's front window collapsed and cascaded onto the sidewalk, a white delivery van screeched to a halt in the southbound lane, directly in front of the door to the market. Several figures burst from the van, rushing through the parked cars and cascading water toward the market's front entrance.

Barber needed to make it difficult for anyone to enter the store, so he decided against taking any individually aimed shots. He placed the 4X ACOG scope's illuminated green arrow just forward of the doorway, and started firing methodically. He never heard the single boom from Wood's .308 rifle, which took down the first man in line to enter the market. The rest of True America's assault team passed through his scope's field of vision, braving the rapid, semi-automatic fire from his MK14 Enhanced Battle Rifle.

By the time the remaining men disappeared into the El Halal Market, two more attackers had been stopped, their bodies crumpled in the doorway. He had no idea how many had made it inside and didn't have time to think about it. Glass rained down upon his head, trickling through his open collar, which meant that the men in the SUV had turned their attention to their sniper nest. There was nothing he could do for the operatives in the market, so he quickly inserted a new twenty round magazine into his rifle and went to work on the attackers using the SUV as cover.

He heard the supersonic crack of Wood's .308 high-grain boat tail hollow point (BTHP) round and saw one of the shooters snap backward, tumbling uncontrollably onto the pavement. Through the thick downpour of water, Barber sighted in on a man near the back of the SUV and depressed the trigger twice. The black clad, masked commando spun in place, flinging his compact rifle out of Barber's view before dropping to one knee. A third 7.62mm round from the EBR passed through the man's head and shattered the rear compartment window. Another boom from Wood's rifle echoed through the room, but Barber never saw the result. He scanned the front of the SUV, which was barely visible through the mist created by the geyser of water shooting two stories high. The wind brought most of the water down on the roof of the building.

A head appeared over the hood of the SUV, followed by a blazing assault rifle. Several rounds from the rifle struck the apartment wall, passing through. Screams erupted from behind him, never breaking his concentration. He steadied the green reticle arrow on the head, conscious of the fact that the man's rifle continued to pour rounds into his position. He applied even pressure to the trigger and was rewarded by the rifle's kick. The head and rifle quickly disappeared.

"That's a kill!" yelled Woods.

In the seconds that followed, a vicious firefight erupted in the darkened market below them, drowned out by the ringing in Barber's ears. Repeated muzzle flashes punctuated the gray fountain of water pouring down onto the sidewalk, competing with the red and blue strobe lights from the FBI SWAT team screeching into position on the street directly in front of the market.

ॐ

The market went dark and Abraham Sayar dove to the floor with his teacup still clenched in his left hand. His right hand already held his pistol. Naturally right handed, he relegated the busy work to his less coordinated hand while "on the job," keeping his dominant hand free to react. This simple, disciplined act would save his team from a quick demise. Dozens of bullets slapped into the posters behind his seat before he hit the ground, showered in shards of glass from the market's front window. Automatic gunfire shattered the market, filling the aisles with a volume of incoming rounds that Sayar had never experienced before. Concentrated, extended bursts snapped overhead and tore through foreign-labeled packaging, exploding the dried contents. He heard a muffled scream from the back of the market, which sounded like Diyah Castillo. The screech of tires took him out of reaction mode and put him on the offensive. They were up against two vehicles on Coney Island Avenue. The first vehicle had been True America's "shock and awe" attempt. The second would contain the breach team.

He unconsciously released the teacup and gripped the pistol with two hands, quickly rolling through the freshly broken glass to a position directly in front of the market's entrance. A cold mist from the fire hydrant's spray hit his face, as blurred figures appeared on the sidewalk. He aimed at the first figure's head and started to pull the trigger, but the man dropped to the ground. The next darkened mass spun in the doorway, punctured by bullets from an unseen shooter. A man in street clothes wearing body armor and a ski mask burst through the door, shoulder firing a drum-fed Saiga shotgun into the market. Lying well below the Saiga's twelve-gauge shot pattern,

Sayar fired a single .40 caliber round from his Glock through the intruder's forehead and searched for another target past the descending body. The lifeless body slumped to the left, pinning the door against the wall.

He watched another body awkwardly fall into the threshold, the victim of FBI sharpshooters. Before he could mentally celebrate, another heavily armed commando jumped through the doorway, dropping to the floor a few feet in front of Sayar. From a prone position, he fired an extended burst from his G36C assault rifle at the area around Sayar's table. The man realized his mistake halfway through the burst and swung the rifle in Sayar's direction. The Israeli born operative stopped the rifle with his left hand and placed the Glock against the side of the man's head, blasting his brains onto the wall next to the door.

An explosion from the rear of the market told him that their ordeal was far from finished. Another team had been detected in one of the homes across the alleyway. He reached forward to grab the semi-automatic shotgun that had fallen against the blood-splattered door, still hearing gunfire on Coney Island Avenue. He'd have to rely on the FBI to finish the job out there.

He holstered the pistol and shouldered the massive shotgun before moving deeper into the market. In a low crouch, he made it a third of the way through the maze of merchandise before the shooting started. Unable to positively identify anyone through the smoke caused by the blast, he held his fire for a few seconds…until automatic weapons fire and shotgun blasts dominated the store. He couldn't imagine that any of his team had survived. The door leading upstairs was open, which meant that Abdul had joined the fight. Two gaping holes and several smaller splinter marks in the door gave Sayar the impression that he hadn't lasted very long.

He lined up the nearest shadow detectable through the smoke, and put the shotgun into action, pulling the trigger repeatedly as he moved swiftly toward the back of the market. He expended the fifteen remaining twelve gauge shells within a few seconds, abruptly stopping the assault team's momentum into the market. Grunts and screams erupted during his sudden charge, as a wall of double ought buckshot blanketed the narrow confines of the storage area, ripping through half of the True America commandos. Return fire followed immediately, barely giving Sayar enough time to reach the cashier counter. He saw a dark red, football-sized smear on a calendar tacked to the wall behind Diyah's stool. The operative was nowhere in sight.

He caught movement in his peripheral vision and hurled himself over the counter. Before he could clear the white Formica barrier, an automatic weapon sent several bullets in his direction. The counter disintegrated around him and he felt his left knee explode, followed by a similar pain in his right ankle. He crashed into a stack of VHS tapes and toppled a recycling bin as his momentum slammed him down to the littered floor.

He heard repeated pistol shots and looked up to see Diyah Castillo sitting low against the wall a few feet away, firing her pistol through the opening in the counter. Her face looked ashen. She stared blankly down the sight of the Glock, firing slow, methodical shots. The drywall around her exploded, as True America's commandos started to take better-aimed shots from the storeroom. She didn't flinch as the rounds hit the wall next to her head.

He reached out and grabbed her bloodied left arm, yanking her toward him as several bullets struck the space she had just previously occupied. Her right arm remained extended and she continued to fire. A ski mask and assault rifle appeared above the counter, the barrel pointed right at his head. Before the muzzle could flash, ending Sayar's life, Diyah's pistol roared, sending a .40 caliber hollow point round through the rifle's EOTech sight. A massive dark splash hit the wall behind the commando's head.

He had managed to bring his own weapon up over Diyah's left shoulder when he saw more movement over the counter. *Too many of them,* he thought, as the slide on Diyah's Glock locked back. Her pistol was empty, and there was no way she would be able to reload it. Her left arm had been destroyed. He raised his own pistol, thinking that this was the end. He hoped their sacrifice would give Sanderson what he needed to stop True America. Before he could pull the trigger, bursts of rifle fire erupted from the front of the market. He was faintly aware of the blue and red light dancing on the market's surfaces and the sound of yelling. The words "clear" and "FBI" rang in his ears.

Aleem Fayed sprinted down the poorly lit, uneven sidewalk, keeping his suppressed MP-9 submachine gun as low as possible. Tariq followed a few steps behind. He couldn't believe their luck, given the fact that the True America operatives had nearly achieved a complete surprise attack. Their radio discipline had kept the impending assault from detection until the very last moment, when the final order had been given from the vehicle they were rapidly approaching. One brief radio transmission had given their electronic warfare team everything they needed.

Tariq and Aleem had been parked just around the block when the attack order had been transmitted. The close proximity of True America's command vehicle put them within striking distance. When the location of the transmitted order popped up on their mobile tablet, they hadn't wasted a second talking about options. They bolted out of their car, leaving the keys in the ignition.

The occupants of this vehicle had been the true purpose of the entire operation. The FBI might capture some of the True America shooters alive in the market, but Sanderson was more interested in getting his hands on someone higher up in the leadership structure. Given the training level of the True America operatives, Sanderson highly suspected the existence of a substantial training compound. If they could discover the location of True America's militant training center, the FBI should be able to rapidly unravel True America's plot. Aleem intended to be the one to deliver this information to FBI.

The two operatives slowed to a quick walk, raising their weapons to a ready position. Tariq's MP-9 had been fitted with an underslung Taser, which would be critical to taking one of the men alive. It would be Aleem's job to identify the leader and kill the rest. They had exhaustingly practiced this abduction technique at the Argentina compound, to the point where they could take down a four-man security team, removing the high-value target within seconds. As they weaved through the thick tree trunks between the parked cars and sidewalk, he could see that they were dealing with two men in an Explorer parked three cars down. The sound of automatic gunfire echoed off the brownstone houses, hitting his ears from every direction.

The driver raised a handheld radio to his ear for a few seconds, before lowering it and shaking his head quickly. The Explorer's brake lights illuminated, followed by the sound of the vehicle's ignition turning over.

"Driver is our target," said Aleem.

Tariq sprinted forward, clearing the trees, while Aleem slipped between two parked cars and approached from the street. As he passed the rear of the Explorer, he barely caught the white reverse light in his peripheral vision. If the car was in gear, this could get complicated when Tariq's Taser pushed 50,000 volts of electricity through the driver's body. If his foot was on the accelerator, they'd have a major problem. It was too late to stop Tariq. He just hoped his partner detected the white reverse lights. Based on Tariq's wide angle of approach, he wasn't hopeful.

As soon as the front passenger's head came into view through the rear passenger window, Aleem fired a short burst, immediately seeing the bloody result on the front windshield. He aimed through the shattered window into the back seat, confirming that it was empty. He continued forward, but was unable to get to the front passenger window. It took him a brief moment to realize that the car was moving forward. He fired a round through the passenger window and tried to aim at the driver's leg, but the car accelerated rapidly, headed straight for a white pickup truck parked several spaces down. He sprinted behind the vehicle with Tariq, who no longer held his submachine gun.

"I tossed it in the fucking car to keep the wires intact," he hissed, anticipating Aleem's question.

The Explorer slammed into the rear of the pickup truck, causing a deafening crunch. The SUV's engine continued to scream, pushing the vehicle against the pickup truck and edging both vehicles forward. The engine's whine drowned out the sounds of gunfire, bringing the neighborhood to life. Porch lights snapped on up and down Westminster Street. They needed to get out of here immediately.

Tariq reached the Explorer first and yanked the driver's door open for Aleem, who grabbed the driver by the left arm and pulled him free of the vehicle, silencing the hideously loud engine. He dragged the convulsing man several feet onto the sidewalk, while Tariq retrieved the MP9 in the dead passenger's lap and disabled the Taser. In the few seconds it took for Tariq to do his job, Aleem searched the man for weapons, finding only a wallet in his rear pants pocket.

"Grab the radio and find his phone," he said.

Five seconds after the Explorer had crashed into the pickup truck, he jogged down the sidewalk with their target in a fireman's carry, while Tariq covered their one block retreat to their vehicle on Argyle Road. Through his own labored breathing, Aleem noticed that the distant shooting had stopped. He hoped Sayar and his team had survived, but given the amount of gunfire they had heard approaching the Explorer, he wasn't very optimistic. Sanderson had been right about the Imam. Killing him had been extremely important to True America's leadership. Important enough to send more than a dozen highly trained commandos to conduct a brazen hit and run attack. His deadline for extracting information from the man slung over his back would be accelerated. There would be no way to keep the FBI's direct involvement a secret, which meant that True America might hasten their timeline upon learning that some of their operatives had been captured alive.

Chapter 23

8:59 PM
National Counterterrorism Center (NCTC)
McLean, Virginia

Ryan Sharpe removed his headset and stared at the main screen. The market operation had been a success, yielding three live suspects for background searches and interrogation. They also had thirteen dead True America militants, which they could identify and research. For an investigation that had essentially stalled earlier in the day, this would breathe new life into the search for the remaining virus canisters. He glanced up at Callie Stewart, who had chosen to watch the operation from the balcony above. She met his glance and nodded before walking into her office, presumably to report to her master.

Her team—Sanderson's team—had lost two of their undercover operatives in the attack. The two survivors had been rushed to The Brooklyn Hospital Center's Level II trauma center with multiple gunshot wounds. According to Damon Katsoulis, the mobile task force's tactical commander, Diyah Castillo had been listed in critical condition by EMTs. She had departed on the first ambulance to leave the scene, immediately followed by her team leader, Abraham Sayar, who was listed in serious condition. Two FBI agents had been wounded in the fierce gun battle, both of them hit by armor piercing rounds fired at the snipers in the apartment. The bullets passed through the building's brick façade, striking a pair of headquarters agents as they entered the sniper's nest to provide additional firepower. Fortunately, the armor piercing rounds had lost much of their velocity punching through centuries old bricks, and didn't penetrate the ceramic plate inserted in the lead agent's tactical vest. The round that struck the non-hardened ballistic material covering his right shoulder was another story. The "through and through" projectile lost some more velocity tearing through muscle and bone, but continued down the hallway undeterred, glancing off the second agent's head before finally lodging in a doorframe on the other side of the apartment. A few more millimeters to the right, and the bullet would have punctured her skull.

Katsoulis had arrived in one of the first vehicles to reach the market, but by the time they rushed through the front entrance, most of the battle was finished. After a brief exchange of gunfire that killed one of the suspects, the last standing True America commando surrendered. They found two more alive in the storeroom, bleeding through multiple wounds. Katsoulis said the inside of the market looked like a slaughterhouse. He had no idea how their undercover operatives had managed to survive a simultaneous, two-sided attack.

According to agents covering the back alley, at least seven heavily armed attackers emerged suddenly from one of the houses behind the market to breach the rear entrance. By the time the agents had assembled to respond as a group, the firefight inside the market had ended. The entire event had lasted roughly forty-five seconds and yielded a fresh start to their investigation.

He still didn't trust Sanderson any further than he could throw Hesterman's massive linebacker body, but he felt a debt of gratitude. Without Sanderson's involvement, they would still be scratching their heads, waiting for a warrant to enter the Imam's mosque. This thought made him wonder about the Imam's fate. Just as he felt his moral center start to wander, he remembered the dark side of Sanderson's involvement. Operating outside of the law always came with a hefty price tag. Sharpe knew this better than anyone.

He had distinctly crossed that line two years earlier, pitting Agent Edwards against Jessica Petrovich. Only a hefty dosage of sedatives and alcohol, presumably provided by Jessica against Edward's will, had saved Sharpe from answering some serious questions about his investigative methods. Luck had intervened, along with something else. Every record of the emails he had sent to Agent Edwards had disappeared. Agent O'Reilly had checked, knowing that the trail would lead back to both of them. She couldn't find a single trace of the emails anywhere.

There was only one possible explanation. The system had been hacked through Edward's computer. For obvious reasons, he couldn't push the issue, although a thorough risk assessment had been conducted on Edward's laptop. Standard procedure for a laptop that had been left "unattended" in the presence of a criminal suspect. The assessment hadn't uncovered a security breach, which further unnerved Sharpe. Why would Sanderson go out of his way to help him like that? Blackmail further down the line, or a sense of duty to protect the good guys? He couldn't begin to guess, let alone spend time worrying about it. Still, the seed had been planted, and every once in a while, it dominated his thoughts. Right now, he couldn't shake the feeling that Sanderson was pulling all the strings.

He patted O'Reilly on the shoulder and walked toward his office. All of their marching orders had been issued. They would start searching for commonalities between all sixteen True America operatives. Travel patterns, purchase history, friends, email, phone records...everything. Interrogation of the survivors would begin immediately. Agent Carlisle eagerly awaited their arrival at the Newark field office, though he would only have one customer tonight. The other two would need medical treatment and rest before they could be questioned.

He hoped they could turn up the heat on the prisoner at the field office. Collating and analyzing data for trends could take too long. He had no doubt it would yield valuable results, but he needed something *now*. Carlisle's interrogation tonight would be their best hope for moving things along quickly. Part of him wished they could divert the van carrying the prisoner to Sanderson's people. An even darker part of him hoped that this plan was already in the works. He knew Sanderson's people were capable of taking down a prisoner transport van without causing friendly casualties. They had done it before. He erased the thought as quickly as he had formed it, angry that he had even let it slip through his moral safeguards.

Chapter 24

11:21 PM
Hilton Hotel
Harrisburg, Pennsylvania

Jackson Greely had penned a few changes to the speech he'd given to the University of Pennsylvania Libertarian Association earlier that evening in Philadelphia. The event had been well attended by university alumni, students and members of the greater Pennsylvania Libertarian Party. He also recognized a few familiar faces from his own organization at the dinner. Typical of his university appearances, campus political organizers had protested his talk, citing many of his "old" talking points as reasons to ban him from the institution. Of course, he steered clear of these topics, playing to the crowd of libertarians who shared many of True America's core beliefs, but shied away from True America's concept of isolationism.

Greely didn't like using the libertarian favorite foreign policy word: non-intervention. Non-intervention was part of True America's philosophy, but Greely and others felt that the concept was misleading. The U.S. would be forced to intervene in order to enforce the isolation necessary for the New Recovery. The international community had become reliant upon U.S. involvement, without realizing the scope of their dependence. Lost behind a tide of resentment, foreign politicians rallied against U.S. foreign policy without giving much thought to the consequences of its absence. When the Aegis shield held over them by the U.S. was suddenly lowered, chaos would ensue, requiring intervention to keep the backlash from reaching North American shores.

Even U.S. sworn enemies in the Muslim world would panic. Without their convenient "bogeyman" to blame for the Middle East's current state of decay, the Imams would be forced to come up with new material to inflame the expanding mass of Muslim youth. They'd still blame everything on Israel, but without U.S. support, even Israel's "defiant" existence in the Holy Land would fade from relevance to many followers. Greely predicted a massive wave of violence from Muslim extremists, as they came to terms with the fact that they would soon lose their only connection to Muslims worldwide. Stand-off intervention might be required for decades to keep this threat at bay, but he downplayed those aspects of True America's core beliefs when speaking to libertarians. Their support would be crucial in the upcoming days, and essential to 2008 election efforts to put the first president outside of the entrenched two party system in the White House since Millard Fillmore was elected from the Whig Party in 1850.

Jackson wished he could have spent more time in Philadelphia. The city radiated a palpable current of political vitality that never failed to energize him. The founding fathers had spent months creating the documents that had shaped this great nation, debating and deliberating with great care. Current politicians barely bothered to read the bills they signed or voted into law. Senators and congressmen utilized entourages of poorly paid staffers or volunteers to sift through the nonsense that none of them seemed qualified to examine on their own. All of this would change. The next few weeks would catalyze the American people and give them the courage to demand a new course of action for the nation.

His cell phone rang and he snapped it off the desk before it could ring a second time. He had expected to hear from Brown earlier. The operation in Brooklyn was of paramount importance to their organization. True America's militant arm could not be connected to the events leading to the inevitable coup. Distanced from the rational, public face of the True America movement, the political leadership would rise to lead the nation into the New Recovery. But the rise would be tenuous, and any ties to Al Qaeda, regardless of the necessity, could foment opposition to the movement at a vulnerable stage. Brown's orders had been explicit. Eradicate the last remaining link between the two organizations.

"Give me some good news, Tommy," he said.

"We have a major problem. Possibly several," said Brown.

In the decade that Greely had known Brown, he had neither seen nor heard even a trace of panic or exasperation from the man. Brown kept his emotions in check, betraying nothing, even to his closest friends. Greely detected a shift in his tone, a combination of fear and dread that immediately set off every one of Greely's internal alarms. He considered disconnecting the call until he could verify that Brown wasn't speaking to him under duress.

"What the fuck happened? This was an easy mop up job."

"Not so easy when...one, you're expected by the FBI; and two, the entire area is covered by SWAT. The teams got inside, but the feds had people in the market as well. Two of our operatives were captured. The rest were killed in the assault."

"This is a fucking disaster!" roared Greely. "Tommy, did they at least kill the Imam?"

"Not that I can tell. My sources can't confirm this one way or the other. I rather doubt the Imam was anywhere near the market."

"What does Estrada have to say about this clusterfuck? What does he know?"

"That's the worst part. Estrada is missing...and I don't think he was taken by the FBI. His truck was found a few blocks away, crashed into a parked car. Davis was still buckled into the passenger sea—"

"They caught Davis too?" interrupted Greely.

"No. Davis was still strapped into the seat, shot through the head. Executed. Someone ambushed the car. My local PD contact said that two Arab-looking men helped the driver of the crashed SUV out of the truck, and carried him down the block running. Do you think it was Al Qaeda?"

"I doubt it. Al Qaeda is out of business from what we can tell. We know they grabbed the last cell in Bayonne this morning. I don't know what to make of it."

"Maybe a cell operating outside of the Imam's network? A cell activated to shadow the operation?" suggested Brown.

"Maybe. Either way, we need to significantly accelerate our plans. If we fell victim to an FBI sting operation, then they have the Imam and he's talking. Where are you right now?"

"I'm on interstate seventy-nine outside of Morgantown, heading to Hacker Valley. I should arrive at the compound within the next two hours."

"Good. I need three things from you in the next twelve hours. First and foremost, get the compound ready to repel an immediate attack. You know what to do. Second, activate our insurance policy in D.C. I know it's a rush job, but the feds are putting the pieces together quicker than we had anticipated. I want him ready by tomorrow evening. Lastly, send another team to deal with Young. Terminate with extreme prejudice, and tell them to be extremely cautious. They might have competition."

"Understood. I'll start making some calls right now. How long do you think we have at the compound?"

"At least twenty-four hours, probably more like thirty-six. Is everything set for tomorrow morning?"

"Yes. They'll start digging at noon," replied Brown.

"Perfect. I'll let you go, Tommy. I need to clear out of here, just in case the FBI decides to suspend the Constitution and grab me out of my hotel room. I'll be in touch shortly. Don't hesitate to call if you run into a snag. We're almost there. Just another week or so, and the country will have a fighting chance to realize a new era of American exceptionalism."

"Well worth the sacrifices, Jackson. I'll see you up north in a few days."

"Sounds like a plan, Tommy. Make sure to get the hell clear of the compound as soon as possible. You don't want to get caught up in that mess.

"I'll be out of there by mid-morning at the latest."

"Good luck, and take a deep breath when you get off this call. I don't need you driving your car into a ditch," said Greely.

He heard Brown laugh, which was a good sign.

"I hear you. Long, deep breaths. Talk to you soon."

Greely started to collect his items and pack his bags for an immediate departure. He'd steer clear of any known associates or regular stops from this point forward. Once he got on the road, he'd call Lee Harding and give him an update. Harding would have to go into hiding with him. Owen Mills had anonymously rented a comfortable house on Lake Wallenpaupack for their absence. From the house, they were perfectly situated for quick trips to the laboratory facility and the distribution hub in Honesdale, each less than twenty miles away.

A perfect hideaway for the two of them until it was safe to emerge and make a statement in support of the New Recovery. Mills owned a significant lakeside estate a few miles south along the waterfront. Lake Wallenpaupack had turned into the epicenter of True America's secret leadership cabal. Decades from now, people might travel from all corners of the country to catch a glimpse of the house used by New Recovery founders Jackson Greely and Lee Harding. Maybe it would become a national landmark.

His most important call would be to Jason Carnes at the laboratory. Carnes had insisted that his people needed a minimum of eight days to get the bottles out of the lab. He needed them to cut that timeline in half. He needed those trucks rolling out of Honesdale as soon as possible. Everything hinged on the trucks delivering their cargo. Once delivered, it was in God's hands.

Chapter 25

12:45 AM
New Brunswick, New Jersey

Aleem Fayed opened the basement door and stepped into the kitchen, closing it softly behind him. He tossed a small digital dictation machine on the kitchen counter and started to wash his blood soaked hands in the sink.

"It's all there," he said, without looking up from his hands.

Once the red tendrils of blood had stopped flowing across the white ceramic basin, he switched the water to cold and took a handful to splash his face. He rubbed his eyes with watery hands, before placing them on the edges of the counter to brace himself for a few seconds of rest. He stared at the soap dispenser behind the sink, just to the left of the tap. He needed more than a few seconds of repose, but his day was far from finished. He turned his head toward the dining room and saw that everyone was staring at him.

"Did you find anything on his phone?" he asked the others, breaking the silence.

He knew why they were staring at him. Screams and crying from the basement had lasted for nearly an hour, as Aleem perpetrated his finest masterpiece of physical and psychological torture. By the time Estrada had finally expired, the True America militant had been so utterly confused and physically strained that he had rambled completely unrelated pieces of information in the hopes of unlocking the key to his survival. Even Aleem felt slightly sorry for the wrecked human being fastened to the metal basement support beam. The man had endured the most twisted hour of his life, dying unceremoniously in an anonymous basement on the outskirts of a New Jersey suburb. Breaking Miguel Estrada had required little physical torture, beyond a few well-placed kicks and punches. Most of the session had been a mental see-saw attack, designed to rip the psychological rug out from under Estrada, over and over again.

It started when he was shoved into the dimly lit unfinished basement and tied to the thick metal column several feet in front of the Imam. Aleem kept him faced away from Hamid Muhammad, until the Imam's muffled screams could no longer be ignored. Estrada was free to rotate around the column, restrained by handcuffs and a long u-shaped Kryptonite bicycle lock. When he finally shifted to face the muffled screams, Aleem ripped the duct tape off the Imam's face and watched as Estrada's face registered recognition and confusion. At this point, Aleem announced that Estrada's abduction had been part of an induction ceremony to bring him into the next level of True America's inner circle, and that the raid on the market had been staged as his final test of loyalty and competence.

As the Imam screamed, Estrada was told that he would be given the honor of killing the Imam with his bare hands, but he would not be released until the Al Qaeda terrorist was dead. Aleem released Estrada from the handcuffs and pushed Hamid Muhammad's chair within striking distance of the militant. It took him nearly ten minutes to pummel the life out of the Imam. Aleem had pulled the chair back several times to keep Estrada from strangling him. He wanted Estrada physically exhausted and emotionally charged for the next turn of events.

When the Imam's pulse faded to nothing, Aleem unleashed a vicious attack on Estrada, dropping him to the floor. He recuffed his hands and thanked him for doing the Prophet's work. Sending the traitorous Imam straight to hell on behalf of Al Qaeda would ensure a quick, painless death he had assured Estrada. He explained how the Imam had double-crossed everyone. He had stolen money from True America, while at the same time giving up the location of the hidden Al Qaeda cells. Estrada knew that part of this was untrue, but any effort to explain how they had tracked the Al Qaeda cells was met with Aleem's fists. He demanded to know where they had taken the stolen virus canisters, but Estrada held out, even after one of his fingers was bent backward to the point of breaking. At this point, tears started rolling down Estrada's cheeks, which told him it was time to change back to the first story.

Aleem completely freed Estrada and tossed a water bottle down for him to drink, congratulating him on passing the final test of loyalty. He would now be taken to meet Lee Harding and Jackson Greely for the final ceremony. Estrada grabbed the water bottle and accepted Aleem's hand, rising back to his feet. He could tell that Estrada wanted desperately to believe that he had passed some bizarre hazing ritual. This was when he slipped up for the first time. He asked if they still needed him for the job in Atlanta. Benjamin Young. Aleem immediately kicked him in the groin and pulled him by his hair back to the basement support column, reattaching the u-shaped lock.

He had *almost* passed the test, stated Aleem. He'd given up mission details under uncertain circumstances, possibly jeopardizing True America's inner core. Estrada apologized profusely and took a drink of water, squeezing the rest of the water over his head. The results of the habanero infused water were immediate. Estrada's sweat pores and eyes absorbed the habanero oil, causing his face to feel like it had caught fire. The pain in his mouth had probably been beyond comprehension for several minutes. Aleem waited for the screaming to die down before informing him that Jackson Greely had once told him something at the training compound that could save his life. Something important that only Estrada could know.

Aleem spent the next twenty minutes using a flaming aerosol can to keep Estrada talking. He gave up everything in hopes of hitting the one thing that might save his life. He had crossed the line of rational thought, which would have never allowed him to disclose some of the intimate details of his association with True America. He'd confirmed several things they had suspected, but never provided details about the bigger plot. Tommy Brown and he had masterminded the simultaneous hit against Al Qaeda, having tracked and observed the cells for over a year. Brown was the tactical arm of the True America militants.

Beyond shepherding one of the cells to the Mount Arlington pump station, Estrada didn't have any further details. His next mission after killing the Imam involved killing a man named Benjamin Young in Atlanta. He didn't have many details about the man. He'd planned to take two other operatives down to Atlanta. He apologized profusely for not knowing more, but assured Aleem that Brown usually gave him future tasking upon completion of each mission. Based on the sheer terror in Estrada's eyes, he had little reason to doubt the man's sincerity.

When he informed Estrada that he worked for an "off the books" government agency tasked to stop True America's plot, the man alternated between rage and self-pity, screaming one moment and suddenly crying the next. Aleem ended his misery with a front kick to the man's neck, crushing his neck against the metal pole.

"Hello? Earth to fucking techno-geeks. Did you pull anything off the phone?"

His comment jarred them out of their trance, prompting Graves to respond.

"He had several text messages containing addresses in Atlanta. Listed separately as 'family home, apartment, escort apartment, escort bar, and hotel gym.'"

"Makes sense. His next mission was a hit in Atlanta. A man named Benjamin Young. Start working up a profile on this guy and download the information on this recorder. Is there anything on the phone related to Hacker Valley, West Virginia?"

"Hacker?" said Anish Gupta.

"Coincidence. Hacker Valley is the location of their training compound. You'll find detailed directions on the digital recording," said Aleem.

"I'll start cleaning things up downstairs," said Tariq.

Graves and Gupta watched Tariq get up from the dining room table and walk into the living room.

"Are they dead?" asked Gupta.

"No. I'm planning on taking them to get a Big Mac and fries after they clean up," replied Aleem sarcastically.

"Fuck, man. This is getting out of control," said Gupta.

"What the fuck are you complaining about? Nobody's asking you to clean up the mess. You think I enjoy this shit? Trust me, I don't. You do your job, and I'll do mine. That's how it works, unless you want out. I'll make the call to Sanderson myself. If you can't do your jobs, I need to find a crew that can. Do you want me to make the call?" asked Aleem.

"I'd rather not be taken by one of you to get a Happy Meal at McDonalds, so I'll stick around," said Graves.

"I don't even like McDonalds," said Gupta.

"The comedy duo of Gupta and Graves." Aleem laughed quietly, shaking his head. "Let's get a data package put together for General Sanderson. We'll clean up the mess and sanitize the house. I'd like to be out of here in less than two hours."

"Sounds good to me," said Graves, standing up to grab the digital recorder from the kitchen counter.

Aleem returned to the sink and ran the water across the entire surface of the basin, washing any trace of red down the drain. He'd use Comet later to remove any remaining traces of biological evidence. Before that, they would remove the bodies, placing them in the trunk of the stolen Honda Accord that sat parked in the garage. Tariq appeared in the dining room doorway, and held up two black plastic body bags.

"Ready when you are," he said, grimacing.

"Let's get this over with. I'll grab the cleaning supplies," replied Aleem, turning off the faucet.

Graves and Gupta focused on their computer screens, avoiding eye contact.

Chapter 26

1:21 AM
National Counterterrorism Center (NCTC)
McLean, Virginia

Special Agent Sharpe stood next to Dana O'Reilly and let her explain her team's findings.

"The mobile investigative team found five vehicles involved in the attack; four located within the immediate vicinity and one found a few blocks away," she said, looking up at Sharpe.

"We'll talk about the missing driver in a minute," said Sharpe.

He probably shared the same concerns about the driver as Dana. It seemed unlikely that additional Al Qaeda elements were involved, which left them with one scenario: Sanderson's people.

"The assault group had been sanitized of any identifying paperwork. Nothing was stashed in the van besides prepaid fuel cards, Visa gift cards and a small amount of cash. The vehicle registrations belong to a corporate entity that specializes in discreet vehicle leases. We'll request the appropriate warrants, but you can guess where that will lead."

"Nowhere, eventually," said Sharpe.

"Exactly," replied O'Reilly.

"We've identified six of the dead men scouring state and federal databases with our facial recognition software. Nothing unusual about any of them. Two military veterans, a paramedic, a truck driver, restaurant manager…average people on the surface."

"Clearly not. What about the suspects in custody?"

"The two in the hospital won't be ready for any kind of meaningful interrogation for at least two, maybe three days. Carlisle has assigned one of his interrogators to each of them, just in case they feel like talking. No ID's on either of them, yet. Carlisle is leaning on the suspect that surrendered in the market. We've identified him as John Galick. Married with three children, ages three, six and ten. Lives in Raleigh, North Carolina, less than ten miles from his alma mater, Duke University. Information technology consultant. No military experience. The only red flag I can find are numerous political posts on My Space and Facebook. The posts smack of True America rhetoric, but they stop cold in 2005."

"Probably when he was recruited," said Hesterman, leaning back as far as his chair permitted.

"You comfortable, Eric?" said Sharpe.

"Not really, but Dana won't give me permission to put my feet up on the desk," said Hesterman.

"The last thing I need is a pair of size fifteen shoes in my way," said O'Reilly.

"I can rest them over here," he said, nodding at the corner.

She just shook her head and continued the briefing.

"So far, he hasn't said a word, but Carlisle is pretty sure he'll have him talking by morning."

"Don't count on it. This group reminds me of another group that gave us a shit ton of trouble, and continues to pull the wool over our eyes. I'll call Carlisle myself and make sure they proceed very cautiously with Mr. Galick. So, why did you really call me down here?"

"Am I that transparent?" asked O'Reilly.

"Considering the fact that you forwarded me this information nearly forty minutes ago, I'd say your deception skills are lacking."

Hesterman let out a muffled laugh from his resting position.

"We…" she said, hitting Hesterman in the shoulder, "think we've uncovered the location of True America's compound."

Hesterman sat upright in his chair, quickly adjusting the seat back to accommodate the undesired change in his posture.

"Demir's agents found a total of six cell phones, five prepaids. One for each vehic—"

"GPS enabled?" interrupted Sharpe.

"No," said Hesterman. "And they were probably purchased nearby. But cell phone number six isn't a prepaid. They found it in a backpack that was stuffed in the rear cargo compartment. We have in our possession a

Blackberry owned by Miguel Estrada. Resident of Everett, Washington. Served on active duty in the Army from 1989 to 2000. Most of his time was spent with the Second Ranger Battalion. Honorably discharged as a Captain. Stayed in the active reserves until 2005, when he formally resigned his commission."

"Looks like True America's commando training kicked into full gear around 2005," Sharpe remarked.

"Yeah. It's starting to look like this has been in the works for some time," said O'Reilly.

"So, the Blackberry was dead and had to be rebooted, which is why it took us so long to figure this out, but it appears that Estrada was a little sloppy with his OPSEC. With the help of our NSA liaison, we were able to trace his Blackberry's travels over the past month, right until it ran out of juice yesterday morning," Hesterman continued.

"Do I even want to know how the NSA could retroactively track a GPS enabled phone?"

"No, and apparently it wouldn't matter if you did want to know. Nobody is offering an explanation. I brought the matter to the NCTC watch supervisor, who gave me a number at Fort Meade. All they asked for was the Blackberry's phone number. Forty minutes later, I received a list of GPS coordinates. Obviously these coordinates are classified," said O'Reilly.

"Obviously. Thanks for keeping me in the loop."

"You were napping at your desk, and Mendoza told us not to disturb you," said O'Reilly.

"I most certainly was not sleeping," said Sharpe.

"I'm just kidding," said Dana, "We all wanted to surprise you with a little good news. Go ahead, Eric."

Hesterman clicked the mouse, and their 27-inch flat screen monitor showed a map of the northeast corner of the U.S., spanning from Connecticut to Ohio. Hesterman started the show by zooming in on New Jersey.

"Are you kidding me? He was less than a half mile from the Mount Arlington pump station. How does that make sense?" said Sharpe.

"It doesn't, unless True America was somehow supporting Al Qaeda, or following them. The coordinates are provided in one-hour increments and we have two hits at this location along Old Drakesville Road. Estrada sat here for more than an hour, which doesn't sound like he was following them."

"We can worry about that later. Where's the compound?"

"Two weeks ago, his Blackberry traveled to an obscure location in West Virginia, northwest of Hacker Valley. Google maps showed a large, natural clearing at the coordinates. The area is heavily forested, and I don't see a road leading to the clearing," said Hesterman.

"Did you request recent NRO satellite imagery?"

"I just finished sending the request when you woke up from your nap," said O'Reilly.

"I wasn't napping."

"I'm sure you weren't. I think the next step is to request live satellite surveillance," she said.

"Agreed. Send me the coordinates, and I'll get the ball rolling with Director Shelby. He'll need to brief the White House," said Sharpe.

"Do you think they'll roll in with military?" said O'Reilly.

"It depends on what they find in West Virginia, but I wouldn't be surprised if they use the military regardless. Our special operations liaison said that SOCOM has assembled one of the biggest Tier One packages he's ever seen at Dover Air Force Base."

"Do you want to talk about the missing driver now?" said O'Reilly.

"Yeah, about that missing driver…two 'Arab looking' men dragged him to safety according to witnesses," said Sharpe.

"Nobody found it odd that they carried him from the scene?" Hesterman asked.

"Apparently not," O'Reilly said.

"I think this was the work of our favorite general, which leads me to wonder about their intentions," said Sharpe.

O'Reilly leaned closer to Sharpe and spoke in a whisper. "I still don't trust Sanderson's crew, but we've definitely benefited from their participation. Maybe it's not a bad thing if they have Estrada."

"That's the last time I want to hear either of you talking like that. We can't play by their rules, and we certainly can't condone what they're doing, no matter how much we benefit. When the internal investigators descend upon our databanks to audit the inner workings of this task force, we'll all have to stand on the red carpet and explain why we turned a blind eye to murder, torture, kidnapping…all of it. We're walking a very fine line as it is. Understood?"

"Yes, sir," Hesterman and O'Reilly responded in unison.

"Good. I'll handle Ms. Stewart and Sanderson. This bullshit ends tonight. E-mail me those coordinates."

"They're already waiting for you at your computer," said O'Reilly.

"Thank you. And by the way, excellent work. Sorry to run, but I need to square away our situation with Sanderson," he said and turned toward the staircase leading to the second level.

He hoped that his ass-chewing would steer O'Reilly and Hesterman away from the inner workings cast by Sanderson's spell. He didn't dare admit to them that he shared the same hope that Estrada was strapped to a chair in some dank basement, awaiting the next round of unthinkable pain and agony. He'd long ago seen the value of Sanderson's tactics, but he couldn't come to terms with it. He'd spent most of his adult life following regulations and strictly observing the rules laid out for him by the FBI. He'd strayed from this straight and narrow path two years ago, in his pursuit of Daniel Petrovich, and it now felt like a huge weight had been lifted from his shoulders.

He wasn't on his way to Stewart's office to put an end to Sanderson's interference. His plan was to harness the power that Sanderson wielded to prevent the death of countless thousands. He'd tasted Sanderson's world and wanted more. He had fought against these urges, knowing that they had no legitimate place in his law enforcement world, but the consequences of failure were too devastating. If stopping True America's plot meant wrecking his own career, he would gladly make that sacrifice. He couldn't make that decision for O'Reilly or Hesterman, so they would be excluded from the covert side of Task Force Scorpion, and he'd have to keep Mendoza in the dark as well. In the unlikely event that the Sanderson association blew up in his face, they would be protected from prosecution.

He ascended the stairs and approached Callie Stewart's assigned office. Before he reached the door, she stepped out onto the catwalk.

"Is DeSantos in there?" he asked.

"No. He's been gone for several hours. Can I help you with something?"

"Let's step into your office. Close the door behind you, please," he said.

Once the door was shut, he sat in one of the faux brown leather chairs near the window. Stewart lowered herself into the adjoining chair.

"From this point forward, we're going to cut the bullshit. I know you have Estrada. Do you have the compound location?"

"I just received the information," she said, clasping her hands.

"Were you planning to share this information with me?"

"Well...it's a little more complicated than that for us."

"Because you don't want to tip Sanderson's hand? That's no longer a concern between us. I'm just going to assume that Sanderson holds a royal flush at all times. I'd like to speak with him for a moment, if you wouldn't mind calling him for me," he said.

"It would be my pleasure," Stewart said, standing up to walk over to the desk.

"I'd like this to be a private call. Let's use your cell phone," said Sharpe.

Stewart slowly dropped back into the leather chair, her facial expression showing no surprise at the request.

"All communications leaving here are monitored by—"

"Not buying it, Ms. Stewart. You're good, but I've worked in counterintelligence for twenty years. I haven't walked up those stairs once since you arrived, and the first time I decide to pay you a visit, at 1:30 in the morning, I'm intercepted at the door?

She dialed the number and waited a few seconds for Sanderson to answer.

"Everything is fine, General. Special Agent Sharpe would like to speak with you."

She passed the phone to Sharpe.

"Good morning, General. I was just talking to Ms. Stewart about how I'd like to proceed from this point forward. No more secrets. I need to know exactly what you know, as soon as you know it. I need to know what your operatives are doing, before they do it. The flow of information at this point is a congested, one-way street."

"One-way street? You haven't exactly rolled out the red carpet for Ms. Stewart. Information is flowing like mud from your end," countered Sanderson.

"Really? Maybe this would be a good time to reboot and debug the NCTC computer system. They'll probably follow suit at the Newark field office. How would you feel about the information flow then? The cyber techs didn't find any security breaches at the Newark field office, but I'm sure your people covered their tracks pretty well. Money buys the best talent, and from what I can tell, you have a lot of money at your disposal."

"I'm not sure sharing information would be in your best interest, as a government employee," replied Sanderson.

"Let me worry about that," said Sharpe.

"Once you stepped into this arrangement, you can't just step out. We're partners.

"I wouldn't go that far. What kind of information did you manage to get from Estrada?" asked Sharpe.

"Details about the compound. From what I can see, your people have the correct location. I assume that General Gordon's Joint Special Operations Command will be given the task to take down the compound. Based on what Estrada disclosed, the FBI would be seriously outmatched and outgunned. Unfortunately for us, planning and intelligence gathering efforts for the operation will remain in-house with SOCOM. Aside from timeline and general information, we'll be spectators. This is where your background will be critical to their success. We need to ensure that they either find—or are prepared to deal with—.50 caliber heavy machine guns. Estrada said they had three at their disposal, with armor piercing ammunition. They also have some kind of armored vehicle, with a mounted MG42. It's more of a body-shop project, but not something our Special Operations forces want to stumble upon. They also have a 60mm mortar with high explosive ammunition. Have you ever come across evidence or rumors that True America was acquiring this stuff? We have to warn them somehow, and I'd rather do it in a way that doesn't tip our hand."

"Your hand," corrected Sharpe.

"*Our* hand. This is our hand now. No going back at this point. Can you connect True America with heavy weapons purchases?"

"I can connect them to a deceased arms dealer who specialized in hard to find, highly illegal weapons. He provided your organization with .50 caliber sniper rifles and a whole host of new weapons."

"Navarre. Perfect. He offered my operatives a whole host of crazy, very dangerous shit. Soviet bloc shoulder fired surface to air missiles. I think you need to insist that your voice is heard. Once a decision is made to raid the compound, schedule a sit down with your SOCOM liaison, Colonel Jeffrey Hanson. He's a good soldier, and will listen to what you have to say."

"What if they go completely behind our backs, or just announce the raid an hour or two in advance?" Sharpe asked.

"We need to make sure that doesn't happen. I have people on the inside that can warn us, and I'd recommend that you cozy up to Director Shelby. He was instrumental in planning the raid that landed over a hundred special operators at my camp in Argentina. Just be careful. He didn't have much of a choice about my unit's participation in Task Force Scorpion, and I suspect he'll turn on me at the first opportunity, and you too if he catches wind of this."

"My agents will need to be on scene immediately to start processing evidence. As soon as the compound is declared clear, it's back in my hands. I'll make sure they don't cut me out of the loop," said Sharpe.

"Sounds like a solid plan. In the interest of full disclosure, I'm working on something else that might interest you. Nothing actionable yet, but highly intriguing. After killing the Imam, Estrada's next mission was to travel to Atlanta and assassinate a prominent D.C. lobbyist named Benjamin Young. Mr. Young's wife and children live in Atlanta. He also maintains apartments in D.C. and Manhattan. Apparently, he's not the most faithful husband and he's developed quite a drug habit. True America leadership wants him out of the picture, so he must be a critical liability. I'd like to know why. I'll have people in Atlanta by mid-morning to start surveillance. I'm hoping to take him off the streets before True America sends another team after him."

"I'll steer clear of that one for now," said Sharpe.

"Good call. I'll keep you apprised of any developments in Atlanta."

"Alright, and, General?"

"Yes?"

"You're not going to screw me on this, right?"

"Ryan, I give you my word that the only agenda item on my blackboard is to put an end to this terrorist plot. My operatives are loyal and share that single goal. You saw proof of that earlier this evening. The operatives assigned to the El Halal mission understood their odds. More importantly, they understood the importance of their mission to our country. Hundreds of thousands of American lives will be lost if we don't stop True America. I debriefed Petrovich and Farrington after they returned from Monchegorsk. The video evidence and accounts of horror publicized by Reuters do little justice to the tragedy that unfolded in that doomed city. Just one of those canisters could turn one of our cities inside out."

"You had people on the inside? In Monchegorsk?"

"I had a small team penetrate the city on behalf of the CIA. The Russians are lying through their teeth about Monchegorsk and they're leveling the city to eradicate the population. You've seen the projected symptoms of the weaponized virus we're facing. Temporal lobe damage to almost everyone infected. Symptom severity varying from fever with disorientation all the way to an uncontrollable murderous frenzy. My team said the streets were overrun with aggressive, zombie-like citizens. That's why they are calling this the Zulu Virus. If this virus is unleashed in a high density population area here in the U.S., our own government's options for dealing with the crisis would shrink rapidly. How do you effectively deal with a thirty to forty thousand person rampage in the suburbs?"

"I guess you go Russian on them," said Sharpe.

"Exactly. My organization is willing to go as far as necessary to stop that from happening in the U.S."

"I wish we could do more, but my hands are tied here," said Sharpe.

"Your task force is doing exactly what it was designed to do, and doing it exceptionally well. You just need the occasional boost from my group to fine-tune your efforts. Working together gives us the best chance to stop this threat."

"I'm not going to lie to you, General. Working with your group makes me nervous," Sharpe admitted.

He had to make sure this was clear to Sanderson. He wasn't sure why, but he needed the general to acknowledge his concerns.

"I won't leave you hanging out to dry, Special Agent Sharpe. I consider you one of my own now," said Sanderson.

"Alright. We're unlikely partners in this mess. Speaking of which, I need to get back to the watch floor. I'm going to hand you off to Ms. Stewart."

"Good luck today and welcome to the team."

Sharpe didn't like the sound of Sanderson's last comment. He handed the phone back to Stewart.

"This doesn't mean you get to hang out in my office and drink coffee," he said to Stewart before departing. "We keep up the appearance that I can't stand your presence here."

"Got it," she said, taking the phone.

"And have your people actively track O'Reilly's computer activity. I can't be the only one around here to suspect that our system has been hacked. She's smarter than both of us combined, and way craftier," said Sharpe.

"Is there any way to bring her on board?" said Stewart.

"Absolutely not. The rest of my people are off limits. That's non-negotiable. If this dangerous liaison detonates, I don't want them exposed. This includes Mendoza."

Sharpe left her office and stepped onto the catwalk, glancing down at the watch floor. The activity level had diminished throughout the center, which was more a reflection of the late hour and the fact that they had been running nonstop for the last forty-eight hours. Most of the agency liaisons were holed up in their offices sleeping, leaving skeleton crews on the floor to monitor progress. His own crew had thinned tonight at O'Reilly's request. She kept enough agents and analysts on the floor to process evidence and information gathered by the mobile investigative team in Brooklyn. She had sent at least half of them away to get rest once they had put the computers to work trying to identify the men and women captured or killed in the market raid.

They had the location of True America's militant training camp, which would effectively propel the investigation forward. He'd pass this information on to the White House situation room as soon as he stepped into his office, and then place a call to Director Shelby. Actually, he'd reverse that order, he decided. Shelby would probably savor the chance to deliver this information. He'd at least give Shelby the option. Career management 101. It sounded petty and ridiculous, but little things like that mattered to the director.

He imagined that this new information would trigger a string of early wake up calls throughout D.C. He'd be lucky to grab an hour or two before the watch floor was back in full swing. Before all of that, he'd need to convince O'Reilly that he'd laid down the law with Stewart. O'Reilly hated Sanderson's crew and represented the single greatest threat to unhitching Sanderson from the task force. He'd lie about Estrada, telling her that Stewart denied involvement. O'Reilly wouldn't believe Stewart's claim, but in the long run, it was a safer move for all of them.

He'd have to maintain the same lie with Mendoza, which might be too big of a stretch. Mendoza had been present during Stewart's confession that Sanderson's people had abducted and absconded with the Imam right under the FBI's watchful eyes. He knew that the El Halal Market operation and the early morning Bayonne raid had all fallen into their laps, compliments of General Sanderson. He'd have to gauge Mendoza's reaction. If his friend pushed back too much, he might have to relent. He didn't like running a web of conspiracy and lies within his own task force, but the stakes were too high to lose Sanderson's support. He turned toward the staircase, ready to start spinning his own web upon reaching the watch floor.

Chapter 27

4:11 AM
C-17 Globemaster III
20,000 Feet over West Virginia

Chief Petty Officer Steve Carroll checked the straps of his oxygen mask and adjusted his wide lensed goggles one more time. He twisted around in the awkward parachute rig and scanned his team. Barely visible in the darkened cargo hold, he verified that all seven members of his reconnaissance team were up and checking each other's gear. He abruptly spun his head around to face the impenetrable darkness beyond the open loading ramp. Barely discernible through the darkness was roughly two minutes of free fall. Invisible hands tugged on his gear, providing him with a final assurance that nothing would come loose during his descent. They were loaded down with an atypical assortment of weapons and sensors, all of which were needed to safely reach the ground.

The jumpmaster located to his left wore an oxygen mask and an oversized headset. Like the rest of the Naval Special Warfare Development Group (DEVGRU) commandos in the oversized cargo bay, he had been breathing compressed oxygen since the flight departed Dover Air Force Base less than an hour earlier. Having just arrived at 20,000 feet, they were in no immediate danger of hypoxia, but mission planners had made it clear to the flight crew and DEVGRU personnel that no unnecessary risks would be taken en route to the objective. Even the ramp had been lowered immediately after take-off, to ensure that a midflight malfunction could not keep his team from jumping.

Carroll felt two solid slaps on his right shoulder, signifying that the final equipment check for his team was finished. He extended his right hand and gave the jumpmaster the "thumbs up" sign. The Air Force Technical Sergeant had given them their one minute warning less than thirty seconds earlier. The red indicator lights on each side of the ramp flashed twice, prompting the jumpmaster to yell.

"Thirty seconds!"

Time seemed to stand still. He was glad time wasn't measured standing at the edge of these ramps. After what seemed to be an eternity, the indicator lights turned green and his team stepped forward in unison. He walked off the edge of the ramp and hit the turbulence caused by the C17's four Pratt and Whitney turbofan engines. The turbulence was expected and short lived as he quickly fell away from the aircraft. The air tore at his suit and equipment as his body approached terminal velocity, fighting to destabilize his "spread stable position." Several seconds later, his body position stabilized and he knew he had achieved his terminal velocity.

He was now in complete control of his free fall. Without changing the position of his upper arm, he hinged his left elbow and examined the illuminated navigation board attached to his left forearm. He would use the information provided by the GPS receiver to guide his team to a position over their drop zone. Examining the rudimentary display, he decided to guide them north. By altering their body positions, they could affect a small degree of lateral movement, which was usually enough to compensate for any distance error caused by the jump.

He pointed his head north and locked his arms alongside his body, while simultaneously bringing his legs closer together. The new body position had an immediate effect, and he rocketed downward. Though nearly imperceptible to Carroll, his body made lateral gains north as most of his momentum carried him vertically down. He held the position for ten seconds and went back into "spread stable" to check the effect of his maneuver. He was relieved to see that they were in a much better position to hit the drop zone when they deployed their parachutes at 2,000 feet. He might even consider a lower deployment altitude given their current position relative to the wide clearing they had chosen. 1,500 feet would give them ninety seconds of glide time to make any final adjustments. His altimeter had been set to warn him at both altitudes.

He altered the position of his arms and deflected enough air to spin his body one hundred and eighty degrees. He now faced his team's formation. He counted seven dark gray shapes packed tightly together in front of him, bobbing and shifting as each commando continuously made small adjustments to stay within arm's reach of each other. He considered one more northerly adjustment, but decided against it. He had traded fall time for accuracy by shaping his body like a bullet in a "tracking" position for ten seconds. By decreasing his stability and eliminating a significant portion of the drag on his body, he nearly doubled the speed of their descent. They were rapidly approaching 5,000 feet and needed to prepare for parachute deployment.

He gave the hand signal to open their formation and watched as the team started to separate. Less than twenty seconds until they reached 1,500 feet. He stared below and saw a few distant lights to the south. The area that contained their drop zone and surveillance target gave him nothing. Black emptiness stared back at him. He watched his altimeter and took one more look at their formation. Plenty of distance between jumpers. He saw each of the three muted flashes provided by his altimeter, and knew they had reached 2,000 feet. He quickly confirmed the altitude and watched the digital readout pass 1,600 feet. He reached down with his right hand and pulled his ripcord right before the altimeter flashed again. He knew that the entire team would follow his lead and deploy their parachutes less than a second later.

The parachute harness yanked high against his inner thighs as the experimental MC-6 parachute arrested his descent from 176 feet per second to 16 feet per second. Within seconds he started steering the parachute with the toggles attached to the canopy lines, searching for the drop zone located beneath them. At a thousand feet, he started to see the differences in terrain. A quick glance at his navigation board confirmed that the lighter patch of gray just below them was the designated drop zone.

The clearing was less than fifty meters long and thirty meters wide, which was why they had chosen the experimental MC-6. The round parachute gave them an advantage over the square shaped MC-5 canopy in more confined spaces, giving them the option of a steep descent. Though each member of his team could easily land an MC-5 in the drop zone below, mission planners took into account the possibility that they might be forced to land somewhere else. No chances were being taken with this operation, and he fully understood their mentality.

As he rapidly approached the ground, he slowed his descent and manipulated the toggles to gain more forward momentum. Despite being a round canopy, the MC-6 was highly maneuverable, and he fully intended to land gently on his feet…deep within Hacker Valley.

Chapter 28

6:15 AM
The White House, Oval Office
Washington, D.C.

The President of the United States rubbed his face with his hands and leaned back in the deep golden couch, waiting for his first cup of coffee to arrive. He warily eyed the two men seated on the matching couch opposite him. The concealed door leading to the West Wing opened, and a Secret Service agent entered, quickly stepping aside to permit the entry of the president's coffee service. A middle-aged man with thin brown hair dressed in a sharply tailored black suit with a crisp white shirt and black tie pushed a silver cart into the room. He efficiently placed the polished silver tray containing three matching silver cups and a large silver coffee pot on the low table between the couches. A few seconds later, an assortment of cream, sugar and other sweeteners appeared on the table. The man started to prepare the president's coffee.

"Thank you, Robert. That won't be necessary this morning," said the president.

"Very well, Mr. President. Will you be taking breakfast in the residence this morning, sir?"

"Yes. I'll eat with my family in about thirty minutes, Robert."

"I'll notify the kitchen. Mr. President. Gentlemen. Please excuse me." He nodded and pushed the beverage cart back through the same door through which he'd entered.

Jacob Remy, the president's Chief of Staff, leaned forward with Harrison Beck, the president's chief political advisor.

"So it's confirmed?" asked the president, helping himself to the coffee service.

"Unfortunately. Our hopes for a convenient bogeyman evaporated last night. The FBI conducted a major sting operation that killed or captured seventeen militants, none of them Al Qaeda. They've identified a possible terrorist training camp in West Virginia, which is under surveillance as we speak. SOCOM is putting together a package to take down the camp if ordered," said Remy.

"It looks like three militants were captured?" the president asked.

"That's right. One surrendered to the FBI. The others were severely wounded by undercover agents inside the market," replied Remy.

"And the special assets used for the operation?"

All three of the men knew what he meant by 'special assets'. Even within the confines of the Oval Office, none of them would speak directly about Sanderson's involvement.

"Two killed, as you know. The two wounded are in stable condition."

"Harrison, what's your take on the situation?"

"This is a tough one," Beck replied. "We haven't confirmed that this is the work of True America militants, but I can't imagine the FBI is too far away from drawing that conclusion. I think we're dealing with a splinter group, likely under the leadership of Jackson Greely or Lee Harding, but we don't have enough information to make the connection."

"I'm not sure we want to," said Remy.

The president nodded in agreement and Beck continued.

"The True America political movement is sweeping the nation and grows larger every day. We all suspect that they'll make an independent bid for the White House next year, and they'll most certainly do some damage to the House and Senate. Projections show them taking at least twenty percent of the House, though these projections are early. Neither party has started to throw any serious money at advertising at this point. I see those poll numbers dropping drastically when the real money hits the streets. Still, their grassroots political campaign has been extremely effective and can't be discounted. Any connection to domestic terrorists will kill the movement. I can't see any scenario in which the True America political arm would condone this militant action. The True America folks on the Hill have very clearly denounced the previous militant rhetoric spouted by Greely and

Harding. The two of them barely make a living giving speeches to NRA dinners and Libertarian rallies."

"Either way, we have to be careful with this, Mr. President. Our best case scenario is that we stop this plot and never really connect this group to True America," said Remy.

Beck chuckled at his comment.

"I don't think we're going to benefit from that kind of a convenient luxury. This reeks of True America, and if it links back to Greely or Jackson, no amount of distance will keep the political movement alive. The FBI has traced one of last night's captured cell phones to the Mount Arlington pump station, connecting them with the Al Qaeda plot to poison the water supply of 35,000 citizens. Then we have the picture of the guy taken at the Al Qaeda safe house—Julius Grimes. He's even been photographed in public with True America. Politically, the biggest challenge we face is not appearing overly eager to connect this to True America and torpedo the movement. We're dealing with a major political phenomena predicted to upset the two party system in 2008, or at least shake up the status quo. We need to be one hundred and ten percent certain that True America is behind this plot, before anybody mentions a possible connection between the two. The last thing we can afford in the early election cycle is the accusation that we're trying to pin this attack on True America."

"Our first priority is stopping any further attacks. I want a link to SOCOM's planning efforts and a continuous executive summary of the surveillance. I'll address General Gordon in the Situation Room later this morning. In the meantime, I'll talk to Director Shelby and make sure he understands the importance of keeping the True America link quiet for now," said the president.

"What do you think about approaching True America's leadership with these developments? Shake the trees a little. If the political arm is in any way connected, they might put pressure on the militant group. If they're not connected, they would likely start their own investigation. This could be a coup in the making within True America," said Remy.

"All speculation at this point. This might be a group completely unconnected to True America. Until we possess more information, we can't approach them like this. They'd ask for proof, and we'd be hard pressed to give them more than a picture of a guy that used to hang out at Greely's old True America rallies. They'd cry foul," said Beck.

"No sense in trying to predict their reaction to hypothetical situations at this point. We'll keep an eye on the political ramifications, but let me be clear about one thing. If True America is involved, I have no problem exposing them," said the president.

"At the right time," added Remy.

"Exactly. I'd love nothing more than to torpedo their movement."

Chapter 29

7:32 AM
Hacker Valley, West Virginia

"Mugs" started moving forward slowly and Chief Petty Officer Steve Carroll settled in for a long morning. After an uneventful landing three miles north of the target compound, they hid their gear and split into four teams of two, each assigned a different cardinal approach to the compound. Their mission was simple, observe and report, but above all, remain undetected. Remaining undetected was the trick. They had moved at a normal pace under the cover of darkness, which allowed his team to cover most of the terrain in two hours, stopping at a point he had previously designated on his map to deploy Mugs.

A few minutes before arriving at the point, he'd started to pick up faint wireless signals on his wrist mounted battle feed, which had been detected by one of the squat antennas protruding from the communications rig in his backpack. This particular antenna was a "receive only" array, processing signal strength, data emission and direction. Based on the information transmitted to his battle feed, several devices were emitting wireless signals in front of them. They hadn't moved close enough to the signals to process a fix, and he had no intention of moving any further. He had no idea how far the opposing sensors could reach.

Mugs would cover the remaining 1,000 meters at a turtle's pace. One fifth of a mile per hour, or roughly 5.3 meters per minute, which was a pace scientifically proven to defeat all known, commercial and industrial grade remote infrared sensors. Mugs would end its journey twenty-five meters back from the point where the forest stopped and the clearing that surrounded the compound began. The drawback was obvious. Carroll and his teammate, Petty Officer First Class Jeff Stanhope, would have to wait more than three hours for the electronic assistance to reach its destination, possibly longer if the robotic device encountered obstacles.

The Micro Unmanned Ground Vehicle (MUG/V), affectionately known as "Mugs" to the SEALs, resembled a remote control tank, with no turret. Roughly the size of a typical 1/8 scale remote control vehicle, the MUG/V contained an internal surveillance package that included four night vision capable cameras supported by infrared illuminators. This provided a three hundred and sixty degree omnidirectional view for the operator. Additional sensors on each side allowed MUG/V to navigate around obstacles when it was programmed for an automated journey like the one that had just commenced. This particular model contained sensors that could detect wireless signals and transmit the data back to Carroll's communications rig, along with the camera feed.

Carroll had his reservations about using Mugs in the rough forest terrain, but he didn't have much choice. The robot could right itself if tipped, and was capable of climbing over medium sized fallen trees, but he was concerned that it might get caught up in thick branches. Mugs had a bad habit of trying to push through thick brush. The density of bushes didn't register as an obstacle that needed to be avoided.

The two SEAL DEVGRU operators disappeared into the surroundings and began the long waiting game that would consume most of their morning. If all went well, they would be able to cautiously advance with Mugs once the motion detectors were disabled. Their robot couldn't jam or disrupt the signals, but the data sent back to his communications rig would be transmitted to a nearby E-8C JSTARS aircraft. NSA techs onboard the command and control aircraft would figure out a way to penetrate the compound's computer network and disable the sensors. If the techs worked fast, they might not have to wait for Mugs to finish the entire journey. Until then, there was nothing to do but remain hidden, and try to keep Mugs from getting stuck.

Chapter 30

12:16 PM
Bonitos Boathouse
Fripp Island, South Carolina

Jessica stared at the young woman like she was holding a wet brown paper bag filled with dog feces over her lunch. The waitress looked to Daniel for support, still holding the phone out for someone to grab. Jessica didn't need to ask to figure out who was on the line. Few people knew they were here, and only one of them would have the nerve to call them. Given the fact that he had tracked them down at lunch on the first day they were together, Jessica was pretty sure this wasn't a social call. She could barely bring herself to look at Daniel, who should have snapped up the phone immediately. She was starting to wonder if this was her husband's intention all along, to let her make the decision. Well fuck *both* of them.

"I'm not talking to him," she said to Daniel, then turned to face the ponytailed, twenty-something waitress. "And if you continue to hold that phone in my face, I'll throw it over the railing into the water."

The woman retracted her hand and bit down on the top of her lip, unsure how to proceed.

"I realize this isn't your fault. I apologize for snapping at you," Jessica said, staring at Daniel. "I'm talking to her, not you. Go ahead and hang up on the gentleman, miss. I'll add a twenty to your tip if you do it within the next three seconds. Three, two..."

The waitress smiled and pressed the disconnect button. Before Jessica could dig the money out of her handbag, the phone rang again.

"I'll make that $500 if you throw it into the water."

"Don't throw the phone over. She doesn't mean that," Daniel said to the waitress. He turned to Jessica. "You want me to take this?"

"Not really, but I have a feeling it's inevitable. I don't want to talk to him. He's not going to get my approval to drag you off on another crazy adventure."

Daniel took the phone from the waitress and thanked her. Before she scurried off, Jessica gave her two twenty-dollar bills and apologized for putting her in the middle of their dispute. She watched the waitress walk quickly away from the table and thought about the difference between the two of them. At her age, Jessica had been learning spy craft at Camp Peary, Virginia, also known as "The Farm." A world apart. One woman ready to cry after being placed in an uncomfortable position while waiting tables, the other training for the rigors of an undercover position in war torn Yugoslavia. She envied the waitress and wished her a simple life that she herself had had.

She caught snippets of the conversation, choosing to focus on finishing her grilled calamari salad. It was a little heavy on the southern spices, but otherwise cooked to perfection. She drank most of her Bloody Mary, staring out at the marina, watching the masts bob up and down, back and forth. She heard enough of the conversation to be satisfied with Daniel's performance. Her suspicions had been wrong.

"He won't be bothering us anymore," Daniel said, placing the phone on the table.

"What did he want?"

"Do you really want to know?"

Jessica considered his question with her own internal query. Were they really done with the Black Flag program? Could they afford to cut ties with the program? That seemed to be the real question they needed to answer. Neither of them could predict how long their current immunity deal would last under a new administration. They were one year away from an election year, and a possible reshuffle of the White House. They had planned to disappear as Jessica and Daniel Petrovich, and reemerge as a "regular" couple somewhere within the United States. Living in another country remained an option, but their options would be limited, unless they were willing to spend a considerable sum of money. Money like that always attracted the wrong kind of attention.

"Where does he want to send you now? Back to Europe?"

"Atlanta, and he doesn't need me. He wanted to speak with you for a reason."

"He found a job for me? He is still aware that I was recently beaten to within an inch of my life and shot in the hand, right?"

"All of that supposedly makes you the best candidate. If not you, he'll have to hire from outside the group."

"A woman with a claw hand, strangled neck and black eye is the best candidate for the job? Why can't he send Diyah Castillo instead? I'd be happy to punch her in the face a few times."

"Diyah's in critical condition, along with Sayar Abraham. The rest of Sayar's team is dead. They were part of an FBI undercover operation in New Jersey. Sanderson's already sent Munoz and Melendez to Atlanta to start surveillance. The target is a highly successful quasi-lobbyist and fundraiser named Benjamin Young. Apparently, he has a weakness for beautiful women."

"Don't they all?"

"He has a specific weakness for the professional ladies," said Daniel.

"Sanderson needs someone to play the role of a prostitute? Wonderful."

She started to get up, but thought about what little she had heard of the conversation. Daniel had flat out refused whatever Sanderson had suggested, quickly ending the call. She had to remember that none of this was his fault. She lowered herself back onto the plastic patio chair and finished the Bloody Mary in one long gulp.

"You know how I feel about work like that," she said.

"The suggestion didn't sit well with me either," said Daniel.

On paper, two years of intense training with the CIA had prepared her to operate undercover in Belgrade. In reality, nothing could have prepared her for the ordeal she had been selected to endure. She had been too naïve and enthusiastic in Virginia to put the pieces together. Too caught up in her success within the Agency to see it coming. From top to bottom, men dominated the Serbian government and paramilitary structures. Women played no role in these corrupt and brutal organizations. This fundamental characteristic of Serbia was so overwhelmingly obvious, that it remained invisible to her. The training continued and she remained blind to the jaws waiting to chew her up and spit her out when she arrived in Serbia. Her handlers only made matters worse for her in the long run.

Beyond the best clandestine training available worldwide, she was spoiled by the CIA. Indulged in expensive clothing, etiquette lessons, and exposure to the finest food and wine money could buy. She emerged from the CIA's clandestine operations training program feeling unstoppable. Highly trained, confident and sophisticated, she could breeze through the casinos of Monte Carlo like James Bond or scale the walls of the Kremlin after sipping a martini with a Russian double-agent. The possibilities were endless for the newly minted agent. Even her undercover name sounded like something out of a Frederick Forsyth novel: Zorana Zekulic.

Her first assignment was to develop Serbian contacts in Paris. Members of Milosevic's paramilitary organizations made a killing in the black market, selling everything from stolen cigarettes to knock-off Polo shirts. The more cosmopolitan criminals traveled throughout Europe, spending time in cities like Paris and Amsterdam, where they could party like rock stars and try to expand Serbia's black market reach. These were typically highborn Serbs, who had vacationed with their families outside of the Balkans and were accustomed to more than Belgrade had to offer.

Family business connections had put them in a position to participate in the paramilitary ponzi-scheme at a high level, but they didn't mix well with the rough crowd that dominated the ranks of most paramilitary groups. Extended stays in the fashionable European cities served many purposes. Survival sat at the top of the list. The more time they spent outside Serbia, the less opportunity their paramilitary brethren would have to cut their throats open in a dark Belgrade alley.

For eight months, "Zorana" had lived the life of a runway model, partying with the "long distance" criminal element of Milosevic's paramilitary regime. Her time in Paris was extremely productive, exceeding CIA expectations. She fine-tuned her newly acquired tastes and broke into nearly every important social circle within the city. As a result of her "hard work," she developed well-placed contacts from three of the major paramilitary groups competing for Milosevic's attention in Belgrade. She repeatedly turned down offers to return with them to Serbia. The CIA wanted her to arrive in Belgrade on her own, not beholden to any particular group. Her handlers would direct these efforts once word of her arrival had spread throughout Belgrade. It would also give the CIA time to assess the success of her cover story, as the name started to filter back to Serbia from Paris.

So far, her "legend" had raised no eyebrows among Serbian expats in Paris, but Belgrade would be a different story. Serbians were suspicious by nature, especially in their own backyard. Her "legend" had been crafted carefully, extensively weaved into her training at the one year mark, where she would start to learn region specific skills that would transform her into Zorana Zekulic.

Zorana had left her parents when she was seventeen to live in Novi Sad with another girl from her small southern village. For two years, she waited tables at night and cleaned houses during the day, saving enough money to travel to Amsterdam. Two months after arriving in the Netherlands, she learned that her parents had been killed by Bosnian guerillas in a rare reprisal attack against civilians in southwestern Serbia.

Zorana Zekulic was found dead a few months later, floating in an obscure canal west of the city, the apparent victim of a heroin overdose and possible strangling. CIA analysts given the task to find a new "legend" had struck gold making these connections. Zorana's death went unnoticed in Amsterdam, since she had never broken into any significant social scene. CIA agents struggled to find anyone that remembered her beyond a hazy "oh yeah, I remember her…she used to hang out at the uh…one of the cafes in De Wallen…I'm trying to think of the name…give me a second" comment. Agents in Amsterdam calculated that any memory of Zorana Zekulic would fade within three months, long before her replacement arrived in Paris.

Paris had been like a dream for Jessica, now living as Zorana Zekulic. Three inches taller, and she could have easily broken into the runway model business. She had already turned down several photo-ops for women's fashion magazines at the request of her CIA handlers. They wanted her to attract attention, but not worldwide attention. Several months later, she was given the "green light" to leave Paris.

Immediately upon arrival, she noticed that the scene was starkly different in Belgrade. Her "friends" had kept their distance in Paris, despite their wealth and overconfidence. In Paris, she held the upper hand. She learned very quickly where she stood among these "friends" in Belgrade—a few notches up from prostitute. The rest of the men didn't differentiate. She spent most of her first month crying in her apartment. She was trapped in the most demeaning role imaginable, with no way out. She had been recruited by the CIA because she was "the very best of the best," and accelerated through the most selective training program in the world. All of that had landed her on the streets, fending off the most vile savages on earth. Looking back, she couldn't believe she hadn't seen this coming. She came from nothing. Why would she have expected anything different?

She looked back at Daniel. He had rescued her from the depths of hell after she had turned her back on him and disappeared in Chicago. He never asked any questions about why she had abandoned him. That was the thing with Daniel; he never judged and he never hesitated to take her back. He understood her on a core level, which both frightened and comforted her. No matter what she did, he'd always be there for her. She couldn't ask for anything else. She loved him fiercely, and wanted to do what was right for both of them, even if it meant small sacrifices.

"What's the risk level?" she asked.

"Low. Young travels between D.C., Manhattan, and his home in Atlanta. True America wants him dead. Apparently, he knows too much about their organization at this point for them to overlook his addiction to escorts and drugs. Sanderson sent your two friends to keep an eye on him. He wants us to talk to Young before they kill him. This involves you luring him from a hotel lobby bar to a hotel room, under our watchful eyes. We'll take care of the rest."

"You'll be there?"

"The entire time," he assured her.

"This may sound crazy, but I don't think we should sever ties to Sanderson yet. He may be the only person that can save us if the immunity deal falls apart. Despite his cold, calculating personality, I sense a loyalty to you that can never be broken. As long as we can work together, I'm in."

"Nothing crazy about sticking together. Are you absolutely sure about this?"

"I'm sure. What's the timeline?" she said.

"Young is scheduled to be in town for two more nights. Sanderson doesn't know very much about his Atlanta routine, but the guy's taken a room at the Ritz Carlton in Buckhead, presumably for extramarital entertainment. The dynamic duo has secured the room across the hall from him. Sanderson wants us to give this a try tonight. He stressed the importance of grabbing him during his normal routine at the hotel. Munoz hasn't detected any third-party surveillance, but it's only a matter of time before True America gets some eyes on Young…or stuffs a gun down his throat. They have already issued Young's death warrant, so Sanderson thinks tonight might be our only chance to do this without drawing attention."

"Buckhead is a four to five hour drive from here and I need to do some shopping. Preferably in a few of the boutique shops on Peachtree Road. We need to get moving."

"We can finish lunch. Sanderson reserved two seats for us on the 2:15 out of Savannah. Puts us in Atlanta by 3:30."

"In that case, I think I'll order the buttermilk fried flounder and another drink while you give Sanderson the good news."

"Sounds like a plan," Daniel said, staring off at the ocean past her.

She could tell something bothered him about the seemingly simple mission. Something he had chosen not to disclose.

Chapter 31

1:46 PM
North Tract
East of Laurel, Maryland

Officer Warren Donahue turned the Laurel Police Department's Ford Explorer onto Hill Road and cruised at a comfortable speed down the dusty service road. Thick foliage from the trees crowded the dirt lane, creating a shaded tunnel around his vehicle. Newly grown weeds lapped at the sides the SUV. In a few more weeks, some of the sturdier species of brush would scrape the paint if they didn't get a crew out here to cut everything back. He checked his watch and thought about the end of his shift. Two hours and counting.

Today's shift had started normally enough, despite the increased manning requirements dictated by the most recent Homeland Security threat assessment. Two hours into his eight-hour shift, Donahue had been recalled to base to pick up a passenger. Sergeant Bryan Osborne had decided that today would be the perfect day to get out on patrol with one of the rookies. Donahue really couldn't complain, Sergeant Osborne had even paid for lunch at Pi's deli.

He spotted the turn for Combat Road and debated whether to take his sergeant further into the vast tract of forest, or turn west toward downtown Laurel. He drove this stretch at least once during every shift, mostly checking for abandoned cars. His route varied, sometimes taking him to the western edge along the Wildlife Loop. He thought it was a waste of time, but the entire loop only took one of their patrol cars out of town for thirty minutes, so his patrol sergeant insisted that at least one of the officers make the trip. As the shift's rookie, the errand typically fell in his lap.

He decided to head back to Laurel and started to guide the SUV left at the worn patch of grass and dirt serving as the intersection.

"Hold on, Warren. Back up and take a right. I thought I saw something down Combat Road," said the sergeant.

"Roger that, sir."

A few moments later, the SUV headed east toward the outer loop road.

"Right there. Looks like a pickup truck nestled in the woods," Sergeant Osborne said as they approached a small turnoff to their left.

Donahue stopped the SUV and stared down the tight path, which was overgrown with thicket and looked barely navigable by vehicle. From this spot on Combat Road, he could see the back of a red pickup truck, which had been fitted with a commercial cap and roof rack. He wasn't sure how the sergeant had managed to spot the vehicle from the intersection. He probably had caught a glimpse of the red paint through the forest, which was another argument for assigning two officers to each patrol vehicle. He wondered how many details like this he missed on a daily basis, being more focused on safely navigating his vehicle. Then again, Sergeant Osborne had been doing this for nearly fifteen years, and had developed instincts and skills that Donahue could only dream of at this point.

"Nice catch, Sergeant. Do you want me to squeeze her down the road to take a closer look?" asked Donahue.

"No. Why don't you park and we'll take a look on foot."

With the SUV parked several yards back from the path, the two officers walked down the rough vehicle path until they approached the back of the pickup. A cursory examination revealed that the vehicle was a late model F-150, kept in excellent condition.

"Kind of seems out of place here, doesn't it?" said Osborne.

"I was thinking the same thing, sir. The exterior is pristine, aside from the mud kicked up from this little spot," Donahue replied.

The pickup had been forced to traverse thick mud to arrive in a dry patch on the edge of the small clearing. Donahue measured the area and determined that the pickup would barely have enough room to turn around.

"I don't know how they plan to get out of here," he said.

The sergeant just shook his head and stepped around to the driver's door to take a look.

"Door's locked. Hood's cool. Just rained this morning, so they couldn't have arrived last night," said Osborne, pointing at the tracks in the mud.

"Should we call this in and have another unit join us for a look?" asked Donahue.

"Nah. We'll head out a hundred yards or so and see if we can pick up a trail. If not, we'll make sure the next shift swings by to check it out before dusk. Probably some yahoo out hunting."

"I don't know, Sergeant. Check out those patterns in the mud over there," Donahue said, pointing toward the far end of the small clearing. "Looks like they carried something here, and put it down. Wheel tracks lead off onto some kind of path."

Osborne joined him at the edge of the clearing and looked back and forth between the pickup truck and the new set of tracks.

"Looks like something heavy. See how it sank into the mud?" said Osborne.

"Maybe we should call this in?" Donahue asked again.

"Alright. Call it in to dispatch, and have them send a unit to assist. Tell them to wait at the Explorer until we get back. We'll poke around the woods for a few minutes and head back to meet them."

While Donahue called it in using his shoulder-mounted microphone, Osborne followed the wheel tracks deeper into the forest. Initially, they had to push through light bushes, which showed damage from whatever had preceded them, but within twenty feet, they broke out onto a worn path. The tracks became less apparent on the dry, packed ground, but freshly broken branches on both sides of the trail assured them that the wheeled contraption had been moved forward.

"What do you think we're dealing with here? Meth lab?" asked Donahue.

"Fuck if I know. Whatever it is, I guarantee they're up to no good."

With Sergeant Osborne in the lead, they casually walked about one hundred feet until the sound of machinery caused them both to freeze in their tracks. Osborne cocked his head as if trying to determine the direction of the noise. At the same time, he released the strap on his holster and drew his semi-automatic service pistol. Donahue did the same, pointing the Glock 22 downward at a forty-five degree angle.

"What do you hear?" he asked, moving closer to the sergeant.

"I don't know, but I don't like it. Sounds like some kind of serious work going on out there. Turn your radio down. We're going to split up and figure this out. Let's stay within sight of each other. Are you familiar with basic hand signals? Eyes on, stop, move out, down, retreat?" he said, mimicking each signal to emphasize his point.

"Yeah, I got those, Sarge. We use the same signals hunting," Donahue said.

"Good. Move slowly and quietly. If you step on a branch, get down. We'll see how they react. If we're quiet, I think we'll be able to walk right up on them."

"Maybe we should wait for backup," Donahue suggested.

"Let's see what we're dealing with first. You head out maybe 50 feet on the left side of the path, I'll take the right side and we'll move forward until we make visual contact. Keep your finger off the trigger. You don't want to trip and fire off a round."

"Yes, sir," Donahue said, taking his finger out of the trigger well.

The two officers split up, fighting through the brush before stopping to establish visual contact with each other. Donahue saw his sergeant wave his free hand forward and start walking north along the direction of the trail. He stepped through the brush, trying not to break any branches or step on anything that looked like it would snap. It turned out to be a nearly impossible task.

Fortunately, the machine working in the distance would likely drown out any noise created as they pushed through the forest. He felt certain of this, since he couldn't hear the sergeant's equally noisy efforts across the one hundred foot divide.

He alternated between watching his footfalls, scanning ahead for the trespassers, and keeping an eye out for the sergeant. As they drew closer to the noise, Donahue recognized the sound of a small generator between the more pronounced mechanical bursts of sound that had originally attracted their attention. Out of his peripheral vision, he noticed that Osborne had stopped moving forward. He turned his head toward the sergeant and saw him lower to one knee. Donahue immediately mimicked the sergeant's action. The sergeant turned and signaled him by pointing two fingers at his eyes, followed by a single finger pointed north. He had spotted someone ahead of them. Three fingers held upward indicated three people. Shit. Three was enough to wait for back up. He anticipated the next signal to be a wave in the opposite direction, but Sergeant Osborne had other ideas.

Osborne raised himself up and pointed his pistol, signaling that they should move forward. Donahue's heart started racing as he watched the sergeant move forward and realized he had no choice but to follow. Every step filled him with dread. The possibility of taking on three suspects in the middle of nowhere was a bad idea, even with back up inbound. They were already too far into the forest to immediately benefit from assistance. He couldn't imagine what these people were doing out here with heavy machinery.

With every step, he prayed that Sergeant Osborne would change his mind. They could even crouch down right here and direct the backup units toward them. Sergeant Osborne stopped again and lowered himself. His signals indicated that the group of men were directly ahead of him. Donahue squinted, trying to pierce the thick leaves and ground brush with his eyes, but was still unable to spot anyone. The next hand signal scared the hell out of him. Osborne wanted Donahue to join him. He didn't relish the thought of crossing the path this close to the suspects, but he liked the idea of safety in numbers. He felt extremely exposed by himself in these unfamiliar woods.

With the racket of machinery covering his own noise, he approached the path as quickly as possible, keeping his eyes focused north. When he peeked around the last tree trunk before the path, he caught a glimpse of movement less than fifty feet ahead of him. They were way closer than he had suspected. The figure stayed within view for several seconds, before disappearing behind an impenetrable layer of brush and crowded trees. Overhanging branches dipped low on the path keeping him from seeing a face, but he could tell the man was Caucasian by his hands. After he was certain that the man had completely vanished, Donahue crossed the path, staying low until he reached Osborne.

"Fifty feet ahead, behind all of the shit up there. I saw one of them," whispered Donahue.

"I saw three guys through a break in the trees just for a second. They're working some kind of portable digger," said Osborne.

"Hey…maybe they just bought the property and are digging a well?" said Donahue, still trying to catch his breath.

"Nobody digs a well carrying an AR-15," said Osborne.

"AR-15s? We have to back off and call in SWAT. They might have more people patrolling the forest," said Donahue.

His heart thumped faster, and he knew that he was coming close to having a panic attack. This was too much for two municipal police officers to handle. Three men armed with AR-15s. This could be anything, from some wacko militia group to drug dealers. They were less than three miles from Fort Meade, so maybe this was some kind of terrorist attack. They could be burying a mortar in the ground to fire on the National Security Agency. The possibilities were endless.

"We can take this crew down quickly. You saw one of them down the path. That'll make everything easy. Quick approach. They'll never hear us coming. We'll achieve complete surprise. Trust me. Nobody will move when we pop up out of nowhere with drawn weapons"

"I'm not trained for this kind of tactical situation," said Donahue nervously.

"Look, Warren," Osborne said, making direct eye contact, "I used to head one of our tactical teams. This will be over in less than five seconds. You have to trust me on this."

Donahue nodded and tried to shake the doubts that weighed heavily on him.

"I'll take the lead. We'll rush up the path and spread out once everyone comes into view. You aim at the guy farthest to the right and alternate with the next one to his left. I'll take the furthest left and alternate with the middle guy. That way they see that we have them all covered. Follow my instructions once they raise their hands and we have them under voice control. You good to go?"

"Yeah. I'm good. Let's do this," Donahue said, trying his best not to sound doubtful.

Osborne patted him on the shoulder. "Good man. How far out is our backup?"

"Hold on," he said and put a call through to dispatch. After receiving a response he said, "They just turned onto Columbus Road."

"Perfect. They're less than three minutes from our truck. We'll have this wrapped up before they step out of their vehicles. Stay close and stay low."

Sergeant Osborne walked briskly toward the path, pointing his weapon at the opening in the brush less than thirty feet ahead. Donahue followed in his footsteps, careful not to point his weapon at Osborne. His finger kept returning to the trigger and he had to make a conscious effort to listen to Osborne's previous advice. An accidental discharge right now could possibly kill both of them. His sergeant reached the edge of the thicket and took a knee, waiting for Donahue.

"Here we go. On three. One. Two…Go!" he hissed, and the two officers sprinted down the path.

ঌ৵

Sergeant Osborne cleared the brush and aimed at the first target that materialized, which turned out to be a dark haired man wearing a long sleeve khaki shirt and blue jeans. He was facing away from the sergeant and cradling an AR-15. Osborne didn't hesitate. The first rounds to leave his service pistol struck the man high in the back before Donahue stumbled through the opening. He shifted his aim to the man operating a portable digging machine and fired three rounds in rapid succession. One of the rounds skipped off the contraption's raised auger bit, saving the operator from a clear shot to the forehead. The remaining two rounds burrowed through the thick muscle of the man's right shoulder and collarbone, barely moving him.

Still in the game, thought Osborne, as he sighted past the auger and focused on another headshot.

Before he could pull the trigger, Donahue's pistol roared to life, spraying bullets into the two standing men. Osborne had counted on this type of reaction from the rookie. He figured that once the shooting started, Donahue would unload his pistol. He could see the panic in the young officer's eyes a few moments earlier. He knew there would be no trigger discipline, just a maelstrom of steel erupting from his officer's gun. Osborne pulled the trigger of his own weapon, hitting the machine operator between the eyes as three bullets from Donahue's pistol stitched across the man's chest. A quick glance at the third suspect confirmed that he was out of the fight, with two holes in the center of his gray polo shirt.

The third man dropped to his knees and toppled to the right, trying to jam the stock of his rifle into the soft forest floor, in a desperate attempt to arrest his fall. When the shooting started, Osborne realized too late that he had underestimated the reaction speed of their suspects. The third man had almost managed to bring his AR-15 to bear on them. Fortunately, Donahue had turned out to be a better shot under pressure than he had expected.

Osborne rushed to the fallen suspect and snatched the assault rifle from his grip, kneeling down to examine the man's wounds. Donahue lowered his pistol and muttered "what the fuck" several times before addressing Osborne.

"What the fuck was that all about? You started shooting without any kind of warning," he said, surveying the scene. "You hit that one in the back, Sarge? Shit. We're fucked!"

From his lowered position next to the dying suspect, Osborne holstered his weapon.

"Calm down. There are three guys with assault rifles. One of them almost put this into action against us. We didn't have a choice," he growled, aiming the rifle at Donahue.

"This is absolutely fucked," stated Donahue, oblivious of the barrel pointed at his head.

"Sorry about this," said Osborne.

"Sorry doesn't undo the fact—"

The sentence was interrupted by a short burst of automatic fire from the rifle pointed at his head. Officer Donahue never changed expressions as his body went slack and hit the ground with a muted thump. Sergeant Osborne jammed the rifle back into the wounded man's arms and drew his handgun, firing three rapid shots into the suspect's head. He stood up and glanced at the scene. A bright red, portable digging machine vibrated on oversized inflatable tires, drumming out the echoes of gunfire. Everyone was dead from what he could tell.

He looked back at Officer Donahue's crumpled body and cursed himself. They had insisted that he would need another officer on the scene to avoid any suspicion, but he had been wary about this idea from the start. He knew it would have to be the rookie. The more seasoned members of the force would have refused to proceed into the forest without backup. They would have certainly never agreed to charge an armed group in the middle of the forest. He needed someone he could pressure into following him. He just wished the young officer had reacted differently, so he could have kept the kid alive.

He'd argued this point extensively with Brown. He saw very little upside to having another officer on the scene, especially an idealistic rookie. He had to make sure every one of the suspects were killed in the gun battle, which meant he had to go in with guns blazing. There was no other way. They couldn't take the chance that one of them might actually surrender. Brown had made this point crystal clear and saddled the sergeant with a severe handicap. They obviously wanted it this way. He had to admit, the scene was compelling. Two local police officers unwittingly stumble onto the scene of a planned terrorist attack, taking out the terror cell, but not before one of the heroic officers is killed in a fierce exchange of gunfire. It made one hell of a story.

He checked his watch. With any luck, their backup had just arrived. He rushed over to Officer Donahue's body and heaved the dead weight into a fireman's carry. He struggled through the forest, screaming for help while trying to ignore the blood and brain matter that gushed down the left side of his uniform. He had to make this look good for the officers that came upon him. Donahue's sacrifice would catalyze a nation into action. Both of their actions would be recorded in True America's secret operational files, to be unceremoniously, yet handsomely rewarded at the appropriate time. The New Recovery would usher in a new era of prosperity, never forgetting the risks taken and sacrifices made by a handful of dedicated patriots.

He stumbled forward a few more steps, before spotting a familiar navy blue uniform shirt racing through the trees. As the voices approached, he found himself able to conjure up tears. The final act of his performance approached, and he wanted to win an Emmy for True America.

Chapter 32

2:14 PM
National Counterterrorism Center
McLean, Virginia

Sharpe had just sat down in his office when his mobile phone rang. He had been looking forward to possibly closing his eyes for a few minutes. The call originated from the daytime NCTC Watch Floor Supervisor, Jason Volk.

"Mr. Volk. How can I help you?" he answered.

"My analysts just picked up some police traffic that might be related. You should take a look at this. I can send it to your computer."

"No. I'll be right out."

He headed out of his office and turned left, making his way to the front of the watch floor. The immense projection screen dominating the front of the room showed a detailed satellite map of the northeast United States. A red marker blinked near Baltimore, Maryland. As he approached Jason Volk at one of the forward most workstations, the map zoomed in on the mark, centering on a location between Laurel, Maryland and Fort Meade.

"That's only a few miles from the National Security Agency," said Sharpe.

"Exactly. Our filters picked up an emergency police bulletin requesting HAZMAT and EMT support at this location, in addition to Anne Arundel County SWAT assets. Not in that order. There is an officer down, along with multiple suspects. Laurel Police Department dispatch initiated the request. Everyone is responding."

"Get me a line to the Laurel Chief of Police, or whoever is in charge over there. Good work on this," said Sharpe.

"Right away. I'll patch it through to your mobile phone," said Volk.

Sharpe nodded, already on his way to O'Reilly's station. Before he could say a word, she turned to face him.

"I'm notifying the Baltimore field office," she said. "They can coordinate a response with the D.C. field office if they need additional resources. HAZMAT and SWAT?"

"Don't get too excited. The entire nation is on edge right now. This could be anything," Sharpe cautioned her.

"That's what I thought, but the nearest pump station is four miles away."

"I'm beginning to wonder if my presence is necessary any longer," said Sharpe.

"We've been wondering that for the last year," replied O'Reilly.

"He does have a connection to the director. That helps," said Hesterman.

"Does it?" she said.

"Is this what the two of you do all day?" Sharpe asked.

"Pretty much. Along with connecting all of the dots for you. Take a quick look at this," said O'Reilly.

She enlarged one of the windows on her flatscreen monitor, which showed a complicated chart. He could see that the x-axis represented calendar weeks for the past three years. The y-axis contained names. He recognized several of them. Miguel Estrada, Julius Grimes and John Galick were the most prominent. The others had been added over the course of the day as his team had identified them.

"We've identified eleven of the seventeen terrorists involved in the market attack. Seven have former military experience. All except Galick were dishonorably discharged from the service. I found evidence of anti-government cyber space rants from nine of the eleven, but nothing within the last year. We managed to develop a background for nine of them, including recent employer data. Some of the employers were kind enough to provide schedule information. Six out of the eleven."

"Looks like this crew vacations together," said Sharpe.

"Either that, or it's one hell of a coincidence going back two years. Six different vacation periods align, but here's the scary part: they're all scheduled for two solid weeks of vacation starting next week, in addition to the days they've taken this week. Estrada quit his job in Seattle a month ago," said O'Reilly.

"Jesus. This is not a good sign. I have a feeling they aren't headed to the Caribbean," said Sharpe.

"Historically, two weeks is the longest period of time that has coincided. Given everything else we've seen this week, I'd say they have something big planned," said O'Reilly.

"How long ago did they submit their vacation schedules?"

"Three of the employers confirmed that the vacations went on the books months ago," Hesterman said.

"It sounds like this was True America's plan all along," said Sharpe.

"I thought we weren't allowed to say this is the work of True America," said O'Reilly.

"My apologies. Politics trumps common sense. What I was trying to say, is that this timeline calls into question the assumption that Al Qaeda's shipments were a last minute reaction to Anatoly Reznikov's poisoning of Monchegorsk. If these vacations were planned months ago, then Tru—the domestic terror network in question knew ahead of time that the canisters would be shipped earlier this week. I don't think Al Qaeda ever intended to target cities in Europe. I think the U.S. had always been their primary target, and True America knew it."

"You did it again," said O'Reilly.

"Did what?"

"Said True America," added Hesterman.

"Sorry. Let's just pretend I never said that."

Sharpe's mobile phone rang, causing his hand to shoot down to his belt. He looked up and saw Jason Volk give him a thumbs up. He pressed a button on the phone's screen and was connected with Laurel's Chief of Police. Less than a minute later, he disconnected the call.

"They found digging equipment in a forest area a few miles south of Fort Meade. City engineers confirmed that one of the water supply mains from the Laurel pump station heads through that area and connects with a pump station in Fort Meade. Three men armed with automatic rifles were killed by police officers at the dig site. One of the police officers was killed in the shootout. They called HAZMAT because of a canister they found on the scene," he told them.

"Canister?" said O'Reilly.

"The description matches canisters recovered from the Mount Arlington pump station. We have an even bigger problem on our hands," said Sharpe.

"There's no way we can protect thousands of miles of water supply pipes," said Hesterman.

"Hundreds of thousands, Agent Hesterman. There could be over 5,000 miles of water main located in Anne Arundel County alone. There's absolutely no way to protect it all. The only option is to stop drinking water from public supplies," said Sharpe.

"Or we put an end to the domestic terrorist network in question," said O'Reilly.

"I need to speak with the director. They need to take down that compound in West Virginia immediately. Start running profiles on the three men killed at the site and prioritize testing of the canister's contents. Push everything to the White House Situation Room, including your assessment of the link between suspects killed or captured in the market raid. I'll be back to brief the entire floor in five minutes," said Sharpe.

He walked back to his office, locking eyes with Callie Stewart, who was standing next to Admiral DeSantos on the catwalk with her arms folded on the railing. Things were definitely about to heat up around here.

Chapter 33

4:05 PM
White House Situation Room
Washington D.C.

The president slammed his fists down on the conference room table in a rare expression of anger. This was a good sign as far as Frederick Shelby was concerned. The administration might finally take the gloves off and kick some True America ass. *Domestic terror network* he had to remind himself. Whatever. As soon as the connection was solidified, he planned to issue arrest warrants for every single member of True America he could identify.

He just needed to keep his enthusiasm in check during this meeting. He couldn't read the president on this one. He knew that politics dominated his decision to deemphasize the connection to True America, but he wasn't sure if this was just a temporary political move while the "fires were hot." He didn't dare ask the president or any of his closest allies. If they caught wind of what he planned, they might shut him down before he could start rounding up this band of traitors. Shelby was no stranger to the political arena, but he wasn't about to let politics endanger America. Too much of that had taken place during his tenure as FBI Director.

"I want this compound taken down immediately. General Gordon, how soon can your forces hit them?" asked the president.

"Maybe we should slow down and wait for Justice to—" started Kathleen Walker, his senior legal counsel, but the president interrupted.

"No. No more waiting around for the next attack. I'm done reacting here. We take the offensive and shut this group down permanently. I don't need a warrant to attack enemies of the United States. General?"

"Mr. President, surveillance teams have been in position around the compound since midmorning, and all of the compound's remote security sensors have been disabled. We've made a few last minute adjustments to the plan based on their intelligence, but I feel comfortable launching a raid tonight. I still need to infiltrate two Delta troops. I can drop them at 9:30 PM, when it is sufficiently dark enough to cover their descent. They'd be in position within a few hours. Barring any unforeseen difficulties, I can support a midnight time-on-target. All other assets are on immediate standby."

"Can we go without the Delta troops?"

"Negative, Mr. President. Surveillance puts enemy compound strength at over one hundred personnel and—"

"Good God. That's a huge number, General," interrupted the president.

"And to make matters worse, Director Shelby has informed me that True America is known to possess heavy caliber machine guns and possibly a functional 60mm mortar. We can't discount the possibility of Soviet era surface to air missile capability either. Delta operators will set up light machine gun positions on all sides of the compound to suppress any of these weapons. They will also provide direct action teams that will be the first to breach the wire and provide direct fire against the barracks buildings. SEALs arriving by helicopter for the main takedown won't have an easy time, but at least they won't come under direct fire from .50 caliber machine guns. We have a few other surprises planned for the compound."

Shelby found it curious that nobody stepped in to correct General Gordon's use of the term "True America."

"Can we use armed drones during the attack?" asked Robert Copley, CIA Director.

"We had a discussion about this earlier, Robert, and decided against deploying the drones in U.S. airspace. Even for surveillance. We feel that this is a slippery slope," answered the National Security Advisor.

Copley did his best to conceal a look that expressed Shelby's first thought. They had no problem using Tier One Special Forces operators on U.S. soil, but a Predator armed drone was somehow out of the question. Politics.

"I want to minimize collateral damage to the compound infrastructure. We need to preserve as much evidence as possible for the FBI. How close can we bring the FBI mobile task force to the compound before the raid? I want them on scene immediately. The attempt at Fort Meade couldn't be an isolated event."

"Undercover Delta operators infiltrated the surrounding towns and suspect an active network of informants. I don't recommend any ground vehicle activity in the area prior to the attack. I'd keep them on Interstate 79 and time their arrival at the Route 15 exit for midnight. A convoy of government vehicles traveling through some of the towns along Route 15 might raise the alarm. It'll take them about an hour, maybe less, to arrive at the compound from that location. I have a two-vehicle Delta team that can escort them. They might need the help, since the road from Route 15 to the compound looks dicey," said General Gordon.

"Can we put them in support helicopters and land them directly at the compound?" asked Shelby.

"Sure, if you can get them over to Dover Air Force Base by 2200 hours," replied the general.

"I can have them at Dover by 1900," said Shelby.

"Then I can arrange to have them dropped at the site once my people have declared it clear of hazards."

"Excellent. I'll be in my office down here for a few hours. Frederick, will you join me?" asked the president.

Shit. Maybe he had looked too eager when the president slammed his fists into the table. Shelby really hoped he wasn't that easy to read. He followed the president and Jacob Remy into the president's private office. Once seated, the office windows obscured at the press of a button. He was finally on the inside after all of his years of service. He just hoped he hadn't been brought in here for an ass chewing. The president didn't waste any time getting down to business.

"How far along has Sharpe come to connecting the attacks to True America?"

Shelby started to think carefully about his choice of words, but decided to trust his gut instinct and forget politics.

"We know this is True America, but to be completely honest, we don't have a solid case yet. I was hoping that one of the men killed near Fort Meade would be wearing a True America t-shirt, but no such luck. They've covered their tracks pretty well up to this point. I'm hoping that the compound raid will break this wide open."

"What if it doesn't?" asked Jacob Remy.

"What do you mean?"

"What if we go in there, and at the end of the day, we don't gather any more evidence connecting this to True America?"

"We'll make the connection," Shelby said. "Their plot is too complicated to cover up completely. We have our best interrogators working on the three terrorists captured in Brooklyn. The compound raid will break the back of their organization. We'll roll up the entire group with the evidence uncovered in this raid. You heard the general's surveillance report: over a hundred terrorists on site. We're going to catch them right in the middle of planning their next phase of attacks. The timing couldn't be better."

"I share your optimism, Frederick. Unfortunately, Jacob is skeptical. He thinks this is a conspiracy involving all True America leadership, and they've planned this for years to coincide with the upcoming election."

"I'd be lying if I told you the thought hadn't crossed my mind."

"Make sure Sharpe's task force gets everything it needs to make this connection, and stand by to dismantle True America when the connection is made. We may have to wait until the timing is right, but we'll take them down. As far as I'm concerned, True America is the most dangerous terrorist organization that has ever walked on U.S. soil, and I intend to remove that threat."

"I'll make sure Sharpe has every resource at his disposal, and I'll make sure to consult with you about the possibility of a wider response to the evidence uncovered at the compound."

Message received.

"Perfect. Until then, I want Sharpe to focus all of his efforts on safeguarding America."

"Understood, Mr. President."

"Thank you, Frederick. I'll see you later tonight."

With those words, Frederick Shelby was dismissed after a not so subtle warning to suppress any connections his task force made between the current terrorist plot and True America. He left the office with a glimmer of hope. Despite the warning, he sensed that the two men wanted nothing more than to crush True America. They just wanted to control the timing for political reasons. Shelby could live with that, as long as it didn't interfere with Sharpe's investigation. He was far from being a political pawn, but he'd learned long ago that positions of great power in Washington D.C. always required you to sell a small portion of your soul to stay in the game.

Powerbrokers ran afoul when they sold too much of their soul to the wrong person, ending up beholden to the Beltway devils. Forced to leverage the rest of their soul in a desperate, yet futile bid to keep a seat at one of the big tables. Shelby planned to be at the table until the day he died, with his soul mostly intact.

Chapter 34

5:49 PM
I-95 South
Laurel, Maryland

Darryl Jackson sat in sluggish traffic that would only get worse as he approached the entrance to the D.C. Beltway. Once on the beltway, he could get out of his car and have a picnic on the roof of his Suburban at this time of the evening. He'd left his house yesterday, immediately after hearing the news of the Mount Arlington attack, and filled his SUV with bottled water and microwaveable meals purchased from the Wegmans Supermarket. He arrived in Princeton for a late lunch with Liz, after which he helped to move the water and supplies into her dorm room.

Sensing her nervousness about the Mount Arlington attack, or possibly the fact that he had shown up unannounced with enough food and water to last her a month, he decided to stay in a nearby hotel for the night. She begrudgingly ate pizza with him in the hotel lobby, before finally convincing him that she was fine. Finding himself unconvinced the next morning, he managed to linger around long enough to feed her lunch before departing too late to dodge D.C. traffic. By the time he said goodbye, he finally realized that he was much more nervous about Liz's situation than Liz herself.

The traffic crawled to a stop and he grimaced. He'd be lucky to get home by nine o'clock. His cell phone rang and he snatched it off the passenger seat. Cheryl. She was the other half of the nervous party.

"Hi, honey."

"Where are you? I thought you'd be here by now," she said.

He detected a thin layer of panic in her voice, which was unusual for his wife.

"I'm stuck in traffic north of D.C. Just south of Laurel. I had lunch with Liz."

"*Laurel?* Jesus. Did you hear what happened? It happened right in Laurel!"

"What's going on, hon? What happened in Laurel?"

"They tried to attack a water pipeline in Laurel. Local police shot and killed the suspects. A police officer was killed. It was pure random luck that they even found these guys," said Cheryl.

"Honey, slow down. Who did this? What happened exactly?"

"Terrorists tried to drill into one of the water mains leading to Fort Meade. They were in the middle of a forest south of the town. The police stopped the attack, but now they're saying there's absolutely no way to safeguard the public water system. They can't guard hundreds of thousands of miles of water main pipe. Some towns are talking about shutting down the water supplies," said Cheryl.

"Who are they? You can boil the water. This is crazy. When did the attack take place?"

"Some time in the middle of the afternoon. The White House has made a statement, but they didn't give any useful details. They can attack us anywhere, Darryl. Are you sure Liz will be alright?"

"She's doing way better than we are. I'll give her a quick call to update her on the situation and make sure she understands what to do. Karl assured me that the virus would be killed by the boiling process. Can you head to Wegmans and try to stock up on bottled water? Just to make our lives easier, until they can start testing the water."

"They can't test the water if the terrorists are picking random locations along the pipeline. They could tap into a water main running through the woods behind our house, poison the entire subdivision. They'd have to test the water at every tap, continuously throughout the day. That's what they just said."

"Who are *they*? Who is saying this?"

"I'm hearing it on Fox, CNN. It doesn't matter, they're all saying the same thing—drink bottled water," she said.

"Then you better get over and buy some, even if you have to wait in line until I get back. Head over to Costco instead. They have a full warehouse sized aisle devoted to bottled water. Bring your phone. I should be home by nine. We'll be fine, honey. I'll call the kids. I love you."

"I love you too. Alright, I'm heading back out. Tell Liz and Emily that I'll talk to them later tonight. And tell them to be careful. No showers, no cafeteria drinks, nothing," said Cheryl.

"I'm on it. Give me a call from Costco with a situation report," he said, realizing he had just slipped into operational mode.

"Yes, sir. Call you soon," she responded, playing right along.

He hung up and stared to his left, across the jammed highway. A few miles east of here, those bastards had tried to poison the National Security Agency, along with thousands of nearby citizens. The location of the attack couldn't be a coincidence. He wondered what their bigger game would be. Taking out the NSA, or at least disrupting it had to play into their complicated plot. Berg had been light on the conspiracy details, but had told him enough to know that there was a major terrorist operation in the works. Maybe the government had the situation under control. How else could they have stopped this attack? Maybe they were in the process of similar raids across the country. After calling his children, he'd give Berg another call. He had to know what they were up against.

He turned his attention back to the creeping traffic and tuned the radio to an AM news station to get some background information before starting his calls. Unfortunately, most of the chatter relayed useless theories and guesswork designed to panic the population. He quickly gained the sense that details were scarce and the government wanted to keep it that way.

Chapter 35

8:22 PM
Ritz Carlton Hotel-Buckhead
Atlanta, Georgia

Daniel stood to greet his guest. He wished their first meeting could be under different circumstances, given the debt he owed the young man. He took Enrique Melendez's hand and pulled him in for a man hug and a pat on the back, which was a stretch for Daniel. He'd never been an expressive kind of guy. He glanced briefly at Jessica over Melendez's shoulder, noting that she remained focused on the Cosmopolitan in her hand, still paying little attention to the man sitting next to her at the bar.

Jessica had kept the seat available for Benjamin Young's arrival, which had been no easy feat on a Friday night in Buckhead. The swank Lobby Bar at the Ritz Carlton proved to be a popular destination for the affluent, after work crowd, which hung around sipping cocktails well past the dinner hour. Gradually, the expensive suits and slacks surrendered to country club chic, replete with muted pastel blazers, tailored dress shirts, tight cocktail dresses, and more wheat-toned gabardine than he'd ever seen in one place.

Young arrived at 7:45, and Jessica lifted her Chanel 2.55 black lambskin bag from the seat as he approached the bar. He took the bait and ordered a scotch served neat, cordially confirming with her that the seat was still available. Daniel had noticed that Young's eyes had followed the handbag. He was impeccably dressed in an expensively cut navy blue suit, with white dress shirt and gray tie. It was easy to tell that he appreciated fine goods and the people that chose them. A faded pink pocket square peeked out of his jacket's left breast pocket at the requisite half-inch height. Thick brown hair, tan skin, chiseled features, blue eyes—he looked like a Brooks Brothers model.

He took notice of Jessica immediately, but didn't initiate any contact. Likewise, Jessica didn't invite any additional attention at first, wanting to let his situation simmer for a little longer. As the eight o'clock hour passed, and Young started to fidget, she began to exchange glances with him. His "date" hadn't arrived, which heightened his anxiety. He touched his nose several times, indicating his need for a little nose candy booster.

Daniel was amazed to see how quickly Benjamin Young unraveled, as the prospect of being stood up by a prostitute became more likely.

"Good to see you again, my friend," he said, releasing Melendez and putting a hand on the chair meant for him.

He had selected a table at the back of the lobby, giving away two of the four chairs to an ever expanding group of well groomed men at the table next to them. The remaining chairs were arranged behind the table to give them both a full view of the Lobby Bar, which would be a necessity given the number of people pouring into the tight room. By 7:55, it had become standing room only, and he couldn't keep an eye on Jessica without moving his head in an obvious manner. Given the recent arrival of two men, who had taken an obvious interest in Benjamin Young, he couldn't afford to tip his hand here in the bar.

"Likewise. Young's eight o'clock appointment was taking a nap in the parking garage. We're clear for at least three hours. Here's her phone," said Melendez.

The stocky Latino took his seat and casually scanned the room, signaling for the cocktail waitress two tables away. Daniel's anxiety level dropped a few notches with Melendez at the table. He'd been nervous using Jessica like this. True America wanted Benjamin Young off the street sooner than later, a fact reinforced by the quick replacement of the original assassination team. The two men standing at the end of the wide, mahogany bar gave away their intentions as soon as they arrived. Sipping club sodas, the two had spent the last twenty-five minutes stealing impatient glances at Young.

Their tradecraft skills were nonexistent, which signified that they were either operating well out of their comfort zone or that they had never been trained for the more subtle aspects of their work. Either scenario worried Daniel. A combination of the two terrified him. There was little doubt that

"Ben and Jerry" had been given orders to kill the man sitting less than six inches from Jessica. The hazard lay in their interpretation of the orders and their professionalism. Had they read the situation correctly and realized that he'd be headed up to his room shortly? Would they panic when his escort failed to show, and try to kill him in the bar? Daniel wished Jessica would double her efforts. Based on the increasing severity of their facial expressions, he calculated that Ben and Jerry would make a bad decision within the next ten minutes, maybe sooner.

He saw Jessica lean over and say something to Young. *Finally*. She could read the situation better than any of them. If he knew Jessica, they'd be out of there shortly. Daniel smiled and faked a quiet laugh, turning to Melendez.

"Time to send Young a text from Natasha's phone. Type this…ready?"

Melendez pulled the phone out of his blazer and held it under the table.

"Shoot."

"Something came up. Sorry. Will call later," Daniel dictated.

"That's it?"

"That's it. The message should frustrate him enough to turn all of his attention to Jess."

"Sending," said Melendez.

Daniel watched Young shake his head upon reading the message. Jessica immediately leaned in and said something, which caused Young to put the phone down on the bar and engage her in conversation. It looked like their mark had conveniently forgotten all about Natasha. Jessica could have that effect on men. He noticed that she had started to touch the bottom of her nose like Young. She was definitely expediting the process. Daniel took a sip of his vodka martini and shifted his gaze to Ben and Jerry, who looked even edgier than before. The mystery text had probably shaved three minutes off their bad decision timeline.

"She'd better hurry this up," said Petrovich.

"You got that right. Those two look ready to start shooting," said Melendez.

"If this gets out of hand, grab Young and get him out of the hotel," said Daniel.

"What about you?"

"I have Jessica."

"Got it," Melendez said.

"We'll get a real drink when this is over. I owe you my firstborn. I'll never forget what the two of you did for her," said Daniel.

"As long as the kid comes with a return option. Fucking scary concept, the two of you having kids," said Melendez, and they both laughed for real, though it was short lived.

Jessica moved her purse and Benjamin Young put his cell phone away. A few seconds later, Jessica swirled her index finger around the rim of her half-finished cosmopolitan and removed the maraschino cherry inside. She slipped the cherry in her mouth, sensuously pulling the stainless steel pick clear of her lips.

"Time to move," Daniel said, and placed a pair of twenty dollar bills on the table.

The cherry trick was their prearranged sign that departure was imminent.

"Are you sure you want to work it this way?" asked Melendez.

"Yeah. I'll babysit them on the way up. Get going," said Daniel.

"All right. See you upstairs," Melendez said and walked through the bar to the lobby.

The plan was simple, but required careful timing. Melendez would leave the bar a minute before Jessica and their mark, taking the elevator directly to the eighteenth floor. He'd join Munoz in the room across from Benjamin Young's suite and wait. Munoz had been watching the suite most of the afternoon, making sure that Young didn't have any uninvited guests. He'd sent Daniel a text message indicating that nobody had approached the suite after he left tonight, leaving him relatively confident that the two men standing at the bar comprised the entire team sent to eliminate Young.

Jessica stood first, clutching her purse and making brief eye contact with Daniel. He quickly shifted his eyes to Ben and Jerry, both of whom had placed their drinks on the bar. Jessica walked past Young before he could stand up. She placed herself close to the bar and pulled him to her left side, ensuring that her new friend would walk out of the bar with a human shield as they passed the two men on their right. It would probably be enough to discourage the two men from taking a hasty shot in the bar, but it involved unnecessary risk.

Jessica clung onto Benjamin Young's arm, and they started walking together toward the spacious lobby opening. Daniel watched Ben and Jerry closely, knowing that the two men would be too focused on Young to notice. He rose from the table as the new couple passed the two operatives. Jessica said something to Young as they passed in front of them. Whatever she said seemed to put their countdown on hold. He saw one them place a hand against the other, in a subtle restraining motion. He'd be willing to bet that Jessica made it clear they were headed to Young's room and said it loud enough for the assassins to hear. Still, he wasn't going to rely upon this assessment. They could follow him to the elevator and shoot him as the doors started to close, or take the elevator up with him. He could think of a dozen scenarios, all of which put Jessica right in the line of fire.

One of the men checked his watch and spoke to the other. Daniel couldn't believe it. They were actually timing how long they would wait. At least they had enough sense to avoid a bloodbath in the lobby. He left the bar, trailing his wife at a respectable distance. He decided to ride the elevator up with Ben and Jerry, so he diverted toward the concierge for a few moments. From there, he could watch Jessica and Benjamin Young and make sure the two idiots in the bar didn't change their minds about a public murder. The two men emerged from the bar just as his wife stepped on the elevator ahead of Young. For a brief second, a shiver of panic ran down Daniel's spine.

The two men looked like they might go for Jessica's elevator. Daniel tensed, ready to sprint across the lobby to intercept the men. Ben and Jerry exchanged words and started to walk rapidly toward the elevator bank. Daniel's right hand drifted along his beltline, pushing the bottom of his suit jacket back. He tried to keep the motion subtle, but they weren't making it easy for him. They walked directly at the open door, closing the distance to thirty feet. The door started to move at twenty feet, which still didn't relieve him. One of them could press the "up" button, while the other blasted away into the carriage.

He firmly grasped the polymer grip of his HK USP Compact pistol and loosened it in the concealed holster. He started to edge toward the elevator bank, hoping to close the distance for a more accurate shot. If either of the men glanced in his direction, there would be little doubt about his intentions. The lead operative reached the elevator buttons a few seconds after the door closed. The illuminated numbers above the elevator door had not started moving, and he looked back at his partner, who shook his head. Daniel eased the gun back into the holster and approached the elevators, pulling out his cell phone.

Once illuminated numbers above Jessica's elevator started moving, the man pressed the elevator button. The closest elevator was on floor three, which should give Jessica enough time to make sure they were in the room before Ben and Jerry appeared on the eighteenth floor. He had no doubt they wouldn't waste any time eliminating Young and any witnesses that could identify them.

He dialed Munoz and waited for the elevator.

"Hey, Jeff. Are the ladies ready for dinner?" said Daniel.

"Yep. We're all set here. Are you on your way up?" replied Munoz.

"I just left the bar. I'll run by the room and grab Jess. See you in a few."

Daniel put the phone in his jacket and nodded cordially at the man who had just stepped away from the glowing elevator button. Instead of returning the nod, the light haired operative started conversing quietly with the wiry dark haired man to his left. He watched them while they argued in harsh whispers for several seconds. The dark haired operative, possibly the leader, ended the argument by telling the blond not to worry. He examined them a moment longer and started to wonder if they had any experience whatsoever with this kind of an operation. The only thing the two of them had going for them as covert operatives was the fact that they were both utterly unremarkable in every way.

It didn't really matter. He could in no way afford to underestimate them, no matter how inept they appeared. He was about to spend nearly a full minute alone with them, packed tightly into an enclosed space. If they were craftier than they appeared, Ben and Jerry might try to kill him in the elevator. Daniel wanted to avoid this at all costs. Skill levels didn't mean much in an elevator.

He followed them into the elevator, moving to the left corner. He pressed the button for the seventeenth floor.

"Which floor?" asked Daniel, before the man could press the buttons on the other side of the open door.

"Eighteenth, please," said the man with the thick eyebrows.

Daniel pressed the button and settled in for the ride, avoiding eye contact in accordance with the universal code of elevator conduct. His peripheral vision served as his only early warning system in this enclosed space. Any quick movements from either Ben or Jerry would be met with extreme violence. Both of them stared at the numbers above the elevator console. Within several seconds, the elevator started to slow, arriving at the seventeenth floor. Daniel nodded at them and walked briskly to the right, toward the stairs. When he heard the doors close, he broke into a full sprint for the exit sign thirty feet away down the hallway.

ↂ

Jessica hung on Young's arm as they walked down the hallway to his suite. She couldn't wait to end this deception. Benjamin Young was an arrogant creep. Once in the elevator, he'd cast off any subtlety and began to inquire about her menu of activities. She'd almost broken out of role in the elevator and put a knife to his throat. She was slightly surprised by his quick change of demeanor. Charming and suggestive in the bar, he'd shown the kind of confidence expected from a man receiving flirtatious advances from a beautiful woman. She could have easily lured him upstairs without the overt hints that she was "on the clock," but they didn't have that kind of time.

The two men at the end of the bar smacked of intense desperation and took few measures to conceal their interest in Young. Daniel had locked eyes on them, confirming her suspicion and advancing the timeline. She needed to get Young out of there within the next few minutes. It didn't require a great deal of effort on her part. Young asked her what she was doing in Atlanta, and she told him that she had recently moved down from Raleigh to find new clients. The follow up question about her clients led to the immediate departure for his suite on the eighteenth floor.

The elevator transformed him into a sex fiend. He put his hands on her thigh, sliding them deep into private territory on both sides of her body. She could feel his hot breath on her neck, as he licked the small of her neck and whispered something about putting his cock somewhere she'd considered permanently off limits. She fought every instinct in her body to keep from tensing, responding with a subtle, sensuous exhale, but nothing more than that. She didn't want to encourage him to the point where he might try to stop the elevator. His hand slid deeper along her inner thigh, and all she could think about was the serrated blade in her purse. Mercifully, the elevator doors opened on the eighteenth floor, putting his disgusting behavior on hold. She couldn't imagine how bad it would get when he closed the door to Suite 1812.

Benjamin Young sported all of the prerequisites that would identify him as a wealthy, well-heeled gentleman: Armani suit with pocket square; $350 haircut; custom leather shoes; Clive Christian cologne; Rolex; diamond cuff links. But beyond this ungodly expensive, thin veneer, he was no different than the body odor soaked, soulless murderers and rapists she'd lived among in Belgrade. He might smell better, but ultimately, he behaved like the rest of them. Countless women and children suffered because of men like Benjamin Young. She hated his type and looked forward to getting him behind closed doors. His reign of terror permanently ended tonight.

They arrived at his door and she stole a glance at the peephole on the door directly across from the suite. Munoz and Melendez were waiting patiently for Young's admirers, which should give her some time alone with Young. He slid the keycard in the door and opened it, inviting her in. As she entered, he spoke quietly but urgently.

"I couldn't tell from our elevator conversation whether you were into anal play or not. Money isn't a problem, in case that's your hang up."

She almost started laughing at the absolute desperation of his comment. This appeared to be all he was worried about. His previous "date" had apparently cleared him for rear entry, and this was his sole point of focus. She couldn't wait to disappoint him. Instead of answering his question, she walked deeper into the suite, placing her handbag on a marble topped counter. He closed the door, and rushed to catch up with her. She felt his hand grip her upper left arm tightly and try to pull her back to face him. He was really concerned about his menu options tonight. She shirked his hand and turned to face him, keeping the matte black, serrated blade concealed along the side of her right wrist.

"I'm not paying you to ignore me," he said.

She just stared at him with a smile, until he stepped forward and reached out to grab her wrist, committing a rookie mistake. She lifted her wrist slightly, just far enough to make it easier for him. Once his hand tightened around her wrist, missing the concealed knife blade by less than a centimeter, she flexed her hand upward, and broke his grip. Before he could react, she stepped forward and rapidly slid her hand over his extended arm toward his throat. As he tried to wrap his arm around her, she pivoted on her right foot, which brought her body flush against Young's back. Her left forearm braced his chin backward as she eased the tip of the five-inch blade against his throat.

"This ass isn't for sale," she hissed in his ear.

"Everything is for sale. Whatever your game is, I'm into it…but without the knife at my throat. This is definitely something new, but it makes me a little nervous."

"Move into the bedroom. Now!" she said, manhandling him toward the bedroom door.

"Look. This is a little rougher than I expected. Maybe I should pay you for your time and we'll call it good. Sorry about the misunderstanding," he said. Jessica could detect fear in his voice.

"There hasn't been a misunderstanding, Mr. Young, and no amount of money is going to buy your way out of this one," she stated, moving him through the door into the bedroom.

"I never told you my last name. Who are you?"

"Time to shut the fuck up. If you say another word without my permission, I'll take a big slice out of that pretty face."

"What is going—"

His comment was interrupted by her left forearm, which exerted incredible pressure on his larynx and prevented him from either speaking or breathing. She shifted the knife and gently placed it near the outside corner of his right eye socket.

"I'll give you one more chance. If you say another word, I'll start cutting. Do you understand me? Nod if you understand me," she said, and he nodded quickly.

The quick movement of his head caused the knife to penetrate the skin on his forehead, a consequence that Jessica had foreseen. Young winced, but held steady, not making a single noise when she released the grip on his neck.

"You need to think carefully about everything you do. Every thought. Every movement. From this point forward, every action has a consequence. Take a seat on the edge of the bed, and don't fall off. This knife stays right here until my friends arrive."

She felt his jaw start to move, as he fought the urge to ask about her friends.

"Very good. A quick learner. You just might survive the night, Ben. Personally, I hope you don't, but if you keep following directions, I think you'll see your family again."

Benjamin Young didn't move a millimeter in response to her comment, which made Jessica smile. Fully compliant in less than a minute. Maybe

Sanderson wasn't full of shit for once. They might even be able to fly back to the coast tonight if Young behaved. If not, they could still enjoy a late dinner and some nightlife in Buckhead. She could think of worse places to be trapped on a Friday night.

ꕥ

Enrique Melendez sat forward in his chair and watched Jessica Petrovich and Benjamin Young approach the door to Suite 1812 on his monitor. The small, flat screen monitor was mounted to the edge of the desk in the living area of their two-room suite. Jeffrey Munoz stood next to the door, holding the second monitor, ready to intervene in the hallway if the situation deteriorated. Melendez seriously doubted that Jessica would require their assistance with Young. He'd seen her in action at the high-rise apartment in Buenos Aires and taken part in her knife training drills. Even with an injured hand, Young would be absolutely no match for her skills. Their job was to take care of the two True America operatives who were most likely a minute or two away from breaking into Suite 1812.

They had drilled through the glass peephole and replaced the lens with a fiber optic camera capable of providing a high resolution, wide-angle view of the hallway, vastly improving upon the image afforded by the peephole. The fiber optic cable fed into a small digital recorder on the desk, which split the signal to the two monitors and allowed them to rewind and review the feed.

Just as importantly, it permitted them to closely monitor traffic in the hallway, without standing with their heads pressed to the door for hours on end. Each monitor was attached to fifty feet of video cable, giving them full range of the suite. This had come in handy for Munoz, who had been trapped in Suite 1811 most of the day, making certain that nobody besides Benjamin Young entered Suite 1812. He'd alternated that duty with babysitting the original occupants of Suite 1811, who lay unconscious on the floor of the bedroom, zip-tied and neatly arranged next to each other with pillows under their heads.

Mr. and Mrs. Hines, a young black couple from Birmingham, Alabama, had checked into the hotel around 4 PM with 8 PM dinner reservations at Restaurant Eugene. Unfortunately, the exclusive Friday night reservation at this chic gastro destination had already expired, and the rest of their weekend getaway would be ruined by a lingering headache, coupled with a hotel-wide police investigation. Mr. and Mrs. Hines had been hit with a powerful, yet relatively harmless neurotoxin, which would leave them disabled for a few hours. A smaller dose of the neurotoxin would be administered every few hours until the mission was completed.

Working together earlier in the afternoon, Munoz and Melendez borrowed the housekeeping master key from one of the carts left unattended in the hallway and made a copy with a handheld scanner. Within thirty seconds, they had swiped the master key, storing the keycard's electronic signature in their scanner, and created four copies with the blank keycards. The Hines' were in the middle of unpacking, when two well-dressed Latino gentlemen suddenly appeared in the bedroom doorway holding small metallic tubes. They wouldn't remember anything beyond that.

"How was Daniel taking her little show?" Munoz asked.

"He appeared to be one hundred and ten percent operational," answered Melendez.

"We'll see. I feel bad for the guy."

"Why's that?"

"He's up against the two of them," stated Munoz.

"Yeah. Tough break for the guy. Alright, they're in the room. Man, I wish I could see through that door," said Melendez.

"You and me, both. She's probably bitten off one of his ears by now."

Munoz's phone vibrated and he took the call.

"Got it. We'll take them down when they reach the door," he said into the phone, then cut the call. "Petrovich just hit the stairs. He'll back us up in the hallway."

Several seconds passed before Melendez saw the elevator doors open. Two men walked out, stopping to check the elevator vestibule before proceeding briskly down the hallway toward Suite 1812.

"They're moving fast," Munoz noted.

Melendez stood up and moved over to the door, grabbing his HK USP Compact from the foot of the bed. The pistol was fitted with a suppressor that appeared longer than the pistol itself. Munoz sat his monitor against the wall, on the small table to the right of the door, and gripped the suppressed Steyr TMP submachine gun attached to the sling over his shoulder. Melendez grabbed the doorknob and watched the two men fill the monitor's screen. The dark haired man standing to the left held a pistol in his right hand and a key card in his left. Melendez nodded quickly and quietly pulled the door open.

Munoz slipped through and stepped to the right, aiming at the light haired man. Melendez moved straight forward, centering his pistol on the top of the dark haired man's back. The dark haired operative managed to turn his head over his shoulder before Munoz hissed a warning.

"Do not fucking move. You each have a weapon pointed at your back. Nod if you understand," he said, and both of them nodded quickly.

Daniel Petrovich appeared in the hallway, near the elevator vestibule. The light haired man turned his head an inch, and Melendez could tell that the dark haired operative had seen him. His pistol hand tensed. He probably recognized Daniel from the bar. This had the potential to go south really fast if Munoz didn't take control of the situation.

"That man is one of ours. You've been under surveillance all afternoon. Listen to me very closely. You will drop your weapons to the floor. Simply release them from your grip. On three. You will not get a second chance to do this. One. Two. Three." One of the guns clattered to the carpeted floor. The other remained in the dark haired man's grip. Melendez shifted his aim and fired a bullet through the man's right elbow. The bullet passed through his arm and lodged in the door, spraying the soft, salmon colored paint with bright red arterial spray from his brachial artery. The suppressed gunshot had the desired effects, dropping the second gun to the carpet and stopping a more lethal chain of events.

Melendez kicked the man against the door, further stunning him, and yanked him back. He locked his arm around the man's neck and placed the end of the suppressor behind his ear.

"The next one goes through your skull," he whispered.

Munoz pulled the light haired operative to the side and pushed him into the wall, giving Daniel room to pass. He turned to room 1812, withdrew another keycard from his pocket and approached the blood-splattered door, glancing down at the pool of blood at his feet.

"Nice mess. A little trigger happy tonight?" said Daniel, inserting the card while furtively glancing in both directions down the hallway.

"He was a fraction of a second from making it a whole lot worse," replied Melendez.

Inserting the key card, Daniel opened the door and stepped inside the vestibule, ready to draw his pistol.

"Is Mr. Young still breathing?" asked Daniel.

"He's fine, but you need to take him off my hands before I start cutting," replied Jessica from another room.

Upon hearing Jessica's comment, Melendez glanced at Munoz and smiled, but his partner didn't look happy. Glancing at the mess on the door and the blood still pumping onto the carpet, he wasn't surprised. There was no way they could wipe this clean enough to avoid unwanted attention. The hallway carpet contained deep red patterns, which helped; however, the carpet pattern was symmetrical and the bloodstains were irregularly spaced. Only the most intoxicated or oblivious hotel guest would walk by without wondering whether Hannibal Lecter was waiting behind the door for them.

Melendez followed Daniel into the room, forcibly shoving the gunman against the wall next to the bathroom doorway, searching him for a second weapon. Munoz followed at a safe distance behind with the second man. Melendez found a small knife strapped to his ankle, along with a wallet, car keys and a cell phone in his trouser pockets. His jacket held two additional magazines for one of the semi-automatic pistols that Munoz had kicked inside of the room when Daniel opened the door. Melendez threw all of these items onto the nearby table while Munoz kicked the door shut with the heel of his shoe.

"Give me a hand here. I need to tie off this arm or we'll lose him. The bullet hit an artery."

Daniel emerged from the bedroom doorway to help.

"Keep him covered," Munoz said, handing the pistol to Daniel.

Melendez reached into his right pocket and fished out a black plastic zip tie restraint. He placed the zip tie around the wounded man's lower bicep area and connected the plastic coupling. He pulled the tie as tightly as possible, causing the man to scream in agony. The steady stream of blood had slowed, but still poured onto the floor. He braced the man's arm against the wall and yanked on the end of the zip tie again, putting all of his strength into pulling the thick plastic band tighter. The man reached around with his free hand, but Daniel was there to grab it and jam his pistol into the back of his neck. Melendez backed up and examined the blood trickling down the man's hand. The flow had stopped, which would give them some time to extract information, or do whatever Daniel had planned for him.

Daniel grabbed the man's jacket collar and pulled him into the sitting area, throwing him down onto one of the tan couches. He handed

Melendez the pistol and pulled his own out of the concealed holster along his waist. Munoz covered the two men while Daniel took a few seconds to screw a short suppressor onto the threaded barrel.

"I hope you brought some cleaning supplies," said Daniel, nodding toward the door.

Munoz tossed the second man onto the same couch and replied, "We have a kit in the other room. We'll do what we can with the mess and I'll stay in the other suite to keep an eye on the hallway. We have enough neurotoxin to knock out the entire floor if necessary. Shouldn't be an issue."

"Perfect. We'll get things started in here," said Daniel.

Melendez appreciated his partner's calm attitude about the situation. Neither of them said a word as they exited the room, careful not to step in the massive dark red stain in front of Suite 1812. Munoz immediately opened the door to Suite 1811 and disappeared, leaving Melendez to close the door to 1812. When he turned to face the door, he grimaced. What a fucking mess.

"Grab the big towels from the bathroom," he said.

***

Daniel stepped over to the sitting area and pulled one of the plush taupe wing chairs away from the large coffee table in front of the couch, dragging it against the wall behind him. He pushed the other chair to the side and kicked the small round end table out of the way, knocking it against a smaller chair near the conference table. The Buckhead Suite offered three distinctly separate living areas for the discerning business guest: a spacious bedroom with a glass enclosed, marble shower; a sitting area occupied by two terrorists, one of whom was grievously wounded and ruining the furniture; and a conference area, featuring a mahogany table with seating for six. Mr. Young certainly spared no expense while he was in town.

"Bring out tonight's guest of honor," said Daniel.

Jessica wrenched a ruffled, despondent looking Benjamin Young through the bedroom door and jammed him into the wing chair against the wall. Daniel backed up a few steps toward the conference table and pointed the pistol at Young.

"If you try to get out of that seat, the young lady here will stab you through your armpit all the way to your heart. The blade's long enough, right?" he said.

Young looked torn, like he wasn't sure if he had permission to respond.

"It might be an inch short. You can talk now. I give you permission," said Jessica, standing next to him.

Daniel winked at her, when he thought Young was distracted.

"I saw that. Alright, alright. Enough already. You guys got me good. Seriously. I'm fucking freaked out of my mind right now. Whoever put you up to this earned their fucking money tonight. This is by far the best joke ever. Really. Can you tell I'm freaked out? No need to continue. I'll pay you double to call it quits," Young said, starting to get up from the chair.

Jessica turned the knife in her hand and brought the end of the handle down on his face, shattering the cartilage in his nose and splitting his top lip. Young shrieked and dropped back into the chair.

"My fucking face! What the fuck is going on here? Who the fuck are you people? I told you this was over!" he screamed.

"Lower your voice," said Daniel.

He nodded at Jessica, who immediately raised the knife in front of Young, causing him to cower in the chair, flailing his hands above him in a sad, useless display.

When he spoke again, he whispered. "Look, whatever is happening here…it doesn't have to happen. I have a lot of money, and I can access even more if necessary. I guarantee I can double or triple what you're being paid now."

"I'm not being paid anything," Daniel said. He turned to Ben and Jerry. "Are either of you being paid?"

Neither of the men answered, prompting Daniel to aim at the dark haired man's head.

"Are either of you receiving a fat paycheck to be here tonight?" asked Daniel.

"Fuck you. I'm not saying a word," replied Dark Hair.

Daniel fired a single Hydra-Shok hollow point round through the man's head, snapping it back against the top of the couch. A dark red stain splashed the tan curtain panel behind him, rustling the thick material. The light haired man scooted away from his now deceased friend, struggling to move with his hands tied behind his back.

"Oh fuck," Young whimpered. "He did not just kill that guy. This is a joke right? He did not—"

Daniel turned his head and arm at the same time, firing a bullet into the wall less than six inches from Young's head. The suppressor reduced the gunshot to a subsonic crack. Jessica gasped. Young's face went blank as he examined the damaged drywall near his head.

"Holy shit," he whispered and closed his eyes.

"Did I shatter the window?" ask Daniel, turning back to the couch.

Daniel hadn't heard the glass shatter, but he couldn't be sure. The decision to kill Dark Hair had been a last second decision. He could tell by the man's defiant expression that he'd be nothing but trouble during the interrogation. His light haired accomplice looked a little softer. The man stared at him quizzically.

"You don't like to talk either?" Daniel asked, raising the pistol again.

"No. No. I'll talk. You asked about the window. I didn't hear it shatter. I didn't hear anything like that," Light Hair pleaded.

"I hope not. If the police arrive before I'm finished. They'll need at least two SERVPRO teams in here to scrape you off the walls."

"It didn't shatter. I think I would have heard that happen. Yes. I know I would have heard that happen."

"You're sure? Sure enough to bet your life on it?"

"Yes. No. We're good," he said.

"I hope so. Next question. How many more can we expect?" asked Daniel.

"What?"

"You're either purposely ignoring me, or you're scared out of your mind. Either way, it's starting to piss me off," said Daniel, closing the distance to the couch while pointing the pistol at the man's head.

"I can't concentrate with a gun to my head."

"Really? You came here to put a gun to Mr. Young's head, but this bothers you? I'm done repeating questions. Are you and your dead partner working alone, or can I expect amateur hour to continue?"

"We're working alone. We weren't expecting any obstacles," replied the man.

Daniel walked over to the conference table and removed both of the wallets. He glanced at the driver's licenses. Both of the men carried South

Carolina licenses. Theodore Kindler sat before him on the couch, still breathing for now.

"Ted? Theo? I like Theo. Let's get the introductions out of the way. Benjamin Young, meet Theodore Kindler. He was sent here to put a bullet through your head."

"Come on guys. This is crazy. Did my wife hire these guys?" said Young.

"She should have," snapped Jessica.

"I couldn't agree more, but this goes way deeper than your extracurricular activities. Would you care to explain this to him, Theo? Tell him why you're here to kill him?"

Theodore Kindler opened his mouth, but the words faltered. He wore a painful look, torn between preventing his own death and maintaining loyalty.

"Don't know where to start? I'd be happy if you simply identified your organization. That'll be enough to keep your brains off the curtains," said Daniel.

"I really can't—"

"Yes you can. I already know the answer. I just want him to hear it from you. Three. Two. One…"

"True America," he grunted, looking disgusted and frightened.

"True America? Why would they want *me* dead? I'm about to close a deal worth a healthy sum of money for their organization," said Young perplexedly.

"Oh, you haven't heard?" Daniel said snidely. "True America is up to something big. Much bigger than a campaign announcement or a string of expensive primetime television ads. Big enough to start tying up loose ends. By our estimation, you're one of the biggest. We took down the first assassination team in New York. You're looking at the substitutes."

"Jesus Christ. What about my family? Who's watching them right now?" Young asked.

He tried to stand up again, but didn't get more than three inches off the chair before Jessica's knife appeared at his throat. He sat back down and Jessica eased the knife away.

"What about my family?" he hissed at Kindler.

"Answer the man," ordered Daniel.

"Our mission didn't involve your family," said Kindler.

Young didn't look convinced. His face showed an unsure anger that Daniel knew had already turned Young against True America.

"If these are the bad guys, why am I being forced to sit in this chair with a knife to my throat?" asked Young.

"Because I haven't decided which side you're on. True America wants you dead. We need to figure out exactly why this is the case. Until then, your brains are just as likely to hit the wall as Theo's," said Daniel.

"This is un-fucking-real. After all I've done for Greely and the rest of those rednecks, they turn around and stab me in the back like this. Fuck them! I'll tell you everything I know. I have records, all kinds of shit. I'm good at covering my ass. We're talking detailed records. I've been diverting large amounts of money earmarked for True America's D.C. office to Greely and Harding. The fuck if I know what they're doing with it."

"Apparently, they used some of it to hire contract killers," said Daniel.

Kindler lurched forward on the couch in a useless gesture of anger, bringing the full attention of Daniel's pistol to his face. Daniel simply shook his head and Kindler settled back into the blood soaked couch.

"None of you get it," Kindler said. "We're not being paid. We're part of the revolution to put America back on the right path. There are hundreds of us. Soon to be thousands…"

One of the cell phones on the conference table vibrated, shaking the car keys. Daniel stared at Kindler and examined his response. He wasn't pleased with what he could read on the man's face. Kindler managed to keep his eyes off the table, but the strain was evident.

"Expecting a call?" asked Daniel.

"It's probably just a standard check in."

"With whom?" replied Daniel.

"I really can't say," said Kindler, avoiding eye contact.

Daniel shot Jessica a glance, which she returned without changing her expression. They were prepared to evacuate the room at a moment's notice.

"Mr. Young, do you have remote access to these records?"

"Most of them. We'd have to visit my office in D.C. to access some of the deeper account specifics. We don't have remote access for regulatory reasons. What are you looking for?"

"Anything related to True America, directly or indirectly."

"And you'll let me go if I give you everything?"

"I won't kill you, if that's what you're asking," said Daniel.

"Can you protect my family? Is there a witness protection program or something?"

"We'll cross that bridge when you provide us with the information," said Daniel.

"How do I know you won't just kill me?"

"This may sound kind of cliché, but you don't."

"That's reassuring," said Young.

The cell phone stopped buzzing, which caused Daniel to glance in the direction of the small pile of wallets, pistol magazines, cell phones and keys in the middle of the table Less than a second later, the second phone started to vibrate, which didn't surprise him in the least. He didn't need to look at Kindler's panicked face to figure out what would happen next. Theodore Kindler launched forward, successfully propelling himself off the couch and onto the coffee table, careening desperately toward Daniel with his hands behind his back.

Daniel extended his hand and fired a single round through his face, stepping aside as momentum and gravity carried the corpse into Benjamin Young. The dead weight slammed into Young, momentarily pinning him to the wing back chair before sliding to the floor. Kindler left a considerable portion of his head in Young's lap, causing him to instantly vomit a brownish-yellow stream onto the lifeless human pile at his feet. He turned his head to the side of the chair opposite of Jessica and vomited again.

"We need to move. Prep Mr. Young for immediate departure. Make sure we have all of his electronics," he said and sprinted for the door.

Munoz nearly stumbled into the room when Daniel yanked the door open. He held a bloody towel in one hand and a spray bottle in the other. The air reeked of bleach solution. Melendez was on his hands and knees scrubbing a soapy liquid into the carpet.

"We've got company. Unknown disposition. We need to move Young to a more secure location. Do you need anything from your room?"

"Just our backpacks. Spare magazines, money, ID. The essentials," replied Munoz.

"Grab the packs and cover the hallway. Both directions. We'll be ready to move in fifteen seconds," said Daniel.

He grabbed one of the killer's discarded pistols from the tile floor bathroom and took two magazines from the conference table. He considered grabbing their cell phones and wallets, but decided against it.

Their mission was to secure Benjamin Young, or more importantly, any useful information he could provide. He returned to the sitting area to find Young on his feet, vigorously wiping his face with a wet towel. Jessica snatched the towel out of his hand.

"You look beautiful again," she said and pushed him toward the door.

"Fuck. Will you take it easy?" complained Young.

"You got everything?" he said, reaching out to grab Young by the shirt collar.

"Two laptops, Blackberry, some kind of crypto key fob, wallet, cash…Mr. Young is ready to roll," replied Jessica.

While she hiked a dark brown leather satchel over her left shoulder and made a last second adjustment to the straps, he pulled Young in close.

"Listen to this woman and don't think for one second that you can escape us. Is that clear?" he said, shaking Young's collar. "Things will get hectic on the way out of this hotel. If you try to run, you're a dead man."

He winked at Jessica behind Young's back.

"Keep him low and behind cover. How's your hand?" he whispered in her ear, kissing the nape of her neck.

"It's fine. Do I really have to babysit him?"

"I agree. I'd feel more comfortable with someone else," interrupted Young, without turning around.

"Shut the fuck up," said Daniel.

Turning toward Jessica, he said, "You're not exactly dressed for a running gunfight. Sorry."

She kicked her high heels onto the floor.

"Next time I'll wear a track suit."

Jessica was dressed in a sleeveless black turtleneck dress, cut at the mid-thigh. Not exactly the best suited outfit for urban escape and evasion, unless you planned to take refuge in a chic nightclub. He wished they had brought a more practical pair of shoes for her. Running barefoot through the streets of Buckhead on a Friday night wouldn't be a pleasant experience. He smiled at her.

"Ready?"

"After you," she replied.

Daniel moved Young out of the way and paused at the door. He replaced the magazine in his pistol with a fresh magazine from one of his inside jacket pockets, giving him thirteen rounds. Glancing through the doorway, he saw Munoz and Melendez crouched behind the corners of the recessed hallway vestibule outside of Suite 1811. Munoz covered the elevator with his suppressed TMP submachine gun, and Melendez watched the long hallway leading to a set of stairs toward the far end of the hotel. Daniel decided against taking the furthest set of stairs. The elevator vestibule was closer, giving them access to a stairwell that led right into the lobby and a quick exit onto the street.

"Stairs by the elevator. Munoz first, then me. Package in the middle. Melendez covers the rear. Move out," he said and stepped into the hallway.

Munoz burst into the hallway with his weapon trained in the direction of the elevators, followed closely by Daniel. They hadn't taken five steps before the elevator bell rang.

"Cover," said Daniel, bumping into Jessica and Young as he stepped back into the vestibule.

The elevator doors opened, and the carriage appeared empty for a moment. A head poked out from the right side, quickly followed by an unsuppressed automatic weapon. Daniel didn't linger long enough to determine what the figure had fired at them. The rounds tore into the drywall and wooden framing around the vestibule, showering the floor and Daniel with fragments. Bullets snapped by as the staccato hammering of the gunfire pounded his ears. Munoz and Petrovich dropped to the ground, simultaneously leaning out to fire their weapons. Their bullets caught the shooter in an attempt to sprint clear of the elevator, throwing him back into the carriage amidst a cascade of mirrored glass shards. Daniel noticed a steady bright red spray pulsing into the air above the body.

A second shooter sprayed bullets down the hallway from a position outside of the elevator, shattering light fixtures and damaging more drywall. Daniel wasn't sure if this shooter had exited the elevator or joined the fight from the stairs. Munoz caught the shooter's head with a short burst of fire from his TMP, dropping the figure to the ground along the left corner of the hallway.

"She's down. Head shot," said Munoz.

The words caused him to glance back at Jessica in a moment of panic.

"Jess is fine. Shooter was female," said Munoz.

"Targets from the rear," said Melendez, immediately firing three rounds down the long hallway.

Daniel jumped to his feet and pressed his body against the wall, moving to the opposite side of the vestibule to reduce his exposure to fire from the other direction. He kept his aim centered on the elevator hallway. Munoz shifted positions across the hallway, barely avoiding a fusillade of bullets. He reloaded the TMP as Daniel watched several bullets puncture the drywall and splinter the painted wood immediately behind both of them. Nothing moved in Daniel's sector near the elevator. Munoz's TMP cracked to life, spitting several tightly controlled bursts at their new assailants. Munoz expended thirty rounds in less than five seconds and pulled another thirty round magazine from the top of his backpack.

"I hit one of them. We need to make a move, man," he said.

"Flashbangs. Both directions. We make a run for the elevator," said Daniel.

Another torrent of bullets pounded their position, missing them by inches and causing them both to hug the wall. Melendez responded with his pistol, but the suppressed snaps of his well-aimed shots sounded pathetic compared to the explosions blasting at them from the end of the hallway. Munoz opened his backpack and removed two black cylindrical objects. He tossed one of them to Daniel, amidst another burst of gunfire. One of the bullets grazed the top of his hand during the throw.

"Mother fucker," said Munoz, grimacing.

"You all right?" yelled Daniel.

"I'm fine. Let's get this over with. Pull!" he said.

They yanked the safety pins out of their flashbang grenades at the same time and threw them in opposite directions. Daniel's landed in the middle of the elevator vestibule and Munoz's landed somewhere near the closest shooter down the long hallway. The M84 stun grenades had a time delay fuse of 1 to 2 seconds. By the time the grenades had landed and stopped rolling, they were milliseconds away from exploding. Daniel didn't wait. He reached inside Suite 1812 and pulled Young into the vestibule. Young fought him, trying to hold onto the doorframe, but Jessica hit his hand with one of the pistols she had grabbed from the bathroom floor. Young let go and they nearly tumbled into the hallway as the flashbangs detonated. Everyone sprinted toward the elevator as Munoz unleashed a long burst from his TMP into the cloud of smoke billowing from the far end of the eighteenth floor hallway.

Daniel reached the elevator vestibule first, sweeping from left to right with his pistol. Through the thin haze produced by the flashbang's magnesium/ammonia nitrate pyrotechnic mix, he saw nothing beyond the corpse at his feet and a bloody lump inside the elevator. The reflective polished copper elevator doors repeatedly opened and closed when they encountered the pair of lifeless legs protruding out into the hallway.

"Clear!" he said.

He walked swiftly toward the illuminated exit sign, turning his head once to confirm that Young and Jessica were following him closely. Munoz and Melendez ducked into the elevator lobby, taking cover behind the corner, while firing controlled bursts down the hallway. Their disciplined gunfire was immediately returned by a wild, three second hammering from one of the opposing submachine guns. Both of the operatives moved back from the corner as 9mm rounds slammed into the elevator doors and skipped off the walls. Munoz signaled with his hand for Daniel to proceed into the stairwell.

Daniel dropped the magazine from his suppressed pistol and replaced it, staring at the door leading into the stairwell. Anything could be waiting for them on the other side. Fuck it. They needed to keep moving. Police would hit the lobby within minutes, if they weren't already on scene. They needed to be down these stairs and merging with evacuating guests immediately.

"Move to the side," he said, directing Jessica and Young to the wall next to the door.

Once they were clear of the opening, he pulled the door open, pointing his weapon forward. He instantly saw two men turn the corner at the bottom of the stairwell leading up to the door. They were armed with pistols and moving too quickly for him to apply any rules of engagement. His left hand flashed to meet his HK USP and the gun kicked repeatedly as he rushed forward through his own shell casings.

His first rounds hit the first man center of mass, knocking him back into the second man. He heard one of their guns discharge in the tight stairwell, as he adjusted his aim while still firing. The remaining rounds from his pistol connected with the second shooter, splashing the painted concrete wall behind the man with a disturbing scarlet pattern. When the slide on Daniel's pistol locked back, indicating that he had expended the magazine, he realized that the first shooter was still alive and well. The man had been spun around by Daniel's bullets and dropped to one knee, but he hadn't collapsed.

His mind flashed with options, none of them good. He could stand his ground, reload and fire; try to close the remaining distance down the staircase and physically disarm the man; or retreat and hope that the man is too stunned to hit a moving target. Already halfway down the stairs, with his momentum moving toward the shooter, retreat was no longer a viable option. Stopping to reload didn't seem realistic either. The shooter's pistol hand was free from the limbs and body of his partner, already extending toward him up the stairwell. The grimace of pain and determination on the man's face sealed Daniel's decision. He charged down the stairs, trying to stay outside of the shooter's pistol arc.

A deafening boom pounded his ears as he collided with the man, viciously hammering the shooter's head into the concrete wall with his left hand, while pinning the pistol against the wall with the other. He felt the man's pistol tumble along his arm, and hit his leg on the way to the carpeted floor. The shooter suddenly lurched upward and kicked out at Daniel, in a last, desperate attempt to survive. The kick caught Daniel off guard, striking his left hip and knocking him clear. The two men scrambled for the closest pistol, which teetered on the edge of the stairs.

Before either of them could reach it, the shooter's head snapped backward and hit the blood stained concrete with a sick thud that could be felt over the ear-splitting echo of the gunshot. He glanced up and saw Jessica aiming down the stairs. A shell casing tumbled down one of the carpeted stairs in front of her and stopped. He really hoped these weren't cops. Jessica didn't deserve to have blood like that on her hands. The burden of unintentionally killing an off duty police officer two years ago in Silver Spring, Maryland still haunted him.

This type of mental reflection didn't fit the psychological profile identified by days of testing and interviews. The stone cold, pathologically practical covert operative thought about the consequences of pulling that trigger nearly every day. Officer Samantha Rockwell had been executing her duties as a sworn law enforcement officer when her path crossed Daniel's. She'd caught him by surprise at the worst time possible, and had been unceremoniously killed in a grocery store parking lot. It was unintentional...collateral damage. Not that it mattered to her husband and three children. Maybe the government psychologists had been full of shit from the very beginning, or maybe an "extremely functional sociopath" can have an emotional breakdown from time to time. Whatever the cause, he needed to convince himself that he hadn't killed another law enforcement agent.

Once again, there had been no time to assess the situation. He'd applied basic rules and assumptions before entering the stairwell. He didn't think the police could have reacted this quickly. If anything, a pair of uniformed officers would reach the scene first, and they would be unlikely to head toward the sound of automatic gunfire. If they'd run into these two on a lower level, most of his assumptions would have been different, along with his reaction. He quickly searched their torsos for badges or identification, finding nothing along their belts or attached to their shirts. He turned one of the bodies on its side and retrieved a wallet, flipping it open. Nothing. If these were cops, they weren't carrying identification.

"Keep moving!" Jessica yelled at him.

He looked up and watched her reach through the doorway to pull Benjamin Young into the stairwell. She didn't seem to have any reservations or concerns about killing these men. He needed to snap out of this funk immediately. He couldn't afford to get tangled in his guilt again tonight. Getting through the lobby might get messy.

Daniel retrieved his HK USP Compact from the snarl of legs and arms slumped against the wall and reloaded his magazine before proceeding to clear the next level. He moved quickly but cautiously down the stairs, paying close attention to corners and doors. Jessica dragged Young down each staircase as he cleared them. On the fourth floor, Melendez rushed past Jessica and caught up with him.

"We took down the last shooter on the eighteenth. Munoz has our back. He told me to give you this. Said we might need it soon."

Daniel took his eyes off the next landing long enough to see what Melendez had pushed against his left shoulder. An olive drab cylindrical object with "M18" etched in white on the side. Munoz certainly didn't disappoint. A smoke grenade was exactly what he needed to ensure the success of their escape plan.

"Keep that close by. We *will* need it soon," he said, continuing downward.

"What's your plan for the lobby?" asked Melendez.

"Something that will hopefully preclude us from shooting our way out."

"I can't wait."

❧

Officer Paul Anthony tried to calm the guest services manager and the two front desk agents that had been called to an impromptu meeting in the far recesses of the lobby, away from the growing mob of new check-ins. One of the front desk agents had remained behind the lobby counter, politely telling the guests that the computer system had experienced a glitch. This had been his idea and the only thing that appeared to stop the flow of check-ins without creating a general panic. Judging by the size of the line and the desperate looks flashed at them by the young black woman behind the marble counter, the computer glitch story had a two-minute lifespan. They needed to think of something quick. There was no way they could let anyone head up onto any of the floors.

Dispatch had received a single phone call from a frantic woman on the eighteenth floor, claiming that a gang war had broken out in the hallway. The dispatcher confirmed an incredible amount of background noise coming from her phone, though the woman's screaming made it nearly impossible to determine what she was hearing. Anthony and his partner, Officer Sandra Kingston, had been located less than a minute away, having just turned north onto Lenox Road from Wright Avenue. By the time they arrived at the hotel, two additional calls had hit northern zone dispatch, confirming automatic gunfire on the eighteenth floor. SWAT was ordered to mobilize a response.

One of the calls had been placed by the guest services manager, and was still in progress when they walked through the revolving lobby door. The dark-haired woman handed the phone to one of the agents and scurried to meet the officers. She explained that calls had started to flood the front desk and she didn't know how to proceed. He gave her the computer glitch idea and asked her to bring two of the agents to this quiet corner where he could work out a plan that would keep guests safe until SWAT could take control of the scene. A second pair of police officers pushed through the left-most set of mahogany encased, glass swing doors and entered the lobby. He waved them over.

"More officers are on the way. The two of you need to instruct guests to stay in their rooms and lock the doors. Both locks. For their own safety, they need to remain behind locked doors until further notice. Don't give them any details. Let them know the police are taking control of the situation and move on to the next caller. Get another agent to help you with this. Do you have an automated system that can leave hotel wide messages?"

"Yes. We use it for emergencies. I can access it from the security office," the manager said, looking dazed.

"I think this qualifies as an emergency. I need you to record a message informing guests to stay in their rooms until further notice. Start sending the calls immediately. We'll handle the check-ins. Where are your security people?" asked Anthony.

"They just started up the rear stairwell before you arrived."

"Recall them to the lobby immediately. Are they armed?"

"One of them. Maybe. I think he took something from his locker," she said, furtively.

"Get them back here now. They'll get themselves and other hotel guests killed if they try anything crazy. Tell them this is a police order, and if they argue with you, come get me. Alright, let's get this place locked down for SWAT."

Officer Anthony examined the luxuriously appointed lobby and made a quick assessment of the situation while the hotel staff swarmed the front desk. He counted three elevators in the elevator lobby adjacent to the front desk. To the left of the entrance to the elevator lobby, an unmarked mahogany door stood next to a fire alarm, resembling the most likely stairway exit. Discreetly placed illuminated exit signs situated deeper in the lobby indicated a second exit accessible from the lobby level.

"Hey! Do the elevators reach the parking garage?" he yelled.

"The one on the right, but guests can't take it directly to the garage. They have to use the other two to arrive in the lobby, then change elevators," the manager replied.

"Is that the front stairwell door?" he asked, pointing to the inconspicuous wood paneled door.

"Yes. The other stairwell is beyond the shops and past the side entrance."

He nodded and greeted the two arriving officers.

"Here's the deal; we have multiple reports of automatic gunfire on the—"

His sentence was interrupted by a double klaxon sound that echoed through the lobby and was followed by a soothing, recorded female voice. Harsh white strobe lights competed with the soft glow of the lobby's ceiling tray lighting.

"May I have your attention please? May I have your attention please? There has been a fire reported in the building. Please exit the hotel using the nearest exit stairwell. Do not use the elevators."

"Shit," he muttered, just as the high decibel, double klaxon penetrated his ears again.

"Get everyone out of the lobby and grab the other responding officers to help. Kingston and I will cover the lobby exits," he said, slapping one of the officers on the back.

"Who the fuck hit that alarm!" he screeched at the front desk clerk.

"I'm trying to figure that out!" she yelled back at him, clearly becoming unglued.

"This is about to become a fucking nightmare for us," he said to Kingston.

"Shit. I think our best position will be to the right of the front desk. We'll have good cover and an angle on the elevator lobby. The stairwell door is right in front of us," said Officer Kingston.

"That's about all we can do. We'll put more officers on the service elevator and rear stairs as they arrive. Let's go."

They jogged over to the front desk as the crowd of new check-ins started to pull their luggage toward the double lobby doors.

"Leave your luggage!" he yelled at them.

His order emboldened the other officers, who actively corralled and hustled them to the door, enforcing Anthony's impromptu "no luggage" rule. Of course, he'd be relieved of this temporary command as soon as their shift's senior patrol officer or one of the sergeants arrived, which should be any minute now. The sooner the better. The prospect of facing automatic weapons with his Smith and Wesson .40 S&W semi-automatic pistol didn't appeal to him. Anthony and his partner would be hopelessly outgunned and their bulletproof vests would offer little resistance to the new breed of high velocity calibers they were seeing on the streets.

As the first responding officer, he felt compelled to remain in the lobby and offer what little firepower he had available to protect hotel guests. It wasn't the best idea, but there was little doubt that it was the right one. If his sergeant wanted to pull everyone out and wait for SWAT, that was his call. Until then, they'd try to cover four approaches with two guns. He turned to the terrified front desk staff.

"Get out of here with the rest of them. Where's your manager's office?" One of the women pointed behind the desk to the right at an open doorway before scrambling around the side of the counter and running for the exit. The guest services manager reappeared in the doorway.

"The alarm was set off on the ninth floor," she said, eyeing her staff as they disappeared with the crowd into the front parking lot.

"Did you send the message to all of the rooms?" he said, shifting his gaze back and for the between her and the four possible approaches to their position.

"No. I can't do that with a fire alarm. Someone reported an explosion up there. The entire hotel might be on fire."

"Fuck," he hissed.

She was right. If the gun battle on the eighteenth had started a fire, the message might confuse guests and keep them in their rooms. Then again, a general exodus down the stairwells could lead to a massacre or a hostage situation. He had run out of good options for handling the hotel's guests, so he sent the guest manager on her way to the exit. He would hold this position with Kingston until they were given different orders. All he could do was continue to move guests out of the hotel. He'd already started that. When the first wave of evacuees arrived, he'd help them onto the street, keeping a close eye out for the shooters.

He grabbed his hand-held shoulder mounted microphone to pass this plan onto the other officers, but something hit the stairwell door hard and caused him to stop. He heard some yelling on the other side, then pounding. Was it locked? He looked at Kingston, who raised her shoulders. The yelling intensified, along with the pounding. The guests pouring out of the Lobby Bar started to push and shove to get through to the hotel's front entrance. Several turned for the hallway containing the shops, and an escape through the side entrance onto Peachtree Road.

The lobby would be clear in a few moments, giving him the opportunity to open the door without exposing guests to automatic gunfire. He had no idea who was knocking on that door, and he didn't want to unleash a bigger problem. The pounding beckoned him as the last of the guests cleared the front lobby door. Two police officers from his precinct pushed through the doors with their service pistols drawn, focused on the stairwell door. They took cover behind the sturdier pieces of lobby furniture as the pounding continued.

Officer Anthony slid past the corner of the front desk, pointing his pistol in the direction of the service elevator to the left. He approached the stairwell door cautiously, expecting it to burst open at any moment. Based on the location of the door handle, he could tell that the door would hinge open in his direction, providing him momentary concealment from any shooters that might emerge. He'd have time to duck into the elevator lobby and return fire. Unfortunately, the elevator lobby was a dead end if they pursued him, though he might be able to use one of the elevators for further cover.

He wouldn't be able to escape without a fire service key. He knew from experience that a hotel fire alarm would automatically engage the elevator system's fire service mode and send all of the elevators to the Fire Recall Floor, where they would remain until the alarms were reset or bypassed by a fire service key. He might not be able to use the elevators to escape, but at least he could rule out the possibility of surprises from the elevator lobby.

He spun into the rectangular shaped area, leading with his pistol. He quickly confirmed that one of the guest elevators was open and empty. The second elevator's doors remained closed, and he had no way to tell where the elevator car might be. God forbid the Ritz Carlton disturb the precious, polished mahogany wood interior to install a floor indicator. He could barely find the buttons that activated the elevators. Maybe you had to be rich to see them. He edged forward, aiming at the open door across from the guest elevators. He "sliced the pie," moving slowly to his right, gradually exposing more of the parking garage elevator car to the sight picture over the barrel of his pistol. Empty.

He rushed back to the elevator lobby opening and nodded to his partner, who concentrated her pistol on the stairwell door. He heard frantic screaming from behind the door and decided that he had no choice but to open the door.

"Hold your fire. No shooting!" he yelled.

The three officers in the lobby nodded, though he didn't get the sense that the order registered. He edged up to the door and reached across the mahogany panel to grip the thick metal handle. The door swung open easily, which almost surprised him more than the thick volume of smoke that immediately billowed from the open doorway and swirled toward the front lobby exits. At least a dozen people initially poured out into the lobby, pushing each other out of the way, coughing and hacking. This group was followed by another surge of guests, assisting each other and yelling. Anthony didn't see any weapons evident, though he admittedly couldn't see very effectively through the thick acrid smoke. He holstered his weapon and rushed in to stabilize an elderly woman, who looked confused.

"Where was the fire?" he asked.

She looked up at him, coughing and squinting. "I don't know. Where's my husband?"

"We'll find him, ma'am," he replied. "Head out the door to get some fresh air."

He singled out a young couple that appeared to be under control. They were headed toward the far right exit, helping another man with a smashed nose. Needing some basic information about the situation, he approached them. As their features became clearer through the smoky haze, he noticed the woman had short brown hair and deep blue eyes, resembling a movie star that he thought he recognized. She was dressed in a black turtleneck dress. Her shoes were missing, but she had probably ditched them in the stairwell. He imagined she'd worn high heels with this outfit. She grasped hands with a serious looking well-heeled gentleman with jet-black hair, who supported a slightly taller, equally well dressed injured man.

The taller man had brown hair and leaned heavily on the other man, unable to put weight on his left leg. His nose was clearly broken, with the bright crimson evidence still pouring down his face and chin onto his crisp white shirt. They were all coughing as they trudged toward the exit. He stepped in front of the group. Nothing about this group set off any internal alarms for Anthony.

"What happened to him?" he said.

They stopped and the black haired man leaned his friend against the wall.

"He fell on the stairs and hit his face. We couldn't see a fucking thing in there, officer. We were waiting for the elevator on five when the fire alarm went off. We hit the stairs, but they were already filled with smoke," he said, coughing into his elbow.

When the man raised his right arm to cough, his suit coat opened, briefly exposing a gun tucked into his right waistline. Officer Paul Anthony instantly felt sick as an incredible surge of adrenaline coursed through his veins. He fought against every panicky instinct telling him to pull his weapon. The man's steely gaze told him that he'd probably never clear the pistol from his holster. He wasn't some brash mafia hit man or wild-eyed gang-banger. Anthony was staring at the real deal. Something he had never seen before. He didn't know how he knew this, but the sudden realization saved his life.

"Officer Anthony?" said the woman, no longer holding the man's hand.

He barely nodded and muttered, "Yes?"

"We're going to walk past you now to seek medical attention. That's really all you should remember about us. Does that sound like a fair assessment of the situation?" she said, smiling.

"What happened up there?" he automatically replied, now scared that he might have signed his own death warrant.

"Nothing worth the life of a police officer. You should help some of the guests now."

He glanced at the mayhem through the thinning smoke and saw several people lying on the tan marble floor, coughing and wheezing.

"I suppose you're right," he said, betraying a hint of regret in his decision.

He heard his sergeant's voice and watched the uniformed police officer push his way through the left-most lobby entrance, along with two plain-clothed officers, both armed with short barreled M-4 Carbines. The sergeant spotted Anthony immediately and started walking over. He now had three police officers focused on his gathering. He detected a shift in intensity from the couple standing in front of him. The man previously leaning against the wall now stood on both feet, his leg wound suddenly healed. Anthony made a decision that he'd professionally regret, but personally cherish. He extended his right hand and placed it on the woman's shoulder, raising his voice over the din of confusion that seemed to envelop the whole lobby.

"Head out into the parking lot and check in with a paramedic," he said, patting her on the back to move them along and through the doors.

He never looked back at them.

"What are you doing?" asked the sergeant.

"What does it look like I'm doing? I'm screening the guests. We have no information about the shooters. They could be up on any of the floors, or trying to sneak out in the stampede!" he yelled over the noise.

"Nice job, Paul. I need you to head outside and organize the rest of the officers as they arrive. I want teams of three or four on each exit screening guests. I'll get you some tactical support assets to beef up your presence." The sergeant turned to the first response tactical officers, not waiting for Anthony's acknowledgement.

He issued orders to the two tactical officers and jogged into the smoky chaos to try and gain control of the situation. Anthony turned to the door, surprised to see that his mystery guests were no longer in sight, and had been replaced by several other desperate hotel guests. He made his way through the people, careful not to jostle anyone, and emerged under the roof of the guest drop-off area. He glanced around, relieved to discover that they had already disappeared. Unless the hotel crashed down on all of them, he'd make it home in time for the morning ritual. He'd kiss his wife goodbye before work and walk his two boys to the bus stop for school. Priceless moments like those left him with no regrets about letting those three vanish.

ত

They fast walked toward Peachtree Road, hoping to catch a taxi within the next minute, before the Atlanta Police Department threw the full weight of their resources into the containment effort at the Ritz Carlton. Daniel could hear multiple sirens in the distance as they approached the crowded six-lane city street. They needed to get as far away from Atlanta as possible. Normally, he fled toward crowds, but tonight was different and their evening was far from over. It would take them a while to find a secondary location safe enough from the public eye to sit down and have an earnest chat with Mr. Young. He sensed that Young would give them everything, but they had to be sure he didn't play them. Sometimes that could get messy, or at least a little loud. Either way, he didn't expect to be on a plane headed back to the South Carolina coast tonight.

"That was beautiful! Who the fuck *are* you people? You just stared down a police officer. I've never seen anything like that. He saw your gun. You know that right?" said Benjamin Young.

Daniel flipped his right hand back and snapped Young directly in the face, connecting with his broken nose. The man howled and cursed, stopping in his tracks before Jessica moved slightly behind him to provide a razor sharp reason to keep moving.

"What the fuck did you do that for?" Young mumbled.

"To remind you that we're not friends," said Daniel.

"Now shut the fuck up and keep walking. I don't want to hear another word out of you unless I ask a question. Got it?"

"Yes or no works for us," said Jessica.

Young simply nodded, clearly struggling to walk after his focused strike. Daniel saw several taxis pass in the minute it took them to arrive at Lenox. His cell phone vibrated and he hoped it was good news from Munoz and Melendez. They had poured out of the smoke filled stairwell a few people back from Daniel's group, prepared to run interference if the police had already locked down the lobby. He'd watched them slither past the sergeant and his two heavily armed police escorts, just as Officer Anthony made a decision in everyone's best interest. One wrong move by Anthony might have led to a bloodbath that no presidential amnesty could forgive, and an even bigger rip in his soul that could never be mended.

"Where are you guys?" he said in greeting.

"Headed northeast on Lenox. Looking to pick up a cab. What's the rendezvous point?" said Munoz.

"I think we should circle the city on the two-eighty-five and meet up at Hartsfield Jackson. We can grab a rental at the terminal and head east into South Carolina. Find somewhere outside of Columbia to stop and have a chat with our friend here."

"Alright. I'll call Sanderson with an update. I don't know what Jessica said to that cop, but it avoided a messy situation."

"Tell me about it. I'll pass that on to her. We'll meet you at the baggage claim inside the north terminal," said Daniel.

"See you there," replied Munoz, ending the call.

Daniel held out his hand to hail a cab, hoping the growing number of blue police lights wouldn't scare off their easiest and most secure form of transportation to the airport. They could always walk down Peachtree Road for about ten minutes to Buckhead Station and take the MARTA to the airport, but one glance at Young's bloodied face and scarlet stained collar shelved that idea. They would need to clean him up before arriving at the airport. Their best course of action might be to head into the side entrance of another hotel along Peachtree Road and take him to a bathroom.

"Let's take a walk," he said, staring down the street at an illuminated "Westin" marquee sign.

Several police cars converged on the intersection of Peachtree and Lenox, screeching around the corner toward the main drive-up entrance to the Ritz Carlton. Two of the cars remained in the intersection, blocking traffic from reaching the main entrance to the hotel. It wouldn't be long before they started expanding their cordon. He turned southeast on Peachtree Road and started walking.

Chapter 36

10:20 PM
Interstate 81 North
Hazelton, Pennsylvania

Jackson Greely's Chevy Suburban hummed past the faint glow of Hazelton. The Chevy's cruise control was set at 70 MPH, which experience had taught him was a safe speed to avoid unwanted attention from the Pennsylvania State Police. Anything over 70 MPH was a complete crapshoot, especially on a Friday night. He hit the deceleration switch once and tucked the speed just under 70. He couldn't afford to have his whereabouts recorded in state police databanks. He'd left Harrisburg after a quiet dinner engagement with local political supporters and headed north for Lake Wallenpaupack. It was time for Greely and Harding to disappear, while events transpired that would change the course of American history.

He and Harding would be arriving at the lake house ahead of schedule, thanks to an unknown entity. Greely agreed with the rest of the council—the FBI hadn't taken custody of Miguel Estrada. They had enough contacts at the Bureau and local law enforcement offices to know that Estrada hadn't surfaced in any of the New York City precincts, hospitals or federal offices. He'd simply vanished into thin air, carried away by two Arab-looking thieves in the night. None of it made any sense, but his coconspirators agreed that they needed to bump up the timeline.

Jason Carnes, head of laboratory operations at their secret facility, had protested, but reluctantly admitted that they could speed up the cultivation process. They would start injecting the virus into the bottle caps late tomorrow, with the intention of transporting the first crates of infected bottled water to the distribution hub the day after that. From there, the convoys would be loaded, assigned drivers and sent to their destinations. Once the convoys hit the roads, the entire organization would go to ground and wait, leaving nothing for the feds to investigate.

His cell phone illuminated and started to buzz. He pressed a button on the steering wheel, which activated the Bluetooth system. "How are we doing?"

"Not good," replied Brown.

"Now what?"

"The team in Atlanta failed," said Brown.

Greely could sense the apprehension in his voice. "What do you mean they failed? What the fuck is wrong with our people? I'm starting to wonder if you've been jerking me off with your reports of how well trained we are."

"Our people are extremely well trained, and I don't appreciate the implication."

"Then how did Young manage to slip away from…how many of your people?"

"Six. He had help. Skilled help. Two of my men were executed in Young's hotel suite. The others were gunned down in the hallway and stairwell."

"Let me guess. More Arabs?"

"No. A hotel security camera showed a man and a woman escorting Young through the lobby. The image is obscured by smoke, which wasn't caused by a fire. Police found a spent smoke grenade in the stairwell. Flashbangs were used on the eighteenth floor. The crew that extracted Young was well equipped, well informed and highly skilled. I'm worried that we've attracted the wrong kind of attention from someone unexpected."

"Fuck!" Greely yelled, pounding the steering wheel. "We need to figure this out immediately. Benjamin Young can connect some dots that we can't afford have connected right now…or ever. We should have killed him weeks ago. Damn it! Fucking Mills didn't want to cut off a big funding deal Young was working on. The son of a bitch has more money than Bill Gates and now we're looking at a serious security breach."

"I know. I have my eyes and ears on the ground in Atlanta. If he surfaces, I'll put a bounty on his head," said Brown.

"He won't surface. He's a ghost now, just like Estrada. How is our insurance policy shaping up?"

"We have two suitable options. The package will be in place within thirty-six hours."

"Make sure nothing goes wrong with this. If the government is somehow involved in Young's disappearance, the success of our plan will depend upon it," said Greely.

"Understood. I'll personally oversee the operation."

"Very well. Any word from the compound?"

"Nothing yet. I just got off the phone with Bishop."

"Alright. Keep me posted. I'm headed north for my forced vacation," said Greely.

"Don't hurt yourself up there. I'll be in touch with any developments."

Greely hit the steering wheel again. He considered calling Jason Carnes and pressing the case for further expediting laboratory operations, but he knew that the laboratory staff had their back up against the wall on this one. Carnes had made it perfectly clear that current timeline cutbacks might ultimately impact the virus's efficacy. He needed to be patient and trust in Brown's tactics. The compound, the attack earlier today and their insurance policy would combine to create a perfect storm in their favor. Even if Young spilled everything to his government captors, there would be no way they could recover quickly enough to stop their plot. He had to focus on the big picture. At this point, small setbacks were like road kill on the highway—squishy little bumps that had no chance of slowing down his Chevy.

Chapter 37

11:58 PM
True America Training Compound
Hacker Valley, West Virginia

Tyrell Bishop stood a few steps outside of the headquarters building and surveyed the compound. The full moon directly overhead cast a grayish-blue light on the silent facility, creating a monochromatic collage of shadows among the structures. He took in the crisp night air with a deep breath. Like always, the valley air was pristine, which added to the bittersweet taste in his mouth. He didn't relish leaving the compound. The place had been his permanent home for the past two years, filling him with nothing but cherished memories. He looked up into the hills and pondered the impending attack, which Brown had assured him would come within the next forty-eight hours. A grin spread across his face. Bishop had no idea what they were up against, but Brown felt confident that they could repel any attack thrown at them by the FBI. The amount of firepower at his disposal could hold off a concentrated Taliban attack.

He had removed their four M2 heavy barrel .50 caliber machine guns from the armory and prepositioned them in buildings near the fence line. Within minutes, he could put them into action against enemies coming from any direction. Brown had told him to expect a coordinated vehicle and helicopter assault, which was a favorite tactic of the feds. Idiots. By the time the vehicles traversed the road leading to the compound, True America would be ready for a fight. He was willing to bet that the FBI helicopter pilots had never come under heavy machine gun fire on a raid before. He couldn't wait to see them turn tail and fly away when .50 caliber tracer rounds reached out to touch them. Without air support, he wondered if the ground forces would press the attack. He hoped so, since the compound held a few more surprises for them.

His favorite was their armored vehicle. Last year, several mechanics and body shop guys went to work on a Ford Bronco, turning it into a light armored vehicle. Fitted with steel plates on all sides and airless Michelin Tweel tires, the "Road Warrior" was impervious to small arms fire. The Bronco's rear compartment roof had been removed to provide a gunner's stand for the fully restored German MG42 belt fed machine gun attached to a swivel mount welded to the truck. Twin protective plates would give the gun operator added protection while mowing down feds with the same gun that had defended the beaches of Normandy. Road Warrior would emerge through the front gate to meet any vehicles that tried to deliver federal storm troopers to his doorstep.

Even a long distance standoff wasn't a feasible option for Uncle Sam. Bishop's arsenal consisted of nearly a dozen .50 caliber sniper rifles that could reach out and touch anyone hunkered down along the tree line. The furthest point from the fence was roughly 350 yards, easy pickings for one of his sharpshooters, not to mention the heavy machine guns. If the feds showed some tenacity and decided to stick around, he could always dust them off with "thumper." Even the most highly disciplined storm troopers would scurry when he started to walk 60mm high explosive rounds onto their position. The baseplate and tube could be set up in less than a minute, providing him with unmatched firepower. The mortar crew's training consisted mostly of "dry fire" drills since ammunition was severely limited, but he felt confident that they could rain hell down on their enemies.

If they failed to stop the feds, Brown had ordered him to retreat through the back fence using one of the compound's ATVs. Brown made it clear that Bishop was too valuable to be captured, and that he was needed to play a critical role in upcoming events. He could take the surviving camp regulars with him. They had enough four wheelers for about a dozen of them to escape if they doubled up.

The new recruits would have to stay and fight it out, no matter what happened. He hoped it didn't come to that, but Brown had made the options clear. If the feds turned the tide too quickly, Hacker Valley would vanish into obscurity, and there would be no point for him to remain behind. If they could repel the attack and force the government to come back with a bigger force, True America could turn this into another Waco, Texas. Greely's spin-doctors in the media would make this a symbol of government oppression. Brown and the higher ups had something massive planned for the upcoming days. Ongoing media coverage of the Hacker Valley siege would play right into that plan, so he was told. The key to that plan was holding the fort.

Through the fence line, he could see that a faint mist had started to penetrate the valley, lightly touching the ground in a few patches to the south. He raised his night vision scope and scanned beyond the fence. The light cast by the moon turned the landscape into day, providing a crisp image across the clearing in every direction. They had some night vision equipped rifles, which would come in handy if the attack took place at night. He highly doubted they would attack under a full moon, on a clear night. Then again, he wasn't facing military tacticians. Lawyers and accountants filled the ranks at the FBI. If he were in charge of the federal attack, he would hit the compound an hour before full sunrise. The mist often transitioned into fog by then, stringing thick ribbons of smoky white clouds across the valley. Perfect cover to approach undetected.

He was about to step down from the doorway and take a walk around the compound when an excited voice nearly scared him out of his clothes.

"They're coming! Ty! They're coming."

He ran into the building and took the first door on his left, entering the control room. The small space housed a table with three monitors and a variety of communications equipment. Two of the monitors showed feeds from various cameras located throughout the compound and along the approach road. The third monitor displayed a virtual security window that relayed information from several dozen sensors placed in the forest surrounding the compound. Immediately upon entering, he could see that motion sensors along the approach road had been tripped.

"Rewind the camera feed," he ordered.

The black haired, bearded man seated at the table clicked the mouse a few times and the digital feed sped back in time twenty seconds. As the image flashed on the screen, Bishop saw a massive convoy of vehicles enter the screen, headed backward toward Route 15.

"Stop it there. Play it forward."

Bishop counted the vehicles as they slowly passed the night vision equipped security camera. Eight vehicles inbound, carrying maybe fifty agents. The lead vehicle had been a stripped down Humvee, probably from a West Virginia National Guard unit. This made sense since none of the vehicles displayed headlights. The Guard drivers could navigate the road with night vision and lead the feds along safely to their target. The convoy was more than twenty minutes out, giving him more than enough time to deploy the compound's defenses. He wondered if they had him under some kind of long-range surveillance. He'd considered the possibility, but his array of motion sensors told him a different story. He'd overseen the placement of this array, and had tested it from every direction. If working properly, nothing could get close enough to watch the compound without alerting him.

Still, he didn't want to completely spoil the surprise. He notified each of the barracks buildings with his radio and set them in motion. Within minutes, he'd have two heavy machine guns covering the approach road from the ground and the other two mounted in fixed rooftop positions. Located on opposite sides of the parade field, the rooftop guns could fire in any direction around the compound, and would be their first line of defense against helicopters. Sniper positions on the rooftops and along the raised earthen barriers inside the fence could similarly fire in any direction, though he would concentrate their placement in the direction of the approach road.

The recruits would man the entire fence line armed with a variety of automatic rifles, equipped with state of the art optics. Once the heavy machine gunners made contact, he'd deploy the Road Warrior if they pressed the attack forward. He really hoped they were stupid and stubborn enough to try and breach the fence line. He'd love nothing more than to see the entire group of FBI agents slaughtered as they crossed 350 yards of open field.

He opened a tall metal cabinet pressed against the wall and grabbed his battle gear, which consisted of an AR-15 with 4X ACOG scope and a full tactical vest loaded down with spare magazines. He already wore his pistol in a drop down tactical leg holster, along with a hand microphone-equipped command radio.

"Stay on the command channel. If you see any movement on the forest sensors, aside from the approach road, you notify me immediately. Understood?"

"I got your back, Ty. I wish I could be out there with you guys."

"You'll get your turn, don't worry. If we have a turkey shoot out there, I'll send someone back so you can empty a few mags."

"Fuck yeah! Save some of those dirt bag pieces of shit for me," he said, as Bishop disappeared.

"All teams report when in position. I want everyone ready in three minutes," he said into the hand mic.

He had a dozen snipers, four heavy gun team leaders, Road Warrior and the mortar team on the command net. Things would get busy, very quickly. The recruits would be led by his regulars, separated into groups of ten. If he needed to contact them, or vice versa, the request would be relayed through a different channel that was monitored by his second-in-command, who was sprinting down the hall toward him.

Paul Thomas had been a competent soldier to have at his side for the past year. Wearing a Marine Corps style "high and tight" haircut that matched his persona, the former Marine staff sergeant got things done around here. He considered Thomas to be an essential camp asset, which was more than he could say about many of the regulars that rotated through the compound.

"Wake your ass up, Marine. We have a whole invasion force coming down that road. Make sure the recruits get into position, and don't leave my side. We may need to shift guys around pretty quickly."

"Roger that," Thomas said.

"I want to get down by the front gate to assess the situation firsthand," Bishop said and started running south, in the direction of the front gate.

On his way across the parade field, he saw activity on the rooftops designated to hold two of the heavy machine guns. These boys worked fast. Dark figures dashed in every direction, following orders barked by men and women who had been trained to lead freedom fighters into battle. The sound of equipment rattling sent a chill down his spine. He had never served in the military, but he imagined that this was exactly how it must have felt to be stationed in the Korengal Valley, at one of those hilltop firebases when the Taliban launched a surprise attack. The feeling nearly overwhelmed him as he reached one of the machine gun positions established beside the gate. He had to stop and catch his breath, woozy from the excitement and adrenaline.

The machine gun was almost fully assembled on its tripod, which had been jammed against the two-foot high berm. When in position, the barrel would clear the top of the raised earth by a few inches, giving the gunners cover from return fire. He doubted there would be any accurate return fire. With two or three .50 cals pouring hot steel into their vehicles, options would be limited for the agents that managed to crawl out of the wreckage. They could either hug the ground or kiss their asses goodbye.

ᘛ

Chief Petty Officer Carroll stared through the lens of his AN/PED-1 Lightweight Laser Designator/Rangefinder (LLDR) and depressed the trigger, firing an invisible, pulsed laser beam at the side of an ammunition can that had been placed next to a sandbag emplacement on the roof of one of the buildings. Within milliseconds, the Joint Fire Support Console connected to the LLDR had calculated the range and elevation to the ammunition can, comparing the data to the GPS signal provided by the chief's sophisticated communications rig. By the time he had released the trigger, the compact JFSC screen presented him with a muted orange, digital readout of the ammunition can's coordinates, which he quickly highlighted and transmitted, along with a brief target description, to the E-8C JSTARS aircraft circling far overhead. A similar process was conducted by DEVGRU teams in three other locations around the compound, aided by laser pointers from at least a dozen weapons aimed into the compound.

Within seconds, precise coordinates for all of the compound's heavy weapons and the single armored vehicle had been relayed by the SEALS to the JSTARS aircraft, where computers eliminated duplicate coordinates and packaged the data for transmission to Gunslinger Three One, a three-gun firing section provided by Fox Battery, 2nd Battalion, 10th Marine Artillery Regiment. The section had been delivered by three Marine CH-53E Super Stallion helicopters, under the cover of darkness, to a remote forest clearing located eighteen miles north of the compound. Their M777A2 Howitzers would fire six M982 155mm high-explosive Excalibur rounds in support of the mission. The Excalibur round was an extended-range GPS guided munition, with a circle error probable (CEP) of less than five meters, allowing for near pinpoint battlefield accuracy. He had to give the Joint

Special Operations Command planners some credit for creativity. The use of battlefield artillery against terrorist forces on U.S. soil had never crossed his mind. Then again, he had never foreseen the authorization to use Tier One Special Operations assets either.

He waited for the final list of targets to arrive, which appeared on his console a few seconds later. The list looked good. Four gun emplacements and one armored vehicle. He typed additional instructions for their "fire mission" on the small keyboard attached to the JFSC and transmitted the data.

He diverted his attention from the screen and glanced through the lens at the bright green image centered on one of the rooftops. One of the men picked up the ammunition can and placed it inside of the sandbag emplacement. The three-man crew had attached the heavy machine gun to a fixed mounting bracket and was in the process of loading the weapon. Panning out, Carroll took in a wider view of the compound. Personnel scrambled in every direction, with the majority of the terrorists manning positions toward the front gate. Suspected sharpshooters armed with optics-equipped .50 caliber sniper rifles started to take positions on several of the rooftops. Lasers calibrated to a frequency only visible to friendly night vision equipment reached out from the tree line and marked the shooters, guiding sniper teams from 1st Special Forces Operational Detachment-Delta and the Naval Special Warfare Development Group to their highest priority targets.

The plan remained intact, as far as Chief Carroll could tell. The fake video transmitted from the JSTARS aircraft to the compound's security feed had catapulted the sleepy camp into action. Unknown to camp personnel, JSTARS technicians had completely hijacked the compound's security systems, disabling the motion sensors and using the camp's own cameras for close-up surveillance. The compound's commander had reacted in accordance with the battlefield intelligence presented by his hijacked sensors and deployed a majority of the camp's defenders to repel nonexistent vehicles approaching from the southern access road. Carroll's surveillance of the compound was interrupted by a low volume tone in his right earpiece, indicating that JSTARS had sent him an update. His JFSC console relayed fire mission data from the artillery battery.

"FM12-001. Two salvos-3 rds. 1st salvo, 2 bldg gun empls-1 rd, vehicle-1 rd. 2nd Salvo, 2 grnd gun empls-1 rd, vehicle-1 rd. TOF 141s. Ready."

He reviewed the fire mission and highlighted "FM12-001" to bring up options on the screen. Without hesitation he selected "Fire." Thirteen seconds later, his screen provided an update for the fire mission. "Rounds complete." The console kept track of the timing and provided him with a countdown to the estimated Time on Target (TOT). He didn't need the computer to keep track of the artillery rounds. The math was simple: Time of Flight (TOF) for the rounds was 141 seconds, and it took the artillery battery twelve seconds to fire a second salvo. Within 156 seconds, all mission critical impediments would cease to exist.

There was no need to transmit voice data to any of the teams on the ground. All team leaders were equipped with a wrist mounted Battle Feed console that relayed the same information. Carroll glanced at his teammate, Petty Officer Stanhope, who was focused on the scope attached to his suppressed Mk11 Mod 0 semi-automatic sniper rifle. Stanhope's rifle utilized a uniquely effective sighting combination, attaching the AN/PVS-27 Magnum Universal Night Sight (MUNS) in front of a Leupold Mark 4 scope.

"One-four-one seconds to impact," he whispered.

"Got it," muttered Stanhope, remaining perfectly still behind the scope.

Several feet away, one of the Delta support teams lay motionless, preparing to eliminate any high threat targets and provide suppressive fire for the assault groups. Each support team consisted of four Delta operators, broken into a machine gun section and a sniper section. The two-man machine gun section operated a night vision equipped M240B belt-fed machine gun, capable of accurately firing 950 rounds per minute at targets up to 800 meters away. The sniper/spotter duo fielded the M107A2 Barrett sniper rifle, which accurately fired the unstoppable .50 caliber 661 grain BMG round to ranges of 1,800 meters.

Five additional Delta support teams ringed the compound, each similarly equipped, bringing the total number of support weapons aimed into the compound to sixteen. In a pinch, Chief Carroll and the other SEAL spotters could pick up their rifles and join the fight, adding four additional guns to the mix. He very much doubted they would be needed. His role was to observe the entire compound and adjust ground fire support to maximize the neutralization of targets. His weapon would be the AN/PED-1 LLDR, unless a real problem developed. Given the number of weapons concentrated on the terrorist force, and the six inbound 155mm artillery shells, he didn't think the assault teams would encounter any resistance. There might not be anyone left alive in the compound. He glanced down at the JFSC console. One hundred and ten seconds until impact.

Master Sergeant Ethan McDonald pressed himself against the concrete foundation of the building and checked his Battle Feed wrist monitor. One minute and twenty-two seconds until impact, which he figured would be about one minute too long at this rate. The compound's militia had reacted faster than any of them had expected, and started to arrive at positions along the rear fence line ahead of schedule.

Twenty minutes ago, his assault troop had breached the fence at the northwest corner and spread out among the five northern most buildings along the fence line, lying flat and melting into the shadows. The troop consisted of eighteen Delta operators, split into three teams of six. Armed primarily with suppressed, night vision-equipped HK416 assault rifles, breaching shotguns and grenades, his troop's mission was to clear the buildings of hostile personnel, starting from the rear of the compound and moving forward.

Mission planners had originally suggested two teams of six operators, figuring that the smaller group would have a better chance at remaining undetected. He agreed with that assessment, until he learned that they would be required to accept surrenders when practical. Taking prisoners would eat up his operators quickly, so he had opted for one more team than mission planners had suggested.

As the first wave of defenders trickled through the buildings to take up positions at the fence, he didn't think they would remain hidden for long. Fortunately, most of them had braced their rifles against the raised berm and scanned the darkness beyond the fence. If one of them glanced back at the unusual dark clumps along the bottom of each building, they would have a problem. With over a minute left until TOT, he couldn't risk detection and the possible discharge of an unsuppressed firearm. They would have to start neutralizing the defenders very shortly. He just wanted to wait until most of them had arrived.

Another terrorist jogged into the open and tossed a smoldering cigarette less than a foot away from McDonald's right elbow. The man kept moving toward the fence without looking back at the orange glow that McDonald had crushed with his fist. They now had eight targets in the open and he didn't think there was any way their luck could persist.

"Take down in three, two, one…mark."

McDonald raised himself to one knee and quickly leaned his rifle around the corner of the building, searching for any stragglers. He heard the suppressed snapping of his troop's HK416 rifles as he sighted in on a pair of men less than fifteen feet away. One of the men spoke into a handheld radio as he walked, oblivious to the fact that his entire squad had just been neutralized. McDonald placed the EOTech holographic reticle in the middle of his face and waited for him to lower the radio. Less than a second later, he fired a single round through the squad leader's nose, rapidly shifting his rifle to acquire the second man's head.

Through the AN/PVS-14 night vision scope mounted in tandem with the EOTech sight, he registered a look of surprise before puncturing another skull with a single .223 caliber bullet. Both men instantly dropped to the ground, spilling their rifles and communications gear noisily to the ground. McDonald waited for three seconds before running forward and dragging one of the bodies behind the building. Without speaking a word, another Delta operator took care of the second body and the dropped equipment, handing the radio to McDonald when he rounded the corner. Other operators surged toward the fence, examining the individual heaps for signs of life. They still had over a minute left on the clock and they didn't need any surprises. He saw one of his men jam a hand against a terrorist's mouth and stab him in the neck with a concealed blade. No surprises.

He issued hand signals changing their posture from defensive to offensive and watched as the troop formed up on the buildings, ready to move deeper into the compound. Right now, they were spread thinly among five structures, covering every approach to their area between the buildings and the rear fence. A few seconds before the artillery rounds hit, they would consolidate into three teams and move forward. Before advancing through the compound, each operator would activate a Pegasus infrared signaling beacon attached to their ballistic helmets. The infrared beacons had been preset to a specific sequenced flash pattern and synchronized to facilitate rapid identification by support gunners in the surrounding hills and inbound helicopter personnel. Machine gunners would start with targets closest to his men and work their way forward, allowing Delta assault teams to move forward rapidly without fear of absorbing friendly fire.

He heard two snaps from a position near the northwest corner building. Before he could activate his radio, his earpiece came to life.

"Single tango. Male. Started wandering along the fence toward the northwest corner. We snatched his body without anyone noticing. He carried a radio. Possible leadership."

"Copy. TOT in forty-two seconds."

The presence of a radio on the man was bad news. They had neutralized two possible leadership positions assigned to the compound's perimeter defense, which would certainly draw unwanted attention. Forty seconds until impact. A lot could go wrong in forty-two seconds.

❧

Tyrell Bishop patted the woman gripping the M2 Browning .50 caliber machine gun's trigger handle on the shoulder. She was sitting down with her legs extended forward, braced against the machine gun's heavy-duty tripod. She looked oddly relaxed in this position, but Bishop could tell by the tension in her shoulder muscles that she was anything but calm.

The two machine gun positions had been placed several yards along the fence, on each side of the main gate, giving the gunners a clear field of fire that extended the entire length of the access road. The .50 caliber bullets, guided by intermittent tracer rounds, would start hitting the federal convoy as soon as it emerged from the forest. He couldn't imagine the vehicles making it halfway to the compound. He considered holding fire until they had closed the distance, ensuring that there would be no way for the agents to withstand the withering heavy machine gun and rifle fire. He glanced at his watch and briefly chuckled. They had another seventeen minutes to get their shit together before the vehicles arrived. He had to hand it to himself. The compound reacted quickly and professionally under his leadership.

He'd received reports from all but one of his regulars. Good ole' Buddy Tyler hadn't passed on a readiness report from the rear fence. There was no real rush, since they had fifteen minutes to spare, but it still annoyed him that Tyler couldn't muster a total of ten men, including himself, and move them one hundred yards from the barracks to the rear fence. There was a reason Tyler had been assigned to guard the opposite end of the compound. Despite his loyalty and enthusiasm, the man lacked a sense of urgency. He really shouldn't have been surprised that Buddy would be the last to report, but he had just talked to him less than a minute ago, which made the situation even more unbearable. The guy had been "five seconds" out from the fence. How long could it take to count nine people and report back? He'd sent John Thibodeau from the western perimeter to check on his progress, but now he couldn't raise Thibodeau. He knew what was happening. Buddy and John were arguing, while he sat on his thumb waiting for one of them to send a fucking report. He turned to Paul Thomas, who was squaring away the other machine gun position.

"Paul!" he yelled. "Can you run back and inform Mr. Tyler that I would like to receive a readiness report before the sun comes up!"

"I'm on it," Thomas replied and took off running north through the compound.

Bishop felt bad sending Thomas on a 400 meter round trip just to deliver a message, but it appeared to be the only way to get anyone to report from the back fence. He'd be back in time for the main show. Thomas was a physical machine, who led daily calisthenics and physical conditioning at the compound. From what Bishop could tell, the man never slowed down. He watched the former recon Marine run parallel with the western barracks along the edge of the parade field.

A massive explosion rocked the compound, obliterating the southern side of the barracks building. The point detonation of 23.8 pounds of TNT encased in high fragmentation steel sent debris flying in every direction, along with a shockwave that lifted the loose soil from the ground nearby, instantly obscuring Bishop's view of the barracks and Thomas. The .50 caliber machine gun behind him roared to life, but his gaze was still transfixed on the explosion. The smoke and dust thrown up by the explosion obscured the fact that a total of three Excalibur rounds had simultaneously hit the compound, neutralizing the two rooftop gun positions and the Road Warrior.

Someone grabbed his shoulder and turned him around to face the machine gun position next to the gate. He could barely hear what the frenzied man was yelling at him over the ear shattering sound of the heavy caliber machine gun's continuous blasts. Why the fuck was she firing? Tracers showered the distance, skipping skyward when they struck the ground. Still in shock, he stared at the light show for a brief second, before he regained enough sense to assess the situation. The woman he had just patted on the shoulder was missing the top of her head.

"Jesus. Get her off the gun!"

Nobody moved toward her, so he lurched forward and yanked the woman off the gun, splattering his face with blood and sticky matter when the rest of her head snapped backward. The gun fell silent, but he still heard machine gun fire. The other rooftop gun must have engaged targets that he couldn't see. Had the sensors missed an earlier convoy? Maybe the one he saw on camera was a backup team. Bishop had no idea what was happening. He remained upright as the rest of the recruits instinctively lowered their bodies in response to the gunfire. He saw a few of them stagger backward and fall to the ground, but couldn't tell what had happened to them. The moonlight permitted him to see detailed shapes, but the rest of the picture remained washed out by the darkness. None of this made much sense to him.

Finally, the familiar snap and hiss of incoming small arms fire reached his ears, propelling him back into his role as camp commander. He saw their situation with full clarity, as machine gun fire raked the defenders stationed along the front fence. Controlled, staccato bursts of gunfire echoed across the small valley, making it perfectly clear to Bishop that they weren't under attack by the FBI. This was something bigger. He could see flashes in the forested hillside. They were barely visible due to flash suppressors, but he could see them. He'd teach these federal sons-of-bitches a hard lesson about combat firepower.

Bishop tossed his rifle to the ground and swung the barrel of the emplaced heavy machine gun toward the forest. He perched his thumbs over the trigger and waited for another flash to appear. His wait was interrupted by the simultaneous arrival of three M982 Excalibur artillery rounds, one of which landed six feet away from his position.

Master Sergeant Ethan McDonald heard the second series of explosions and waited a few seconds for any shrapnel to pass. The Excalibur rounds had landed nearly 200 meters away, which was well outside of the typical 155mm high explosive shell's casualty radius, but he'd seen too many anomalies in his twenty-two year career to discount the possibility of taking a wild fragment from any artillery strike. While waiting, he received a quick radio transmission confirming that all targets had been destroyed.

He passed a hand signal back to his team, transmitting the order to advance to the other team leaders through his helmet microphone. From this point forward, each team would work independently to clear structures and provide their own security. If they encountered any unusual resistance, he would consolidate teams into a larger group to handle the threat. Given the distinctive echo of .50 caliber sniper rifle fire, combined with uninterrupted bursts of machine gun fire from their Delta brethren in the forest, he doubted very much that their work would be interrupted. He tapped the operator in front of him on the shoulder and the entire team moved in unison through the gap between buildings, shifting their weapons to cover every conceivable angle that posed a threat to them.

The troop's plan had been hastily rehearsed at Dover Air Force base, on a cluster of buildings sharing a similarity with the compound layout. Hundreds of airmen had been evacuated from an isolated grouping of two-story barracks buildings, while McDonald's team practiced the mechanics of the operation they would now execute. Based on details provided by DEVGRU surveillance teams, the five buildings situated along the rear fence should be empty of compound personnel. The center most building, which McDonald brushed against rushing forward, had been identified as the armory. If the door was locked, and couldn't be breached by shotgun blasts, they would rig a claymore mine to detonate if the door was opened from the inside. A similar procedure would be followed by the teams flanking McDonald's. Each of those teams was responsible for either clearing or booby-trapping the rest of the structures.

McDonald's team would move to the next row of buildings as soon as the armory was neutralized. The headquarters building lay just ahead of the armory, and the SEALS hadn't detected any side or rear doors. His team would have to go in through the front door, exposing themselves to the vast parade field. They would be exposed to fire from a 180 degree arc while crossing the front of the building to reach the entrance. He heard the deep thumping of rotor blades in the distance, which signified the arrival of two MH-53J Pave Low III helicopters, carrying twenty-four DEVGRU operators. The helicopters should be overhead in a matter of seconds, and would present a serious problem for anyone trying to fire on his Delta troop.

He flipped down the AN/PVS-14 night vision scope mounted behind his EOTech holographic sight and stacked up with three members of his team on the armory door. Another operator rushed forward and fired three Hatton breaching rounds from a short barrel, pistol grip shotgun into the door handle. The soldier in front of McDonald kicked the door with the bottom of his boot, smashing the door inward on its hinges before rushing inside.

McDonald entered behind him and peeled off to the right, immediately clearing the "fatal funnel" created by the doorway. In room clearing situations, most bullets funneled into the breach as defenders instinctively tried to plug the gap. Normally, they used a diversionary device to briefly incapacitate defenders and allow the team to clear the "fatal funnel" unhampered. They had decided against the use of flashbangs in the armory for one primary reason: mission intelligence suggested the presence of recreational muzzle loading rifles and cartridge reloading equipment in the armory. Gunpowder and the magnesium based pyrotechnic substance used by the M84 stun grenade didn't play well together, especially within confined spaces. He had been nervous enough about the limited amount of kinetic sparking created by the Hatton rounds upon hitting metal.

They activated powerful rifle mounted flashlights upon entry and scanned the armory. Most of the racks stood empty. He quickly spotted several flintlock rifles and a variety of bolt-action World War II era rifles. A shorter rack held at least twenty submachine guns, mostly Uzi's and MP-5 variants. Upon initial visual inspection, he didn't see any conceivable hiding place for an adult. The racks sat flush against the wall, and the oversized wooden workbenches stood tall enough to easily scan underneath. He swept the darkened room one more time with his flashlight.

"Form up," he said to the team, taking a moment to pass on a situation report through his headset.

"Armory secure. No sign of 60 mike-mike."

"This is Overlord. 60 mike-mike neutralized by Overwatch."

"Understood. Proceeding to Hotel-Quebec," said McDonald.

"Front door is open. No movement detected inside. All rooftop threats neutralized," replied Overlord, one of the SEAL surveillance teams in the forest.

"Three-one controls access to armory," another voice reported over the digitally encrypted radio feed.

Three-one was one of the Delta sniper teams located to the west of the compound. The first number determined the team designation and location. "Three" represented one of two teams firing laterally across the compound. The second number indicated the type of support. "One" signified that they were snipers. If any non-friendlies approached the armory, they would be taken down by .50 caliber sniper fire. Apparently the snipers had run out of high value targets. He wasn't sure if this was a good or bad sign.

The team formed up again without prompting, and they moved down the western face of the headquarters building, rapidly approaching the front corner. The point man paused briefly at the edge of the building, scanning the area for movement. The dirt and debris cloud caused by the Excalibur rounds hung in the air, obscuring their view across the parade field. Nobody on the team carried any thermal imaging equipment that could see through the haze and night vision would be utterly useless in this situation. He decided that speed would be their best ally here.

"Bobby, you got anything?" he whispered.

"Negative. But I can't see shit," replied his point man.

He held up a closed fist long enough for the team to see. The fist changed to a flat hand, which he moved rapidly back and forth.

"Go. Fast," he said and slapped the point man on the shoulder.

The point man took off, and the team dashed toward the small concrete stoop in front of the entrance door, which stood less than twenty feet away. They left one operator at the corner to cover the approach to the front door. He had closed three-quarters of the short distance to the door when Staff Sergeant Robert Chamberlain appeared to stumble. The sound of a suppressed weapon from his rear and a double tap gunshot from the parade field immediately followed. Chamberlain collapsed and tumbled forward under his own momentum, colliding clumsily with the side of the building. McDonald could see a dark stain on the wall where he had hit.

"Man down," he hissed into his headset.

❧

It didn't take Paul Thomas long to figure out that they were seriously fucked. An incredible explosion had rocked the top of the barracks building, showering the parade field with debris. A large, twisted chunk of smoldering timber had fallen several feet in front of him, stopping his sprint toward the rear fence. Engulfed in dirt and smoke, it took him a few seconds to realize that the machine gun position located on top of building across the parade field had been simultaneously hit by a separate explosion.

The Road Warrior had been disabled by a third explosion that landed less than fifty meters away, in the southeast corner of the parade field, but the impact had been close enough to the other that it never registered to him as a separate hit. Thomas had defied the statistics of battlefield artillery. Located just outside of the fifty-meter kill radius, he had been saved by the fact that the Excalibur round had landed on the opposite side of the Road Warrior, which had absorbed most of the shrapnel sent in his direction. It didn't register with Thomas that he had been spared by the very vehicle he had secretly deemed as one of Bishop's more asinine ideas.

Thomas dove to the ground behind the smoldering timber and assessed the situation. He could hear short bursts of machine gun fire from every direction, competing with the sound of one of their .50 cals at the front gate. The heavy caliber gun continued to pound away at something. So much for short, controlled bursts of fire. He knew it was a stupid idea to put that crazy bitch on the gun, but Bishop had insisted. Equal opportunity or something like that. None of that mattered now. They were in a fight for their lives.

The sound of small arms fire intensified from every direction, and he could tell that the compound was putting up a spirited defense. The .50 caliber machine gun stopped firing, which unmasked something he hadn't been able to hear. Repeated, single booms echoing throughout the compound. He knew that sound very well from Iraq. He lifted his head above the thick piece of blackened wood and watched a body sail horizontally into the parade field from the top of the armory, still spinning as it struck the ground. One of their snipers had been hit by a .50 caliber sniper bullet, which had imparted enough kinetic energy to toss his body off the roof like a rag doll. Thomas stayed low, not wanting to tempt the snipers firing with impunity from hidden positions in the valley.

The second salvo of Excalibur shells landed just as he pressed his body flat against the ground. Thomas once again defied the odds, avoiding the shower of steel fragments released from the artillery round landing near the Road Warrior. He remained in a prone position, scrambling to process his options. He considered running into one of the buildings, but figured that the doors were under observation. They'd send a Hellfire missile right through one of the windows, instantly vaporizing him. This could be the only explanation for the accuracy of the strikes he had witnessed. Drones overhead.

This thought spurred a separate line of thinking. Predator drones were equipped with thermal imaging equipment for nighttime strikes. Sitting here would have the same result. He might have a better chance in one of the structures. If he could get inside the command building, he could send a warning to Brown before they overran the camp. He had to act fast. The cloud of debris would clear up soon, making him an easy target for snipers. He raised his head slowly, along with his AR-15 rifle, scanning for threats near the command building. He started to rise up on one knee, when he detected movement down the side of the command structure.

A small team of soldiers moved briskly along the wall, approaching the front corner. He recognized their fluid tactical movements immediately. Special Forces. There was no way he was going to make it into that building. He lowered his head and glanced behind him, in the direction of the front gate. He could see that the forward machine gun positions had suffered the same devastating fate as the rooftop emplacements. *Fuck.* He wasn't going to make it through this one. His luck had finally run out. He closed his eyes for a second and paused, before peeking at the soldiers. They had already started to move toward the front door. Without thinking, he quickly raised his head and sighted in on the lead soldier. He placed the illuminated green crosshairs of the C79A2 3.4X combat optic at center mass and fired two rounds, shifting the sight picture to the next soldier in the line.

ര·ശ

Sergeant Gabriel Castillo searched for movement. He stared past the parade field at different points in the distance, never fully focusing. He allowed his mid-peripheral vision to do most of the work, knowing that the light sensitive rod cells responsible for peripheral vision could detect motion better than the cone cells that dominated center vision. Several dark clumps of oddly shaped wreckage littered the field, presenting a considerable challenge for one man.

Something moved in the pile of glowing rubble on the far left side of the field. He sighted in on top of the debris heap through his night vision scope and fired a round instinctively. As the rifle recoiled into his shoulder, he still hadn't formed a detailed picture of the target. All he knew was that the round shape he had identified didn't belong to the debris.

His night vision flared bright green, which meant that the target had probably fired a round at the same time. He didn't have much time to process any of this before hearing the words "man down" in his headset. He flipped the night vision scope down and fired three rounds at the hazy silhouette of a human head still poking above the top of the pile. Overkill, but he had to be sure. The target had been quick enough to acquire and hit one of his teammates before he could react...and there had been no problem with Castillo's reaction time. He wondered if there were more like this one in the compound.

❧

"Stinger lead, this is Overlord. We have a man down near the LZ. Recommend Stinger two-one deploy medical team with the assault group. Prepare for immediate cas-evac, over," said Carroll.

He watched the first of two MH-53J Pave Low helicopters cruise at rooftop height over the headquarters building. He hated to break the pilot's concentration on approach to a hot LZ, but the Delta operator might require immediate evacuation to save his life. The casualty report had been passed seconds ago, with no clarifying information. The helicopters could deploy the SEALS as planned, leaving the second Pave Low on the ground for a few moments to deal with the casualty.

"Copy. Stinger two-one will remain in LZ for evac."

Done deal.

"Delta One. Overlord. Pass casualty to Stinger two-one medical team for immediate evac."

He didn't expect a response. Delta One had just stormed the headquarters building.

❧

McDonald hovered over Staff Sergeant Chamberlain, searching his unresponsive body for the wound. As the third operator in line stopped to help, he grabbed him by the sleeve and yanked him toward the door.

"Stack up," he said and called Castillo over from the corner.

"You did the best any of us could do. Stay with him and cover us," he said and continued the quick search.

He started with the head and quickly determined that Chamberlain had not suffered from a headshot. Neck was fine. Upper chest…not sure. No way McDonald could tell in the dark. He listened to the broadcast from Overlord to the approaching helicopters. They'd take care of Bobby.

"Make sure the second helicopter takes him out of here," he said and stacked up behind the last man crouched outside of the door.

The lead Delta operator didn't wait for orders or hand signals. As soon as McDonald reached the stack, he tossed a flashbang inside the door. The seven million Candela flash illuminated the field in front of the building, followed by a thunderous 180-decibel explosive sound. Anyone standing inside the doorway would be incapacitated long enough for his operators to engage safely. With their rifle-mounted flashlights illuminated, they disappeared through the opening and assessed the structure. A long hallway ran from front to back, with two doors on each side. Not a word was spoken as they lined up on the first door to the right. The position of several antennas over the front right corner of the building suggested that this might be their communications room, making it their highest priority.

A flashbang detonated in the room, prompting the Delta operators to enter. As the last man in the stack, McDonald immediately pivoted upon entering the room and covered the doorway across the hall. He had seen enough upon entry to know that he would not be needed. A bearded man in a camouflage patterned jump suit yelled for mercy, with his hands over his head. Within seconds, McDonald's team had slammed him to the ground, secured his hands with plastic zip ties and placed dark green duct tape over his mouth. The man tried to yell through his taped mouth and nose making loud grunting noises, prompting one of his men to lean down and threaten to cut his throat if he didn't shut up.

The man quieted down and McDonald heard his men ask a series of yes or no questions to determine if any other personnel had remained in the compound. The man wasn't one hundred percent sure that the building was clear, but he was the only one assigned to the communications center. The sounds of the interrogation were suddenly drowned out by the overpowering chop of the Pave Low helicopter's rotor blades and the intermittent buzz saw bursts of its 7.62mm miniguns. Dirt and loose debris from the open field flew through the front door, filling the hallway and swirling darkness. DEVGRU had arrived.

"Pack him up. We need to clear these rooms!" he yelled.

Less than ninety seconds later, McDonald's team emerged from the front entrance. The first helicopter had already departed, firing long bursts from both of its side mounted miniguns at the remaining terrorists along the front fence line. Stinger two-one sat in the middle of the field with its rear ramp down. SEALs hustled down the ramp and formed up near the buildings flanking the field. The first contingent of SEALs had already disappeared into the compound, presumably headed toward the front fence. Based on the volume of fire directed by the helicopters toward the south, he assumed that most of the remaining enemy personnel were clustered along that fence line. A sudden increase in small arms fire to the south confirmed his suspicion. The SEALs had already reached the front fence line.

Two Air Force Pararescue operators lifted a medical litter holding Chamberlain's inert form, and started through the pelting dirt storm kicked up by the Pave Low's rotor wash. McDonald sprinted over to them.

"What's his status?"

The Pararescue in front turned to him and shook his head. "He's dead. Rounds punched right through his side plates and out the other side. AP rounds. Sorry."

McDonald nodded as they carried his good friend away. *Fuck.*

"Overlord, this is Delta One. Man down classified as KIA," he reported.

"Understood. Delta Two and Three have finished clearing structures on your immediate flanks," Overlord responded.

"Roger. Delta units will secure the northern half of the compound and continue clearing," said McDonald.

"Copy. Six-two will assist."

The second wave of DEVGRU SEALs, known more affectionately to the public as "SEAL Team Six," would join his men and secure the compound behind the first wave of SEALs. He couldn't imagine the fight lasting much longer. The compound militia had their back up against a fence, and nowhere to run if they could find a way over it.

He jogged back to his team and broke the bad news. Nobody said a word. They simply nodded and formed up to continue their mission. He'd assign Delta Two to guard the prisoner and any others they collected. He didn't think it would be a good idea to leave his own team in charge of this scumbag's safety. They showed little reaction to Bobby's death, but he knew what they were thinking; the same thing he was thinking. His team would be much better off clearing structures.

Less than seven minutes later, they had cleared all of the structures not taken down by DEVGRU during their assault on the front part of the compound. Beyond the heavy drone of helicopter rotors in the distance, the valley had fallen silent again, punctuated by the occasional cry for help from the fence line. He hoped the men and women watching this in D.C. didn't ask him to turn around and help the traitorous fucks they just massacred. He wasn't feeling very charitable toward them right now.

Chapter 38

12:56 AM
White House Situation Room
Washington D.C.

Frederick Shelby spoke into his headset and turned to the president a few seats away.

"Mr. President, I just finished speaking with Kathryn Moriarty, my lead agent at the scene. She arrived by vehicle convoy and has been briefed by the advance party. Their initial assessment is not encouraging, sir. One of the buildings cleared by 1st Special Operations Forces Detachment appears to have been dedicated to training groups to conduct pipeline attacks. The floor in the northeast corner of the room has been removed to expose bare dirt and there is evidence that the ground has been disturbed. They found generic pipeline schematics that could be used for training and one set of equipment similar to what we found at the Fort Meade site. The building has its own ramp and loading bay, giving my team the impression that it had been used to store more equipm—"

"How much equipment?" interrupted the president.

"The back room where they found the spare set was large enough to comfortably fit at least twenty-five of these drills. Lockers along the wall hold shovels, a variety of smaller drills and picks, in addition to components to create two additional virus injection devices."

The president looked at his Chief of Staff, Remy Jacob, and then back at the table.

"General Gordon, Commanders, I can't thank you enough for what your people have done tonight. This has been an unprecedented evening. Unfortunately, I need them back at Dover Air Force Base, ready to roll out at a moment's notice. Based on this initial assessment, we might very well need them again."

"Thank you, Mr. President. We'll have our people in the air, en route to Dover within the hour," General Gordon replied, turning to the U.S. Air Force General behind him to ensure the orders were clear.

"General Gordon, I'd like to reach out to the family of the Delta soldier lost tonight. Due to the sensitive nature of this operation, I'm afraid the circumstances of his death will probably never receive the type of public recognition and respect he deserves. Let Jacob know when it is appropriate to arrange a private phone call or meeting with the family."

"Thank you, Mr. President. That will mean a lot to the family," said General Gordon.

"It's the very least I can do for operators like Staff Sergeant Chamberlain. I know that most of their operations and missions never see the light of day. Now if you'll excuse me, I need to coordinate a public response in light of these developments. We'll adjourn to the main conference room."

He stood up and turned to the lead Secret Service Agent. "Agent Souza, will you inform the watch supervisor that I'd like to convene in five minutes?"

"Right away, Mr. President." The agent spoke into the microphone hidden in the left sleeve of his suit coat jacket.

"General Gordon," the president said, "when you're finished here, please join us."

"Yes, sir."

Director Shelby followed the president's entourage out of the small conference room, navigating the surprisingly packed halls past the watch floor to the main conference room. As the group approached the busy room, the president stopped and said something to a member of his security detail, then followed the agent to a door several feet down the hallway. As Shelby tried to walk into the conference room, a different agent addressed him.

"The president would like to speak with you. First door on the right," he said, cordially, betraying no emotion.

"Thank you," said Shelby.

Shelby braced himself for the proverbial kick in the balls. He wasn't sure why, but he couldn't imagine that a sudden, private audience with the

President of the United States on the eve of a national disaster would be a career enhancing moment. He walked toward the door and was met by the Secret Service agent, who invited him into the tiny room and stepped outside once he entered. The door closed behind him.

"Sorry to ambush you like this, Frederick. I wanted to personally thank you for getting us this far. Task Force Scorpion has exceeded all expectations. I would have congratulated you along with General Gordon, but I didn't want him to feel like I was tacking on my condolences to a list of congratulations."

"I appreciate hearing that, Mr. President. I will immediately pass your compliment on to Agent Sharpe."

"If possible, I'd like to address the task force by video conference tomorrow morning. Just a few minutes. I don't want to disrupt their momentum."

"I think we can arrange that. Let me know when you would like to address the troops. Most of them have been working nonstop for seventy-two hours. This will invigorate them. Thank you, sir."

"They're standing at the vanguard. The least I can do is provide a little pep talk and thank them for what they've done so far. Have your agents started to interrogate any of the captured personnel?"

He wondered where this would lead. For a moment he had actually believed that this meeting was a genuine gesture of appreciation from the president.

"Not to sound grim, but my agents are working with Special Forces personnel to triage and stabilize the survivors. They had a few surrenders, but most of the compound's defenders went down fighting. Tier One operators have an uncanny tendency to hit their targets. The airspace is still under military control, so the situation is a bit of a mess. I promise you that this is one of their highest priorities."

"Make it the top priority. I want to know how closely linked this compound is to True America. As for the survivors, I'll make sure General Gordon understands the importance of facilitating the immediate treatment and safe evacuation of the suspects," said the president.

"I understand, sir. I'll call Moriarty and have her interrogation team go to work on anyone capable of speaking. Our best interrogators arrived with her convoy," said Shelby.

"Perfect. From this point forward, report any and all links to True America directly to myself or Jacob Remy. The political ramifications of True America's involvement require special handling. Any premature accusations or links could be interpreted as a political attack. We need to be one hundred and ten percent sure about any links drawn between the ongoing terrorist plot and True America. I want you to compartmentalize the interrogation findings to Moriarty and Sharpe. Sharpe can use the results to shape his investigation, but I want to minimize the number of people with access to the source information. Our case against True America needs to be airtight. If not, True America's pundits will ignite a powder keg of backlash against the administration right before an important election year."

"I'll make sure that safeguards are implemented to compartmentalize this information," he said.

"Thank you, Frederick. This whole situation is a nightmare, with the potential to blow up on more than one front. I'm not looking forward to our next meeting. I've made a decision that will go down in the history books, and make me the least popular person in the United States."

"Mr. President, some of the best decisions turn out to be the most unpopular. You have my support."

"I appreciate that, Frederick, and will not forget it. Unfortunately, the American people have a tendency to focus on the shitty ones. And this is going to go down in the record books. If you would take your seat, I'll be with everyone in a few minutes, after I take an Alka Seltzer."

"That bad?"

"Worse."

Chapter 39

2:12 AM
Lake Wallenpaupack
Pocono Mountains, Pennsylvania

Jackson Greely sat on the spacious deck overlooking the lake and stared at the full moon's reflection on the rippled lake. A light breeze rustled the dark shapes of several massive pine trees flanking the property and swept across the elevated wood structure. He zipped his jacket all the way to the top, closing the flannel lined collar and preventing the chilly wind from stealing a little more of his core body temperature. Temperatures in the Poconos still dipped well into the lower forties in early May. He couldn't sleep thinking about Benjamin Young's abduction. Or was it a rescue? Six more of their operatives were killed, bringing their total losses to just over twenty in less than twenty-four hours, not including the three men sacrificed outside of Fort Meade. Heavy, unanticipated losses, but nowhere close to a showstopper.

He glanced back at the tall bank of windows facing the lake, resentful that Lee could sleep peacefully at such a critical juncture in True America's revolution. Then again, Jackson had done most of the heavy lifting since they started to put the pieces together. Not all of the lifting, but certainly the lion's share. Lee enjoyed the publicity and rarely shied away from the camera or an audience, but he wasn't comfortable making hardcore decisions on his own, or even suggesting them. That was Jackson's role. Lee's role was to support Jackson and keep the rest of their executive group in line. This was in no way an easy task, but it allowed Lee to sleep on the eve of True America's rising.

Greely's cell phone illuminated the table next to him. A phone call at two in the morning could only mean one thing: Trouble. He recognized one of Brown's numbers and answered it immediately.

"Good news, I hope," he said.

"That was fast. Trouble sleeping?" said Brown.

"What do you think?"

"I think you'll be pleased to know that the compound has been hit. Comms are down and some of our local contacts have reported helicopters in the general area," replied Brown.

"Good. Let's just hope that Bishop and his second in command were killed."

"It doesn't matter either way," suggested Brown.

"You're probably right, but I'm starting to get an uneasy feeling. I'd feel much better knowing that our insurance policy was ready to roll."

"It'll be ready. Perfectly timed in my opinion," said Brown.

"I hope so. I'll sleep better knowing that we've removed the last obstacle."

The call ended and he leaned back into the Adirondack chair. Who was he kidding? Once the bottles were delivered, he'd be glued to the television twenty-four hours a day waiting for the results. He'd be glad to lose the sleep.

Chapter 40

7:08 AM
The Jacksons' Residence
Fredericksburg, Virginia

Darryl Jackson leaned his hands against the brown granite kitchen island and stared at the television for a moment before turning to his wife.

"Guess where you're headed today?" she said.

"Princeton."

There was no other choice. He'd let his daughter, Liz, convince him that she'd be fine with the water and food he'd brought on his trip. She'd listened to his exhaustive list of do's and don'ts, taking copious notes. Even Karl Berg had slightly eased his fears, stating that Princeton was an unlikely target based on the information he possessed. Darryl had countered with the fact that Mount Arlington hadn't exactly been a high value target, but Al Qaeda had targeted it nonetheless. Berg told him that Al Qaeda was out of the picture and that the new threat matrix had shifted radically. Strategic targets like Fort Meade were the new focus. When he asked Berg if he would be drinking water from his tap at home tonight, the CIA agent had paused and said, "Nobody should be drinking water from their tap in my opinion, but as long as she follows the rules, she's not in danger." He reminded Karl that everyone drank water down in Virginia too.

The president's address changed everything. Now, Darryl was less worried about the water and infinitely more concerned about a sudden breakdown of order across the country. Princeton was relatively isolated in the grand scheme of things, but it was damn near impossible to travel there without crossing through some of the most heavily urbanized areas of the country. If her school cancelled finals, he might not be able to reach her if the situation deteriorated. Based on what the president just told the entire nation, he expected it to deteriorate.

"...attack against Fort Meade, home of our National Security Agency, had been conducted by a domestic terrorist group with the capacity to strike again in multiple locations. Given the nation's expansive water distribution network, consisting of nearly 880,000 miles of piping, it would be impractical, if not impossible to secure the system against immediate attacks. Effective immediately, I am asking the American people to bear with their local and regional governments until reasonable safeguards are established to ensure that your drinking water is safe.

Many towns and counties may elect to stop the delivery of water, and we are encouraging them to do so. FEMA and Homeland Security experts have assured us that this is the most effective way to prevent intentional contamination of your water. If you must consume water from a tap, it is imperative that you take precautions to sterilize the water. Simple sterilization procedures will kill the virus. Immediately following my broadcast, the Department of Health and Human Services will outline these procedures and other steps you can take to prevent infection in the unlikely event that your water is contaminated.

Rest assured that we have committed the full weight of our federal law enforcement agencies to bringing these heinous terrorists to justice and preventing further attacks. The insidious attack at Fort Meade was perpetrated by a sadistic, fringe group, far separated from the free and democratic society that we enjoy as Americans...and they will be stopped. The next few days may be filled with doubt, but I trust that we will all conduct ourselves as heroes and citizens in the face of this crisis..."

Sure. Everyone would behave charitably and walk calmly down the streets...once they had secured water for themselves and their families. If he couldn't "persuade" his daughter to return home immediately, he would camp out in Princeton and cover her back.

"I'll load up the truck and get moving. Will you be okay here if I need to stay there until she finishes finals?"

"I'll be fine. I bought enough water yesterday to last a month. What should we do about Emily?"

His older daughter was in her third year at U.C. Berkeley and would not finish her final exams until May 15th, nearly two weeks away.

"Karl said that the threat appeared to be isolated to the East Coast."

"Did he give any more specifics?" Cheryl asked with a raised eyebrow.

"No. But he said they had no indications that the threat would spread west," he said, aware of the fact that Berg hadn't exactly given him an airtight case to present to Cheryl.

"That's not what I gathered from the president's address."

"The president can't make sweeping promises in the face of a biological weapons attack and run the risk of being wrong."

"Neither can we. I get the feeling they have no idea what they're up against."

Cheryl had her hands on her hips and that look on her face that would send most men scrambling for cover.

"I'll call in a few favors out west. If I can't get Emily home, I'll fly out myself."

"Thank you, honey. I'm going to load up my Land Rover on the way to work," she said.

"Bring a sheet to cover it up. I have a feeling that bottled water is about to become a valuable commodity."

"Alright. I'm out of here," she said, stepping over to kiss him.

He could hear her phone buzzing in her purse. She had a long day ahead of her as Deputy Superintendent. They'd probably cancel school until Homeland Security could convince them that the water was safe.

"Be careful out there."

"Me? You're the one that can't stay out of trouble. You and Karl Berg."

"He really misses your home cooking," said Darryl.

She looked at him with soft, patient eyes. "You really miss him. Don't you?"

"He's a good friend."

"Well, if he can promise to keep you out of jail, I might be persuaded to extend a dinner invitation. Don't get excited. He'll have to eat the first meal out on the deck."

"I love you. Karl Berg or no Karl Berg," he said, embracing her.

"Good. Because if I so much as sense that he's asked you for another favor, the offer will be rescinded and never reissued." Cheryl broke their contact and backed up a few feet.

"You'll make a great Superintendent one of these days. Tough as nails."

Once his wife left, Darryl descended into the basement to pick out a few items for his trip north. The kind of items that would be illegal to transport through the D.C. metropolitan area without one of the specialized permits he carried. Twenty minutes later, he emerged with a dark blue nylon gym bag filled with his personal insurance policy should law and order cease to exist.

The home phone rang, and he searched for one of their cordless handsets. After several rings, he finally found one of them buried in the couch. He thought the hidden phone phenomena would end when his daughters left for college, but Cheryl had apparently taught them everything they knew about misplacing remote controls and phones. If anything, the problem intensified when they left. He saw from the caller ID that it was the guilty party herself.

"What took you so long? You had me worried for a minute."

"Oh, I don't know. Maybe I had a little trouble finding the phone you had buried between the cushions. What's up?"

"Don't bother stopping for water. The stores are mobbed. I couldn't even get close to Wegmans. I can't imagine Giant will be any better," she said.

"Give it a try. I don't want to take any from the house, if you can't find more," he said.

"You'll need it if you're staying in a hotel. Take what you need. I can boil water from the creek if I have to."

"Alright. Let me get moving here. I'm anticipating a mess trying to get through D.C."

"Business as usual. Drive safe. I love you," she said.

"I love you too. I'll give you a call from the road."

BLACK AND WHITE

Chapter 41

8:13 AM
National Counterterrorism Center
McLean, Virginia

Special Agent Dana O'Reilly disconnected the phone call and removed her headset.

"Well fuck you too, Deputy Dawg," she mumbled.

"What was that?" said Hesterman from his new napping position at their workstation.

"Nothing. Just some uncooperative dickhead."

She had placed a call to Laurel, Maryland's Chief of Police, following up on a hunch. Something about the shootout in the forest didn't make sense to her. She couldn't put her finger on it, but it triggered her need to apply "Occam's Razor" to the situation in an attempt to try and make sense of her inexplicable discomfort with Sergeant Bryan Osborne's report.

"Occam's Razor" was a principle designed to urge one to select the hypothesis or theory that made the fewest assumptions. Though on the surface it favored parsimony and economy, the principle didn't assert that the simplest available theory should be applied. The "razor" wasn't an arbiter between theories. In scientific circles it served as a guide. For O'Reilly, it was an interesting way to approach competing theories, especially at 8:15 in the morning, when the stimulant effect of coffee had ceased to have any impact.

Maybe it wasn't something specific in Osborne's preliminary report that triggered her hunch. Perhaps it was the entire situation that didn't appear to make sense to her. Occam's Razor in reverse. Sergeant Osborne had chosen today of all days to ride with one of his newest police officers. Officer Donahue had taken him on a ride through the winding, gravel roads of a large park east of urban Laurel, which happened to be part of the officer's patrol. Osborne spotted a vehicle parked deep in the woods from an intersection nearly one hundred feet from the dirt turnoff. Officers responding to their call for backup saw Donahue's SUV parked on Combat Road, but had trouble finding the right path at first. Somehow, Osborne had spotted the vehicle from the intersection. Finally, Osborne called in backup, but decided to investigate with a rookie.

He said they stumbled into the group, and the men reached for their rifles, but one of the men had been shot in the back. Backup officers said the generator was running when they arrived, which made it difficult to believe that the two officers had simply stumbled into the group and got the drop on them. There were too many coincidences and discrepancies to take Osborne's report as gospel, which left her wondering. What had really happened out in the North Tract?

She believed that Osborne had heard the drilling equipment, possibly spied the three men, and decided to play Rambo with his partner. Osborne would have realized this error in judgment as soon as his partner fell to the ground sans intact skull. The discrepancies in the forest could be explained by Osborne's need to present a slightly different version of events, one in which he didn't get his partner killed with backup officers a few minutes out. But this still left O'Reilly pondering the rest of the coincidences leading them deep into the forest.

She was working too hard to explain Osborne's actions, which led her back to Occam's Razor. Was there a theory that cleared most of these assumptions and put Osborne in the forest with his partner, on the path to a deadly engagement with domestic terrorists? There was only one. Sergeant Osborne had known they would be there. Just the thought sent a chill down her spine. If true, this theory had far reaching implications that could undermine their current investigative efforts.

The questions spun around her head like a vortex and called into question everything they had uncovered. What else had been staged for them and why? This epiphany had led her to place a call to Laurel's Chief of

Police moments ago, kindly requesting Sergeant Osborne's vacation schedule for the past two years.

The conversation had started kindly enough, but quickly tanked when she disclosed the request. The chief didn't give her an earful as she expected, but very firmly expressed his distaste. She sat there and listened to his speech about loyalty, their code of honor and the difficulty of making daily life and death decisions under pressure. She didn't bother to remind him that she was a sworn law enforcement officer, just like him, and had been shot through the forearm by a .223 caliber bullet making one of these pressured decisions. She was a woman, calling from a desk, muddying the waters. No point in pressing the issue.

She'd bring it up with Sharpe a little later, and see if he could apply a little downward pressure on the Laurel Police Department. It was worth checking. Until she eliminated this theory, Occam's Razor would never be satisfied. Osborne's forest shootout wasn't the only thing bothering her.

"Eric?"

"Yes," Hesterman said, not bothering to open his eyes.

"Anything new on the guys in the compound?"

"Two more died at Scranton Regional, leaving eighteen. Of those eighteen, only six are conscious. Other than that there's not much to report. Only one of the regulars appears to have survived the assault. Jake Skelly. He's the guy they grabbed in the communications room. He hasn't said a word to Carlisle or anyone."

"He checks out clean, right?'

"Yep. Just like the operatives in Brooklyn. Clean record. Current driver's license from Missouri. Nothing in the system. We'll know more about him in a few hours."

"And the rest?"

"This is the interesting part. We've identified sixty-three of the remaining suspects from personal identification located on the bodies or in the barracks buildings. It looks like True America was in the midst of a recruitment drive. I found eleven of them on our own list of "persons of interest to the government." A few others have overt ties to extremist websites and blogs, posting regularly. I imagine we'll find more links once we start issuing warrants and start digging."

This was one of the other big issues bothering her. None of the True America operatives identified by Task Force Scorpion had any recent connections to anti-government websites.

"This group's profile doesn't match up with the operatives killed or captured so far. Something's off here."

"Maybe not. If you took a trip back in time two or three years, this is exactly the kind of group you might find hanging around the compound. If we hadn't hit the compound when we did, this group would have been instructed to cut all extremist ties and devote all of their upcoming vacation time to training sessions in Hacker Valley."

"I don't know. Why would they start training a new cadre of operatives in the middle of a major operation?"

Hesterman finally opened his eyes and rubbed them with the back of his hands. "What are you thinking?" he said, inching his chair over to O'Reilly's.

"I can't put my finger on it, but I'm starting to see too many inconsistencies and one too many lapses in our investigation."

"Here?" he said, staring around the watch floor.

"Even here. The Imam's snatched right out from under us, never to be seen again. True America operatives carried away into the night less than a block from a major FBI crime scene. Anonymous phone calls leading us right to the Al Qaeda cells. I'm getting the impression that Sharpe's holding something back. I have no idea what it might be, but I'm willing to bet it has something to do with Stewart. She seems awfully content watching over us from her perch. Don't look up at her."

Hesterman stopped his head from turning all the way.

"She just stands up there, doing nothing."

"That's exactly what Sharpe wants her to do around here. Nothing."

"I wonder, though…"

"What is that supposed to mean?" asked Hesterman.

"I don't know. I'm going to talk to Sharpe about my call to the Laurel police chief. I just asked the chief to provide me with Sergeant Osborne's vacation record for the past two years and he flatly denied the reque—"

"You did *what*?" Hesterman said, incredulously.

"Yeah. Nothing about Osborne's statement makes much sense to me. Maybe I'm losing it. Either way, if Sharpe ignores this, it's time to start watching over your back."

"Do you need back up in there?"

"Nope. I'll be fine." She watched Special Agent Mendoza approach Sharpe's door with two cups of coffee. Perfect. She could play them off each other.

O'Reilly stood up from her computer station and prepared what she would say.

❧

Sharpe had taken his second sip of coffee when O'Reilly appeared in his doorway and knocked on the frame, announcing her obvious presence.

"Come on in, Dana. You want to grab a coffee first?"

"No thanks. The coffee doesn't seem to have any effect on me anymore, beyond sending me to the bathroom every thirty minutes," she said.

"Then grab a seat. Your visit is perfect timing, since Frank was about to fill me in on the recent developments from Hacker Valley."

Frank Mendoza slouched in one of the faux leather chairs under a standing lamp, holding his coffee in two hands in what looked like an effort to keep it warm. The coffee cups stocked in the break room weren't insulated and didn't include tops. All of the equipment installed in the Operations Center was state of the art, with the exception of the coffee machine. Even the complimentary juice machine had a touch screen, allowing the selection of several dozen beverages, including carbonated choices. The coffee maker was a stainless steel, two-pot Bunn classic, taking up twice the amount of space necessary and brewing up the same coffee served to government employees for the past four decades. Amazingly enough, the machine looked new.

"I wish there was more to report, but Dana's team will start making calls to businesses and households shortly. We'll send teams out for interviews. How many were identified? Sixty three? It's a lot of legwork. Nobody likes to talk over the phone to a faceless FBI agent. This takes the highest priority, and we'll have help from other agencies, so we're expecting to start collecting detailed information by noon. More pieces to fit into the puzzle. I'm hoping we'll start seeing a useful pattern here shortly. We have a lot of information," said Mendoza.

"I agree, though I'm a little disturbed by the pattern developing at the compound. That, coupled with something else," she said nervously.

"What is it?" said Sharpe.

"It doesn't fit. Does it?" said Mendoza.

O'Reilly looked at him surprised. "No, none of it does."

"What are the two of you talking about?" said Sharpe.

"We've identified sixty-three of the suspects at the compound. Too many of them have overt ties to extremist groups. Eleven of them showed up on the lists you ordered us to start compiling over a year ago. None of the operatives that we've captured recently held recent ties to any domestic extremist groups. They'd all gone quiet on that front three to four years ago."

"A new batch of trainees?"

"On the eve of their magnum opus?" she retorted.

"It struck me as odd too. I was waiting to hear more about their backgrounds," said Mendoza.

"What are you suggesting?" Sharpe asked.

"I'm not sure, but I've also found some inconsistencies with Sergeant Osborne's report. I called the Laurel police chief to ask about Osborne's vacation schedule for the past two years, but he—"

"Dana, would you close the door please?"

O'Reilly looked annoyed by his request and sudden interruption.

"Of course," she said, pulling the door free of its magnetic hold.

"You called the Laurel police chief, implying that Osborne might be involved in today's incident?" asked Sharpe, before she could continue.

"Yes. I didn't think it would be a big deal. Of course, he wouldn't share the information. Maybe it wasn't the best decision on my part."

"I trust your judgment, Dana. I could have told you there was no way he would release the information, especially without a warrant."

Sharpe knew there was no way he could keep them in the dark any longer. He detected a confrontational edge to O'Reilly's mannerisms, which was out of character for her. Something was bothering her, and his guess was that she had finally started to put all of the pieces together. There were too many unexplained coincidences and logical leaps to go unnoticed by either of them for long. He regretted not bringing them into the fold earlier. No matter what he told them now, they'd feel betrayed, possibly not trusted. If he didn't do it now, it would only be worse when they came to the inevitable conclusion on their own.

"Hold up for a minute. We need to bring someone else in on this conversation," he said.

O'Reilly took the remaining empty leather chair and raised her eyebrows at Mendoza. He merely lifted his shoulders from his relaxed position in the other chair. Sharpe sent a text message and waited for the knock at his door.

"Dana, Frank, I need you to know that this has nothing to do with the utmost level of trust and confidence that I have in both of you. I was simply trying to mitigate the potential damage to your careers."

He paused, avoiding their eyes for a moment, until someone knocked on the door and entered without waiting for Sharpe's permission to enter. Callie Stewart closed the door behind her and turned to Mendoza and O'Reilly. She looked as confused as his agents.

"What the fuck is she doing here?" said O'Reilly.

Sharpe watched the look of bewilderment harden into a look of betrayal. He had no idea how he was going to proceed, so he jumped right in.

"I've been cooperating with Sanderson's people without your knowledge since the morning of the 26th. Sanderson's operatives have been critical to moving our investigation along, in ways that we could never implement without their help."

"Jesus Christ," uttered Mendoza.

"I thought I could insulate the two of you, but I was just deluding myself. There are some developments that support your theory, Dana, and require the highest levels of secrecy within the task force. I trust the two of you implicitly."

"It doesn't feel like it," said O'Reilly.

Stewart started to talk, but Sharpe cut her off with a severe look and an outstretched hand sporting his index finger.

"I understand that, and I'm sorry beyond words for keeping you in the dark. I really thought I would be doing you a favor. I made this decision to protect you. The backlash for working with Sanderson outside of the agreed upon parameters would be devastating. You know how the director feels about them," he said.

"Like I do?" said O'Reilly, glaring at Stewart.

"We've worked together for over four years, Dana. I should have known better."

"That's the first thing you've said so far that makes sense," O'Reilly said.

"Frank, you're being awfully quiet. I'm really sorry," said Sharpe.

"For what? Trying to protect us? I can't hold that against you. I just wish you had brought me onboard earlier. What about you, O'Reilly?" "I don't trust Sanderson, or his people, so it probably wouldn't hurt to have a few people looking over your shoulder, making sure you're not being manipulated. Other than that, just some hurt feelings, but I'll get over it…as long as I'm not required to be nice to Ms. Stewart."

"I don't expect anyone to be nice to Ms. Stewart. As a matter of fact, I expect you to continue hating her. Just keep in mind that I see us on the same team. I'd like to spend some time catching you up on a few things," said Sharpe.

"May I say something?" asked Stewart.

"No. Unless you have something to pass on to me that's new," said Sharpe.

"It can wait."

"Thank you, guys. Seriously, I can't express my relief. I'll make this up to you later. I promise."

"You owe us big time. So, why did you have me close the door when I mentioned my call to the police chief?"

"Long story made short—the missing driver of the SUV in Brooklyn ended up in Sanderson's custody. His name is Miguel Estrada, and he led a sizeable contingent of True America tactical operatives. Most of them were killed in the Brooklyn raid. He was also present at Mount Arlington to confirm that Al Qaeda hit the target and call it in to the police."

"The phone they found in the SUV was Estrada's," said O'Reilly.

"Exactly. Estrada screwed up with that phone. It gave us the compound and his link to Mount Arlington. Apparently, Estrada was a key field commander, but not part of the inner circle. He received instructions, with little explanation. He'd helped arrange the Al Qaeda takedown with a man named Brown and a woman that he couldn't identify. Brown might be an alias, since I couldn't match a Brown with the description he gave us. Jamaican born, U.S. citizen with Army Special Forces experience."

"What happened to Estrada?" asked Mendoza.

"I don't know, and I don't want to know. All I care about is receiving accurate information from Sanderson's conduits. I think we can all agree that the stakes are too high to dismiss the help he can provide outside of our rather restricted channels."

"I wouldn't be standing here if I didn't agree," said Mendoza.

"Same here," added O'Reilly.

"Estrada's next mission was to take a team down to Atlanta and dispose of a man named Benjamin Young. Sanderson's team intercepted the assassination team and took Mr. Young into protective custody."

"I knew there was a connection," said O'Reilly.

"A big connection. Young did the majority of True America's lobbying throughout corporate America and the elite political circuit. He raised millions of dollars for their political action group, scraping off a sizable portion for himself and Jackson Greely's militant cronies. He wasn't pleased with their ultimate reward for his lucrative services. He gave them everything in exchange for a secure place to hide his family until Greely is stopped. He's soon to join Sanderson in Argentina."

"That's about as secure as it gets," said Mendoza.

"And the sergeant in Maryland?" asked O'Reilly.

"We don't have detailed information about the sergeant, but Young relayed a comment made by Greely. Young was concerned about FBI surveillance at one point, but was told specifically that he had nothing to worry about. When Young pushed the issue, Greely said they had people in the right places."

"He could have been bullshitting Young. Trying to keep him calm. Playing him until the last possible moment," said Mendoza.

"I doubt it. Given Greely's paranoia, I think he would have severed ties with Young, or killed him sooner, if he had any doubts about the FBI," said Sharpe.

"Do you have any reason to suspect that the task force is compromised?" asked O'Reilly.

"I have no reason to assume it isn't, which is why none of this information extends beyond the four of us. From this point forward, Ms. Stewart will not be seen talking in private to any of us. If someone is watching, this meeting will look suspicious enough. Continued meetings will raise an alarm. Stewart can relay the information to me, and I'll meet with the two of you. We obviously can't make any major course corrections to our investigation, but we've been creative with planting clues here and there," said Sharpe.

"Where do we go from here?" asked O'Reilly.

"We keep piecing together the puzzle with all of the evidence we have. We've gained solid ground here, and I have no intention of kneecapping the task force. With the information we've collected and the personnel captured, I fully expect the task force to produce results that Sanderson's people can't replicate in the field. Putting the two sources together will give us the best chance of shutting down this conspiracy before it's too late."

"What if it's already too late?" asked Mendoza.

"It's a possibility, but if O'Reilly's hunches hold merit, then the attack on Fort Meade was a feint, and the compound loaded with armed rednecks was staged. I hope you're right, Dana. The thought of the forty-nine remaining canisters of this virus being dumped into various municipal water supplies is devastating. But if they're not using the virus to poison the water, what on earth are they planning? Something worse. At least your theory buys us more time. Let's hope you're right."

"Sorry, Ms. Stewart. You had something to say earlier?" said Sharpe.

"Save the 'we're all in this together' speech for the rookies," said O'Reilly.

"That wasn't my plan. I just received some interesting information that has a direct bearing on the case. Our people just cracked Young's proprietary database wide open. We have access to detailed information about his clients,"

"I thought he was cooperating?" said O'Reilly, her anger and outburst forgotten.

"He is, but Young couldn't remotely access deeper tier information. You have to be inside the building at a terminal to do this. We have some cyber security specialists that were able to hijack the system using his outer layer access. We can now see who has received all of the money Young has funneled to Greely. One of the names raises a disturbing possibility. Combined with O'Reilly's suspicions, I'd say it was extremely disturbing. Are any of you familiar with the name, Owen Mills?"

Sharpe had never heard the name, and given the non-reaction from his colleagues, neither had they.

"Doesn't surprise me. I'd never heard the name before either. Mills is the CEO of Crystal Source water, based out of Honesdale, Pennsylvania. They draw their water from the Poconos. Crystal Source is one of the biggest bottled water distributors in Pennsylvania, northern New Jersey and mid-state New York, servicing businesses, homes and of course, selling their bottles of water nationwide. Anyway, accounts owned by or associated with Mills have received nearly thirteen million dollars over the past three years. A Honesdale based construction company was the recipient of a one-time payment of nearly five million dollars. Young said he diverted this money from contributions earmarked for True America's political action group."

"How much money is going to this political action group?" said Sharpe.

"From private donors? It's almost impossible to say. At least it was impossible until about an hour ago. Based on the amount he was sifting, I'd say True America pulls in a ton of money," said Stewart.

Sharpe gave this new information a quick turn through his hazy, sleep-deprived brain and formed a possible conclusion. He wanted to hear what everyone else thought about this revelation. Clearly, Stewart had a specific reason for bringing up Mills. Other accounts related to Jackson Greely or Lee Harding had to be involved.

"I'd like to hear everyone's thoughts," said Sharpe.

"Is it fair to assume that other payments went to Greely or Harding?"

"Yes, but not in the thirteen million dollar ballpark. I think it's fair to assume that Mills is a major player in True America's militant arm. Why would they send him so much money?" said Stewart.

"Maybe he's providing them with a safe haven somewhere in the Poconos. The compound in Hacker Valley smells fishy to me," said O'Reilly.

"That's a possibility. Mills owns an incredible amount of property in the Poconos," said Stewart.

"Could this be a massive stunt to drive up the price of bottled water? Is that an insane theory?" said Mendoza.

Sharpe leaned back in his seat and took in the silence that Mendoza's questions had created. Jesus. Could this whole thing be about money? It suddenly made sense to him. True America used Al Qaeda to get their hands on the Zulu Virus. They'd probably funded the entire operation from start to finish, including the use of Reznikov to create the virus. Estrada watched Al Qaeda approach the Mount Arlington pump station and placed calls to the police and local media. He ensured that the attack couldn't escape widespread attention. True America had taken extreme measures to erase any ties to Al Qaeda or illicit funding. They sent a team to attack Fort Meade, which was conveniently thwarted in a tragic shootout that was no doubt reported to the media the second it happened. Finally, the compound was filled with high profile anti-government radicals and staged to give the impression that twenty-five additional drill teams were on the loose. All of this was designed to force the government into taking drastic steps to secure the nation's municipal water supply. Steps that would skyrocket the demand for bottled water. Was it really that simple?

"It's not insane, if you think in terms of the conspiracy O'Reilly suggested," said Sharpe.

Stewart shook her head.

"I still think they're going to use the virus somehow," she stated.

"I'd like to pursue every possibility, but I barely have enough people on the task force to process the leads and evidence produced by the compound. I doubt Director Shelby would be willing to drastically expand my resources based on a string of evidence illegally obtained by a tier of operatives kept secret from him," said Sharpe.

"Sanderson would like to send the Atlanta team north to the Honesdale area. While they're traveling, our cyber people could do some digging into the Scranton based construction company. Ground assets can take the investigation to the next level upon arrival," said Stewart.

"What exactly does that mean?" O'Reilly asked.

Stewart looked to Sharpe for guidance.

"Exactly what it sounds like. The gloves are off. I'm giving both of you one last chance to back out of this," replied Sharpe.

"I'm in," said Mendoza without hesitation.

"I'm good," O'Reilly stated.

"Alright. Let's send Sanderson's team up to Pennsylvania. How big of a team are we dealing with, Callie?"

"Four, plus a mobile electronic support team. I can have that electronic support team in place within a few hours. We're probably looking at getting the core team in place within six to eight," replied Stewart.

"Let's do it. Business as usual here, unless the team in Pennsylvania uncovers something that changes the game. If that happens, I'll figure out a way to shift assets in that direction. Until then, we process what we have. Good?"

Everyone nodded and Stewart started for the door. Mendoza and O'Reilly moved sluggishly, leaving him with the impression that they wanted to talk in private without including Stewart.

"Ms. Stewart, keep me apprised. I'll be out on the floor in a few minutes."

She took the hint and swiftly departed, closing the door.

"Are you sure you can trust her?" asked O'Reilly.

"No. But Sanderson hasn't given me any reason to doubt his intentions. Have you seen the preliminary law enforcement bulletin regarding the Ritz Carlton attack? I suspected a connection there too. Six gunmen dead, two of them killed execution style in a suite on the top floor. The hallway outside of the suite looks like a war zone. Sanderson's people took one hell of a risk extracting Young from that hotel."

"I don't trust them," O'Reilly said, "and it's not because I'm still pissed about not being able to fully extend the middle finger on my right hand."

Sharpe was fully aware of the damage caused by the .223 bullet that shattered O'Reilly's forearm and tore sinew and ligament on its strange path up her arm toward her hand. She hadn't let it go, nor should she. Even Mendoza didn't dare make light of the fact that he missed seeing that middle finger colorfully deployed on a daily basis.

"Sanderson's plot two years ago was diabolical in every way," she said. "Meticulously planned and brutal. I don't know how he suddenly turned into a semi-legitimate arm of the U.S. government. I have the feeling that it was his plan all along. A manipulation of the highest order."

"You'd be correct in that assumption," said Sharpe, not intending to give further details about the failed attack on his compound in Argentina.

"All I'm saying is to be careful."

"Thank you, Dana. I'm doing what I can. I need you guys to keep an eye on the situation. If you see something spiraling out of control, or you suspect that we're being played, I need to know ASAP. And don't send me anything over the network. Do it in person," said Sharpe.

"Do you think Sanderson has hacked the system? I've checked for signs, but if their people are as good as it sounds, only a system reboot will kick them out."

"No need for that…yet. Plus, this would be a bad time to shut down the system. Just assume that anything you put into the system or say over the phone can be overheard."

"What about our cell phones? Computer microphones? All of that could be used to eavesdrop," Mendoza reminded them.

"We'll get creative if that becomes necessary. Time to break up this little mutiny. We might have other eyes watching us," said Sharpe.

"Fuck. This is ridiculous. We're not even secure at NCTC?" Mendoza griped.

Sharpe shrugged his shoulders. "Business as usual, people. Business as usual. Any last requests before we break this up?"

"Can you call Laurel's police chief and get Osborne's vacation records?" said O'Reilly.

"Maybe we should take a less conspicuous approach. I'll see if Stewart's techies can dig that up through their network. No point in drawing more attention," said Sharpe.

"Business as usual, my ass. Watch your back, sir," said O'Reilly.

"I'm trusting the two of you to take care of that."

Chapter 42

9:25 AM
Laurel Police Department
Laurel, Maryland

Sergeant Bryan Osborne sat in his Honda Accord and stared out at a row of white police cruisers. He still hadn't recovered from the adrenaline high that nearly caused him to break out into a full sweat in front of his chief. Chief Wilson caught him minutes before he planned to step into the parking lot and pulled Osborne into his office. He'd finally been cleared to take paid administrative leave, pending a review of the circumstances surrounding the shooting in the North Tract, and had been making the rounds through the station. He thought Wilson had a few more words of wisdom and encouragement. The ensuing conversation had caused his vision to shrink momentarily.

Chief Wilson told him about an FBI inquiry into his vacation schedule. The agent, a snippy female from somewhere in D.C., didn't explain her reasons for the request. Wilson figured that the FBI didn't appreciate the fact that basic police fieldwork had managed to upstage them, and they were looking for any reason to knock the department down a few notches. He had no idea how Osborne's vacation schedule played into their little game, and he had no intention of providing the FBI with any information about his police officers. They didn't deserve this kind of political maneuvering less than one day after an officer had been killed in the line of duty three feet away from Osborne. He said he might consider filing a complaint with the FBI if the agent called again.

He then proceeded to tell Osborne to keep his nose clean while on administrative leave. What the fuck was that supposed to mean? He didn't really care. He was glad to get out of the station without vomiting. How the hell did the FBI sniff out his trail so quickly? Maybe it was nothing. Standard procedure in a federal case? He didn't like it either way. He'd spent three out of his last five vacation periods at the compound in West Virginia. There was no way they could know that, but it still unnerved him. It was too much of a coincidence. He'd have to buy one of those prepaid phones and report this to Brown. He started his car and drove slowly out of the parking lot onto 5th Street, heading southeast to the Best Buy on Baltimore Avenue.

Chapter 43

9:52 AM
Lake Wallenpaupack
Poconos Mountains, Pennsylvania

A single loon cut through the glassy water just off the small dock extending from the property's rocky shoreline. Lee Harding sat at the end of the floating dock in an Adirondack chair, holding one of the sporting rods they had found in the immense post and beam rental house. Jackson Greely followed the gravel path to a point where a small wooden ramp met the rocks. When he stepped on the dock, the loon suddenly took flight, skipping along the water until it had gained enough speed to achieve flight. Harding turned his head and nodded a greeting.

Jackson took the empty chair and set his coffee down on the chair's wide arm.

"I just heard from Brown. Sergeant Osborne's chief took a call from an FBI agent asking questions about his vacation schedule. Apparently the chief told them to piss off," said Jackson.

Lee muttered an obscenity and met Jackson's stare.

"That was fast. I assume you accelerated the timeline of our insurance policy?"

"We cash in on the premium tonight. That should buy us more than enough time to get the convoys on the road. Once the convoys depart, they can connect all of the dots and it won't matter," said Jackson.

"Tell Brown to get rid of Osborne. The FBI isn't likely to accept the chief's response. They'll obtain the records. It's fair to assume that the feds have connected the operatives captured or killed by their employer's vacation schedules. I wonder what else they're working on?" said Harding.

"It won't matter after tonight. They'll be in the middle of redeploying the entire task force based on what they found at the compound, when all hell breaks loose. Confusion will reign supreme for days."

Lee nodded in approval.

"And the lab?"

Jackson was starting to get a little annoyed by Harding's barrage of questions. He didn't even have his cell phone handy...which wasn't a shocker given that he only fielded calls from Jackson. King Harding sat on his throne and accepted reports from his subordinates. He shouldn't think like this. The two of them had been friends for a long time, and Harding's aloofness wasn't a new development. He'd always been a "hands off" leader. Jackson was the direct opposite, with a leadership style that bordered on micromanagement. He'd long ago learned to identify competent and trustworthy people to help him compensate for this intensive, "hands on" approach. Brown was one of those people. Anne Renee was another. Maybe Lee's easy affect was due to the fact that Jackson took care of everything. He'd never been forced to adapt his style.

"Carnes is bitching up a storm, but he's pretty sure we can get the bottling wrapped up tomorrow morning if they work through the night. Shipments will leave late tomorrow afternoon if all goes well," he said.

"I can't believe we're this close. One week from now, things will start to change. The stage will be set for the New Recovery," said Lee.

"We still have a long way to go, and most of it will be out of our direct control," Jackson corrected.

"True, but the time has never been riper. The mortgage crisis is in full swing. Mortgage backed securities. Credit default swaps. Collateralized debt obligations. The big banking collapse is flying just below everyone's radar. The nation needs new leadership to weather this manmade crisis. True America will step in to fill the void."

"We just need to get the convoys on the road," said Jackson.

They both stared out at the tranquil lake, still unspoiled by summer boaters.

"Has Young resurfaced?" asked Lee.

"No. I don't expect he will."

"Let's hope the FBI doesn't have him. He's enough of a weasel to roll on us."

"I'd be relieved if the FBI had him," said Jackson, causing Lee's head to snap up.

"What do you mean?"

"The team that aided his escape in Atlanta was outsourced. Highly skilled and untraceable. I'm hoping Mr. Young hired them. If not, we could have a big problem," said Jackson.

Chapter 44

10:15 AM
The Westin Princeton
Princeton, New Jersey

"No way, and that's final," said Darryl Jackson.

He started pacing back and forth in front of the two double beds in his hotel room. There was no way he would drive back down to Fredericksburg and do what Berg had asked. The streets were jammed with cars, all with the same goal in mind—to find bottled water. Traffic along the Beltway alone would add two to three hours to his trip.

"Are you telling me that the CIA doesn't have access to a stockpile of weapons at The Farm? That's a two hour drive for you."

"Not with this traffic, and I can't raid whatever armory you believe exists over there," said Berg.

"But it's alright for me to drive six hours or more through traffic to grab shit out of the Brown River armory? Not to mention the fact that Cheryl will divorce me if I abandon Liz," said Jackson.

"Liz will be fine. We're starting to think that the Fort Meade attack might have been a complicated ruse," said Berg.

"For what? A bigger attack? It doesn't sound like you know much of anything at this point."

"All I know is that we're sending outside assets up to Pennsylvania, well outside of any legal boundaries. If these suspicions are correct, this team will need specialized weapons and equipment. I'm cutting them forged FBI badges as we speak. Don't worry, if the shit hits the fan, I have your back," said Berg.

"Pennsylvania doesn't have any waiting period for rifle purchases. You can pick up some sweet equipment on the spot."

"Oh. I wasn't aware that you could buy suppressed weapons over the counter in Pennsylvania now, or fourth generation night vision rifle scopes. They overlook federal licensing for automatic weapons too?"

"This isn't fair, Karl. I can't leave Liz unattended. Cheryl will never forgive me if something happens," said Jackson.

"Princeton is a safe town. Well insulated. You'll be back in Princeton by tonight," said Berg.

"I'll be lucky to reach Fredericksburg by six this evening, and it will probably take me a few more hours to pull off the gun heist and—"

"Nobody's stealing. You're authorized to draw weapons from that armory," interrupted Berg.

"I'll be sure to tell that to the board of directors, after your people throw them into a river to cover their tracks."

"The team didn't have a choice in Kazakhstan. You know that," said Berg.

"Uh huh. So, I steal roughly thirty thousand dollars' worth of gear and get back in my truck for the seven-hour drive to Scranton. Thirteen hours in a car, transporting stolen assault weapons across at least three state lines. By myself."

"We're sending a jet to meet you in Fredericksburg. It's a company jet," said Berg.

"You can swing a Lear jet at the last second, but a few assault rifles are beyond your reach?" said Jackson.

"We don't keep that kind of firepower stateside. Seriously."

"How the fuck am I going to check out a dozen weapons?" he snapped, suddenly raising his voice. "I'm still getting bent over my desk for the Kazakhstan mess. You know what? I'm going to change your name on my phone. Every time you call me, the screen will read 'BOHICA.'"

There was silence until Berg spoke.

"BOHICA? Enlighten me."

"Bend Over Here It Comes Again," said Jackson.

"Very funny. So you'll do it?"

"Yes. I'll do it. But there better be drink service on that airplane."

"I'll make sure they have something you'll like. And a nice bottle for Cheryl," said Berg.

"Don't even go there. If she finds out about this, we're both screwed."

Chapter 45

11:42 AM
Columbia Metropolitan Airport
Columbia, South Carolina

Daniel followed the signs for Hertz and turned the minivan into the designated parking lot across from the terminal. He found a parking space marked for Hertz returns and stepped out of the vehicle. They had no bags at this point. Everything had been stashed in a dumpster outside of the Ramada in Lexington immediately prior to their departure for the airport, including Benjamin Young's computers and disassembled phone. Sanderson's cyber techs had taken everything they needed from his equipment.

Young had been surprisingly cooperative throughout the evening, due to a combination of outrage and fear; he was both indignant over True America's betrayal and intimidated by Jessica's presence. He eagerly rolled over on his former clients and provided a wealth of information and connections. Young's "soft" interrogation lasted until three in the morning, when Daniel finally zip tied Young to the bed and turned him over to Munoz and Melendez. Jessica and Daniel retired to a separate, adjoining room and collapsed. The two of them had spent the morning at the Columbia Center Mall, buying casual clothes for everyone, while Munoz made everyone's travel arrangements.

Young was headed to Dallas to meet his family and fly to Buenos Aires. He'd spend an indefinite amount of time at Sanderson's training compound, safe from True America's reaches and immediately available for questions. His family had left their house in Buckhead before police arrived and travelled to the Hartsfield-Jackson Airport, where they boarded a late night flight to Tampa, Florida. The flight continued to Dallas at 6:25 in the morning. They would be waiting in the airport when he arrived.

The rest of them would catch the 2:25 PM flight to the Wilkes Barre/Scranton Airport in Pennsylvania. Both Daniel and Jessica had been too tired to argue with Sanderson when he called to present his case for their continued participation in the mission. On a deeper level, neither of them wanted to argue. They had already accepted the fact that Sanderson was still their most loyal and potent ally. They would see this mission through to the end and leave him on good terms. Solid terms. When Daniel spoke into the phone, repeating Sanderson's request, Jessica simply nodded her approval.

He opened the door and helped Young out of the van. Daniel had spent a few thousand dollars at Banana Republic to outfit everyone, including Jessica, in some variation of khaki slacks with an untucked shirt. This suited Young just fine, though he complained about wearing the same shoes from the previous night. Only Jessica received new shoes, since she was still barefoot from last night. Her feet had taken a beating on the streets of Atlanta.

"This is where we say goodbye. I'm sure you'll miss us," said Daniel.

"That's an understatement," said Young.

"Make sure to follow directions precisely in Buenos Aires. Alright? They'll make sure nobody followed you off the plane and remove any irregular local law enforcement attention. Follow the script and they'll reach out to you when the time is right. Do everything they say. You will not be allowed to see the final route to the compound, so be prepared to have a bag placed over your head, or something to that effect. Kids too."

"Jesus. Come on. This sounds crazy," said Young.

"You want to head back to Atlanta?" said Jessica.

Young shook his head.

"Follow the script. You'll like it out there. Plenty of hiking, fishing, clean air. Lots of family time," said Daniel.

"No cocaine, though," added Jessica.

Young looked at Daniel. "She's a real treat."

"You'll be staying in our place, which will afford you some luxury out there."

"The two of you are married? I knew it. I feel sorry for you, man. Holy shit."

Daniel cocked his head slightly, which changed Young's expression instantly. He went from cocky to scared shitless in the blink of an eye.

"She's pretty nice to be around, unless you're an arrogant cokehead that spends more time with hookers than your own wife and kids. Be careful what you say in Argentina. My wife is a legend around that compound."

Young stared at him for a second and quickly averted eye contact like a submissive dog.

"Take out as much cash as possible in Dallas, and use the cash to purchase as many prepaid credit cards as possible. Keep a few hundred on you for transportation. Do this right before your flight. Use these cards once you arrive in Buenos Aires. You won't need money at the compound. Now get out of here. Your flight leaves in forty-five minutes. I don't want see you again."

Stumbling with haste, Young nearly fell over, barely regaining his balance in time to turn and walk briskly toward the walkway leading into the terminal.

"You're welcome, fuckhead!" said Daniel.

Young turned nervously and started to open his mouth, but thought better of it. He scurried across the parking lot. Once he disappeared into the terminal, Daniel turned to the rest of his crew. They were still reclined in their seats, trying to gain any rest possible before the flight.

"Now what?" asked Melendez.

"We eat something and try to catch some sleep in the terminal. Sounds like we have another long night ahead of us."

"Like last night?" said Jessica.

"We don't know yet. Fayed should know more when we arrive."

Tariq Paracha and Aleem Fayed had already left for Pennsylvania with one of Sanderson's "electronic warfare teams." The general loved to pick dramatic sounding names. He supposed it was better than "cyber geeks." Fayed and Paracha would pick them up in Scranton and take them to Honesdale, where Sanderson had arranged a secluded rental on a nearby pond. They had a shipment of equipment arriving at the airport later in the evening, which would require their attention, along with some late night planning based on Sanderson's intelligence. For all Daniel knew, they might go right into action against True America tonight.

"Let's give Young a few minutes to get through check-in. I can't stand to look at him. Thanks for the compliment. I didn't know I was held in such high regard," said Jessica.

"I would have punched him in the nose again, but that would have been counterproductive. He'll be lucky if it doesn't start bleeding again on its own during the flight," said Daniel.

"I would have loved to see that punk take another smack," said Melendez.

"We all would. Do you think he'll make it?" said Munoz.

"I don't know. He seemed genuinely worried about his family, so I give him good odds. This could be a cathartic experience for Mr. Young," said Daniel.

"But instead of Dr. Phil, he gets to experience Dr. Sanderson," said Jessica.

"Sounds like a reality TV show in the making," said Melendez.

Chapter 46

2:53 PM
Loring Terrace Apartments, Apt 2A
District Heights, Maryland

Reggie Taylor struggled violently for a few seconds and settled. There was little use. Any time he tried to stand, at least two pairs of hands held him down and another punched him in the stomach. They'd barely said a word to him since throwing a bag over his head and pulling him into the van. It happened so fast, he barely resisted at first.

He'd been walking down Loring Drive, trying to convince the Popcorn Shrimp Combo from Long John Silver's to stay down. He'd overdone lunch again, which hadn't come as a surprise. His new work schedule at the National Counterterrorism Center had wreaked havoc on his sleep and corresponding appetite. He normally worked the 4:00 PM to midnight shift, which was bad enough, but recent events had increased staffing requirements, splitting the security section into two twelve-hour shifts. He'd spent the past three days working 8:00 PM to 8:00 AM, which had been miserable. He'd take the bus home, eat some cereal and pass out, only to wake up starving a few hours later. It was hard to break those natural biorhythms.

He never heard the van pull up. Traffic was common on this street and the school buses were due to arrive at the Loring Terrace complex soon. Hundreds of kids would be dropped off at various points around the vast network of three-story buildings, transforming the well-manicured area into a busy neighborhood. District Heights didn't have the best reputation as a D.C. area neighborhood, but he had never felt threatened walking around during the day. Some of the areas were fairly sketchy at night, but the Metro bus dropped him off at the entrance to his apartment complex. Loring Terrace was peaceful and quiet after midnight.

Getting jacked in broad daylight had never crossed his mind, which was why he didn't offer much resistance until his face had been pressed into the metal floor of the van. Suddenly realizing that this was far more serious than a mugging, he went haywire for a few seconds, which earned him a brief but severe beating. He'd calmed down long enough for them to tie his hands and duct tape his mouth, before rampaging to little avail. He struggled again, until one of his captors slipped a garrote around his neck and pulled tight for a few seconds. He got the message.

They drove for a few minutes and stopped the van, pulling him onto the pavement somewhere nearby. With the garrote around his throat, they quickly guided him through a door and up a set of stairs. He recognized the smell through the thick bag over his head. Musty wood paneling. His suspicions were confirmed when they walked him down a hallway and pushed him through another doorway. The faint scent of his wife's perfume penetrated the bag, followed by all of the familiar smells of his home. That's when he lost it. They had brought him back to his apartment, less than twenty minutes before his kids were due to arrive. He had to get out of here to warn them. He had to do something. He tried, but it had been useless. Even with the garrote removed, he couldn't build up any momentum to stand. Instead, he wobbled on both knees in the middle of his living room, thinking of a different strategy. Someone yanked the hood from his head, and he stared in disbelief. He had been jacked by two white guys, a Mexican woman and a Jamaican. What the fuck?

"Mr. Taylor, this brings me no pleasure, but I need to show you something," said the Jamaican.

He pointed at an open laptop computer on the coffee table and nodded at the woman. Fuck, they weren't wearing masks. They planned to kill him. The Hispanic woman pressed a few buttons, and a digital feed started playing. His heart sank. They had his wife and two children. How was that even possible? He watched and listened in horror as someone placed a mean looking, stainless steel knife against each of their throats as they whimpered. Rage welled up within him momentarily, replaced quickly by a sense of hopelessness. Who were these people? He mumbled "what do you want" through the duct tape. The Jamaican said "enough," and the woman stopped the recording.

"Your family is fine at the moment. We contacted the kids' schools and your wife at work about two hours ago. You'd been hit by a car, and they needed to come immediately. We even sent an unmarked police car to round them up. Sometimes I shudder to think how easy it is to take an entire family off the streets without raising an eyebrow. We need you to do something for us. It's a very simple task. We'll release your family upon completion of the task. I promise you that. If you refuse…we'll tell you where to find their remains. You'll probably be late for your next shift. Can I trust you not to scream if I remove the duct tape?"

He nodded. Screaming hadn't crossed his mind. He'd follow their rules and pray to God that they were telling the truth about not hurting his babies. He couldn't imagine what it must be like for his wife, Danni. She was in the same room with the kids. For Reggie, it was real enough seeing the digital file, but she could probably feel their breath in the dark, scared out of her mind that these might be her last moments with them. One of the white dudes ripped the duct tape from his mouth, searing his lips.

"What do I have to do?" he uttered breathlessly.

"Look the other way for three seconds," said the Jamaican.

"At the center?"

"Yes. You look the other way, and I release your family. It's as simple as that."

"You want me to let someone into the Operations Center? What are they going to do?"

"You don't need to worry about that. All you need to do is focus on your family. I promise you they will be fine if you follow our instructions. Three seconds of inattention, and you don't say a word to anyone. That's it."

Taylor thought about the consequences for a few seconds. He didn't like the idea of letting someone off the street into the operations center, but what choice did he have?

"The place is locked down tight. I can try to slip someone through my checkpoint, but there's a good chance they'll be stopped inside the center. Another guard might stop them right there if they don't have a badge. My checkpoint is for internal NCTC traffic only, people already cleared to be in the building. You can't bring someone in from the outside and hope to get them through my station without attracting attention."

"We're not using someone off the street. You'll recognize the person, and so will the rest of your crew. He's a regular around there, but he doesn't have access to the operations floor for the current operation, so we need your help. Just three seconds of your time. If you do as we ask, your family will be released, regardless of the outcome. Can you do this for us?"

"What will happen to me afterward?"

"I can't say. They may never figure it out, and if they do…you didn't really have a choice, did you?"

He shook his head. It didn't sound so bad, whatever they had planned. A little corporate espionage? It didn't matter.

"As a matter of fact, you can go to the authorities as soon as your family is released and tell them everything. You might lose your job, but nobody will blame you for looking the other way. Nobody with a family, that is. Frankly, I don't see them figuring it out…it's highly possible that your name will never come up."

Taylor felt less conflicted. How bad could it be if they thought that his moment of "inattention" might go unnoticed?

"I'll do this, but I can't control the situation beyond my station. If your man gets through my checkpoint, you have to honor your word," said Taylor.

"Don't worry. He'll get through fine, as long as you don't get cold feet, or decide to do something rash at the last second. Don't think you can fuck us over on this. The stakes are too high for you. Understood?"

"Yes," Taylor said, nodding emphatically.

He hoped their man sailed through without drawing any attention. There was no way this group could figure out if he raised the alarm upon arrival and arranged a sting operation inside the operations center. They were blind once their man entered the building, and even blinder when he walked through Taylor's checkpoint into the Operations Center. If the man didn't succeed, he'd never see his family again.

"Tell me what to do."

Chapter 47

8:11 PM
National Counterterrorism Center
Washington D.C.

Traffic in and out of the Operations Center was nonexistent at this point. The administrative section of the building had cleared out by six-o'clock, leaving either NCTC personnel assigned to support the ongoing task force or authorized task force members. The Operations Center kept a three-section, eight-hour rotation, fully staffed twenty-four hours a day to support Task Force Scorpion. He wasn't supposed to know the name of the task force, but everybody working security knew more than they should about what was happening in "Ops."

Reggie Taylor glanced around at his colleagues. A total of nine security officers had been assigned to the Operations Center entrance. Two for each of the three checkpoints, and one search team comprised of two officers. The supervisor sat in a glass encased office directly behind Taylor, but he knew from experience that the supervisor's desk didn't provide the proper angle to see his screen from a seated position. Standing up was a different story. He'd told the Jamaican that their inside man needed to back off if anyone was standing in the supervisor's office. Taylor's screen would clearly indicate that James Fitch was not authorized to access the Operations Center.

He'd been slightly relieved to learn that Fitch was their man. Fitch had worked at the Liberty Crossing building since its inception as the Terrorist Threat Integration Center in 2003, along with Taylor. They had both been present for its renaming as the National Counterterrorism Center one year later in 2004. Fitch had accessed "Ops" to do network repairs or related IT work several dozen times during Taylor's daytime shifts, so his presence wasn't unusual. At 8:00 PM on a Saturday night, though, he wasn't sure. Still, it was better than dressing someone up in a colonel's uniform and trying to squeeze them through the Operations Center's dedicated personnel entrance.

The dedicated personnel entry gave permanent Ops analysts, technicians and managers quick access from the parking lot. This group comprised the majority of traffic handled by these checkpoints, usually around shift changes. Anyone using that entrance would raise an immediate alarm trying to use his checkpoint. They had chosen wisely with Fitch. Better yet, Fitch had chosen wisely. There was little doubt in Taylor's mind that this son-of-a-bitch IT fucker had specifically targeted him because of his young children. He had to remind himself to push these thoughts aside. They would serve him no purpose tonight. He couldn't afford to screw this up. All he had to do was let Fitch pass.

He'd be fine. Fitch would very likely attract no attention at all. When Ops needed server related support, the Operation Center's deputy supervisor authorized access through the system, without notifying security. The whole process was transparent to the guards. When Fitch or any of the NCTC personnel swiped their card, it would either permit or deny access. The security officers simply enforced the system's output, which completely eliminated the human factor at the gate. Guards couldn't be sweet talked, rushed or intimidated into letting someone through, regardless of their rank or importance…unless someone was holding a knife to your child's throat.

He glanced down the hallway leading into the general administrative building, trying not to look anxious. The Jamaican told him to expect Fitch around 8:15 PM. He was thankful for that. He wanted to get it over with as quickly as possible. Taylor glanced calmly at his watch.

"Long way to go, Reggie," said one of the guards seated across from him at another checkpoint.

"I know. These longer shifts are killing me. I get antsy as soon as I put the uniform on," he replied, not knowing if what he just said made any sense.

He was scared out of his mind. Movement in his peripheral vision brought his attention back to the hallway. A figure moved through the automatic doors, walking briskly toward the security station. He recognized Fitch immediately. Short brown hair, glasses, khaki pants, white button down shirt covered by an NCTC windbreaker. He thought the jacket was an odd choice for someone trying to avoid attention, but this small observation was drowned out by his relief that the guy wasn't carrying a briefcase or anything that would guarantee that he would be stopped. He should sail right through, if he wasn't carrying anything that triggered the metal detector. Something as stupid as a cell phone or a screwdriver would set the damn thing off, and he didn't control the metal detector.

Fitch approached Taylor's checkpoint and sailed through the metal detector without an issue. *Almost there. Come on baby.* He fought the urge to look over his shoulder. He was told that Fitch would abandon the run if Taylor's supervisor stood in a position to see the security monitor. Fitch's eyes furtively shifted in the direction of the supervisor's office behind Taylor. He kept walking. The two men never made eye contact, but Taylor could tell that Fitch was under considerable strain from the one brief glance he stole. Taylor wondered what the Jamaican might be holding over Fitch's head. He didn't know a single fact about the IT guy's personal life.

Fitch swiped his card and waited. Taylor pretended that he didn't see the "access denied" box appear next to Fitch's picture and data profile. He nodded and pressed the green button mounted at his station, which opened the small gate and admitted Fitch, exposing the single greatest flaw in the Operations Center security system. Instead of linking the gate directly to the system, designers had opted to keep the gate operation in human hands. They had their reasons. If the automatic security system interface crashed at the wrong time, Ops personnel could be denied entry during a critical operation. They thought of several additional scenarios to justify the decision, all of which made sense.

Fitch nodded at one of the guards who had taken an interest in his arrival. Taylor held his breath in terror, depriving his limbs and brain of the oxygen rich blood it desperately needed to support his sympathetic nervous system's activation. He started to experience tunnel vision, which triggered panic. Doubt filled his mind, causing his index finger to stray toward the red alarm button. There was no way they would let his family go. What was he thinking! He had no idea what they had convinced Fitch to do in there. He had to stop this. His family was already dead. He knew it.

"Taylor. You all right?" someone said.

He turned his head toward the voice and his vision expanded. He was breathing again.

"Yeah. I'm fine," he responded.

"You look like shit, brother. Eating at Long John Silver's again? That place will turn your stomach upside down," said his friend at the next checkpoint.

"I can't resist the popcorn shrimp. Melt in your mouth goodness," he mumbled blankly.

"Yeah, until it comes out the other end a few seconds later," the security officer laughed.

Taylor couldn't have recited his friend's name if his life depended on it, because it didn't. Everything depended on Fitch getting inside Ops. He smiled and faked a short laugh, glancing in Fitch's direction. Taylor watched the technician open the door leading into the Operations Center's blackout vestibule, disappearing inside. He'd done it. He just hoped that Fitch would go about his nefarious business quickly. The Jamaican said that his family would be back in their apartment by 9:00 PM if Fitch gained access to the Operations Center. His watch read 8:16 PM. He settled in for the longest forty-four minutes of his life.

ය

Callie Stewart had grown tired of observing the watch floor from her usual perch on the catwalk, so she had taken to mingling with the military liaisons on the left side of the watch floor. Admiral DeSantos had introduced her to Colonel Hanson, SOCOM's liaison, who accepted her based on the SEAL's word. She had been able to spread her influence to a few of the technicians, even managing to cozy up to NCTC's Assistant Director, Karen Wilhelm. She had little ulterior motive beyond making her time in the Operations Center a little more tolerable. Of course, her eyes and ears were always open for new intelligence. Old habits were hard to break.

Over the past three days, she had mapped out the relationships between everyone on the floor, paying close attention to mannerism, posture, glances…all of the subtle, below the surface connections that defined the true essence of the microcosm surrounding her. She was less interested in the overt drama, since most of it was window dressing. Once she had mapped out this web of connections, she could anticipate and predict their behavior based on something as innocuous as a pair of folded arms or a stolen glance. Right now, Karen Wilhelm was annoyed. She had just placed her hands on her hips, which was one of her many "tells."

Stewart followed her glare and settled on a man she had never seen before in the Operations Center. He wore a loose blue windbreaker with some kind of yellow logo on the front. She could only read "N" from her angle, but she assumed it read NCTC. He glanced around stiffly as he tentatively approached the other side of the watch floor and started to navigate the cluster of workstations that housed most of the FBI's task force. Karen Wilhelm started walking in his direction from her desk on Stewart's side of the center. When Stewart turned her head to examine the object of Wilhelm's curiosity, she noticed that his left hand was inserted into the left bottom pocket of the windbreaker. Purely out of instinct, she started to walk briskly toward the man. Something was off.

❧

Special Agent Mendoza prepared another cup of burnt coffee and diluted it with three Coffee-Mate creamers. He figured this cup would probably give him heart palpitations, but at least that would keep him awake. The day had dragged on forever after Sharpe's revelation about cooperating with Sanderson. Knowing that they were possibly pursuing false leads, while Sanderson's people assembled in Pennsylvania, had made the exhausting process nearly unbearable. It reached a boiling point when Sharpe finally confirmed that Sergeant Osborne's past few vacation periods matched up with vacations taken by operatives killed or captured in Brooklyn. Julius Grimes, the operative caught on camera near one of the Al Qaeda safe houses fit the same pattern. Sharpe twisted some arms behind the scenes to get Laurel's chief of police to cooperate, without drawing attention within the task force. They still wanted to keep this a secret while Sanderson's crew pursued the next lead.

He walked out of the small break room, intending to step into Sharpe's office for a few minutes, when he noticed a man wearing an NCTC windbreaker walking toward O'Reilly and Hesterman's work station. The guy looked lost, edging his way forward. When the man reached into his left pocket, Mendoza placed his coffee on the edge of the nearest workstation desk.

What he saw next left him with little time to make an impossible decision. When the dark haired man removed his hand from the pocket, he clutched a small, highlighter sized object in his fist. A thin black wire extended from the bottom of the black device back into his pocket. There was little doubt in Mendoza's mind about what was hidden under the man's windbreaker. He didn't hesitate. Mendoza's Glock 23 flashed out of its holster and centered on the man's head. He heard a female voice scream "no" and something about a "dead man" right before he fired. The .40 caliber bullet struck the man at the very top of his spine, exiting through his right eye socket and turning him off like a light switch. Callie Stewart flew into view, screaming "don't shoot!" as the man's body crumpled to the floor. She wrapped both of her hands tightly around the limp hand holding the detonator, pulling it inward to her chest and dropping to the floor next to him. Instinctively, Mendoza aligned the Glock's sights on Stewart's head. She had her hands on the detonator.

"Drop the detonator!" he screamed.

If she didn't separate her hands immediately, he'd kill her. He only hesitated for this long because Sharpe trusted her.

"It's a dead man switch. Don't shoot!" she screamed.

He processed her statement, wasting precious milliseconds evaluating the variables. If she was telling the truth, Callie Stewart had just saved the Operations Center from a suicide bombing. If she was lying, she had just bought herself enough time to finish the job. He had hesitated long enough for her to set off the explosives, but she didn't move. She'd been telling the truth. He started to lower his pistol. Three rapid gunshots erupted at point blank range from the workstation next to her. The bullets struck her in the upper back and neck, spraying blood onto the dead man at her knees. He lurched forward in horror as her body wavered and fell. He never saw her hands come apart.

*

Special Agent O'Reilly had figuratively hit a wall with her research into the backgrounds of the eighty-five men and women they had identified from the compound raid. She didn't see any point in continuing to try to find a pattern that might help forward the investigation. Most of them had recently participated in some kind of anti-government survivalist activity, running the spectrum from bravado forum posts on anti-government slanted websites to misdemeanor criminal harassment charges for threatening elected officials.

She didn't believe that True America would round up over a hundred of these nut jobs for a weekend recruitment drive in the middle of one of the deadliest domestic terrorist plots in U.S. history. Sergeant Osborne's vacation schedule sealed it for her. She was going through the motions until Sanderson's people gave them something substantive to investigate. All indicators pointed to Pennsylvania as their best hope of stopping True America, or at least moving the investigation closer. Unfortunately, there was little to do on their end, especially given the methods and personnel used to obtain the information. Not to mention the possibility of a True America sympathizer within the task force or NCTC. For the first time in years, she was truly frustrated by their inability to take action. She started to type a message to Sharpe on her computer, but stopped. She'd brainstormed every possible way around this and ended up empty handed. It was time to give it a rest.

She noticed Karen Wilhelm walking in her direction at an unusually fast pace. Her peripheral vision detected another rapidly moving object, which turned out to be Callie Stewart in full sprint. O'Reilly twisted her head and torso far enough around to see one of the IT guys standing less than ten feet behind her, wearing an NCTC windbreaker. She recognized the guy. Fitch. Stewart screamed, still barreling through the workstations, when Fitch's head suddenly exploded. Her face was hit by warm splatter, causing her to close her eyes and raise her hands. She heard Mendoza's voice over the deafening echo of a single gunshot, followed immediately by Stewart's frantic voice, screaming something about a dead man switch. Three rapid gunshots drowned out Stewart's desperate plea, causing O'Reilly to reach for her own weapon. She swiveled her chair and opened her eyes. All she saw was Hesterman's massive form bent over her.

Special Agent Sharpe finished reading the last few lines of O'Reilly's initial report regarding the suspects found at the Hacker Valley compound. He completely agreed with her assessment that something didn't add up. A figure loomed in his doorway for a moment, causing him to look up from the computer screen. He saw Mendoza hover near his door with a cup of coffee and walk away. He needed to talk to Mendoza about finding a way to slip a portion of Benjamin Young's information into their investigation. He'd asked O'Reilly to come up with a few ideas, but even the craftiest agent in the building couldn't conceive of a way to do it covertly. Mendoza was his last hope.

A single gunshot shattered his train of thought, and he leapt up from his chair, drew his service weapon, and rushed to the door. He had a clear line of sight to Mendoza and observed him locked into a firing stance with both hands on his gun. Stewart was on her knees past Mendoza, with her hands clasped tightly around something he couldn't quite see. As he neared the door, he saw an arm extended downward from her grip. Mendoza and Stewart yelled at each other, and he immediately understood what had happened.

His moment of clarity was interrupted by three rapid gunshots that hit Stewart. He reached the doorway, only to be blown back into his office by an incredible force that shattered the entire office. If he had been sitting at his desk, he would have been shredded by the floor-to-ceiling glass that was blown inward by the initial shockwave. Instead, he was thrown onto his back, next to his desk, hit by four ceramic ball bearings; none of which severed an artery or punctured a critical organ. Mendoza had been standing directly between Sharpe and the suicide vest, absorbing most of the fragments headed in his direction. He stared upward at the ceiling, unable to hear a sound or utter a word. A few seconds passed before he tried to raise himself onto one elbow. The pain in his shoulder was unbearable and he collapsed back to the glass-covered floor. He felt the entire office shake beneath him and wondered if the building was about to collapse.

ര

Major Hillary Carson witnessed the bizarre events unfold on the Operation Center's watch floor before she was tossed like a rag doll into the concrete wall behind her. She had just stepped onto the raised catwalk from the spiral staircase embedded within the wall and leaned over the railing to look down at her workstation. She worked with the Deputy Assistant Secretary of Defense's liaison group, spending most of her time on the floor wishing they had something valuable to contribute to the investigation. She quickly realized why the Deputy Assistant Secretary of Defense for Homeland Defense and America's Security Affairs was never present in the Operations Center. Their group served no functional role on the task force, other than to allow someone somewhere to check off the box requiring her office to be included in any task force investigating an active threat to homeland security.

She had been headed to their small office on the second level with the intention of lying down on the couch for a few hours. She'd send whomever she found in the office to the watch floor. She was the senior ranking member of their contingency when the Deputy Assistant's Secretary's own assistant wasn't present. He'd left around 7:00 PM, presumably to have dinner, and she didn't expect to see him for a few hours.

When she leaned against the railing and surveyed the watch floor, she immediately noticed the creepy looking guy in the NCTC windbreaker. She'd been assigned to NCTC for nine months and had never seen one of these jackets, not that it was truly unusual or out of place. Every agency in D.C. seemed to have an exclusive line of dark blue, yellow-stenciled outerwear. From her bird's eye view, she could see that three people had taken an active interest in the same guy. Karen Wilhelm and Special Agent Mendoza started to converge on his location, along with Callie Stewart, the sharply dressed woman that everyone seemed to despise.

Stewart's arrival at the Operations Center had sparked a flurry of whispers and controversy among the FBI agents. She quickly came to understand why they were so uncomfortable with her presence. Stewart worked for the formerly disgraced General Terrence Sanderson, and everyone in D.C. knew that story. Stewart's presence was an enigma to everyone but Special Agents Sharpe and Mendoza, who looked like they had been forced to swallow some bitter medicine when she arrived. As soon as Carson learned of Stewart's affiliation with Sanderson, she checked the FBI's wanted lists. Sanderson had disappeared from both the Top Ten and Most Wanted Terrorists lists, along with his associates, Daniel Petrovich and Jeffrey Munoz. Formerly disgraced was the operative term.

Callie Stewart broke into a sprint when Agent Mendoza drew his pistol and fired. The man in the windbreaker dropped to the deck just as Stewart dove at him. She grabbed the man's hand and a quick argument ensued with Mendoza. She couldn't hear what they were yelling, but Mendoza turned the gun on Stewart. Before he could fire his weapon, one of the agents seated at a workstation directly behind her fired three quick shots that killed her instantly. Carson heard one of the bullets strike the glass to her left, distracting her for a moment. She never saw the explosion that destroyed the Operations Center and slammed her against the wall next to the stairwell opening. If the blast had flung her two feet to the left, she might have been tossed down the metal staircase.

Dazed by the blast, she crawled over to the edge of the catwalk, unable to stand, and stared at the destruction. A few of the hanging pendant lights still functioned, swaying back and forth and competing with the inadequate emergency lighting to create dancing shadows among the smoldering wreckage. The FBI's side of the watch floor had been leveled, leaving toppled desks and a tangle of chairs. She couldn't make out too many details through the smoke and paper debris raining down, but she could see that the blast had cleared everything within a twenty-foot radius of the suicide vest and ignited small fires nearby.

She saw bodies slumped over desks in contorted positions or lying twisted on the floor. A few of them still moved. Sparks showered down onto the carnage from the damaged video displays lining the floor, mounted to the bottom of the catwalk. A lone workstation caught her eye on the other side of the Operations Center, where the damage had not been as severe. A man appeared to remain upright in his chair, as if nothing had happened. There was no way for Carson to know that the NCTC analyst had been instantly killed by a ball bearing that had punctured his skull.

Security personnel started to pour into the center a few seconds later. She could see that they were paralyzed by the utter devastation that lay before them. They paused upon entry, clearly debating where to start. One of the men motioned the sign of the cross and dropped to one knee. Just as his knee touched the floor, the Operations Center rumbled and the catwalk lurched two feet downward. Carson clung to the railing until it stabilized, quickly deciding that she had to get out of here.

She crawled into the stairwell just as the catwalk dropped a few more feet and broke free from the bolts that kept it fastened to the wall. The metal supports directly underneath that section of the catwalk had been critically weakened by the blast, putting incredible downward strain on the bolts. When one bolt failed, the rest followed, snapping that corner of the catwalk free from the wall. Instead of dropping directly onto the floor below, it careened outward into the middle of the Operations Center, tearing one section after the other free from the wall, as it swung toward the security guards and finally slammed into the office next to the security doors.

The stairwell felt stable for now, so she decided to stay in place and wait for emergency responders. She remained conscious the entire time, listening to the groans and wails of survivors. In her mind, she kept replaying what she had seen before the explosion. Mendoza had almost stopped Stewart from detonating the bomb.

❧

Reggie Taylor nearly released his bladder when the frosted glass doors leading into the Operations Center vestibule exploded, showering the security checkpoint with glass fragments. The inner vestibule door had resisted the initial blast of the shockwave, absorbing a significant portion of its energy, which saved their lives. The glass left most of them with multiple lacerations, but lacked the speed necessary to deeply penetrate their bodies. He froze at his station, unwilling to process what had just happened. As most of his colleagues raced toward the source of the explosion, Taylor couldn't move.

He couldn't believe this was happening to him. He had unwittingly allowed a suicide bomber into the Operations Center. Fitch's windbreaker made sense now, along with the Jamaican's assurances that they would know if Fitch got into Ops unhindered. He no longer had any doubt that they planned to release his family. Their operation within NCTC wasn't a covert data theft or file corruption that needed to remain a secret. There was no reason to hold them any longer. He briefly considered fleeing the building, but couldn't bring himself to turn his back on the wounded survivors he had just helped to maim.

He stood up from his seat and checked on one of the guards who had propped himself against the opposite wall. His leg looked badly shredded, bleeding profusely onto the floor.

"Go help the others. I'll be fine," the man said.

Taylor looked down the hallway toward the administrative building, and saw the automatic doors open. Security personnel poured through the doorway, sprinting in his direction.

"Alright. Make sure one of them gets you out of here. You're losing a lot of blood," said Taylor, before proceeding to the shattered vestibule.

He stepped through the newly created openings and stopped with the rest of the security team just inside the vast space. What he saw caused him to drop to one knee and cross himself.

"Father, Son and the Holy Spirit," he muttered in disbelief.

A muffled explosion shook the room, bringing him to his feet just as a section of the catwalk disengaged from the wall near the far right stairwell. The metal creaked and screamed for a few seconds, before the entire catwalk structure on the right side of the Operations Center swung across the room, gaining momentum as more sections separated. The guards scurried back toward the security checkpoint, clearing the vestibule as a massive collision rattled the floor. Once the catwalk settled, they hesitantly walked back into the apocalyptic nightmare that had just minutes ago been the world's most technologically advanced counterterrorism center.

As the desperate cries for help and deep moaning finally reached Taylor's ears, he wished he had been crushed by the twisted metal catwalk.

Chapter 48

8:28 PM
White House Situation Room
Washington D.C.

"Director Shelby, please report to the Watch Floor supervisor."

He stood up from his newly appointed, temporary office just outside of the main conference room and straightened out his jacket. After the president's little talk with him this morning, Jacob Remy had slithered over to sweeten the pot even further by assigning him one of the small conference rooms to use as a temporary FBI office. They really wanted him to play ball. He had been tempted to point out the fact that this office should have been offered to him four days ago, when Task Force Scorpion had been commissioned by Shelby to resolve this emergent terrorist threat.

When he opened his office door, two Secret Service agents took control of him, steering him toward the main conference room. Their guns were drawn and pointed toward the ceiling. His first thought was that he had been placed under arrest.

"This way, sir. The Watch Floor supervisor needs to speak to you immediately."

No further explanation was given. He could see at least three heavily armed Secret Service agents blocking the entrance to their destination. Their bullpup configured FN P90 submachine guns were held parallel to the floor, sweeping in every direction. He wasn't being arrested. Something had happened. Something big.

"What's going on?" he asked the agent behind him.

"We're in lockdown. NCTC was hit by a suicide bomber. Possible inside job. We're securing all high value targets within the Situation Room."

"Where's the president?"

"You'll be briefed once inside. Please keep moving, sir," the agent replied.

When they arrived at the door, one of the agents entered a code into the keypad on the wall behind him. His escorts pushed him past the three agents, wedging him against the door, which opened less than a second later. A Secret Service agent inside grabbed him by the shoulder and guided him inside, shutting the door behind them. A tall, blond haired man dressed in a dark brown suit approached him immediately.

"Director Shelby, George Hafferty, Watch Floor supervisor. The Operations Center at NCTC has been hit by an apparent suicide bomber. I know you have—"

"How big of a bomb? I need to talk to someone over there right now."

"Absolutely, sir. We're still trying to sort out the reports. From what we can tell, the bomb was hidden under a jacket. Maybe a suicide vest. I don't know how to say this, but the bomb apparently detonated in the middle of the FBI work stations. We don't have any real numbers, but first responders told us to expect massive casualties. I'm really sorry."

Frederick Shelby had visited Task Force Scorpion earlier in the day, and could picture each agent seated at his or her assigned workstation. He knew every face assigned to the task force, and had taken the trouble to learn something about each one of them prior to his visit. If the bomb had been as powerful as Mr. Hafferty suggested, most of them had probably been killed. Hesterman, O'Reilly, Mendoza, maybe even Sharpe. He felt a bitter anger rise up his throat, threatening to choke off his breathing. He was seething.

"My agent-in-charge? Ryan Sharpe. Did he survive?"

"I don't know yet. We've just started collecting information. I have a direct line to NCTC director, Joel Garrity. I spoke with him moments ago. He'll be your best conduit for information, sir."

"Thank you, Mr. Hafferty. Get him on the line, please," said Shelby.

The door he just entered opened again and deposited the Secretary of Homeland Security, Marianne Templeton, into the room. He nodded at her before following Hafferty. On his way to the mobile Watch Floor hub assembled in the far corner of the room, he took note of the people in the room. He counted four Secret Service agents, two guarding each door, along with at least six personnel hovering around the four workstations comprising the mobile hub. Beyond him, Ms. Templeton appeared to be the only person worth protecting within the Situation Room.

"Get Joel Garrity at NCTC on a secure line for the director," said Hafferty.

Less than five seconds later, one of the analysts stood up from his chair and backed away, holding a telephone handset out to Shelby. Shelby took the phone and remained standing, stretching the cord. His first priority was to establish continuity of operations. As cold as this would sound to Garrity, the immediate survival of the investigation took priority over the casualties.

"The line is secure, sir," the analyst said.

"Joel, what happened?"

"We're still trying to piece it together, sir. I have some digital feedback showing a man in an NCTC windbreaker involved in some kind of controversy on the watch floor. Agent Mendoza shoots him in the middle of the FBI workstations, and that's where it gets confusing. A woman charges onto the scene at about the same time, dropping herself onto the bomber. An agent seated nearby shoots her in the back, and the bomb goes off immediately after that. I don't think anyone on the floor survived."

He would ask more about the woman in a moment.

"Joel, this may sound heartless considering what happened, but—"

"Continuity of operations," interrupted Garrity.

"Yes. I need you to transfer everything on your servers to FBI headquarters. I'll have one of our techs contact you immediately to—"

"They didn't tell you everything? The primary server and its backup were hit by a secondary explosion linked to the first. The investigation from this end has been wiped clean. Someone really wanted to put Task Force Scorpion out of business," said Garrity.

"What? The servers were hit too?" Shelby said, glancing up at Hafferty, who shrugged his shoulders.

"What about Ryan Sharpe? Was he on the floor?"

"No. He was found unconscious in his office. He's been evacuated from the facility," said Garrity, amidst yelling in the background on his end of the phone.

Garrity interrupted the call to yell something back. When he resumed the call, he sounded defeated.

"The entire catwalk just collapsed on some of my people. Look, I'll get back to you right away with more information. We're trying to salvage something from the server rooms, but it doesn't look promising."

"One more thing! The woman that was shot. Who was it?"

"I think it was Callie Stewart. One of the DIA's liaisons," he replied.

"Listen carefully, Joel. I need you to interview anyone that is still conscious there. I need to know what happened on the watch floor right before the bomb detonated. This is critical. I'm sorry to push this on you given the circumstances. We've both lost a lot of good people tonight," said Shelby.

"A lot of good people. I'll be in touch shortly."

Shelby handed the phone back to the analyst and took the nearest seat at the conference table, pondering what Garrity had said about the digital camera feed. Mendoza had presumably shot the bomber before he could detonate the bomb. Callie Stewart happened to be close enough to drop down onto the bomber and was subsequently shot by another agent. Why, at that very moment, had she been close enough to intervene? Sharpe had told him this morning that she steered clear of the watch floor, rarely descending the stairs unless summoned. Shelby didn't believe in coincidences. Her convenient appearance could only mean one thing.

Marianne Templeton approached him from the opposite side of the table.

"What happened, Frederick?" she said.

"We've been played."

Chapter 49

8:44 PM
The Brooklyn Hospital Center
Brooklyn, New York

Ashraf Haddad sat in one of the institutionally painful chairs placed against the wall of the hospital's intensive care unit waiting room. He'd spent the past two days living in this room, punctuated by visits to the cafeteria and the occasional walk around the common areas of the hospital to keep from going crazy. General Sanderson had asked him to keep an eye on Castillo and Sayar, to make sure their best interests were represented and that they were afforded the best possible care available for their recoveries. Castillo's situation had been touch and go for thirty-six hours, but as of this morning, ICU doctors had upgraded her condition from critical to serious. Sayar remained in serious, but stable condition, and was expected to make a full recovery. The hospital staff seemed reluctant to give a long-term prognosis for Castillo, who had suffered multiple gunshot wounds. The hesitance tempered Haddad's optimism about her status upgrade.

He glanced at his watch. One hour remained until he would check on them again and close up shop at the hospital. He had a queen-sized bed at the nearby Sheraton hotel calling his name. After spending the past three years in training with Sanderson's Middle East group, he wasn't about to pass up the opportunity to spend some quality time with one of the Sheraton's Sweet Sleeper Beds. Now that both of his friends were out of immediate danger, Sanderson had suggested that he get some rest. He wasn't about to argue with the general's assessment.

Haddad noticed a group of three men wearing suits approach from the west corridor, walking purposefully toward the waiting room lobby. Their presence immediately raised his internal alarm. A more hurried group of men emptied into the northern hallway, just beyond a set of double doors, and turned in his direction. He recognized two of the men walking briskly toward him from the west wing as FBI special agents that had previously visited the hospital. He started to weigh his options carefully, not that he had many. When the first agent pushed through the swinging double doors holding an MP-5 submachine gun, he decided against anything drastic. He reached onto the small table to the right of his chair and pushed his Starbucks coffee out of the way to retrieve his Blackberry phone. He thumbed several buttons and replaced the phone, picking up his coffee.

He took a long drink of his thick, extra-shot cappuccino. He had a feeling he wouldn't be drinking good coffee again for a while. He placed the cup on the table and read the return text message before all hell broke loose.

"Rcvd."

Chapter 50

8:49 PM
Wilkes Barre/Scranton International Airport
Avoca, Pennsylvania

Daniel Petrovich had just turned their Jeep Grand Cherokee onto Terminal Road from Interstate 81, when his phone illuminated the minivan's center console.

"Can you see who that is?" he asked Munoz.

Munoz grabbed the phone and examined the screen. "Sanderson," he said and answered the call.

Daniel listened to the terse exchange.

"Understood. We'll be standing by," Munoz said, ending the call. "Get us back on the highway. We might be compromised."

Daniel scanned the upcoming street signs and saw that they would have the opportunity to turn off Terminal road directly onto a northbound ramp.

"Compromised by whom?"

"The Feds. Sanderson doesn't have all of the details yet, but the rules have changed in a big way. Something happened."

Daniel turned the SUV onto the northbound ramp and accelerated to match the sparse interstate traffic.

"Is this related to Atlanta?" Daniel asked.

"He's not sure. All he knows is that one of our operatives at the Brooklyn Center Hospital transmitted the federal arrest code, and he can't get through to his liaison at the National Counterterrorism Center. The cyber team tapped into NCTC called him at 8:17 to report that they had been dropped from the system. He's trying to reach some of his other contacts within D.C. Nobody's picking up."

"This isn't good. What's our exposure here?" said Daniel.

"Minimal. Fayed and Paracha are ghosts. Everything they arranged is sanitized. This car. The house. The FBI can trace us to this airport, but no further than that."

"I thought Sanderson and this guy Sharpe had agreed on this under the table?" said Daniel.

"They did. Maybe the director discovered the collaboration and pulled the plug on Sharpe. Any of a dozen things could have gone wrong, leaving us exposed."

"We have to assume the FBI knows that we're headed to Honesdale. Sharpe has no reason to keep that a secret if he's been relieved or incarcerated. For all we know, Sharpe fucked us over and the president is planning a full-scale invasion of the city. All I know, is that we're not going anywhere near that airport, and we're sure as shit not setting foot in Honesdale until this is resolved."

"I'm not going to argue with that logic. There's a Wal-Mart right outside of Scranton that should be open twenty-four hours. We can pick up new phones there," said Munoz.

"God bless Wal-Mart."

Daniel's phone illuminated a few minutes into their drive north. He snatched it from Munoz.

"What the fuck went wrong?"

"One of these True America lunatics somehow gained access to the NCTC Operations Center and detonated a suicide vest," said Sanderson. "Pretty much wiped out the entire task force. A secondary bomb destroyed the servers. The FBI thinks Callie Stewart helped the bomber."

"Who the fuck is Callie Stewart?"

"She was my liaison to Sharpe's task force. They somehow have it in their heads that she was involved. The director of the FBI is on a rampage. He ordered the arrest of our operatives at the hospital. The very men and women that risked their lives for the task force. We need to be careful. Warrants have been issued for all of us, and we're back on the terrorist watch lists."

"Jesus. How many were killed in the blast?"

"At least twenty, with up to fifty additional casualties," said Sanderson.

"How do you want us to proceed? I don't mean to sound grim, but if the task force is history, then nobody knows we're here. We should be clear to make a move against Mills."

"You never disappoint me, Daniel. Practical to a fault. I concur with your assessment. Take whatever measures are necessary to stop True America. I'll arrange to have your weapons and equipment delivered to a location of your choosing. I'm serious about this, Daniel. Do whatever it takes to drag these psychotic traitors down. No rules of engagement on this one," said Sanderson.

"I've never had much use for rules," replied Daniel.

"That's why I recruited you. Let me know when you've selected a location for the transfer. And get new phones. There's a twenty-four hour Wal-Mart in Scranton."

"Am I the only asshole that doesn't know about this Wal-Mart?" said Daniel, throwing the phone in Munoz's lap.

"So, we're still a go?" asked Munoz.

"Yep. We just need to find a secure place to receive the gear."

"Wal-Mart parking lot?"

"Sounds like a plan to me," said Daniel.

Chapter 51

9:06 PM
Wilkes Barre/Scranton International Airport
Avoca, Pennsylvania

"This isn't funny, Karl."

Darryl Jackson gripped the handle next to the Lear jet's exit hatch and stared out at the line of unlit private hangars less than fifty yards away. The tarmac was dark and their aircraft had sat conspicuously in the middle of it for the last thirty minutes.

"I understand your frustration, but there's been a development."

"There's always a development when you're involved. What kind of fucking development are we talking about here? They were supposed to be here fifteen minutes ago!"

"Darryl, they can't risk coming to the airport. I can't get into it right—"

"And I won't get off this muthafuckin airplane, carrying my guns, until your ass starts explaining some shit!" said Darryl Jackson, sounding more and more like Samuel Jackson by the second.

"NCTC was hit by a suicide bomb," said Karl.

"What are you talking about? How does this keep these assholes from coming to the airport?"

"The FBI thinks Sanderson's people were involved."

"I'm out of here. No fucking way I'm turning over this gear to a bunch of fugitives."

"Darryl, please listen to me. The task force was wiped out by the blast. They lost everything and pretty much everyone. The backup servers were hit by a secondary explosion. True America crippled their efforts with this attack. The timing can't be a coincidence. True America shut them down like this for a reason."

"Then why doesn't the FBI take care of this?"

"Only a small group of agents within the task force knew about this covert operation. It's strictly off the books. Nobody else knows that Sanderson's people are in Pennsylvania. There's little chance that the FBI is watching the airport, but this mission is too important to take that risk. At least three of the operatives assigned to the mission traveled under their real identities."

"Are you fucking kidding me? The FBI could be all over this airport. How long could it take for them to track them here?"

"Sanderson's people were arrested in Brooklyn at 8:47. The nearest field office is Philadelphia. All they have in Scranton is a resident agency stuffed into the Post Office Building. It'll take them a little while to move the necessary pieces from Philly to Scranton. I can have you back in the air within thirty minutes if you'd quit arguing with me."

"If I'm arrested, Cheryl will hunt your ass down. No place on earth will be safe for you."

"If you're arrested, I'll gladly present myself to her for mercy," said Berg.

"You're better off running, because there will be no mercy. You'd better hope this works out. She just agreed to have you over for dinner," said Jackson.

"Then you better be careful out there. There's more at stake here than I imagined. Is everything ready to roll on your end?"

"Yes. Three large duffel bags filled with goodies waiting to be transferred."

"Perfect. I've arranged for a car service to pick you up on Hangar Road, right behind the hangars. I'm looking at the airport on Google Maps. The first hangar in the long row is a white structure. There's a parking lot between that hangar and the next. The car will meet you on the road at the end of that parking lot."

"You're going to make me carry this shit?"

"Are you ever going to stop complaining?"

"Just make sure the plane is here when I return. This thing better be taking me right to Princeton," said Jackson.

"What about your car back in Fredericksburg?"

"Princeton. I expect a car to be waiting for me."

"Anything for you. Thanks, Darryl. Seriously."

"No problem. Just do what you can to keep me out of jail," said Jackson.

"I'll do my best. You're a little too soft for hard time."

Darryl leaned out of the hatch and surveyed the hangars, looking for the parking lot Berg had referenced. He could barely identify it in the darkness that swallowed the private section of the airport. The absence of lighting might work in his favor, especially since the airport's tower was visible from the hatch. The fewer witnesses to this transfer the better.

Chapter 52

9:44 PM
White House Situation Room
Washington D.C.

The president leaned across his desk and nearly screamed at Frederick Shelby.

"You exceeded your authority, and you know it!"

"Mr. President, Sanderson's liaison to the task force helped the suicide bomber. This has been confirmed by the video feed and the testimony of an Air Force Major. Special Agent Frank Mendoza stopped the attack and Callie Stewart stepped in to make sure the bomb detonated. I was opposed to bringing Sanderson's people into this on any level. The details of his involvement in Europe and Russia are sketchy at best and unverified. I suspect that he's been playing us all along."

"I don't care if the video shows Sanderson himself lighting the damn fuse. You were well aware of the special circumstances surrounding our relationship with Sanderson. We still have a Black Hawk helicopter sitting in front of his goddamn compound! You don't go around me on things like that!"

Frederick Shelby considered the president's words and the tone in which they were delivered. He was clearly more concerned about the possibility of a scandal than the lives of the agents and counterterrorism professionals lost in the terrorist bombing. He knew that the president wasn't a callous, unfeeling man. He'd seen evidence to the contrary on numerous occasions. Still, Shelby had to remind himself that the president was a politician, and politics relied on reputation and image more than actually doing the right thing, or anything for that matter.

The director didn't have that option. He had to produce quantifiable results in a timely manner, or find another job. He looked up at the president and chose his words carefully. The president was more than just a simple politician. He had beat out every other politician for the grand prize. Shelby had to be cautious here. He was talking to a first term president, who faced an uphill battle for reelection. A little contrition would go a long way right now.

"I have to apologize, Mr. President. The heinous act clouded my judgment. I lost thirteen agents in that blast, and there's a good chance that a few more might not survive the night. The investigation has been torpedoed, and I want to kill the son-of-a-bitch responsible. I didn't intend to put you in an untenable situation."

"I'm sorry to hear about your agents. I know you assigned the most talented agents to that task force. The results achieved so far reflect this. This is a heinous act, Frederick, and I've assured General Sanderson that if I find him to be responsible, we will sever all ties with him."

"You've spoken with him?"

"He contacted my chief of staff within an hour of the bombing, demanding to know why his agents had been arrested in Brooklyn. We didn't have an answer for him. When we finally figured out what you had done, I called him personally. I didn't apologize or make excuses. I told him we had reason to believe one of his people was involved and that his unconditional pardon didn't cover him beyond the day of the failed helicopter raid. Surprisingly, he agreed and said that he understood our actions. He disavowed any involvement with True America," said the president.

"Of course he did."

"He never made a threat or suggested that he would renege on our deal. I didn't get the impression that he was lying."

"He's a slippery character, Mr. President. I wouldn't trust anything he says. I have video evidence and a witness from the blast site that put Callie Stewart's hands on the detonator. This is a difficult fact to ignore."

"I don't intend to ignore it, but for now we need to move the investigation forward. We can build a stronger case against Sanderson along the way. Where do we stand?"

"In a pile of rubble, mostly. Our headquarters' technical division is collecting data from the mobile computers and the Newark field office. The NCTC team processed and analyzed field data collected. This information was stored in the NCTC servers. They formed conclusions and shaped the investigation with this data and parsed it back out to the mobile teams as requested. Unfortunately, it was a fairly compartmentalized operation. Most of the data was lost in the blast, along with the agents who could explain any new leads or theories in development."

"Nobody survived?" The president shook his head with a look of sorrow.

"Ryan Sharpe, the task force leader survived, but he's severely injured and remains unconscious. He was partly inside his office when the bomb detonated and got lucky. Only one of the other agents survived, but she's in worse shape than Sharpe. Video shows Special Agent Eric Hesterman purposely shielding Special Agent Dana O'Reilly from the blast. She was spared any lethal fragmentation, but suffered from massive internal injuries due to the pressure effects of the bomb. Hesterman was nearly vaporized."

The president swallowed hard and exhaled deeply.

"I'm sorry…I can see why you put the hammer down on Sanderson. Can any of the surviving NCTC analysts help?"

"Special Agent Kathryn Moriarty is on her way back to D.C. with a dozen agents. She'll direct all efforts to rebuild the task force from the ground up. That will be one of her first priorities. Most of the analytical work was done by the FBI, but there was considerable collaboration with permanent NCTC personnel. We can piece the investigation back together, but it will take time," said Shelby.

"Time is running out. Do we have any more active field operations planned?"

"No. We're still collecting evidence from Hacker Valley and the Fort Meade site. I do have something to suggest, but it falls under the Sanderson category," said Shelby.

"As long as it doesn't involve another raid in Argentina, I'm open to suggestions."

Shelby wasn't sure if that was meant as a zinger, or it was just the president's way of saying that Sanderson himself was off limits. Either way, he didn't appreciate the comment.

"At least three, but possibly four of Sanderson's operatives landed at the Wilkes Barre/Scranton International Airport early this evening. Both of the Petroviches and Jeffrey Munoz are confirmed to have arrived, along with an unidentified Hispanic man," said Shelby.

Jacob Remy interjected for the first time during the meeting. "They were directly involved in Sanderson's 2005 fiasco regarding the Black Flag program files."

"I remember the names now. That seems like an odd place for Sanderson's inner core to surface," said the president.

"I agree, which is why I'd like to deploy a significantly large investigative team to figure out why they chose Pennsylvania for their corporate getaway."

"How significant?" asked Remy.

"I'd deploy every agent on the east coast if I could, but given the circumstances, I'll settle for Task Force Scorpion's mobile team. Forty agents. Tactical and investigative. I'd be happy to take whatever assets the Philadelphia field office could spare," said Shelby.

"You mean they're not already en route?" said the president.

"The task force or agents from Philadelphia?" asked Shelby.

"I figured as much. Get whatever you need up to Scranton. I want to know what they are doing up there. I don't want things to get messy with Sanderson, but if he's responsible for the bombing, or in any way connected to True America's plot…he's a dead man."

Chapter 53

10:37 AM
Wayne County
Pennsylvania

Daniel Petrovich sat in the front passenger seat of the Jeep Grand Cherokee, tensing for the next pothole in the road. Munoz seemed unable to avoid them. They had driven along these roads for the past forty minutes, each turn depositing them onto a smaller, less comfortable stretch of isolated, tree covered dirt road. Fortunately, they were moving along slowly to accommodate the Ford Transit van following them.

The windowless white van carried the electronic warfare team, which had already proven themselves to be invaluable. Graves and Gupta, two wisecracking cyber geniuses, had swept through Honesdale Construction's unsophisticated computer network and found payments linked to the five million dollars Benjamin Young had shifted to the company's account. The company had multiple projects, both small and large, ongoing and scheduled around the time of the deposit, so they went to work digging. Most of the projects appeared to be legitimate, and included several town awarded contracts along with a dozen or more commercial business expansions.

One project drew their attention, simply because it lacked a physical location. The other projects listed either an address or town grid lot number, but this one lacked any geographic reference. A little more electronic snooping uncovered a list of drivers used for the project, which is how Harry Welsh ended up sitting crammed between Jessica and Melendez in the back seat. Welsh, age thirty two, had worked as a heavy vehicle driver at Honesdale Construction for nearly six years. He'd listed his mother as next of kin on the company's record sheet, and his recorded address in Pittston put him nearly eighty miles from his mother's address in Middletown, New York. They assumed he was unmarried, which suited their purposes. The last thing they needed when they knocked on his door at 6:00 AM, posing as FBI agents, was a headstrong wife demanding to verify their identities with children crying in the background.

Karl Berg had provided them with six sets of forged credentials matched to Sanderson's operatives, complete with badges and picture identification. Daniel had never really seen an FBI identification case up close, but these looked real and felt authentic. If anyone had questions, they would be happy to pass along accompanying business cards with the Philadelphia field office number, which would be answered by someone in the inconspicuous white van that followed them from a distance.

Harry Welsh had answered the door red eyed and disheveled, clearly woken out of a severe Sunday morning hangover. He barely examined their credentials and didn't seem fazed by their outfits. Daniel and Munoz had purchased several black nylon jackets at Wal-Mart to lend some uniform credibility to their group appearance and to conceal their pistols. It worked with Welsh, though Daniel was convinced that the man was seeing double. As he swayed in the doorway, they thought about leaving him alone and moving on to the next driver, but Welsh insisted he could get them to the site and Daniel didn't feel like wasting any more time.

According to Welsh, he'd made over a hundred trips out there, sometimes at night, and could drive it blindfolded. Several wrong turns later, Daniel was about to dump him on the side of the road when he finally spotted the dirt road off Route 590. Based on the numerous, recent tire tracks on the seemingly obscure, unmarked road, Daniel decided to give him a little more time. When he started calling out turns well in advance, they felt more confident that the man had found his way.

"How much further?" said Munoz.

"About another quarter-mile. It's a pretty big place, you know," said Welsh, followed by a deep, guttural burp. "Sorry about that. The road is fucking with my stomach."

Daniel turned his head and met Jessica's glare. She didn't look happy to be seated next to Homer Simpson. Welsh's gaseous discharge refreshed the stale beer smell that had persisted in the SUV since he was stuffed into the back seat. Their short trip on the interstate had provided them with enough air turbulence to clear the stench, but they had no such luxury moving along at ten miles per hour on these roads. Daniel's handheld radio crackled and Graves' voice filled the van.

"We're picking up some faint wireless signals to the north. We should proceed on foot from here," he said, and Daniel acknowledged.

Munoz slowed the van in the middle of the road, blocking traffic in both directions. The Ford Transit stopped twenty feet behind them, depositing Fayed and Paracha.

"What kind of fence can we expect?" Daniel asked Welsh.

"I just hauled construction material up here. They didn't have a fence at that point."

"You think it's a quarter-mile? Does this road run straight north?"

"Straight as an arrow," said Welsh.

"Alright. Let's gear up," he said, and they all stepped into the damp Poconos air.

The operatives met between the two vans.

"Do the two of you mind keeping an eye on Mr. Welsh? We'll head about fifty meters into the forest and turn north toward the site," he said to Fayed and Paracha.

"No problem. We'll make sure nobody gets in or out. Our guys in the van are trying to access the security system. They're pretty sure we're dealing with cameras. High bandwidth wireless output," said Fayed.

"No motion detectors?" said Munoz.

"Not as far as our guys could tell. There might be a hardwired system close to the structure, but these are the only signals so far. I think we should move up another two hundred meters to be sure."

"We'll unload here and set out, while you reposition," said Daniel.

Munoz tossed the vehicle keys to Paracha, who snatched them out of the air.

"Mr. Welsh, Agents Paracha and Fayed will keep you company until we return. We should have you home in an hour or so. This is probably just a wild goose chase, but you never know. You'll be safe here," said Daniel.

He turned and walked to the Cherokee's rear lift gate, raising it to expose two black nylon duffel bags. He pulled out dark green load bearing vests (LBV) for the four operatives that would approach the compound. The vests had been loaded with thirty round magazines for the Mark 18 Mod 0 rifles each of them would carry. The Mark 18 was a modified M-4 carbine, fitted with a more compact 10.3 inch barrel, which was better suited for close quarters battle. These preselected versions had been equipped with EOTech holographic sights. Welsh nearly stumbled off the road when Daniel started to distribute the rifles.

"Fuckin' A, man. What are you expecting in there? Osama Bin Laden?" he said, clearly amused with his own comment.

Worse, thought Daniel. Aloud, he said, "Never hurts to be prepared."

Melendez reached into the same duffel bag and removed a thick suppressor, attaching it to the barrel of his rifle. He had already removed the EOTech sight, preferring to trust the iron sights for any long-range shots that might need to be taken. He would be their designated sharpshooter during the compound breach. All of them removed their black jackets and donned hunter camouflage patterned hoodies and ball caps, also compliments of Wal-Mart. Once they had tightened the LBV's over the camouflage hoodies, they all adjusted their earpieces and conducted a communications check. Everyone would be on the same channel for the raid, including the electronics team. Satisfied that they were ready, Daniel assembled them on the side of the road.

"Melendez, I want you on point. Pick a spot roughly fifty meters out and head due north. The rest of us will follow twenty meters back. Line abreast formation. Jess on the right, Munoz on the left. I got the middle. When we reach the fence, if there is one, we'll breach together. Sound good?"

Everyone nodded and Melendez removed a small handheld GPS unit, which he quickly configured as a compass. Moments later, their scout disappeared into the thick forest.

"We look like hillbillies. I can't believe our friend hasn't figured it out yet," whispered Jessica.

"He's still about seven Pabst Blue Ribbons away from sober. We could have shown up in clown suits. We're just lucky he found this place," said Daniel.

"You get to ride with him on the way back."

"Thanks," he said.

They pushed their way through the persistent ground cover to catch up with Melendez.

The approach to the compound proved difficult. Stubborn, newly grown underbrush obscured their vision, nearly eliminating any clear line of sight beyond twenty or thirty feet. Upon repositioning the vehicles, Graves was able to fix the locations of four wireless signals, none of which were located in the team's path. Graves felt confident that the signals belonged to four wireless cameras located along the road. He still couldn't discount the possibility of a fence linked motion detection system. At this point, security for the compound appeared to consist of four separate wireless feeds, which weren't tied to a central system. There was little Graves could do to help them without a computer network to manipulate. If the fence was hardwired into a standalone security alarm, they could expect immediate resistance.

Forty minutes into their patrol, Melendez reached a point where he could observe the fence. They all moved into a tight formation around Melendez and surveyed what they could see of the grounds. Daniel could see a tall chain link fence, topped with a single coil of concertina wire. It was difficult to tell from his angle, but it looked like the fence backed right up against the forest. Large branches appeared to rest on the concertina wire in a few places, flattening the coils. This basic observation convinced him that the fence was neither electrified, nor rigged with motion detection equipment. The constantly moving branches would have shorted the fence and driven security personnel insane with false alarms.

"Looks like about fifty meters of open ground," he said.

"Maybe a little less. I don't see any cameras mounted to the building, but I'd need to get closer to verify. Too many blind spots from here," said Melendez.

"Alright. Let's move up to the fence and observe for a few minutes. Keep low."

The small group slithered through the brush on the forest floor to a point along the fence. Now Daniel could see everything. Devoid of windows, the building's frontage spanned over one hundred feet. Two black Suburbans, parked side by side, faced a closed loading bay at the far eastern end of the building. Daniel couldn't see a gate from his angle, but he could discern a well-worn driveway leading away from the loading bay. A single, closed metal door was located to the right of the loading bay, made accessible by a short concrete slab stairway. The building's walls were constructed of featureless, gray cinderblocks, holding up what appeared to be a flat, metal roof. He could discern no pitch whatsoever to the roof, which struck him as unusual given the vast size of the one story building. If the interior craftsmanship resembled anything close to the lackluster exterior appearance, Honesdale Construction owed Mr. Mills about four million dollars.

"I don't see any cameras," said Munoz.

"Neither do I," said Jessica.

"I think we should move down the fence until we can see the western side of the building. If it's clear, Melendez will provide cover while we move to the corner. Melendez follows when we reach the building. We'll then move along the exterior to the back," said Daniel.

He passed the plan over his radio to Fayed, while Melendez and Jessica cut the fence with powerful, short-handled tin snips. Once the fence was opened, Daniel slipped through and sprinted for the corner of the building, followed closely by Jessica and Munoz. Daniel moved a few feet down the western side of the building, keeping his rifle's red holographic sight trained along the structure. He heard Jessica and Munoz pile into position behind him, followed by Munoz's voice in his earpiece. Melendez joined them a few seconds later and moved swiftly in front of Daniel, continuing his job as the team's point man.

Melendez extended his arm and held an open palm to Daniel as they approached the northeast corner of the building. At the sight of Melendez's hand, the rest of them stopped and crouched. He watched the young sniper approach the corner carefully, removing his camouflage baseball cap before taking a quick look along the northern wall. By Daniel's rough estimation, the side they had just traversed matched the front of the building in terms of length. The only difference between the two sides had been the complete absence of any openings on the eastern facade. They had just slid silently along a blank cinder block slate.

Daniel removed his own cap and tossed it to the ground, waiting for Melendez's assessment. Their pointman backed up against the wall and crouched. He pointed to his own eyes with his index and middle fingers ("I see"), then held his hand up showing three fingers, keeping his ring finger down along with his thumb ("seven"). The next hand signal indicated they were "enemy," accomplished by a simple thumbs-down. Finally, he stretched his arm upward and formed a pistol shape with his index finger and thumb, representing "rifles." Seven men armed with rifles. Not something you'd expect to find in the middle of the Poconos on a Sunday afternoon. He recalled Melendez.

"What are they doing?" he whispered.

"Digging. I see several bodies nearby. All of the weapons were slung around their backs. I did see a few with just pistols. No body armor. Everyone's dressed casually."

Jessica leaned in to hear what they were saying, while Munoz kept his rifle pointed at the front corner.

"Who were they burying?" asked Jessica.

"I saw a few lab coats stained bright red. The others looked like the gunmen. Looks like a cleanup job," said Melendez.

"Yeah. Tying up more loose ends. I need to get a look at the situation," said Daniel.

Daniel switched places with Melendez and crawled to the corner, easing his head toward the edge. As his view expanded, the stretch of ground between the northern fence line and the rear of the building took on a disturbing familiarity to another time and place. A different life. Men smoking cigarettes, their instruments of murder tossed casually over their shoulders. Nervous laughter. Nobody quite sure who might end up in the ground. In that other time and place, men like these rarely did the digging. That was reserved for the desperate victims that had somehow convinced themselves they were digging a hole for someone else. He watched the men in front of him carefully.

Only five of the men sank shovels into the soft ground near the fence. The other two stood behind them, conversing and laughing. He counted five AR-15 type rifles equipped with optics slung over the diggers' backs. The two "supervisors" carried pistols in tactical thigh rigs. Melendez had missed the fact that one of them carried an MP9 submachine gun on his left side. Admittedly, it was hidden from view. Daniel burned the image in his mind and returned to their tight group pressed against the cinderblock.

"Burial party. The five men armed with rifles are occupied with digging. Unfortunately, they're more or less facing this direction. The other two have their backs turned. One with a pistol. The other with a pistol…and an MP9. You're slipping, Rico," he said, patting Melendez on the back.

"The usual plan?" whispered Munoz, never looking away from the far corner.

"In this case, I don't think we can afford to improvise," said Daniel.

"Do you mind sharing with the rest of us?" said Jessica.

"I forgot that you ditched most of these classes. We bag two of them. Highest ranking and lowest ranking. The rest are targeted for rapid termination. The leader knows the most, but is willing to say the least. The follower knows the least, but is willing to say the most. The two usually hate each other. We play them off each other," said Daniel.

"What if they all go for their guns?" said Melendez.

"Then we have ourselves a good old fashioned shootout. Gunfight at the OK Corral," said Daniel.

"I'm your huckleberry," said Munoz.

"See? He does have a sense of humor, Rico," said Jessica.

"I never said you didn't have a sense of humor," insisted Melendez.

Munoz turned and grinned. "Let's just get this over with."

"Rico and Jessica shoot from the corner. You and I will sprint along the back wall, focused on the two men with pistols. We'll hit the guy with the MP9 and try to force the other guy to surrender. The two of you will tear into the digging crew. We'll be yelling for them to drop their weapons as we move. If you see hands raised skyward, keep them covered until we swing into place behind the group. Less than seventy five feet to targets. Good to go?" said Daniel.

"Sounds easy enough. We'll pop two of them and see what happens," said Melendez, nodding at Jessica.

Daniel and Munoz stacked up on the corner. As soon as they disappeared, Jessica and Melendez would take their place and start to engage targets. He edged up to the corner and took a quick peek, exposing less than an inch of his head to allow his right eye to verify that the scene looked the same. Nothing had changed, so he nodded. Less than a second later, he felt a solid squeeze on his right shoulder, indicating that the team was ready. He checked the M4's safety one more time out of habit and spun around the corner, sprinting along the wall. He wanted to get as far as possible before anyone noticed.

ᘛ

Michael Brooks stood facing his security crew as they slid their shovels into the ground. He hadn't decided if they would be buried in the same holes. It really all depended on how much space remained in each hole when they finished piling the bodies into the ground. Brooks really didn't feel like digging. He had a busy day scheduled and didn't need the delay. Plus, they might come in handy at the distribution center. Anne Renee said they could use some more help, especially given the compressed timeline. He swatted at a fly that buzzed by his head. He really hoped this group would finish their work within the next few minutes. The flies were already swarming around the pile of bodies littering the ground behind his men. He hated flies.

Jason Carnes, whose corpse formed part of the tangle, had never seen it coming. Even when Brooks' men corralled the laboratory group out of the back door for "instructions," he had ignored the dubious looks from his own people and even went so far as to make excuses for the few lab technicians that had already vanished. Two of the techs had tried to escape in one of the delivery trucks early this morning. Their absence was discovered a few minutes before one of the early morning convoys departed for the distribution center and the trucks were searched. They were found jammed between crates, cowering in fear. They had every reason to be afraid. Their bodies were hidden outside of the gate, until it was time to "sanitize" the facility.

The last convoy of delivery trucks carrying crates of freshly packaged bottled water to the distribution center had left the compound around 8:00 AM. Carnes' lab crew spent the next hour shutting down the packaging equipment and sterilizing laboratory equipment. Brooks started to sense that the techs were stalling, hoping that the security detail would leave. He decided to expedite his last remaining task at the facility, by directing everyone outside to receive instructions for their follow up assignment to the distribution facility.

Twenty-three men and women filed out of the door and milled around waiting for him to speak. His assistant, Jason Ryband, stood next to him and started to shoot into the group without warning, catching Brooks by surprise. Brooks had been waiting for his security detail to walk out of the back door and form a hasty line abreast. Instead, Brooks drew his own pistol in a desperate measure to keep Carnes' people from reaching him. His security team heard the shooting and ran through the door, firing at the runners, or anyone not huddled into a group that served no purpose other than to absorb bullets. It lasted less than twenty seconds. The digging followed, after a few distrustful glances from the security team. Brooks watched the shovels carefully, noticing that the men were not straining to move the dirt. Frankly, he was surprised they agreed to dig at all. He started to open his mouth to address this discrepancy, when one of them suddenly grabbed his rifle and tried to swing it around.

The movement startled Brooks, causing him to scramble for the pistol in his thigh holster. A fucking mutiny was underway. Before he could get his hand on the pistol, the security guard's head snapped back. The hiss and snap of passing bullets filled his ears, followed by thunderous explosions that drowned out every sound around him. He removed his hand from the pistol and glanced over his shoulder. His assistant lay face up on the ground, wheezing and rasping through a hole torn in his throat. When he turned back around, only one of his men remained standing. The others twitched or lay motionless on the grass. He didn't dare look for the source of the gunfire. Instead, he raised his hands slowly above his head, nodding at his last guard to do the same.

❧

Daniel jogged over to the presumed leader of the group, keeping his rifle trained at the man's head. Through his peripheral vision, he could see the rest of his team moving toward the second surviving guard. They had a leader and a follower. Not bad for three seconds of work. Munoz announced that he would clear the doorway and make sure they didn't have any surprise visitors from inside the building.

"Clear and restrain," said Daniel.

Jessica sprinted over and yanked the leader's pistol from his thigh holster and tossed it into one of the shallow graves. She patted him down for any other weapons, removing a small folding knife from his back pocket. She stepped over to the second gunman and cut his rifle sling with the knife, letting his rifle fall to the ground. Aside from the K-Bar knife attached to his belt, she didn't find anything concealed. She tossed the knife to the ground and proceeded to zip tie their hands behind their backs.

"Over here," Daniel motioned to the two prisoners.

The two men hadn't said a word since the ambush, which surprised Daniel. These two might be harder to crack than he expected. Normally, someone was demanding answers or exhibiting some kind of useless bravado. These two were either scared out of their minds, or they were cool customers. He'd soon find out. The two begrudgingly moved to where he had pointed his rifle, roughly ten feet behind where Daniel currently stood. He wanted them to have a nice view of the festivities.

"Pay close attention," growled Daniel, as they walked past him.

Daniel walked up to the man who had been armed with the MP-9 submachine gun. A wet rasping sound passed through the hole in his throat, which bubbled and overflowed with blood. His eyes looked ghastly, even for Daniel. He held his M4 CQB rifle in one hand and placed the barrel in the man's mouth.

"Can you tell me what's going on around here? What's the purpose of this facility? Were the virus canisters stored here? I'm sorry, I can't hear what you're saying," said Daniel, addressing the mortally wounded man sprawled out on the ground.

"Who's he talking to?" said the leader, finally breaking their code of silence.

Daniel pulled the trigger, firing a single 5.56mm M885 projectile through the back of the man's skull into the ground.

"What the fuck! Oh, Jesus Christ!" yelled the follower.

Daniel turned to the two of them.

"I have absolutely no use for anyone that can't…or won't answer my questions."

He walked over to the last remaining guard who appeared alive. He kicked the man in the side of his ribcage, where he had suffered from a messy exit wound. The 5.56mm projectile had a nasty habit of tumbling around inside the human body, bouncing off bone and finding its own unique pathway out. He could see three entry wounds in the center of the man's chest, which put this particular exit nearly ninety degrees off the original trajectory. The man emitted a guttural, animal sounding moan in response to the kick.

"I can't imagine this guy answering any questions."

Daniel kneeled down and picked up the discarded K-Bar knife, raising it high before slamming it through the man's neck.

"Fuck this!" the follower screamed, struggling to break free of Jessica's hold on his collar.

"This is psychotic. Who the fuck are you?" said the leader.

Daniel rushed up and placed the sticky blade under his chin.

"But executing twenty people and rolling them into a shallow grave is perfectly normal? You've been hitting the Greely-Harding Kool-Aid a little heavy," he said and shifted over to the follower, grabbing him by his hair.

"Do you really think this fucker was going to let you leave this place alive? I've seen people dig their own graves before. Once they figure it out, they start to shovel half loads in an attempt to put off the inevitable. I've been watching you dig for a while now. How long does it take to dig a fucking hole?"

"He's full of shit, Douglass. Nobody was planning to shoot you," said the leader.

Daniel released his hair.

"I wonder what he told them," said Daniel, pointing to the fly encrusted pile of bodies with his bloody K-Bar knife. "So, here's the deal. I'm going to take a little tour of your facility. When I'm done, I'll be back with lots of questions. You don't want to be the first person to stop answering my questions."

❧

General Terrence Sanderson answered his phone immediately.

"Daniel, I presume everything is moving along smoothly up there?"

"Not by any measure. I think you need to call the president and have them converge on the distribution hubs. From what I can tell, they're bottling up the virus and transporting it nationwide. We caught the last of the security crew here tying up loose ends, Milosevic style."

"Have they confirmed this? What are the targets?"

"We've been working over the two that we captured. They confirmed that thousands of bottles were transported from this site to one of the distribution hubs over the course of the last twelve hours. They both claim to have no knowledge of what went on inside the industrial grade laboratory we found in this place. This site resembles a miniaturized, standalone version of a bottled water plant. They have at least three thousand square feet dedicated to assembly and packaging. Now I know where most of Benjamin Young's money was spent," said Daniel.

"The bottles were poisoned? I didn't think this was possible. The virus wouldn't survive suspended in the water for very long. Are you sure this was their plan?" Sanderson questioned.

"I'm not seeing any other conclusion to be drawn. We found the original virus canisters shipped from Europe. They sure as hell did something to the bottles that left this facility. Whatever they're planning for those bottles, I guarantee it won't be random. They've carefully crafted the events leading up to this sudden demand for bottled water. You need to convince the president to shut this whole fucking town down," said Daniel.

"That won't work. First of all, I'm back on the shit list. They won't believe a word I say, especially with Director Shelby whispering in their ears. Secondly, the bottles might already be on the way to their intended targets. Unless someone confesses on site, the FBI has no way to force this information out of them. This water will disappear into the population as soon as it hits the shelves. Give me specific targets, and I'll try to call the president."

"The president could go on national television and tell the American people not to drink Crystal Source water! How hard can this be?"

"He'll only do that if he believes me. You know how this works. If I call him up right now, rambling about poisoned bottled water linked to a bottled water company, I'm going to have a problem with credibility. Especially when I try to explain how we obtained the information. Anyone that could prove we were working in good faith on behalf of the FBI task force is either dead or unconscious. Right now, we are once again enemies of the state. Get over to the distribution hub and unfuck this situation. Please."

The line went silent for a few moments.

"Alright. We'll close up shop around here and try to figure out which hub they're using. Things sound a little tense down there, General," said Petrovich.

"We're leaving the compound. Headed to more populated areas east of here. I'm not taking any chances."

"It wasn't a bad run while it lasted," said Daniel.

"A minor setback. I'm nowhere close to finished," said Sanderson.

"There's no place for someone like you or me in the system they've created. They'll congratulate you with one hand, and put a gun to your head with the other."

"Don't lose the faith, Daniel. We're their last line of defense. It's worth the trouble. Can I count on you to see this through to the end?"

"Have I ever disappointed you, General?"

"Just once I wish you'd quit answering my questions with another question. Is that too much to ask?" said Sanderson.

"Yes."

"Enjoying yourself?"

"Not really."

"Get me some targeted information, and I'll make the call."

"We're on it," said Daniel.

Sanderson disconnected the call and walked up a short path to meet with his operations officer. Standing on the covered porch of the headquarters lodge, Parker looked disturbed.

"What's wrong?" asked Sanderson.

"I just lost all satellite connectivity. They're shutting us down," said Parker.

"Can they do that without Argentine cooperation?"

Parker shook his head.

"Shit. What's the impact to our organization?"

"We're temporarily cut off from our EW teams in the States. We'll probably lose our sat phones next. We need to get out of here immediately and reestablish our entire communications network. We've been transmitting from a fixed position known to the U.S. government for at least a week, which has given them plenty of time to sniff around our system. I've been careful with our data management. All of our U.S. feeds were one way, which is impossible for them to intercept. I scrubbed the return data in case they had somehow managed to piggy back the satellite we were using. Our network hacks are still intact. The team in McLean has full access to FBI headquarters."

"Issue backup SATCOM to each vehicle and clear out. I'll meet up with you in Neuquén," said Sanderson.

"We'll be ready to roll in fifteen minutes. I guess we should be thankful for the cloud cover," said Parker.

"Let's hope it's cloudy all the way to Neuquén. Start working on a plan to take us to the coast. Neuquén's bound to shrink really fast if the Argentine government gets involved. Senior Galenden told me he had to back off this for a while. We're more or less on our own."

"We'll be fine. We have the best team possible on the job up north," Parker assured him.

Sanderson pondered the ex-SEAL's statement. Daniel's sense of duty was confused. He had long ago ceased buying U.S. patriotism wholesale. His dedication to Jessica overshadowed all of his motivations, which was why Sanderson always framed their conversations around what was best for their future together. It wasn't a disingenuous tactic. Daniel could smell his bullshit for miles, so there was no point in trying to psychologically sway him. Framing it for their benefit allowed him to continue conversations that Daniel would normally dismiss.

He thought about Daniel's tone near the end of their most recent phone conversation. Petrovich resorted to humor when he was undecided. He also tended to quickly agree with Sanderson when he had no intention of following instructions. Daniel remained an enigma to this very day, which gave Sanderson no comfort. Unfortunately, there was little he could do to control the situation. If Daniel walked off the mission with Jessica, he still had four extremely capable operatives to continue the mission. He didn't want to think about it. He had enough to worry about on his end.

❧

Daniel walked over to the two men sitting side by side on the laboratory floor. They were both tightly cuffed to a large, stainless steel workstation, using two pairs of metal handcuffs found in Brooks' desk.

"Good news. You're free to go," he said.

Douglass Kemp expressed a look of relief, which was not shared by Michael Brooks, head of security.

"Not really," Daniel added, instantly deflating the man.

Douglass had been quick to identify Brooks' position after a few minutes of impromptu waterboarding on one of the lab tables. He'd been unable to identify the destination of the convoys leaving this site, but he'd professed that the delivery trucks were filled with crates of water processed in the assembly line next door. He'd also confirmed that the trucks were unmarked and had run nonstop since three or four in the afternoon yesterday. They had pressed him about potential targets, but it was evident that he knew little beyond what he had seen firsthand at the site or had learned from his equally uninformed fellow security guards. He had no solid concept of True America's greater plot for the next few weeks, only that he'd go down in the history books as part of the New Recovery.

Daniel told him that he might make medical history. This comment managed to raise Brooks' eyebrows, which gave Daniel some hope that he might not have to resort to cutting them open. Brooks had shown considerable resilience against waterboarding, leaving them with little choice. They didn't have all day to identify and exploit his psychological weaknesses, though Daniel had an idea. If it didn't work, he'd turn this over to Aleem Fayed and Tariq Paracha. Sanderson had assured Daniel that the two of them would produce results.

"Here's where we stand. Douglass has nothing more to tell, and Michael plans to hold out as long as he can. Michael knows he'll eventually tell us everything, but he's clinging to the notion of loyalty and honor. I can appreciate that, but I assure you that these notions will be crushed just as quickly as your testicles. Just one of a hundred painful, non-lethal examples of the misery you'll endure for your masters. The end result is always the same," he said, walking over to Fayed and Paracha.

"I'll turn you over to my friends here, and your screams will fill this building for hours, eventually replaced with the begging and the sobbing. But here's the twist—they're going to be really careful this time. I want you to survive, Michael. I want you to sit here on this floor for the next week or two with your new best friend. Thirsty, Douglass?"

Daniel took a bottle of Crystal Source water sitting on the table above them and stepped back, slowly twisting open the cap in front of them. He brought the bottle to the trembling man's lips and paused when Michael Brooks yelled, "Don't drink that, Doug! Who knows what they did to it?"

"That's true, Doug. Maybe we should take one out of a fresh crate. Fresh water please!" said Daniel.

Melendez stepped into the room carrying the shrink wrapped case and slammed it down in front of the two men. Daniel ripped open the plastic on one of the sides and started digging through to one of the bottles in the middle. He pulled one out and opened it, holding it out toward Douglass.

"Now here's a fresh one. Found the crate sitting inside the loading bay. Probably left behind for the security guys. Nothing like a clean bottle of Crystal Source after a long day of digging graves. Right, Michael?"

"Don't do it, Doug. They could have poisoned all of the bottles," said Brooks.

"You think we poisoned all of the bottles and then somehow packaged them up to look like they came from the Crystal Source bottling factory? That sounds like an insane conspiracy, Michael. Right? You better get used to this stuff. It's all we're leaving behind for you. Go ahead, Douglass."

He held it closer to the man's lips.

"Douglass, listen to me. They're fucking crazy. We're dead no matter what."

Daniel removed the bottle of water and poured it over Michael's head. He watched the man blow out of his nose and press his eyes and mouth shut until the water ran its course.

"Wow. Did you see that, Doug? He almost had a panic attack."

Daniel dried his head with a towel handed to him by Paracha. He waited until Brook's opened his eyes again, then opened another bottle and put it up to Kemp's lips. The man closed his eyes and mouth, twisting his body and turning his head away from the bottle.

"Damn. Now Doug doesn't want the water. Too bad he already drank a ton of it."

Melendez reentered the room carrying a transparent plastic bag filled with at least ten empty bottles. He kicked the half empty case of water along the floor through the doorway.

"We used these bottles to waterboard Mr. Kemp. Don't worry, Mikey. We used the tap water on you."

Kemp looked despondent and utterly confused. Brooks looked horrified.

"Do you want to tell him what's going to happen, or should I? This may come as a complete shock to you, Mikey, but I led a CIA sanctioned special operations team into Russia a few weeks ago. I saw what happens first hand in Monchegorsk. You have no concept of what your organization just unleashed on this country…but you'll get to experience it firsthand, chained to this table. It's going to be a long week for you Michael. Watching Doug and waiting."

"What is he talking about, Mr. Brooks?"

Michael Brooks stayed silent.

"Mr. Brooks?"

Brooks stared off into space. A quick slap from Daniel brought him back into the conversation.

"Doug., the water you swallowed and took into your lungs was infected with a weaponized form of viral encephalitis. A demented scientist from Russia's premier virology lab designed this particular strain to maximize the amount of damage inflicted on the brain's temporal lobe. At first, you'll start to experience typical flu-like symptoms. Weakness, chills, cough, congestion…the usual stuff. A few days later…"

Daniel shook his head slowly back and forth.

"What?" said Kemp.

"The hallmark symptoms of this virus are rage, aggression, violence, murderous impulses. At least that's what I saw in most of the infected population. The destruction of the temporal lobe results in irreversible brain damage, and permanent regression to these savage instincts. Mr. Brooks had every reason to keep you from drinking that water. You're chained to the table next to him. He doesn't want to wake up in a few days to find you gnawing on his head."

Douglass Kemp tried to distance himself from Brooks, but Daniel had attached their handcuffs to the table less than a foot apart. No matter how hard the two of them tried, they would always be within biting distance.

"History in the making, Doug! You'll be the first to experience the start of True America's New Recovery plan. Turning American citizens into rabid zombies."

"They sent this into the population?" Kemp yelled at Brooks.

Brooks glared at Daniel, shaking his head.

"Thousands of bottles are headed to one of the distribution plants. I need to know which one. Right now, my plan is to free one of Doug's hands, leave the two of you several jugs of tap water, and never return. What are your thoughts about that course of action, Michael? Do you think Doug will put the jug to your lips and let you drink? Or will he bash your skull against the table out of principle? Maybe he won't be able to kill you in cold blood. He'll help you drink, still hopeful that someone might be coming, which they won't be. Then, one day within the next week or so, he'll bite your face off and spit it out in your lap."

"You'll let us go if I tell you?" said Brooks.

"No. I'll drop Mr. Kemp off in town, where he'll seek medical treatment. High dose, intravenous acyclovir should kill the virus. We'll let him know when he can come back out here to get you, or send someone else. Mr. Kemp's choice. If he attempts to warn anyone before that, we'll bring his three children here to the laboratory and cuff them to this little stretch of table with Daddy and Uncle Mike. Thanks to your excellent record keeping, we know where his ex-wife lives. You won't fuck with us, will you Mr. Kemp?"

"No, sir. I won't say a word. I'll go about my business like this never happened. Why would you have my ex-wife's address in a file?"

"Leverage, Doug. That's what security people do. They collect information to use against you," said Daniel.

Brooks shook his head and said, "Don't listen to him, Doug. He's clearly insane. How long will I have to wait?"

Daniel looked at his watch.

"If you stop wasting my time, I'll be done within a few hours. The rest will be up to Doug. He doesn't look happy."

Brooks looked around at everyone. Doug refused to meet his eyes. He stared at Daniel for several seconds and glanced away before he started talking.

Chapter 54

1:08 PM
Washington Hospital Center-Observation Unit
Washington D.C.

Frederick Shelby knocked on the hospital room door and entered. Special Agent Ryan Sharpe sat upright in a sturdy hospital bed, staring out the window. His right cheek was bandaged with a thick gauze pad stretched in several directions by surgical tape. A similar bandage covered his forehead. Beyond that, Shelby could see that his left arm was in a thick cast, supported by a stainless steel bracket mounted to the top of his bed frame. His leg lay in an unsupported cast above the blankets at the foot of the bed. He turned his head and forced a thin smile at the sight of the director.

"You're looking a little better than last night. Still look like crap, but at least you're awake," said Shelby, taking a seat under the raised television. "I'm really sorry to hear about Frank. He was one of our best agents. I struggled to decide who should run that task force."

Sharpe smiled a little more, which was a good sign. Sharpe had contacted him as soon as he regained consciousness this morning. Shelby didn't want to descend upon him like a vulture, but they were having an impossible time trying to piece the investigation back together without the help of key task force personnel. O'Reilly was still unconscious, having been shielded by Hesterman, who was killed instantly. Digital playback clearly showed the two hundred and twenty five pound ex-linebacker from Michigan intentionally hovering over O'Reilly less than a second before the bomb detonated. Mendoza was gone, along with most of the FBI agents sitting near O'Reilly. From what Sharpe had told him a few days ago,

O'Reilly had arranged the work stations so that the more important agents sat close by. Nobody within twenty feet of her survived.

"You probably made the wrong choice. He pretty much ran it anyway. I need to talk to you about something," said Sharpe.

"Don't go and try to blame this on yourself in any way. This was a coordinated attack by True America, with a little help from General Sanderson. There was nothing you could do to stop it."

"Sanderson had nothing to do with the attack. I can assure you of that."

"I watched that Stewart traitor rush over and finish the job. Mendoza had stopped the attack. She set off the bomb. One of the survivors confirmed this," said Shelby.

"That's not what happened. I clearly remember Stewart yelling something about a dead man's switch. She held onto that detonator for a few seconds, while Mendoza lowered his gun—"

"She was just buying time. I saw the tape. She yelled something at him, which made him lower his gun. Probably threatened to blow the place up. As soon as he lowered the pistol, she blew the place sky high."

"No. Another agent shot her. She lost control of the detonator," said Sharpe.

"She set it off, Ryan. Sanderson's people got to one of the security guards earlier in the day. He let the bomber through the checkpoint. He described how a highly professional and brutal group snatched him off the street and kidnapped his family. They threatened to kill his wife and children. Sound familiar? This has Sanderson written all over it. I've already arrested his people in Brooklyn. We're looking for the rest."

"There is absolutely no way that Stewart or Sanderson had anything to do with that bomb. I've been working behind the scenes with them for two days, trying to catch up with True America. Nearly all of the information we've obtained has been hand delivered to us by his operatives."

Shelby thought Sharpe's sentence hadn't made a lot of sense. It had sounded like he just claimed to be working with Sanderson.

"I'm sorry. I didn't fully understand what you just said."

Sharpe spent the next ten minutes explaining everything that had happened since the Brooklyn raid, up through the successful rescue of Benjamin Young. Shelby stood up and paced the room for a few minutes, while neither of them spoke a word. He couldn't believe what he had just heard, but oddly enough, it all made sense. If any other agent had told him that story, he would have arrested them on the spot, but Sharpe was different. He had spent the last two years searching for Sanderson, and had every reason to distrust him. He couldn't dismiss Sharpe's assessment.

"Where did you leave things with Sanderson?"

"He'd sent one of his teams north to investigate a possible lead," said Sharpe.

"He didn't happen to send them to Scranton, did he?"

"How did you know that?"

"Because Jessica and Daniel Petrovich boarded a plane to Wilkes Barre/Scranton International Airport yesterday afternoon. I've already redeployed the mobile task force to Scranton. Guess who was on that same flight?"

Sharpe shook his head.

"Jeffrey Munoz. If Sanderson sent these three to Scranton, we're talking about more than just a reconnaissance mission," said Shelby.

"What are you going to do?"

"About what?"

"About Scranton."

"Wait and see. It sounds like this might be under control," said Shelby.

"And me?"

"There's an upcoming retirement at the executive level in the National Security Branch. Associate Executive Assistant Director. If things don't completely go to shit in the next few days, I'd like to offer you that position."

Sharpe squinted and lightly shook his head.

"I have a reputation for doing things by the book, Ryan, but if you closely examine my career, you'll see a subtle pattern emerge. My greatest successes have always been surrounded by unproven accusations of irregular procedure. Sometimes you have to bend the rules to get things done around here. I keep an eye out for agents that have the salt to walk that line. Let's hope Sanderson comes through for you. If this blows up in my face, I can't bring you along for that ride."

"I understand. Thank you for the kind words regarding Frank."

Shelby nodded and took in a deep breath.

"Have you heard from Sanderson since last night?"

"No. I tried the number he provided, but it didn't go through," said Sharpe.

"Let me know if you hear from him. I don't want the task force to interfere with his efforts," said Shelby.

"I'll let you know if I get through."

Shelby turned and walked out of the room. He was infuriated with Sharpe, but had long ago learned to channel his anger in a constructive direction. Offering him a promotion seemed like the only logical decision. The nation's security depended on his ability to find and promote agents like this Sharpe. Most agents were afraid of their own shadows and spent more time analyzing the political ramifications of their decisions than actually making them. He hated being kept in the dark, but couldn't blame Sharpe for withholding this secret. He had every reason to believe Shelby would relieve him on the spot and have him arrested for treason.

Instead of heading home for a few hours, he decided to head back to the Situation Room. He needed to be in place when Sanderson's people started putting their skills to work in Pennsylvania. He also couldn't wait to break the bad news to the president. From what Sharpe and his team had determined, the terrorist plot had been sponsored and planned by a splinter cell within True America, without any connection to the mainstream political action group. He wouldn't play any part in the president's plan to dismantle True America, unless they could establish an evidence-based connection. From what he could tell, a connection didn't exist. He loved stirring up controversy.

Chapter 55

1:32 PM
Crystal Source Distribution Plant-White Mills
Honesdale, Pennsylvania

Daniel Petrovich leaned across the Jeep Grand Cherokee's center console and presented his FBI credentials to the gray haired, uniformed guard at the passenger vehicle gate. The weathered man's light blue eyes widened at the sight of his badge. He leaned closer to the driver's window and peered into the back seat. Melendez and Jessica held up their own credentials, which seemed to satisfy the guard. Daniel smiled from the front passenger seat. Before either of them could speak, five massive Crystal Source semi-trailers trucks passed through the commercial gate on the other side of the glass enclosed guardhouse, headed for Route Six. He wondered if the trucks carried any of the virus-laced water. He waited for the last truck to pass before speaking.

"I'm Special Agent Harris with the Philadelphia field office. I need to speak with the distribution center manager, Bob Wilkins, immediately. Al Qaeda extremists have made a specific threat against this facility. Is his office nearby?"

"Holy cow! He's right in that building there. See that door on the far left? His secretary sits in there. She's not in today, but pretty much everyone else is. Do I need to close the gate once you're through?"

"No. You're fine for now. We have agents watching the roads, but I really need to talk to Mr. Wilkins about specific personnel employed at the facility. Keep this to yourself for now. Mr. Wilkins will notify the security manager about the new procedures to be implemented. Personally, I'd like to see a few more guards at this gate,"

"I've been saying that for years! Jesus. This is some scary shit. We have several Arab guys working here!"

"Damn right it's scary. Our mission is to make sure that important sites like this remain in operation. Keep up the good work. We'll get you those reinforcements," said Daniel.

"Let me get the gate! Park anywhere in that lot," he said, and pointed at a building across the road, surrounded by a full parking lot. The guard ducked back into the security shack and activated the gate. Munoz started to drive the Cherokee away.

"One of them works in the same building!" yelled the guard.

"One of who?" said Daniel.

"One of those Arabs!"

Daniel gave him an enthusiastic "thumbs-up" through the passenger window, visible over the top of the SUV. Munoz guided them into the parking lot, looking for an empty space. The security guard wasn't kidding about everyone being in today, which didn't surprise him. This might be the busiest day in Crystal Source's history. Daniel and the rest of the team hadn't seen a bottle of water in stock since they arrived in Scranton. As reported by news agencies, the price of most brands had nearly doubled in the past day, leading to accusations of price gouging. Daniel wondered what the American public would think about the fact that the owner of a major regional bottled water company had a direct hand in creating this frenzy.

"Good thing we left our two resident Al Qaeda lookalikes in the van," said Daniel.

The van was parked a few hundred meters down the road, tucked behind a shuttered business. Graves and Gupta would monitor local and state police channels, having already decrypted all of the P25 digital radio protocols in use within the greater Honesdale area. Disturbingly, they had picked up radio traffic indicating a significant FBI presence in Scranton. Daniel had considered sending the van west to collect data directly from the FBI, but they all agreed that the van would serve them better in a direct support role. If the situation inside the distribution center deteriorated, Fayed and Paracha might have to take control of the gate while Graves and Gupta tried to confuse responding police units.

Daniel glanced beyond the parking lot at the massive industrial buildings lining the street. The amount of activity inside the sprawling complex on a Sunday didn't surprise him given the national panic for bottled water. He had to give True America some credit for this insidiously clever plan. They had managed to prevent millions of Americans from drinking publicly sourced water and drive them right into their open arms. Another convoy of trucks passed the parking lot, headed for the open road. Two convoys in less than three minutes. Crystal Source had three distribution centers located within Honesdale city limits. The sheer volume of bottled water heading out into the population was impressive. He was willing to bet that Owen Mills had been well prepared to take advantage of this sudden windfall. Why not make a little money before you jumpstart the New Recovery?

They had considered the option of tracking down Mills first. He lived in a sprawling lakeside estate south of Honesdale. It was a tempting diversion that they couldn't afford. They had wasted enough time with Michael Brooks at the laboratory. He admitted that True America had manipulated events to drive up bottled water sales, but claimed to know nothing beyond that. It didn't matter as long as he provided them with the right distribution center. He had been willing to spend some time with Brooks to acquire this information.

Their fake FBI agent trick was unlikely to work on more than one site. If their first choice had been the wrong one, it would have taken them forever to figure it out. By then, the word would have spread to the other facilities, turning the next visit into a risky venture on several levels. Even worse, a simple phone call to the Philadelphia field office could unravel their deception with devastating results. From what Graves and Gupta gathered over state police frequencies, over fifty FBI agents had taken up residence in Scranton, including a large tactical team contingency. Brooks' information would prove to be invaluable, if the man hadn't lied. They'd soon find out.

"Jessica and I will deal with Bob Wilkins. If I get the sense that he's involved in the plot, I'm dragging him out of the office. Be ready to secure him in the back seat. I don't have a plan for this one. From what Brooks and Kemp told us, unmarked delivery vehicles have been moving in and out of this facility all night. If Wilkins isn't in on this, I can't imagine this hasn't raised some serious eyebrows in his office. He'll be able to lead us straight to the source. Keep an eye out for any interested parties. If True America is running their endgame out of this facility, they'll have eyes everywhere."

Melendez reached over the back of his seat into the rear cargo compartment and pulled out a compact polymer constructed P90 submachine gun and handed it forward to Munoz. Designed by Fabrique Nationale, the P90 represented a revolutionary shift in the design of compact, powerful assault weapons. Weighing less than seven pounds fully loaded, the weapon's length measured just less than twenty inches. Modular in design, utilizing a unique, proprietary top-mounted magazine feed system, the P90 could be handled unhindered in the tight confines of a vehicle or building. An integrated Ring Sight system provided quick acquisition, day or night, for Fabrique National's high velocity, armor piercing 5.7X28mm ammunition. Melendez pulled three more P90's from the rear, along with a smaller nylon bag containing two dozen 50 round magazines for the submachine guns and suppressors.

Jessica and Daniel exited the vehicle and stood on the driver side for a minute.

"You know what to look for. If he tries to sound any kind of alarm, I need you to put that knife into action. Scare some sense into him, but keep him alive," said Daniel.

"What's your plan?" Jessica asked.

"I'm going to lay it all on him. We'll know by his reaction."

"I'll be ready."

He stared at her, taking his mind out of its mission focused, system-processing mode for a second. He had no idea what they would face inside Bob Wilkins' office and beyond, but he could guarantee that the closer they came to the source, the more dangerous this would become. He didn't want her here. Bullets didn't show favoritism. They flew fast and straight until they hit something. Even the most unskilled, panicky shooter got lucky on occasion. Combat was all about the odds to Daniel. If you showed up, there was always a chance it could be your last appearance. There were always precautions you could take to improve your chances, but you could never fully eliminate the odds against you. The only guaranteed way to beat the odds was to avoid showing up altogether. They didn't have that option.

"Take a picture, it'll last longer," Jessica said, smiling.

"Be careful in there," he replied.

She flashed the black Tungsten carbide coated blade hidden along her left wrist and raised an eyebrow. He nodded at his colleagues in the SUV and walked toward the building, glancing around casually. He didn't see anything obviously out of place, but then again, he didn't expect to see someone leaning against the side of the building smoking cigarettes and pretending to read a newspaper.

They stepped inside the building and saw the empty desk that presumably belonged to the absent receptionist. Jessica minimized the amount of noise the door made by easing it closed. The greeting room contained a green vinyl couch centered on a low coffee table, which was flanked by two similarly appointed chairs. A few particleboard bookcases lined the walls, filled with technical manuals and a few random paperback books and topped with haphazardly spaced, framed award certificates. Beyond the receptionist's simple faux mahogany desk, he could see two low, cream-colored file cabinets. A thick CRT monitor sat on the corner of the desk, next to a stainless steel swing arm desk lamp. Altogether, it looked like the lamp and computer monitor had been the only additions made to the reception area within the last two decades.

They waited a few seconds to see if anyone would respond before walking toward the open doorway leading deeper into the building. He could hear voices from the hallway and telephones ringing. As they approached the door, a thin, balding man with wisps of white hair clinging stubbornly to the sides of his mottled skin appeared in the opening. He wore a pressed pair of basic khaki pants and a white, short-sleeved button down shirt with a light blue tie. A faded brown stain stood out prominently on the left breast pocket of his shirt.

"Thanks for coming by, but all sales appointments are going through corporate headquarters over at the Park Street facility. I can give you the number, but I don't know if you'll have much luck with a walk-in order today. I'm pretty sure they're all booked up as you can imagine. You drive up from Philly?" the man said.

"We have an appointment with Bob Wilkins," said Daniel.

The man's friendly demeanor faded as he folded his arms.

"I'm Bob Wilkins, and I don't appreciate sales reps who try to play games. Who are you two with?" he said, raising his eyebrows and crinkling his expansive forehead.

"Bob, can we talk privately?" asked Daniel.

Daniel held out his FBI credentials, while Jessica put herself in a position to reach through the door and grab him if necessary. Wilkins noticed her quick repositioning, his attention now torn between Jessica's close proximity and the badge.

"It has to do with the unusual vehicle traffic here at the White Mills facility, which started last night around five and has run pretty much nonstop since then," Daniel explained.

Bob Wilkins moved further into the room and closed the door behind him.

"It's better if we have a seat and pretend you're from the Villanova University concessions. I'm not sure what's going on around here right now."

They all took seats around the coffee table.

"Is this serious?" asked Wilkins.

"Extremely. What have you noticed beyond the vehicle traffic?" said Daniel.

"Look, I've been a loyal employee here for thirty-three years. Maybe I should talk with a lawyer first, or at least have one present."

"Why? Are you directly involved in something that might require legal representation?" asked Jessica.

"No, not at all. But I run this facility and I'm responsible for everything that goes on here," protested Wilkins.

"You're not under investigation, Mr. Wilkins, and we don't have time for lawyers. I have a tactical team waiting outside, ready to move within minutes," said Daniel.

"What? What are you talking about?" he said, trying to look past Jessica through the front door.

"We know for a fact that a terrorist cell is operating somewhere on this campus. All I need you to do is show us where."

"I don't know anything about a terrorist cell. How would I know where they are located?"

"They're using your facility and your vehicles to mass distribute biological weapons. I think you have a pretty good idea where we might find them," said Daniel.

"D-5. Son-of-a-bitch," Wilkins whispered.

"What does that mean? D-5?" asked Jessica.

"D-5 is one of the most isolated loading bay complexes. Mr. Mills shut this one down after the demand for water skyrocketed. Said he would be using it for special customer deliveries."

"Did he give any specific information about the deliveries?" said Jessica.

"Nothing, and I didn't ask questions. I'm too close to retirement to rock the boat. I figured he was sending shipments to preferred customers or private ones. It's his company. He can do whatever he wants. I just didn't appreciate the impact it had on my operations. He's taken over twenty of my drivers out of the rotation, plus several trucks…not to mention an entire bay complex. Then he cuts me completely out of it and puts some woman I've never heard of in charge out there. Anne Renee or something like that. I told him I'd be happy to run the show, but he didn't want to hear it."

"The woman isn't someone from Crystal Source?"

"I have no idea. Never seen her before at any of the management meetings or retreats. Every time I go over there to talk to her about coordinating gate traffic, I'm told she's busy."

"Have you noticed anything else out of the ordinary?"

"Yeah. None of the trucks are from Crystal Source. I saw a few Dasani rigs. You can't miss those. Arrowhead and Aquafina rigs too. I have no idea why these trucks would be at our facility."

Daniel looked at Jessica and shook his head.

"So much for narrowing this down," he said ruefully. He turned back to Wilkins. "Mr. Wilkins, I need you to take us to D-5."

"I don't know if that's such a good idea. They have a lookout or something posted outside. It's a long way from D-4 to D-5. Nothing in between. I never get past the guy outside."

"We'll take care of that. Do you have any idea how many people they have inside?" Jessica asked.

"I've never been inside, but they'd need at least a dozen to keep up the pace of trucks leaving the complex. Forklift operators and drivers to deliver the pallets of water. Aside from some of the drivers, the rest of the personnel were supplied by Anne Renee or Mills himself," said Wilkins.

Daniel thought about something he had said earlier. "Are the Crystal Source trucks equipped with GPS? Can you track them?"

"Absolutely. We track the entire fleet from one of the rooms down the hallway. All of the routes are preplanned. If a driver has to vary due to road closures or an accident, they call it in and we reprogram their route. It's pretty high tech. I have a bunch of smart people running that. Each distribution center tracks its own shipments," said Wilkins.

"I'm willing to bet they've been disabled, but it's worth a shot," said Daniel.

"You want to try and locate those trucks? I know which ones they are," said Wilkins.

"Not yet. Let's take a look at D-5 first."

Five minutes later, Wilkins, Jessica and Daniel drove off in Wilkins' Ford Taurus sedan, with the Jeep Grand Cherokee trailing a short distance back. Daniel crouched low behind the back of the front passenger seat, cradling a suppressed P90. The plan was simple. Jessica would accompany Wilkins into the building, with the hope of identifying Anne Renee. Jessica would grab the woman and Daniel would take down the lookout. Melendez and Munoz would then drive to the back of the loading bay to prepare for a two-pronged assault. Every attempt to take prisoners would be made where practical. They needed information regarding any of the trucks that had left the loading bay since yesterday evening.

⁂

Anne Renee Paulson's radio chirped.

"Now what?" she said in front of the two security guards stationed just inside the first bay.

The guy outside was starting to drive her crazy, and she was one false report away from replacing him with one of the less jumpy men watching the bays. The operation had gone off without a hitch. The unusual arrangement had drawn some attention and protest from the facility manager, but Owen Mills had squashed that pretty quickly. Aside from a few impotent visits by that aging idiot Wilkins, nobody had bothered them. She had one more convoy to deploy, and then they would close up shop and disappear. Unlike the laboratory, there would be no need for a "clean up." She was the only person in the warehouse that had any true concept of what they were loading onto the convoys, and even she had no idea where they were headed.

Mills had given her six locked metal containers, numbered one through six. She had been instructed to hand the appropriately labeled box to the lead driver right before departure. The driver would open the box, in front of Anne Renee, with a key personally provided by Owen Mills at some point yesterday. Mills had handpicked the lead driver for each convoy over a year ago and sent them through extensive training courses at the Hacker Valley compound. They were experienced semi-truck drivers, holding current operating licenses for the rigs they would drive, and they understood the importance of ensuring the delivery of their precious cargo. The rest of the drivers came from Crystal Source, and had no idea what they were transporting.

Anne Renee discovered that each box contained a handheld GPS receiver, which she presumed to be preprogrammed, an Iridium satellite phone with charger, and a sealed folder. Each driver activated the equipment and verified that it functioned correctly. She assumed that they would call a phone number for further details regarding their delivery. She had no idea what the folder might contain. Possibly the paperwork for the final transfer of the bottled water? Contracts and delivery agreements? She didn't care. Her job was to get all six convoys on the road without incident. Her radio echoed the voice of Sean Thompson.

"Ms. Paulson, Wilkins is here again, and he brought some woman with him. Says it's really important that he speaks with you."

"I don't have time to talk with Mr. Wilkins. I'll stop by his office when we are finished with Mr. Mills' business. Let him know that," she said.

"Alright."

There was an awkward, silent pause, as she shook her head and waited to hear that Wilkins and his guest were leaving. She stood with her back to the door leading into the front office guarded by Thompson, staring at the bustling facility. Two forklifts moved back and forth from the furthest bay, transporting crates to the bays accommodating the back of each trailer. They had almost loaded most of the final convoy—four semi-trailers filled with crates of Crystal Source water. Another hour of work and they would all drive out of the White Mills distribution center and go their separate ways. Anne Renee was supposed to meet Brown later to receive instructions for the next phase of the New Recovery plan. According to Lee Harding and Jackson Greely, she would play an important role. She had no idea if she would see any of these people again, or what the next phase entailed.

"Ma'am," came the guard's voice again, "Wilkins says the woman is the Distribution Center's Operations Manager. There's something wrong with one of the trucks we dispatched earlier. He's pretty pissed off."

She shook her head and cursed before transmitting. "Alright. Let them into the office. I'll meet them inside," she said and pocketed the radio. She looked at both of the security guards. "There's too much at stake here to take any risks. If they won't leave immediately, be ready to kill them where they stand. No mercy. Keep your pistols concealed for now."

Anne Renee opened the door just as Bob Wilkins and a strikingly attractive, well-poised woman walked through the entrance. The woman had an exotic quality, accentuated by her short brown hair and well tanned skin. Like herself, this woman looked out of place in Honesdale, Pennsylvania, especially at an industrial site. Despite the fact that she had only stepped into the building once, and had never met anyone beyond Wilkins, Anne Renee highly doubted that Bob's mystery guest worked in that shit hole of a building he called home. Her presence was a disturbing development, but one Anne Renee could rectify quickly. One hour. All she had to do was keep this place together for one more hour, regardless of how many bodies piled up in the front office.

&

Jessica couldn't hear what the guard was being told. His handheld radio was equipped with an earpiece. The guard didn't carry himself like any of the operatives they'd encountered in Atlanta, and even looked slightly less competent than the security personnel at the laboratory. She started to wonder if Brooklyn and Atlanta True America had made a serious dent in their supply of seasoned operatives. Then again, this guy was just a lookout. The real threats would be contained inside the building.

The bulky guard nodded his head a few times and responded to the voice in his earpiece.

"Go ahead. Ms. Paulson will meet you just inside," he informed them.

They walked up the gray wooden stairs onto a raised platform just outside of the entrance. The guard watched them carefully. When they reached the door, Jessica let Wilkins lead the way. He knew the building and Ms. Paulson would be expecting to see him first. She didn't expect handshakes to be exchanged, so she shifted her knife from the left to right hand. She could fight with the knife in either hand, but heavily favored her right hand for throwing. She didn't expect Paulson to be alone.

As Wilkins stepped through the threshold of the door, Jessica heard a thump from her immediate left. She turned her head casually, hoping not to attract attention from anyone inside. The guard collapsed against the cinderblock wall and slid to the raised concrete platform, trailing a crimson strain. She caught movement out of her peripheral vision, and knew that Daniel had opened the rear passenger car door. Wilkins had advised them to park to the left of the door, since it would be out of sight from inside the office. Everything was moving quickly. She turned forward and stepped into the dank office. She could tell by the musty smell that the office hadn't been used in years.

Just as she walked through the entry, a door in the left rear corner of the office opened, revealing a woman with blond hair worn in a modern-looking bob. She wore a gray fleece jacket over a white collared blouse, along with wheat brown slacks. She was immediately followed by two serious looking gentlemen dressed in casual business attire and wearing unzipped, hip level jackets.

She didn't like the odds. Daniel had her back, but a lot could go wrong in a few seconds. Hopefully, Bob Wilkins wouldn't panic and freeze. They had instructed him to drop to the floor if anyone flashed a gun. Wilkins didn't like the sound of this. He reiterated his earlier observation that he had expected to see more agents and continued to protest on the ride over. He was sharp enough to realize that they were going up against heavy odds.

"Who are you?" said Paulson, directing her glare at Jessica.

"Jessica Petrovich. Thank you for seeing us," she said, extending her left hand and willing her to take it.

Paulson regarded her for a moment and nodded to the two men on her left, "Do it."

Jessica didn't waste a fraction of a second trying to interpret her remark. She'd been prepared for the likelihood of a summary execution attempt and had already rehearsed her options. However, she hadn't anticipated the speed with which Paulson could draw her weapon. In the brief moment she had to initiate her plan, Jessica realized that the small space between them would get messy.

She reached behind her back as far as possible and snapped it forward, releasing the blade as she lurched for Paulson's hand. An overhand throw would have generated more momentum, but she didn't have time to raise her hand. As the knife penetrated the closest guard's throat, just above the Adam's apple, she swept Paulson's black semiautomatic pistol to the left and pivoted, grabbing the top of her shooting wrist with her right hand as it continued across from the knife throw. This briefly put her in a vulnerable position, with her back against Paulson.

Instead of fighting Jessica's grip, the woman kneed Jessica in the lower left back. The intensely sharp pain caused by the blow to her kidney forced Jessica to release her grip on Paulson's wrist. Desperate, Jessica launched herself backward into the woman, slamming her into the bookshelf along the wall. Jessica jabbed her elbow back sharply, catching Paulson in the throat and causing her to drop the pistol. Another elbow shot separated them, allowing Jessica to spin and face her. Expecting to defend another round of attacks, she squared her feet and raised her arms as her body turned; however, Paulson had decided to retreat. The woman threw herself backward, catapulting through the doorway leading into the loading bays and screamed for help.

ꕥ

Daniel knew she would make her move quickly, so he hustled out of the car as soon as Melendez dropped the guard standing next to the door on the platform. He had timed the shot perfectly with Wilkins' entrance. The old man had been out of sight when the contents of the guard's head painted the wall. Wilkins was already nervous enough, and his actions could affect the outcome in that room. Daniel sprinted up the stairs and listened to the voice activated feed sent from a microphone hidden inside Jessica's jacket collar to their earpieces. Once he heard Jessica's greeting, he mentally counted to two and opened the door. Jessica planned to grab Anne Renee if she took the handshake, or pounce on her within a few seconds if she refused. Either way, his mission was the same: fire controlled bursts from the P90 into anyone except for Jessica or Anne Renee.

Tucked into the P90, he immediately assessed the situation and chose his targets. The closest guard had drawn his pistol, but was pretty far from pointing it in a useful direction. *Primary threat.* The second guard had raised both hands to his neck in response to Jessica's knife. *Secondary threat.* He didn't see any firearms involved in the melee between Jessica and Anne Renee. *Under control.* He placed the closest guard's head in the center of the

P90's integrated Ring Sight and pulled the trigger back for a controlled burst. The P90's unusually high rate of fire sent six 5.7X28mm SS190 full metal-jacketed rounds into the man's head, which was overkill for this armor-piercing caliber. He shifted the sight to the other man and applied less pressure to the trigger, firing one round, which had the same effect. The P90 had a double trigger action, instead of a selector switch. Pulling the trigger back past a certain point activated its fully automatic action. By the time he had finished clearing the room, Jessica had disappeared through the open doorway leading deeper into the facility, chasing after their high value target.

"Jessica's in pursuit. Move around the back," he said out loud, hoping that Munoz was already driving the Cherokee toward the loading bay side of the building.

Daniel didn't wait. He rushed through the room, pushing aside Bob Wilkins and leaping over the guard with the blade embedded in his neck. When he reached the doorway, he didn't burst through like his wife. He leaned inside, aiming the P90, and formed an image. The loading bay connected to the office contained several pallets of Crystal Source water bottles piled along the wall closest to the opening. A forklift driver, oblivious to the drama behind him, backed his yellow machine from the rear of the semi-trailer. He could see the far end of the loading bay complex through large openings at the back of each bay, designed to allow the forklifts to move from bay to bay with ease. Jessica stood in the middle of the second bay, sprinting toward the next opening, ignoring everything but Anne Renee Paulson, who was wrestling an M4 rifle from one of her guards.

One of the men Jessica had passed on her way to the second bay drew a pistol and started to run in her direction. Daniel placed the man's upper torso at the top of the T-shaped reticle and pulled the trigger, firing a burst. He immediately switched to Anne Renee, who had grabbed the M4 and had swung its barrel in Jessica's direction. He didn't weigh his options with Jessica at risk. Jessica was in the open, with little hope of getting behind cover in time. He depressed the trigger, firing a short burst that mostly hit Anne Renee in the upper chest and neck. His next burst struck the guard next to her, who had barely recognized the threat to their facility before several armor piercing bullets punctured his face and eliminated any future possibility of forming thoughts. The guard's body collapsed to the concrete floor next to Anne Renee, who had fallen to her knees with a confused look on her face. She wasn't dead, but it was clear that her body wasn't sending commands to her limbs. She had already released the rifle's pistol grip, dropping the M4 to the dull concrete.

Jessica reached the wall separating bays one and two, kneeling behind it. She glanced up at him and cursed. They had lost their high value target, which could be a problem. The sound of yelling started to increase from the bays further down the long access corridor in front of Daniel. All along the back of the complex, members of True America started to realize that something was wrong. A woman peeked around the same corner hiding Jessica and fired some kind of submachine gun on full automatic at his position in the doorway. The bullets slammed into the doorframe and flew through the opening, puncturing the opposite wall and shredding an empty bookcase.

Daniel leaned in with the P90, just in time to see the woman's head disappear behind the wall. He signaled for Jessica to lie flat. Once she cleared the spot where he had calculated the shooter to be located, he depressed the trigger and held it back, perforating the wall above Jessica with the magazine's remaining rounds. At a rate of 900 rounds per minute, the fifty round magazine could be expended within three seconds, with little loss of control. His weapon fired for roughly two seconds, each armor piercing round passing easily through the cinderblock and showering Jessica with chunks of the powder covered debris.

Through the soccer ball sized hole blown through the cinderblock, he saw a body lurch forward. A bloodied hand flopped into view past the corner. Before reloading, he drew his USP Compact and slid it to Jessica. He noticed that she didn't attempt to stand up. After what he had just done to the woman behind the wall, he didn't blame her. If the woman past Jessica had been using similar ammunition, Daniel would be lying on the floor bleeding from multiple holes. Her 9mm rounds severely damaged the cinderblock barrier in front of Daniel, but failed to penetrate with the needed velocity to do more than spray cinderblock pieces into his face. He suspected that the True America operatives were using hollow point ammunition, which would mushroom upon impact and impart their energy over a wider area, further reducing their penetration power. Still, there were no guarantees in the world of projectile ballistics. He'd seen and caused his share of anomalies.

He replaced the P90's fifty round magazine and sprinted across the bay to Jessica. Gunfire erupted when he left the doorway, but most of the fire was directed at his previous position. He heard the snap and hiss of several near misses, as less experienced shooters poured rounds behind him. By the time they decided to adjust their fire, he had already cleared the open area between bays. When he reached Jessica, she was lying prone, covering the three men who stood with their hands in the air near the forklift. A massive gunfight erupted deeper within the loading complex.

❧

Melendez climbed back into the passenger seat of the Cherokee and slammed the door shut. He had just pulled off a headshot with a single, suppressed 5.7X28mm round, at a range of 42 meters using the P90's unmagnified Ring Sight. Given the fact that he had limited experience with the weapon, he was rightfully proud of the accomplishment. They had parked the SUV just out of sight around the next loading bay complex, in a position that allowed Melendez to open the door and brace the P90 against its outer edge. Munoz had parked the vehicle perfectly. The P90's reticle barely cleared the corner of the building, but gave him an unobstructed line of fire to the guard. Munoz had stood behind him to make the determination regarding Wilkins' position. A light tap on the shoulder indicated that Wilkins had entered the building and would not see the man's head splatter the wall. The 5.7 round performed as advertised.

The SUV lurched forward before the door closed, slamming Melendez against the headrest. Munoz drove across the wide expanse of crumbling asphalt that separated the two loading complexes. The large space between buildings was designed to accommodate the semi-trailers that would be navigated into position along the multiple loading bays behind the building. He drove diagonally across the asphalt, ignoring the faint markings indicating a proposed traffic flow. They needed to be in position at the corner of the building within seconds in order to effectively support Jessica and Daniel. Melendez could see the cab of the first semi-rig beyond the corner and hoped that the driver was inside the building. They had no idea how far the conspiracy penetrated, but they assumed the drivers would be heavily armed.

The car reached the corner and Melendez piled out, following Munoz into position at the corner. They both heard Daniel give the order to move, followed seconds later by the thunder of automatic gunfire. They turned the corner and stared at the first trailer. He could see the next trailer through the space underneath. Their quickest route to the last bay would be underneath the trailers. The gunfire intensified inside the first bay as they approached the trailer. Melendez caught some movement in his left peripheral vision and shifted the P90 to meet the threat. A man jumped down from the driver's door with an MP-5K in his right hand, but collapsed to the asphalt in a heap. Melendez had fired an extended burst from the P90 at his center mass before sliding under the trailer behind Munoz.

Glancing up at the bays as they moved through the fleet of trailers, they could tell that it would be a tight fit squeezing through the openings between the trailer sides and loading dock. They ducked under the second to last trailer, coming up on the last bay. A quick movement to their left brought both P90's up to their shoulders. Neither of them fired at the bearded, pot-bellied Grizzly Adams lookalike standing with his hands in the air.

"Federal Agents. How long have you been with True America?" said Munoz, flashing his badge.

"What? I've lived in America all my life. Look. I'm getting paid double for this haul. I don't ask questions, as long as they're just loading water in my rig. If Mr. Mill's has paranoid friends that want to guard their water shipment, that ain't none of my business," said the man.

The sound of automatic gunfire and individual pistol shots rang out, slightly muffled by the thick rubber seal linking the back of the trailer to the bay.

"Could you move your rig up a few feet so we can get into the bay? We'll make sure our people know whose side you're on. Stay in your cab until we come back for you," Munoz requested.

"No problem. I got nothing to do with this shit." Grizzly Adams ran back to his cab faster than either of them thought possible.

The diesel rumbled to life and lurched forward a few feet. Munoz and Melendez climbed into the bay undetected and started to clear the complex.

❧

Jessica couldn't believe how badly she had fucked up their one chance at grabbing Anne Renee Paulson. She had underestimated the woman on every level. The knee shot to her kidney had come a fraction of a second before she could throw her elbow, stunning her long enough to lose physical contact. Then she had recklessly chosen to pursue her through the doorway into the open bay area. She'd left Daniel with no choice but to kill her. She really hoped her decision didn't jeopardize their ability to track the shipments.

An incredible overpressure filled her ears, followed by repeated blasts which caused her to press both of her palms against the side of her head. Muzzle flashes extended beyond the wall in front of her, heating her face. Someone had just emptied an entire magazine on full automatic less than a foot from her face. The ringing in her ears continued when the gun fell silent. Daniel signaled for her to go prone, which she immediately acknowledged by diving to the cold concrete floor, facing away from the corner. She never heard the fusillade of bullets puncturing the wall where she once knelt, but she felt the jagged pieces of cinderblock pepper her back and strike her head.

A black semi-automatic pistol slid in front of her, which she grabbed without wasting the time to acknowledge her generous benefactor. She rose to one knee and aimed at the men near the back of the open trailer in bay one. None of them appeared to be armed. From the looks on their faces, they didn't appear to have any interest in weapons. Their hands flew skyward. A few seconds later, she saw Daniel burst through the doorway, headed in her direction. He reached her unscathed, despite the maelstrom of bullets that struck the bay wall behind him. She felt his comforting hand on her shoulder and could tell he was trying to tell her something.

She looked at him and shook her head. "I can't hear anything," she said, which came out at full volume.

Daniel nodded his head and pointed at the three men. She understood.

&

Daniel grimaced when Jessica yelled at him. The machine gun blasts had induced a temporary hearing loss that could last most of the day, producing a ringing or buzzing sound that would gradually diminish. This could become a considerable liability for their team if they decided to raid Mills' lakeside mansion. Satisfied that Jessica had this group under control, he spun around and faced the corner, determined to draw this battle to a quick end.

He raised the suppressed P90 and peeked around the corner, drawing fire from a guard hidden behind a forklift parked two bays down. The small caliber rounds struck the wall in front of Daniel, spraying his face with sharp fragments and causing him to flinch. The gunfire was relatively accurate for fully automatic bursts, but not accurate enough to suppress Daniel. He placed the shooter's head at the top of the Ring Sight's T-shaped reticle and pulled the trigger back far enough to fire a short burst of three rounds. The result was immediate, knocking the shooter back through the red cloud that had exploded from his head. He was starting to get the hang of this exotic weapon.

He detected movement to the left and aimed at a point two feet in, along the inner wall separating bays two and three. He'd seen something low profile peek around the corner. A quick peek from someone being cautious. He depressed the trigger again, holding it down for a second, sending roughly a dozen rounds through the cinderblock wall. A figure stumbled into the open past the corner, holding a standard Heckler and Koch MP-5 in one hand. Daniel couldn't see the entry wounds, but knew the man was finished. He let the man crumble to the concrete without taking further action to hasten his fall.

"Bay six clear. M and M clearing bay five," he heard in his earpiece.

From the far reaches of the loading complex, he saw two men take position along the furthest opening. They started cycling their weapons immediately through targets located in the furthest bays. Daniel couldn't hear their weapons from this distance, but he could tell they were actively clearing the bay. Specifically designed for the P90, the attached Gemtech suppressors reduced the sound produced by the weapon to the gun's own internal mechanism. Standing several feet away, it would sound like someone rapidly pulling the charging handle. At fifty feet, it would draw little attention from someone not attuned to the sound of suppressed firearms.

Determining that the opening directly in front of him was clear, he extended his torso around the corner, peering into the bay. Aside from several dozen pallets of bottled water set against the wall, the bay looked clear. He saw some movement deep inside the semi-trailer, behind a stack of secured pallets, but nobody fired at him from that direction. He motioned for them to come out of the trailer and waited.

"Bay five clear," he heard in his earpiece.

"Bay one clear. Clearing bay two. Watch inside the trailers. I found a few hiding," replied Daniel.

He saw M and M move cautiously through bay five. When they reached the opening to bay four, automatic gunfire thundered throughout the complex. The long bursts of fire concentrated on the corners hiding the two operatives. Dozens of projectiles tore the cinderblock barrier apart; cracking it in several places and exploding jagged pieces across the concrete floor. He was really glad they were using standard ammunition. The industrial grade walls separating the bays continued to prove effective cover against 9mm projectiles.

The men in the trailer walked out with their hands on their heads. Daniel sprinted around the corner and approached them, keeping an eye on bay three. He didn't see anyone in the brief second he was exposed.

"Face against the wall, on your knees. Fingers interlaced."

He circled behind the men as they quickly moved against the wall. Once they were flush against the wall, he frisked them for weapons, finding a 9mm Beretta pistol on the first man. He tucked this into his belt and completed the search of the other two, yielding nothing but a stainless steel multi-tool.

"True America?" said Daniel, slapping the first man's head.

The light haired man nodded and Daniel went to work with the oversized zip ties stuffed into his front jacket pockets. He secured the man's wrists and ankles, connecting the two zip ties together with a third, effectively hog-tying the man. He pulled the scruffy looking guy to the concrete.

"What about the rest of you?" he hissed.

"I was offered overtime. Been working since last night. Same with Benny," he said, nodding at the other guy.

"Don't move from this spot or I'll kill you. Understood?"

The two men nodded.

"Bay four clear."

One more bay to go. Daniel arrived at the corner in time to see two men take up position behind a stack of empty pallets to fire on Munoz and Melendez. He fired extended bursts at both men, instantly dropping them to the ground behind the blood sprayed wood. Each of the terrorists' upper torsos had absorbed roughly half of the P90's remaining twenty-eight rounds, which tumbled upon entry, fragmenting bone and jellifying their chest cavities. They were dead before their bodies started to fall.

Daniel detected movement to his left. Something moving fast. His world exploded a millisecond later.

 බ

Melendez hit the corner hard and dropped to a prone position. He didn't want a repeat of what happened in the last bay. He had been hammered by the repeated impact of cinderblock chunks, as the bullets pulverized the reinforced wall in front of him. The combination of stinging fragments and the prolonged sound of automatic gunfire caused him to instinctually crouch, knowing on some level that the wall wouldn't resist the 9mm onslaught much longer. He wasn't sure how many of the bullets had made it through, but a sizable hole remained when the guns fell silent. Large enough for him to use as a firing port to clear his side of the room.

He heard the mechanical sound of a suppressed P90. Two long bursts. He slid into a firing position at the corner of the wall and leaned his weapon in to take a quick look. Two men immediately filled his view, both carrying drum fed shotguns. Melendez fired a quick center of mass burst at the man aiming the shotgun in his direction and retracted his head. The first shotgun blast disintegrated a 2x2 foot section three feet above his head. The rest of the 12 gauge 00 buckshot went high as the mortally wounded shooter lost the ability to control the shotgun. Still, he managed to fire the entire thirty-round drum, even as he fell backward. His efforts brought down half of the cinderblock onto Melendez and punched several dozen holes through the roof. Because of the devastating shotgun blasts and hailstorm of concrete, he assumed that both shooters had unloaded on his wall.

ബ

Jessica felt the vibrations and miniature shockwaves produced by the automatic fire deeper inside the loading complex. She could also hear a low thumping sound over the persistent buzzing and ringing. Her sudden deafness left her feeling exposed. She constantly looked around, painfully aware of the fact that she couldn't hear someone walk up to her. She glanced back and forth between the blasted cinderblock corner and the three men. They looked terrified of the gunfire.

"Stay right here," she said, knowing that she had probably yelled this at them.

Against her better judgment and training, she left the men alone and scrambled for the opening. She reached the corner in time to see the wall next to Daniel explode, knocking him backward. The explosions continued, vaporizing sections of the wall, but sparing Daniel any further concussive damage. He scurried backward along the floor, losing his grip on the P90, as a figure shouldering a Saiga shotgun attempted to round the corner. The man repeatedly discharged the shortened semi-automatic shotgun as he walked, emboldened by the sheer firepower at his disposal. He appeared oblivious to Jessica's sudden presence.

She lined up the HK USP Compact's three-dot sight on the man's head and fired a single shot that stopped the firing. The man stumbled forward, discharging the weapon into the concrete one last time, before falling onto the clumsy shotgun. Daniel lay on his back, fumbling with an unfamiliar Beretta, which he finally extended toward the fallen shooter. He stared at her in disbelief and winked, which was the extent of the acknowledgement she required for saving his ass. She smirked, shaking her head, and turned to deal with the men she had left unattended. Thankfully, they hadn't moved a centimeter.

Daniel's ears rang, but he had no problem hearing Munoz.

"All clear in bay three. You okay in there?" yelled Munoz through the opening.

"I think so. How the fuck did you miss the guy with the Saiga?" yelled Daniel, making no effort to stand up.

"Two guys with Saigas. The other one fucked up Melendez. They came out of nowhere," said Munoz, showing his face through one of the holes in the wall.

Daniel sprang to his feet and retrieved the P90.

"Jessica's deaf. Help her out with the prisoners and get Wilkins back in here. We may need him," he said, pointing at Anne Renee's contorted body.

"Shit. I'm on it," Munoz said and ran toward bay one. Daniel reloaded while walking toward Melendez. A gray, cement powder encrusted form lay still among the rubble.

"I'm fine," Melendez said, lifting his head from the pile.

He spit a few marble sized chunks from his mouth and shook the debris from his head. Daniel offered him a hand and examined the bay. Four men dead and two huddled inside the back of the semi-trailer with their hands on their heads.

"Any live ones in bays five and six?"

"Negative. We cleared anything that moved," said Melendez.

"How did you get in?" Daniel said, glancing at the tightly sealed docking connection around the open trailer.

"The driver pulled forward a few feet to let us in. He must have been one of Wilkins' regular drivers. The driver of the first truck was definitely True America. He jumped down from his cab with an MP-5K."

"Go back out and get him. We need to talk to a driver," said Daniel.

"Got it."

Melendez rushed through the bays, trailing concrete dust. Daniel ran to the back of the trailer truck and ordered the two men forward. He hustled them at gunpoint toward bay two after a quick search. When he arrived in bay two, he found all three of the men pressed firmly against the wall. He was slightly surprised to see that the two unsecured men hadn't fled during the shotgun attack. He pointed at the hog-tied terrorist.

"Drag him by his legs into the first bay," he ordered, then turned to toward the room and yelled, "I want all of the prisoners assembled against the wall in bay one."

Daniel planned to spend one minute determining who would leave with them. He couldn't imagine they would be able stay here for much longer. The gun battle inside the warehouse was sure to have attracted attention. He expected to hear from Graves shortly. When he reached bay one, he directed the seven men to stand with their backs to the wall. The True America prisoner was thrown against cinderblocks by the warehouse loaders, one of whom kicked him in the stomach. He'd start this without Melendez and the driver. They really needed to get out of here.

"Everyone look up at me. I don't work for the FBI or any federal agency. I have no rules or restrictions holding me back, so don't fuck with me. True America is finished. Jackson Greely, Lee Harding and Owen Mills will be dead before the sun goes down. No mercy will be shown. This is how my organization works. The bottled water loaded onto these trucks carries the same weaponized encephalitis that destroyed a city in Russia and led to the president's national address yesterday morning."

All of them mumbled and protested. The man restrained on the floor spoke up.

"I didn't know the water was poisoned. I was dragged up here to help."

"With a Beretta pistol?" said Daniel.

"That's my own pistol. I'm a local volunteer for True America. I was asked to show up at the loading bay, so I tucked the pistol into my belt when I left last night. It was a little weird getting a call to come here after dark on a Saturday night."

"I know this guy. He's not a trouble maker," vouched one of the men in the line.

"I'm really not interested in a list of civic achievements. I need to know everything this group can tell me about the convoys that left here," said Daniel.

The man on the ground spoke up again.

"You need to check the locked box back there on that folding table. Ms. Paulson took one of those outside right before each convoy left. She came back empty handed."

Munoz stumbled back into the warehouse through the office door. "Wilkins split. We need to get out of here immediately."

"Melendez. What's your status?" said Daniel into the comm.

"Got the driver. Checking the other cabs. Looks like the rest of them took off," replied Melendez over the comms channel.

"Understood. Get him into the Cherokee. Search the driver with the MP-5K and take everything. Munoz, search Paulson's body for anything. We move in thirty seconds."

Daniel stepped over to the True America operative on the ground and pulled a small knife. He cut the zip ties restraining the man's legs and pulled him to his feet. He pointed to Jessica and signaled that he wanted her to take custody of the prisoner.

"Fuck with me one bit, and I'll cut your throat," he said, pushing him toward Jessica. "Melendez, bring the car around."

"Give me a minute to search this body," replied Melendez.

"You have about twenty seconds," said Petrovich.

A new voice cut into his earpiece.

"I'd recommend driving through the gate within the next sixty seconds. Honesdale dispatch just sent three cars to investigate reports of shots fired at the facility. I'll try to divert them, but this is bound to attract state troopers, which will inevitably drag the FBI into the picture," said Graves.

"Roger. Police en route. Fayed, I need you to intercept a gray Ford Taurus. Should be passing your position shortly. You're looking for a thin, gray haired gentleman named Bob Wilkins. We need him to identify the drivers assigned to the convoys and help us access company records. Take him to the house."

"I see the Taurus. What the fuck happened in there? He's driving that thing like a bat out of hell," said Fayed.

"Make sure you grab him. He's our best shot at locating the convoys," said Daniel.

"Copy. Out."

Munoz finished searching Paulson's body, retrieving a cell phone, car keys and a few spare magazines for a pistol.

"Toss me the car keys," said Daniel.

Forty five seconds later, they were split up between the Cherokee and Paulson's Mercedes SUV, travelling toward the gate. Munoz and Melendez had the True America operative in the Cherokee with the lockbox, while the Petroviches ferried Grizzly Adams. They sailed through the commercial gate unopposed, driving within the speed limit as they navigated toward Route Six. They passed several Honesdale police cars headed to the White Mills Distribution Center, followed closely by Pennsylvania state troopers. He hoped the contents of the box would shed some light on what Jackson Greely and the rest of his True America lunatics had planned for this supposed New Recovery.

Chapter 56

2:14 PM
The White House Oval Office
Washington, D.C.

The president stared at the phone for a second and glanced at Jacob Remy, who shrugged. The Situation Room's senior watch officer had requested the president's presence in the main conference room. Normally, this request would be passed through his National Security Advisor, or someone a little higher up in the chain-of-command.

"Patch the watch officer through," he said out loud.

"Mr. Lee, you're connected to the president," said his secretary.

"Mr. President, I apologize for this unorthodox request, but we've had a major development. Major General Bob Kearney needs to speak with you. They've figured out what happened to the remaining canisters, but it's complicated, sir. He's standing by."

"Tell General Kearney that I'm on my—"

"Pardon the interruption, Mr. President, but he said that you'd want to talk to him before entering the Situation Room. General Sanderson was involved."

Jacob Remy stood up from his comfortable chair and gave the president a concerned look. He nodded a second later. The president had no idea where this would go, but he was fairly certain it would be painful. Kearney had vouched for Sanderson's NCTC liaison, who appeared to have been a True America undercover operative. His Washington D.C. career would hit a wall if the evidence officially supported Shelby's theory that Sanderson had planted a traitor on the task force.

"Alright. Put Major General Kearney on," said the president.

"Mr. President, General Kearney. Sorry for the subterfuge, but I have a situation that requires special handling."

"What do you mean by that? Sanderson's situation is already complicated enough."

"Are we on speaker phone, Mr. President?"

"Yes. I'm with my advisor, Jacob Remy. The room is clear."

"We've discovered six convoys suspected of carrying bottled water contaminated with the Zulu Virus."

"Convoys? Bottled water?" he said, glancing at the pitcher of water on the silver tray at the edge of his desk.

"It appears that True America never intended to poison municipal water supplies. Sanderson's team tracked the canisters to a hidden facility in Pennsylvania, where they were used to lace bottles with the virus. Thousands of bottles headed to different targets. They managed to stop one of the convoys at its point of origin in Honesdale, Pennsylvania at one of the Crystal Source spring water distribution plants."

"Have they figured out the convoy's target?"

"Yes, sir. The shipment was manifested and scheduled for delivery to the United Nations Headquarters in New York City. The delivery paperwork looks authentic."

"Good God. The General Assembly is scheduled to start a two-week session tomorrow. Do we know any of the other targets?"

"Negative, sir. The lead drivers of each convoy were given sealed boxes with preprogrammed GPS units, a satellite phone and delivery paperwork. Only the driver knows the target."

"Where is Honesdale?"

"Near Scranton, sir."

"Have you notified Director Shelby? They have an entire task force in Scranton."

"I've been debating that," said Kearney.

"What? I'm not sure I'm hearing you correctly, General. What exactly is there to debate?"

"This is why I wanted to talk with you offline. Sanderson's team has unfinished business. The FBI task force could interfere," said Kearney.

"Go ahead."

Jacob Remy was shaking his head slowly, expressing the same sentiment that the president was feeling. It had been a big mistake to let Sanderson work his way into the task force.

"One of the convoys is untraceable. It left Honesdale this morning around nine—"

"How is this one untraceable?"

"Sanderson provided the NSA with a list of cell phone numbers for the drivers that were provided by Crystal Source's operations manager. Only the lead driver for each convoy is with True America. The rest are employees diverted from the company's normal distribution schedule. We know that six convoys left the facility. NSA has been able to locate phones in five of the convoys, including the one sitting in Honesdale. The missing convoy was smaller than the rest, consisting of three trucks. NSA is getting no hits from the convoy. Bad luck, really."

"Or they're all equipped with SAT phones. They might all be involved with True America," said the president.

"That's a distinct possibility, sir. This might be their most important convoy. The others consisted of six vehicles each. Either way, tracking that convoy may no longer be important. The convoy left at nine. If its target was located in either Washington D.C. or New York City, it may have already delivered the water. Sanderson's team has volunteered to take the necessary steps to identify the convoy's destination. If the FBI descends on the bottled water facility too quickly, they'll render the Sanderson option unviable."

"The fact that you're speaking vaguely gives me the impression that I don't want to know the details of Sanderson's operation."

"That's correct, sir. All we're asking for is a few hours."

"We? Are you working for Sanderson now?"

"Terrence has been a close friend of mine since West Point. I trust him without question or hesitation. His methods are unconventional and he's not afraid to twist arms."

"He twisted mine pretty hard. I didn't appreciate that," said the president.

"The bruises and twists are a small price to pay for the results he consistently delivers. I trust him, Mr. President."

"I can't exactly order Shelby to stand down to give Sanderson's team some time to work their magic. How do you propose I handle this in the Situation Room meeting?"

"May I suggest a much smaller meeting for now? We can deal with the convoys still on the road using SOCOM assets. Local law enforcement can be called in separately to handle any situations precluding military intervention. We can get a jumpstart on the convoys while we wait for Sanderson to provide the missing convoy's destination."

"Who is tracking the convoy right now?"

"The National Security Agency. They're tracking the convoys live using cell phone GPS locator data and satellite imagery."

"Shelby will go haywire when he finds out this was done behind his back," said the president.

"If Sanderson's team works fast, we might be able to sneak this past him," said Kearney.

"Little has gone smoothly over the past week…and nothing gets by Shelby. This is guaranteed to get ugly," he said and paused.

He didn't look at Remy. This was his decision to make.

"Tell Sanderson that I'll hold off notifying the FBI, but I won't order Shelby to cease and desist if he catches wind of this. General, will you do me a favor and discreetly bring General Gordon to the Oval Office? Notify your source at the NSA. I want them video conferenced into the meeting. Coordinate with Mr. Lee in the watch center to transfer the NSA's feeds to the screens in my study. Be up here in five minutes," said the president, disconnecting the call.

"This is like dealing with the devil," he sighed.

"Preventing a biological attack on the United Nations General Assembly is worth shaking hands with Satan himself," said Remy.

"This is clearly a politically motivated attack on world stability. Right in line with some of True America's hardcore rhetoric, and their mainstream talking points."

I think we go after them immediately. Shut the entire organization down," Remy suggested.

"Greely and his band of nutcases just made that a little easier for us, didn't they?"

"I have a feeling that the rest of the targets will seal that deal. We'll have to move fast to take advantage of the public outrage and prevent their political action group from generating any significant momentum. I'm seeing another primetime television address," said Remy.

"Let's not get ahead of ourselves here. We still have five convoys to stop," said the president.

"I'll bring Beck up to speed and have him prepare a comprehensive strategy that we can implement as soon as we've safeguarded the American people," said Remy, referring to the president's chief political advisor.

"Sounds good. Let's get the study reconfigured to handle this. I want this sealed off from the rest of the staff. Just you, me and the two generals. We'll bring in others as we need them. I have a plan that might help us deal with Shelby, in the short run and the long run," said the president.

"Good. I was beginning to worry about him," said Remy.

"I've always worried about him."

Chapter 57

2:19 PM
Lake Shore Drive
Lake Wallenpaupack, Pennsylvania

Daniel stared out of the window at the lake. He would have preferred a nighttime attack on Owen Mills' lakeside compound, but the clock had started ticking when Anne Renee Paulson's body hit the warehouse floor. Her cell phone indicated that she had called a local number hourly since yesterday afternoon. Her last call had been placed at 1:15, roughly twenty-five minutes before the attack. He expected an inbound call to her phone any minute.

Fayed had suggested leaving the phone for Jessica to answer. Graves and Gupta had a headset microphone that could imitate hundreds of situations and modify her voice. They could mimic severe interference, which might have been enough to keep her contact from becoming overly suspicious. Daniel decided against this option, mainly because Jessica hadn't recovered a fraction of her hearing. Plus, Paulson and her contact might use a code word to start their conversations. He didn't want to tip their hand, especially since they would arrive at Mills' gates in less than two minutes.

Instead of regrouping at their rental house on Cadjaw Pond, they drove the three vehicles south on Route 6 for a few minutes before turning off on an unmarked dirt road. From there, they split into two teams and abandoned the Jeep Grand Cherokee.

Jessica joined Graves and Gupta in the van, along with Wilkins and the two men from the warehouse. With her hearing compromised, she didn't protest the decision. Her team would return to Cadjaw Pond and start to put all the pieces of the puzzle together. The two electronic warfare specialists had everything figured out by the time they arrived at the house fifteen minutes later. Wilkins helped them access Crystal Source's server network to acquire a list of known cell phone numbers for the convoy drivers identified. They also checked the Crystal Source trucks for active GPS signals. As suspected, the built-in GPS trackers had been disabled.

Once this information was passed on to Sanderson, they abandoned the safe house near Honesdale, leaving the men restrained in separate rooms.

Daniel and the rest of the team transferred their equipment to Paulson's Mercedes-Benz GL Class SUV, and spent the next ten minutes gearing up for the inevitable assault on Mills' lakeside mansion. Mills was the key to unraveling the entire conspiracy. He had hand delivered the metal boxes containing the target information to Paulson, and at some point, he had given each driver a key to open the box. They had found the key to open the last box on the driver that Melendez had shot. All of this had been carefully planned to keep the target information compartmentalized. Even Paulson may have been kept in the dark regarding the final target selection.

If anyone knew where the convoys were headed, it had to be Mills. Only Mills could have arranged the deliveries, which he would have kept quiet. Mills clearly had some hefty political connections somewhere. Securing a one-time contract to deliver water to the United Nation's Headquarters Building couldn't have been easy. Then again, when bottled water was currently the only safe and trusted drinking option on the table in the United States, it may have been a slam-dunk for Mills. It wouldn't surprise Daniel in the least to learn that Mills had been in active negotiations to deliver water to the U.N., when the crisis "conveniently" erupted.

Five more convoys were likely headed to similar, but unknown targets. The NSA was tracking four of them. Their mission was simple: acquire the missing convoy's final destination as quickly as possible. Based on the information available, the convoy in question had left the warehouse around nine in the morning, and could have already delivered its cargo to a target as far away as Washington D.C. This possibility precluded the best assault options, like a water approach at dusk, or a multiple point perimeter breach. They had barely carved out enough time to survey the compound.

Located at the tip of Boulder Point on the western bank of northern Lake Wallenpaupack, Owen Mills' estate occupied a vast stretch of the most desirable real estate on the lake. With sweeping views of the water spanning east to west, his lone mansion commanded most of the point. A single looping road swung down from Lake Shore Drive, closely following the shoreline and passing several luxury homes on its journey to the front gate of the estate. The road turned inland at that point and crossed the small peninsula, depositing cars back onto Lake Shore Drive. A formidably tall, yet elegant black wrought iron fence spanned the peninsula, actively discouraging tourists from taking a closer look at the massive house in the distance.

From Ledge Point, a smaller peninsula to the east, they had spent close to fifteen minutes observing Boulder Point, counting guards and looking for patterns. Their first obstacle would be the gatehouse. Manned by two armed guards and located one hundred feet from the eastern shoreline, the stone shack guarded the only road leading to the mansion at the southernmost tip of the small peninsula. The property itself was relatively featureless, with the exception of several thick pockets of towering pine trees. One of the pine tree clusters stood between the gatehouse and the main structure, hopefully obscuring the view between the two structures. They planned on using Paulson's car to approach the gate without raising any alarms. Once the guards were neutralized, they would ditch the car and approach on foot. Taking the car any further would attract too much attention.

Beyond the gatehouse, several lone guards armed with assault rifles patrolled the property. Unfortunately, their observation detected no discernible patrol pattern. None of them came any closer than three hundred feet from the wrought iron fence, giving Daniel the impression that Mills didn't want to attract the wrong kind of attention. Even the guards at the gate kept their weapons concealed inside the shack, though Daniel could see the barrel of an AR-15 through one of the windows. Clearing the patrols wouldn't be a problem. He was more concerned about what waited for them inside the house.

The guards patrolling the estate looked better trained than what they had encountered in the warehouse. They were heavily armed with optics enhanced assault rifles, outfitted with body armor and apparently taking their jobs seriously. They constantly communicated using hand signals or talking into their shoulder mounted microphones. It appeared that Mills had reserved the best operatives for his personal security detail. On the eve of True America's greatest moment, he supposed this was appropriate. Or maybe Mills had VIP guests, which raised a completely different realm of possibilities. The men on patrol didn't look like Secret Service agents, but they could easily pass for civilian contractors assigned to a VIP protection detail.

"There's the turnoff for Boulder Point Road. We're about a minute from the gate," he said, applying the turn signal and easing the car over the dashed yellow line.

Despite the fact that they were about to jump headfirst into a battle against a numerically superior force, he started wheezing in laughter. He couldn't help it. With one of Jessica's blond wigs jammed over his head, Munoz looked like a transvestite prostitute that had long ago given up trying to maintain the pretense of being a woman. Before leaving with Graves and Gupta, she had tossed it into the back of the Mercedes, thinking it might come in handy approaching the gate. Anne Renee Paulson had blond hair. Laughter erupted from the van, causing Munoz to slam on the brakes and spill everyone forward.

"How about a little fucking professionalism?" he hissed, slamming them all back into their seats by rapidly accelerating.

"Just be glad we're not taking pictures. You look beautiful, by the way," said Daniel, igniting another round of snickering.

"Fuck you, Petrovich."

Munoz continued along Boulder Point Road until the gatehouse appeared over a slight rise in the road. Melendez lowered the rear passenger side window. If the guards reacted before they reached the gate, Melendez would raise himself out of the window and fire his suppressed P90 over the top of the SUV. He was their long distance insurance policy.

"Here's where we find out if that wig was worth it," said Daniel.

Munoz just nodded, having already settled into his meditation. Daniel would hold the wheel while Munoz lowered the window and held a suppressed pistol in the other, timing the approach so that he could fire point blank into the furthest guard's head upon pulling parallel to the shack. Fayed would shoot the other guard from the rear driver side. Daniel watched one of the guards nonchalantly grab his shoulder handset and presumably relay information regarding Anne Renee's arrival. He didn't detect any signs of panic or alarm among them. A quick scan of the estate in front of them confirmed that none of the patrols were in sight and that the guard shack was partially obscured by the cluster of pines he had spotted earlier. Their approach had been perfectly timed by Munoz.

Daniel held his own suppressed pistol between the front passenger seat and the door, just in case. The decoratively spiked front gate started to swing inward as the Mercedes pulled up to the two guards. Even as both of the driver side windows descended, neither of them looked interested in the vehicle. Daniel gripped the wheel just before Munoz raised the pistol and fired a single .40 caliber bullet through the guard's forehead. The two shell casings hit the front windshield and deflected onto the dashboard.

Munoz threw the blond wig in Daniel's lap and accelerated through the gate, barely missing the slow moving barrier. He heard a whirlwind of activity from the rear seating area, as Fayed, Paracha and Melendez traded out their compact P90's for more suitable long range weapons provided by Karl Berg's contact. They would close the main house on foot, possibly traversing up to 800 feet depending on how far they could drive the SUV. The P90's effective range remained well inside of 200 yards, which could put them at a significant disadvantage if they needed to engage targets at the house. The vehicle slowed and Munoz eased it off the blacktop next to an untamed row of yellow forsythia bushes.

"That's as far as we can go without breaking into sight."

Everyone dismounted at once and more rifles were exchanged with Paracha, who handed them out from the depths of the SUV's third row of seats. Melendez held out a suppressed M1A SOCOM 7.62mm rifle and a combat load bearing vest for Daniel. He took the vest, sliding it on before grabbing the rifle and slinging it over his shoulder. He snapped the olive drab vest shut, checking it for loose pouches or anything that could snag on the bushes. They had pre- rigged all their gear on the dirt road off Route 6, swapping 7.62mm and 5.56mm magazines between vests, based on weapons assignment.

Daniel and Melendez had chosen the longer range M1A, a close relative of the venerable 7.62mm M-14 rifle, which saw extensive action in Korea and Vietnam, and continued to serve as a battlefield sniper weapon. The SOCOM was designed using lighter materials and featured a shorter barrel, which increased the operator's maneuverability in close quarters battle, but reduced the effective sniping range of the rifle. Still, a skilled shooter could easily hit targets at 400 yards with the steel sights, reaching out even further with magnified optics. He didn't foresee any problems with the delivery of highly accurate fire to cover the assault team's approach.

All of their weapons were fitted with suppressors. Fayed, Paracha and Munoz carried the Mk 18 Mod 0 rifles used earlier in the day at the laboratory. Equipped with unmagnified EOTech sights, they would be more reliable inside the house or on the immediate grounds. Their directive was to advance quickly under direct cover fire from Daniel and Melendez.

Once Daniel snapped his vest together and fitted his headset, he started jogging toward the trees directly ahead of them. He wanted to be in position when the three men crossed the open area. He loaded his rifle on the move. Melendez sprinted west, looking for a position located roughly one hundred yards across the point, where he could scan for targets on the far side of the house. Spread apart among the trees, the two of them could effectively clear the entire approach to the house and eliminate patrols. He reached the pines and raised his rifle, scanning for targets among the thick tree trunks. He easily trampled the thin layer of newly formed spring brush, reaching the edge of the tree line and staring out at the expanse of ground leading to the house.

He counted two patrols in plain sight, and located another possible sentry at the edge of a cluster of smaller trees near the house. The house itself was massive, measuring at least one hundred and fifty feet across. He stared at the stone laden, modern post and beam structure, which featured five chimneys protruding from the green metallic roof. He was truly impressed with the sheer size and quality of design. Apparently, bottling the earth's water and selling it was a lucrative business.

The western end of the two-story vaulted-roof house angled north, featuring a four bay garage. Several SUVs and trucks crowded the driveway in front of the garage, possibly belonging to security personnel or guests. He didn't see any obvious luxury vehicles among them, or the telltale black Suburbans used by most government agencies. This might purely be a True America gathering, which suited him best. There would be no survivors.

He stared through the rifle's ACOG scope at the windows along the front of the house. Not surprisingly, the front of the house contained few windows. Like most lake homes, windows were an afterthought on the landward side, deferring to vast ceiling to floor glass facing the water. Beyond the three patrols in front of him, he spotted one additional guard standing under the home's covered porch entrance. He highly doubted anyone was stationed in one of the small windows. This might be easier than he had originally predicted. He crawled forward a few more feet to clear brush and extended the rifle's bipod, resting it on the soft ground. He now had a perfect one hundred and eighty degree view of his killing field.

"Overwatch One is set. Confirm four targets in front of the house, including the front porch," he said.

"Overwatch Two is set. Three targets in range on western side. I'll take the front porch."

Daniel didn't protest. Melendez was an excellent shot. Several seconds passed before he heard Melendez again.

❧

Melendez sighted in on the sentry standing on the front porch and eased his breath. Firing a single 7.62mm bullet accurately through a sixteen-inch barrel at a target more than 700 feet away wouldn't be easy. At this range, the M1A's standard twenty-two inch barrel would be more appropriate, but their mystery benefactor had opted for a conservative mix of multipurpose weapons. A wise decision given the uncertainties that existed yesterday. He couldn't complain, though he'd much prefer to take down the closer patrols, then move a few hundred feet closer to compensate for the short barrel. Unfortunately, the guard standing at the top of the steps was in the ideal surveillance position, representing the greatest threat to their element of surprise. He'd have to go first.

Daniel aimed at the stationary guard's nose and raised the rifle's barrel less than a millimeter to compensate for the distance. He'd be happy to land the shot anywhere between the man's throat and forehead. Any lower and the bullet could strike the man's ballistic vest. Any higher and it could deflect off his skull. Either of those scenarios would drop him temporarily, but could give him a chance to raise the alarm. Daniel needed a clean shot that would either instantly kill or paralyze the target. He nudged the ACOG's vertical crosshair directly in the center of guard's head and added another ounce of pressure to the trigger. The rifle bucked into his shoulder, sending the round downrange.

Melendez brought the ACOG's sight picture back to the door, centered roughly on the space previously occupied by the guard. Before firing, he had taken a mental picture of the background, lining up fixed objects with the hash marks just beyond the target. He could see a significant scarlet mess on the wooden door twenty feet back from the front of the porch. A mess like that could only mean one thing. He confirmed the fatal headshot and passed the report.

ꙮ

"Front door target is down," crackled his earpiece.

Aleem Fayed started running toward the house. He was looking at traversing about three football fields at a full run, loaded down with gear. As one of the Middle East operatives, his training focus had been field craft and close-in engagements. As he hit the fifty-yard point, he was glad that Sanderson had pushed their physical training so hard. Fayed had never ceased to bitch up a storm on one of their ten mile conditioning runs, or during the course of an unannounced hike in the woods. Sanderson and Fayed clearly had a different concept of the word "hike." Realizing that he still had a full minute of running in his immediate future, Fayed promised himself never to complain again.

He could feel the burn in his legs from the sprint, but his lungs still felt strong thanks to Sanderson's routine. He'd need that lung capacity when he reached the house. Daniel's plan didn't include a short break to regain their breath. They would go to work on the house immediately, assuming they reached the house intact. The two guards in the distance were still standing as he closed the distance, forcing him to wonder why Daniel hadn't started firing. If he approached any closer, one of them was bound to hear him and turn around, which could eliminate the element of surprise.

The guard closest to their small group was located fifty yards away, slightly offset from their path. He was faced away from them, walking toward the house, but that could change at any moment. He heard Daniel's rifle cough, sending a bullet somewhere downrange, but the sentry in front of him didn't fall. A guard Fayed hadn't spotted dropped to the ground at the edge of the tree cluster near the house. Now he was screwed. He raised his rifle and stopped, sighting in on the guard along their path. There was no way he hadn't seen the other guard's head explode. A snap passed Fayed's head, and the heavily equipped sentry in Fayed's sights dropped his rifle, reaching up for his neck with both hands. The guard sank to his knees as another bullet sailed overhead, eventually striking the furthest lookout in the forehead, just above the binoculars he had raised to his face. Daniel's voice came through his earpiece.

"Assault, the path is clear. Advise if you see more targets."

Fayed leapt forward, quickly acknowledging the fact that Daniel had perfectly coordinated his shooting, prioritizing the targets according to threat level against the assault team. He felt a little better running blindly across Daniel's killing field. He just hoped that True America didn't have someone with similar skills.

❧

Jackson Greely took a sip of the amber liquid from the heavy crystal tumbler and savored it in his mouth for a brief moment before swallowing. The warmth spread immediately, from his stomach to his head. This was some of the best scotch he had tasted in a long time. He stared at the exquisite crystal decanter sitting on the silver tray. His gaze shifted to the sparkling lake beyond the infinity pool next to their table. They sat in all weather, European country style chairs arranged around a low teak surfaced table. Greely wasn't accustomed to this kind of luxury, but he could certainly get used to it. Lee Harding looked equally at ease in these surroundings. Brown had looked unsettled all afternoon, which prevented Greely from fully relaxing.

"This is superior scotch, Owen. Very nice," he said.

"A family favorite. Glengoyne Seventeen Year. Simply one of the finest scotches in production. Of course, I'm a bit partial to the distillery."

"I thought your family was Irish?" said Harding.

"We are, but my great grandfather traveled to Glasgow several times a year on business and discovered their distillery just north of the city. He fell in love with their scotch and struck up a deal with the Lang Brothers to import it into Ireland, but this eventually ran afoul thanks to rising troubles in Northern Ireland, though he did make a tidy sum of money in those few years and maintained a good relationship with the Langs. When he brought our family over to America, he settled in the Syracuse area. He spent most of his fortune struggling to establish an import business for his beloved Scottish whiskey, a business better suited for the east coast. He'd made some small investments in Canada, which paid off big time when prohibition hit. The whiskey market in Canada soared overnight, as you can imagine. Crystal Source water sprang to life a few years later, no pun intended."

"That's an incredible American success story," said Greely.

No wonder the family was wealthy. Like the Kennedys' vast empire, the Mills dynasty had its roots in bootlegging. Greely's great-grandfather had worked in the Ohio mills, earning an honest living while trying to keep his family alive. There was a stark contrast between Mills' version of the American dream and Greely's.

"Indeed it is. But it pales in comparison to the legacy we will leave the American people. Gentlemen, by my watch, the last shipment has departed. Here's to America's New Recovery," said Mills, raising his glass.

They all toasted to the New Recovery and downed the remainder of their drinks. Jackson turned to Mills.

"Still haven't heard from Anne Renee?"

"Not yet. She should be on her way. We get shitty reception all along the lake," said Mills.

"Have you tried to call her?"

"She usually checks in once an hour, or whenever a shipment leaves. The last shipment left at 1:20. She called a few minutes before that. We're fine," he said.

Greely gave Harding a skeptical glance, before turning to Brown, who hadn't said a word.

"You look nervous," said Greely.

Brown put his glass down on the table. "Anne Renee is sharp. If Brooks mentions anything about executing Carnes and the rest of the lab people, she'll make a run for it. It was a bad idea to mix those two together at this point."

"Brooks won't say a word. He's been on the inside from the beginning. Part of the club," said Mills.

"You could say the same thing about Carnes," said Brown wryly.

The black handheld radio sitting in front of Mills chirped, followed by a transmission.

"Mr. Mills, this is the front gate. Ms. Paulson has arrived with Mr. Brooks."

Mills grabbed the radio. "Excellent. Let her through. Make sure they are shown to the pool terrace."

"Understood," the guard responded.

"See? Nothing to worry about. How about another round of drinks? I'm bringing out the cheap stuff after this," Mills chuckled.

"I'll make sure Anne Renee and Michael find their way down to the pool," said Brown.

This statement struck Greely as odd. For some reason, he didn't like the idea of Brown alone with Paulson and Brooks. Something about Brown definitely fueled his paranoia.

"Security can take care of that," said Mills, pouring generous amounts of scotch into each glass.

"I want to get a read on these two before we invite them to share drinks. I'd rather not get shot in the face," said Brown.

"If you're so worried, just take care of them now," said Mills.

"In front of the other operatives? That's a guaranteed death sentence. We stick to the plan, unless I sense a real problem. Don't worry. Brooks has a shitty poker face. If they're planning something, I'll know it right away," said Brown.

"Fuck. Now you have *me* paranoid," said Mills.

"We have plenty of security around here. We're safe," said Greely.

He gestured to the three casually dressed guards standing between the pool and the beach less than a hundred feet away. Unlike the patrols, these sentries were dressed in casual business attire and didn't wear body armor. Short-barreled AR-15 rifles were slung around their backs as they surveyed the lake.

"I'm still checking them out," said Brown.

"Suit yourself," added Mills.

Brown stood up and walked up the stairs to the deck, navigating his way to the screen doors beneath a massive two-story wall of wide glass windows framed by stone.

"I wish your wife didn't have a problem with firearms," said Greely, "I feel a little exposed sitting here unarmed."

"Are you worried about Brown? His loyalty to the cause is second to none. Trust me on that. He's just being cautious. Nothing wrong with that," said Harding.

"I suppose not, which is why I'd feel better with my Colt," said Greely.

"Sue Ellen will not allow them in the house, which is why I own several houses," said Mills, laughing at his own joke.

"I can't imagine she feels too comfortable about all of this firepower on the estate," said Harding.

"I convinced her that kidnapping threats have been made against the family because of the water crisis. She loves those kids more than life itself. As long as the weapons stay outside of the main house, I could land a battalion of Marines on that beach."

ঌ৩

Brown strode across the slate floor of the Vista Room and headed right for the Grand Entry. All of the rooms in this house had a fucking name, and he'd already forgotten most of them. Mills had subjected them to a tour of the estate, once they had all arrived earlier today. Prior to this morning, none of them had been invited to Mills' exclusive Lake Wallenpaupack estate. They'd always met in his "lesser" homes or at retreat locations throughout the region.

Wallenpaupack. Brown promised himself that if he ever had enough money to buy a lake house, it wouldn't be on a lake with such a stupid name. He felt like a douchebag even hearing someone else say it.

He hoped to hell that he didn't run into Mills' trophy bride. More like old trophy, though you couldn't tell by the amount of work she'd had done on her face, which is why he hoped to avoid her. She was teetering on the edge of looking like one of those cartoonish Hollywood freaks that got a little bit carried away with collagen injections and skin tightening. She wasn't there yet, but give her a couple more years and she'd be forced to take drastic action to continue looking thirty years old. According to Mills, the two of them had been high school sweethearts. Mills had recently celebrated his fiftieth birthday, which put Sue Ellen in her late forties. Once she hit fifty, the gains achieved through simple plastic surgery and Botox would start to diminish, forcing her to either accept the aging process or continue the madness and risk looking like Donatella Versace.

Brown stopped at the far end of the Vista Room, at the custom crafted, arched doorway leading deeper into the house, and wondered if he should have taken the smaller opening on the other side of the fireplace. The house had so many rooms and hallways that he imagined unattended guests could disappear, only to be found hours later. It was truly an outrageous spectacle, and frankly didn't square well with the workingman focus of True America's manifesto, though he was quite sure that Owen Mills wouldn't hesitate to waste an hour of anyone's time explaining how his success embodied the true potential of America's resurgence to greatness.

Somehow, inheriting a multimillion dollar company from your parents was considered an American success story in his world.

Before stepping out of the room in search of the Grand Entry, he couldn't resist looking back at the sweeping panoramic view of the lake through the virtual wall of windows behind him. He estimated the view to span one hundred and twenty degrees from the two-story fieldstone fireplace at the back of the room. He shook his head at the king's view of Lake Wallenpaupack before continuing.

He had chosen hallways wisely, seeing the front door in the distance. He hoped Anne Renee hadn't figured out her fate. She'd be hard to track down if she vanished. The arrival of Paulson and Brooks closed the loop on their involvement with Al Qaeda. The guards brought to the Mills' estate for the "exclusive" VIP protection detail were all that remained of the teams assigned to steal the virus canisters from Al Qaeda cells in the New York Tri-State area. They couldn't completely erase True America's links to Al Qaeda, but they could take steps to prevent detailed testimony regarding the unsavory relationship.

Paulson had been intimately involved with the plan to fund Al Qaeda's overseas efforts to acquire the virus, which was enough to put her in the ground. Her direct coordination of their plan to steal the canisters from Al Qaeda and "redistribute" the virus ensured her execution. Greely had recruited her through a military contact, but he had never grown fond of her. Brown had detected from the beginning that Greely was simply using her intelligence background to fill a temporary role within the organization.

Mrs. Mills would leave with the kids for their house in St. Kitts early tomorrow. After they departed, Greely, Harding and Brown would host a celebratory picnic on the estate for True America's most loyal and valuable members, none of which would leave the property alive. He didn't look forward to loading over twenty bodies onto a truck.

Brown approached the door and noticed something he hadn't seen before. A hand-sized red splotch adorned the center windowpane on the left side of the double pine door and daylight shined through two small holes in the door. It didn't register with Brown until he drew closer and saw that one of the holes was splintered. He immediately grabbed his radio and sprinted to the wall next to the bloodied window.

He was fucking right about those two, but he didn't think they'd have the nerve to take on his entire security detail. He wondered if they had managed to turn any of the estate's security detail. The New Recovery could end right here at the estate if Paulson managed to recruit any of the guards. He needed to get his hands on a weapon. That stupid Mills bitch had put a moratorium on firearms in the house, and her equally fucking stupid husband had agreed.

"All patrols, this is Brown. Shoot Paulson and Brooks on site. They've gone rogue. Secure the VIPs in the guest house."

His radio wasn't squawking as many replies as he had expected. Either most of the security team were already dead, or they had turned and were converging on the pool. He thought about warning the men near the beach. They would rush to protect the men sipping scotch by the pool, but would never expect the other guards to fire on them. This whole situation was about to explode, which made him think briefly about his other option. Get the fuck out of here. He thought about it for a second, but decided to do some reconnaissance first. If Paulson and Brooks were acting alone, he would be running away for no reason.

Brown opened the heavy front door and crawled through the opening, scrambling to the crumpled guard located at the foot of the covered porch. The guard lay face down in a contorted position, with his head hung over the top step. He saw no blood on the porch. The guard's AR-15 was nowhere in sight, which really worried him. He stayed low, continuing to the top of the stairs, hoping to find a pistol in the man's thigh holster. He reached the man and started to turn him on his side. What he saw on the stairs stopped him cold.

The granite stairs leading to the driveway were soaked bright red, in a fan shaped pattern starting where the man's head touched the top stair. The back of the man's head was completely missing, which struck him as odd. He glanced behind him at the door and saw the remnants of the sentry's brains and skull fragments on the door. The splintered hole he saw on the inside of the door represented a bullet that had passed through the guard's head with enough energy to penetrate two inches of thick wood. He hadn't been shot in the head with a pistol. This was the work of a high-powered rifle. *Shit.* He started to dig for the guard's pistol, but spotted the barrel of a rifle protruding from the evergreen bushes a few feet away. He ripped open a few of the pouches on the dead sentry's vest and looted two spare rifle magazines before he lurched forward and grabbed the rifle. Dashing back inside the house, he didn't stop until he reached the perceived safety of the room next to the two-story entry hall.

He sat back against the wall and tried to process the scene. Nobody had taken the rifle. If Paulson or Brooks had taken down the guard, they would have grabbed the rifle. The guard had either been shot at close range with an assault rifle or hit from a distance with a sniper weapon. Based on the exit wound characteristics, he was leaning toward the high-powered sniper theory, which led him to the worst possible conclusion. They had professional company on the estate. His range of options had just shrunk considerably.

"All units report," he said, and waited a moment, but received no response.

He swallowed hard and stood up, planning to work his way back to the Vista Room. Escape was no longer an option…and neither was capture.

❧

Melendez fired two rapid shots at a muscular black man that had come barreling around the southwest corner of the house in a full sprint. The 7.62mm rounds caught him by surprise, striking him center mass, but failing to penetrate the hardened ceramic trauma plates inserted into his vest. The kinetic energy of the rounds spread throughout the plates and stopped him cold and knocked him off balance. He stumbled backward, taking his hands off the only thing that could have saved him at this point. Before he could regain his footing or grab the rifle hanging from his three-point sling, Melendez dropped to one knee and fired a single round between his eyes. The massive guard grunted once and landed on his back, his arms and legs no longer receiving any coordinated or recognizable directions from his frontal lobe or cerebellum.

He took a deep breath and ran for the corner of the house, glad the guard hadn't seen him first. He'd have to take the backyard approach a little slower, spending more time searching for concealed targets. Someone had obviously sounded the alarm, and not every guard would run helter-skelter into the open. He reached the corner and surveyed the backyard. Past the tennis courts, he saw the edge of an infinity pool, which was partially obscured by a metal rack filled with several kayaks. Three guards wearing polo shirts and khaki pants sprinted from the wide beach toward the pool. Melendez raised the M1A SOCOM and fired at the lead runner, tumbling him onto the well-manicured grass. Shifting his aim, he watched the other two guards careen forward, losing control and crashing to the ground in lifeless heaps. He hadn't fired these rounds.

"Back patio is clear. High value targets secure," said Fayed over the radio.

Melendez scanned the area between the house and the waterline, searching for a concealed shooter. It looked clear.

"West side clear. Approaching the pool from the west," he said, making sure Munoz and his crew didn't accidentally fire on him.

"Assault team securing targets. Approach clear."

Melendez took off running.

⁂

Daniel passed a short hedgerow on the eastern side of the house and searched for the single guard watching the southeastern shoreline. Unlike the sentries stationed between the house and road, this one hadn't moved more than ten feet while they watched from Ledge Point. He located the heavily armed sentry exactly where he expected. The man raised his hand to block the sun as he scanned the lake. Daniel edged forward a little further, completely exposed. He kept an eye on the guard as he approached the corner of the house. He wanted to make sure the sentry's sudden collapse wouldn't attract attention. Their position on Ledge Point didn't provide them with much information regarding the disposition of True America's guard deployment behind the house.

He reached the corner and crouched, taking a careful look beyond. He saw a large deck with stairs leading down to a patio. Three men sat comfortably around a low table drinking from tumblers. He recognized them immediately from their online research. Mills, Greely and Harding. Beyond a blue slate infinity pool, he counted three additional guards near the foot of the dock on the beach. This might require some timing.

The guard to Daniel's left suddenly turned and started running for the house. They locked eyes, but Daniel had years of experience on the man, which translated into quickness and zero hesitation. A lethal combination on the battlefield. He fired two shots before the man could process the fact that Daniel wasn't part of their guard detail. Both projectiles hit him in the face.

Realizing that someone had sounded the alarm, Daniel leaned around the corner and aimed for the guards past the pool. He saw them drop from sight, leaving thin vapors of red mist above their vanishing heads. He aimed up at the deck, finding it clear of threats. Munoz and his team emerged from one of the sliding doors below the deck on the ground level, aiming at the three high value targets still holding their drinks, relatively oblivious to what had just transpired. Jackson Greely placed his glass on the table and stood up, searching for the guards near the beach. He stumbled backward, spilling Lee Harding's glass out of his hand and nearly landing in his lap. Mills ran for the house with the drink in his hand, knocking one of the chairs out of the way. He was intercepted by Paracha, who butt stroked him in the face with his carbine, knocking the CEO of Crystal Source to his knees and breaking his nose. He grabbed the overweight man by the collar of his tailored shirt and yanked him to his feet, pushing him back toward the pool.

Daniel jogged forward to join them, anxious to get this over with. With any luck, he could be headed south with Jessica by nightfall. He heard Melendez report his approach from the west, and glanced up at the deck to make sure they hadn't missed anyone. Satisfied for the moment, he turned all of his attention to the three psychopaths being searched by the assault team. He missed the Jamaican's appearance on the deck by less than a second.

&

Brown eased through the Vista Room in a low, tactical stance, scanning with the barrel of his AR-15. So far, he had detected no movement in the house, which led him to believe that the teams had flanked the mansion and converged on his coconspirators. He heard a scuffle outside, followed by the sound of patio furniture screeching against stone. A few harsh voices joined the activity, followed by the sound of Mills crying out in agony. He wondered why agents hadn't flooded the house. Why didn't he hear the sound of helicopters or support vehicles?

The backyard was quiet beyond guttural voices and the occasional protest from Mills or Harding. All of these thoughts and observations floated through his head as he stepped quietly toward the open door. Through the massive wall of picture windows facing the lake, his view of the rippling, dark blue water transitioned into sandy beach and rocks, exposing the three guards sprawled in the grass. Everything had been so quiet. He was impressed. A sudden realization washed over him. This could be the same crew that had abducted Miguel Estrada and stopped the assassination team assigned to kill Benjamin Young in Atlanta. A glimmer of hope flashed in his mind. He might be facing a small team.

He flipped the G33STS Magnifier down, exposing the EOTech sight. He anticipated engaging targets at close range in the backyard, and would have no use for the 3X optic attachment. The edge of the infinity pool appeared over the deck, followed by Mills and Harding. A dark haired, dark skinned man stood next to Mills. A little further and the whole scene would come into focus. Four men armed with rifles stood around the three founders of True America. Brown thumbed the rifle's selector switch to "auto" and aimed at two of the operatives standing in tandem. Lee Harding's torso was clearly visible behind them, which didn't make an impression on Brown one way or the other.

He depressed the trigger for a sustained burst, shifting the EOTech's red holographic sight image to the next target. A 7.62mm bullet penetrated his right eye and exited his skull before he could aim the next burst. Brown could still see out of his other eye and was vaguely aware that his body had ceased to function. He never felt the fusillade of bullets fired from the pool patio.

ಹಿಹ

The smell of scotch floated in the air between the confused men. Daniel leaned over the table to pour the three terrorists another round of drinks. They would need a little something to numb them for what he had planned. The crystal decanter exploded in Daniel's hand, followed by the thunderous explosions, as 5.56mm bullets ripped through the air, shattering everything in their path. He felt a sharp pain in his left shoulder and realized he had been spun ninety degrees to face Munoz and Fayed, who pointed their smoking rifles upward at the deck. Daniel saw a dark figure drop out of sight below the railing, followed by a cascade of glass from one of the immense picture windows high above him. The glass fragments tumbled over the side of the deck, bringing him back to his senses.

He turned back to their three prisoners. Lee Harding's head lolled to the left, his arms and legs lightly twitching. His glassy eyes stared lifelessly forward, drawing Daniel's attention away from the small red hole visible above his right eyebrow. Jackson Greely looked unharmed, staring blankly at Harding's grotesque post mortem display. Mills started to stand, but was pushed back into his chair by Fayed, who stared past Daniel with a look of dismay. As Daniel's hearing recovered and the initial shock of being shot faded, he heard the desperate rasping sounds of the man who had been standing right behind him when the automatic fire started. He didn't need to turn around to know that Tariq Paracha had absorbed most of the steel fired from the deck.

Fayed shoved the table aside as Daniel wheeled around to see Paracha on his back, clawing at his blood soaked neck. He could see two other entry wounds, one in his upper chest and another high on the front of his left thigh. The vast amount of blood pooling on the stone under his hips signaled to Daniel that the bullet passing through his thigh had likely severed or nicked his femoral artery. Combined with a neck shot, there would be little they could do for Tariq. They hadn't been equipped with a first aid kit, let alone a trauma kit.

"Watch them and keep an eye on the house. We can't afford any more surprises," said Daniel.

Melendez, who had just arrived, joined his counterpart Munoz and aimed toward the house, searching for movement. Daniel placed his rifle next to Paracha and put his hands under the dying man's back, kneeling behind his head. He lifted Paracha's upper torso onto his knees to elevate his chest and head. When he removed his arms from under Paracha, they were slick with dark, red blood. He held them up for a few seconds, before wiping them on the side of his khaki pants. All they could do at this point was make him feel a little more comfortable. He'd be unconscious in less than a minute. Fayed crouched next to Paracha and spoke.

"We'll make sure this was worth it," said Fayed, squeezing Tariq's shoulder.

"Fucking right we will," added Daniel.

Paracha tried to talk, but they heard nothing more than an incoherent rasp.

"Take it easy buddy. Take it easy," he said soothingly.

The operative's hands started to ease away from his neck and Daniel felt his body relax. When his arms fell to the stone, Fayed closed his eyes and glared at Mills and Jackson. Daniel tracked his murderous stare, while he eased Paracha's body to the stone and retrieved his rifle.

"Fayed, take Melendez and clear the house. Bring me Mills' family," he said, and leaned in to whisper in his ear. "They'll pay for this. Don't worry."

Fayed nodded with a hard look on his face and climbed the deck with Melendez, disappearing into the house.

"You're hit pretty bad," said Munoz.

"I hadn't noticed," Daniel said, walking up to Harding's corpse.

He took hold of Harding's shirt with both hands and lifted him out of the chair, swinging him over the splintered teak table and splashing Jackson Greely with bloody brain matter. The table collapsed under the weight, spilling Harding onto the patio in front of an empty chair. Daniel stepped over Harding and took a seat, resting his feet on the dead man's chest. He stared at the two men, noting that each of them shook slightly. Greely's face had been decorated with clumps of deep scarlet matter and Mills' nose still streamed blood. Despite the shock of having their world collapse around them, they looked surprisingly composed. He'd quickly change that.

"Gentlemen, I've been at this for nearly forty-eight hours. I'm tired and I've just been informed that I'm bleeding, so let me save you the bullshit. We don't work for the FBI, CIA or Department of Defense. We work for an independent organization that has no rules or boundaries. This is a point you need to understand before I ask the million-dollar question, because there won't be a referee to step in and save you," said Daniel, shifting his rifle from Greely to Mills.

"And there's really no point in trying to resist. True America is finished. We found the facility used to contaminate the bottled water and we stopped the last convoy at the distribution center. We're tracking four additional convoys, which will be intercepted within the hour."

Greely stole a glance at Mills, who tried to pretend he didn't see it.

"Don't get excited. We know there's one more convoy. We just don't know how to find it. That's the million-dollar question we've been sent to ask, before the federal task force sitting in Scranton descends on Honesdale. By my watch, we have at least another ninety minutes. The president gave us ample time to obtain this information. Even if we have to do this the hard way, I can't imagine needing more than ten. Your friend here makes a nice leg rest," said Petrovich, shifting his feet.

Screaming erupted from the house, causing Mills to stand. Munoz barked at him to sit back down, raising the rifle over his head to ensure his compliance. Daniel turned to see Fayed shove an attractive blond woman and two middle school aged girls toward the stairway leading down to the patio. Mills' wife was dressed in black designer jeans and a tight pink blouse. Her daughters were dressed more conservatively in jeans and brightly colored sweaters. Fayed yelled at them as they protested.

"Line them up on the edge of the pool!" yelled Daniel.

"You need to leave them out of this! You son of a bitch!"

Mills tried to launch out of his chair, but Munoz had anticipated his outburst and smashed the butt of his rifle down on his left shoulder, cracking his collarbone. The sound of the bone snapping could be heard over the metallic crash of the rifle. Mills' wife grabbed both of her daughters' hands and tried to run over to her husband, but Fayed snatched the dark haired daughter out of her grip, stopping Sue Ellen Mills in her tracks. Melendez grabbed the woman by the neck and strong-armed her over to the pool, followed by Fayed with both of the terrified girls.

"How do you want them?" yelled Fayed.

"Line them up side by side, like a firing squad."

Daniel lifted himself up from the chair, careful not to put any pressure on his left arm. He winced and exhaled, despite his efforts to ignore the pain. Munoz came up next to him.

"You alright?" he whispered. "You're losing blood."

"I'm good for now. Small entry and exit wound. Passed right through."

He knew that Munoz was right. Judging by the amount of blood soaked into the light brown chair cushion, he was about ten minutes away from fading into unconsciousness. He felt all right at the moment; a little dizzy from the initial blood loss, but most of his attention was still focused on the pain. The sharp searing sensation had been joined by a dull, agonizing ache that had spread through his arm and into his chest. The bullet had missed the coracoid process of his scapula, a small hook-like bone connected to the clavicle, likely passing through the ligament connecting the two and causing a cascade of muscle tightening and ligament inflammation throughout his body. Once on his feet, he could barely raise his left arm, but retained the function of his elbow and forearm. His fingers felt tingly, but he could still tightly grip the M1A's hand guard.

"This whole thing is bigger than all of us. You're patriots. I can tell you've served the nation honorably, but your country has lost its way. We're going to change all of that and put America back on its feet. Back on the track to a New Recovery," said Jackson Greely, gesturing grandly to the sky.

"By poisoning the U.N. and detonating a suicide bomb at the National Counterterrorism Center?"

"This is a historical day for our citizens. Deep down inside, I know you agree," he added.

"Have you lost your fucking mind? True America is gone. Can't you see that? Not only your little nightmare group, but the whole movement. There's no way the mainstreamers will survive the bad press associated with your plot. The Republicans and Democrats will make sure of that. This might be the first time in years that they actually agree on something. It's a real shame actually. True America was on the path to providing an alternative to the two party system. I heard they might have fielded a viable presidential candidate next year."

Jackson Greely didn't respond. Daniel looked at Mills, who looked deflated and scared.

"Things were cooking along nicely until you put this plan into action. Something to think about while you're rotting in prison," said Daniel.

"It would have taken forever," stated Greely.

"And you might have missed out on the chance to sit at the big table. Where is the last convoy headed, Jackson? The least you can do is salvage a speck of dignity from this mess you've created."

"You can kiss my—"

A single gunshot erupted from Daniel's rifle, catching Greely under the nose and blasting the back of his head into the bushes behind him. He remained upright in the chair for a moment before toppling sideways. Mills' wife and two daughters screamed uncontrollably as Owen Mills tried to launch himself at Daniel.

"Time to rearrange the furniture. I want him turned to face the ladies," he said.

Daniel slung the rifle over his shoulder and walked behind Mills, grabbing him around the neck with his forearm.

"Swing the chair around," he told Munoz.

Once Mills faced the pool, Daniel released his forearm and leaned close to Mills' right ear.

"I can't kill you, because you appear to be the only one left that can identify the convoy. Tell me where it's headed, and my team will leave your family, unharmed."

"I can't dishonor the people who sacrificed for our cause. I won't."

"That's a lofty thing to hear from someone living in a 15,000 square foot lakeside mansion. I think you're full of shit, so I'm going to help you understand the true meaning of the word sacrifice. You get to pick which one of these courageous ladies pays the ultimate price for the cause you're defending."

"You fucking psychopath! My family has nothing to do with this!"

Daniel slapped him and screamed back. "They have everything to do with this! Your suicide bomb shattered dozens of families!"

"What is he talking about, Owen?" yelled Sue Ellen hysterically.

"They had to be sacrificed for America," said Mills.

"You're pretty big on sacrificing the people dedicated to your cause. Hacker Valley, the laboratory staff, Benjamin Young. Am I missing anyone?"

Daniel turned to the family standing beside the pool. "Stand them up straight!"

"Daniel, maybe we should just focus on Mills," Fayed said quietly.

"I'm done with fuckers like this. Sitting back sipping scotch while his expendables make history. I need to make sure none of his DNA leaves the estate," said Daniel, pointing his rifle at the two daughters.

The girls screamed and Sue Ellen Mills nearly fell into the pool trying to escape Munoz's grasp to get between Daniel's rifle and her children. He was starting to feel really lightheaded, and could barely raise the rifle with his left arm.

"We need to get you some medical attention," whispered Fayed, "you're starting to worry me."

Daniel cleared the haziness. He was going to finish this right here, right now. He wasn't sure why this was taking him so long.

"I'm fine. Mills, by the count of three, or I get to choose," he said.

"I can't *do* that," Mills screeched.

"Do what? Pick which one we shoot or tell me where the convoy is headed?"

"I can't do either," he sobbed.

"Honey, just tell them what they want to know. Please!" his wife pleaded.

Daniel engaged the safety on his rifle and threw it to the stone patio behind him. He removed his pistol from a concealed belt holster and aimed it to the left of Sue Ellen's head. He had no intention of shooting her, but he was losing control of the situation. He was also starting to feel short of breath, which he knew was a symptom of progressive blood loss. He wouldn't be able to stand for very long. Maybe he wasn't getting enough oxygen to his brain to make these decisions. He didn't know. All he cared about was extracting the information and getting back to his life with Jessica.

For a brief moment, he lined the pistol's sights up on Sue Ellen's face. Maybe shooting her in the face would get Mills to reveal the convoy's destination. He didn't want to do that, but his finger added pressure to the trigger. He became tunnel focused on her and no longer heard the kids screaming and crying. Mills' pleading faded as he moved the trigger closer to its eight-pound pressure release. He could no longer guarantee that he wouldn't shoot her. Munoz's face appeared in the pistol's sight picture.

"Danny, you don't have to do this. Fayed can handle it," said Munoz.

Jeffrey Munoz had placed himself between Mills' wife and the barrel of the gun. Daniel squinted and realized that he needed to let this go. Munoz had stood in formation next to Daniel on their first day at Sanderson's experimental training camp in Colorado. He was one of the few surviving members of the original Black Flag program, and one of the few people that truly understood how Daniel's mind worked. Now he owed Munoz another favor. He lowered the pistol and turned to Fayed.

"He's all yours. Melendez, secure the family comfortably in the house."

"Thank you. Thank you," muttered Mills.

Fayed patted Daniel on the shoulder and approached Mills. Daniel stared out at the lake, shaking from the realization that he had been pulled back from the edge of the darkest hole he had ever seen. If Munoz hadn't intervened, he would have worked his way down the line until Mills started talking. He might not have stopped at that point. Jessica would have never forgiven him for executing children. He wished he could blame what almost happened on the blood loss, but he knew better.

Sanderson had awoken a menacing darkness deep inside of him. He'd drawn on its energy to survive his undercover assignment in Serbia, but it came with a price. It would never go dormant again, and it was always there, faintly whispering to him. Today it had risen up and screamed at him. Fayed stood behind Mills and placed his hands on the man's shoulders, pressing downward. He leaned down and spoke loudly enough to jar Daniel back into the moment.

"Don't thank him yet. Here's how it works. If you don't tell me the convoy's destination right now, I'm going to march you naked into the kitchen and sit you down on the front burner of that beautiful, stainless steel Viking stove. Then, I'll turn the oven to broil and stuff your legs inside, jamming them in place with the door. We'll spend the next ten minutes testing the front burner settings, while broiling the flesh off your feet. I'm not kidding about this."

Mills looked horrified and gasped for breath.

"What is the convoy's final target?" said Daniel.

Deflated and scared, he blubbered, "The Capitol Building. I…uh…donated several million dollars to the right campaigns and called in the favor. Three semi-trucks with Arrowhead Water logos delivered the bottles fifty minutes ago. Restaurant Associates accepted the shipment. They handle the Capitol Building's dining and concessions. Can I see my family now?"

Daniel nodded to Fayed, who removed his hands from Mills' shoulders. Owen Mills stood on shaky legs, taking a few steps forward. He avoided eye contact, taking a path around Daniel that brought him close to the pool's edge. Daniel raised his pistol and fired two bullets into the CEO of Crystal Source, knocking him into the pool. He landed on his back, with his arms extended sideways. A crimson geyser exploded upward from the pool as his body disappeared underneath the dark water. He didn't wait to see if the body resurfaced. The dark whispering went silent for now.

"He deserved a lot worse," said Fayed.

"I agree, but we don't have the time. The feds will show up at any second, and I had no intention of losing any of these guys to an army of lawyers. Grab Tariq's gear. Berg's guy took a serious risk getting this gear to us. We roll in thirty seconds," said Daniel.

"I'll meet the team out front," he said and started removing Tariq's vest.

"Should we bring him along? I hate to leave him here, scattered among these criminals," said Daniel.

"Tariq's corpse is the last thing we need to be hauling around in a car. Sanderson can straighten this out with the FBI," said Fayed.

"Speak of the devil," said Daniel.

He removed a satellite phone from one of the magazine pouches and answered the call.

"Good timing. We just finished cocktails."

"Don't fuck with me right now. I can never tell if you're fucking with me. Did you get the information?"

"Still on the run?"

"Daniel, I need to make a few very important phone calls. Important to you and important to me. Cut the shit for once," said Sanderson.

Daniel could tell from the sound quality that he was on the road. For some reason, the image of Sanderson fleeing in a gypsy caravan made him happy.

"The Capitol Building. Delivered fifty minutes ago by three semi-trailers with Arrowhead logos. Tariq is dead."

"Jesus. I'm really sorry to hear that. Fayed's Middle East group took a beating. Alright. You need to stay off the grid until further notice. Escape and evade. We're still on the FBI's shit list," said Sanderson.

"I assume you can fix that?"

"I'm working on a plan."

"You need to work fast, because I'm going to require hospitalization within the next fifteen minutes. I've lost too much blood to ride it out."

"Get yourself to an ER. I'll have this squared away soon enough."

"That would sound more encouraging to me if I didn't suspect you were driving at breakneck speed toward some dingy hideout in Neuquén right now."

"Have a little faith. When have I ever let you down?"

Daniel didn't say a word. He waited for Sanderson to speak.

"Alright. Don't answer that question. You'll be back in South Carolina with Jessica by…tomorrow," said Sanderson.

"I've heard that before."

Chapter 58

2:36 PM
The President's Study-The White House
Washington D.C.

Frederick Shelby walked with two Secret Service agents through the walkway connected to the Oval Office by a hidden door located at the eleven o'clock position facing directly north of the president's office. The other hidden door led to his secretary's office. Shelby was surprised when the agents continued past the door and took him toward the hallway leading deeper into the West Wing. He passed two officers from the Secret Service's Uniformed Division manning a security checkpoint at the entrance to the hallway. With a simple nod, the agents passed through the checkpoint, along with Shelby.

The agents opened the first door on the left, which led into the president's study. Shelby nodded at the agents and entered, surprised to see Major General Bob Kearney and Lieutenant General Frank Gordon, both wearing headsets, seated in front of two flat screen monitors and a small array of computer equipment. The president sat at his desk facing the screens, with Jacob Remy watching over the generals' shoulders. The door closed behind him.

"Director Shelby, please take a seat. There's been an interesting development. General Sanderson has been running a ghost operation that tracked the virus canisters to a laboratory in Pennsylvania, just outside of Scranton. It appears that your instincts were right. Here's what we know.: Owen Mills, the CEO of Crystal Source water and a major donor to True America, partnered with Jackson Greely and Lee Harding to destabilize our government."

Frederick Shelby took the seat offered to him. The president had skipped to the part he didn't know, and suspected that Sharpe had withheld during their hospital chat. Sharpe still didn't trust Shelby, which was perfectly fine with the director. A little distrust increased your longevity on the Hill. He was mostly interested in how Sanderson had managed to earn the president's trust again so quickly. More importantly, Shelby wanted to know who Sanderson had used to neatly wrap this present and hand it to the president. Of the five people sitting in the president's study, only one stood out as odd. General Kearney. He nodded with interest and let the president continue.

"They feigned an attack against the public water supply, which drove bottled water demand through the roof and tanked the public's confidence in our ability to defend against domestic terrorist attacks. Apparently, they used most of the virus to contaminate thousands of bottled water containers, shipping them to various targets along the east coast. One of the targets was the United Nations General Assembly. Sanderson's people stopped that convoy. Another convoy delivered several thousand bottles of contaminated water to the U.S. Capitol Building roughly one hour ago."

"On a Sunday? Directly to the Capitol Building? Mills must have some serious connections," Shelby said, shaking his head.

"Apparently so. Deliveries are normally cleared by the Capitol Police at an offsite delivery center, during the week. I'm sure Mills took advantage of the bottled water shortage to arrange the delivery. With the House and Senate in session, this had the potential to destabilize the legislative branch and trigger a coup. Picture every Congressman and Senator sipping from one of True America's poisoned bottles. Can you imagine the worldwide impact if these attacks had been successful? This could have shattered the world order."

Shelby bit his tongue. The plan itself was diabolical, but he could see where the president was going with this. Destabilizing the government. Coup d'état. World order. All big words he would use on camera to make True America sound like the greatest threat to humanity since the Nazis. More like the greatest threat to the monopoly his political party now enjoyed in D.C.

"We're tracking four additional convoys right now. One of them is headed up Sixth Avenue in Manhattan. The NSA is tracking this live. NYPD is already following the trucks in unmarked cars. We'd like to determine the convoy's ultimate destination before Emergency Services takes them down. We have another convoy passing through Parsippany, headed east along Interstate Eighty. Probably headed to New York City. The two remaining convoys are further out, headed south along Interstate 476. One just outside of Philadelphia and the other approaching Allentown. We think these are headed toward the D.C. area. General Gordon has a helicopter strike force headed for the northern most convoy. Philadelphia police will stop the other before it enters the city."

Since his agency's law enforcement services clearly weren't needed at the moment, Shelby didn't pay much attention to what the president said. His mind scrambled to process the bigger picture. Shelby did his best not to grin, as the sheer audacity of Greely's plan unfolded in his mind. He couldn't think of two groups reviled by more Americans right now than the United States Congress and the United Nations.

Unleashing the Zulu Virus on them was a horrifying and repugnant act of terrorism, but on some deep level, Shelby was willing to bet that the attacks would have resonated with many Americans. According to polls, the number of Americans who closely identified with True America's core message grew larger every day. A major part of their message centered on the sad state of politics in D.C. and the need to enforce a more isolationist foreign affairs policy. This was a desperate gamble by Greely and Harding. Despite most Americans' daily grumblings about politicians, the horrific reality of their act would have driven True America's support base into the ground. The success of Greely's plan to send America a wakeup call would have destroyed the mainstream movement.

"Director Shelby?"

"Sorry, Mr. President. I'm just trying to absorb the scale and complexity of their plot. This is unbelievable."

"It's hard to comprehend. By now, you're probably wondering why I've called you in here. Today's events will require special handling by someone I can trust. Sanderson has given us the location of the laboratory used to contaminate the bottles. It's about an hour out of Scranton. I want your people to get there first. You can coordinate with the Pennsylvania Department of Health to get a HAZMAT team to assist your people onsite. I also want the FBI to take charge at the White Mills distribution plant in Honesdale. Sanderson's people stopped the final convoy at one of the warehouses and left quite a mess. State and local police have already responded to the scene, but I don't trust them with the evidence. This is too important."

"I'll send teams to each location immediately, Mr. President. What about Mills or Greely?"

The president looked at Jacob Remy for guidance, and also locked eyes with General Kearney.

"Owen Mills, Jackson Greely and Lee Harding are dead. Owen Mills owns a massive estate on Lake Wallenpaupack, right outside of Honesdale. Their bodies can be found near the pool toward the back of the estate. No local police response has been detected in that area, so it appears that Sanderson's attack on the estate went unnoticed. I'd like to keep this as quiet as possible for now."

"How many bodies are we talking about? I can't imagine they were hanging out alone," said Shelby.

"About twenty. One of them belongs to Sanderson's team."

"Twenty bodies? Exactly what are my people expected to do at the estate?"

"Keep local law enforcement away until we can get a Special Operations strike force up there. Send a small group," said the president.

Shelby understood immediately. Later today, General Gordon would land several helicopters at the estate, creating enough mayhem to explain the sudden appearance of twenty bodies. He'd play along with that, in the interest of national security.

"That sounds easy enough."

"There's one more thing. I need you to remove any and all pressure from Sanderson's people."

"Already done, Mr. President. I revoked the warrants and released the agents being held in Brooklyn. I've also removed them from the wanted lists. After examining the evidence gathered by Task Force Scorpion and speaking with Special Agent Sharpe, I've concluded that Sanderson had been working in good faith, on the nation's behalf, despite his methods. The digital recordings of the NCTC watch floor confirm that Callie Stewart indeed sacrificed herself, along with others, while trying to stop the suicide bombing," said Sanderson.

"Frankly, I'm relieved to hear that this is your independent conclusion. We've invested an inordinate amount of trust in Sanderson's word."

"Don't get me wrong, Mr. President. Sanderson is a dangerous character. I don't fully trust him, but based on the evidence, his organization's assistance was instrumental to stopping the final stage of Greely's plan. My task force was on the verge of a breakthrough, which is why NCTC was targeted. They had unofficially concluded that the Fort Meade attack had been orchestrated to fail, and that the Hacker Valley compound had been filled with weekend warriors having little to do with True America. Sanderson's information serves to reinforce the taskforce's belief that Greely's splinter group was behind everything. Mills; the bottled water connection…it all makes sense. I imagine the remaining four targets will directly support Greely's extreme version of the True America manifesto."

"In my opinion, the True America manifesto is a clear and present danger to the stability of the United States," offered Jacob Remy.

Here we go, thought Shelby. The idea of a splinter cell didn't sit well with the president's Chief of Staff.

"I agree. Which is why I think we got lucky in Pennsylvania. The last thing this country needed was a public trial of Greely, Harding and this Mills character. They would have become martyrs for the True America political movement. Sanderson did us a huge favor. I just hope he left us enough evidence to track down the rest of Greely's people. I'd like a solid link back to the NCTC bombing. The families of the victims deserve the closure."

Jacob Remy looked like he was about to make a point, when General Kearney turned around and made an announcement.

"Mr. President, NYPD just stopped the Manhattan convoy at the GE Building loading docks. The driver was killed in a brief firefight."

"Thank you, General."

Frederick Shelby added this target to his mental calculation. Was NBC the target? NBC owned more than half of the seventy-story building, housing most of its corporate offices and studios there. Greely despised the media, on both sides of the political spectrum. Shelby wouldn't be the least bit surprised if the next convoy stopped at the News Corporation Building to deliver some contaminated water to Rupert Murdoch's empire. Knowing three out of the six locations, he could probably guess where the rest of the convoys were headed. He'd be willing to bet his job on the likelihood that one of the convoys was headed to lower Manhattan. Greely and Harding had clamored for the public overthrow of Wall Street, well before it was cool to hate Wall Street executives. The convoy headed to Allentown would probably turn east on Interstate 78, unless General Gordon's commandos reached it first.

"General Gordon, how long until your air units intercept the northern most convoy?" asked the president.

"Just inside of twenty minutes. We're trying to coordinate this for an open stretch of road with limited traffic. It might happen after Allentown."

"Thank you, General. Jacob, Frederick. will you follow me into the Oval Office for a moment?"

Shelby followed Remy into the Oval Office, past a seasoned regular Secret Service agent. When the door shut behind him, the president turned and leaned his back against the front of his desk. There was no invitation to sit.

"What exactly did your task force uncover regarding Hacker Valley? I was told by General Gordon that the compound was filled with heavily armed domestic terror cells. This is important. I'm about to level some heavy accusations against True America, and I need us to be on the same page. What leads you to suspect that Hacker Valley was some sort of diversion?"

"Very few of the militants—"

"Terrorists," corrected the president.

"Very few of the terrorists captured or killed fit the profile of an active True America operative. This could have been a recruiting drive for True America, but I feel pretty confident in my assessment that the compound had been stuffed with anti-government weekend warriors in order to send us in the wrong direction. I also have strong reason to believe that the attack on Fort Meade was orchestrated to make it look like our public water supply was in jeopardy. The sergeant involved in the shooting has disappeared and his vacation schedule fits the profile of every True America operative we've recovered. And I don't think it's a coincidence that NCTC was hit soon after Special Agent O'Reilly placed a call to Laurel's Chief of Police to check the specifics of his vacation."

"This is all very compelling, Director, and I'm sure you'll get this all sorted out later, but right now you're missing the bigger picture."

"I don't understand, Mr. President," Shelby said, fully understanding exactly what was headed his way.

"I'm not convinced this is the end of True America's plot against the government, and I have no intention of waiting around for round two. Starting tomorrow, we will systematically dismantle True America."

"I'm not sure there's anything left to dismantle. Their training compound has been destroyed. Their plan has been stopped cold; most of the experienced personnel have been killed or captured and the three ringleaders are dead. Do we have new information from Sanderson or the CIA?"

"Don't play word games with me, Director. I expect your agency to assist the Department of Justice in the execution of warrants against all of True America. I've authorized the Attorney General to start the process. We'll begin right here in D.C. while the embers are still hot."

"I don't appreciate your analogy, Mr. President, and I think you're jumping the gun on this. There's not enough evidence to sustain your course of action in the long run. At least at this point. I can assure you that my agency will conduct an extremely thorough investiga—"

"I'm not waiting around for six months while you assemble data and question thousands of witnesses. We need to strike this organization down now."

"While the public is still outraged and confused? I'll restructure Task Force Scorpion to address these investigative needs, and put them to work immediately. We'll figure out exactly what happened, starting with Al Qaeda in Europe."

"I don't feel like I'm making myself clear…"

"Mr. President, you have made yourself abundantly clear. I have just been trying to tactfully steer you away from a disastrous course of action. You cannot take advantage of the situation to flush True America down the toilet. This is a political attack and little more."

"The movement's founding fathers tried to poison thousands of Americans in an unholy alliance with Al Qaeda!" the president shouted.

"And these founding fathers have been pariahs within the mainstream True America movement for years. They've been an embarrassment…relegated to speaking to libertarian gatherings at the Howard Johnson's, or ranting about government intervention at county fairs. They're irrelevant within the movement. This whole nightmare was dreamed up by two dried up, desperate hacks unable to come to terms with the fact that the movement they started thirty years ago has been succeeding without their help for the past decade. Take a look at the targets. The United Nations. Congress. NBC. This is nothing more than two highly persuasive lunatics taking one last swing at a revolutionary wet dream they had in the seventies."

"It's still their movement, and I have no intention of waiting around for the rest of Greely's snakes to bite," barked the president.

"Don't expect my agents to participate in a political coup."

"If I can't count on you to rally FBI support, I'll find someone who can."

"Good luck, Mr. President. Oh. If I remember correctly, we still have a Black Hawk helicopter sitting on the ground inside Argentina, among other things," Shelby reminded him.

"Are you threatening me?"

"Not at all, Mr. President. I'm just reminding you of the multitude of domestic and international laws you've violated over the past few weeks, directly or indirectly. If that's it for now, I'd like to contact my task force in Pennsylvania. We wouldn't want any local cops arriving at Mills' estate before the Special Operations road show arrives. I'll show myself out," he said, and turned for the hidden door leading to the hallway.

Chapter 59

2:44 PM
Interstate 78 East
Allentown, Pennsylvania

Staff Sergeant William Gaskey revved the GAU-2/A 7.62mm Minigun, spinning its six barrels at nearly ten revolutions per second. His spade grips had been rigged with a sealed thumb switch, which powered the gun drive motor without engaging the feeder system or ammunition booster motor. With the barrels rotating, he could depress either of the two triggers attached to the grips and instantly deliver a virtual wall of steel. The electrically driven, air-cooled machine gun could fire up to fifty 7.62mm rounds per second at a sustained rate, utterly devastating anything in its sights.

Two days ago he had put the gun to work against a terrorist compound in West Virginia. Today he would use the gun to stop a semi-trailer on the highway. A convoy of trucks had just run a hastily assembled local police roadblock near Allentown, headed full speed through civilian traffic. The past week had been the strangest of his career. He much preferred Combat Search and Rescue (CSAR) missions or Special Operations pickups in Iraq or Afghanistan. Something didn't sit right with him about using these helicopters on U.S. soil.

"Starboard gun. On my command. Two second burst into the lead truck. Direct your fire at the cabin," echoed his headset.

"This is Sierra Gun. Two second burst. On your command," he replied.

He felt the twenty ton MH-53M Pavelow bank to the right and drop at the same time, commencing its gun run. His stomach tightened in response to the sudden downward pitch, and he tightened his grip on the gun handle, ready to disable the tractor-trailer. The interstate suddenly appeared in his view, along with two dark green semi-trailers, spaced evenly along the road. Three of the five trucks in the original convoy had stopped after the lead truck crashed and rammed through two Allentown cruisers at the first roadblock. According to the latest intelligence, only the lead driver was affiliated with the terrorists, so they would limit the engagement to the first truck.

The interstate behind the trucks was clear of civilian traffic. Several police vehicles trailed the convoy at a safe distance. He assumed the pilots had confirmed that the interstate was clear of oncoming traffic. The helicopter dropped nearly even with the road and sped ahead of the first truck, veering left for a few seconds, before turning hard right on what appeared to be a collision course with the lead vehicle in the convoy. He placed the driver's side door in the center of his gun's iron reticle.

"Starboard gun. Two second burst. Fire."

❧

Brandon Osborne put his book down and closed his eyes. He'd been in the car for over an hour and was already bored out his mind. They were headed to see his grandparents in Phillipsburg, which wasn't too much further down the interstate. They normally visited for a mid-afternoon lunch, but his grandparents had a church function lasting until two, so they had decided on dinner. Their late start meant that Brandon wouldn't get back to Scranton until nine. He'd miss half of his Sunday night Call of Duty Three game. Every Sunday night, starting at eight, at least a dozen of his school friends played Call of Duty Three in multiplayer mode through Xbox Live. They usually played until ten, but sometimes continued beyond that. Brandon could think of no better way to start his school week.

He knew this drive well, since they made the trip at least twice a month. He really enjoyed these trips, especially when his grandfather hit the Pabst Blue Ribbon a little harder than usual. The World War II stories started to surface and they increased in detail and color in proportion to the empty cans sitting on the kitchen counter. He had fought on Guadalcanal and several Pacific beaches with the 1st Marine Division, somehow miraculously avoiding tropical diseases and Japanese bullets until Peleliu.

His luck had run out on the approach to the beach. He was hit in the shoulder by a Japanese shell fragment while manning the amphibious assault vehicle's .30-caliber machine gun, and never made it to the beach with his platoon. He called it bad luck, but Grandma always reminded him that he might not be here today if he had made it to the beach. Over half of his platoon was killed in the fighting on Peleliu, which lasted over a month. He always wondered what his grandpa would think of the Call of Duty games. He'd probably think they were nonsense.

Brandon felt the minivan start its turn on the side of an elevated hill that overlooked Central Valley and a bright red farmhouse. A deep rumbling, followed by a muted buzz saw sound filled his ears, causing him to look out of the back window of their minivan. He saw the front of a green colored truck disintegrate into a storm of sparks, glass fragments and twisted metal. A massive helicopter crossed in front of the truck, obscuring his view of the carnage for a second. Just as the helicopter cleared the truck, his view was cut off by the hill on the inside of the turn.

"Holy fucking shit! Did you see that?" he yelled.

"Brandon! Watch your mouth! What the hell is wrong with you?" his mother yelled from the front seat.

"Did you see that?"

"See what?" his father demanded, glaring at him through the rearview mirror.

"A helicopter just crossed the road at ground level. It shot a semi-truck to pieces! You have to go back!"

"I've had enough of those video games. All they do is talk about helicopters and shooting. I don't know what has gotten into you, but you can forget about that stupid video game tonight!" said his mother.

"I'm not making this up," he said, scanning the skies out of the minivan's windows.

"I don't want to hear another word from you until we reach your grandparents' house," said his father.

A few minutes later, they approached a roadblock that spanned both sides of the interstate and consisted of at least twenty police cars. Heavily armed police officers clad in camouflage and body armor removed three layers of spike strips set on the road at least fifty yards in front of the roadblock. They signaled for the minivan to proceed, and as they approached the cars, one of them moved back to let them through. His father lowered his window.

"What's going on, Officer?" he said to a trooper wearing the traditional gray Mounties hat who approached the car.

"We have a high speed chase out of Harrisburg just past Allentown. Couple of crazies robbed a convenience store. We're expecting them soon, so I need you to move out of the area. You're clear to proceed, sir."

"Were they using helicopters to track the car?"

"What makes you say that?" asked the trooper.

"Nothing. My son thought he spotted one. Good luck, Officer."

The state trooper nodded and the minivan eased forward.

"What kind of a helicopter did you think you saw?" said his dad.

"A massive gray helicopter with fuel pods and a nose refueling probe. Dad, I'm not kidding about this. It tore the cab to pieces," Brandon stated emphatically.

"You don't seriously believe this, do you?" his wife countered.

"I don't know," his father said. "*Something's* going on back there. Take a look in the distance."

Brandon turned his head again and saw a thick black column of smoke rising above the hills they had just driven through.

Chapter 60

8:33 PM
Wayne Memorial Hospital
Honesdale, Pennsylvania

Jessica sat up in the vinyl chair placed in Daniel's sparse hospital room. Daniel had been transferred from the emergency ward less than an hour ago, after they were reasonably sure that his condition had been stabilized. The bullet had passed through his shoulder unhindered, tearing through a few ligaments, but causing no foreseeable long-term damage. The real problem stemmed from his blood loss, which had been categorized as a Class III hemorrhage, requiring aggressive fluid resuscitation and blood transfusions immediately upon arrival. By the time she'd reached the ER, Daniel was still deep in shock and nearly incoherent. The ER doctor estimated that he had lost more than thirty percent of his blood in the "shooting accident."

She heard footsteps approaching the room and tensed slightly. Jessica's hearing had slowly improved over the past several hours and the ringing had almost subsided, but her ears were still a long way from a full recovery. She was slightly tense, since the ER staff said that Daniel would have to provide a statement to the police. This was standard procedure for any injury involving a firearm. Fortunately, the local police were thoroughly occupied with some kind of major incident at a local business, and couldn't take the statement until tomorrow. She had a plan to get him out of here before the police arrived.

Sanderson had assured them that everything had been squared away with the FBI, but they were leery of local police involvement. Neither of them was one hundred percent sure what a background check might reveal about Daniel's involvement in the regrettable incident in Silver Spring, Maryland, two years ago. Their presidential immunity agreement didn't extend to local and state government, though they had been reasonably assured that most jurisdictions would comply. Still, she'd prefer not to test those waters while Daniel was relatively immobile. A short blond nurse entered the room, holding her hand out to stop whoever had followed her.

"Hold on, gentlemen. Mrs. Petrovich? I have two FBI agents who would like to speak with you and your husband. I can request that they return tomorrow morning if you want," she said.

"My husband has had a long day. He needs to rest. I'd prefer if they came back tomorrow," she said, worried that something else had changed in D.C.

"We were sent by Deputy Director Sanderson," interrupted someone from the hallway.

She recognized Melendez's voice.

"Alright. You can let them in," said Jessica.

"Are you sure?" responded the nurse.

"Very sure. Thank you for running interference," said Jessica.

"My pleasure. Go ahead, gentlemen, but if you get out of line, I'll have you removed," said the nurse, winking at Jessica.

Melendez and Munoz stepped inside the room and walked past the empty bed closest to the door. They were dressed in the same clothes they had been wearing that morning.

"You guys are getting a little brazen with the FBI badges," she said.

"We're thinking about joining the FBI. Sanderson should be able to hook that up from what I understand."

"I'm sure they'd be really happy to have you after the stunt you pulled in Stamford. Plus, the badge thing would get old really quick," said Jessica.

"Sanderson and Director Shelby apparently have an understanding," said Munoz.

"I'll believe that when I see the two of them shaking hands," said Jessica.

"How's he doing?" asked Melendez.

"Much better. He'll need some surgery to repair the ligaments damaged by the bullet, but beyond that he should be back on his feet by tomorrow."

"Good deal. We were worried," said Munoz.

"Thank you for bringing him to the ER, instead of the house. Another fifteen minutes driving around could have killed him. He'd lost too much blood at that point. The two of you are making a career out of saving our asses," she said.

"It never seems to end," said Munoz.

"You just make sure those kids of yours hear the stories about Uncle Jeff and Uncle Rico," said Melendez.

Munoz looked at him like he was crazy.

"What the fuck kind of a comment was that?" Munoz muttered.

"Do you know something I don't know?" said Jessica.

"No. I was just saying, that if they ever have kids, they should…I was just making a joke. Fuck."

"Uncle Rico and Uncle Jeff? Did we miss the wedding?" said Daniel, without opening his eyes.

"Well there he is. Back from the dead when there's a joke to be made," said Melendez.

"Please excuse my partner…my colleague. Damn it, Melendez!" said Munoz.

"The two of you do make a nice couple," said Jessica.

Munoz shook his head. "I'm going to miss having the two of you around, despite the incessantly inappropriate humor."

"Who says we're going anywhere?" said Jessica.

"Sanderson doesn't expect you to return to Argentina," replied Munoz.

"Sanderson's right about that. I have no intention of living the rest of my life on Gilligan's Island, but I never said we were finished."

"What about kids and living a peaceful life in a nice family community? Didn't I hear you talk about that before?" said Melendez.

"In due time, Rico. We still have a few loose ends to tie up," said Daniel.

"Srecko?" said Munoz.

"Among others. Until then, nobody is allowed into our residence. We'll be back sooner than you think," said Daniel.

"Sounds good. We're going to hit the road. We have a two-hour drive to Harrisburg in a stolen Suburban packed with automatic weapons and an Osama Bin Laden look-alike. Did I mention the truck was driven by Mexicans? I'm not optimistic about our chances," said Munoz.

"I'm glad I was shot. Make sure to say thank you to Berg's guy," Daniel smirked.

"This is like the start of a bad joke. Two Hispanics, a black and an Arab meet up to trade machine guns in a Wal-Mart parking lot," said Jessica.

They all laughed for a few moments.

"We'll see you in a little while," said Jessica.

Once they were alone, Daniel turned his head slightly and stared at Jessica.

"I need at least a solid month of vacation before heading back down to Argentina," he said.

"A month? I was thinking more like six months."

"Six months sounds nice. I assume we won't be here in the morning?"

"They're headed right back here after they deliver the weapons. The FBI will need to remove you for national security reasons. I doubt the night shift will ask any questions."

"Back to South Carolina?" he asked.

"That could work. I'm sure they have adequate medical facilities in Charleston."

She walked over and kissed his lips, staying there for a few moments before leaning back. He exhaled and closed his eyes.

"I love you."

"I love you more. Rest up. The Mexican connection will be back around one in the morning," she said.

"Two Latinos and Osama Bin Laden traveling through Pennsylvania with the nation on red alert? I hope you have a backup plan."

"I still have my badge and a few wigs in the Cherokee. You'd be surprised how persuasive I can be."

"I'm pretty sure Nurse Ratched has you pegged."

"I checked. Her shift ends at midnight."

Chapter 61

7:00 AM
FBI Headquarters
Washington D.C.

Frederick Shelby sipped his straight black coffee and leaned back in the plush black leather executive chair behind his desk. He raised the volume until the CNN commentator's voice could be easily heard from his desk. The moment of truth was seconds away. He'd either continue his day as FBI Director, or be summarily dismissed by the White House. He'd already spoken with his lawyer, a good friend and senior partner at an established Washington D.C. law firm that boasted one of the most successful and robust Public Policy and Law divisions in the country. If summoned, his lawyer would accompany him on the trip. He was apparently no stranger to the inner sanctums of the hill.

"My fellow Americans, I am pleased to inform you that the terrorist threat against our nation's public water supply has been eliminated by federal law enforcement agencies, working in close conjunction with key military units. I understand that the past week has been filled with uncertainty. This attack threatened all of us in a place we consider the safest—our very own homes. Thanks to the tireless effort and courageous sacrifice of our nation's heroes, I can assure you that your town's public water supply is safe. My administration agrees with the Department of Homeland Security's assessment that the threat has been neutralized, in all of its forms, and that your local municipality can commence regular water service effective immediately.

"I know you have many questions, and they will be answered in as much detail as possible during the upcoming weeks. Here's what I can say right now: A rogue, domestic terrorist group acquired the deadly virus from Al Qaeda operatives in the United States. Both the domestic terrorist group and the Al Qaeda cells involved have been neutralized. This represents a major law enforcement victory, in that Al Qaeda's operations in the United States have been destroyed. We'll release more information about the domestic terrorist group in the weeks ahead, though it appears that most of the group was killed or captured during counterterrorism operations yesterday. On a somber note, I can confirm that this group successfully detonated a suicide bomb at the National Counterterrorism Center on the evening of the 28th, killing 26 people and injuring 62 more. This attack was directed against the task force actively engaged in hunting them down.

"The FBI, supported by the White House and the Department of Justice, will conduct a thorough investigation of the events leading up to the attack, and the declassified results will be released to the public when they have been assembled. I'd ask that you join me in a moment of reflection, for the men and women who gave up their lives safeguarding ours."

The president bowed his head, and Shelby followed suit.

"God bless you, and may God bless the United States of America," said the president.

He turned off the flat screen monitor mounted on the wall in front of his desk and folded his hands. He was impressed with the president. No direct mention of the bottled water conspiracy or the final targets. Police officers successfully stopped the convoy approaching Philadelphia, without killing the driver, who identified the Chinese embassy as the target of the southernmost convoy. Delivery paperwork and a preprogrammed GPS confirmed the driver's statement. New York City Emergency Services officers stopped the second Manhattan convoy at the News Corporation Building, just as Shelby had predicted.

The last convoy's destination remained unknown, since the lead truck was destroyed after a Special Operations helicopter fired over one hundred rounds of 7.62mm ammunition into the cab, causing the rig to swerve off the road and explode. He still wasn't sure exactly why the president had authorized General Gordon to obliterate the truck and destroy critical evidence, but figured it had something to do with his dramatic departure from The Oval Office. Both the president and Jacob Remy looked panicked by his final outburst. The destruction of the truck represented one less piece of evidence connecting the plot to Greely's splinter group, which didn't support the White House's spin against True America. It didn't really matter. The FBI would go to excruciating lengths to investigate the events and provide a concise, detailed account of how Greely's cabal had acquired biological weapons from Al Qaeda and come so close to successfully executing their wild plan.

The president could do whatever he wanted with the results of the investigation, if he was still the president when the final report was issued. Detailed investigations took a long time. Long enough for the American public to forget. Within three months, the outrage would have faded, and the events of the past few days would no longer hold the political capital required to launch an attack on the mainstream True America movement.

His direct line rang and he examined the caller ID. He smiled and picked up the phone. He didn't bother to identify himself.

"Frankly, I expected a little more fight from the president," said Director Shelby.

"Then I guess you made a lasting impression yesterday," said a deep male voice.

"They'll recover sooner than you might expect. Give them a few days to reorganize…or a few hours," said Shelby.

"I have no doubt they'll be back at our throats shortly, but this gives us more time than we had originally anticipated. I assume the investigation will be a lengthy process?"

"It took the 9/11 Commission nearly nineteen months to release their report. I don't anticipate taking that long, but we can't afford to rush this kind of an investigation. From what I can tell, Greely's plot had roots extending all the way back to Al Qaeda cells in Europe. As you might imagine, I would demand nothing short of the most exhaustive and detailed investigation into a terror attack of this magnitude," replied Shelby.

"And we would expect nothing less from our nation's top law enforcement agent. I foresee an incredible future for your agency, Director. Especially if we continue to build our momentum leading into the 2008 election. With our focus on reshaping the domestic landscape, we see an expanded role for the FBI…especially in the wake of repeated attacks against our nation's great people."

"With more resources and less legal red tape, we could have stopped this conspiracy in its infancy," said Shelby.

"I couldn't agree more. Stopping this heinous attack despite the obstacles placed in your way is a tribute to your leadership. Leadership this nation can't afford to lose."

"I appreciate hearing that, and look forward to the days ahead."

"As do we. Thank you for your continued, dedicated service, Director," said the voice, emphasizing the word continued.

"My pleasure. I'll keep you posted."

After disconnecting the call, Shelby leaned back in his chair and stifled a laugh. The politics disgusted him, but he was willing to ride this train a little longer. He had played a long shot, but if True America's candidate won the 2008 election, he'd be in a position to make history for the FBI and the United States. The payoff on this bet was too tempting to ignore, even in the twilight of his career. For the first time in years, he felt there was hope for this nation. He picked up the phone and summoned his secretary. He had a vacancy to fill within the FBI. Associate Executive Assistant Director Ryan Sharpe would lead the National Security Branch's investigation into the events leading to the recent attack against the United States.

Chapter 62

7:42 AM
Central Intelligence Agency
McLean, Virginia

Karl Berg walked into his office and picked up the phone on his desk. He dialed the secretary assigned to him and informed her that he had just arrived. He took a moment to look around his office. Thanks to the events of the past month, he still hadn't found time to unpack even one of the boxes he had dragged here upon his promotion to the National Clandestine Service's (NCS) liaison to the Intelligence Directorate's Weapons, Intelligence, Non-Proliferation and Arms Control Center in late March. He'd spent less than a month in that position before Thomas Manning summarily promoted him to a position that hadn't previously existed within NCS, working as Audra Bauer's deputy assistant. He would retain his duties as the Intelligence Directorate liaison, which appeared to be the only official tasking that came with the promotion at this moment.

This would give him time to put up some shelving and start unearthing his treasures. With the Zulu Virus threat finally under wraps, he could start unpacking his boxes. Apparently, he wouldn't have to move again. His promotion didn't come with a new office in the "executive" zone, which suited him fine, though he had been pleasantly surprised with Thomas

Manning and their director. He had expected handcuffs instead of a promotion.

He got up and started to survey the stacks of boxes covering his vinyl couch and black lacquer coffee table. The line from his secretary buzzed and he answered it.

"Good morning, Mr. Berg. I have Darryl Jackson on the line?"

"Thank you. Put him through."

The line beeped.

"Darryl. How's my favorite go-to guy?"

"If you know someone else with access to weapons, please feel free to start using him. I'm fucking exhausted from cleaning weapons all night."

"They had a rough time up there," said Berg.

"I could tell. One of the rifles was covered in blood. How bad was it?"

"One KIA. I can't thank you enough for the help. You're one of the unsung heroes in this drama."

"That seems to be the story of my life. Hey, are you going to answer my wife's email or what? She still hasn't figured out that I've been flying all over the country delivering illegal arms shipments. Her invitation could be revoked at any moment," said Jackson.

"I'm kind of hurt that she didn't call. An email invitation to dinner seems impersonal," he joked.

"A phone call? I don't think she planned to talk to you at dinner! I just assumed she'd seat you on the deck. Baby steps, my friend. She doesn't forgive easily."

"As long as she's serving me the same food you're eating, I'll eat in the garage. I'll send her my acceptance as soon as we get off the phone and pick out a rare Bordeaux."

"Cheryl collects vintage Bordeaux."

"I guarantee she won't have this bottle. It was never for sale," said Berg.

"Sounds like you're good at taking baby steps. I have to go. I'm still dealing with the fallout from the Kazakhstan fiasco, which could be smoothed over if the CIA ponied up the money to replace the weapons that were lost…in the direct interest of national security?"

"I'm sure something could be arranged," said Berg.

"Then let's arrange it. I have two daughters in college, and can't afford to buy Brown River several new rifles."

"A shipment of rifles shouldn't be difficult,"

"Maybe I should take cash. I don't need one of your buried Cold War stashes."

"That hurt my feelings, Darryl."

"I'll fax you the bill. Catch you later, Karl."

Karl Berg hung up the phone and sat on the edge of his desk, staring at the boxes again. His office could always wait.

The End

To sign up for Steven's New Release Updates, send an email to stevekonkoly@gmail.com

Please visit Steven's blog for more on *Black Flagged* and future projects. www.stevenkonkoly.com

A bonus excerpt from the next book in the *Black Flagged* series and an excerpt from *The Jakarta Pandemic* immediately follow:

Excerpt from *Black Flagged Vektor*

(To be released in the Spring of 2013)

Chapter 1

10:25 AM
Mountain Glen "Retirement" Compound
Green Mountains, Vermont

Karl Berg walked briskly down a wide, raked gravel path bordered by cedar planks. The main walkway cut directly through a rough landscape of knee high grasses and watermelon sized rocks. Several subsidiary paths branched off into the thick pine trees and led to modest residences hidden just out of sight. He easily found path number five, which was marked by a solid looking post displaying the number. He stopped for a moment and took in his surrounding.

He stood in a round clearing the size of three football fields. A natural stream ran through its northern edge, visible from Berg's position near the center. At the opposite end of the field behind him stood a massive post and beam lodge, which contained the facility's gourmet kitchen, common dining area, recreation room, indoor pool and exercise facilities. Fifty meters to the left of the lodge sat a white, one-story building that housed the compound's backup generator, water distribution system and main electricity breaker. An attached two bay garage held several ATV's for patrolling the grounds, plowing snow and transporting "guests." He had just walked out of the only other non-residential structure in the compound. The security station.

Resembling a two-story colonial style home, the station housed fifteen security specialists and contained the state of the art equipment used to keep track of the compound's "guests." Bristling with antennae and fitted with an odd dome at the apex of the roof, the house served as the compound's nerve center, monitoring every aspect of the "guests" lives. From heartbeats to toilet flushes, dozens of active and passive measures were taken to ensure each guest's compliance with the rules.

The guests stayed in "residences" situated beyond the thick tree line that surrounded the clearing. Hidden from overhead view by towering evergreens, each residence was "bugged" and monitored by several cameras mounted in nearby trees. Motion detectors tracked movement inside and outside of each structure, guiding the sophisticated array of night vision and thermal imaging equipped cameras assigned to each guest. Patterns were recorded, analyzed and anticipated. Anything out of the ordinary was immediately investigated by a mobile security team.

Guests were allowed free run of the compound, as long as they didn't bother another guest or interfere with the staff. Violations resulted in lockdown. Each guest villa could be locked and unlocked remotely from the security station. The final immediate security precaution consisted of a reinforced, twelve-foot tall, razor wire fence that encircled the entire compound. Located three hundred meters beyond the edge of the clearing, the entire fence line was monitored by cameras and motion detectors. If one of the compound's guests, or an outside party decided to scale the fence, security personnel could deliver a substantial electrical charge to the section of fence under attack. Beyond the fence, the last deterrent to an escape was isolation. Located deep within the Green Mountains, accessible by a single road that wound through thick pine stands and rough terrain, anyone finding themselves on the other side of the fence would face a fifty mile trek through unforgiving wilderness to reach the first signs of civilization.

For such a small "guest" population, the Mountain Glen facility cost taxpayers an unimaginable sum of money. The compound had been designed as the final "deal" for enemy foreign nationals willing to provide information critical to U.S. national security. Enemies too dangerous for release were offered a lifetime "retirement" in exchange for their knowledge, which would be vetted and confirmed. Each case was carefully reviewed by the Director of the CIA, prior to their permanent placement. If the information turned out to be bogus, or failed to live up to advertised expectations, the "guest" would be evicted.

Permanent placement was contingent upon full disclosure of the information promised, which involved a significant element of trust. Few prospective guests turned their back on the deal after spending a few days at Mountain Glen. Fresh air, mountain views, babbling brooks, gourmet food, first class accommodations. Most of them had already tasted the alternative while in U.S. custody. Only the most stubborn or distrustful chose to spend the rest of their lives trapped in a dank, poorly lit prison cell, pissing and shitting into a rusty coffee can that was emptied once a day.

He turned down the path and let the pristine air fill his lungs. Cold pine air. Quite a difference from the crowded confines of the Beltway. He couldn't imagine anyone turning down the offer to stay here. The temperature dropped a few degrees as he passed through the green curtain of pines. He could see a small post and beam structure with a green metal roof situated in a clearing fifty meters ahead. He searched the trees while he walked, trying to spot any of the cameras or sensors. He felt exposed walking to Reznikov's villa alone.

He approached the front door cautiously, scanning the windows for signs of life within the house. Security has assured him that Reznikov was awake. Breakfast had been delivered thirty minutes ago. He thought about that. They delivered breakfast at Mountain Glen. Reznikov certainly didn't deserve a place like this, but what other options did they have? The door opened before he could knock.

"Come in my friend. Breakfast is waiting," said an invigorated looking Anatoly Reznikov.

"I already ate," said Berg, stepping across the threshold prepared to defend himself from a hand to hand attack.

"Nonsense. Please. This is my treat. Welcome to my mountain dacha."

"It's not yours yet. We're still a long way from securing your stay, which is why I'm here," said Berg, following Reznikov through a short hallway to kitchen table.

From the table, they had a view of the pine wall at the edge of the back yard, and the snow covered peak of a mountain rising above the pines. The view wasn't what caught Berg's attention. A one third empty bottle of Grey Goose vodka sat on the kitchen counter, next to a small shot glass.

"Looks like you've made a remarkable recovery," said Berg.

"It must be the mountain air, and a little gift from the staff. Join me in a toast."

"A little early, don't you think?" replied Berg.

"Never to early to celebrate. Plus, it's almost noon—"

"It's 10:30," interrupted Berg.

"And I need to warm up for our chat. You won't be disappointed," said Reznikov.

While the mad scientist pulled another shot glass out of a cabinet, Berg placed his leather satchel on the pine floor and sat down at the kitchen table. He surveyed the feast prepared for him by the lodge's kitchen staff. He hoped they were just rolling out the red carpet to loosen Reznikov's lips. Fresh fruit, lobster benedict, smoked salmon and toasted bagels with cream cheese, orange juice.

"Please help yourself. They just showed up with all of this. Can you believe it? Only in America. I should have come to your country earlier. Maybe I wouldn't have turned out so bad," he said and poured two full shots of vodka.

He set one of the glasses in front of Berg and took a seat across the table.

"A toast. To taking down VEKTOR Labs."

Berg hesitantly raised his glass. He eyed Reznikov warily, as the Russian downed his glass of clear liquid. Berg followed suit, grimacing at the sharp burn. A few seconds later, he felt a little less worn out from the previous day's travels.

"Where did you stash your beautiful assistant? I had hoped she would be part of the package. I didn't notice any women here."

"I'm sure they keep a few blow up dolls on hand for the guests," he said, placing the shot glass down on the table.

"Such hostility. Not exactly the kind of environment that makes me want to share the intimate details of my former employer," said Reznikov.

The Russian reached behind him to retrieve the vodka bottle from the counter top behind him.

"Perhaps you'd rather have your head stuffed into a diarrhea filled toilet bowl three stories below the surface of the earth?"

Berg raised his hands to simulate a balanced scale.

"Fresh mountain air, nice view, gourmet food, spa-like amenities," he said, raising one hand and lowering the other.

"Or…daily beatings, concrete pavement sleeping arrangements, one meal a day and toilet bowl scuba lessons. Don't fuck with me here."

"Easy, my friend. I get it," said Reznikov, pouring another shot.

He started to move the bottle over to Berg's side of the table, but Berg grabbed it from his trembling hand. On closer inspection, Reznikov didn't look as robust as he was acting. Mention of a permanent prison cell underground had quickly flushed the color from his face.

"I'm not your friend, and you'll get this bottle back after we've made considerable progress."

He placed the bottle on the floor and retrieved a legal pad from his satchel, along with a digital recording device.

"Don't put the bottle on the floor. Radiant heat. Feels wonderful, but you almost have to wear socks," said Reznikov.

Berg removed the chilled bottle from the floor, placing it on the table, shaking his head. Radiant fucking heat? What was next? Daily massage therapy?

"So. Where do you want to start?" said Reznikov.

"From the beginning. How did you become involved with VEKTOR?"

"The roots of that decision reach back to my childhood. Are you in the mood for a story?" he paused.

"As long as it has something to do with VEKTOR," said Berg.

"It has everything to do with VEKTOR, and how Russia's bioweapons program long ago eclipsed their nuclear weapons program," he whispered.

Three hours later, Berg emerged from the villa with a distant look on his face. He followed the gravel path through the forest to the main clearing, hardly paying any attention to his footing or his surroundings. The warm, late afternoon sun barely registered on his face. If Reznikov had told the truth, the United States and its allies faced the greatest threat to world stability since the Cold War. A secret race to develop bioweapons of mass destruction, and the Russians had a thirty-year head start. The reckless plan that he'd suggested to Sanderson didn't feel so outlandish anymore. The bioweapons program at VEKTOR Labs had to be destroyed.

&

Anatoly Reznikov peered through the shades of his front window at the vanishing shape of Karl Berg, the enigmatic CIA agent that had miraculously rescued him from a quick death at the hands of his former masters. The past week had been confusing, hazy and punctuated by severe fluctuations in his mental state that kept him unable to focus. He'd spent most of the time feeling utterly helpless, certain that he would be brutally interrogated and discarded. The pessimistic side of him had taken full control of his emotions, which came at little surprise to him. He'd tried to drink himself to death in Stockholm, and failing that, had put a gun to his head to finish the job. And that was just the beginning of a two-day roller coaster ride marked by repeated cardiac arrest, torture and beatings while strapped to a bed.

Only a sheer miracle could explain his sudden moment of clarity on the jet ride back to the United States. It had probably just been a natural fluke. A random release of chemicals, possibly dopamine, to relax his anxiety long enough for him to wrestle control of him mind. Maybe it had been triggered by the sight of Karl Berg sipping scotch, or the sharp smell of aged liquor filling the cabin. It didn't matter. Within the short span of time it took for Karl Berg to walk down the business jet's aisle, he had formulated a plan that was guaranteed to set him free. Free from all of this.

Earning a transfer to this facility was just the first step in his plan. As soon as his mind had devised the plan, he wondered if it had been his fate all along to fall right into Berg's lap. He couldn't think of a better scenario now that his mind had cleared enough for him to see the bigger picture. He'd been despondent about Al Qaeda's betrayal and his subsequent failure to recover more of the virus canisters, but this new turn of events would take his original plan to the next level. He just needed to place a single phone call to activate part two of his plan.

He hadn't lied to Berg. On the contrary. He had told the agent everything, except the part about how he had successfully stolen samples of every weaponized virus and bacteria created at VEKTOR. He hadn't been dismissed from VEKTOR for attempting to steal viral encephalitis samples. By that point, he had already stolen samples of everything he had seen in the bioweapons division. He had been caught trying to access a section of the laboratory off limits to everyone except for three scientists. Rumors started circulating that the small group had created something nobody had seen before. He took the bait and attempted to sneak into the lab. At that point, security features at VEKTOR relied more on humans than technology, and large sums of money helped him circumvent most of the security surrounding the isolated laboratory cell. Or so he had thought.

Seconds from crossing the point of no return, he was warned off by the only security guard not infiltrated by FSB agents. Without stepping foot in the off limits section, they couldn't shoot him on the spot like they had planned. Instead, FSB agents backed off and allowed him to continue work at the lab, under close supervision. A week later, he received an offer to lead a lab group at their sister institute in Kazakhstan. He knew it was a setup, and the rest was history. He'd escaped with his life and bioweapons samples worth millions of dollars. Fate had given him one more chance and he didn't intend to waste it. One call to some very nefarious "friends," and he could take leave of this place, free to sell his weapons to the highest bidder. And the icing on cake? VEKTOR's bioweapons division and all of its key personnel would be likely be targeted by Berg's people. He'd finally avenge his parents' murder at the hand of Russian security forces. Revenge was sweet, especially when it required no effort on his part.

Chapter 2

9:15 PM
Viggbyholm, Sweden

Mihail Osin stared at the glowing windows of 14 Värtavägen and considered his options. He hadn't detected any movement inside the one-story house, but the interior lights had greeted them upon their silent arrival at the edge of the property's thick evergreen screen, and he couldn't ignore the possibility that their target might still be present. Even snagging one of the safe house's "keepers" could put them back on the path to finding Reznikov. Unfortunately, his own experience with the use of foreign safe houses didn't leave him optimistic. Reznikov's abduction had occurred over two weeks ago, which was an eternity to keep a high value target in such an exposed, but well concealed location.

The CIA made a wise choice with this house. The neighborhood was surprisingly rustic and eerily quiet for a suburb less than fifteen kilometers from the center of Stockholm. Close enough to the city for quick access, yet isolated enough to ensure natural privacy. Hidden in plain sight. Judging by the amount of time it took the Russian Foreign Intelligence Service to uncover the location, the CIA had gone to great lengths to bury this place in the open.

His team of four operatives had been dropped off on the street behind the safe house a few minutes before dusk. Their van quickly departed the area, and joined a rented Volvo sedan parked at a church less than two minutes away. The two-man team in the Volvo had conducted the initial reconnaissance of the neighborhood, quickly determining that street parking was either prohibited or discouraged in the residential areas of Viggbyholm. They hadn't seen a single car parked on any of the nearby streets, and had a difficult time picking out a discreet spot along the road behind the house to drop the team unseen. Parking one of their vans on the street for any length of time or lingering nearby would simply invite disaster. Sitting in the church parking lot after dark probably wasn't the best idea either, but it was the only non-residential parking zone with quick access to the safe house.

Mihail shifted knees and removed a hand-sized black electronic device from the open nylon backpack next to him. The device had two stubby antennae and muted orange LCD screen. He examined the LCD screen, which cast a barely detectable orange glow on his face. The multi-channel, wireless radio frequency (RF) detector showed a few faint wireless signals in the 2400-2480 MHz range used by off the shelf, commercial home wireless routers. He was more interested in anything using the 800-1000 MHz frequency range, which included specific sub-ranges most commonly used by wireless motion sensors. Anything lower than 800 MHz would similarly pique his attention. The RF detector had passively collected data since their arrival twenty minutes earlier, twice detecting a short frequency burst at 910MHz, which was one of the most common frequencies associated with the local GSM-900 cellular network. The short transmission also resembled what he'd seen before when a cell phone regularly registers to a local cell tower. At this point, he felt satisfied that the neither the yard nor the house was protected by motion detectors. He stood up and signaled for the team to move forward, placing the detector in the pack before slipping it over his shoulders. He disengaged the safety on his PP2000 submachine gun and stepped into the backyard.

Three of the four Spetsnaz operatives converged on the back door from different points in the yard, while the fourth operative slid along the right side of the house, looking for the power line connection. Mihail listened intently near one of the illuminated windows, but heard nothing beyond the distant hum of a car motor. He decided that they would try to pick the lock and deadbolt, instead of forcing the door open. He desperately wanted to avoid making noise in this neighborhood. If nobody was present in the house, he wanted time to inspect it for anything useful. While one of his operatives worked the locks with a small tool kit, he listened underneath a different window. The house was still. By the time he returned, less than one minute later, the two locks had been silently opened.

He lowered his PN21K night vision monocular into place over his right eye and spoke softly into the microphone attached to his headgear. Two seconds later, the house darkened and the lead member of his team burst through the door with enough force to dislodge any chain lock barring their entrance. Mihail followed the second man through the door and they fanned out, scanning the darkness with their goggles. Once the doorways leading out of the kitchen were secured, he whispered orders for the team to go silent and listen. Roughly two minutes later, he raised his night vision goggles and ordered the fourth operative to return electrical power to the house.

When the lights reenergized, they could plainly see what the rough green images cast by their night vision had indicated. The house had been cleared of everything, "sanitized" all the way down to the toilet paper rolls. He recalled the fourth member of his team, and they spent the next five minutes checking closets, opening drawers and prying at wallpaper in a futile attempt to find anything. Each operative returned to the kitchen cradling his submachine gun and quickly shaking his head. Nothing. He opened his backpack and scanned the radio frequency detector. He found a strong reading at 1621 MHz, which had started a few minutes ago. This was an L band frequency used for satellite communications. Someone knew they were here, and would very likely receive a video feed of their foray through the house.

He signaled for the team to evacuate the structure, recalling the van once they were outside. On their way to the front of the house, he ordered the power to be permanently cut from the house. He checked the RF detector again and saw that the device hidden in the house continued to transmit, indicating an independent power source. He thought he had committed an error restoring power, but it wouldn't have mattered if he had kept the power off. The big mistake had been assuming that they might find anything useful in a sanitized CIA safe house. Now someone knew for certain that they hadn't lost interest in Anatoly Reznikov, which meant it was time to exercise the least desirable option on the table. As they waited for the van in the shadows, Mihail pulled out his encrypted cell phone and placed a call to SVR headquarters. As he had anticipated, their night had just begun.

Chapter 3

1:26 PM
CIA Headquarters
McLean, Virginia

Karl Berg reviewed the last few slides from the PowerPoint presentation he would present to Thomas Manning in ten minutes. He had been awake much of the night putting together the first draft of his urgent appeal for the CIA to take action against Vektor Laboratory's bioweapons department. With Reznikov's inside information, they could send General Sanderson's Russian Group to destroy the facility and eliminate key personnel involved in the program. Reznikov felt confident that a small, properly equipped elite force could successfully execute the mission, given the right tactical intelligence...which he would provide.

Audra Bauer joined him for part of the morning, helping him smooth most of the slides. She had already spoken at length with Manning about the threat posed by Vektor labs. Israeli intelligence assets have repeatedly warned the CIA that the Iranians continue to aggressively pursue research positions within Vektor, despite Israel's best efforts. From the CIA assessment of the past decade, Iranian scientists seemed to die from sudden natural causes at a startlingly higher rate than their counterparts in other nations. A scientific career in the fields of biology, chemistry, or physics currently ranks as one of the most hazardous occupations in Iran.

The Israelis have little doubt that the Iranians intend to steal bioweapons samples from the lab, or collaborate with Russian scientists associated with the program. Recent grumblings from their Mossad liaison left Manning and Bauer with the impression that Israel was no longer satisfied with the CIA's backseat approach to the Iranian's unquenchable thirst for weapons of mass destruction. Manning had dodged three meeting requests from the Mossad liaison since the President appeared on national television to explain the domestic terrorist attack on the nations' water supply. They both knew what Wiljam Minkowitz would say. Time for the U.S. to step up.

Berg's job wouldn't be to convince Manning of the necessity to target Vektor. Manning was already primed to take their efforts to the next level. His presentation was designed to convince Manning that they could win the Director's approval, which would ultimately impact their chances of winning over the President. Without the President's approval, Berg would have to make some difficult choices. Drop the topic entirely, or take the operation "off the books." He didn't think an unsanctioned black op would be feasible in this situation. Novosibirsk was the third largest city in Russian, nearly 200 miles beyond the Kazakhstan border. Getting Sanderson's team to the target wasn't the problem. Evading the massive military and police response from the Novosibirsk Oblast would be impossible without significant, targeted intervention. The feasibility of this operation depended upon White House support, which shouldn't be entirely difficult to win given the fact that a weaponized virus from Vektor labs nearly decapitated the government.

His STE (Secure Terminal Equipment) desk set rang, indicating a secure call from the operations watch center. He picked up the handset, which triggered the automatic negotiation of cryptographic protocols within the removable Fortezza Crypto Card inserted into his phone. Unique identifiers built card's cryptographic processor verified that Karl Berg was on one end of the call and that the operations watch center was on the other. STE technology represented a major improvement over the STU-III system, where the cryptographic processor was built into the phone, and provided no unique identification procedures. With the STE system, Karl Berg could insert his card into any STE phone and conduct a secure, encrypted conversation.

"Karl Berg," he answered.

"Good afternoon, Mr. Berg. I have a Flash Alert data package designated for your eyes only. How do you want me to proceed?"

"You can send it through my secure feed. I don't have time to review the package in the ops center," said Berg.

Berg knew where the package had originated, but he was dying to see the contents.

"Understood. You now have access to the package."

"Thank you," Berg said, and disconnected the call.

He navigated to the CIA Operations intranet gateway and entered a long string of passwords that enabled access to his secure feed. He found the data package in question, and opened it.

A separate screen opened, showing eight data sets, all of which contained a hyperlink. He opened the one showing the longest period of time, which ended three minutes ago in Sweden. "19:17.24GMT/13:17.24EST-19:23.53GMT/13:23.53EST."

The hyperlink activated a data recording captured by one of the motion-activated, night vision capable cameras hidden in the Viggbyholm safe house's fire detectors. Located on the ceiling of each room, the cameras provided a searchable three hundred and sixty degree view within each space. The recording showed a three-man team enter the kitchen from the door leading into the backyard and proceed to wait for two minutes. Each operative wore latest generation Russian night vision monocles and carried the same type of submachine guns used by the Zaslon Spetsnaz team in Stockholm.

After two minutes, the house lights came on, momentarily blinding the camera as the smart-sensor switched camera lens inputs. Definitely not your garden-variety operatives. He guessed they were some variation of SVR Spetsnaz. A forth operative joined them through the back door, and they proceeded to searched the house. Berg toggled through the other hyperlinks, which showed the team conducting a quick, yet thorough investigation of the empty house. He returned to the first link, which was still running, and almost missed the most important part of the data feed. The lead operative removed a small, black electronic device from his backpack and immediately ordered the team's evacuation. Less than fifteen seconds later, the scene went dark, replaced by the green image of an empty kitchen. The team leader knew that their raid didn't go unnoticed.

Berg sat back in his chair and considered the situation. He hadn't expected the Russians to forget about Reznikov. Given what the crazed scientist had told him over vodka shots and gourmet food, he was surprised that they hadn't heard more from the Russians. Of course, the Russians were still dealing with the staggering fallout caused by Reznikov's manmade disaster in Monchegorsk. Compound that with Reznikov's link to the terrorist plot in the United States, and the Russians didn't really have a basis to object on any level. Everything leads back to a program that supposedly didn't exist.

As predicted, the Russians would dig around quietly for Reznikov. But how long would their efforts remain below the surface? The Spetsnaz team in the video didn't look like they would have passed up the opportunity to take down anyone found in the house. The big question was where would they go next? If Berg was pulling the strings, he'd start with the Stockholm embassy.

Three members of the CIA station knew critical details about Petrovich's operation. One of them was temporary assigned to his staff, while she awaited her next assignment, which took her out of play. This left the Stockholm embassy's CIA Station Chief and her Assistant Station Chief. The Russians wouldn't dare touch the Station Chief, but if pressed, they might make a move on the station's second-in-charge. This was the only move that made sense.

Given the sensitivity of Reznikov's circumstances, it would be reasonable for the Russians to assume that the details of the operation had been restricted to the most senior CIA officer at the station. In this case, neither the Station Chief or her assistant knew the identity of the target, but this wasn't something he could pass on to the Russians to dissuade them from taking regrettable action. All he could do was warn Emily Bradshaw that the Russians were actively prowling the streets of Stockholm. He opened a different internet directory and located the station chief's after hours contact information.

Excerpt from *The Jakarta Pandemic*

Prologue

Alex checked his watch for the tenth time in less than twenty minutes. 5:50 p.m.

Where are they?

He had started to lose his patience early, which came as no surprise. He had been lying under the McCarthy's play set for nearly an hour, as a vicious Nor'easter dumped thick waves of snow on him. This would be enough to test anyone's patience…and physical limits.

He lowered his night vision scope for a moment and rubbed his eyes. Now, even the green image in the scope added to his discomfort. He just hoped that Charlie was keeping a better watch over the stretch of ground that defined the ambush site.

He'd better be, or they could stumble right through here undetected.

Alex had doubts about spotting them with his night vision scope. The near absence of ambient light combined with a blinding snowstorm continued to degrade the already grainy image formed by the inexpensive first generation night scope.

He twisted open the green ceramic thermos and poured the last of the hot tea prepared for him by Kate. He sipped the steaming tea from the thermos cap, placed the cap down next to the rifle in front of him, and took another look through the night vision scope. He could still see the Hayes' house, but the image was even grainier. He knew the batteries were not the issue; he'd just changed them. Soon enough, he'd have to rely solely on Charlie to spot them in time to spring a coordinated ambush. If not, he'd have to take the three men down himself, which wasn't optimal, but was still well within his range of capabilities. He didn't want to think about what could happen if they slipped by him. Nothing would stand between these psychopaths and his family.

As long as I see them before they're right on top of me, I'll be fine.

Alex swigged the rest of the warm tea and replaced the lid. He tucked the thermos into his backpack and checked his rifle again. Looking through the Aimpoint scope, he saw that the red dot still glowed brightly in the center of the sight. He pulled back on the AR-15's charging handle and ejected the bullet loaded in the chamber, leaving the brass cartridge in the snow where two other bullets lay. He'd ejected one bullet every half-hour to ensure that the freezing temperatures had not affected the weapon's mechanical action. A malfunction tonight would spell disaster.

He suffered a sudden, violent, and insuppressible full body shiver, which rendered him useless for a few seconds. He couldn't last out here all night, and he knew it. He looked through the night vision scope again, and the green image confirmed that he was still alone. Staring through the scope, he wondered how it was possible for things to have spiraled so far out of control.

So far gone, in fact, that he now found himself lying under a neighbor's play set in a blizzard, eagerly waiting to kill. He never thought twice about doing this in Iraq. It was his mission. He didn't really have any problem with it here either, and he could rationalize this act on several levels. He had to do it: for the good of the neighborhood, and probably society in general, but most importantly…for the immediate safety of his family.

And in the end, that was all that really counted for Alex.

ARRIVAL

Chapter One

Friday, November 2, 2013

Alex was jarred awake by a loud pulsing vibration. He squinted in the darkness and labored to turn his head toward the source of the persistent buzzing sound.

Shit, my iPhone.

The phone's display illuminated a half empty glass of water on the nightstand. He watched, still helpless, as the phone moved closer to the edge with each vibration. Breaking through the murk of a broken sleep cycle, he reached for the phone to check the caller ID. *Maine Medical Center.* A jolt of adrenaline shot through his body, and Alex headed out of the bedroom to the hallway.

"Alex Fletcher," he answered in a whisper.

"Oh…Alex. It's Dr. Wright. I thought I'd get your voicemail."

Dr. Wright was the head of the Maine Medical Center's Infectious Disease Department.

"No problem, Dr. Wright. I usually don't keep my phone on the nightstand. Just happened to end up there tonight," he said, closing the door to the master bedroom.

"I'm glad you're awake, Alex. I'm fairly confident we've seen our first cases of the new pandemic flu tonight. Cases started rolling into the ERs early this evening."

"You said 'ERs'. More than one?"

"Yes. Three cases at Maine Med. Two came from Westbrook and one from Falmouth. And one case at Mercy, patient walked over from somewhere in the west end. I also have a confirmed case at Maine General in Augusta and possible cases at Eastern Maine Med up in Bangor."

"Confirmed as what?"

"Confirmed as nothing I've ever seen before. That's why I think we're dealing with this new virus out of Hong Kong," Dr. Wright said.

"That's more than six cases. How did this pop up here first and not Boston? It doesn't make a lot of sense."

"Boston has been hit with several dozen cases, possibly more."

"What do you mean? I didn't see anything on the news, or on any of the websites. We've been keeping an eye on this," Alex said.

"I don't know what to tell you, but I know for a fact that Boston has been slammed. A friend of mine at Mass General called to tell me to get ready. He said that area hospitals in Boston saw dozens of cases trickle in overnight Wednesday, with more showing up as the day progressed. Several dozen more by the time I talked to him."

"Why didn't the media catch this yet?" he asked.

"Well, between you and me, and I don't have to remind you that this entire conversation never happened—"

"Of course. Absolutely, Dr. Wright," Alex said instantly.

"We have been instructed by the state health department to report all cases directly to them so they can coordinate resources and notify federal health agencies. I assume that direction filtered down from DHS. They also asked us not to notify the media, in order to avoid a panic. I can understand part of that logic, but if you ask me, I think they're trying to keep this under wraps because they're not prepared. Unfortunately, this is the only direction we've received so far from the state or feds. Or maybe that's a good thing for now. Aside from rushing us more useless avian flu detection kits, nothing else has been done. Alex, I have to let you go. I have a long night ahead of me."

"Sorry to hold you up. Thank you for the call, Dr. Wright. I really appreciate the heads up, seriously. The preliminary case fatality rates in Asia look high."

"Yeah, we're not taking any chances. This is different than the avian flu, which was bad enough. It makes the swine flu look like a common cold. And thanks for making a trip over here yesterday, especially considering the fact that the state's anti-viral stockpiles will fall under federal control if the flu spirals out of control. Your samples will really come in handy."

"Could you use some more? We've been instructed to keep our distribution of TerraFlu to a minimum, but I have no problem hooking you guys up. Really."

"I'll take whatever you can give me at this point, but I don't want you to get in trouble with Biosphere, Alex."

"I'm not worried about them. What time works for you tomorrow? My schedule is pretty clear, so I can make a trip over any time."

"How about 12:45? I plan to be back from the hospital at that point. My first patient is at one. We could take care of it then," Dr. Wright said.

"Works for me. See you at 12:45. Good luck tonight," Alex said and waited for a reply, but the line was already dead.

He headed back into the bedroom and looked over at Kate, who was soundly asleep. He walked over to her and kissed her on the forehead. She barely moved.

He left the bedroom and walked to his home office, activated his computer, and checked the *Boston Globe* and *Boston Herald. Still nothing.*

He checked the International Scientific Pandemic Awareness Collaborative (ISPAC) website and navigated to their pandemic activity map. The map had changed dramatically since he'd last seen it and was now interactively linked to Google Earth.

Color-coded symbols represented reported flu locations, and when you passed the mouse over one of the new icons, basic information appeared in a text box, which could be further expanded for more detailed information. Light blue: cases of interest, yellow: initial outbreak, orange: small-scale outbreak, red: medium-sized outbreak, violet: large-scale outbreak.

He zoomed in on North America.

Cases in Canada, Mexico, Central America...wait, wait, look at this, Los Angeles, San Diego, and San Francisco. He looked at the East Coast and saw no colored icons. Alex adjusted the map to focus on southern California and placed the cursor over the yellow Los Angeles icon.

"Los Angeles. Population 4,089,245. Isolated outbreaks. 190+ cases reported. Uncontained. Isolated outbreaks among ethnic Asian populations."

In a separate desktop window, he navigated to the *Los Angeles Times* homepage. He looked for the California/Local section. *Here we go.* He found an article and began to read:

Hong Kong Flu Hits Asian Community.

"Cedars-Sinai confirms at least a dozen cases of Hong Kong flu. Mainly confined to Asian community. UCLA Medical Center confirms several cases. Mainly Asian community. East LA Doctor's Hospital sees its first cases late in the evening on October 31. Community leaders decry nearly one day delay in reporting cases to the public. Employee at Cedars-Sinai contacts Los Angeles Times with information about suspected flu cases. Cases were being kept isolated from other patients and under a tight information seal. Times reporters launched an immediate investigation into all area hospitals, uncovering several dozen more cases."

Looks like a cover up.

Alex put the cursor over the yellow San Francisco icon. *"San Francisco. Population 853,758. Isolated outbreaks. 100+ cases reported. Uncontained. Isolated outbreaks among ethnic Asian populations."*

He then moved the cursor south to San Diego and placed it over the yellow icon.

He changed the view to China and saw that dozens of southern coastal cities were shaded either orange or red; Hong Kong and the surrounding areas were shaded violet. He passed the mouse over one of these areas. *"Greater Guangzhou city. Population 12,100,000. Massive outbreak. 8,000+ reported cases. Uncontained. Containment efforts focused on Guangdong Province."*

8,000 plus cases in one city? I thought there were only 26,000 altogether in China yesterday?

Alex passed the mouse over a few more cities in the area around Hong Kong and saw similar text fields. He quickly added up the other numbers and calculated roughly 77,000 reported cases in southern China.

He zoomed out of China and settled on a world view. Colored dots appeared to sweep outward in a concentric wave from Southeast Asia. A solid perimeter of blue dots extended from Japan, through South Korea and Vladivostok, then reached across northern China and connected with Pakistan and India. India was covered in blue dots and yellow dots; orange icons appeared centered over several major cities within India. Oddly, Java Island contained no dots. He placed the cursor over Java.

"Java Island. Population 150,000,000. No reports."

Something's up over there.

Beyond Asia's ring, blue-colored dots littered every continent, concentrated on nearly every major city. He almost wished he hadn't seen the map. He felt his stomach churn as a wave of anxiety blanketed him. Still, he walked back to the bedroom and lay down next to Kate, feeling secure lying there with her. He closed his eyes and started breathing deeply in a futile attempt to induce sleep.

Chapter Two

Friday, November 2, 2013

Alex's body shuddered, and his eyes flashed open. He searched the bright room to confirm that he was still lying in bed with his wife, Kate, in their Scarborough, Maine, home. His heart pounded through his shallow breath. He touched his forehead with the back of his right hand and wiped the sweat on his gray T-shirt, leaving a dark stain near the neck.

Jesus. I don't ever want to see that bridge again.

He turned his head to look at his wife. Kate's face was turned away; she had the covers pulled up over her neck, and all he could see was her jet black hair.

Thank God she didn't wake up. I don't need her starting in on the VA counseling again.

He'd successfully dodged a phone call to the Togus Veteran's Hospital for the better part of nine years.

He sat up in bed slowly, careful not to wake Kate. The sky to the east was clear, and the room was aglow with pre-dawn light. Alex slid out of bed, walked over to Kate's side, and kissed her on the forehead. Her head stirred slightly, and she settled back into the pillow, her mouth forming a nearly imperceptible smile. She looked peaceful buried under the covers, and he watched her for a few more moments, trapped by her tranquility. Kate slept soundly every night. His heart was still thumping rapidly as he walked quietly to the master bathroom.

Several minutes later, in his home office, he sat down to check for any updates to the flu situation and navigated to his internet homepage. He scanned the national and international headline summary section of the homepage and shook his head slowly.

China Acknowledges Deadly Disease Within Border; China Imposed Quarantine To Keep Deadly Disease Out; Unknown Disease Spreads Through China; China Admits WHO (World Health Organization) Teams To Outbreak Areas; Deadly Disease Outbreak In China.

No surprises here. Only took them two days to acknowledge what the rest of the world already knew.

He clicked on an *Associated Press* article and shook his head again.

Fucking Chinese.

❧

Alex exited the kids' bathroom dressed and freshly showered, having lost his bid for the master bathroom. He quietly descended the hardwood stairs and eased into the kitchen unnoticed. The smell of coffee overtook him as he surveyed the area. A small sauce pot simmered on the stainless steel gas range, cooking what he really hoped was something other than Kate's lumpy oatmeal. A red toaster just to the left of the stove promised to deliver a more suitable breakfast alternative. A glass of orange juice, two open bread loaves and several containers sat in disarray on the black granite kitchen island. Kate moved quickly between the island, refrigerator and stove.

Kate was dressed in a knee-length navy blue skirt and a pressed French blue shirt. Her navy blue suit coat lay folded over the back of one of the black high-back stools at the kitchen island. Her hair, arranged in a tight ponytail, starkly contrasted her deep blue eyes and fair complexion. Compared to Kate, Alex looked like he just returned from a Caribbean vacation, owing to a mix of Sicilian and Irish genes. His black hair was not as pure as Kate's, but his eyes shared the same deep blue color. The toaster popped.

"Toast's ready!" Kate said, as she turned around and saw Alex. "Oh, hey. Good workout?"

"Not bad. Quick one. I didn't get up in time for a run…up a little late last night. I got a call on my cell from one of my infectious disease doctors," he said.

"What time?" she asked, eying him warily.

"Just past midnight. He thinks this mystery flu has already hit Portland," he told her, putting both hands on the island.

"What makes him so sure? We haven't seen anything on the internet, or the news."

"I think we might be a day behind the West Coast. After I talked to him, I saw some articles published out of LA referencing possible cases, and the ISPAC website lists LA and San Francisco as having several dozen confirmed cases of the new flu. Dr. Wright also said that the cases didn't resemble anything he's seen before. I think he tried to run some lab tests and came up empty."

"Did he say that?" Kate pressed.

"No, but he definitely said the cases didn't resemble anything he's seen before. I don't think he was talking about symptoms."

Alex heard some mumbling from the great room and glanced toward the sound of the voice. He saw that the family room LCD TV was fully operational, set to the Military Channel. Their twelve-year-old son, Ryan, scurried into the kitchen to collect his breakfast. He was already dressed for school, in faded blue jeans and a red long-sleeved rugby shirt. Ryan shared the same hair color as his father, but little else. He was born with emerald green eyes and his mother's fair skin.

"What's up, Mr. Man?" Alex said to his son.

"Not much, Dad. Hey, are you picking me up today after cross-country?"

"Yep, 4:45, right?"

"Sure, but around back so I don't have to walk around to the school pickup circle."

"I certainly wouldn't want to add another hundred yards to your workout."

"None of the parents pick their kids up at the circle, Dad."

"You are as right as your mother."

"You're in a slightly antagonistic mood this morning," Kate said.

"Yeah, I feel like pushing it today," Alex replied.

He smiled at Kate and raised his eyebrows. Ryan continued past his dad and pulled a plate out of the cabinet over the coffee maker. He slathered a piece of toast with butter and raspberry jam.

"Did you see what's going on in the Orient?" Alex asked.

"Nice. Could you find a few more politically incorrect terms to slip into your conversations? Don't listen to your dad, Ryan," she said, turning back to the range.

Ryan looked up at his mother, then shifted his glance to his dad. Alex raised his shoulder and mouthed the words, "I don't know."

Ryan returned to the family room and the volume from the great room TV increased.

"Mom, can you get my juice for me?" Ryan yelled over the noise.

"Can you grab that for his royal highness?" Kate said to Alex.

"Surely, my royal queen," he replied and delivered the glass to his son.

"Hey, should I teach Ryan the Chinese national anthem? Me Chinese…me play joke?" Alex asked.

"You could probably skip it, and we'd all be fine. So what's happening in China?"

"They finally admitted to a full-scale outbreak of some mystery virus in the south, and they also claim to have imposed their one-way travel ban because they were confident the disease didn't originate in China. They were trying to keep it out," he said, shaking his head.

"How does that make any sense? So they tried to keep the virus from entering their own country, but did nothing to keep it from spreading outside of China?"

"Apparently, they're convinced the epicenter is somewhere else. Hey, give them a break. At least they didn't keep it a secret for three weeks like in 2008. I read an Associated Press article, and one of the Chinese officials sounded proud of their new transparency efforts, like they did a much better job handling the issue this time."

Alex lowered his voice. "It's unbelievable really. Just like in 2003, when they put their first astronaut into orbit. Who gives a shit? It took them forty years to finally steal enough information about our rocket program to put a human in space. Congratulations. And now? Well, now they only sit on information critical to mankind's survival for two days, instead of weeks. I don't think we can ever trust them. I have a bad feeling about this one," he said.

"Whatever it is, we'll be fine," Kate answered.

"Hey, I'm gonna eat and run. Emily's in the shower, so she should make the bus. I promised the folks at the Mercy ER that I would stock them up with TerraFlu, so I want to hit them early. I guarantee that Biosphere is going to ask us to stop signing over samples," he said, pulling a coffee mug from the cabinet.

"Is that a big deal? I mean, aside from making your day easier than it already is."

"Very funny. Samples are scarce already, but eliminating them in the face of a pandemic crisis will not be perceived as a cool move by Biosphere."

"Can't the doctors just write a prescription for the pharmacy?"

"Sure, and at this time of year, the pharmacies should be well stocked with anti-virals, but most of the offices are looking for any reason to stop seeing reps, and they barely tolerate us as it is. It'll get ugly quick if Biosphere restricts samples."

"They won't buy off on the 'greater good of the community' speech? Stockpiling drugs for the national pandemic response?" Kate asked.

"Would you?"

"Probably not," she admitted.

"Especially when they know for a fact that they won't see any of it when the shit hits the fan. Health and Human Services will swoop down and grab it all for selected treatment centers," he said.

"Sucks to be you today," Kate taunted.

"Let's hope not," Alex said as he walked over to fix some breakfast.

"Seven o'clock. Turn on the *Today Show*," Kate said to him.

Alex found the remote and turned on the kitchen TV, just in time to see Matt Lauer appear on the screen. "Someone better say something about the fact that the Chinese sat on this for two days."

"*Good morning, on Friday, November 2nd. The news dominating the thoughts of all Americans today comes to us from Southeast Asia, where the evidence of a growing pandemic virus is mounting. Earlier this morning, Chinese government officials verified that an unidentified flu strain has caused several major outbreaks in the southern coastal regions of China. They have also confirmed that the cases are not caused by a strain or variant of the H5N1 avian flu. This announcement sparked uproar in the scientific community, where fear of another pandemic is rising.*"

"Turn it up, honey, I can't hear over that frigging Military Channel," Kate said.

Alex raised his voice, "Ryan, can you turn that down? We're trying to listen to something important about the world over here."

Kate responded first, "Are you seriously going to get into it with him again? Just turn up the volume, please, we'll miss the whole segment by the time you two figure it out."

Alex shook his head and raised the volume so he could hear Matt Lauer clearly.

"Thomas McGreggor from the Department of Health and Human Services joins us this morning to shed some light on these developments. Mr. McGreggor, welcome."

"Thank you, Matt."

"Now, one of the Department of Health and Human Services' major roles is to implement the national strategy to prevent or slow a pandemic's entry into the United States, and to limit the domestic spread of the disease."

"That sounds like a monumental task, and frankly, some experts just don't think it's possible for a single department to accomplish these goals. They all seem to agree that the national plan is solid, but argue that very few of the recommendations in the plan have been implemented. The statistics are sobering. Some experts cite a compliance rate of less than ten percent with the plan's recommendation at local levels, and it appears that little money is flowing down from Washington. Critics also suggest that most of the money is heading overseas to fund the WHO."

"Certainly these critics like to point fingers at Washington whenever they can, but a pandemic is a complex emergency, requiring an effective and coordinated response on many levels. The bulk of the costs occur once the pandemic strikes, and when this occurs, each state will receive disaster level funding to ensure continuity of pandemic response operations."

Matt shifted in his seat.

"I don't know if I agree. Let me read directly from the DHS manual. 'Ideally, states develop a multilayered strategy that delineates responsibilities at all levels of society to ensure the viability of government functions and services, such as energy, financial, transportation, telecommunications, firefighting and public safety.' This sounds like an expensive proposition. My parents' hometown can barely scrape together enough money to

repair winter damage to its roads. Where will towns and cities get the money to implement these preparations?"

"Well, first, I don't agree with the statistics that claim only six percent of the national plan is implemented. We've seen amazing progress throughout the nation, without reliance on more federal money. An appropriate level of funding is available at all levels for implementation of the plan."

"I hope you're right, because the situation in China has health officials concerned that the world might be on the verge of a deadly pandemic."

"Matt, the United States is in good hands. Since 2008, our nation's pandemic response capability has been vastly improved. From vaccination production and research capability, to anti-viral stockpiling. We learned a lot from the avian flu and applied those lessons to the national plan in place today."

"So given the events unfolding in Asia, what is DHS's primary concern at the moment, and what part of the national plan is being implemented?"

"We are working in close coordination with the CDC and WHO to receive real-time information regarding all aspects of the crisis. Our number one priority will be to prevent this disease from entering and spreading in the United States. Currently there is no indication that the disease has spread to the United States, though we have activated passive foreign traveler detection protocols. Customs officials have been alerted to identify and track any foreign travelers that appear ill."

"Is this for real?" Alex said to no one in particular. "It's already here. How could he not know that? Full of shit."

Kate silenced him with a hand signal, so she could hear the rest of the segment.

"Will these travelers be detained?" Matt asked.

"Not under passive protocols. Active protocols require a massive personnel increase, as you can imagine, and will be implemented when it is certain that a pandemic grade illness is headed to our borders."

"Has DHS considered the possibility that the disease has already entered the U.S. in considerable numbers? For nearly three days, travelers have left China for the U.S. and hundreds of other locations abroad, and the ISPAC website indicates that it may have already hit the west coast."

"We've definitely considered this, and fortunately, the number of passengers traveling to the U.S from China within a three day period is small. We are tracking all of these passengers and taking steps to ensure that if any of them are sick with this disease, they will be identified immediately. We feel confident that the disease is limited to China right now. Right now, we are taking the appropriate steps given the information available. And thanks to the Chinese government, the information is flowing much more efficiently than in 2008.

And to address the ISPAC website, none of their figures are official CDC or WHO statistics. If the flu arrives in the U.S., we'll know first."

"You've gotta be shitting me," Alex said, clicking the TV off.

Kate stifled a laugh. "That guy didn't sound very convincing," she commented.

"If this guy represents the government's attitude toward the situation, then we're screwed."

"Looks like your day is most assuredly going to suck," Kate said, wearing an overly fake sympathetic face.

"Yeah, I really need to get rolling here."

Please visit Steven's website for more information on *The Jakarta Pandemic*, the *Black Flagged* series and future projects:

www.stevenkonkoly.com